SIRA

OTHER TITLES BY MARÍA DUEÑAS

The Time in Between

SIRA

MARÍA DUEÑAS

Translated by
Simon Bruni

AMAZON **CROSSING**

Previously published as *Sira* by Editorial Planeta in Spain in 2021. Translated from Spanish by Simon Bruni. First published in English by Amazon Crossing in 2023.

Published by Amazon Crossing, Seattle

www.apub.com

Amazon, the Amazon logo, and Amazon Crossing are trademarks of Amazon.com, Inc., or its affiliates.

ISBN-13: 9781662501012 (paperback)
ISBN-13: 9781662501005 (digital)

Cover design by Emily Mahon

Cover image: © Leonardo Baldini / ArcAngel; © kzww / Shutterstock; © Roger Viollet Collection / Contributor / Getty

Printed in the United States of America

SIRA

PART ONE

Palestine

1

That typewriter didn't shatter my destiny. I had been wrong when I was still young and ignorant to think it would, when I hadn't yet filed away in my mind words like violence, grief, devastation, or rage, and so could not have anticipated the lacerations that life had planned for me. No, my destiny wasn't changed by an innocent device intended to join letters together. If only it had been. But the future had a different trial in store for me: eight hundred pounds of explosives deposited under a hotel in Jerusalem. Something infinitely more sinister.

The summer of 1945 took us to the Near East. Behind us we left a hungry and submissive Spain and a massacred Europe beginning its painful efforts to rebuild. A year and a few months before, through mutual persuasion and in order to protect me from the unwelcome hazards of my role as collaborator with the British secret service, Marcus and I had married in Gibraltar one windy March day, with the Iberian Peninsula to one side and North Africa to the other: lands that were worlds apart yet intimately close and that meant so much to us.

In lieu of a typical wedding, we settled for a mere formality that was as brief as it was austere. The Rock had been militarized from its tunnels to its peak and was almost devoid of a civilian population, having been evacuated at the onset of the Second World War over fears of a German invasion. There were no flowers or photographs or even rings in that office in the Convent, the governor's official residence. Marcus showed his genuine papers: a diplomatic passport in the name of Mark Bonnard, his real identity—the surname Logan was merely cover used in turbulent times. After the required *I do*s, I swore the formal oath of allegiance to the king in my shaky English, and I was immediately issued another document with my new particulars. Sira Bonnard—previously Arish Agoriuq, before that Sira Quiroga—was now a brand-new British subject. My final words were almost a whisper: "So help me God." Maybe nobody else noticed, but the moment I said them I couldn't help but feel moved. Despite the stiffness of the proceedings, the words confirmed the existence of an alliance that could overcome adversity and turmoil, borders and distances.

Back in Madrid, the marriage certificate and my new passport were left in the care of the embassy, and Marcus and I continued to lead seemingly separate lives, always seeing each other in secret, him carrying on his activities—comings and goings in defense of his country's interests—and me reporting information I'd extracted from the wives of Nazi officials in my guise as a sought-after seamstress who'd arrived in the capital as if sent from heaven.

When Germany surrendered in early May 1945 and ceased all its military operations, I closed the shop that the British had set up for me on Calle de Núñez de Balboa and moved in with Marcus. It wasn't easy for me to leave my trade, the work that had filled my days and had brought me satisfaction and pride, contacts and an income. In light of recent events, however, giving up sewing came as a relief. The job I'd held since childhood had turned into a thankless occupation owing to a clientele of undesirables to whom I had to show my most fraudulent and hypocritical cordiality. The fabrics and patterns ended up feeling as heavy to me as gravestones, the thread became rope that strangled me, and the act of simply trying my garments on the bodies of women I despised became a revolting task. Giving up the deception, forgetting about all those women, and no longer having to hide anything eased my anxiety and restored my peace of mind.

Still, I was aware that Marcus's and my time together in the simple apartment on Calle Miguel Ángel would be brief. The Third Reich's collapse and the Allied victory also marked the end of my hitherto secret husband's mission on the Iberian Peninsula. It was time to rethink our futures, and our interests were pointing us in different directions.

Marcus was keen for us to move to England, to contribute to restoring his homeland's prosperity. I too was anxious to leave Madrid with its blackouts, noisy propaganda, black bread, and reprisals: where every home had a dead person to mourn, where people still slept with rancor under their pillows, and children's heads were shaved so lice wouldn't feast on them. No, I didn't want to stay in that dreadful environment. I wanted my children to be born in a place without the remnants of horror on the streets, without desperation on people's faces. And so I suggested returning to Morocco, to its luminous warmth, close to the past and to my mother. I longed to escape the scenes of our furtive existence that had been so full of concealment and lies, to forget who we had been and to begin to be how we were: undisguised, free from falsehoods, mysteries, or fears.

Both our wishes, however, went up in smoke a few weeks later, when we were still getting used to walking together without always being on the alert, and while we still found it hard to grasp that we could do simple things in public like go to the movie theater on Gran Vía or dance at Pasapoga until the early hours. The order that Marcus received was categorical. He was needed for a new post in Palestine under the British Mandate. *To start immediately, spouse welcome,* he read out loud to me. A new role under the umbrella of the Secret Intelligence Service. He said no more. I preferred not to ask.

I was disconcerted but tried hard not to show my disappointment. The ladies in the Sección Femenina, had they been aware of my attitude and had my husband not been an Englishman, would have been proud: there I was, a well-bred Spanish woman living up to the model of the self-sacrificing spouse that the new Francoist regime imposed—willing and obedient, the angel of the home, the perfect wife. After all, I was just a seamstress who no longer sewed, while Marcus, thanks to his efficient performance of his duties, had become a valued asset in the service of his government. The truth of the matter, however, was that, beyond my marital obligations, time had only strengthened the volatile love that had sprung up between Marcus and me in Tétouan, Morocco, back when I was nothing more than a frightened little girl and he was a young operative who walked with a stick, masquerading as a journalist.

The machinery that drove the still-great British Empire had now, in essence, ordered a move that didn't fit with Marcus's intention to resettle in his own country, let alone with my ambition to return to Africa. But since insubordination had no place in our principles, we packed our clothes and belongings into two trunks and a few suitcases, and in late June we set off for a new place in the world, with a brief stopover in London—just enough time for Marcus to receive instructions and for us to visit his mother and see with our own eyes the sad reality of another grieving capital.

The prospect of facing Lady Olivia Bonnard, whom I had not met till now, triggered a disconcerting anxiety in me. After years of handling myself soundly with all manner of human specimens, I suddenly felt insecure.

"Should I address her that way, with the *Lady* in front?" I whispered to Marcus as we arrived. I took in the white stucco facade of the house: faded, flaking, and yet still splendid. Marcus winked at me with an expression I was unable to interpret. Perhaps, in teasing me, he thought to calm the nerves of a new wife facing the perennially unnerving figure of a mother-in-law. Or perhaps he was just forewarning me of the type of woman who awaited us in that residence on the Boltons, in the Brompton area of Kensington, a district whose elegance had not shielded it from the bloody onslaught of German planes.

House and owner seemed the perfect match: at once damaged and formidable, in harmony both in their bones and their guts. Both somewhat in decline but dignified and upright. Impressive. Fortunately, I'd spent years honing my skills in the art of pretending and had learned to move with grace in circles that crawled with people and eccentricities of every hue. This enabled me to hide my initial nerves, and I managed to keep my composure at that first tea, in that wild and beautiful garden. Feigning confidence, I deployed all my charm, brought out my best manners, and limited myself to the occasional composed smile and brief remark. I behaved, in short, like the most delightful of all possible wives.

In her correspondence, her attitude toward me had rotated between the minimum courtesy befitting her class, one or two gestures of disdain, and an ethereal indifference. In person, her demeanor was nothing like I had expected: I'd presumed she would be stern and restrained, in keeping with the time of hardship that the country had suffered and continued to suffer. But I'd gotten it completely wrong. Olivia Bonnard was a different kind of woman.

With her angular face and a long braid streaked with gray that rested over her left shoulder, her body wrapped in a worn velvet robe, and as she chain-smoked the American Chesterfields that Marcus had obtained for her on the black market in Madrid, Lady Olivia contrived to dent my morale more than once. She didn't hide the haughty looks my imperfect English evoked from her, and on a couple of occasions she pretended she couldn't remember how to pronounce my name: Saira? Sirea? Seira? Every so often she broke off midsentence to bend down and stick a piece of cucumber sandwich into the mouth of one of her dogs, the three of them half-crazy, one lame, all of them old.

Evidently, she was uncomfortable accepting as her daughter-in-law a foreigner who had neither lineage nor fortune and who'd originated in an uncivilized, backward, Catholic country where brothers killing brothers had become a bloody habit.

One person she *did* pour her affection onto was Marcus, her eldest son, her only living descendant in a dwindling family now reduced to just the two of them. In typically British fashion, there was little physical contact between them: no hugs, no kisses, no frivolity. At one point she ruffled his hair with her bony fingers—that was all. But their connection was obvious: they exuded complicity, and they were alike in the greenish color of their eyes, the veins on their necks, even the shape of their ears. As they were stringing together topics of conversation in a clipped English that I found hard to follow, at several points in her unstoppable monologue she let out a piece of gossip with elegant sarcasm that made him roar with laughter. He was more relaxed than I had seen him, with his long legs crossed on the overgrown grass and his eyes half-closed against the summer sun in the garden of his childhood, the hardened and skeptical spy made childlike for a few moments under his mother's protective wing.

"The war's been hard on her," Marcus mumbled when we got back in the car that would take us to Croydon Airport, as if making an excuse for her. We looked at her through the window. She was watching us leave from the top step, stoic between the dirty pair of stuccoed pillars that held up the porch, uncommonly majestic under her old robe, with her defective dogs at her feet, a cigarette between her lips, and that singular head of hair. The Victorian morality she'd been brought up with prevented her from expressing her feelings openly—she merely waved a goodbye—but I could sense that, as her son left, a knot like a tight fist was blocking her throat.

The widow of Sir Hugh Bonnard, Lady Olivia had lost her only daughter to meningitis before the girl was out of adolescence, and the youngest of her sons, an RAF pilot, had died in combat at the beginning of the Battle of France. Though she'd done nothing in her life until then but engage in the idle pursuits typical of her class and sex, her pain and the infectious patriotism of the time had made her shake off her indolence and open her home to whoever needed it, and she'd become eager to help as much as possible. She'd even sold off some of her furniture, many of her bronzes, pieces of jewelry, paintings, porcelain, furs, and rugs, and used the money she obtained to meet the needs of the poor wretches that the goddess of good fortune had forgotten. Marcus had already told me about it in Madrid, albeit in a purely informative vein. Now he did so again, speaking from his core as our vehicle's route showed me the ravages of the bombings that had taken place all around us. The magnificent Bladon Lodge close to their house had been reduced to a leveled area covered in rubble; the nearby Anglican church St. Mary The Boltons had been left without its organ, its stained glass windows, its roof. Even the iron railings that once encircled the park had been removed to be melted down and made into armaments.

News of the war's end had filled Londoners with jubilation: more than a million souls flocked to the central areas of the city after the announcement, arriving in packed buses and trucks, on carts, walking, running, cycling, on the Underground. Planes flew over the city in celebration, the Thames tugboats sounded their horns, and church bells rang furiously. Crowds had gathered, people yelling till they were hoarse, singing, laughing, clapping, and waving flags, with paper hats on their heads, forgetting all formality, freed from panic. On Piccadilly Circus, young men in uniform formed long congas with radiant young women dressed in their Sunday best; droves of youngsters rolled up their trousers and took to the fountain in Trafalgar Square; the king, queen, and Prime Minister Churchill on the balcony of Buckingham Palace had received impassioned cheers and joyful applause.

By the time Marcus and I arrived on our brief visit in their city, however, there was little trace of that victorious collective euphoria. Almost two months had passed, and harsh reality had taken hold. Almost six years of war had left Britain impoverished, devastated, and exhausted. In addition to the hundreds of thousands of soldiers who'd fallen or were badly wounded on the various fronts on the continent, the Luftwaffe's bombs had killed more than sixty thousand civilians on the British Isles, almost ninety thousand had been wounded, and huge numbers of people were homeless, jobless, breathless. The Blitz had swept away more than forty thousand properties in London alone, reducing them to rubble, twisted iron, scorched timber, and ash. Everything was in short supply: food and shelter, building materials, coal, clothing. The treasury's coffers were empty, and the accumulated debts were vast; dejection oozed from everywhere.

I felt immense relief when we boarded our BOAC passenger jet to leave the island that was so alien to me and that I was nonetheless irremediably tied to now because of passport and husband. I didn't even look back through the window; I just gripped Marcus's hand and closed my eyes tight when we began takeoff. With him by my side, I was safe, and everything would be bearable.

Our first stop, on one of the empire's traditional routes, was Malta. From there we continued on to Cairo, and, finally, the next day, we landed at the little Lod airbase, which had been built by the British a decade earlier, on Palestinian soil.

How could I have guessed, as we descended the stairs from the Avro York onto the Holy Land, that twenty months would pass before I would return to that London in ruins?

How could I have anticipated the stretches of troubled road ahead that Olivia Bonnard and I would end up traveling together? Without Marcus. Without making peace. Without understanding each other.

2

Just four passengers got off the plane with us; the rest were continuing to Karachi. On the runway, a stocky and obsequious Arab was waiting to drive us to Jerusalem. It took us almost two hours to reach the city. Now and again we came across British military vehicles: night patrols in a territory that was silently arming itself. Marcus kept quiet almost the entire time. I didn't insist on talking—I knew his silences. He was thinking, reflecting, slowly getting his bearings. He was arriving shortly after the end of the Great Revolt in a Palestine that was under his country's colonial mandate, at a time when it was still unclear whether, and in what form, the tensions between Arabs, Jews, and the British would return. Our duration of stay was indefinite, requiring maximum discretion and extreme caution. That was all I had to understand. I was to know nothing of his operating methods, his protocols, his contacts, or his efforts. It wasn't because of a lack of trust in me; it was simply how things were done. As if a pane of glass separated Marcus and me into different airtight compartments.

"No one's foreseeing good times," he muttered as we passed the umpteenth vehicle full of his fellow countrymen in uniform. He wasn't wrong. In 1917, His Majesty's government had agreed, as set forth in the Balfour Declaration, to support the aspirations of the Zionist Jews who longed for a permanent settlement for their people: *a national home.* This was a diffuse and ambiguous concept that meant hope for some and suspicion for others. Did a permanent settlement mean the creation of a new Jewish state within Palestine? Or perhaps a place for the Jewish minority within an Arab state? Nobody had stopped to go into specifics about this at the beginning.

We remained silent in the car, but in the previous weeks and during our outbound flights, Marcus had given me a snapshot of the place where we were to be based for an uncertain amount of time. After the Great War, under the auspices of the League of Nations, the British Empire had begun to exercise its colonial mandate over Palestinian territory, moving in its troops and civilians—often whole families—who brought with them their institutions and their manner of organizing life, their ways, their language, their arrogance, and their interests. At the same time, an increasing number of Jews from central and eastern Europe had been settling there, fleeing pogroms, persecution, hostility, and disdain; sick of being cast out from professions they were more than qualified to do; sick of being looked down upon and having stones thrown at them. Running from all of this, Jews had been arriving in Palestine in successive waves since the late nineteenth century. In the time since the British Mandate had begun to be exercised, however, the numbers had multiplied, and the local Arabs—who'd made up the majority of the population for centuries—had gradually begun to feel threatened and started to put up resistance.

The Jewish population, meanwhile, kept on growing, bringing in money and buying land, determined to stay put within the confines of the territory biblically known as Eretz Israel. By the late thirties, they made up a third of the region's population, and by the midforties, they approached half. And still they continued to come. And the more that came, the greater the strain on the populations' coexistence. The high-pressure situation had exploded in 1936 with Arab protests that culminated in uprisings and violence from both sides.

In response to the Arabs' demands, in May 1939, the British had issued their White Paper, a document that laid out an intention to reject the partitioning of Palestine into two states, to limit Jewish migration, and to drastically restrict Jews from buying land. A few months later, the second great war would break out in Europe.

Though some small rebel groups continued to mount attacks during the war, the global conflict gave rise to a period of relative peace in Palestine, one that ended no sooner than the Allies had achieved victory. The end of that war did not bring peace to Palestine as it had to Europe. On the contrary, it led to the intensification of hostilities between Arabs and Jews, between Jews and British, between British and Arabs, all of whom were living together and mixing badly. After Germany's surrender, the survivors of the Holocaust were more anxious than ever to flee a bloody Europe that had exterminated them by the millions, to settle permanently in the Promised Land, and to build the national home to which the British had pledged support almost three decades before. Friends, family, and fellow Jews were waiting there, ready to welcome them.

The British administration, however, in its commitment to maintaining harmony and protecting the rights of all, refused to relax its strict immigration quotas. Jewish refugees systematically challenged the restrictions, arriving illicitly by the shipload. The Arabs, in the meantime, felt increasingly betrayed by the British, harassed by the Jews, and resistant to the inrush of survivors of a war between Christians in which they themselves had played no part. The outcome was mutual frustration and hostility, positions that became increasingly radical in the absence of any prospect of the parties coming to an understanding.

When we arrived tired and hungry at the American Colony that night, we found only dim lights and a staff member asleep on his feet. I was accustomed to the grand hotels of Madrid where I often went to fulfill my work commitments, and this place did not seem to me a typical guest establishment; rather, it was more like a converted mansion, akin to a large stone villa, a portion of which was for some reason used as a hostel to accommodate visitors. But it was too late to stop to investigate such subtleties. Marcus and I simply devoured the tray of cold delicacies they offered us and went straight to sleep, holding each other, exhausted and silently restless.

As had happened so often before in our endlessly eventful relationship, when I woke the next morning, Marcus was gone. With bare feet and disheveled hair, I went to the balcony, opened the wooden shutters, and allowed the light to stream in—pure, clean light. Our room overlooked a leafy courtyard, and the gurgle of the central fountain reached my ears along with an exchange of female voices in a language that seemed familiar even if I couldn't understand it. One of the women let out an exclamation, and the others laughed through the bougainvillea, large plant pots, and palm trees. A moment later they showed themselves: three young employees dressed in white with shawls covering their heads, carrying piles of bedclothes in their arms. They reminded me of sweet Jamila, the girl who'd cleaned at the smuggler Candelaria's guesthouse in Morocco; Jamila of those Moorish days that were now long past and yet were, at the same time, always so present in my memory.

The three of them turned around when another resounding voice suddenly silenced them. From one of the lateral arches, a woman of mature years entered the courtyard. Tall, energetic, broad-shouldered, with a prominent bust, and white hair gathered in a bun, she was impeccable in her day dress. Mixing English and Arabic, she gave orders in a powerful tone. The girls nodded obediently, and each returned to her duties. Once she was alone, the woman bent down to pick up some jasmine leaves that had fallen into the fountain's water. As she straightened her body, I thought she glanced up toward my balcony. Then she retraced her footsteps. The echo of her heels on the flagstones could still be heard when she was out of sight.

She had indeed seen me. She'd confirmed that I was awake. I knew this just ten minutes later, when another employee knocked on my door and handed me a note:

Sira

Mrs. Bertha Spafford Vester requests the pleasure of your company for breakfast at half past nine.

I looked at the time. It was ten past nine. Twenty minutes later, I arrived in the dining room still undecided about which of my identities it would be most advisable to use to introduce myself: the seamstress from Madrid, the Moroccan who'd collaborated with the British, or the wife who was prepared to go to the ends of the earth with her husband. After all, they were all more or less true.

"Whenever possible, I like to welcome our guests in person."

As I sat opposite her at a corner table, with a linen tablecloth, delicate crockery, and silverware between us, I realized that she was more advanced in years than I'd initially sensed. She was probably almost seventy; older than my mother, I thought. Older even than Lady Olivia, and completely different from them both, at least in appearance. I accepted coffee.

"It's Turkish, magnificent," she said emphatically.

I accepted toast and bitter marmalade.

"We make it here," she explained, "with our own oranges. The eggs are ours, too. How do you like them? Fried or scrambled?"

I continued to observe her while she gave orders to a dark-skinned waiter. Her eyes were blue, and she wore pearls on her neck and ears. Over her ample bosom she sported a burnished serpent-shaped brooch.

"We're Americans, independent Christians. We're not a large community, but we have been active for decades, particularly in social and philanthropic causes," she explained as she spread butter on her bread. I understood that she was referring to the American Colony's endeavors that she led. "My parents left Chicago at the end of the last century. The death of my four elder sisters, drowned in a shipwreck when they were still young girls, left them deeply disturbed. They decided to settle in the Holy Land in search of peace for their poor souls. I was just two when they brought me here. They're no longer alive, neither is my husband,

and my six children are scattered around the world. Now it's just me in charge of the institution, helped by a willing and committed group of accomplices."

We'd each finished our first cup of coffee, dense and sweet. A delight, sure enough, compared to the ersatz version Marcus and I had drunk in those days in Spain. Without asking me, she went ahead and served us some more.

"We run a children's hospital and have fertile land," she went on as the black liquid trickled into the porcelain, "and a workshop for Arab girls and a number of soup kitchens."

It was evident that presenting her credentials was first and foremost on my hostess's mind. Describing her colony's goals must have been the calling card with which she greeted anyone who stayed under her roof.

"We bought this house on the Nablus road where we are now from the powerful Husseini family, and to begin with, decades ago, we all moved in to live a communal life. Then we decided to convert it into a hotel whose profits we would reinvest in our other humanitarian activities."

She paused, chewed on her toast, and drank some more.

"We also pester the authorities and Jerusalem's privileged on behalf of those most in need. We leave no stone unturned to try to win them over to our cause."

"And what is your cause, Mrs. Vester?"

"If you're asking whether we're pro-Arab or pro-Jew, you should know, my dear, that our colony has never taken sides. We work only for the common good. Politics are completely alien to us."

Despite her somewhat excessive explanations, I liked Bertha Vester from the start. She was direct and clear, with an English I found accessible even with her American accent. Whereas Marcus's mother had employed a sharp cadence, Mrs. Vester strove to make sure I could follow the thread of the conversation easily.

The dining room was almost empty when we finished breakfast, only a young mother with two children and an older couple reading newspapers remaining. As we stood, I was struck by a gust of memories of another equally hospitable woman, albeit one with a very different style: Candelaria, in the Moroccan city of Tétouan, whom I'd known when I was no more than a naive young woman who'd been abandoned by a crook. Almost ten years had passed since then, and that modest guesthouse in the La Luneta district bore no resemblance to this magnificent villa in the prosperous Sheikh Jarrah neighborhood. Neither was the demeanor and manner of my friend the smuggler anything like the refinement of this regal lady. Nor was I the same: I had in the years since experienced shady affairs and diverse people that had opened my eyes to the best and the worst of the human condition, and these had taught me to sense the places where cruelty hides and from where integrity and decency emerge.

I was about to thank my hostess for breakfast when she spoke up before me.

"Is there some matter that requires your immediate attention in your room?"

I shook my head emphatically.

"I must go to the bank to deposit some checks. I'd be delighted," she proposed, "if you'd accompany me."

The driver was a Sudanese man, and the car a Ford as American as its owner. As the two of us sat in the back on the drive into the center of Jerusalem, she pointed out the notable places we came across: St. George's Anglican Cathedral, the walls of Jerusalem, the Damascus Gate, the Russian post office, the New Gate, the French Hospital, the Chapel of St. Vincent de Paul, a police station . . . I took it all in, uncertain. What would this strange place bring for Marcus and me? Would we be moderately happy here? Able to find our niche? Would we manage not to get involved in local tensions, or would we end up being dragged into them?

At the beginning of my hostess's and my journey, most of the people I saw were Arabs—men, primarily. Some were dressed entirely in their traditional attire; others wore European-style suits, their heads covered with a scarf that was tight on the forehead—the kaffiyeh, as I would later learn it was named. Some wore the fez of the well-to-do classes, the same hats I remembered from my time in Morocco years before.

As we moved into the modern area of the city, the Arabs were less visible, and Jews took their place—not the ultraorthodox kind with bushy beards, black overcoats, bare ankles, and large hats, but urban men dressed in tailored suits that they could just as well have worn to walk the streets of Amsterdam, Berlin, or Warsaw. There too were women in floral dresses, their arms bare; boys in white shirts with the sleeves rolled up; and girls with crimped hair and light-colored summer blouses. A mixture of people, in short, who wandered the sidewalks in a seemingly normal manner, crossed the roads, got on and off buses, stopped to speak to someone on a corner or sat outside a café to read the *Palestine Post* or a newspaper in Hebrew. I also saw, in disharmony with the apparent tranquility of the scene, large numbers of British soldiers in khaki uniforms, with their short trousers above their knees and long socks, their berets tilted to one side. And police in His Majesty's service, too. Police in droves.

The streets that unfurled in front of us were well paved, with wide sidewalks and harmonious buildings. Most of the structures' exteriors were made from a sand-colored stone, beautiful and well coordinated in accordance with the colonial mandate which—as it did in everything—intervened in the areas of architecture and urban design. From the outset, the British had ordered that buildings be constructed using stone from the nearby quarries. Large canvas awnings protected the exteriors of offices, movie theaters, hotels, stores, agencies. In this area of the city, most of the posters and signs were in English. Many were in Hebrew. None were in Arabic.

My hostess's bank appeared in front of us: semicircular in shape, with an arched entrance and a sparkling Union Jack flying over it, gently waving the empire's colors under the morning sun. BARCLAYS BANK (DOMINION, COLONIAL, AND OVERSEAS). The capital letters gleamed on the facade. We got out of the car. I moved slowly, looking around me, trying to take everything in, still unable to understand the rules of the game, how the pieces moved on this new board.

"Collect us at one at the King David, please, Mustafa," she ordered the driver, bending to make herself heard through the open window.

The King David, she'd said. I didn't know what Bertha Vester was referring to then. It was the first time I'd heard the name that would echo in my soul for the rest of my days.

There were several dozen customers in the bank, almost all of them British. Our summer hats, dresses, and gloves provided a colorful counterpoint to the monochromatic male majority surrounding us. My hostess said her hellos, and the responses were always affectionate. *Good morning, Mrs. Vester. Good morning, my dear friend. Isn't it a wonderful day?* She didn't introduce me to anybody, as it was neither the place nor the time. The bank offered to call for the manager to attend to her personally, but she declined. Her transaction was quick; we barely had to wait, as if this was a recurrent activity and she was an important figure they always treated with deference.

We were about to leave the building when we almost bumped into an individual who was entering impetuously, rushing with arms piled high with papers. In fact, his shoulder and mine brushed against each other. He was tall and stocky with plentiful brown hair and a light-colored cotton suit, the jacket somewhat creased, the tie a little loose.

"Watch where you're going, Soutter!" my companion warned without giving him the chance to apologize. "Why're you always in such a rush, my dear?" Then she questioned him, citing the initials of an organization whose name I did not know, but that I soon would. "Can't PBS cope without you for a single minute?"

3

A quick scan of the impressive lounge was enough for me to spot him. Marcus was sitting at one of the tables on the left side, in conversation with two other men. He seemed relaxed, but that didn't mean anything; even in the tensest and most complex situations, he rarely lost his cool. In one hand he held a whiskey on the rocks, in the other a cigarette. His face bore an expression that didn't change when he saw me. Receiving this reaction, I did the same.

This was how we had operated over the years: each time we met in a public place, neither showed the slightest sign of knowing the other. It was a precaution—basic protocol. As if we'd never had anything to do with each other. As if we'd never shared our fears and our skin, our worries, loyalty, and caresses. In all likelihood, there was no need to be so cautious here. He and I were not living in the pro-German Madrid of the period that had followed the civil war, a time when Franco had continued to pander to the Nazis while confronting the British with bare fists. Even without agreeing in advance, probably out of sheer habit, that afternoon Marcus and I followed our usual code. Simulated indifference. Calculated inadvertence. Neither one of us taking the slightest notice of the other, as if we both were physically transparent.

In contrast to the quiet charm of the American Colony, the King David Hotel was a grandiose place. The Palace and Ritz Hotels, which I'd frequented, seemed modest by comparison. This was of a different class, a tribute to opulence that married authentic Near East style with a lavish ambience. The six-story rectangular building had been funded with Jewish money of Egyptian origin and built by Arab labor with stone from a quarry near Jericho. It was decorated with white and green- ish marble, its walls adorned with biblical scenes, and Byzantine lamps hung from the ceiling by chains.

An attentive European waiter whose nationality I was unable to identify led us to one of the few remaining empty tables, located near one of the large windows open onto the garden. Some distance from Marcus, thankfully.

"Jerusalem's most iconic sights are of a unique nature, as I'm sure you know," said Bertha Vester, discreetly fanning her neckline. "To visit them and understand them, however, requires a certain amount of devotion. This modern area outside the walls is probably the best place to begin your stay."

She ordered a glass of fruit juice. I joined her.

"Everyone gathers here daily to talk endlessly about politics and money, and to inform themselves and scheme about the world and the Near East in general, this troubled Palestine of ours in particular. Businessmen, dis- tinguished tourists, top executives in corporations, journalists, merchants, traffickers, assorted opportunists. And of course, a great many wealthy local Jews and wellborn Arabs. They're all here," she announced as she swept her gaze around the large space. "Let's say the King David is the most cosmopolitan public place in Palestine. And entirely neutral. For the time being."

Three military officers passed us—high-ranking ones, I deduced from their stripes and their bearing.

"Overflying all of them, as you'll see, are the British, of course," she added, responding to a greeting from one of them with a polite nod. "The army has set up headquarters here, and the secretariat has installed the mandate's civilian government as well. They all came before war broke out in Europe, during the bloody Arab Revolt, for safety and convenience. They've taken up almost half of the hotel—the entire south wing. Though naturally, only officers and high-ranking officials frequent these rooms. The troops have their barracks and clubs elsewhere, and the clerks, typists, telephone operators, and support staff access the building via the back doors and use the service stairs."

A svelte, dark-skinned waiter, dressed as if attending an operetta, brought us our drinks on an embossed copper tray that he handled with skill.

"Sudanese attendants to serve them, and Arabs to clean the floors and wash the dishes. Long live the empire!" Bertha Vester added with a sarcastic wink.

I held my glass to my lips and, without taking my eyes from her, drank slowly. Then I deposited it on the table, also slowly. My years of painstaking work with the secret service had taught me not only to listen with the closest attention but also to use my silence to keep others talking.

"But life out there is tough, my dear. You'll see for yourself that the English and the rest of the expatriates live here as if Jerusalem were a cruise liner. They mix with the same people in the same places at the same times, all of them moving at the same pace, seemingly imperturbable. And meanwhile, in the outlying areas and villages, in the fields and settlements, there is hardship. And hate, my dear. An intense hate that grows and grows."

Another skill I had acquired during the course of my covert work was the ability to divide my attention without anyone realizing it. Which was how, while I listened to my hostess so closely that I didn't miss a single syllable, I also watched Marcus and the people he was with finish their drinks and get up. One of the strangers picked up his hat and shook Marcus's hand. The other gestured to one of the waiters and indicated where in the hotel they were going. Given the time, I presumed it would be the restaurant for lunch.

"My husband," I said then in a low voice, gesturing faintly at him with my chin.

It was the first time I'd used that adjective with that noun in front of someone. There had been no reason before for me to do so—those words had never left my mouth, as Marcus and I always kept ourselves hidden, distorting realities, covering feelings. I had just broken my opacity unilaterally, the permanent discretion I'd been forced to maintain. But what did it matter, if Bertha Vester was accommodating us together in her home, where we shared a room and bed, a bathroom, a wardrobe?

She must have read something, however, in my tone or expression.

"Sometimes marriages break the mold," she declared with the intuitive wisdom accumulated over seven decades.

We both now had our eyes fixed on Marcus as he walked away, mine on those solid shoulders that I leaned against during turbulent nights and that gave me security on uncertain days. He was walking alongside the other man, in conversation.

"It's always easier," my companion went on, "to tie oneself to an equal, a person from one's own world. Yet for all that, sometimes, for some strange reason, we board ships that must inevitably sail through storms."

Marcus and his associate disappeared through a set of enormous cedarwood doors.

Bertha continued. "I know what I'm talking about, my friend. I know from experience. My husband was of Swiss-German origin. At the beginning of our relationship, when my mother found out we were seeing each other, she decided the family would return to Chicago for a time. Not for a single day of those two years did I stop thinking about him, about Frederik Vester. In the end my family came back to Palestine, and she accepted him. He fit in easily and we were a happy couple until a heart attack tore him from my side three years ago."

She looked out at the garden, as if reflecting for a moment. Through the glass we could see beautiful roses, fountains, paved paths, and manicured cypresses.

"But we could just as easily have been disgraced."

Her blue eyes returned to mine. She breathed a deep sigh, her chest and the large brooch rising.

I remained silent, contemplating my hands, which sat on the marble tabletop—the hands of an only child who'd been born to a single mother, hands that were tired after years of sewing since my childhood of scarcity. My own experience of marriage was minimal, and in my immediate environment I lacked examples to corroborate or contradict my companion's view. My parents had not married each other. My father did marry, a woman I never met, and as far as I knew they hadn't been very happy together, but I never delved into the reasons why or who was to blame. At the church in Tétouan, my mother, Dolores, had said *yes, in good times and in bad, in sickness and in health* to a retired postal worker, a quiet widower who gave her company, financial support, and affection. But hers was a pairing quite unlike mine, the closure of a circle rather than the beginning of a new chapter in life, one that Marcus and I hoped would bring us lasting happiness.

As Bertha Vester and I headed to the exit, just before we were swallowed up by the big revolving door, she gestured at a shiny wooden counter on which lay magazines, maps, tourist leaflets, and a rotating stand full of postcards.

"Perhaps you'd like to send your loved ones a picture of this land, one as holy as it is complex."

4

I did send those postcards. Later, as the days and weeks and months passed, I corresponded with letters. Letters to my mother, at the respectable address she enjoyed as a Tétouanese wife. Letters to my father, at his apartment on Calle de Hermosilla in Madrid. To my friend Félix, who'd moved to Tangier after burying his odious mother without shedding a single tear. To Candelaria in Morocco, and to my friend Rosalinda, also in Morocco, but whose address was forever changing. Long letters for each of them that, despite the many words I strung together, never said an awful lot. I only related flashes, small details and anecdotes, as if my eyes belonged to a dimwitted and supremely frivolous tourist. The sweetness of the watermelons, the eternal haggling in the souks, the shocking sight of the ultraorthodox Jews hitting their heads against the Wailing Wall.

I never mentioned the rougher side of the city, not one word about the outbreaks of violence—as if Jerusalem were a spa town and I was on an endless honeymoon. Why would I describe the complexities and conflicts that entangled this part of the world without offering any hope of resolution? What was the sense in mentioning Marcus's commitments and my efforts, his uncertainties, my fears?

The summer ended with an unwelcome state of affairs. Under Clement Attlee's Labour Party, the new British government was sticking fiercely to its decision not to allow a mass influx of European Jews to settle Palestinian lands. The local Jews had responded with open rejection of the approach. Most channeled their obvious unrest through resolute but peaceful protests and demands; there were, however, other ways to express their disagreement. Three covert paramilitary groups—Haganah, the Irgun, and Lehi—had hitherto perpetrated violence separately. Now they'd set aside their differences to join forces in rebellion against the British Mandate. Their targets were police posts, radar stations, oil refineries, railroads. Neither Arabs nor Christians ever knew where the next attacks would come from, nor what targets the groups would single out.

Marcus and I remained at the American Colony for the time being, away from the bustle of the city. The departure of other guests meant that we were able to move to a larger room, practically an apartment. Bertha Vester and her attentive staff continued to take care of us. They fed us, washed our clothes, put a car with a driver at my disposal, invited me to join in on activities and events. Even so, perhaps because I had no specific function to serve, or maybe because of the strangeness of our surroundings, despite my best efforts and the passage of time, I struggled with my role as an expatriate wife, and even more so with being an inactive one.

The arrival of autumn brought storms of sand and dust from the desert. With them came gunfire and arrests, street riots, weapons passing from hand to hand, and the detonation of homemade explosive devices. Then there were the first rains, purifying, welcome, healing afflicted minds and parched soils. The days shortened, and the city seemed to draw inward. And there I remained in the middle of it all, the seamstress who no longer sewed, the conspirator who no longer conspired, the unoccupied wife of an Englishman with slippery duties who spent more time out working than by my side. This was my existence: trying to keep a foot in each camp, to balance like a tightrope walker.

One aspect of this was that I wanted to enjoy living in the Jerusalem that was so meaningful to three creeds. To that end, I'd made various visits to the Old City. My feet had trod the Via Dolorosa and the narrow, stepped streets in the different neighborhoods; my eyes had contemplated the Holy Sepulchre and the Cenacle, the Tower of David, the Dome of the Rock, the Armenian Cathedral of Saint James. I'd learned to distinguish the various communities and could now identify them by their language, their worship, their clothing. The Greek priests with their beards and miters. My Franciscan compatriots and their brown habits fastened by a modest rope with three knots. The Orthodox Jews with their black coats, enormous hats, and ringlets hanging down in front of their ears.

Moving through the maze of streets in the heart of the city, I had also seen the ordinary people—Muslims and Jews and Christians; children, women, men—going about their everyday tasks, their routines, their buying and selling of bread, oil, figs, chickpeas, candles, fish. Intermingling with these age-old inhabitants, I had seen bronzed, young Jewish settlers in khaki striding enthusiastically; pilgrims and visitors newly arrived from a thousand parts of the world; skinny goats, donkeys laden with goods; Bedouins; blond English girls in school uniforms; and many other varied people coming together and separating, amalgamating and dispersing on the streets, little squares, and alleyways like colored pieces of glass in a kaleidoscope.

Yet despite my efforts, I couldn't shake the constant restlessness that I wished to avoid and that clung to my bones. Marcus went out early and often returned tense. Sometimes he was gone for two or three days, to Tel Aviv or Jaffa or God knows where, always insisting before he left that I mustn't worry about him, that I myself should be careful. When he was with me, however, he tried to ease my worries, take the sting out of my fears. Some nights—a minority of them—we retired early to our room at the American Colony, and he told me as much as he could about his activities, sometimes even a little more than was prudent, and then we made love unhurriedly and whispered promises and plans into each other's ears. On other occasions—the majority of nights—he suggested going out. I did not doubt that his motives were sincere when he insisted on infusing my days with a bit of entertainment: dinners, dances, sights, people. But it was also true, I knew, that this lively night-life was helpful to his mission. His job was to absorb information one way or another, and it could be found hiding just about anywhere in the early-morning hours.

Often we went to Fink's Bar, a smoke-filled place brimming with a variety of faces, drinks, and languages. Other nights we spent at the clubs in the Semiramis Hotel or the basement of the Jasmine House Hotel, which Marcus called the press ghetto, because it was where the British and American correspondents stayed. What we tended to do most, however, was go to private residences where crowded gatherings were held. There were dinners in the Arab neighborhoods of Katamon or Talbiya and occasionally in the Jewish district of Rehavia. Cocktail parties or soirees in the villas of lawyers, intellectuals, or businessmen connected to Europe in some way—Marcus's fellow countrymen or transient foreign residents. At all of them, always there were excuses to keep discussing, drink in hand, the matter of Palestine and its uneasy future.

On occasion, back at the American Colony at two or three or four in the morning as I got into bed, Marcus would take off his jacket and tie, roll up his shirtsleeves, turn on the little desk lamp, and sit down to work, focused and determined, wakeful. I often watched him from the bed, trying not to be dragged under by sleep. I liked seeing his silhouette against the yellowish light from the bulb—his arms bare from the elbows, his hair somewhat disheveled by this time of the night—until finally, lulled by his pen's scratching on the paper, I would close my eyes, without knowing how long he would sit writing or what words he would use to express the concerns his brain was processing.

The beginning of November finally saw the arrival of the new high commissioner of Palestine: Sir Alan Cunningham. He was one of the recipients of the exhaustive collection of documents Marcus was amassing for the government in the filing cabinets of the office he'd been assigned at the King David Hotel, where his compatriots from the secretariat were stationed. Sir Alan was an imposing army veteran who had just been given a mission full of obstacles and problems. His reception at Government House, the headquarters of the British Mandate of Palestine, was attended by high-ranking officials, decorated military men, diplomats from all over the world, representatives of large corporations, and prominent local citizens, as well as by the leaders of the Arab Higher Committee and the Jewish Agency, of course. And us: Marcus in formal dress, and me enveloped in one of my own designs.

We were received by an honor guard from the Highland Light Infantry, with salvos and hurrahs for the king and empire, in the gardens of the Mount of Olives residence as evening fell over the Old City, the change of light causing its golden domes to glow and drawing magical shades of color from the stones. The letter of appointment was ceremoniously read out in the three languages, inside the large ballroom. The most senior judge of the mandate's supreme court, dressed in formal attire and a long wig, swore in the new high commissioner. Sir Alan would be the seventh head of the British administration. No one anticipated he would be the last.

As the military band blasted out the chords of "God Save the King," I couldn't help but remember another reception, held at the high commission in Tétouan eight years before: the first time, and the last before now, that Marcus and I had gone to an official gathering together. At that reception, the Spanish politician Ramón Serrano Suñer—Franco's brother-in-law—had wanted to meet the Spanish military and political leader Juan Luis Beigbeder. For his part, Beigbeder had gone to great efforts to smother Suñer with attention, not suspecting that a few years later the Cuñadísimo, as Suñer was known, would give him the almightiest kick in the backside. In Jerusalem now it was all very different: the British were in a whole other class when it came to colonial power. The pomposity and stateliness were of another scale, and the protocol was infinitely loftier than the one that had been adopted by Spain's humble Moroccan protectorate.

I couldn't contain myself. My voice reached Marcus's ear as a whisper.

"How long will he stay?"

His answer was just one word.

"Indefinitely."

I bit my lip to stop myself from asking, *And what about us?*

I couldn't wait to leave that convulsive land. To go anywhere else. As soon as possible.

5

Two weeks later, the charismatic Katy Antonius invited us to one of her parties. Katy's parties were the best in Jerusalem, no question about it, Bertha Vester informed me. Even so, I didn't have the slightest interest in attending. I hadn't been feeling well for a couple of days. I would've far preferred one of our quiet nights in the American Colony, just Marcus and me, eating whatever the kitchen had available. Or without even bothering with dinner.

I said this to him as I finished putting my makeup on, curling my eyelashes in front of the mirror, wearing my deep-red gauze dress and Morocco leather shoes. I still had a few clips in my hair, marking the waves. Behind me, he had just fastened his cuff links. He took me by the shoulders and turned me around.

"And what will I do without you, just me alone among all those people? I need you there."

My response was a weak burst of laughter; I didn't have the strength for more.

"Liar," I whispered.

One by one, he started removing the clips that held up my hair.

"I'm not lying. You always manage to have whoever you want eating out of your hand," he said slowly, his breath touching me.

He took off the first clip and threw it onto the floor, where it made a metallic tinkling sound on the tiles. Several locks of hair fell onto my left shoulder.

"You come across as a strange and beautiful wife hanging from my arm . . ."

He unclipped the second, there was another clink, and the locks now fell on my right shoulder.

"You examine the scene with precision, pretending you're admiring the decor or ambience . . ."

When he removed the third, more hair fell down my back.

"You select your target and analyze it meticulously . . ."

With the fourth and last clip, a curtain of hair fell over my face. He combed it aside with a forefinger.

"And in half an hour you've completed your mission."

I couldn't help but give a wry smile, despite my weariness; I knew full well there was an ulterior motive behind his flattery.

"And this evening, my darling, who is it you want me to target?" I asked.

"A Jewish couple. I believe the Valeros will be there."

We often acted in this way in public—coordinated, complicit. While he was pursuing a target under the guise of a friendly social event, I lent a hand. He always equipped me with a wealth of information beforehand.

"Of Sephardic descent," he continued in an almost telegraphic tone as he put on his jacket. "He is a doctor. From a wealthy family of local bankers whose ancestors arrived from Spain centuries ago."

I turned back to the mirror, sunk my fingers into the hair that Marcus had just undone, and finished styling it.

"The Sephardim have been living amicably alongside the Arabs for generations, doing business together, cultivating smooth relations with few ups and downs. But in recent times, since the arrival of waves of Ashkenazi Jews from central and eastern Europe, the Sephardim have become a minority. Which is why I'm interested in getting to know some of them. To see whether they still have some influence."

I uncapped a stick of lip rouge.

"What exactly do you need?"

I ran it over my lips, the upper first, then the lower. Behind me, Marcus had stuck his hands in his pockets and was looking at me appreciatively. I closed my mouth to seal the rouge and opened my lips again.

"An invitation to dinner at his home, for instance?"

The American Colony's driver took us to Karm al-Mufti, Katy Antonius's impressive mansion on the slopes of Mount Scopus, quite near our accommodation. We drove through a cast-iron arabesque gate and found ourselves in a torchlit garden. When we climbed out of the Vesters' Ford, the music from inside the house was reaching the porch. As soon as we were inside, a dark-skinned servant in an eye-catching velvet tunic took our coats; another in the same garb held out a tray of drinks; a third tempted us with appetizers and dried fruit. Marcus knew me well: in the time it took to politely decline both the cocktails and the food, I had already scanned our surroundings. More or less.

A hundred or so bodies were moving around the reception room among antique rugs, Damascene tapestries, and French art-deco furniture. European women in evening gowns were settled onto ottomans and armchairs with their legs crossed, each with a pink gin in hand. Arab women, some of them dressed in beautiful kaftans and others à la mode, smoked long cigarettes with crimson-colored filters. Colonial bureaucrats in strict black tie, officers of His Majesty's Armed Forces in mess dress uniform, and Arab men of all ages were present, some in long white tunics, most in urban three-piece suits. Intermingling with them all—surrounded by shelves crammed with books, large lanterns, beautiful engravings, and expressionist paintings—were diplomats and intellectuals of varied nationalities, transient aristocrats, reporters on the job, well-heeled exiles, and a handful of people I struggled to categorize. However, apart from one or two journalists, there were scarcely any

Jews. The growing tension between the various groups wasn't conducive to festive gatherings, and Katy Antonius was a fiercely pro-British Arab.

From a gramophone, the voices and out-of-time maracas of the Andrews Sisters filled the room with the melodious rhythm of "Rum and Coca-Cola." In the air floated cigarette smoke, heated conversations, and occasional bursts of laughter. I understood immediately that this was an infinitely more stimulating scenario than that of the many formal parties I used to attend in Madrid—reserved affairs lit with low-wattage bulbs, perhaps because my country was still healing from the wounds of a war, whereas Palestine had the rather brash effervescence of a people who did not yet know what was to come.

A woman of short stature wrapped in organza approached us with her arms extended. Her face was friendly and her voice somewhat shrill. She was past forty and wore her hair short, curly, and dark, except for one white lock that fell over her brow. Hanging from her neck was a long string of baroque pearls.

"Welcome, welcome, my dear friends . . ."

We barely knew each other, had met on only a few occasions and hardly exchanged a word. But she had seen us recently at the Government House reception, where she must have sensed that Marcus played an interesting role among his people and so had decided to bring us into the fold. The warmth with which she welcomed us that evening would have made anyone watching think we had been friends for decades.

"Come in. What a pleasure to have you with us, darlings. You make a fabulous couple," she said joyfully. "You grow more handsome by the day, my esteemed Mark. And you, my dear, are as striking as ever in that divine dress. I'm dying of envy that we don't share the same dressmaker. Come, darling, we're all longing to know your view on how Spain has been faring since the little general took over . . ."

Katy Antonius was one of Jerusalem's Christian Arabs, the group that to the British mind held the most moderate stance in the conflict.

They were not, at a little over a hundred thousand, a majority of the population. But they were educated and well traveled, many of them respected professionals, almost all of them living in affluent neighborhoods. They were almost always dressed in western attire, they were lovers of horses and tennis at the YMCA, and their children attended any one of the British universities, the tolerant American University of Beirut, or Victoria College in Alexandria. The Christian Arabs held many prominent roles in the mandate's administration, and some of them believed that the solution for the Palestine territory was not to form independent states, but quite the opposite—these individuals said that everything would be resolved if Palestine became a real British colony. Our host, Katy Antonius, who was both the daughter of a wealthy Egyptian publisher and the widow of the Lebanese historian George Antonius, had been brought up in the Greek Orthodox tradition and educated at a London school for distinguished young ladies, and she fit the mold of the group to perfection.

With sparkling verbosity, she grabbed me by the waist and took me deeper into the large room, leaving Marcus behind. Our host had decided to make me the main attraction of the evening: an unlikely Spanish woman to add color to the party. I would have given the world to be able to escape back to my room and curl up under the blankets.

"Allow me to introduce you to some friends. But eat something first, darling. What would you like? Tell me . . ."

I tried to refuse while she gave an imperious gesture to one of the servants. A full tray appeared in front of me.

"This is hummus, but I'm sure you know it."

Of course I knew it; I knew everything she was offering to me, and usually I enjoyed it. At any other time I would have accepted gratefully. But not now. I didn't want anything now. I had been feeling unwell all day, and the dense smoke in the room, or perhaps the heat from the mass of bodies, or some other cause, was increasing my discomfort by the second. Katy Antonius, however, hospitable to excess as she was, seemed unprepared to let me go.

"We call this fatayer, this one's filled with cheese. It's delicious. Try it, darling, try it . . ."

I began to feel an intense heat. I noticed my hands sweating, and my back. What was the name of the couple I was supposed to approach? If I concentrated on them, perhaps I'd be able to keep my nausea at bay. Valero, that was the name, but where were they? My discomfort grew, and my inexhaustible hostess wouldn't stop talking.

"And these are kibbeh, made with lamb. Go ahead, try it, my dear, they're fresh from my own kitchen."

I had no choice but to give in. I took one of the croquette-shaped morsels and, with extreme caution—as if I were about to ingest a vial of cyanide instead of a mixture of bulgur, ground meat, and spices—I held it to my mouth. I took a small bite and chewed as well as I could. Around me, American music was still playing as if coming from a parallel universe, and conversation was still floating in the air. From one of the huddles of people there came a sudden eruption of laughter.

I was incapable of swallowing, despite my best efforts. And worse still, my stomach not only refused to allow entry to the tiny piece of food, it was now threatening to throw up everything it already had inside. In this desperate state, I tried to whisper something but, judging by Katy's reaction, the sounds never took shape.

"I beg your pardon?"

I tried again.

"I don't know what you're saying, dear. Are you all right? You're very pale . . ."

No, I wasn't all right. I needed to get out of there immediately.

"Perhaps you'd like to go to the bathroom, my dear? It's at the end of that corridor—"

She didn't manage to finish the sentence. Leaving the rest of the kibbeh in her hand, I headed hastily in the direction she'd indicated.

Until, abruptly, something blocked my path. A body. A large body of a man who was at that moment breaking away from a group in search of another drink, or maybe he was leaving the party already, or simply escaping a conversation that didn't interest him.

A memory flickered in my mind. This man, this shoulder. This very man, his shoulder, and I had already seen one another in a similar moment. In Barclays Bank, I remembered in a flash. He had been going in, I had been coming out, we'd bumped into each other.

"We seem destined to collide. Please forgive my clumsiness. Let me introduce myself. I'm Nicholas Soutter, from—"

By the time he'd finished uttering the three letters in "PBS," I'd lost control, and my vomit had spattered the bottom of his trousers and shoes.

6

We were taken aback by the discovery that I was pregnant. It wasn't part of our plans, wasn't expected. A child on the way, good God. I wasn't a girl anymore—I was over thirty. At my age many women had already made a whole family. My apprehension was huge: so far from home, in a turbulent Palestine, with Marcus forever active and often absent.

What's more, bitter memories of another time scratched at my soul: Tangier, the Hotel Continental, my former lover Ramiro fleeing, my confusion when I read the letter that finally opened my eyes to his true interests and feelings. The bus to Tétouan, my unstoppable hemorrhage, Commissioner Vázquez, and the unjustified suspicion that fell upon me. Almost a decade had passed since that summer of 1936, I had long since ceased to be the naive young woman I once was, and Marcus was nothing like Ramiro Arribas. The father of the child that was beginning to grow inside me was an honest man—not a fraud. Even so, I couldn't help but feel the heartbreak of those terrible days again. The uncertainty. The dejection.

Marcus, as ever, reacted ably. At once, his pragmatic mind laid out the situation rationally so that he was able to see it from the most convenient angle.

"We were going to embark on this adventure at some point. And there's an excellent British hospital in Jerusalem," he assured me. "There's no risk to your health, the American Colony's food is completely safe, and Bertha Vester is willing to put us up until the end of time . . ."

I stopped him with my fingers on his lips. There was one other certainty that I needed.

"But we'll go before it's born, won't we?"

He pulled me to his chest, as if wanting to pass on to me some of the strength he exuded, and which had been so scarce in me of late.

"I don't know, Sira. I don't know yet."

The sickness I felt at the beginning, the nausea that had made me vomit on Katy Antonius's marble floor and on a stranger's feet, gradually disappeared as December progressed. Hanukkah, the Festival of Lights, was being celebrated in Jewish households, with a candle lit each day on the hanukkiah, the nine-branched candelabrum. Meanwhile, preparations for Christmas were underway in Christian homes. Everyone was exchanging heartfelt greetings in the hope that the season and the coming year would bring the peace that the country so badly needed.

Bertha Vester arranged for a large tree to be set up in the American Colony's main reception room and invited me to take part in decorating it, as if this were something to be excited about. Back when I was growing up in Madrid on Calle de la Redondilla, all we had done was set out an incredibly humble earthenware Nativity scene above the stove; during my years in Tétouan, I had never been in the mood for festive embellishments; and back in the Spanish capital as an adult, in my apartment on Calle de Núñez de Balboa, I had been forced to put up a few decorations each year to please my customers. But I had never had a tree. For me—a humble girl from traditional Madrid, a young seamstress in Africa, and a sham dressmaker from a good neighborhood—a pine full of sparkles made little sense. Still, I agreed to do it out of courtesy.

Two days later, the invitation came to bake Christmas pastries. I agreed again, with no interest or desire to do it. The third summons was to sing carols. That was where I dug my heels in. I didn't miss the daily grind of the workshop or my clandestine work, but I did miss being active, feeling useful in some way. Hanging up paper chains and colored baubles, making gingerbread cookies, and singing Christmas songs were far from what I wanted to be doing in this new phase of my life.

"I understand, dear," said Bertha Vester when I turned down her offer with vague excuses. "In your state, one needs rest. All the same, if you feel better and decide to join us, we'll be leaving at half past three."

No, it wasn't rest I needed. Pregnancy wasn't debilitating me—I had zest; I felt strong. The problem was something else, something I struggled to find the words to describe. It was a sort of melancholy, a permanent feeling of restlessness. Or maybe it was just my jumbled hormones.

I ate in my room—Marcus rarely came back for lunch. At two o'clock or so I lay on the bed and tried to sleep, but I was kept awake by a dog barking in the backyards, or voices from the courtyard, or maybe the faucet dripping in the bathroom. Or perhaps I simply wasn't tired. I looked at the time: twenty minutes till three. I decided to read. Lately I had been braving novels in English that weren't too complex. But the lines in Daphne du Maurier's *Hungry Hill* danced in front of my eyes. I couldn't concentrate. I checked the time again: five minutes past three. I rested my hands on my belly, searching for a pulsing or a movement, though I knew full well I wouldn't feel anything. It wasn't yet possible to physically perceive the tiny baby. What name would we give it? Would it have Marcus's nose, my dark eyes, his knobby knees, my narrow feet, his hair color? His solidity? My fears? There were no answers to my questions, and I turned on my side and fixed my eyes on the alarm clock again. Ten minutes to go before it was half past three.

I was still pulling on my gloves when I reached the lobby just as Bertha Vester was about to leave, accompanied by two other guests, Americans of mature years like her.

"I'm so glad you decided to join us, dear. It'll be a very special concert. You won't regret it, you'll see."

I didn't even know exactly where we were going, and I merely admired the scenery as we drove south from Sheikh Jarrah. As we traveled along the route, enveloped in unpleasant weather, I saw children playing on the roadside, Arab women with bundles of firewood on their backs, a goatherd with his kaffiyeh on his head, determined to bring his starving herd into line. We passed the Damascus Gate before heading along the beautiful Street of the Prophets, lined with consulates, foreign schools, small hospitals, and splendid villas. We turned off onto a street I read was QUEEN MELISENDE'S WAY. Finally we stopped in front of a large building of the same stone and similar appearance to everything the British erected. High up, the everlasting Union Jack was flapping furiously in the wind.

We'd reached Broadcasting House, and other cars were arriving or had parked moments before. Dozens of children, all with meticulous side parts in their hair, climbed out of the cars along with their mothers. The youngsters dashed up the broad staircase. The ladies, wearing felt hats and fur stoles around their necks, with elegant purses in their hands, stopped to greet one another—polite and agreeable. Most were Marcus's compatriots, the families of high-ranking officers and prominent officials. Boys from Saint George's School, girls from the English Girls' College, and the most international wives in all Jerusalem, as Marcus often joked—families that had a nanny from southern England, a Russian maid, a Cypriot gardener, a Berber cook, and an Armenian driver in their service. *Perhaps I should try to be more like them,* I thought as I observed the women: adapting to their husbands' comings and goings, fully aware of their own supporting role, with a perfect knowledge of the accompanying etiquette, protocol, promotion ladders, and appointments, experts in charity work and in the art of hosting a dinner.

For good or bad, however, among all these impeccable spouses, I was an odd entity. I was married to one of their own group, but I neither spoke nor dressed nor ate nor moved as they did. I did not understand their codes, know the ins and outs of the colonial administration, or grasp the most routine housekeeping norms. And so I waited for these ladies to take the front rows of the auditorium, prepared to listen to their children's hymns. Bertha Vester gestured at me to sit beside her, but I signaled my thanks and pointed at the exit. I wanted to stay at the back, by myself, in case I needed to make a quick escape. Or so I led her to believe—a lie like any other.

The curtain was raised to reveal a piano to one side of the stage, a plump, blond-haired conductress with baton in hand, and a choir of forty or fifty children under the age of ten. After that age, children were usually sent to England to continue their education at boarding school. In the darkness of the room, as the first notes of "Silent Night" were played, I again rested my hand on my belly. Would I be able to separate myself from my child when it reached elbow height, like these refined English ladies did? Or would I become a loud, opinionated, possessive mother like the women of my country and status?

My solitude at the back didn't last long. One by one, or two by two, latecomers crept into the hall, quietly taking up seats here and there. Just two or three were still free when someone sat down to my right. The choir finished "O Come, All Ye Faithful," and the entire auditorium broke into applause.

"I trust you're recovered now."

I turned at once and saw a man beside me. Despite the dim half-light, I recognized him right away. It was the gentleman whose feet I'd spattered with vomit. Between the morning when we almost ran into each other in Barclays Bank and the disastrous incident at the party, I'd seen him in the distance at a few events, but we'd never been introduced.

I tried to smile by way of a greeting but only managed a tense grimace. Flashes of that uncomfortable scene returned to my mind, and I remembered him saying his name at the critical moment, but I couldn't recall it now. While Katy Antonius and some other guests had virtually carried me to the bathroom and the servants had swiftly bent down to clean up my mess, he must have gotten out of the way. Then Marcus had been informed, and we'd left immediately. The next day, or the one after, or at some indeterminate moment, it had occurred to me that I should perhaps find out who the man was, locate him, offer him my apologies. But I never did. And now I had him there again, right next to me, almost brushing against my arm with his arm, as the audience enthusiastically accepted the choir conductor's invitation to all sing another carol together.

"Why won't you sing? You're not moved by all the Christmas warmth?" he whispered.

I detected a hint of irony in his voice, but preferred to be discreet.

"I don't know the words," I said simply. "I'm not British."

"I can't stand it," he confessed, unabashed. "I just came for a few minutes to keep up appearances." A pair of heads whose faces wore bad-tempered expressions turned slightly in the row in front, and I fought back laughter. He lowered his voice to an obliging volume. "May I offer you a cup of tea? That way you can apologize for ruining my best shoes."

His name, the one I couldn't remember, was Nicholas Soutter. Or Nick, as some colleagues of his called him when they said hello. He worked in that very building we were in, for the Palestine Broadcasting Service—the PBS, as it was known—the British Mandate's official broadcaster. He informed me of all this himself while we walked the length of a couple of corridors. He stepped aside at the entrance to a spacious office with two large windows and a desk stacked with papers and files. At the other end of the room, under a sizable framed world map, there was a small sofa, a coffee table, and two armchairs. He invited me to make myself comfortable. A young secretary in a pleated skirt appeared. He asked her to make us some tea, and she nodded before making herself scarce.

"I'm glad we share a common indifference toward Christmas carols," he said as he sat down opposite me.

I stretched my lips faintly, a neutral expression that could've meant anything. Even I didn't know for what absurd reason I'd decided to leave the children's concert to blindly follow a stranger to his office.

He leaned forward to stub out his cigarette, pressing it hard against the bottom of the ashtray as I watched him. Rather less frosty than the senior officials of the Mandatory Administration, infinitely less stiff than the military officers. More in the mold of the correspondents who argued at the top of their voices as they consumed entire cases of Cyprus brandy in the basement of the Jasmine House Hotel. But somehow unlike them, too.

"You'll have to forgive me putting my oar in—I simply had to find out who the beautiful woman I keep bumping into everywhere was. Once I knew, a number of times I was on the verge of phoning you at the American Colony or trying to reach you via your husband."

I remained imperturbable. My years collaborating with the British had taught me to behave like them when I was unexpectedly embroiled in a situation the nature of which I had little control over. Motionless, impassive, waiting.

"Yes, we know each other," he went on. "Mark Bonnard and I have met a few times and have some mutual friends scattered around the world." He paused, as if suddenly remembering some specific thing, an anecdote, a scene, or a particular moment. "A good chap, your husband," he concluded, holding out his cigarette case.

I declined. He lit another cigarette and inhaled deeply. His words came from his mouth enveloped in smoke.

"Genuinely, I'm glad we finally meet. Know that you'll always be welcome here at the PBS. I don't know if you've ever heard of us. We transmit on medium wave."

"I don't listen to the radio much," I confessed. Though, in fact, I was lying. Since I'd arrived in this place, the truth was I hadn't listened to it even once.

"Here at the Palestine Broadcasting Service, we cater to the various communities with programs in English, Arabic, and Hebrew. We're part of the BBC family, an entirely public broadcaster. No advertisements or commercial interests. The station was founded in 1936 with the intention of not covering politics, but rather devoting ourselves to educating and uplifting the population, and to promoting culture and understanding. Those are ultimately the orders from London—to modernize, through our programs, the uneducated, rural Arab population, to provide the urban, professional Jews with cultural material they find stimulating, and to ensure that the British don't die of boredom."

Out of sheer habit after so many years in action, I continued to study him while I listened. He must have been about Marcus's age, and he was roughly the same height. The likeness ended there. Marcus was slender, wiry, and flexible, brown-haired and of a fair complexion. His character was measured and his features well proportioned. Whereas Nick Soutter was stout and dark haired, with round features and prominent eyebrows, more spontaneous, more expansive, almost explosive.

"That's the mission," he went on. "Which is why we have independent programs, and a lot of both Arab and Jewish staff. Between you and me, I very much doubt that this paternalistic attitude, as well intentioned as it is, and such categorically separate programming can somehow have a positive influence on coexistence. If anything, the reverse is likely to be true. If you ask me, this approach only magnifies the differences, but that's another story I won't bore you with."

No, it didn't bore me. Quite the contrary.

"And you never stray from local matters?" I asked. "The daily life, the events inside this bubble?"

"We do, it goes without saying. In fact, as programmer, it's what I try to do—open up new horizons, broaden our scope. Which is why I'm always looking for new contributors to talk about matters of interest besides our bitter present."

"What kind of matters?"

"You tell me. Anything that inspires our listeners. Just now we had a doctor talking about penicillin. A few weeks ago, it was a classical historian who was visiting the area, and last month the chef from the King David was telling us about French cuisine . . ."

"Anything on Spain?"

He took a moment, looking serious this time. "What're you saying?"

My expression was apparently so eloquent that it made him burst out laughing. From the back of his throat.

"Are you proposing that you work with us, Mrs. Bonnard?"

"It just occurred to me. Forgive my boldness."

"No, no, not at all . . ."

"Perhaps it's a bit brazen of me, but I suddenly thought it might be interesting to your listeners to learn something about my country."

We began to hear voices in the corridor. It sounded as if the repertoire of carols had reached its end and the audience was flooding out. I stood, and he quickly did the same.

"I won't keep you any longer. They must be looking for me," I said, holding out my hand. "Think about it in your own time, no strings attached. I'll understand if my offer seems out of place, but you know where to find me if it interests you."

I tried to make my handshake emphatic, as if I were brimming with self-confidence. After my feigned coolheadedness was over, however, I was bewildered by my own show of nerve.

7

Nick Soutter wasn't the dithering type. I found this out the next day when I received his call first thing in the morning. Though it was his job to work with words, he wasn't prone to wasting them, and with me he used only the number of words necessary, not one more. Not one fewer.

"I accept. I trust you. We'll start in January."

With this new commitment looming, Christmas of 1945 got underway. At the doors to the Church of the Nativity in Bethlehem, the Christmas Eve crowds clamored to be allowed in, but a tight cordon of British policemen with scowling faces denied them access. Only those people with official passes were given entry. We, of course, were among the lucky ones. We struggled through the crowd, me with a scarf up to my nose, fiercely gripping Marcus's arm while protecting my belly; him with a strained look on his face due to the tense and noisy atmosphere. *Gloria in excelsis Deo, et in terra pax.*

A seething mass of Christians remained outside. Many were protesting, pushing, demanding at the top of their voices the access that was being denied to them. Others were spilling into the nearby streets, yelling, singing, rejoicing. Both reactions were in marked contrast to the devotion and spirituality I had expected to find in that setting. In their traditional dress, bearing torches, were Copts arrived from Egypt, Maronites from Lebanon, Anatolians from Asia Minor, Syrians, Ethiopians, Armenians, and Palestinians from all over the country. Plus thousands of Westerners who formed a caravan of vehicles that stretched for miles and did not budge an inch. A biting wind was blowing. Stands and food stalls were set up, lighted with kerosene lamps. The smell and smoke from barbecued kebabs wafted in the air.

Inside the church, in the somber light from a cluster of hanging lamps, amid the pomp and ceremony of the religious service, the toing and froing of the Latin Patriarch, the priests' colorful chasubles, the military stripes, corduroy suits, uniforms, and submachine guns, there was barely room for anyone else. Once again, the diplomatic corps, senior officials, army officers, and prominent foreigners had taken precedence over the locals. A few years before, I was told, there'd been free access—riotous, popular, and chaotic. Not anymore. Due to the growing tension, every possible precaution was being taken.

I had never been a practicing Christian beyond attending the Sunday masses of my childhood at the Church of San Andrés in my neighborhood. As life had unfolded, the little belief I once possessed had been depleted, until I was left clinging solely to the earthly world. Even so, that night, amid the psalms, the sound of the organ, and a dizzying aroma of incense—in this city where, they say, a woman gave birth almost two thousand years ago to a boy they wrapped in rags—I tried hard to find a glimmer of faith deep inside me with which to pray for us all. For those who sooner or later would leave this place, for those who would stay forever in a turbulent Palestine. For my parents and friends, wherever they were, for my ruined and starving country, for my husband's exhausted England. For Marcus, for me, for our child.

New Year's Eve, in contrast, was a night of opulence. The King David Hotel, in whose wings Marcus and his fellow countrymen—civilian and military—had their headquarters, welcomed several hundred privileged individuals with bottles of Laurent-Perrier, oysters and other delicacies, streamers, confetti, and orchestral music. Entry, once again, was closely supervised. Inside, however, everyone seemed to forget for a few hours about the violence, the terror, and the desperate attempts to find a rational compromise between three groups of humans that seemed condemned to eternal discord. As if we'd been transported momentarily to a parallel universe, Marcus and I danced to the rhythm of swing and toasted a happy 1946. Carefree for one night, a little tipsy perhaps after a few glasses of champagne, neither the hardened operative nor the beautiful dressmaker could imagine how terribly unhappy the coming year would end up being.

On the morning of January 6, I found a package in our room, by the door. Marcus, as usual, had gone out early. He never misplaced anything; in that aspect of life, as in almost everything, he was extremely precise and methodical. Never a shirt unhung, nor a book open, nor an envelope left visible. Never even a solitary sock lost under the bed. Nothing. Even so, every day, I perceived traces of him all around: his body's warmth lingering between the sheets, drops of water from his shower on the curtain, his damp shaving brush on the bathroom shelf. That day, without warning, he'd also left a sizable package with a brief handwritten note on top. *A gift from the Wise Men,* it said. With a sudden welling of nostalgia, I remembered the Three Kings Day mornings of my childhood, the modest gifts I'd found by the fireplace: a pack of sugared almonds, two pairs of socks, a ragdoll my mother had stitched together from trims pilfered from her work. Feeling as excited as if I were a seven-year-old again, I pulled away the boards, straw, and cardboard that the gift was packed in. Inside, I found a shortwave radio set.

"Your husband isn't at the office today, Mrs. Bonnard," the friendly voice of Esther Klausner, his secretary, told me when I called.

Phoning Marcus at his office at the King David had been my first reaction, to thank him, to tell him how much the gift meant to me. I knew that it was his way of encouraging me about the radio pieces on Spain. He was pleased to see me taking on a new project for myself, something that would give my days substance, so I wouldn't just be a silent wife in the shadows.

His absence from the secretariat that day didn't surprise me, as it wasn't unusual not to find him there. Sometimes he worked on-site, but very often he was out on his own, meeting people, moving in different circles, observing everything, in motion.

And so I asked the operator to put me through to the PBS.

"Mr. Soutter's in the control room at present," I heard from the other end of the line. "If you wouldn't mind leaving me your details, he'll return your call shortly."

I gave my name to the female voice, which I supposed belonged to another young, competent Jewish secretary, one of the many who worked in a multitude of roles within the mandate's machinery. Half an hour later, the telephone rang. It took us just a few seconds to agree to a meeting.

Nicholas Soutter was waiting for me in Café Atara at eleven. He was sitting at one of the windows reading the *Palestine Post*. On the table in front of him was an ashtray with a couple of cigarette ends, a black coffee with a spiral of lemon peel floating in it, and an open notebook, an uncapped pen lying across his dense lines of notes. It was a busy time of day, with a lot of men and quite a few women there, just like in all the cafés nearby—the Vienna, the Europe, Kapulsky's, the Alaska—all owned by Jewish settlers from central Europe and similar in style to the coffee houses the proprietors had left behind in their countries of origin once they were no longer able to bear being marginalized and insulted, or when they'd had to narrowly escape the arrests and persecution in the lead-up to the war. There were also some Arab cafés not far away, the main difference being that women didn't go in those.

He stood when he saw me, casually folding the newspaper. I pulled out the chair so that I could sit, and he signaled to a waiter. In the few minutes it took for them to serve us, while we talked he waved to three or four people and exchanged words with three or four others.

"This place is like my second office. Whenever I can, I slip away from Broadcasting House and set up shop here. I work, organize, meet whoever I need to meet, and from time to time, if it's a quiet day, I chat with the waiters. That fellow, he's a musician," he said, gesturing at a slim man balancing a tray of drinks. "Before the war, he played the flute in the Berlin Philharmonic. And this one approaching is a Polish philosopher who's written several books. The chap behind the counter owned a lamp factory in Prague with more than fifty workers."

I already knew that this was the unfortunate situation of many of the Jews who had arrived in recent times. Educated, highly trained, capable people had been forced to leave their homes behind and were now surviving however they could, doing whatever jobs they could find.

"It's also a way to take the pulse of the city and its people. You can't imagine what's bubbling up under this layer of apparent normality."

I could imagine it perfectly. Much of the shadowy side of my work in recent years had taken place in tearooms, restaurants, and hotel foyers, passing on information, reporting details with complete precision and efficiency. So it would've come as no surprise to me to learn that in full daylight—among coffees, slices of cake, pastries, and cups of thick hot chocolate—all kinds of plots and conspiracies were the subjects of whispering. The only reply I gave, however, was a cynical expression of innocence. In this man's eyes, I was just an appendage to a fellow Englishman, a slightly exotic wife of leisure.

"Right, let's get down to business . . ."

Four fifteen-minute programs were what Nick Soutter was proposing in response to my offer. Four short pieces on Spain, prerecorded, to be aired on successive weeks. Art, geography, some history, cuisine, customs, traditions—whatever I wanted. Delivered in English, of course. In my own voice, complete with my strong accent, occasional mispronunciations, and any unexpected mistakes I made along the way.

"Don't worry if you slip up, it'll add authenticity. Exactly as you're talking to me now, it's delightful. It's only a shame they can't also see you."

The Sira of old wouldn't have been able to stop herself turning bright red. The Sira of now simply stirred her tea, containing a half smile: it had been a long time since a stranger flirted with me so brazenly. Or perhaps Nick had not even intended to flirt. I watched him again a moment later as he exchanged a shalom with a gray-suited man passing by.

In his unconventional way, Nicholas Soutter wasn't unattractive, with his strong neck and broad shoulders, his abundant brown hair, the first grays appearing at his temples. He was a long way from being a handsome man; he didn't have the well-proportioned, elegant features that Marcus had, let alone the seductive beauty of Ramiro Arribas. But in his round face, his sturdy chin, his prominent nose, his large teeth, and the thick brows over sharp eyes, there was a strange magnetism, something different.

"And current affairs?" I asked when he returned his attention to me, apologizing for the interruption to our conversation. "Should I touch on politics, or would you prefer me to skirt around it?"

His fingers drummed on the marble tabletop.

"There's nothing I'd like more than to delve deep, but I'm afraid we can't." He frowned at me. "What's your view on the situation in Spain, if you don't mind me asking?"

I didn't mind him asking. I was surprised at his directness, but it didn't bother me in the least.

"It saddens me deeply" was my only reply. I didn't see the need to say any more.

"I can imagine. You and everyone else, though some are trying not to broach the subject."

The finger-drumming became a rhythmic hammering with his left fist. As if the thought he was forming was making him edgy.

"Our war was bloody, too," I added. "And we're still suffering the consequences."

"I'm sure," replied Nick. "Did you live through it there, in Madrid?"

"No, I was in Morocco at the time. But I heard what it was like from my mother, from friends, people who did suffer it at close quarters. I returned at the end of the war, so I witnessed the aftermath."

"There's also your relationship with your husband," he said, probing further. "I imagine that because of it, you're also aware of the Franco regime's attitude toward Britain and Germany during the world war?"

My response was clear.

"I'm aware through my relationship with him, and from my own experience."

He looked at me again with a flash of curiosity, but neither did I add more, nor did he keep asking.

"Though we're operationally independent when it comes to programming, at the PBS we're obliged to abide by certain criteria set by official sources, and our orders, ultimately, are not to take aim at Franco's Spain."

Three English ladies passed us on their way to their table, wrapped in furs and woolen overcoats—wives of colonial servants of the empire. They greeted both of us, and we replied in kind. I knew them from other gatherings—an event at Government House, some charity tea, perhaps a concert—but I couldn't remember their names. Nicholas Soutter didn't pay much attention to them. They may have been surprised to see us together. No doubt we'd given them a topic of conversation to add spice to their morning get-together.

"They've started to get very twitchy in London about the rise of communism after the war," my companion continued. "So provided your Generalísimo keeps the communists in check, the British will let him be."

He said "Generalísimo" in Spanish with such awful pronunciation it almost made me laugh, though the subject was not funny in the least.

"Anyway, I don't want to keep you," he said. "Let's get things in order . . ."

We finalized the details, stood, and headed to the exit. I noticed he didn't stop to pay for our drinks and guessed he was running a tab.

"Call me if you have any questions," he said, holding out his hand. His grip was firm, confident once more.

We were on the pavement of Ben Yahuda Street now, and Mustafa was waiting for me with Bertha Vester's car.

"I will, Mr. Soutter."

"Please, call me Nick."

I made a face that could equally have meant "I will" or "I won't." As the car started, I watched him through the window's glass. He was making his way through the crowds: men wearing kippahs or felt hats, women with baby carriages, old people walking, news vendors. He disappeared from view on his way toward Zion Square, walking with a spring in his step and another cigarette in his mouth.

8

From the start, I knew I couldn't just sit down in front of a microphone with a jumble of ideas floating around in my head, and it was essential that I prepare in advance. The bulk of my writing experience had been noting down the information I heard come from the mouths of my German customers at my dressmaker's studio and subsequently transcribing the reports and secret messages for the British. I'd never worked with my own ideas or concepts before, only with my hands, eyes, and fingers. Surprisingly, however, my dressmaking skills showed me the way. When it came to creating a new piece—whether it was a sophisticated evening dress, a cocktail dress, or a simple muslin blouse—there were fundamental steps I needed to bear in mind. I needed to have a clear vision before I began my work; I had to choose the right fabric, take accurate measurements, cut the material with total precision, sew with skill, and check the garment for mistakes. The approach I would take now was similar, for all intents and purposes. Only this time I would work with words instead of fabric, and instead of customers, I'd have listeners.

From a stationer's on Mamilla Road, I bought three notebooks, a box of pencils, and a modern pen the shopkeeper called a Biro, which would allow me to write without an inkwell. For several mornings in a row, I went with my stock of equipment to the impressive YMCA center opposite the King David. It was said that the center had been built by the same architect who designed New York's Empire State Building and that a generous donation of a million dollars had been used to construct it stone by stone, with its high arches and domes, magnificent tower, modern facilities, and library. It was the latter that interested me. From among the thousands of volumes on the shelves, my attention fell solely on the *Encyclopaedia Britannica*. With my scant education, coming from a home that not a single book had ever entered, I now threw myself into the task of reading, rereading, translating, and checking, copying, crossing out, and making lists—sometimes tearing pages from my notebooks and scrunching them into compact balls. I kept going like this until I had a mass of information on my country that seemed coherent, moving from geography to gastronomy, the seas that washed against our shores, the music we played, and the monarchs who'd reigned over us with varying degrees of glory.

I set up a second camp on a little olive-wood desk in the reading room at the American Colony, where I was surrounded by tapestries, rugs, and watercolors. Day after day, I devoted my time to organizing everything I'd gathered at the YMCA, adding it to my own knowledge, and giving the resulting material my own personal nonencyclopedic tone. I called Nick Soutter almost every day, and when I couldn't reach him, he would, sooner or later, always return my call. His ideas were clear, his guidance sound, and all my doubts and insecurities were instantly resolved. Sometimes he even responded with a loud burst of laughter. At the end of every conversation, I promised not to bother him again the next day.

"Don't even think about it!" he would say. By then we'd given up on ceremony. "Call me as often as you like, Sira. Listening to you is a joy in these times of dismay."

In the afternoons, I stayed in to listen to the PBS programs in English, and sometimes to listen to the BBC, absorbing methods and styles—the manner in which the presenters modulated their voices, their pauses, the way they alternated slower sequences with livelier ones.

At the end of the day, Marcus became my audience. We went out less at night now. January was a bleak month, the tension continued on the streets, and everyone seemed to have become more reclusive, as if anticipating something. And so, in our rooms, I rehearsed word order, pronunciation, rhythm, and cadence. My English had improved markedly in the months we'd been in Jerusalem—how could it not when I had no one to speak my own language with? Nonetheless, I still slipped on the vowels, tripped over the consonants, and put my foot in the holes of the vocabulary at times. Thank goodness my patient husband volunteered to listen and correct me, like a dedicated teacher with a student who'd been skipping classes for seven years. He laughed when I pretended to sit in front of a microphone, using a hairbrush in place of the device. "Quite the opposite, Sira," he said when I asked him if he was fed up with playing Pygmalion. "Hearing you is like a balm for the spirit in these uncertain days."

Both Nick and Marcus had good reason to feel discouraged by the general atmosphere at that time. The year had begun with little prospect of change, and beyond the warmth of the American Colony and of our rooms, and outside the peace of the YMCA library and other private or exclusive locations, apprehension could be felt everywhere. The Jewish extremist groups continued their bloody activities. Sometimes it was the Irgun that was responsible, acting on the orders of Menachem Begin. On other occasions the attacks came from Lehi, the self-proclaimed "Fighters for the Freedom of Israel," who in reference to their founder Avraham Stern were commonly known in English as the Stern Gang. Haganah were also active as the unofficial army of the Yishuv, as the Jewish population was known, backed by the Jewish Agency. Yet no matter who was perpetrating the atrocities, the harsh reality was that the groups were all united under the banner of the Jewish resistance movement, mobilized with a firm and specific commitment to attack the British, both personnel and infrastructure. Their shared goal was to establish the State of Israel as an independent nation. And Britain was in their way.

At any time of day or night, we might be startled by a burst of gunfire or a grenade going off. The attacks against official buildings were constant. Every few days there was news of more sabotage: another ambush, another offensive, or yet another munitions heist.

All the same, everyday life continued with apparent normality. People went to work, shops remained open, American films arrived at the cinemas, and cooking pots bubbled in kitchens. I finally agreed to meet Nick Soutter on January 18 to rehearse and finalize the details of my broadcast, and the recording itself would take place the next day. Alone in front of my wardrobe, as I was every morning, I unhooked a plain navy-blue two-piece suit. When I tried to do up the jacket, I noticed for the first time that my waist was different. It unsettled me to find my body changing, expanding, making space for the child that was growing inside.

A PBS car collected me at the American Colony and dropped me at Broadcasting House a few minutes before ten. I got out clutching my notes, trying to keep my nerves under control. In recent years, back when I was working for the SOE—the Special Operations Executive—in Madrid and in Lisbon, I had at times found myself in extremely delicate circumstances and had handled sensitive information in risky situations. Now that I faced a task that held no complexities, that was nothing more than a harmless adventure, I still couldn't help feeling anxiety writhing like a snake within me.

I reported to the reception desk, and Nick Soutter came out to receive me within two minutes, looking so vibrant and purposeful that my unease instantly vanished. Through corridors, galleries, offices, and studios, he showed me the various departments and sections of the PBS. Occasionally, he introduced me to the organization's supervisors. Azmi Nashashibi, controller of Arabic programs and a member of one of the most powerful families in Jerusalem, bowed before me like a

Casanova and kissed my hand. Edwin Samuel—director of the service, a British Jew, and a nobleman, and fully dedicated to all three of these facets of his life—offered me a formal greeting that sounded sincere. The producer Ruth Belkin, a Russian Jew who was short in stature and mature in age, promised me she would be at my rehearsal, as well as by my side in the studio the next day. I was pleased to see plenty of women at the desks, the first time I'd seen a workplace with so many female employees. They were a minority, and they may not have held the most senior roles, but I felt a stab of healthy envy whenever I saw them working—dynamic, involved, efficient.

"We have more than a hundred employees in total, including producers, scriptwriters, presenters, actors, administrative personnel, and technical staff, plus the orchestra and occasional contributors like you, of whom there are also many," Nick told me. "We air on medium wave in three languages, we have staff from three different religions—some reporting to the colonial administration and others not—and every day we receive hundreds of letters from listeners, offering praise, criticism, suggestions, or complaints. We're always walking a tightrope, trying both to avoid friction and to keep everyone happy."

Finally we reached the studio where my talks would be recorded. Ruth Belkin gave me instructions on different aspects of working with the microphone: breathing, posture, distance. She also taught me the signals they would give me using only their hands. Then I started the rehearsal. With Ruth, Nick, and an Arab technician in front of me, I began to read my text—written in a language that was foreign to me—about the "old bull's hide," which is what we on the other side of the Mediterranean called that country of mine. When I looked up from my papers fifteen minutes later, I was met by applause. It was just six hands clapping, but I welcomed the praise as if I'd been awarded a prestigious prize.

And so we agreed to make the final recording the next day.

"At ten, like today?" I asked.

"At ten," Nick confirmed.

Ruth checked the schedule and corrected her boss.

"No, we'd better start earlier, in case there're any setbacks."

"Nine?" I suggested.

Marcus and I ate breakfast together the next morning. Fried eggs, sausages, and plentiful coffee for him; just a cup of tea and three bites of toast for me. We walked out together to the two cars waiting for us at the door. I was profoundly glad for that moment—moved, almost. Had it occurred in some other part of the world, the scene would've been my ideal for married life: leaving the house and starting our day together, each with our own inspiring work ahead of us. Marcus kissed me briefly, wished me well, urged me to be careful. I was aware he would've preferred me to stay at the hotel writing postcards, reading novels, listening to the radio, or watching Bertha Vester's jasmines grow. Respectful of my decisions as always, however, he kept this wish to himself and whispered "good luck" in my ear.

The two vehicles started in unison. Marcus's went ahead; mine, a Morris from the PBS, followed close behind. We descended to the Damascus Gate, and there our paths separated. My driver took a right turn onto the Street of the Prophets, and Marcus's continued in the direction of Julian's Way. I checked my watch: twenty minutes past eight. It was cold, and a day of winter sun—bright and biting—lay ahead. Huddled in the back seat with my coat collar up, wearing my hat and leather gloves, I continued to go over my scripts: the contents, my pronunciation, those tricky Ss that slipped through my teeth. There was barely any traffic, either cars or pedestrians. We overtook a fire-wood-laden cart pulled by an old donkey. An even older Arab walked beside it, dragging his feet, wearing a ragged djellaba, his kaffiyeh on his head.

At the Italian Hospital we turned onto Saint Paul's Road before heading down Queen Melisende's Way. At the end stood Broadcasting House with its two stone stories, flowerless mimosa plants at the entrance, its grand staircase. Some lights were on inside, but it was still early and very quiet outside. The car moved slowly, and I still huddled in my coat and warm gloves, focused on my notes about my homeland.

It was then, as we arrived at the entrance, that something unexpected flashed across our path: a shadow, a rapid, slippery human presence. The driver slammed on the brakes and yelled. I was thrown forward and instantly wrapped my arms around my belly.

The explosion was brutal. The car rocked as if shaken by a furious giant, and my ears thundered. Dust and smoke enveloped us, bursts of submachine-gun fire, gruff yelling, and the sound of people running. The driver turned and grabbed me unceremoniously by the head, pulling off my hat and pushing me down as he roared something in Arabic and tried to reverse to get away.

I stayed curled up on the back seat, eyes open, dumbstruck, frozen, and at the same time strangely serene, my arms coiled around my torso and my legs folded on top of me. The gunshots, the raspy screaming in Hebrew, English, and Arabic, the running, the engines of other cars, tires skidding on the gravel, the sirens that sounded in the distance, growing ever louder—none of it, not any of it, mattered. My detachment was stubborn; my calm had one purpose. The only thing I cared about was that my arms stayed where they were, that they kept protecting my child, giving it warmth, courage.

9

In fits and starts, roaring and swearing, the driver finally managed to escape the infernal section of the road outside Broadcasting House and get back to Saint Paul's Road, where we met an accumulation of anxious onlookers, cars at a standstill, and police vans trying to force their way through, sirens blaring. With my throat dry, I asked him to take me to the King David, and as soon as he stopped in front of its facade, I rushed toward the revolving door. The car was covered in a thick layer of dust, my hair was disheveled, and I ripped my stocking as I got out. I was just about to go inside when Marcus dashed out from the other side of the door, panic written on his face. News of the incident had traveled fast, and he was on his way to find me. He held me against his body, asked me if I was all right two, three, four times. He stroked my back and neck as I sunk my face into his chest. He suggested going straight to the hospital so I could be examined.

"No, no, no . . . ," I repeated, clinging to him.

My voice sounded choked. He insisted, but I continued to refuse.

"Let's go in" was all I whispered. "I just need some quiet and a drink of water."

We sat in a corner of the lobby until the deafening sound in my ears began to fade. In some primal way, out of pure organic instinct, I knew my child was still clinging to my insides.

Midmorning, Marcus took me back to the American Colony. He also spoke to Nick Soutter and told him what had happened to me. Nick came to see me in the afternoon. He arrived with a bottle of burgundy, a tired face, and a crumpled suit. By way of a greeting, he stretched out his arms in a gesture of helplessness and muttered a rough "sorry." He was in no way to blame for the atrocity, but he felt in some way responsible because he'd arranged for me to come at the exact time of the attack. Feeling touched, I gave him a hug that he didn't turn down, but which he no doubt found odd.

We went to the reading room, to the corner where a few days before I'd sat to prepare my radio talks. I said nothing about those hours at the olive-wood desk. There was no need for him to know how much the little project had meant to me, how much I'd enjoyed feeling active again, even if it had been such a minor undertaking. What did all that matter now?

"It would've been more gentlemanly of me to bring flowers or chocolates, but I didn't have time," he said as he left the wine on one of the side tables. "This is all I could find. I pinched it from a colleague."

He settled himself opposite me in the leather armchair by the fireplace. The fire was lit, creating a cozy atmosphere there among the tapestries, thick curtains, and Persian rugs. Our states of mind, however, were bitterly cold.

"Your husband told me you're pregnant. I had no idea," he mumbled a little awkwardly. "I'm very glad that nothing . . . that you weren't—"

I cut him off with a gesture. I didn't know if Nick Soutter had children. I didn't know if he'd ever been through the ordeal of creating a life that ended up being cut short. And above all, I had no desire to talk about something so personal with him. I still bore the shock of my circumstance in my bones. Marcus's and my child was arriving at the worst time, in a land thrown into confusion, a harsh and alien place. I was nonetheless terrified of losing it.

One of the waiters, Assim, arrived at that moment with a tray and served tea in silence. When we resumed our conversation, Nick simply outlined the attack's impact on PBS staff and the building.

"The Stern Gang has claimed responsibility. Luckily, there were no victims."

Though the young man who'd planted the explosive device had managed to escape, a second suspect had been identified.

"But they achieved part of their objective by blowing up the electrical substation." Nick filled his mouth with air and blew out hard. "It's not the first time something like this has happened," he added. "Last year they attacked the broadcasting station in Ramallah, and before the war, three bombs went off one after another during Children's Hour. One destroyed the control room, another ruined a corridor, and the third killed the young woman who was presenting the show as well as a technician."

Without delving further into the painful details, Nick gradually steered the conversation toward less distressing subjects: the radio and his universe there, his previous posting in Cairo, his various comings and goings and changes in direction.

"I'm sure it's not easy being a foreigner tied to someone in the service of the empire," he said then.

"I never imagined this would be my fate."

Though I hadn't intended it, my tone sounded brutally honest— touched with bitterness, even. I was alluding to how hard it was for me to be powerless, with Marcus absent much of the time and my life spent within the four walls of a hotel, in this violent land.

"Not all wives are prepared to go with their husbands to these postings," he replied, his eyes fixed on the rug. "Mine, for instance, flatly refused."

He ran his hands through his hair and rubbed his scalp, strain showing on his face. His voice took on a deeper, rougher, drier tone.

"And now we're paying the price."

I tried to imagine what Nick Soutter's wife was like, what had become of her, where she was while he was keeping me company in Jerusalem. Just then Marcus came in.

They greeted each other warmly, united in adversity. We suggested to Nick that he stay to have dinner with us, but he turned down the invitation, mentioning his unpresentable state as well as some vague commitment. The excuses were unnecessary, in any event. His day had been dreadful, and no doubt he preferred to go his own way. To have a few drinks at Fink's Bar, in all likelihood. To forget the horror and warm the soul, without his wife, before returning to the solitude of his apartment.

To prevent further potential attacks, an Arab Legion detachment integrated into the British forces was posted on the Broadcasting House roof, all of the men armed to the teeth. The site's perimeter was secured with barbed wire, visits from external personnel were kept to a minimum, and staff were given special working hours and passes.

While the authorities took all these measures, and while the terrorists went after new targets, I spent three days shut away in the American Colony without even leaving our rooms, barely speaking to anyone, except to Marcus when he returned each night, and even then saying very little. For three whole days I lived in virtual isolation, my mind returning again and again to a thought that almost became an obsession: leaving. Quitting Palestine, looking after the life that was growing inside me, keeping it away from calamities and danger. The aggression between Arabs, Jews, and the British had nothing to do with me—I'd already suffered my own country's war, had already collaborated voluntarily with the British in theirs. I'd done my fair share. I was saddened by the situation in which stateless Jews, Arabs threatened by fierce Zionism, and my husband's fellow countrymen—equally despised by both groups—found themselves. But neither I nor my baby had any part in this cruel mess.

Hour after hour hidden away in our rooms—lying on the bed looking up at the ceiling, going out onto the balcony overlooking the courtyard, sitting in an armchair, staring into nothing, or looking in the mirror without seeing myself—I formulated, discarded, devised, and scrapped plans until I was left with just one: return to Tétouan, the white city where life was slow and easy, free of the demands of Madrid, of its sorrows and hardships. From what I understood, there wasn't much housing in Tétouan anymore. After our civil war ended in 1939, many people left mainland Spain for Spanish Morocco in search of a new future. But perhaps my mother could put me up for a while in the apartment she shared with her husband on Calle Mohamed Torres. Or maybe Candelaria had a free room in her guesthouse, the tiny box in the back where I'd stayed a decade before, the one with the leaks and the junk in it, the coarse woolen mattress, and the doorless wardrobe with wire hangers. It didn't matter where I went. I'd get back on my feet, somehow. That time in Tétouan had been even harder than this one, and I'd managed to get through it.

In my head, I went over the question of where I would stay and other unknowns again and again: what I'd do when my child was born, whether I'd open a new dressmaking studio or find a different job to support us. I didn't share any of these thoughts with Marcus, however. I took it for granted that he wouldn't come with me. I couldn't ask him to give in to my fears, and his priorities were clear. At that difficult time, his responsibilities were as unequivocal as his sense of duty and commitment to his country were fierce. No, I wasn't going to get him caught up in my anxieties; he had enough of his own problems to deal with related to his duties, whatever those were.

And so each evening when he returned, I tried to assume my usual identity: well dressed, made up, in love, charming, attentive. I didn't even ask him about his work, preferring to save him the trouble of having to lie to me. As if nothing had happened, we talked about trivial things, shared the dinners we were served: Ali the cook's stuffed pigeons, fish from the Sea of Galilee, even the bottle of burgundy that Nick Soutter had brought me. We enjoyed it all sitting opposite each other, chewing with apparent normality. At no time, however, did we hold hands on the tablecloth or rub ankles under the table. We were both aware that a kind of breach was opening up between us.

My lies and seclusion lasted three days. On the fourth, I swung into action as soon as Marcus was out of the door. I was already awake when he untangled himself from my body and got up, as ever, without the need for an alarm clock. But I stayed lying in bed on my side, feigning the sleep that had eluded me since before dawn. Keeping my eyes closed even though I was awake, I heard him move around with his usual stealth. The bedsprings, hinges, and door handles were barely audible; not even the soles of his shoes made a sound. Before leaving, he bent down and stroked my neck.

I shuddered inside, but kept up the pretense. It took everything I had to contain myself—I had to clench my fists, dig my nails into my palms, and clamp my teeth together to keep from throwing myself at him and begging him to give up his responsibilities, take my hand, and come with me to find a light-filled place in some other part of the world.

10

Before going out, I emptied one of our drawers and searched in the bottom. We kept money there, in an envelope inside a folder. There were pounds sterling, a few hundred. A wad of fifty-dollar bills. And two thousand of the new pesetas, the ones issued after the war. I didn't know how much I was going to need. I took all of it. Just in case.

I asked Mustafa, the hotel's driver, to take me into Jerusalem again, to the busy streets and crowds of people. On the way, apprehension gripped my insides. Behind every rise, in every van, I sensed a threat. In every young man we crossed paths with, I saw a terrorist. But nothing materialized between the American Colony and my destination.

A worker was setting up large notice boards with advertisements: the Thomas Cook & Son agency was opening for another day of business at its premises near the Jaffa Gate. Almost thirty years had passed since General Allenby captured Jerusalem on behalf of His Most Gracious Majesty, dismounting from his horse as a sign of respect and passing through the magnificent entrance to the walled city on foot to mark the beginning of the mandate. At the time, all of Jerusalem had welcomed the arrival of the British in Palestine: Arabs because they were at last free from Turkish rule and saw the way cleared for independence, and Jews because they hoped they would finally be able to establish their homeland. Now both groups longed for the British to go back where they'd come from so they could shape the country's future themselves. Even if getting what they wanted meant a bloody war.

That winter morning, however, in the area around that entrance to the Old City, only ordinary people could be seen. Peasant farmers setting up their stalls of fruit, vegetables, live chickens, and eggs; an old man, stooped over, sweeping at the door to his shop; hawkers selling religious souvenirs; kerosene deliverymen; children from three different faiths on their way to school.

There were already three early birds ahead of me at the travel agency: a man in a Borsalino hat and a couple of young Americans carrying equipment in cases and canvas bags. I supposed they were archaeologists, geologists, topographers, or specimens of some other rare species. Behind the counter, under a sign that read WORLD TICKET OFFICE, two agents attended to them while I sat and waited on one of the side benches. With my handbag on my knees, hands on top of it protecting the money, I spent the time examining the walls, which were covered in posters and maps. Advertisements for excursions to Galilee, the River Jordan, Mount Sinai, the Judean Desert. Interpreters and guides, mule drivers, and tents and bicycles for hire.

Others arrived at the shop: a plump Arab in a red fez and western suit, a pair of Benedictine nuns, a fellow who just studied the posters through the thick lenses of his glasses. After a few minutes, a lone woman who seemed in a hurry came in. When she saw the crowd of customers, her face conveyed her annoyance.

I imagined she was more or less my age, and English, like so many people in Jerusalem then were. Judging from her appearance, however, she didn't seem like the wife of a military officer or a secretariat official; those women didn't tend to wear morning outfits that consisted of a masculine jacket, flannel trousers, and sturdy shoes. The woman was attractive in her own way. She sat beside me and mumbled a dry "good morning" before taking from her handbag a small notebook, held closed with an elastic band that also gripped a pencil. She crossed her legs and began to write, resting the notebook on her left thigh. Without altering my posture, I looked at her out of the corner of my eye.

She was sharp nosed and fair haired, with curly locks gathered at her neck in a loose bun. A ringlet fell over her face, and she tucked it nonchalantly behind her ear. I tried to decipher what she was writing, but it was impossible: her pointy letters formed sort of half words. She'd filled half a page when she looked up. The attendants were still with the first customers; no progress had been made. Irritated, she spun the pencil between her fingers for a moment, then tried to carry on with her notes, but her annoyance made her jab it into the paper. So ferociously that she broke the point.

She cursed through her teeth and began to rummage through her bags in search of something with which to continue writing but found nothing. For no reason whatsoever, almost unconsciously, I opened my bag, dodged the envelope of money, and felt in the bottom. There I found the Biro: the modern cylinder with its own ink reservoir that had been sold to me at the stationer's on Mamilla Road, back when my naive broadcasting aspirations were still intact.

I took it out and offered it to her. She turned her head and looked at me, without yet taking the instrument.

"You're not English, are you . . ."

"No, but my husband is."

"Oh," she replied. Then she did take the pen, after which she muttered a terse "thank you" and carried on writing. Five or six lines later, she stopped and looked at me again. "Where from?" She sounded surly, almost demanding.

"Madrid, Spain," I said.

"Oh," she murmured again. This time, her comment betrayed a trace of surprise. "How long have you been in Palestine?"

I answered without hesitation. I'd been counting the days.

"Almost eight months."

"And do you have any idea how things are going there?"

A few days before, we'd received the weekly delivery of Spanish newspapers we'd ordered before leaving, which arrived through a friend of Marcus's at the embassy. So I was more or less up to date with what was happening in my country, which was, in all honesty, not much.

I kept to myself those trivialities that she wouldn't understand: the bullfighter Manolete's triumphs, the success of the animated film *Garbancito de La Mancha*, the popularity of the song "Mi vaca lechera." The recital by political prisoners at the Carabanchel Prison of Juanito Valderrama's coplas. Neither did I mention that the privileged members of Madrid's high society had lunched at the exclusive and recently opened Jockey restaurant, while most of the population remained subject to the rationing of basic goods such as legumes, sugar, and oil. Or that, thanks to the newly available disinfectant DDT, it seemed that bedbugs and fleas were gradually being reduced.

I summarized the news of moderate interest in a few brief sentences.

"All foreign ambassadors have left."

"And who says so?" she asked.

"*ABC, Ya, La Vanguardia . . .*"

"All press close to the Franco regime, I assume."

"Do we have any other?"

She concurred with her chin, appearing serious, without joining in my sarcasm. The man in the hat finished his paperwork at the counter and an employee with a bushy mustache raised his hand to invite me to approach. I stood, though I would've preferred not to do so. I didn't like the idea of this inquisitive stranger being at my back, listening, perhaps. I didn't know who she was. She could've been a lay missionary, the wife of an employee of a foreign company, or simply a passing tourist, and I would probably never see her again. Still. What I'd come to do at the travel agency was a private matter. I was less than keen on my business reaching her ears.

I made my inquiry, trying to speak no more loudly than necessary.

"Travel to Spain?" the agent repeated with surprise in his tone. "To Spain? Europe?"

That was exactly what I wanted. Options for reaching Spain. I didn't care what they were. Once it was clear in my mind how I'd get there, I would figure out how to make my way to Tétouan on my own.

The agent frowned and scratched the back of his neck, thinking. Clearly my destination wasn't among the most popular. He consulted a map.

"Would Gibraltar do?"

I nodded. Gibraltar would do perfectly. My mind cast back to the day of our wedding: the austerity of the ceremony, the fierce east wind blowing through the strait, our almost nonexistent honeymoon at the Rock Hotel, so short lived it lasted just an evening, a night, and the next morning. While the agent ran his fingernail over a list of companies and destinations, something stirred inside me. My marriage to Marcus had begun in Gibraltar, and perhaps it would also end there. I had no idea how he would take my departure, whether he'd be understanding or consider it a disloyal and treacherous desertion.

The mustachioed man checked a second guide, then a third.

"Jerusalem to Cairo by train or perhaps by air, then Cairo to Alexandria to Famagusta, Cyprus, and on to Valletta, Malta, and lastly, by sea to Gibraltar. That's your best option. Next departure, March 5. Sixty-five pounds sterling. Would you like me to book the journey now, or would you prefer me to note it down for you?"

I quickly did the sums. The travel would take only a few days. And I had the money with me. The man stood motionless looking at me, waiting for an answer. I turned my head: more customers had come into the shop. I also saw that the anonymous woman with the pointless pencil was now being seen to by the other attendant.

"Madam?"

I couldn't do it. My resolve, or my courage, failed me. I looked at him without answering. I noticed he had some gray hairs in his mustache.

"Best I write it down, so you can think about it?"

When he was done, I just folded up the piece of paper, muttered a weak "thank you very much," and turned away. I headed to the exit in a state of dismay, quickening my pace in anger. At my cowardice. My lack of integrity.

I had just made myself comfortable in the back seat of the car and was about to close the door when a hand grabbed the top of it, stopping me.

"I didn't give you back your Biro," the impolite stranger said, holding it out to me.

I took it and muttered a thanks.

"Forgive my tactlessness, but I thought I heard that you're planning to travel to Spain. Will you leave soon?"

I held my tongue, though I wanted to ask her, "What does it matter to you?" In any case I wasn't given the chance: she kept talking.

"It's just, there's something I'd like to propose, if there's still time."

I looked at her without hiding my displeasure.

"I haven't decided yet about going," I replied bad-temperedly.

She didn't appear to give two hoots about my unfriendliness. Undeterred, she kept on.

"Have you ever worked?"

I didn't understand the question. Or rather, I understood it literally, but it seemed so intrusive that I hesitated for a moment.

"For a living, you mean?"

She nodded, her eyes still fixed on mine. Hers were of a strange dark blue, almost metallic hue.

"I've worked, yes. For years."

I immediately regretted my response. I hadn't given her any specific details, hadn't mentioned my work as a dressmaker, let alone my covert collaboration efforts. But I scolded myself, even so, for not keeping my mouth shut.

Oblivious to my musings, she put her hand in her jacket pocket. She didn't find what she was looking for there and tried another. Finally, she took out a rather dog-eared card.

"I'm Frances Nash. Canadian reporter," she said, offering it to me. Then she started to tie a gray scarf at her neck with a tight knot. "I'd like to speak to you, if I may. I'm in a hurry now but if you leave me a message at this number, I'll come see you at whatever time and place is most convenient for you."

Without waiting for an answer, she headed off in the direction of an open-topped jeep parked a few yards away. There was no driver waiting in the unprotected vehicle, and she sat behind the wheel herself. Even before our sturdy Ford set off on the journey home, the stranger had stepped on the accelerator and was headed toward Jaffa Road, enveloped in a cloud of dust.

11

I went back to the American Colony, furious with myself for my lack of courage to buy the tickets that would ensure my safety and that of the life I carried in my belly. When Marcus arrived hours later, a little earlier than usual that night, I concealed my irritation behind the excuse of some nonexistent pains.

"I don't think staying shut up inside all day helps."

I didn't argue or contradict him, but the knowledge that I was using silence to suppress the truth only caused me to feel angrier. To hide this, I avoided looking him in the eye and began to tidy clothes on a shelf in the wardrobe.

"How about we go out for dinner?" he suggested.

He'd sat on an armchair near the balcony, legs crossed and voice serene as he watched me. If I'd stopped for a few seconds to pay a tiny bit of attention to him, I'm sure I would've noticed a shade of suspicion in his demeanor. But I carried on with what I was doing, making myself appear engrossed in the absurd task of stacking handkerchiefs.

"To Hesse's? La Régence?" he persisted. "I hear they've found a new chef. It seems they stole him from Shepheard's in Cairo. Shall we try it out?"

I finally turned around, putting on my "good wife" disguise in a flash. I half smiled, moved closer, stroked his cheek, barely touching him. The word "traitor" resounded in my head.

An attentive manager showed us to our table just an hour later. To reach the King David's nightclub, we'd first had to go through the half-empty streets of Jerusalem, through the hotel's strictly controlled entrance, and down two flights of stairs. While the upper floors housed dozens of military and civilian staff, all plugging away at the mandate's official affairs, on the main floor—in the Arab Lounge, the foyer, the large restaurant—both locals and foreigners endlessly debated politics, terrorism, and business. La Régence was a nightspot that offered a relaxed atmosphere, where the grim activities of the floors above could be forgotten for a few hours.

It was dimly lit, its walls covered with tapestries, and the ceiling was rather low. A pianist was stringing melodies together. In one corner was a dance floor, still empty: it wasn't yet nine o'clock. The rest of the place, however, was packed with transient businessmen, diplomats, and conspirators; wealthy traders, reporters, rich tourists visiting the Holy Land; and Arab and Jewish hosts wining and dining their guests. I recognized a handful of faces, and Marcus knew more than a dozen. But we didn't stop to speak to anyone; we simply waved our hellos.

We sat some distance away from the crowd, by a broad pillar, not stopping to think that it was one of the architectural braces that held up that wing of the building. The maître d' delivered our menus, written in French and bound in deep-red leather.

"Do you remember our first dinner, at the Hotel Nacional?"

The question surprised me. Marcus wasn't given to nostalgia.

"Of course," I mumbled. I lowered my gaze to the menu to avoid his.

No, I hadn't forgotten a single instant of that night when he first arrived in Tétouan masquerading as a reporter, with a broken body, supporting himself with a bamboo walking stick, his face covered in wounds. I had just opened my business in partnership with Candelaria and was passing myself off as a discerning dressmaker. Behind that facade there had been a frightened and lonely young woman, one who'd been forced to live in a strange place. Marcus had promised to arrange my mother's evacuation from Madrid in exchange for a long interview with High Commissioner Beigbeder, which was offered to him by my friend Rosalinda Fox. As soon as our food arrived, Rosalinda had been unexpectedly summoned away.

"You ordered sole," he said now, remembering.

I could only smile with a touch of melancholy, without parting my lips. Yes, sole. And he'd had roast chicken. And two or three glasses of wine. Followed by two helpings of custard for dessert. His calm disposition had borne it all. My nerves, on the other hand, had given me a knot in the pit of my stomach.

He closed the menu after a quick glance and left it on the table.

"You barely touched it," he added.

He had come into my life in disguise. He hadn't ever intended to publish his conversation with Beigbeder, in any medium, he'd just wanted to size him up, to speak to him as an officer gathering intelligence for his country, though it would be some time before I was to know this. Still, from the outset, his presence became for me something firm to hold on to during uncertain times.

"Afterward, I took you home."

He had been intent on doing so, yes—the first time of many he'd done just this. To my home on Sidi Al Mandri in Tétouan, or on Núñez de Balboa in Madrid. And if I'd moved a thousand times before we lived together, he would have accompanied me, night after night, to a thousand front doors.

Now, instead of one of the Spanish waiters at the Nacional, it was a Sudanese waiter at La Régence who brought us our dishes. *Courgettes à la turque* for me, while Marcus preferred some rare meat. While I chewed my stuffed zucchini without any appetite, I looked back at his candlelit face. The young Marcus Logan of nine years ago both was and was not the same Mark Bonnard I had in front of me that night. He still had, on the left side of his face, near the ear, a couple of scars that bore witness to those old wounds. At the corners of his mouth some folds were now forming—proof of the passing years—and his first gray hairs had appeared, intermingling with his light-brown ones. His flexible, sinewy body, however, had barely changed. He was as solid as ever. And he'd never failed me, while I, without speaking a single word to him about it—disloyal, ungrateful, and entirely behind his back—had for days been scheming to leave him.

"You no longer need me to go anywhere with you," he said then.

I looked at him aghast: we weren't floating on the melancholy air of another time now. We'd abruptly descended to our bitter present. I wanted to say something, but he raised his hand to stop me, appealing for time before I opened my mouth.

"It goes without saying that I haven't followed you, Sira. I'm not keeping watch on you or trying to control you. It's just, this morning I heard you were at a travel agency, and I put two and two together." He shrugged, as if expressing resignation over his behavior. "It's what I do every day with things that matter rather less to me than you do. You know my work."

I nodded silently. Anything I may have wanted to ask about was superfluous. It mattered little now who had told him they'd seen me. It could've been anyone who'd done it, whether innocently or maliciously, with the utmost candor or out of an unhealthy desire to meddle.

"You've been putting on an act, but it's obvious you're hiding other feelings. I know everything that's happening in Jerusalem has been a shock, all the aggression, the bitterness. I often berate myself for making you come here with me. In my defense, I can only say that, after the war, no one anticipated Jewish insurgency reemerging so radically and violently. Which is why I don't blame you for wanting to leave. Nor do I feel betrayed. It's not your fault."

At some point I left my cutlery on the plate. I was overcome with a terrible feeling of weakness, as if all the blood had suddenly been drawn from my body. I hadn't planned for things to go this way; my intention had been to explain my decision in a convincing, well-considered way, not for him to find out first through God knows what channels.

"It's understandable you're afraid," he went on. "Anyone would be, not least of all someone in your state. It's natural you can't bear it. It happens all the time to wives in similar situations when they're forced to follow their husbands to complex places. You're not the first, nor will you be the last, don't worry. Some are used to it, or perhaps they knew beforehand what was involved in marrying a military man or a public servant in a particular field."

The pianist had stopped playing, and now the voice of a female singer softened the atmosphere. But we were in our own bubble, a desert island in the middle of a storm, cut off from the music, the waiters, the customers.

"However, it's different in your case. You're a foreigner even among other foreigners. Your situation's twice as complex because you can't feel the safety of being among your compatriots. No friends, no job. The rules and norms are alien to you. You can't even speak your own language to anyone. And on top of that, you're carrying a life inside you. Wanting to run away, get the two of you to safety—it's understandable. Responsible, even."

I nodded again, swallowing.

"But I can't leave, Sira. As much as I would like to, I can't go with you, but I don't want you to think that means I don't care. I don't know how long the British have left in this place where no one wants us, but we have a mandate to fulfill, an obligation conferred on us by the League of Nations that prevents us from unilaterally walking away. And while my country needs me, I must stay."

Someone walked past and greeted us with apparent warmth, but the words didn't reach my ears. The waiter approached to remove the crumbs from the tablecloth with his silver brush. Seeing our faces, he took a tactful step back and disappeared.

La Régence's entertainers probably continued performing their lighthearted themes, conversation probably flowed from every corner, and there must have been the occasional burst of laughter, the clinking of dishes. My mind, however, didn't register any background noise. Only Marcus's voice. And around us, a vast silence.

"All I ask you is that, when you leave, you don't disappear."

I wanted to protest, to tell him that would never happen. But the words got stuck in some hollow within me and didn't leave my throat.

"Don't take our child from my life when you go back to your people."

He picked up his knife and fork again, his eyes returning to his meat. He'd said everything he needed to say to me. Before the metal touched his filet mignon, however, I finally managed to react: I stretched my arms over the table and grasped his wrists.

"My only people are you, Marcus."

My fingers gripped the edge of his jacket, and at the precise moment I felt his bones through the fabric, I knew that I wouldn't leave. However hard things got, however painful the circumstances were, however fiercely the winds blew, we would face all that fate had planned for us, together.

I had been wrong to think I wasn't brave enough to buy my ticket for the ship; it was the exact opposite, in fact. No, it wouldn't have been brave to disappear, to run away from my problems. The courageous thing to do was to stand firm beside the person who needed me to be unfailing, to share my life with him, to offer him encouragement. No, I wasn't going to leave, I wasn't going to separate my child from its father. My place was by Marcus's side, and not because my marital vows said so, but because of love, responsibility, commitment.

Dinner lasted until the early hours. In the end we both opened up about our worries and doubts, placing them like playing cards faceup on the table. We left La Régence with our arms around each other's waists while the vocalist sang "You Are My Sunshine." As we walked along the corridor toward the street, Marcus whispered the song lyrics in my ear.

How unsuspecting we were, how foolish. We didn't have the slightest idea we were leaving the King David's jugular, the very center of the horror.

12

Following directions, I located the Public Information Office on King George V Street inside a modern, functionally designed building. I waited for the young woman behind the counter to finish her telephone call. I was struck by her skill at holding the receiver between her shoulder, jaw, and ear.

"I'm looking for Frances Nash," I announced when she hung up.

I took out the card the stranger had given me outside the travel agency the previous day, before she drove off in her jeep. I repeated the name and tried to show it to the receptionist.

"She told me I could find her here."

The telephone started ringing again, and the young woman spoke to me with her hand over the receiver.

"I don't know if Mrs. Nash is in. Go through to the common room and look for her, if you like."

I hesitated. My attempt to find her had really only been a sort of acid test. I'd decided to stay in Jerusalem and to embrace all that that entailed. And I'd sensed that in order to strengthen my resolve, the first thing I had to do was lose my fear of getting around. Everyone was carrying on with their lives: going to work, taking buses, buying bread and olives, visiting friends, making love, going to the cinema. Yes, I'd sustained a tremendous shock outside Broadcasting House, one that had ended my radio adventure. But I wouldn't let it stop me from doing other things. Without anywhere in particular to go, with no one to meet and no prospect of anything else to do, I had decided to contact the stranger who'd approached me near the Jaffa Gate. I didn't have the slightest idea what she might want from me, but at least this was a connection to the outside world. Or a simple excuse to keep the foundations of my decision to remain in Jerusalem from wobbling.

I headed in the direction the receptionist indicated until I reached a large and bright room where there were a couple of dozen desks, some with people sitting at them, others empty. Some of the occupants were working, typing away or speaking on telephones. Others were chatting with one another, in twos, in threes. I noticed a couple of women among them, but saw straightaway that none of them was the one I was interested in.

No one turned their attention from their work to ask me what I wanted; I guessed strangers coming and going was normal there. I decided to approach the nearest desk, which was occupied by a man and a woman. He was seated on a swivel chair with his jacket hanging on the back, and she perched on the edge of the desktop.

"Excuse me. I'm trying to find Frances Nash."

They looked at me without much interest. She scanned the room.

"She doesn't appear to be here."

The man, meanwhile, was studying me curiously.

"Pardon me, but aren't you Mark Bonnard's wife?"

He stood and came closer.

"Douglas Gallagher, of the *Daily Mail*. We've met at one or two gatherings . . ."

Sure enough, Marcus had introduced me to this man with the sharp eyes and untidy appearance. At someone's home in Rehavia or Katamon, or perhaps at the Yasmina's bar.

"We spoke about my work in Spain during the civil war, remember?" he said, holding out his hand. "I worked for the *Daily Express* in those days . . ."

Then I remembered: some time ago, he and I had chatted for a while in the home of the Arab lawyer Henry Cattan. At the time, he had told me he'd been one of the last reporters to leave Barcelona, as well as the only foreign journalist to have covered the fall of Madrid to the Nationalist forces. We had spoken that night until I managed to shake him. The conversation had been interesting, certainly, but at some point he'd rested a hand on my thigh and left it there, as if forgotten; I got out of there as quickly as possible. He was just as unshaven now as he'd been then, and his memory was intact.

"Of course," I replied with my falsest cordiality. "Delighted to see you again."

"Fran Nash isn't here right now. This is just a shared room, where correspondents come and go, unscheduled. It's likely that no one will know of any particular time when your friend will show up," he said. "Or even whether she'll come at all today."

The reporter fell silent for a moment. Perhaps he was remembering the feel of the silk dress over my leg.

"But if you'd like to wait for her, I can take you to the bar," he suggested. He looked at the time with a gratified expression. "It's almost twelve, a good time for the first drink of the day."

I made my escape with excuses of other nonexistent commitments and headed down the two flights of stairs to the ground floor. As I reached the big foyer at the bottom, I saw Frances Nash walking into the building, her silhouette outlined in the threshold of the wide-open double door. A pair of curly locks had escaped her knot and were falling over her forehead again. Once more she was wearing clothes with a masculine cut, which, probably unintentionally, lent her a strange air of elegance. She was carrying a large leather bag slung crossways over her shoulder.

A look of satisfaction—triumph, almost—came over her face the moment she saw me. She approached with agile strides and waited for me to descend the last steps.

"I just lost a bet with myself, but you can't imagine how pleased I am."

The early drink I hadn't accepted from Gallagher, I ended up having with Frances Nash, in the snack bar that the Public Information Office itself had opened. I didn't know what she wanted from me. I knew nothing about her. But I let myself be led by her and was ready to listen.

"Ever since the war ended, the new director hasn't known how to win the correspondents over to the British cause," she said as we settled into armchairs upholstered in velvet. It was still early, and only two or three tables were taken. "One of his great ideas," she added, "was to set up the press center upstairs, as well as this fabulous place."

She gestured at our surroundings with a lighthearted expression I couldn't decipher—sarcasm or appreciation. A waiter was putting clean glasses on the shelves behind the bar, and through the windows we could see the constant flow of pedestrians and vehicles. It was a pleasant place, with its arabesque carpet and heavy curtains, but I still didn't understand what the connection was to the news agency upstairs. Infected by the contagious spontaneity with which she spoke, I decided to ask her outright.

"Are you telling me they hope to buy foreign journalists with whiskey, gin, and beer?"

She burst out laughing. Behind her unpainted lips I discerned large teeth that seemed strong and healthy. She was in a rather better mood than she had been when we were waiting in the travel agency.

"I wouldn't say they're trying to buy us, exactly, but they certainly want to lure us here to keep us outside the influence of the Jewish Agency and its very adept press office." She paused to thank the waiter for the pink gins he brought us. I barely wet my lips, but she savored her first sip with delight. "During the war," she went on, putting her drink down on the glass tabletop, "the foreign media didn't care that much about what was happening in Palestine. But now that there's a new order in the world and the tension's growing, there are more and more foreign correspondents here. Someone told me the other day that there are eighty or so of us."

I knew some of them already through Marcus, the British ones, mostly, like the Gallagher fellow from a few moments earlier. And Americans, too. I knew a few of them by sight.

"The Jewish Agency," she continued as she rested her arm on the back of her chair, "is razor sharp and saw from the start how they had to deal with the press at this pivotal time for their people. So while the British carried on operating as they had during the war—only paying attention to the bureaucracy of passes and authorizations, the official reports, bulletins, and mind-numbing meetings with military men and mandate officials—the Jewish Agency's press department reacted quickly and fell over themselves to engage with any foreign journalists who showed their faces around here."

She drank again; I didn't. I just listened. Though there were many obvious differences between the two, she reminded me of Rosalinda: self-assured, with strong opinions, uninhibited and open. They looked nothing like each other—Frances Nash didn't have my friend's refinement. Her angular features were less harmonious than Rosalinda's, her hair was less well tended, and her general style was far from refined: short fingernails, no trace of makeup, no adornments or accessories. And yet something about them was the same. For a few naive moments I suspected that perhaps a very different kind of blood ran through the veins of His Royal Majesty's subjects. I didn't remember ever having met a Spanish woman who was so bold, efficient, and decisive. Maybe, I concluded, that was because nobody had ever silenced the English's thoughts.

"The Jewish Agency's press bureau provides us with everything we need," she went on. "As soon as there's an incident—an attack, an accident, anything—before the dust has even settled they've issued a press release. One that gives their own partisan version of events, of course, but is filled with detailed and comprehensive information. The moment one of the Jewish leaders makes a statement or gives a speech, copies are made available in English. If a publication requests an interview with one of the agency's heads, they give it within days—hours, sometimes. If we want to visit a kibbutz or a settlement, they take us there, with a car, driver, and interpreter thrown in. They even place their own offices at everyone's disposal, complete with telegraph cable, telephone lines, and any resources we need. In short, they know how to appear prompt, fast, and efficient in their relations with those outside their organization, and it's appreciated, of course."

Two men walked past us. I guessed they were colleagues of hers. "Hi, Fran," they said. She returned their greeting with an elegant wave. I still hadn't the faintest idea why she was telling me all of this, but I didn't mind listening to her. Not at all. She spoke with ease and aplomb, I was able to understand her without difficulty, and I had nothing better to do that first midday of the rest of my life.

"Where was I?" she asked after another sip of her cocktail. It was a rhetorical question—in contrast to my total ignorance, she knew perfectly well where she was going with her chatter. "Oh yes. As I was saying, as soon as Dick Stubbs, the new director of the British Public Information Office, arrived in the autumn to take up his post, he realized how obsolete and ineffective its services were and decided to completely overhaul them. The British are going through their most difficult times in the Holy Land, and they don't want the news that reaches the world from here to be slanted in favor of the Jewish cause and therefore critical of the mandate. It's enough to have to deal with the sheer number of Jewish or openly pro-Zionist correspondents that are sent here from overseas."

I couldn't contain myself and interrupted her rather impolitely.

"And you—"

"Call me Fran, OK?"

"All right. And you, Fran, where do you stand?"

"I personally think that both sides—Arabs and Jews—are to some extent right in each and every one of their grievances. As are the British, of course. But picking sides is not my job, Mrs. Bonnard."

"Call me Sira."

"Right. Sira. My job isn't to decide who is most justified. What I try to do is state how things are, undistorted, with no manipulation or sympathy for one side or the other. Again, the fact is that the Jews are generally receiving much more favorable treatment in the global press than the Arabs and British are, thanks in part to the good work of their press bureau, and that's what the new director of this organization is trying to rectify. Hence all the facilities for the reporters, which are intended to keep us from depending solely on the Jewish Agency's generous offerings. It's why they set up the open-access room you must've seen upstairs, why they took on more staff and instructed them to perform with the utmost diligence all that must be done. They've since established a smoother relationship with us correspondents, in every way. Sometimes they even provide us with authorization to accompany the military on missions or as they intercept the ships loaded with Jews that continue to reach the coasts."

"Plus this bar," I added.

"Plus this bar," she confirmed. And she finished off her drink.

We sat in silence for a moment, until she finally decided to abandon her explanations and get to the point. Her change in tone and subject was abrupt.

"Télam. Heard of it?"

I shook my head.

"Telenoticiosa Americana," she elaborated in my language, with dreadful pronunciation. "A new news agency. Do you know Argentina?"

I indicated again that I didn't.

"But the Spanish they speak there is similar to yours, I imagine."

I recalled the singing voice of Carlos Gardel, and that of Celia Gámez, who sang tangos before she became known for her Nationalist song "Ya hemos pasao." The little I knew about that far-off country ended there. But yes, I understood the song's Falangist lyrics completely.

It was almost lunchtime and the place had gradually filled up with small groups, as well as some tinier ones. If everyone there was a journalist, the British press office's new policy was certainly working. We remained at our table; Frances had ordered some sandwiches and I hadn't refused when she suggested having lunch together.

After the first mouthful, she moved on from her geographical inquiries.

"I want to work with them," she said of Télam, "and I need someone to translate my pieces from English into Spanish. Accurately and, above all, immediately."

I almost burst into laughter. So that was it. After her long preamble intended to acquaint me with the world she moved in, finally she'd cut to the chase. She needed a translator: her proposal was that I take on the job. My vague suspicion had been that she'd gotten wind of my flair for dressmaking, or perhaps that she was aware of the work I'd done with the SOE using patterns and false stitching.

"I'm not a translator," I said simply.

"But you could try. I don't work for a particular newspaper, you see. I write freelance for a Canadian corporation, the Southam Company, which owns several publications. I'm not their correspondent exactly, but I based myself here in Palestine when the war ended, offered them my services, and they've taken almost every piece I've written since then." She shrugged as if she was about to say something obvious. "We're part of the Commonwealth, you know, and British affairs are always of interest to us. Canada also already had more than a hundred thousand Jewish citizens before the rise of Nazism, and since the Holocaust, tens of thousands more have emigrated from Europe, so there's growing concern about everything happening in this place they call Eretz Israel: this land where they long to build a state."

She paused and asked if I was following her. I confirmed that I was.

"Good. So that's how I'm operating, and I must admit I'm not doing badly. I have my autonomy, I don't have to follow guidelines or orders, they pay decent rates, and I maneuver however I want. The downside, however, is that being freelance means always having to walk a tightrope. Which is why I think it'd be useful to have something else to fall back on if the rope ever snaps, or if I slip, or if the wind begins to blow in an unfavorable direction."

She raised her eyebrows, as if asking again whether I was still following. I must have looked less certain now.

"In a word," she said, "I need more work. That's more or less what I'm trying to say. I need to open new channels, find other partners. And that's where Télam comes in."

We were interrupted again by hellos and goodbyes from people passing by. "Good to see you, Fran," and "See you soon, Nash." She dismissed them all with brief waves. It was clear she wanted to stay focused on our conversation.

"Before I go on, tell me, do you know how news agencies work?"

After my long relationship with the British, I was well acquainted with them. But I decided to remain modest in my response.

"I can't remember if Spain has one," she admitted.

"There's the EFE agency," I said.

EFE—pronounced like the letter f in Spanish, whose name was not an acronym, and whose meaning and origin was uncertain even to those who worked for the agency—had been set up by the Nationalist politician Ramón Serrano Suñer in Burgos toward the end of the civil war. At the time, he was still ordering people around amid the creation of the new Francoist state, whether proposing or rejecting ministers, as he did with Beigbeder, or going to great pains to maintain strict control through his powerful Ministry of Governance. I was aware of all this because, back in Madrid, Marcus had often complained about the brazen way EFE altered news from outside Spain when they translated it: censoring it, ignoring it, or dressing it up however they wanted before release. The politician's eventual fall from grace had been meteoric, but the agency he founded was still operational and pursuing its interests with agility.

"EFE, that's right," she confirmed. "And it's state run, I think, so it's comparable to Télam, which is also mostly government owned. In any case, it's an agency that could begin to gain traction. Argentina's still rich compared to the European countries. Its coffers are full because it remained neutral in the war and exports tons of meat and grain to the UK. So far, for international news they've used Associated Press and United Press International, the big US agencies. But they want to end their dependency on those American giants, and they have the funds to do it. With that goal in mind, they're looking for a correspondent in Jerusalem, perhaps because their expansion plan is that ambitious, or maybe too because there are hundreds of thousands of Jews in their country who want to know what's happening with the Zionist efforts, the shiploads of refugees, and all the tension that exists here."

While she took another bite of her sandwich, I processed what she was suggesting. If the journalism world was alien to me, Argentina was even more so, though for decades my fellow Spaniards had been migrating there to escape hunger. At the same time, unfortunately, I was well acquainted with the complexities of Palestine.

"My problem," she explained without having yet finished swallowing, "is that I need to be sure I can send my reports straight to them in Spanish. I need to find a way as soon as possible so they don't send anyone from outside, and so none of my colleagues get ahead of me. I'm aware that for a lot of them this contract would be nothing. I can't see the refined Geoffrey Hoare of the *Times*—who drives around in a Wolseley with his Fred Astaire manners as if he were a minister—or the *New York Times*'s haughty correspondent Clifton Daniel fighting over the job. But a lot of others, like me, have weaker ties, and they can see a not inconsiderable opportunity in this, too. The first obstacle, however, is the same for everyone."

"That none of you speak Spanish."

"Not a word. I guess many others might have a translator at their agency's headquarters in London or New York, or they might be able to hire one of their own accord. There must be options, but all of them would slow down the process and the news would lose its immediacy."

I tried to think of someone else who could provide the service, to prove her wrong. Certainly not the Spanish consul. The vice-consul, perhaps—he was young and spirited—but no, not him, either. I didn't know whether there were diplomatic representatives or residents from other Spanish-speaking countries who might do it. There may have been Sephardic Jews around who still spoke Ladino, the Judeo-Spanish of the Ferrara Bible, but they would probably struggle with twentieth-century Spanish. There also existed members of various religious orders, but I was equally doubtful of their availability.

Oblivious to my ruminations, she put her idea forward with force.

"There's nobody else, Sira. What I propose is that we work together hand in hand and become partners. I'd write the news using the same material I use for my Canadian company. It wouldn't involve much more work for me. You would translate it quickly into Spanish, and I would take care of getting it to Télam. When they pay me, we'd share the money."

Almost a decade before, in the autumn of 1936, when I'd settled in Tétouan with my spirits crushed and drowning in debt, the smuggler Candelaria had proposed that we open a dressmaking studio together. She had laid out the plan to me at her guesthouse one rainy afternoon: to fund our business, she was counting on selling a load of pistols, an operation I ended up taking charge of. A few years later, in September of 1940, Rosalinda Powell Fox asked me to collaborate with her country's secret service. She arranged to meet me in the storeroom of Dean's Bar in Tangier, among stacked crates and sacks of coffee, Billie Holiday playing in the background on a gramophone. She'd proposed that I collaborate with the Allies for the common good of our countries.

Now I was in broad daylight in Jerusalem's modern district, in a snack bar that had been recently opened by the British in a naive attempt to restore balance to a disturbed and elusive order. In front of me was a Canadian journalist I knew nothing about. She wasn't talking about selling pistols or passing on secret messages. Nevertheless, her offer took me aback as the others had. Perhaps fearing that she'd been too direct, instead of waiting for my reply, Frances Nash tried another angle.

"You told me you've worked before. May I ask doing what?"

My reply was half-truthful.

"I was a dressmaker. I had my own business."

"Did it go well?"

"It went very well," I had to admit. "But it was only temporary. I closed shop when the war ended."

"Don't you miss it?"

I didn't say yes or no. She looked at me with sharp eyes again, as if trying to peer into my brain and read my thoughts.

"We could try," she suggested. "See if it works. Forgive my forwardness, but yesterday I noticed that you didn't end up buying a ticket. I guess you're not going anywhere anytime soon."

I did forgive her forwardness. Or at least, I let it go.

"I didn't have a good day yesterday."

"Nor did I," she admitted. "And I'd like to apologize. I was brusque because I was flustered. I was in a mad rush to buy a ticket, all for nothing because . . ." Her expression turned weary. "My husband . . . my ex-husband has a knack for driving me crazy, and . . . Anyway, let's focus. Tell me, why're you finding it so hard to accept my offer?"

I could have given several reasons, all of them valid. But I chose just one.

"I'm expecting a baby."

She looked at me in disbelief.

"And? Whatever could that stop you from doing? Pregnancy is a fabulous thing, my friend. It gives you strength, lucidity. It lights up the soul."

Never in a million years would I have guessed that this singular woman was a mother. She seemed to anticipate my assumption and was ready to set the record straight. She rummaged in her big leather bag and found a wallet. She leaned toward me and opened it, holding it in front of my eyes.

"My girls," she announced with a hint of pride. Two curly blonds smiled in the portrait, displaying not a trace of shyness. "They're twelve and ten, boarding in Cairo with the French nuns at La Mère de Dieu School. Their father, my—"

She broke off. Someone had just come into her field of vision.

"Hi, Nick!"

She greeted him in a friendlier manner than she had her other colleagues, gesturing to him to come over to the table. As he approached, and as it registered that I was the one sitting with Frances Nash, I glimpsed a trace of confusion on his face.

He stopped near our armchairs and addressed me first, asking how I was. In a neutral tone, he said it was nice to see me. Then he turned to the journalist.

"You're a wicked woman, Nash."

She responded with a burst of laughter.

"You were quite right, Soutter. Sira Bonnard's a formidable woman. I've filled her in on my proposal. I just need her to say yes. I'm waiting."

He opened his mouth to protest, even jabbed the two fingers with which he held a cigarette at her, wordlessly reproaching her for something. As ever, he wore his tie a little loose, he had files under his arm, and his manner was rushed. He held back and said nothing.

Frances, on the other hand, spoke.

"Our mutual friend is ultimately responsible for all this. It was he who told me about you. About a beautiful Spanish woman who had been going to work with him on the radio, only it all came to an abrupt end. He praised your natural talent, your magnetism. You made an impression on him, and believe me, he's not the kind to be easily captivated. Crossing paths with you yesterday in the Thomas Cook agency was one of those glorious gifts of coincidence that fall from the sky every so often."

The confession didn't amuse Nick Soutter one bit, and he didn't hide his annoyance. Someone called to him from the bar, he said a quick goodbye to us, and we were left watching his broad shoulders, his firm step, as he walked away.

"Paradoxically, the thing that unites Nick Soutter and me is separation," Fran Nash concluded, sitting back in her armchair. "But don't go thinking we're in a relationship. That's not the case at all. We're old friends from our time in Cairo, and right now we're both going through the ordeal of seeing our marriages break down. It's not a nice situation for either of us, so, from time to time, we talk at length over a bottle of whiskey and take our demons out for a bit of air."

13

It was a week before I finally received the call. I had been unsure it would ever come. Some days I eagerly awaited it; others, I hoped it would never happen.

"Ready?"

I swallowed.

"Ready."

"Perfect. We start tomorrow."

I sat at the desk in my room, resting my palms on it. Fran Nash had just confirmed that she'd finally received approval to send her reports as a Télam correspondent in Jerusalem. Or rather, *our* reports.

We had planned it all out. We'd completed some samples and found that we could work together well. In preparation, I'd borrowed a Webster's dictionary from Bertha Vester's library, and I already had a bilingual one that Marcus had used since he arrived in Spain at the start of the civil war. It was extremely well thumbed, but it would do the job.

If Marcus was surprised, upset, or worried about the Canadian journalist's proposal, he never showed it. "Are you sure?" was all he asked. "Then go ahead."

Unsurprisingly, the first report I tackled had to do with the Jewish insurgency. Specifically, it was about an Irgun attack on a British police station, in which four people had been killed and several injured. It was neither long nor beautiful; it was simply a handful of lines that gave a brief account of an event. There were no explanations, only an outline of the background, and few clues to frame the report in context. Bare, concrete information, without a hint of embellishment. It took me less than half an hour to finish the job, with only a couple of terms I had to look up in the dictionary to confirm my intuition. Then I went over it at least seven times, swapped some word or other for a synonym, crossed out two or three more, changed the order of a sentence. When I was sure it was ready, I rewrote the whole thing, folded the sheet of paper into thirds, put it in an envelope, and called from the balcony to the young Arab who was waiting in the courtyard with his bicycle resting against the fountain.

In half an hour Fran Nash would have it on her desk. In forty minutes she would be sending it by cable, and my words would cross seas and deserts, mountain ranges and an ocean to reach Buenos Aires, number 140 on Calle 25 de Mayo. There, on a third floor, in an under-staffed office with new furniture, very close to the national bank and a stone's throw from the Casa de Gobierno, someone would receive the cable from far-off Jerusalem and disseminate its contents to the media all over the country. One thing Fran and I didn't foresee: that our story would end up being eclipsed by the intense coverage of the general election taking place in the country at the time—the one that would give Juan Domingo Perón his first victory. We only knew that our news would arrive there, ready for whoever was interested in it.

The release would be signed by Frances Quiroga. That was the name we'd decided to use—our "nom de plume," my colleague said. With "Quiroga" we would be giving the correspondent a Spanish voice and, at the same time, I would be rescuing the surname I'd lost both in my new married life and in my previous life as an impostor. "Frances," for its part, was ambiguous, somewhat masculine, and in all likelihood the Télam directors' minds would be more at ease if they were unaware that a woman was behind the reports.

"And that way," Fran had concluded, "I also avoid exposing myself too much."

She showed up at the American Colony that afternoon without warning. To celebrate our debut, she announced. Then she asked where the bar was.

"There isn't one," I replied.

Our hotel had been founded as a Christian project, a quasi-missionary institution. In time it had also come to be a comfortable hostel, but Bertha Vester hadn't wanted to change certain aspects of its essence.

"Let's go, then. Come on, get your coat."

We bumped along to the city in Fran's old jeep, the one that some division in some army probably had deemed unusable after the war. It was bitterly cold in the vehicle, and I spent the whole journey gripping my belly in fear, scolding myself for being so careless. Fran might not have cared if she left her daughters motherless if she overturned in a ditch, but safeguarding my child was my primary concern.

"Don't be such a scaredy-cat, Quiroga!" she yelled as she swerved around a pothole.

She dodged some children who waved us goodbye, then a handful of sheep. After that, she headed into the modern area of the city and finally parked in Zion Square in front of Café Europe's large windows.

"They serve the best Sacher torte in Jerusalem here," she told me. "The pâtissier was the owner of one of Vienna's great pastry shops. Looking at your face, I reckon you'll be glad to trade our toast for a good dose of sugar."

After we'd sat down and been served, she said, "Can I ask you a question?" The query came as I was holding my fork to my mouth. "Have you honestly never worked as a translator before? Or a writer, or . . . ?"

The chocolate cake hit my tongue with a flavor that must have been delicious, but I barely registered it. Even stronger than my sense of taste was my doubt about how honest I should be with her.

"Though my Spanish is limited," she said, "I think I can make a superficial assessment of your work. I'm struck by your"—she paused for a moment, as if trying to find the best way to express herself—"concise use of language, your attention to detail. You don't seem like a beginner."

How much important information had I gathered from my German customers in Madrid? How many of those conversations had I scribbled down afterward in my notebooks? How many nights had I spent redrafting those notes into succinct, unadorned sentences, leaving only the bare substance? Perhaps hundreds or thousands of messages—I had never stopped to count them—later transformed into miles of dots and dashes. But day after day, night after night, that's what I had done, almost five years of my life spent laboring with silent dedication.

"It might be because of writing all my dressmaking notes," I suggested with false innocence.

The SOE had been dissolved as soon as the Axis powers were defeated, and my work as a covert collaborator had ended then. Other than to Marcus, I had never spoken to anyone about it again. And I still did not intend to.

Fran Nash gave me a skeptical look.

"Your husband works for the intelligence service, doesn't he?"

He did, of course. He'd always done so. First, in Spain, for the British intelligence service MI6. And now for the Defence Security Office, the colonial branch of MI6's sister agency MI5. In the service of His Majesty and under direct orders from Sir Gyles Isham. Fran could probably verify all of this quite easily. But no one was ever going to hear it from me.

"You'll have to ask him that. He's looking forward to meeting you, by the way."

She laughed.

"For a simple dressmaker, you're very good at dodging questions, Quiroga. Ah well, we all have a skeleton or two in the closet. The trouble is, skeletons open the door sometimes."

"And what skeletons do you have, if you don't mind me asking, partner?"

She laughed again, but when she was done there was a trace of melancholy at the corners of her mouth.

"At least a dozen."

She looked through the window. The light outside had dimmed, and people were coming out of the offices and establishments on Zion Square, which was as busy as ever. A British policeman was there, directing the traffic. On the streets, girls, men, boys, and women were finishing their shopping and heading to the bus stops, or lining up outside the cinema, or walking in different directions to their homes located in neighborhoods to the west, south, or north—areas inhabited by Jews from diverse countries of origin, separated by large open spaces full of thistles, stones, and dry earth.

"I've just turned thirty-four," she confessed when she turned back to me. "It's taken me more than a decade to put my own signature to my writing, but I've been involved in journalism since I was twenty-one, when I started working as a proofreader at Toronto's *Globe and Mail*. That was also when I had the absurd idea of falling in love with a married journalist seventeen years my senior who also happened to be my boss." Her expression conveyed bitter irony. "I guess you know how stupid and blind love is sometimes. I crossed the Atlantic with him when he was offered a post as Near East correspondent. We settled in Cairo, rented a beautiful home, joined the Gezira Club, and became entangled in the capital's vibrant social life—much livelier than Jerusalem's, by the way. And we also brought two daughters into the world, though from the start he'd shown hints that there was another side to him. We spent both the most turbulent and the least turbulent days of the war in Cairo, and from there he also traveled around—Bucharest, Tripoli, Beirut, Athens—constantly coming and going, alternating his work with gloomy spells of depression, lovers, and boozing. I lost count of the hundreds of reports I wrote for him and sent off with his signature while he refused to get out of bed, or spent entire days in the garden, dozing on a hammock, hung over or just dejected."

She spoke without pausing, and with a naked openness. I simply studied her metallic eyes, her sharp-featured face.

"I put up with it for as long as I could. But for my mental well-being, I knew it had to come to an end, and I set the deadline myself: when Germany fell, I would say goodbye to my marriage. I organized myself and prepared the girls. They're smart and were fully aware of the situation despite their age. They agreed without any drama to board for a while with the Catholic nuns, God bless them, while their mother went out into the world and filled her lungs with air again."

She paused, as if the sudden memory of her daughters wouldn't allow her to merely touch on the subject in passing and as if speaking of them required a little more thought.

"I try to go see them once a month," she said. "They always welcome me as if Santa Claus had arrived. I never hear a single word of complaint or reproach. I'm certain it's been the best thing to do for all three of us and infinitely more bearable for them than to live with a frustrated and resentful mother who was slowly wasting away. The day I left them at the school, in order to keep my heart from breaking, I had a big send-off at home first, and the next morning I got on the train. Now I live in a little studio apartment at the Austrian Hospice. I have barely any furniture and zero comforts or domestic help, but apart from the girls and a handful of friends, I don't miss my other life at all. I feel good, free, alive. The one thing that hasn't changed is that the father of my children is still furious with me for leaving him. The stupid idiot doesn't know that his malice only spurs me on to something better every day."

What an admirable woman, I thought. Admirable in her courage, in her astonishing fearlessness. Or so I believed, until I ventured to ask her plainly.

"Doesn't everything that's happening ever scare you?"

"It terrifies me," she admitted. "From day to day, what might happen later. But you've got to learn to live with the dread, my friend. If you don't, you'll go to pieces."

14

The rest of that winter of 1946 passed while I grew the life I carried inside me, listened to my radio, and translated news about disagreements and atrocities, which included few reasons for optimism. Depending on her workload, sometimes I met with Fran Nash and we chatted for hours. At other times, she was tied up with her responsibilities, or she went to see her daughters or traveled to the Jewish kibbutzim, the Arab villages, Tel Aviv, or wherever, and I wouldn't see her for weeks. The muezzins continued to call Muslims to prayer at the mosques, the Christian church bells rang to summon the faithful every day, and from the nearby ultraorthodox neighborhood of Mea Shearim, at dusk each Friday I heard the Sabbath's beginning announced.

Alongside these everyday routines, security measures in Jerusalem were growing ever tighter. The Anglo-American Committee of Inquiry had been set up some months before to address the problems of the refugees clamoring for permission to enter the country, and it finally made its resolution public: a hundred thousand Jews must be admitted to Palestine with immediate effect.

Britain now faced a hellish dilemma: If it obeyed the committee's instructions and accepted a mass influx of refugees, it would please the Jews and the United States but earn the hostility of both local Arabs and Arabs in neighboring countries whose territories were crossed by the Suez Canal and were home to coveted oil fields. If Britain refused, on the other hand, to admit all the Jews, it would satisfy the Arabs but go against the Americans, whose sizable loans the United Kingdom depended on to rebuild its economy. Meanwhile, with the hours of daylight increasing and temperatures on the rise, new boats kept appearing on the Mediterranean horizon packed with survivors of the gas chambers who were in search of a new future. Some managed to disembark in secret, but many others were left at the mercy of the winds, crowded on ramshackle vessels, vulnerable and racked with uncertainty.

In the end, the scales tipped in favor of the second option, and the Labour prime minister Clement Attlee announced that Britain would continue to limit the influx of refugees. The retaliatory terrorist attacks by Jewish insurgents against the British immediately became more radical— raids, sabotage, kidnappings, robberies, and direct attacks on institutions and named targets. The insurgents stole weapons, ammunition, and anything that could cause damage: gelignite, dynamite, TNT, cans of petrol.

The police and His Majesty's Armed Forces responded by hunting down the perpetrators with unrelenting might. They scoured cities and settlements, set up mobile checkpoints everywhere, and combed kibbutzim, villages, anonymous suburban homes, and slums. They searched in passages and alleyways, on roofs, in basements, warehouses, and back rooms. The authorities had plenty of particulars: names, nationalities, ages. Czech, Polish, Russian, Austrian, Iraqi, German; nineteen, twenty, twenty-two, twenty-five years old. Pictures of the insurgents were pinned to police station walls, and rewards offered for information on their whereabouts: two hundred, three hundred, five hundred pounds. But no one said a word. Nobody cooperated. Jews refused to be involved, to report their own, showing a fierce solidarity that made plain their opposition to the policy that turned their people away, back to Europe's refugee camps.

At dawn each day, young Jewish men and women—children, even—went out onto the streets to scatter pamphlets and stick satirical posters on lampposts, writing in chalk on exterior walls messages that decried the despicable subjects of treacherous Britain. They often addressed the Arabs, too, in their own language, promising them that they would be welcome in the future Jewish state the Jewish people would never stop fighting for.

The British authorities began to protect their facilities in Jerusalem with barricades made of sandbags and concertina wire. Foot soldiers in khaki uniforms with tommy guns and berets policed the streets; soldiers in jeeps, tanks, and armored vehicles patrolled around the clock. Sirens blared with sinister eloquence. Two consecutive blasts signaled the imminent threat of a terrorist attack, at which point traffic would come to an instant halt and everyone would try to take cover. One drawn-out hoot would later announce that the danger had passed, and life would resume.

When attempts to find the culprits met with limited success, curfews were imposed in the Jewish neighborhoods to facilitate the search for weapons and fighters. The protests were constant: the British were punishing an innocent majority for the atrocities of a handful of extremists. Even so, at the designated time—normally six o'clock—the Yishuv, the Jewish population, remained confined to their homes, leaving streets deserted and businesses closed. They were even forbidden from going into their own gardens, from leaning out of their windows. Men, women, children, the elderly; employees, business owners, shopkeepers, and the unemployed: the order applied to them all. It was the PBS—the mandate's public radio—that announced the curfews with official formality, reminding the population at regular intervals. Meanwhile, the police drove around these districts repeating through loudspeakers, both in English and in Hebrew, the strict ban on going out.

Sometimes I saw crowds of mothers running home as the last half hour ran out, dragging their children, anxious they wouldn't make it in time and would be arrested, something that happened frequently and without the slightest consideration for those who were caught outside. More than seventy thousand Jews lived under these severe restrictions, confined day after day to their homes, bunched together in small apartments, well-to-do villas, or modest low-rise houses built from concrete blocks. Silent and obedient inside their homes, with blinds lowered and front doors locked. Reading the newspapers written in the language of their prophets, listening to the radio with the volume on low if they were lucky enough to own such a set. Humiliated, frightened, whispering to one another in the dark. That was when the armed police patrols went into action with torches, searchlights, and dogs. Whatever house they called on, whatever the hour, the people inside were required to let them in.

The curfew was lifted first thing in the morning, announced by radio and megaphones. The blinds went up, the shops and workshops opened again, and the Jews' lives carried on as they started another day of hard work and normal activities, interspersed with acts of resistance. The Zionists' fighting spirit was inexhaustible; they bore everything with their sights set on the creation of their own state.

As spring took hold in Palestine, with poppies covering the nearby mountains and the air beginning to warm with the hot sandy wind known as the khamsin blowing in from the desert, I continued to translate the news that went to Argentina with increasing frequency as the unrest intensified. I also sewed clothes for my child, now that my body was growing rounder: tiny garments made with small stitches in cotton and cambric, baby wraps and sheets. Our social life did not ease off—it was as if the British and the other foreigners were trying to soothe their nerves and ward off the specter of fear with a busy schedule of gatherings, meetings, soirees, and dinners. In public venues and in private residences—between drinks, cigarettes, and plates of mezze—everyone talked and discussed, suggested, interpreted, remarked, rebutted, and predicted.

Passions remained equally alive, unashamedly public at times, as if the tension had made the frosty English lose their decorum and reserve. Word had it that the wife of a high-ranking official in the secretariat was having an audacious affair with an attractive Arab of the powerful Nusseibeh family. That the director of the British Electric Company was refusing to end his extramarital involvement with his Jewish secretary. That Lieutenant General Sir Evelyn Barker, General Officer Commanding of the British Armed Forces in Palestine and Transjordan, was hopelessly in love with the great Katy Antonius, and that each night they danced cheek to cheek, and each morning he wrote her a passionate love letter on army letterhead.

Frivolities aside, the fact remained that the terrorist threat hung over everyone we mixed with. And Marcus—though he tried, with me, to be the same person he always was and to hide his worries from me—made it obvious in other ways that he knew everything was plunging into a dark void. He ate little and smoked a lot. His cheekbones were accentuated, and the tiny creases at the corners of his mouth that signaled the onset of middle age had almost become wrinkles. He never went out without a pistol anymore. Each day he left and returned at a different time, taking a different route, in a different car. He slept badly, got up in the early hours, and to avoid disturbing me, snuck into the room that adjoined the bedroom. But my sleep was also fragile during those days when it was starting to get hot, and my belly now had a heavy solidity. I struggled to find a comfortable position and often needed to go to the bathroom in the middle of the night.

Through the crack under the door, I would see the light in the other room as he wrote and reflected his way through his insomnia with the balcony doors open. It upset me that I couldn't help him with anything, and I would be overcome with deep anguish and hold my belly. And so there in the dark, I squeezed my eyes shut and prayed to Jehovah, Allah, and the Christian God alike to do something to bring peace and sanity to this land. Sadly, my prayers fell on deaf ears.

Early on June 17, the telephone rang in our apartment. Marcus quickly dressed, reassured me with great difficulty, and rushed off. Haganah, the military arm of the Jewish Agency, had just blown up every bridge that connected Palestine to its neighboring countries. The structures that the British Armed Forces' vehicles so frequently crossed had been dynamited simultaneously in a symbolic act, a straightforward reminder to the mandate's authorities and Attlee's government of the Jewish insurrection's capability.

With the tension and passions at a boiling point, High Commissioner Cunningham—the official whose formal arrival we'd witnessed some months before—asked for authorization from London to carry out a crushing counterattack. After a few days of secret preparations, on Saturday, June 29, the British launched what they called Operation Agatha—the Black Sabbath, as it would come to be known in Jewish memory.

At a quarter past four, before sunrise, the British forces headed to their targets. The first priority was to seize the Jewish Agency's premises, but that wasn't the only objective. Throughout that Saturday and for days after, thousands of soldiers and policemen arrested thousands of Jews all over Palestine, for suspected links to terrorism. Weapons and reams of documents were also confiscated. The high commissioner spoke on the radio, and later I learned that it was Nick Soutter who'd had to run the broadcast. The arrests weren't targeting the Jewish community as a whole, Cunningham insisted, only those who were involved in the campaigns of violence and those responsible for instigating them.

The operation continued until July 11, at which point the British troops returned to their barracks, leaving the Yishuv hurt and perplexed. The next morning, the streets were once more filled with children throwing handfuls of nails on the roads to puncture the police vehicles' tires. Young people with their faces hidden behind scarves stuck up posters on every visible surface. *Nazi British. Fascist Hooligans. Exterminators.* They called the police *the British Gestapo*; the army *the British SS*. There were also references to the Exodus verse: *a life for a life, an eye for an eye, a tooth for a tooth* . . . Other pamphlets announced that the Zionist resistance had only just begun.

In the hot and dusty air of early summer, there floated an ominous question: How long would it be before the reprisals against the British began?

15

A week or so later, once the commotion of Operation Agatha had settled slightly, we went to see off a colleague of Marcus's, a veteran who was retiring from active service and whose name is lost in the fog of my memory. The Saturday night gathering was organized by another colleague and his wife at their residence in Talbiya. There would be twenty guests, two dozen perhaps, more men than women as always, all of them British except me, but I was used to my uniqueness by now. Some were of mature years, others less so; some with partners, others without. The men wore white dinner jackets, and we women left our shoulders uncovered. I'd had to let out another dress that afternoon so it would fit.

We were welcomed with compliments and congratulations for my pregnancy, everyone insisting I looked radiant in the final stretch before my baby arrived. The admiration on some of the gentlemen's faces when their gaze caught my neckline left little doubt that the appreciation was real. We had drinks in the garden surrounded by palms, figs, and cypresses. For a moment I thought that at some future time I would like to live in a place like this with Marcus and our baby and any other children we may have, in a home as beautiful but in another part of the world, far from here, somewhere where we didn't hear stray gunshots while the cocktails were served or bursts of machine-gun fire accompanying the trays of canapés. While we sat at the table, everything projected an air of apparent normality: the service, the food, the polite tone of the guests, the understated elegance. I, on the other hand, continued to be amazed by the stoicism of these people.

At first the conversation fanned out in various directions, but it wasn't long before it centered on one subject, the usual one of late: Britain's role in Palestine and the possible solutions to a crisis that seemed to have an impenetrable heart and an ever-tougher skin. All I felt about the departure of the fellow Englishman in whose honor the dinner was being held was envy, pure and heartfelt envy.

We'd planned to spend Sunday at the pool at the Semiramis Hotel. Marcus could relax in the water while I rested in the shade of a white canvas parasol, drinking fruit juices or iced tea. Something came up at the last minute, however. He didn't say exactly what, but he had to go. Selfishly, I was glad. I struggled to get in and out of the car; my pelvis, my kidney area, my lower back all ached. At this point, everything seemed unbearable.

He was back at the American Colony by the midafternoon, but not to rest: within half an hour he was receiving someone, then two other men joined them. Unusually, he decided not to gather with his colleagues in the library and instead invited them into our apartment, where they would have more privacy. I didn't need to be asked, and I opted to make myself scarce.

I gripped the banister as I waddled downstairs to the ground floor, then I crossed the central foyer to the large lounge and settled myself down under one of the fans. I had a Graham Greene novel in one hand and my workbag in the other. For a long while, however, I opened neither. I just sat in the armchair with my eyes closed and my head tilted back, thighs apart and arms hanging down, receiving the cool air that the wooden blades blew my way as they revolved wearily. There was nobody in the room, luckily—the position of my body was improper, unseemly, even. With slightly bitter irony, I wondered whether I would ever get back my waist, my ankles, my elegantly crossed legs.

The baby was due soon. The last week of August had been the estimation in my most recent examination by the doctor who saw me at the Government Hospital, an austere Scotsman from whom I never received the slightest waft of empathy, only cold remoteness. Despite his calculations, I wasn't convinced my body could wait that long, with my big, low belly as hard as stone.

The men who'd met with Marcus finally left at dusk, as quietly as they'd arrived. When he appeared in the library looking for me, jacket-less, his shirt creased and his sleeves rolled up, I saw immense tiredness on his face. I suggested having dinner in the courtyard. He murmured excuses, but I ended up persuading him.

At dinner I pretended to ignore my discomfort and focused on one thing: making sure we had a few moments of pleasure, as if we were an ordinary couple in everyday surroundings. The courtyard gave us the false sensation of being in a little paradise, soothed by the trickling fountain, illuminated by lanterns that cast dancing shadows on the walls' golden stones, enveloped in the aroma of orange trees and jas-mine. The pressure from my belly on my pelvis was unbearable, and my poor back was screaming for me to let it lie down, but my willpower won, and I kept up my spirits. Even the whistling bullets seemed to give us some respite, allowing us to chat undisturbed about the minor details of our family in the making. Would our child be a blond boy with Anglo-Saxon features, or a little Spanish girl, slight and dark? Will we name him Mark or opt for Gonzalo, after his maternal grandfa-ther? Will we call her Olivia, after her extravagant grandmother from London, or María, after the woman who gave birth to a divine child two thousand years ago, or Sira, after me, a name borrowed from an obscure saint?

"We'll decide when we see its face," Marcus concluded.

He raised his glass of wine and at last gave a tired half smile, and although at that precise moment I felt a sharp stabbing pain at the very bottom of my abdomen, I clenched my jaw and managed to take the pain without showing it.

Before long we went up to our room, each step a struggle for me. We went to bed with the balcony door open onto the night, Marcus at my back, holding me, both of us unaware of what that moment meant, both oblivious to its significance.

"Don't go . . . ," I murmured.

Dawn had just arrived, weak light filtering through the shutters. I was still in bed—I'd been getting up late recently so the days wouldn't feel so long. He was standing beside me, ready to leave just like any other morning. He pulled on his jacket. I made him bend down and stretched my bare arm out to the back of his neck, sinking my fingers into his hair. He kissed me on the lips, pushing a lock away from my face. Then he lifted the sheet and rested a hand on my belly.

"I'll come and have lunch with you," he whispered in my ear.

I fell back asleep, his words floating in the early-morning haze.

16

I got up around ten and opened the shutters to let the day into the bedroom. With my eyes still half-closed, I rested my hands on my hips and arched my back. The heat was already fierce, and the grunts, squeals, and brays of the animals from the pens out back reached my ears. I started to fill a bath, like I did every morning. While the water ran from the taps, standing barefoot on the cold tiles, I raised my arms to gather up my hair. From the side, I contemplated my ample, naked body in the mirror. Only later did I piece together what was likely happening while I was making these preparations.

As I readied my bath, in some back room in one of the outlying Jewish neighborhoods, eight young men were taking off their everyday clothes. The short-sleeved shirts and khaki trousers were thrown onto their pallets or hung over the backs of chairs. In place of these ordinary clothes they put on blue overalls, like the ones the Arab deliverymen generally wore.

A mile or so away, at the King David Hotel, in the areas still open to the public and guests, the staff were diligently performing their duties. Max Hamburger, the refined Swiss manager, was overseeing the arrival and departure of guests, recording surnames, job positions, and other relevant details. Two floors up, the housekeeping manager was allocating towels, sheets, and pillowcases to the rooms. In the kitchens in the basement, half a dozen cooks, twenty or so kitchen porters, and a troop of waiters were working unflaggingly on preparations for lunch.

In the same building, in the areas that had been converted into offices for the secretariat and the headquarters of the British Armed Forces, the activity was as frenetic as on any other Monday, with the sounds of orders given and replies made, conversations, typing, telephones ringing. There were the constant comings and goings of colonial officials, military personnel, and staff from corridors, offices, and meeting rooms. Some arrived and others left, some informed and others were being informed, some read documents and others prepared them. The flow of people from outside the organization was also constant, ordinary citizens coming in to do their paperwork and sitting down to wait.

In his office, Marcus had just asked to be put through to Beirut to speak to his superior, Sir Gyles Isham, who'd traveled there a few days before. Looking extremely thin in his light linen suit, his face contorted, he was smoking his ninth cigarette of the day to ease the wait.

At about half past ten, I was still in the bath, my neck resting on the edge to keep my hair dry. My belly rose above the surface like half a watermelon, a half-moon, half an alabaster sphere, hard and taught.

At the same time, the young Jews dressed in overalls started loading seven large metal milk churns into a van. Each churn measured a yard or so in height and two handspans across. The main body was cylindrical, narrowing into a neck and widening again at the rim. All had two sturdy handles and lids with clasps to prevent spillages. Each one held seven gallons and usually weighed seventy-seven pounds when full. The young men also loaded a few hessian sacks, of the kind commonly used to carry chickpeas, pistachios, pine nuts, or lentils. That day the shipment was something different: inedible metallic devices.

In the King David's kitchens, the maître d' Naim Nissan, an Iraqi Jew who'd at one time served the royal family in Baghdad, checked to see that everything was going as planned. He tasted sauces and dressings, inspected breads, cheeses, desserts. Two, three, four, five floors above, the Sudanese housekeepers were making the beds in the suites and rooms. In her cubicle behind the reception desk, a young telephone operator was noting down the first dinner reservations.

In the secretariat's area in the south wing, the female members of staff had stopped work momentarily to enjoy their midmorning tea break: twenty-something Arabs, Jews, some British, a few Armenians, a handful of Greeks. Competent and high spirited, they all wore their clothes, hair, and makeup in the western fashion. While they drank tea and ate shortbread, they breezily discussed their bosses, nail varnishes, and Hollywood heartthrobs.

In his office in the same area, Marcus had finally managed to reach Beirut and was speaking to his direct, and now absent, superior. From two hundred and fifty miles apart, they were exchanging opinions without much agreement.

At around eleven, fresh out of the bath and wrapped in a big white towel, I barely managed to contain the urge to get back into bed. I resisted and turned on the radio. The PBS was airing one of its programs in Hebrew, so I tuned in to Radio Cairo. Catchy, lilting Egyptian music was playing. I left it on.

At the same time, the van loaded with fake Arabs, diabolical sacks, and metal milk churns was heading down Julian's Way, approaching the King David and turning down the lane that led to the hotel's service doors, where deliverymen usually unloaded their goods. While the main entrances were closely guarded, there was no one at the service doors to order them to halt.

In the King David's elegant barbershop, barbers were cutting a wealthy Arab's hair and trimming the mustache of a British colonel. In the lobby, two porters were helping a couple carry their luggage to the door. In the staff canteen in the basement, the waiters and kitchen porters were about to sit down at the table. In the garden, the old gardener Shlomo was watering the rosebushes.

After their rest, the secretaries had gone back to their places in the south wing. The heat didn't appear to affect their performance. Some typed decisively, others wrote down memoranda dictated to them. Some were taking calls, and a few were filing reports or passing on to their superiors documents ready to be signed.

Still in his office, Marcus had just hung up the telephone after speaking to Sir Gyles Isham. He stood and approached the window. He looked out toward the YMCA tower with his hands in his pockets. His thoughts, however, were somewhere else. The Bakelite fan was on full blast, but he was sweating.

At half past eleven or so I opened the wardrobe doors and took out underwear, a blue skirt with an elastic waist, and a white cotton blouse, cool and sleeveless. On the table was the breakfast tray they brought me every morning, but I hadn't touched it. The tea was cold, the toast dry, and a couple of flies perched on the sliced fruit. Something strange and unpleasant had been gnawing at my body and soul since I got up. An ominous feeling.

I dressed and tuned back to the PBS. The cultural slot in English was now broadcasting a show about female Victorian writers. Lately they'd been repeating these programs, recorded a long time ago. They no longer aired external contributors on the public radio, making do with their own staff. I had been the last guest, at the beginning of the year, and in the end I hadn't managed to broadcast a word. I sat down to listen without much focus, not in the right frame of mind for daughters of the vicar, wuthering heights, moors, and the countryside. For some reason, however, I wanted to let the radio waves enter my head and didn't want to leave the room.

Just then, at the King David's service entrance, the eight young Jews with the van were joined by a few more comrades, who until a few minutes before had been hiding, skillfully camouflaged, in the urban landscape. Dressed from head to toe in Arab clothes, they went unnoticed by the sizable police and military presence. They all began to do what had been planned, without needing instructions. Their movements were meticulously choreographed. In pairs, they unloaded the milk churns from the vehicle and dragged them to the door. The fact that these contained not milk but explosives made them rather heavy. Other comrades, meanwhile, opened the hessian sacks and distributed their contents. Tommy guns. Sten guns. Some pistols.

The ones with the weapons ran to the kitchens and the staff canteen. The sounds of orders, shouting, scuffles, the crash of crockery, and a couple of gunshots could be heard through the swinging doors. The men responsible for the milk churns stuck to their task. One by one, they dragged the churns along a corridor until they reached La Régence, the club where Marcus and I had gone for dinner months before, where I had made the decision to set aside my fears and stay in Jerusalem by his side. The table we'd sat at that night was kicked away. There, by one of the pillars, they positioned two of the milk churns full of TNT and gelignite. The other churns were distributed around the rest of the room, directly under the secretariat's offices, against the pillars that held up the south wing's entire structure. The men connected detonators to all of them. As soon as they'd finished, they turned off the lights and ran. It was a quarter past noon.

Minutes later, a call was received at the French consulate near the King David. A young, nervous female voice passed on a message. In the name of the Jewish resistance movement, she announced, a bomb was about to explode inside the neighboring hotel. The subordinate rushed up to the consul general's office. Though threats came frequently, the senior official decided to give credence to the warning and trigger the emergency protocol: they opened all the windows, closed all the curtains, and evacuated the staff. It was twenty-seven minutes past noon.

A few minutes later another call was received at the offices of the *Palestine Post*. From the back room of a nearby warehouse, the same voice delivered the same warning. The operator tried to pass the message on to the police station, but for some time no one answered there. It was now thirty-two minutes past noon.

In the King David's kitchens, the terrorists had fled, setting the workers free, and confusion and hysteria had ensued. Amid the commotion, between the chaotic exchange of languages, opinions, and versions of events, a kitchen porter mentioned having seen some Arabs dragging milk churns through the corridor. No one seemed to hear him.

Some of the workers went up to the lobby to spread the word. But the information was muddled, and by now everyone was more than used to false alarms—their warnings fell on deaf ears. The Sudanese waiters continued to serve bowls of olives and cocktails table by table, imperturbable with their turbans, gloved hands, and bronze trays. Colonial servants, decorated military men, wealthy citizens, visitors, tourists: none of the regulars seemed prepared to miss their aperitif because of yet another threat.

Marcus, still standing at the window, thought about making another call to let me know he wouldn't be returning to have lunch with me after all. Distracted and apprehensive, he couldn't shake the feeling that something that Monday wasn't quite right.

Meanwhile, I was trying to amuse myself by leafing through a back issue of *Tatler* with the radio still on in the background. I was turning a page when I heard the boom, loud enough to make the windowpanes shake. I winced, held one hand to my heart and another to my belly.

I didn't know it yet, but the entire south corner of the King David Hotel had just been blown to pieces. The eight hundred pounds of trinitrotoluene had turned into fifty-five thousand gallons of gas, which heated the air to fifty-five hundred degrees Fahrenheit.

The milk churns melted. The pillars disintegrated. The iron framework liquefied like wax. The upper floors shook as if they had a life of their own. First the walls swelled, then they shuddered, then they convulsed inward, and finally, with a deafening roar, they turned to rubble, sheets of fire, and clouds of black smoke.

The six floors built from stone and reinforced concrete collapsed. They dragged down furniture, radiators, appliances, piping, individuals' belongings. And with them, scores of human beings.

17

The first contractions came shortly after the explosion. Straight to the kidneys, sharp as daggers. They still hadn't subsided completely when I managed to pick up the telephone receiver. With my throat suddenly dry, I asked to be put through to the secretariat, but it was impossible to connect: there was no signal at all from its switchboard. I breathed anxiously through my nose as terror traveled through my bones. Marcus. Marcus. Where was Marcus?

I'd been told that labor came on more progressively than forcefully. What was happening now in my body, however, seemed like something quite different. And that explosion. The explosion. I was used to hearing grenades go off, bursts of machine-gun fire, and bangs of every size. I'd even experienced an explosion close-up at Broadcasting House a few months before. But this blast had been on another scale, a monstrous aberration.

The next contractions made me pace up and down the room, from end to end and back again, unable to keep calm or stay still. Once they eased, I lifted the receiver again and asked the receptionist for Bertha Vester. She went out an hour ago, Mustafa took her to the optician in the Ford, was the answer.

I tried to keep my head, to breathe at a steady pace, as I'd been advised. But fear and anguish prevented it. With my hands on my lower back, I approached the balcony. A dense cloud of smoke was rising above some part of Jerusalem, dark gray, almost black, a chilling contrast against the bright summer sky. I began to hear sirens from afar, first one, then several, and the thick smoke continued to soar. Standing there, gripping the railing, looking into the distance, I felt a hot liquid run down my inner thighs. Over my knees, my calves, my ankles, onto the floor.

Alarmed, my heart pumping frenetically, I allowed all the liquid to come out of me; it was impossible to stop. Leaving wet footprints on the tiles, with great difficulty I made it back to the telephone. I asked to be put through to the secretariat again with no success. Then I asked for the King David's main switchboard. Nothing. "Marcus," I whispered again. "Marcus, where are you?" Then I tried the press office, hoping to find Frances Nash, but the line was busy. "Keep calm, Sira," I repeated to myself. "Slow down. No Marcus, no Bertha, no Frances, either." I reviewed my situation, trying not to completely lose my cool. Perhaps, I thought, I could call the Government Hospital directly. Which I did, to no avail.

My terror grew as I realized everyone seemed to be unreachable. Then it occurred to me that maybe Said, the employee tasked with shopping and making deliveries in the American Colony's van, could take me to the hospital, in the vehicle that was as likely to transport eggplants and sacks of birdseed as it was chickens or lambs. *He's not here either, madam* was the reply. The sirens, meanwhile, continued to blare.

With the contractions, I was alternating between painless moments and unbearable ones—my wet skirt was sticking to my legs, the heat was dreadful, I was still sweating. I was clearly about to give birth, I had no one to turn to, and I felt a dark certainty that Marcus wouldn't be by my side as I delivered, either. I went out onto the balcony again, treading through the waters my body had expelled. Across the court-yard, at the end of the garden, I saw the cleaning staff and other workers looking awestruck in the same direction as me, toward the smoke climbing from the center of Jerusalem, clotted and ominous. I tried to yell, to catch the attention of one of the girls. I knew them all: Amina, Lamya, Malak, Sharifa. They all touched my belly constantly, teasing me affectionately about my size. Perhaps because they were shouting too, shaken by the explosion, or because my voice wasn't loud enough, or because the distance between us was too far, they didn't hear me. Nobody paid attention to my yelling, or even turned around.

"Dios mío, Dios mío, Dios mío." Oh my God, I babbled to myself as I went in from the balcony again. *"Dios mío, Dios mío, Dios mío . . ."* Until I stopped dead in the middle of the room, standing with my legs half-open. A familiar voice had just reached my ears. I looked around in confusion, then I rested my eyes on the radio. That was where it had come from. The voice was Nick Soutter's. I approached the device, my gaze fixed on it. In a sober, solemn tone, the PBS head of news was reporting the devastating terrorist attack that had occurred at the very heart of the British administration in Palestine. They'd destroyed the secretariat's headquarters, the King David Hotel's entire south wing, he said. There were many casualties, their identities as yet unknown.

My howl must've been so ferocious, so broken, that two of the Arab girls soon banged furiously on my door and came in without waiting for permission.

"Nicholas Soutter, PBS," I wailed as soon as I saw them. "Call Nicholas Soutter at the Palestine Broadcasting Service." I pointed at the radio, turned clumsily toward it, and slapped the wooden casing as hard as I could. "Call Nicholas Soutter, for the love of God, call him for me."

An indeterminate amount of time passed, half an hour, an hour, maybe. The contractions continued to come every six or seven minutes. A newsreader who wasn't Nick continued to announce emergency measures: curfew was imminent, approaching Julian's Way was forbidden, streets and access roads were blocked, establishments were being closed. Lamya was holding my hand, Sharifa was fanning me with a magazine, and the two of them were saying things to me in Arabic that I didn't understand. Whenever the contractions returned, I pulled myself away, stood, and paced the room like a caged madwoman.

Nick Soutter didn't arrive, but two women did come on his behalf: Ruth Belkin, the middle-aged PBS producer, and a young woman who, seeing me, reacted as if she'd seen a three-headed monster. "Come on, come on," the older woman ordered, taking control right away. They helped me down the stairs, through the ground floor, and out into a car while I yelled at them to tell me about the explosion, the King David, my husband. The stranger sat at the wheel, and Ruth got in beside me on the back seat. "Breathe, breathe, in and out, in and out," she insisted, keeping her cool. Lamya and Sharifa stood watching, surrounded by their workmates, their faces tense, wringing their hands.

As soon as we moved away from the American Colony, I realized we were going in the wrong direction, toward Mount Scopus and not the city center.

"Take me to the Government Hospital," I pleaded, screamed, perhaps.

"No," said Ruth. "We're going to the Hadassah."

"Government Hospital," I shrieked. The British hospital had my medical record and the unpleasant doctor.

Ignoring me, the stranger kept driving in the same direction, in silence. She finally stopped outside the Jewish medical complex, after subsequent contractions prevented me from continuing to object. Days later, I would learn that the two women had decided not to take me to the Government Hospital because when they passed it on their way to the American Colony, they saw scores of ambulances, police vans, and private cars arriving with the injured, the mutilated, the burned, the dead.

Everything that happened afterward ended up merging in my memory in a scrambled sequence. The hospital staff tore off my soaking clothes, put some kind of open gown on me, and laid me on a wheeled bed. There were only women around me: midwives, nurses in spotless uniforms trying to soothe me while they opened my legs, women telling me to calm down while they inserted their fingers into my vagina. There may not have been many of them—just two, three, four—but their outlines multiplied in my mind. I didn't understand why they'd brought me to this place; the pain was appalling, the terror immense. I didn't know whether Marcus was alive or dead. "Find out how my husband is," I begged them whenever the contractions gave me a moment's respite. I mixed English with Spanish, my sweat melded with my tears, my begging and wailing with my sobs. "Ask for Mark Bonnard at the King David. Ask for Marcus Logan."

They pushed the trolley along a white-tiled corridor and went through some white doors into an even whiter room. The contractions now came practically one after the other. They put me under a strange round lamp, enormous, metallic, the light so bright it blinded me for a moment. One of the women—a midwife, I assumed—approached the head of the trolley and spoke with authority, but I didn't understand anything she said.

Then she gave an order, and a nurse held her hand to my nose along with some device that was attached to a small cylinder. I guessed they wanted to sedate me, and I batted it away. They held my arms and I continued to resist, shaking my head, sweating through every pore. I felt locks of hair stuck to my face.

They didn't manage it, in the end. Within seconds, I felt a tremendous need to push and roar, to roar and push at the same time. The child inside me was getting ready to come out, begging to be let through. The midwife dove between my legs. I felt her manipulate me and thought she was going to break me in two. I was beginning to reach exhaustion, and they urged me to push harder. I did, with all my strength, once, twice, a hundred times. Some of the pushes made me lose myself, and I struggled to find the way back.

My son came into the world warm, slippery, eyes open. I yelled at them to give him to me, though the midwife hesitated before agreeing.

I held him tight, purple, sticky, hot. I touched him, smelled him, kissed his head, contained my anguish so that I wouldn't pass my premonitions on to him. I looked at him, and he looked at me with his almond-shaped eyes, recognizing me. I tore my gown off and offered him my breast.

There were puddles of blood and towels stained with a dense red on the delivery room floor. The harsh sun filtered through the slats of the blinds; the medical instruments seemed like a butcher's tools.

I called him Víctor, because his little life arrived in the world as a victory, amid suffering.

PART TWO

Britain

18

We arrived in London in early February, in the middle of a dreadful winter.

Demoralized by the lack of solutions for keeping the terror under control, the mandatory authorities in Palestine had decided to impose martial law and ordered the repatriation of all family members and nonessential civilian staff. I'd tried to refuse, and I'd even managed to meet with High Commissioner Cunningham. I'd cited my Spanish nationality, the absence of any formal ties with the British following Marcus's death. I'd been alone ever since, clinging to his memory and devoted to my son.

There was nothing to be done. Officially, I was a British subject, an Englishman's widow, and the mother of a British child. Therefore, I had to be evacuated with the rest: the order was unequivocal, and no delays or exceptions were permitted. Within twenty-four hours we would be assigned a means of transport. Within forty-eight we would depart.

We were allowed to take only the bare minimum, a maximum of one item of luggage per person. Many people abruptly left behind the fruit of decades of putting down roots: a spouse, friends, and loyal servants; trees they'd planted, walls they'd painted; smells, tastes, and sounds they would never experience again. Others, like me, left behind loved ones buried under austere gravestones. After the horror of the King David, Bertha Vester had offered me the alternative of a private burial in the little cemetery her colony maintained on the slopes of Mount Scopus. I had been about to accept—why should I care where they laid to rest the broken remains they hadn't allowed me to see, if Marcus was no longer alive? In the end, I managed to find some clarity somewhere in my torment, and I opted to do what I believed was more in keeping with the circumstances: he'd died serving his country and he belonged among his own, in the Anglican cemetery on Mount Zion, surrounded by his compatriots.

In a different way and with a different destination, now I was saying goodbye to this wicked and brutal Holy Land. The urgent plan to remove British civilians was named Operation Polly. Initially, many families had been assigned trains to Cairo and then ships to English ports. They were the first to leave but, ultimately, proved to be the least fortunate because poor organization and adverse seas delayed boarding and they had to wait in Egypt, housed in barracks. Other families were allocated Royal Air Force Halifax aircraft, and the authorities arranged civilian flights for the rest of us, some direct to London, others to airports relatively nearby. Víctor and I were flown to Paris and from there taken to Calais on buses. We crossed to Dover by ferry and, once there, traveled by train to London.

Our plane was filled with young and older mothers, and girls and boys by the dozen, euphoric to be climbing onto an iron bird for the first time. There were also babies aplenty, crying because the pressure plugged their ears or because, with their miniature intuition, they sensed that something was changing in their lives forever. Such was the case with Víctor. On my lap, in row nine, in the window seat, he was inconsolable for the entire flight, as if already furious at the world at his six and a half months, unable to understand anything. I was tearing him from his home at the Austrian Hospice in the Old City, from his olive-wood cradle, from the muezzins' chants and the church bells that had lulled him to sleep every day. I was separating him from the warmth and the soft Arabic of our beloved Sharifa, the dear girl who'd come with us when we moved from the American Colony. From the explosive personality of Fran Nash, our neighbor on the floor above; from Nick Soutter, who lifted Víctor to the ceiling, making him burst out laughing; from the journalist friends who came to the building when the bars were closed. My son was saying goodbye to all of this without knowing it. And to his buried father.

Victoria Station seethed with relatives there to collect the travelers. The reunions sparked shouting, children's tantrums, exclamations, warm greetings, one or two sobs of emotion. Marcus's mother, Olivia, came to meet us. Ever since I'd told her of her son's death and of Víctor's birth, she'd tried everything to persuade me to leave Jerusalem and move to England. But I always said no. For my tiny baby's sake and for Marcus's memory, for myself and my grief, I didn't want to leave the place we'd shared; I wasn't afraid anymore.

It took a long time for Olivia and me to recognize each other in the crowd; neither of us looked the same as we had when we'd met that one bright summer afternoon. She now wore a fur overcoat and an eye-catching hat of thick felt; her distinctive plait wasn't on view. For my part, I'd forgone any trace of sophistication months ago. Now that my social life was reduced to almost nothing, and thanks to Fran Nash, I had discovered that trousers were infinitely more comfortable than skirts. I had also swapped my silk stockings for socks and dismounted from my high-heel shoes in favor of low ones with laces. Marcus's old sweaters, emptied of his presence, had been added to my wardrobe, and I even took apart his tweed jackets and adjusted them to fit my body, as if doing this would make him feel close to me still. I couldn't even remember the last time I'd put makeup on, and I always wore my hair gathered up with a barrette at the back of my neck. Almost nothing was left of the glamorous-foreigner look with which I'd naively hoped to win my mother-in-law's approval on my first visit to London.

We hesitated for a few moments in the middle of the packed platform when we were finally face-to-face, she looking magnificent, me holding my boy in my arms. But there was no doubt, in front of me I had the mother of the man who was the love of my life, the person from whom he'd inherited the features and mannerisms I missed so much. I was the one who provided the icebreaker: I whispered her name without title and opened an arm. When we let go, her eyes came to rest on Víctor, on his half a year of life. He looked a lot like Marcus, with greenish eyes, light skin and hair. She swallowed when she saw him, bit her lip, held a gloved hand to his cheek. Tired, puzzled, her grandson swiveled his neck and huddled against my shoulder, shying away.

"There's plenty of time," she whispered as she drew back her hand. "Plenty of time. What matters is you're finally home, thank God."

It was snowing when we came out of the station, and it had already been dark for hours. The entrance was crammed with taxis and private cars ready to collect the many families who'd arrived from far-off Palestine after an exhausting three days of travel. It was bitterly cold, so I covered Víctor's face with the lapel of my coat and pressed him against me. Olivia started to make her way confidently through the mayhem of running engines and exhaust fumes. We followed. Behind us, a porter carried our suitcase and an overnight bag. It was all we had.

We approached a luxurious Bentley, and the driver rushed to open the doors for us. I wanted to pay the porter who'd helped us, but Olivia stopped me and took care of it. She also took the lead in the conversation during the journey. I just listened and replied with a few words from time to time. There was hardly any traffic once we were away from the throng outside Victoria Station; very few pedestrians were walking the dark, snow-covered streets that freezing night. When we arrived, Víctor was asleep.

The exterior of the house in the Boltons seemed less imposing than I remembered, perhaps because of the lack of light: only a dim streetlamp cast yellowish shadows on the portico. The front door opened right away, and from it emerged a housemaid somewhat advanced in years who I remembered vaguely from my previous visit. I got out of the car with my baby in my arms, trying not to wake him. Olivia gestured grandly for me to head inside, and I obeyed, greeting the servant as she held the little wrought-iron gate open. I was starting to climb the porch steps when I realized that Víctor had lost a shoe. I turned to ask them to please look for it, and then I saw something that shocked me: while her housemaid was unloading my luggage, Marcus's mother was paying the driver with some notes. It was clear he wasn't the household's driver. I turned back, and none of them noticed that I'd seen.

The hall in front of me was in semidarkness. I stepped forward, took a deep breath, and blew out hard. A dense cloud of moist air came from my mouth.

"Here we are," I whispered.

I hadn't the slightest idea what it would be like staying in this house that was so different from any of the places I'd lived before now. Amid this uncertainty, however, one idea held firm in my mind: we would leave as soon as possible.

We spent the next hour in the half-light settling in.

"Would you prefer to put the boy in a separate room?"

I must've looked at Olivia as if she were mad because she understood the answer was no without a word from me. She gave us a bedroom with two big windows protected from the freezing night by thick curtains. The room was large and clearly beautiful, but disrepair was obvious everywhere: a door on the enormous wardrobe didn't close, the walls were dotted with the imprints of missing paintings, the chinoiserie wallpaper had peeled in some sections. Still, the room had a fireplace with a good fire going that they must've lit for our arrival, and we positioned Víctor's cot next to what would be my bed. When I laid my son down, I felt a deep sense of relief tinged with dejection.

I probably should've made the effort to go downstairs with Olivia and talk for a while, to show at least a modicum of gratitude for her hospitality and the trouble she'd gone to. But I wasn't in the mood to recall the incredibly long journey, nor to describe the bleak Jerusalem we'd left behind, let alone stir up our memories of Marcus. And so I accepted her offer to have her servant bring up a bottle of warm milk for Víctor and something to eat for me. I said good night to both of them and shut myself in my room.

I woke when Víctor's hunger arrived with screams and threats of crying. I'd brought him into my bed in the middle of the night to keep him warm after the fire went out. The room was still dark and freezing. I mustered my courage, leaped out of bed, yanked the curtains open to peep outside, and quickly got back under the blankets. I was beginning my first day in London with the city covered in snow. I tried to play with my son for a short while, hoping to distract him, but he flatly refused. It was time to get going.

Twenty minutes later, I carried the boy downstairs in search of breakfast for the two of us. When I reached the last step, the housemaid came out to show us where to go. "Milady's waiting for you in the dining room," she announced in an accent that seemed strange to me. She was over sixty, with a clunky body and plain face. Her black uniform was faded in some areas, and over it she wore an apron and bonnet of a questionable white, and a thick cardigan. As I followed her, I realized that one of her legs was slightly longer than the other.

The great Lady Olivia Bonnard was reading the *Times* at the head of the table. Now she resembled the mother-in-law I met more than a year and a half ago, wrapped in layers of striking woolen shawls, hair gathered in a plait that fell over her shoulder and down to her chest. Once again, her appearance surprised me: among the English ladies of her age I'd met in Palestine, I'd never seen any like her. They were all infinitely more sober and conventional in their choice of clothes, their style, their hair. One of her dogs was curled up in a ball at her feet. I supposed the other two had died of old age.

My place was set on one side, to her right. And for Víctor there was an old high chair made of dark wood. I imagined it had been salvaged from a dusty attic and found it touching to think it might be the same one Marcus had used as a boy. Olivia, however, soon put me right.

"Oh no, my dear. Nothing of the children's is left. I found this last week along with a pram, at the church jumble sale."

The fire was lit, but the early hour and the size of the room hadn't allowed it to warm up yet. I immediately regretted not putting more clothes on us, and neither had we managed a bath. When I'd tried, I had discovered that only icy water came from the taps in the bathroom that adjoined the bedroom.

As if reading my mind, while closing the newspaper, Olivia announced, "It's going to be a difficult winter, dear. It started to snow in the last week of January, and the forecasters insist that, for the time being, it doesn't look like it will stop."

The table was exquisitely laid with porcelain crockery decorated with delicate flowers, silver cutlery, linen napkins. I soon discovered, however, that all the resplendence was in stark contrast to the frugal nature of the food. From a nearby sideboard, we helped ourselves to a small mound of scrambled egg, a scrawny sausage, and a tiny handful of mushrooms. No pastries. Not even a suggestion of fruit. Some bread, very little butter, with jam expertly spread over a glass dish to give the impression of plenty.

"The war is over, but the country has not recovered," my distinguished mother-in-law explained. "There are restrictions on everything and for everyone. Gas, coal, electricity. Even newspapers, would you believe, are allowed to print only four pages in each edition. And food is rationed, of course. We must go as soon as possible to request your rationing coupons."

I allowed a few moments of silence while I chewed. I answered after swallowing.

"That might not be necessary."

She raised her eyebrows with a mixture of surprise and curiosity. I straightened out her confusion right away.

"We don't plan to stay, Olivia."

She frowned ever so slightly.

"And may I ask, where do you intend to go, darling?"

"To Morocco."

The journey from Jerusalem had given me the chance to reflect and make decisions. We couldn't go back to Palestine, and I had to decide where we would start a new life. Between the choices of Madrid and Africa, perhaps because our exhausting journey had coincided with the harsh winter, the scales tipped toward the south, so that my boy would grow up under its benevolent sun.

"Morocco . . . ," she slowly whispered. She pursed her lips and nodded, as if my idea were supremely brilliant. An expression that communicated obvious sarcasm.

"Yes, Morocco," I said firmly. "My mother lives there, and I have friends there."

"And for how long do you expect to visit them?"

"It won't be a visit. I've decided we're going to settle there. Permanently."

She held her teacup to her mouth. I had the impression that, as the rim brushed her lips, her hands were trembling.

"You have ties here too, Sira," she said with restraint as she returned the cup to its saucer.

She looked at Víctor, who was sucking on a piece of bread with delight. Oblivious to us, he was sitting in his little throne and observing the ancient dog with curiosity.

"This boy is the only descendant of a family that has been serving Britain and the Crown with dignity, responsibility, and integrity for generations. When the time comes, he will inherit this house and will honor the Bonnard name, and to do so he must be appropriately educated. I doubt that an impoverished Spanish colony in Africa will be the best place for that."

I had no intention of arguing. I had neither the desire nor the strength. So I let the matter go, with the excuse of passing another piece of bread to my son. As soon as he grabbed it with his little hand, he threw it at the dog and burst out laughing when he hit it on the head. Olivia and I both smiled, pretending that the tension had been defused. At least for the time being.

19

Not even those born before Queen Victoria was widowed could remember there ever having been such a brutal winter. Over five successive weeks, there wasn't a single night when the temperature rose above freezing. The gas came out at very low pressure, the coal deliveries were meager, and there were power cuts every day that lasted for hours. In homes and in public buildings, candelabras and candlesticks were put back in use on many nights. Even indoors, we spent the whole day with our gloves on, dressed in two pairs of socks and several layers of clothes. Animals froze to death on farms, and fresh fruit and vegetables were almost luxury goods. Deliveries were complicated if not impossible to make, and the food rations we received in exchange for our coupons were even more diminished than they had been during the war. Factories, businesses, offices, and schools were closed; public transport and trains were barely operating; the army was working hard to clear the snow from the streets, roads, and railways; and German prisoners of war were even made to lend a hand. Half the country came to a standstill, and hundreds of thousands lost their jobs.

Since it was impossible to travel in this dreadful weather, Víctor and I had no option but to prolong our stay in London, shut up in the Boltons, in a house my mother-in-law ran with an unyielding hand. Olivia recruited a young nanny with curly brown hair—a small, timid girl named Philippa—and put her up in the house. I didn't need her, in principle, but I didn't want to deprive the poor girl of a roof over her head. Uncomplaining, I adapted to Olivia Bonnard's routines: breakfast in the dining room at eight o'clock, watery coffee in the lounge at eleven, a frugal lunch at one, tea at four, supper at half past seven. On the first Sunday after my arrival, she suggested that I accompany her to the nearby parish church, St. Mary The Boltons, and this became our habit, even with the snow above our ankles, the two of us bundled up for warmth. She introduced me to the vicar and his wife, to neighbors and relatives. She showed Víctor off to all of them proudly, openly expressing her joy at having us at home.

On Tuesdays her friends came to play bridge. She received other visitors often—whether spontaneously or by prearrangement, I couldn't say. And every Thursday, without fail, a diverse group of people appeared—eight, ten, a dozen or more, sometimes—to talk while they smoked and drank whatever they'd brought between them: whiskey or sherry, French red wine, gin or brandy.

The gatherings went on for as long as the bottles lasted. Generally, the talk centered on society matters: high-flying gossip and detailed political analyses that usually tore Prime Minister Attlee and his left-wing cabinet to shreds, portraying them as the malign perpetrators of the recent nationalization of the coal mines, power plants, and railways, and the Bank of England.

I suspected that these gatherings, which were as full of conversation as they were devoid of food, had in other, less hostile times included lavish dinners brought to the table by three servants. Perhaps then, the honorable Hugh Bonnard hadn't yet been struck dead by a heart attack before he was fifty-four, and the family's three children, led by Marcus, had still run rampant through the house, healthy, slender, and full of promise. Now, only the mother was left, wrapped in her extravagant woolen shawls. The dining room wasn't opened for the guests anymore because there was nothing to offer them, and the one remaining servant went to bed at eight o'clock or so, no more duties or obligations to be met, leaving behind a handful of ashtrays and the faint light from a few candles as the only preparations for the visitors.

During those days of bitter cold when we barely left the house—staying between those refined mansion walls screaming for a lick of paint, a plumber to fix the pipes, or some new wallpaper—my son and I moved about like silent ghosts, present but uninvolved. My relationship with my mother-in-law remained courteous, with little warmth but without major mishaps, as fluid as any contact between two strangers from radically different universes could be.

From the start it was clear that Olivia Bonnard was utterly indifferent to me, her only interest being my marital bond to her son and my role as the breeder who bore her grandson. She never asked about my background, my family, or my country, about my life before—or my relationship with—Marcus. It was clear that I was the opposite of what she would've hoped for her firstborn's wife: a foreigner with no social status or wealth, from a dubious and backward nation. Intelligent as she was, and in her own interests, she tried not to openly show her disdain. I did, however, sense her profound affection for Víctor, a warmth without kisses and cuddles that, with my mother's instinct, I perceived to be sincere.

One of the ways I passed those endless hours of spare time was to explore the house from top to bottom—from the laundry room, empty pantry, office, and big kitchen in the basement, to the attic that once housed the domestic staff, now nonexistent except for Philippa the nanny and old Gertrude. I looked for some trace of Marcus in his childhood or youth, anything to bring me closer to him, but all I found were a couple of tennis rackets with warped wood and broken strings. Over the course of the war, Olivia had taken in distant relatives, friends, and acquaintances and had even let some of her rooms to strangers. She'd parted with furniture, decorations, and other possessions, having had no option but to give up nonessentials in favor of an almost military functionality. She'd even ended up selling her husband's large library.

Of those who'd lived in the house in the past, now only memories remained.

Almost every week, I received news from Fran Nash in Jerusalem, long letters that I devoured shut away in my bedroom, repeating paragraphs out loud to my son, as if he could process them with his little brain. In one, she told me she'd found a young Andalusian Franciscan to replace me as her translator for Télam; in another, that my apartment at the Austrian Hospice was being rented by an American couple, also journalists. She also wrote about acquaintances, her daughters, films she'd seen, with flashes of irony and anecdotes. To avoid upsetting me, she hardly touched on the violence of the Jewish resistance.

Less often but also regularly, I received letters from Bertha Vester, written on elegant ivory-colored paper with the American Colony's emblem on it. Though I'd left her hotel to reorganize my life, we maintained a pleasant correspondence. I also received messages from acquaintances in Fran's circle who'd become almost friends after Marcus's death and my move to the Old City. And of course, Nick Soutter often wrote to me in his assured hand, recounting the ups and downs of the PBS where the Jewish staff, led by Edwin Samuel, had walked out of the mandate's public radio station en bloc and left of their own accord. At the end, he always devoted a couple of lines to Víctor, calling him *old chap*, *old chum*, addressing him as if they were friends. Half-joking and half-serious, he asked him to take care of me.

I read and reread all those letters as if they were the only thing that connected me to my past. When I rewound my memory, Jerusalem was almost all I remembered, as if my whole existence had begun there. Madrid, Tétouan, Tangier, my young years, and my work as a dressmaker seemed so far back that sometimes I felt as if they hadn't belonged to me but to some stranger. The time I'd spent in Palestine—first with Marcus, and then the months afterward, living with his absence—was my truest reality. My dearest friends now belonged to those times: the ones who had been with me on the nights of pain and sleeplessness after his death, who'd held a hand out to me so that I wouldn't sink completely into the dark waters of suffering. They were the ones who, in this glacial London and inhospitable house, I missed so much, and my days passed with them in my thoughts, as I waited for the bad weather to end so we could head for the sun and get away from these icy and alien surroundings.

I was rereading a letter from Fran that had arrived that morning while Víctor was taking a nap, when Gertrude knocked on my bedroom door. The rest of the house was so uncomfortable because of the temperature that I spent long hours shut away in there. The room was big enough for me to have set up a little kitchen in the corner with a portable stove, for heating the feeding bottles and a teapot. Gertrude had also provided me with a small paraffin heater, at night she brought us hot water bottles to heat the sheets, and from time to time she found us a couple of bananas or a packet of biscuits. Deep down, I thought her generosity was more about annoying her mistress than it was about making me feel at home—their strange relationship was forever swinging between affection and dislike, between veneration and hostility.

"Milady asks if you could go down, madam," she announced in the strange accent I was now growing accustomed to.

One of her eyes was narrower than the other, and I often wondered whether it was blind. Despite her aloof look, old age, and dragging foot, she flew like a bullet into her work. She washed and ironed Víctor's nappies in a matter of hours, saw to my room and clothes despite my protestations, and such was her skill that she could turn the meager food that came into her kitchen—liver, small eggs, insipid cabbages, tins of soup, and even whale meat—into something moderately nice.

Given the domestic isolation, the lack of belongings, and my efforts to ward off the cold, my appearance was somewhat unkempt: flannel trousers, a thick Shetland wool sweater with a cowl neck, and one of Marcus's old jackets. Underneath, out of sight, I wore several undergarments in layers. My hands were protected by knitted mittens that

I took off straightaway. My hair was gathered in a ponytail tied with a handkerchief. There wasn't a drop of makeup on my face, or a trace of the lipstick that, to keep up morale, the British authorities had encouraged women to wear during the war years.

I found them sitting on armchairs in front of the fireplace, drinking one of the watery, grayish coffees that were commonplace at the time in the absence of good beans. Both Olivia and the stranger were examining some big rolls of paper spread out on the table. They looked up when they heard me arrive, and he stood politely. He was middle aged, slim, and well dressed, with glasses and a badly receding hairline. When I greeted him I saw that he hadn't taken off his scarf. Olivia introduced him to me as "the architect Mr. Baker," or Barker, or something like that—I didn't manage to retain it.

"We have a difficult challenge on our hands, my dear, and we'd like your opinion," she said. "Do we divide into two, four, or six? What do you think?"

I didn't know why they needed my thoughts on something that was neither my responsibility nor of any interest to me, but I sat with them and feigned involvement. The plans were of the residence on the Boltons where we now were, and they were proposing various ways of separating out the space. One option was to convert it into two adjacent homes. Another, into four independent stories. The third option was to create six apartments.

"This house is too big, and it makes sense to do something with it," Olivia explained. "It hasn't been renovated for decades, and the expense of a complete refurbishment would be unconscionable."

"Measures of this kind are being taken all over London," the architect added. "The shortage of housing is a serious problem due to the huge number of buildings the German bombings wiped out."

They showed me how the possible distributions would look. Even in the case of the most drastic option—the one with six separate units— the resulting dwellings, if not exactly grandiose, would undoubtedly be more than acceptable. If I had to make some comparison, I'd have said that each would be much more spacious than the humble rented home on Calle de la Redondilla where I'd grown up.

"A lot of friends and acquaintances, people like us, are doing the same thing. We must adapt to the times, we must—"

"The results are excellent. They can install central heating—"

"A modern kitchen—"

"Stainless steel taps . . ."

I looked up from the plans. Something clanged in my head as I listened to them give their perfectly choreographed arguments. As it happened, they were both right. On the one hand, the family house had too many empty rooms; on the other, its decline laid bare the lack of financial liquidity. It was obvious that Olivia Bonnard had very little to live on.

The Bonnards had never belonged to the aristocracy. Neither did they have an abundance of properties or estates. The fact that Marcus's father had received the title of "Sir" and Olivia had accordingly adopted the rank of "Lady"—whether by right or not, who could say—didn't mean that they'd descended from nobility; the title was merely a form of address that had been conferred on Hugh Bonnard as a judge of the High Court of Justice. Both came from long lines of lawyers and public servants of various kinds, a well-to-do, respectable, and cultured class of people who'd educated their sons at Harrow School and the Oxbridge colleges, and had married off their daughters to similar families. An upper middle class that had lived more than comfortably while the winds were fair and had been forced to tighten their belts when the storms blew in. Etiquette and good manners defined the class, as did their distinctive way of speaking and their many routines and conventions. But at this point, ready money was in short supply.

As far as I knew, Olivia still maintained ownership of the magnificent Victorian mansion: stuccoed facade, four floors, and an unsurpassable location on the Boltons, between South Kensington, Chelsea, and

Earls Court, almost equidistant between Kensington Gardens and the Thames, and overlooking communal gardens that I hadn't yet had the chance to enjoy because of the wretched snow. Even so, and although the idea of restructuring the property seemed entirely logical, that afternoon, with the plans in front of me, I was overcome with the feeling that I was missing something.

While I tried to put my finger on that elusive suspicion, the architect went on making his case, describing the advantages of each alternative. Until, to sum up, he pointed at a specific part of the plan with his silver propelling pencil and looked straight at me.

"Though, if I had the choice, as you do, I'd go for the four-unit option, keeping the first-floor rooms with views of the gardens for myself."

I almost burst out laughing. So that was it. All at once it was clear. Having run out of ways to persuade me, my enigmatic mother-in-law was trying to stop us from leaving by tempting us with a future home. Independent from hers, but on her property. Separate from her, but adjoining. Like an extension. Or a sort of appendage.

20

We were into March by the time the temperature had begun to improve, the snowfall and frosts had eased off, and I could finally venture out onto London's streets. After several weeks of being snowed in, I had a buildup of things to do. One was to track down some clothes for Víctor, who never stopped growing and had arrived in London with the bare minimum. Another was to try to buy some provisions to offset the cost of our stay. I'd offered to contribute to the housekeeping many times, but Olivia, with the headstrong pride of a magnanimous matriarch, had flatly refused me.

Getting hold of a map was another pressing need. And lastly, I had to find somewhere to buy tickets for our departure. Besides, over and above all of that, I was longing for some fresh air, and not just in a physical sense—for that I went out to the back garden of the house with my son well wrapped up in my arms. The first time I'd done it, I felt a sharp stab of pain: right there, more than a year and a half before, Marcus had been there in the garden with Olivia and me, relaxed, his legs stretched out on the lawn and his face raised up to the summer sun, attractive in his linen suit, satisfied because his mother and his wife had finally managed to meet each other. None of us, on that radiant summer afternoon, could have imagined that the flight to Palestine we'd take that night would be a one-way trip for him.

There in that beautiful garden, neglected and now rendered lifeless by the rigors of winter, I went for short strolls with my boy, back and forth to the brick wall at the end, again and again, several times to allow the oxygen to enter our pores, noses, eyes, and ears.

I announced my intention to go out on the first morning that I saw pale hints of sun come in through the windows. We were still keeping up the early-morning ritual of breakfast at the great walnut table in the dining room, a meal that consisted of tea and little of substance. I often wondered why Olivia clung to this somewhat grandiloquent practice when there were only cobwebs in her pantry, but I supposed it was her way of not succumbing to despair.

She looked up from the *Times*, peering curiously at me over her reading glasses.

"Are you going anywhere in particular?"

"I have to do some shopping."

She turned the page, read a few lines, then paused again.

"Would you like me to go with you?"

"There's no need, thank you."

She continued to read with her glasses on the tip of her nose. As ever, she was wearing one of her knitted shawls and the plait over her shoulder.

"Would you like to borrow my fox fur coat?"

I almost burst out laughing. Four words came to mind: *Not on your life!* But I managed not to say them and just repeated, "There's no need, Olivia, thank you."

She was of course aware of the meagerness of my wardrobe, which was limited to the little I'd managed to fit in a single suitcase: my most everyday clothes, my boy's, and some things of Marcus's. Fran Nash had offered to send our trunks containing what we were forced to leave behind, but I'd told her it wasn't necessary. Those things all tied me too much to a time that was behind me, one I'd rather not reminisce about. I missed only my radio, but I got used to its absence.

That was how my first contact with London began, with me alone, curious, amazed. The area around the Boltons was obviously privileged, but the bruises of war were visible: mud-filled holes in the road surface, smashed curbs, and mounds of dirty snow mixed with rubble. On my way through residential streets almost devoid of pedestrians and traffic, I saw a great many elegant houses with damaged exteriors. Some had windows boarded up as a substitute for glass, and the paint was flaking off almost all of them, leaving patches where it had been. I imagined that many of these houses would also end up being converted into apartments. Wandering aimlessly, driven only by the energy in my legs, I soon reached a main road where the scene was different: more cars, more people, buses, movement. FULHAM ROAD, I read on a sign.

A couple of hours later, I was back with my slender provisions. Not without effort—going into shops, asking for what I needed, going back out, and trying others—I'd found some wool with which to knit sweaters, hats, and socks for Víctor; gauze for nappies; two rubber teats and a bottle. The bare essentials, in other words. Best not to overload myself before we set off for Morocco. Laying my hands on any food at all had been harder still. Everywhere I went I was asked for rationing coupons, which I didn't have with me. Olivia had secured them in the end, but Gertrude was in charge of them. All I eventually got hold of was a bottle of sherry and, at an exorbitant price, a couple of cans of processed meat.

I saw lines everywhere: pale, often dejected-looking people standing silently outside butcher's shops, bakeries, greengrocers, and department stores. The only item I found without difficulty was a secondhand map of London, with which I planned to try to locate my old friend Rosalinda Powell Fox. I knew nothing of her current situation and hadn't been able to reach her for a long time, which seemed very strange. At the end of the world war, I'd surprised her in Lisbon, where her club El Galgo was still open and where she lived in a large apartment on Avenida da Liberdade—I'd met her there years before during my shady

Portuguese adventures. Shortly after Marcus and I settled in Palestine, she'd returned to England, and at her husband's request, they'd tried to rebuild their relationship, moving into a country house in Surrey. But it lasted barely a few months. Once she realized that prolonging their unhappy marriage would only bring them suffering, she left Peter Fox and moved to London. That was when she wrote her last letter to me. At the time, she was in the process of opening a new club, quaintly named the Patio. The return address was 9 Tilney Street, which is where I would head with the help of the map before I left England, in search of my mercurial friend who'd slipped through my fingers.

Having completed almost all my tasks, all that remained was to find a travel agency. I'd decided to tackle that the next day. On my return to the Boltons, I was received as if I'd crossed an ocean. Víctor threw himself into my arms with a cry of jubilation, Gertrude tried to identify the contents of my bag with her good eye, and Olivia studied me. Young Philippa, as timid as ever, stood behind them with her hands together.

"It looks like the world has started up again" was my mother-in-law's greeting. But I sensed something hidden between the lines. Some displeasure. A trace of discontent.

"You have post," she then announced, raising her eyebrows and glancing sidelong at the silver tray where the letters were deposited each day. "From Jerusalem, I believe."

I supposed it was from Fran Nash or Nick Soutter, or maybe one of their journalist friends, or perhaps Bertha Vester or Katy Antonius, who also wrote to me on occasion. But no. The envelope bore the official stamp of the British Mandate.

I passed the boy to Philippa. Once my hands were free, I tore the envelope open, immediately regretting that I hadn't taken it up to my room to open it calmly and carefully with my paper knife. But I couldn't contain my emotion: anything to do with official matters of the British in Palestine still unnerved me.

Olivia must have sensed something because she didn't budge from my side. The letter consisted of two typed pages written in a bureaucratic language that I barely understood. It mentioned services, payments, departments, addresses of offices in London. But its purpose eluded me.

"I think it's something about Marcus," I muttered, holding it out to them.

I followed Olivia as she headed to her desk, squinting at the pages. When she finally found her glasses, she sat and read the contents slowly to herself.

"Indeed," she confirmed when she'd finished. Then she folded the letter along its creases with her long, knotted fingers. "They're recalculating the pension you'll receive after his death. They say there could be readjustments, compensation, perhaps. They request you go to their offices in Westminster so they can explain—"

I didn't let her finish. I shook my head. All this took me back to the weeks after the attack at the King David, the cumbersome, often incomprehensible formalities to which I had to subject myself shortly after giving birth, still bleeding heavily, tears still running down my face, my breasts sore, full of milk.

No, I didn't want to go through that purgatory again. But I knew the matter couldn't be ignored. My son and I needed Marcus's pension to live on; for the time being, we had no other financial means. Aware of my insecurity, Olivia seemed resolved.

"Would you like me to take care of it, on your behalf?"

"Please," I murmured gratefully.

"Leave it to me. It won't be a problem. Oh, by the way . . ."

I assumed she wanted to change the subject to make me feel better. But no. She did in fact have something specific to tell me.

"There was a call for you."

I looked at her, feeling doubtful and incredulous.

"From the BBC. They received a package addressed to you, also from Palestine, by internal mailbag. I don't know why they can't send it here, but they want you to collect it in person."

Unlike the other news, this information raised my spirits. The sender could only be Nick Soutter, sending some of my things at Fran Nash's request, perhaps, or something for Víctor, who he'd taken such a shine to. Either way, that package didn't represent a thankless administrative process like the one outlined in the letter. Rather, it was something that had arrived from a friend, and that was good enough for me.

"Where is it?"

"Where's what?"

"The BBC."

"Broadcasting House? In Marylebone. At the end of Regent Street, near Park Crescent. Opposite the Langham Hotel, if I'm not mistaken. But you could insist they send it to the house. Would you like me to call and—"

I didn't let her finish.

"I'll go tomorrow."

21

That night, by the weak light of an oil lamp, I managed to locate Rosalinda Fox's most recent address on the map. Kneeling on the threadbare rug at the foot of my bed, poring over the spread-out map, I let out a cry of satisfaction. There it was: Tilney Street, in Mayfair, part of a grid of little streets to one side of Hyde Park. That had been my clue: *very near the park,* she'd said in her last letter. She hadn't clarified whether it was her family's property, or whether she rented it, or if she was staying there as somebody's guest. I marked the map with a cross. To my satisfaction, I also saw that it was located on the way from the Boltons to the BBC.

The first thing I did when I awoke was look out of the window to make sure the snow hadn't returned. Through the glass, I saw the same ashen sky I'd seen the previous morning, but nothing was falling from it, and I took that as the signal for me to get going. Without overdoing it, I put a modicum of effort into getting ready. I wasn't attending a special event, but I was going somewhere to do something in a city whose streets were passable at last, a marked contrast to the confinement I'd just lived through.

From my lean wardrobe, I opted for my most presentable outfit: cheviot trousers, a pale pullover, and a burgundy-colored overcoat, the only clothes from my refined past that had fit in my suitcase. I put on some light makeup, tidied my hair, and knotted a scarf of Egyptian wool around my neck.

At the breakfast table, Olivia greeted me with an expression halfway between appreciative and suspicious. I could easily have gotten her to help me with my tasks. After all, they were trivial matters: locating a friend and collecting an unexpected package. But I wanted to stand on my own two feet, even if I got lost and confused and took an age to find my destination. She was already going to take care of the unpleasant business of Marcus's pension, and that was enough. I preferred not to involve her in the rest of my affairs. I needed privacy, needed to leave her sphere for a short time.

I was aware that she tried hard every day to control herself, often biting her tongue to keep her opinions and instructions to herself. Even so, it was obvious that she didn't approve of what I was doing. She was unhappy that I didn't leave Víctor with Philippa for most of the day, and that I instead carried him on my hip from room to room. She didn't like me speaking Spanish to him. She didn't like it when I let him suck on hunks of bread. She didn't think it was proper to let him crawl about freely on the rug in front of the fireplace. She disapproved of me not changing my clothes for dinner. She didn't welcome me treating Gertrude with something like familiarity. Nor did she like that her male friends, when they arrived at the house, gave me approving looks out of the corners of their eyes. Above all, she still hadn't come to terms with the prospect of me leaving England with her grandson.

"You're not going to put on a hat?"

I thought of the hatboxes I'd left in my apartment at the Austrian Hospice, filled with the beautiful creations from my days as a refined dressmaker. Despite the feigned innocuousness of her tone, the question was uncalled for. She was well aware that, other than a wool beret, I hadn't been able to bring any hats.

"Postwar pragmatism, I suppose," she mumbled, returning her gaze to the newspaper.

I smiled with false innocence.

"Precisely."

I could've looked for a cab, but I preferred to walk. I had plenty of time, and Víctor would be fine. With his good nature, he had hit it off with Philippa, and he got on well with both Gertrude and my mother-in-law. In any case, the later I returned, the more time Olivia would have to put all her energy into him, to speak to him in her language, to let her old dog lick him, to daydream, perhaps, about the prestigious boarding school for wellborn boys she longed for him to attend.

I went out with the map folded up in my coat pocket, though I hardly needed it. It was a long way to my destination, but the route was quite straightforward. I admired the surroundings, walking along Old Brompton Road before joining Brompton Road. I reached the Brompton Oratory and saw the majestic edifice of the Victoria and Albert Museum on my left. I passed Harrods department store, which I was dying to visit, but this wasn't the time; I just gazed at its opulent shopwindows and kept walking. I was now in the exclusive Knightsbridge neighborhood, and soon I would arrive at Hyde Park Corner, where the imposing Wellington Arch would signal that I had to turn up Park Lane. I was heading for the Dorchester, because in her last letter Rosalinda had mentioned that she often went there. *How marvelously convenient it is,* she'd said, *living near one of London's most exclusive hotels.*

It was the kind of place she loved to go for tea or a cocktail. As I later learned, during the war the Dorchester had welcomed the upper crust of the conflict: President Eisenhower with his secretary-driver-lover during the Normandy landings. The British foreign secretary Lord Halifax, who occupied eight rooms with his wife while finding time to be unfaithful to her in a suite with the splendid Baba Metcalfe, who in turn was having an affair with Mussolini's ambassador. However, I didn't much care about any of the hotel's eminent guests. All I wanted to do was find an elusive friend, the woman who'd shaped my future.

Tempted by her comments, I decided to peek at the sumptuous lobby. I'd barely taken a few steps when my stomach knotted. The

Dorchester's lobby was nothing like the King David's foyer in Jerusalem. There was no trace of Orientalist decor, their customers were not wearing exotic clothes, nor did I see any Sudanese waiters. There were only light-skinned Western faces and employees attired in sober uniforms. Even so, something similar was in the air of this elegant space where people trickled through, negotiating, conspiring, or conversing: businessmen meeting their counterparts, big-spending American tourists, groups of elegant ladies chatting with ivory cigarette holders between their fingers, perhaps some undercover intelligence officers already on the alert for the imminent Cold War. And here and there—coming out of a lift, having a late breakfast, or inquiring at the concierge's desk—I also saw elegant, attractive high-society couples, clearly in love. Couples like Marcus and I had once been, before fate dealt us its cruelest blow.

Standing in the middle of the lobby, feeling as insignificant as a grain of sand in the Palestinian desert, I scanned my surroundings while trying to hide my unease. There was no trace of Rosalinda, and there was nothing else I needed in that place. Better to leave as quickly as possible.

Sure enough, I found Tilney Street behind the hotel. Number 9 was a small, three-story Victorian brick building. It wasn't an attractive property, but it was respectable, judging by its location and good state of repair. I rang the bell, and a flushed housemaid opened the door. I presumed she'd been doing strenuous work when the bell interrupted her. *Mrs. Rosalinda Fox? Mrs. Rosalinda Powell Fox? Mr. Peter Fox?* She shook her head at all my questions.

A female presence then emerged from inside, the woman speaking with a commanding voice. I introduced myself to the lady of the house, explaining my quest while she looked at me with some suspicion. Once she'd gotten over her wariness, she invited me into a drawing room that was decorated to excess with drapery, porcelain, and ornaments.

"I never met your friend Mrs. Fox," she explained, offering me a seat. "When we returned, she was gone. Like so many Londoners, we spent the war in the countryside, in Sussex, at my parents' house. The bombings, children, all that, you know."

She spoke at length, relating unnecessary details, and I began to fear I would never get away. Her surname was Tembler, or Tembley, or Tembluy, as far as I could make out. She was extravagantly well dressed and wore her reddish hair gathered up with elaborate waves at her temples. In my plain flannel trousers, my pale woolen pullover, and my beret, I must have seemed to her like a timid prude or a missionary.

"My husband agreed to a year's lease with Mrs. Fox, but she decided to leave sooner and didn't give a reason. Nor did she leave a forwarding address."

She struggled somewhat to get up after having sunk into the heap of soft cushions. The postwar pragmatism my mother-in-law had mentioned was clearly not this woman's style. She went to a desk, opened a drawer on the lefthand side, and took out a stack of letters.

"Would you mind taking these?"

I hesitated, but Mrs. Tembler or Tembley or Tembluy didn't seem prepared to accept no for an answer. She straightened her short arm, holding nine or ten letters out in front of my face until I accepted the offer.

As I left, I looked at the letters. Two were mine, one sent from the American Colony and another from the Austrian Hospice. Four were from various people I didn't know, all with addresses in England. The sender of the remaining three was Juan Luis Beigbeder, the letters in plain envelopes without official letterhead, with Madrid postmarks on stamps that featured Franco's head. I was imagining their journey through the relentless censorship when I noticed that the three envelopes were clean open at the top.

I looked back at the house before setting off again. "Where've you disappeared to, Rosalinda?" I whispered pensively to the facade. There was nobody else to ask, in London or anywhere else.

I wandered the streets, captivated by the most elegant sights of the Mayfair district. In time, I reached the magnificent Regent Street with its rows of formidable buildings and shopping arcades, a mass of red double-decker buses belching out black smoke; its department stores, restaurants, and tearooms; its crowds of people with an urban, contemporary, industrious appearance. In this part of the West End, almost miraculously devoid of scars from the bombings, the city unfolded before me in an infinitely more prosperous, opulent, and beautiful state than that of my poor Madrid. Both cities had been ravaged by their respective wars, but the impact wasn't the same because they'd set off from very different starting lines. For centuries, London had been the capital of the biggest empire humanity had ever seen, the legendary epicenter of a global economic, political, cultural, and technological superpower. The Madrid I'd left behind was something else: traditional, shabby, and tightly packed, with its many beggars, its modest shops, its people in mourning, and its lack of splendor. A one-horse town, some said disparagingly. Even so, alone and bewildered as I was in the middle of that strange metropolis, I felt a slight stab of nostalgia.

I crossed Oxford Circus and soon reached the BBC, a stone-clad art-deco building with six, seven, maybe eight floors, behind a curved facade. There was a sculpture of a bearded fellow and a naked boy over the entrance, and a tall antenna on the roof. At first glance, the architecture reminded me of Barclays Bank in Jerusalem, but with its dimensions multiplied.

Inside, the building was a hive of activity, with staff, deliverymen, and visitors milling around. I approached a desk, but with only the vague information I gave them to work from, they were unable to help me. They directed me to another room, and from there to another corridor, and from there to another office, before finally I was shown to yet another department where they were able to give me a response.

"Oh yes, the package from Palestine," a young woman with glasses and buck teeth said in a singsong voice. "Wait in the corridor, if you don't mind."

I'd seen a lot of women as I walked back and forth through the building. They often seemed to have administrative roles, but there were others in various posts. As had happened in other industries, the shortage of men during the war had led to a great many women being hired here. Across the country, women had become factory workers, clerical staff, bus and ambulance drivers. Within the BBC, in addition to the usual secretaries, telephone operators, and announcers who worked there, women had become sound engineers, broadcast operators, and other technical workers.

I watched some of them come and go while I waited on a bench against the wall, until the friendly girl poked her head out to check if I was still there. Seeing me, she turned and said something to a person behind her. The person came out to meet me.

She was slim, blond, and dressed in a simple navy-blue two-piece suit that didn't hide her good looks. She must have been my age, perhaps a little older.

"Mrs. Bonnard?"

I detected a slight sharpness behind her polite tone. And in her eyes, a deep curiosity.

"A porter has taken your package to the main entrance. You can collect it there." She looked me up and down rather brazenly. Nothing went unstudied: my hair, my face, my clothes, my shoes. "I understand it arrived from Jerusalem recently." We remained a couple of paces from each other. I'd stood up, but she hadn't come any closer than necessary.

"That's right."

She took a long time to reply, as if she was also assessing my accent.

"Forgive my curiosity. I shouldn't be here. I run another department that has nothing to do with deliveries from the colonies."

As she spoke she made a brief gesture, as though indicating a floor above us in the building, the place where her responsibilities lay, whatever those were. Reciprocating her strange attitude, with my trained eyes from another time, I scrutinized her, too. She was certainly attractive, with a look of diligence about her. She wore her hair above her shoulders, with waves at the tips. Her eyes were blue and her face narrow.

"But there was a mistake," she added. "When they recognized the sender, they notified me, assuming I was the intended recipient. However, I realized straightaway that it wasn't addressed to me, but to another woman. And I couldn't resist the urge to meet you."

She continued to keep her distance as she finally identified herself.

"I'm Cora Soutter. Nicholas Soutter's wife—though for how long I will remain so, I don't know."

22

As I left the building, a biting wind belted my face and rumpled my hair. It was starting to rain, and I tried to find a taxi, but they were all taken. Around me people quickened their pace, gripping umbrellas and holding their hats down on their heads.

I pressed the package I'd just collected against my body. It wasn't very big, but it was too large to walk with comfortably under one arm, especially in bad weather. And I had no idea how the buses or Underground worked. The magnificent city I'd perceived earlier suddenly seemed harshly inhospitable.

I went back into the BBC building, sat on a bench in the lobby, and brushed the drops from my shoulders, sleeves, and hair. I set the box down beside me, the sender's name now smudged by the rain. After my encounter with his wife, the excitement I'd felt at anticipating that Nick Soutter had sent it now turned to confusion.

I looked around me, watching the people in the hall, coming and going, leaving and entering. All of them minding their own business, nobody so much as glancing at the uncertain stranger with the package beside her. I knew intuitively what its contents were, I just needed to make sure. And, though I was aware that this wasn't the right place or time, I couldn't stop myself. I took the little scissors I always had with me out of my handbag and used its points to remove the package's seals. As expected, the first thing I found was a note from Nick, which I left unopened for now. I continued to cut the string and packaging until tears welled up in my eyes as I brushed a familiar surface with my fingertips.

It was my radio. My wireless, as the British often called it. The Murphy A46 from Marcus that the Three Kings had delivered to our room at the American Colony, the one that had kept me company for so many hours in his absence. For months, in our bedroom, it had seen us coming and going, watched over us as we slept. Then, after the Irgun terrorists blew up the King David, after my son arrived fatherless in the world and we moved to the apartment at the Austrian Hospice because I couldn't bear the idea of staying where Marcus and I had lived together, the radio had gone with me. When we were forced to leave Jerusalem in such a hurry, as hard as I tried, I'd been unable to fit it in my suitcase. It was the only material possession I'd regretted leaving behind, placed in the care of my friends. I had left them in charge of getting rid of my belongings, my few pieces of furniture, my old clothes, the hats whose absence annoyed my mother-in-law so much. I'd pleaded with them to keep my radio. The rest of it, they could sell or donate or burn, for all I cared.

To shake off my melancholy, I looked up and fixed my eyes on the opposite wall. A directory was there, in the form of a mural, listing the names of all the building's offices in large block capitals. I focused on reading it, not because it interested me particularly, but to distract me from a rising feeling of dejection. As far as I knew, Nick Soutter's relationship with his wife had been in tatters for years, strained by divorce proceedings. Now, after he'd gone to the trouble of sending me my most beloved possession, his wife had called me in to size me up, without hiding her disrespect.

I continued to study the directory, an absurd defense mechanism intended to combat my nostalgia, until I came to a sudden stop. *Overseas Services*, I read. And under it, between various sections indicating other global regions, one name attracted my attention like a magnet: *Spanish Service*. Without stopping to think about it, I stood and picked up my package again, bulkier now that it was open, with the paper and card torn, the straw and packing tape hanging loose. At the reception desk they gave me directions: two floors up, on the right.

What I found halfway down the corridor was a locked door. I checked the time: almost one. Whoever occupied the office could have been having lunch somewhere else. I was about to turn back when I heard voices. I continued on and stopped at the next door, which was open. A sign announced my unexpected destination: *Latin American Service.*

Two men were deep in conversation, uttering words and sounds that reached my ears like caresses. One was speaking overseas Spanish; the other, my inland Castilian. Listening to them stirred my emotions. I'd been away from my world for almost two years, far from my language and from any trace of human beings remotely like me. But I composed myself—it wasn't time for sentimentality. I'd made a decision, and perhaps these strangers could help me.

"Excuse me, *señores.*"

Their conversation came to an abrupt halt, their heads turned, and their eyes fixed on me with a look of surprise. The man sitting behind the desk had plump cheeks and dark, slicked-back hair; he seemed the stouter of the two. The other, in front of him, was slighter. He'd controlled his brown curls with plentiful gel and was sporting a small mustache. They looked fortyish. The desk between them was covered in magazines, bulletins, and newspapers.

"There's no one in the office next door," I said.

"They must've gone out for lunch, but we're *La Voz de Londres*, too."

La Voz de Londres. Of course. *The Voice of London.* My father was forever mentioning it. He listened to it at night in his living room on Calle de Hermosilla, in his dressing gown, with a glass of brandy. *Estación de Londres de la BBC emitiendo para España*—the BBC's London station broadcasting for Spain—was responsible for the transmission that he regularly discussed with his friends at the Gran Peña community center over a drink the next day.

"We broadcast for Latin America and they for Spain, but we're like brothers. So if there's anything we can help you with . . ."

I swallowed while they waited for me to speak.

"I came to offer myself as a contributor," I managed to say.

They looked at me for a few seconds, then the stout one with the soft cadence marked by hues from other lands spoke.

"Thank you for your interest, *señorita*, but we're fully staffed at this moment in time."

"I can offer you something different."

He cleared his throat awkwardly.

"I'm sorry, really. You see, we have no—"

I broke in.

"I got back from Jerusalem recently. Everyone's worried about what's happening there."

I indicated the newspapers they had in front of them with my chin. Sure enough, the tensions in the Holy Land were featured on all the front pages.

"I can tell your listeners about it firsthand."

Not allowing them the chance to continue putting me off, I dove in and kept talking.

Using a mixture of truths and half-truths, I told them about my links with the Palestine Broadcasting Service. What did it matter that my undertaking hadn't materialized in the end? At least I had been taken on and I'd tried. I gave them names of references, details about the PBS and the conflict, and remarked that I had been the only Spanish resident in the area in recent times, aside from a couple of diplomats and a handful of monks. If I'd managed to persuade Nick Soutter to have me talk about Spain in Palestine, perhaps I could persuade these strangers to do the reverse.

"I stayed there until they repatriated me with Operation Polly."

The repatriation of British families and nonessential personnel was no secret. That someone like me had been among those people *was* out of the ordinary.

"My husband is . . . was . . . my husband was English," I explained. "I had to come away with my son. They didn't give us any alternative."

George Camacho. That was what the Colombian head of the service turned out to be called. And Ángel Ara, the Spanish man, was his deputy. The very moment I'd interrupted them, they had been discussing an upcoming recording of *Don Quixote*, which would be the first to be broadcast on the airwaves. But the exploits of the man from La Mancha took a back seat for the time being.

Nick Soutter had waited a day before taking me on at the PBS. These two expatriates were being equally cautious.

"What you're proposing is certainly interesting, but—"

"You can think about it," I cut in. "I don't need an answer right away."

"Good, in that case . . ."

"Why don't I call you tomorrow? At this exact time, let's say."

Still hesitating, he agreed.

"In the hypothetical case you're accepted, bear in mind it would be an ad hoc contribution, with no possibility of a permanent role."

"Something like that is what I had in mind. I'm just passing through London."

"You'll also have to adapt to an established standard, a fairly strict one."

"I'll take all that into consideration."

"And we would need to request formal authorization from higher authorities."

"I completely understand."

Having run out of provisos, he took a card from a leather box and held it out to me.

"Call me, then," Camacho concluded as he stretched out his arm. "We'll think about your offer . . ."

When I went out onto the street for the second time, it had stopped raining, but the sky remained leaden, and the same strong wind was blowing. I was still carrying my radio, the packing paper flapping and threatening to be carried away by the wind.

23

Olivia brought me news about the business she'd offered to take care of on my behalf.

"They're reviewing the King David casualties. They must establish the precise pensions due to the families. We'll have to wait for assessments, reports, perhaps even court rulings. It will take time."

"How long?"

"Difficult to say." She took a long drag on her cigarette, then added, "Several weeks at least. Perhaps months."

"And is it necessary for me to stay here until the formalities are finished?"

"It seems so. You'll have to accept and sign the settlement in person."

"Couldn't I leave everything in place before I leave London? Through a power of attorney or some kind of official document that . . . that . . ."

I stammered, fizzled out. Aside from the subject being a painful one, I didn't know the administrative terminology in English, the intricacies and formulas involved.

"I doubt it."

"Or I could deal with it myself somehow from . . ."

She raised her eyebrows with the rather disdainful irony so typical of her.

"From Morocco?" she asked with exaggerated surprise, as if I'd suggested yelling my messages from a field of African prickly pears.

"Through the British consulate in Tangier, I mean. A proper diplomatic office."

The bluntness of my reply cut through her sarcasm.

"You have to see to everything yourself, and it has to be from here, darling," she said, stubbing out her cigarette impatiently. "If you won't take my word for it, you can try to persuade them yourself."

We held each other's gaze for a few tense seconds.

"I don't doubt you," I murmured. "Quite the contrary. I'm sorry."

After dinner, now that my radio was restored to me, I tuned in to the BBC's Latin American Service. There was a variety of music, news from London and Europe delivered in a mixture of accents, the announcement for the future dramatization of *Don Quixote*. There was even a tango that transported me back to the time when the nonexistent Frances Quiroga sent his reports to the Télam agency in Buenos Aires. I wondered whether Fran Nash signed them with the same name now that a Franciscan monk had taken over my translations.

Once the programs had ended, with my son asleep and the bedroom in semidarkness, I finally decided to open Nick Soutter's letter. I'd been putting it off all day, perhaps because my mind still held the fresh image of his wife before me in the corridor: sharp and haughty, blond and insolent.

Nick Soutter and I had spoken a lot during my grief, sometimes in the company of Fran Nash, sometimes just the two of us. We had spent long hours together at the Austrian Hospice—they with their respective separations, and me with my heartbreak—baring our souls while Jerusalem grew ever bloodier. I was aware, therefore, of Nick's two children, whom he saw only once every six months. Perhaps that separation was why he showed such enormous affection for little Víctor. I also knew he'd met his wife in Bombay, back when they both worked at All India Radio, in the service of the empire. After they were married with children, they'd returned to London together just before the start of the war. He'd gone alone, however, to his post at Radio Cairo after the war was underway, and he'd done the same with his next position, at the PBS. He'd never specified to me what happened between them when they returned to their shared homeland, but it had been during that time that they grew apart. Later, there had been an attempt to mend their differences, but with no success, and now divorce was looming. What Nick had never spoken to me about in detail, however, was her. She was temperamental, he'd mentioned. She didn't have an easy disposition. But he'd never bad-mouthed her.

Unlike his previous letters, which were full of warmth and familiarity, this one said nothing particularly interesting or personal or novel, just a short note to accompany the radio. Perhaps he'd foreseen the package ending up in the hands of his unpredictable wife. In any case, none of it mattered very much now. Our friendship was encapsulated in another time, and missing it was senseless because those days of closeness and confidences were in the past. I would probably never see him or Fran Nash again. After leaving Palestine, my only constant would be my son. And so, rather than sink into nostalgia for times past and people absent, I made myself focus on the now. And the fact was that my present was at a standstill. I was stranded in someone else's home on the Boltons, waiting to tie up some bitter formalities that would delay our departure and keep me tied to London.

At noon the next day I took George Camacho's card from my bag. While Olivia and Gertrude waged fierce combat for the umpteenth time with the jammed boiler, I headed for the telephone to call the director of the Latin American Service. The idea of spending another stretch of time tethered to my mother-in-law, stringing together days and nights with absolutely nothing to do under her roof, was about as appealing as a long prison sentence. So I decided not to waste any more time—if I had to stay, I'd better not squander the opportunity that chance had placed before me.

With a knot in my stomach, I waited to be put through. His answer almost made me scream.

"We're interested," he said. "Come and see me as soon as possible, please."

I went back to Broadcasting House within the hour. From the moment I went through the door, I looked closely at all the faces and bodies that crossed my path. Luckily, at no time did I see Cora Soutter again.

George Camacho received me wearing a pinstriped suit and was alone this time. He offered me a seat, tea, coffee, a pastry, water, biscuits. I looked at the biscuits out of the corner of my eye and would've gladly stuffed a handful into my pocket, but I kept up appearances and only accepted a chair. We sat opposite each other, and for a moment I was reminded of the other radio man who'd welcomed me into his office at another place and time. But whereas Nick Soutter was expansive, resounding in voice and demeanor, unceremonious and a compulsive smoker, my Colombian host was exceptionally courteous, with a serene voice and no signs of an interest in tobacco.

"First of all, allow me to give you the overview. The Latin American Service broadcasts on shortwave to all the Spanish-speaking countries of Central and South America, and we also have Portuguese programs for Brazil. We've been operating since 1938. I had the honor of reading the inaugural bulletin in front of our ambassadors, and at the risk of sounding smug, I can tell you that we were incredibly well received from the start. Throughout the world war, we became a reliable source of information for millions of listeners in the Americas—from the Atlantic to the Pacific, from Patagonia to Mexico."

I was itching for him to get to the point, but it was pleasant to listen to the preamble in his flowing, melodic Spanish. What he was telling me was certainly interesting, but I would've enjoyed it just as much if he'd recited the Lord's Prayer fifty times. It was the sounds that captivated me, the familiar words, the sentences strung together with nouns and verbs that were close to me. His accent, different from mine, added something more. I was surprised to realize only then how much, how very much, I'd missed hearing my language.

Oblivious to my feelings, he continued his introduction.

"As your offer is one that combines current affairs with international politics, as well as with matters of cultural and historical significance, we've given it very serious consideration. And as I said on the phone, the answer is yes. We'd like you to prepare some informative pieces and will guide you every step of the way."

I nodded silently, trying not to show my satisfaction.

"Three episodes would be an excellent start, and we'll pay you five guineas each. You'll work directly with Ángel Ara at Bush House. You met Ara yesterday. He'll work alongside you at every stage of the project. And as for the content, we are of course interested in illustrative perspectives on the conflict, but also in the events of your life there, your own experiences . . ."

Nick Soutter, back in Palestine, had also suggested three segments; it must be the standard within the organization and its satellites across the empire. The difference was that my friend, in that meeting we had in Café Atara in Jerusalem, had asked me to speak about my impoverished country in a neutral, undemonstrative way, whereas now, Camacho was proposing something quite different. My *own experiences*, he'd said. I almost let out a bitter burst of laughter. He wanted me to focus on my own wretched, terrible, bloody experiences.

I stopped him. Better to save him the trouble.

"If I have to talk about myself and what I went through, I'm afraid we're not going to be able to reach an agreement."

He sat looking at me, his next sentence ready, his mouth half-open. He closed it again, cleared his throat, adjusted the knot on his tie.

"All right," he said gently. "In that case—"

I cut in again.

"But if you allow me to leave the details of my own life out of it, we can start immediately."

24

My unexpected assignment at the BBC took me physically and mentally out of the tiny world I lived in with Olivia. Her pushiness, however, never let up. And neither did her plans.

The same silent chauffeur who'd collected us from Victoria Station would be taking us to the dinner at the Hodsons' residence in Belgravia. She explained the situation as we headed to the car.

"Bernard, our lifelong driver, moved to Swansea with his daughters at the beginning of the war, which is when I decided to donate the Bentley to the Royal Hospital. Everything's simpler that way."

In an artificially neutral tone, as if we were discussing some trifling matter, she always delivered the perfect explanation to justify her hardships to me. If she had no gardener, it was because she adored tending her own flowers; if she lacked a cook, it was because Gertrude was a magnificent replacement; if the central heating was weak, it was not for want of coal, but because nothing beat a good fire for warming the bones. I never dared contradict her. Once more, I simply said nothing.

She'd told me about the invitation a few weeks before, and the knowledge of it had lodged in my intestines, as weighty and irritating as an indigestible lunch. I hadn't turned it down, however, and had even feigned some moderate interest, had prepared to make an effort. After all, this was a chance to encounter Marcus's old world, and I felt that refusing to participate would, somehow, be untrue to his memory.

Now the day had arrived, and I had little choice of what to wear. I had only one evening dress among the few clothes I'd brought from Jerusalem, probably the plainest of my former wardrobe. In my understated clothes, makeup, and hair, I looked at myself in the mirror before going out. It was the first time I'd dressed up since Marcus's death, and the last time I'd worn this dress was at a Government House reception, at the start of my pregnancy. For one fantastic moment, I imagined I was going to see his image reflected behind me, his sharp profile at an angle as he adjusted his bow tie or fastened his cuff links. I pressed my eyes closed to stop my mascara from running and breathed deeply. No, in that big, shabby bedroom there was no one but me, getting ready for a gathering with some people I didn't know.

Olivia looked me up and down when I came down the stairs wrapped in sober tobacco-colored crêpe. I didn't expect any compliments from her, and I didn't receive any, of course. Instead of her explicit approval, she delivered one of her typical comments.

"Some good diamonds, my dear, would be the perfect accessory."

I never wore jewelry. I'd owned some magnificent pieces during one brief period of my life. They'd belonged to my paternal grandmother, the great Doña Carlota, whom I never met—the one who'd ended my parents' relationship in one stroke after her son, the promising young pup of a wealthy and respectable family, started seeing my mother, Dolores Quiroga, a simple dressmaker. But those valuable pieces soon left my life, swiped by Ramiro Arribas, the rat who changed my future forever. Since then, I hadn't the slightest bit of interest in jewelry.

After a short journey through almost empty streets, we arrived outside a row of elegant houses plastered in white stucco, with porticos and great balconies spanning their fronts. The invitation was from a family who'd been friends with the Bonnards for decades. One of the sons had been a school friend of Marcus's. Now high up in the colonial administration of Kenya, he was spending a few days in London and had suggested getting together.

An ancient butler announced us in a metallic voice. Through double doors, the warm opulence of the reception room appeared before us: pleasant lighting, polished wood furniture, curtains, upholstery, and thick carpets. I saw, distributed around the room, a group of refined humans, some standing by the fireplace, others seated on sofas and armchairs. A beautiful woman sat on the arm of one chair, her slender legs crossed under folds of chiffon. The conversations sounded light and agreeable. The same butler began to make his way around the room, one gloved hand holding a tray of appetizers, the other behind his back. For a few seconds, the memory of my sorely missed friend Rosalinda Fox fluttered inside my head. *This is how the British upper crust live, my dear,* she would've said with an ironic wink, *when their bank accounts, jewelry cases, and strongboxes aren't full of cobwebs.*

Our hosts greeted us with genuine affection; Olivia hadn't lied when she mentioned the long friendship between the two families. The gentleman was a stooped, skeletal old man quite a bit shorter than his wife, a well-built lady with blue eyes and a prominent bust. The Hodson couple and Olivia were the only people there who'd been born before the turn of the century. The rest were in their late thirties or early forties—the men, elegant in dinner jackets, the women stylish in evening dresses, some chosen with more success than others. Wellborn, well bred, all of them, that much was obvious. Well fed, well served, well spoken, well educated, well traveled, well read. Members of the same class and way of life, with their parameters and measuring sticks, their conventions, standards, and manners.

As the sherry, gin, and whiskey flowed, I became the center of attention without intending it: everyone was longing to meet the widow of their old friend, dearest Mark Bonnard. The greetings swung with graceful poise between the perfect compliment and the most heartfelt condolences. And among these guests, as had happened so many times before, I also detected a certain curiosity at my incongruous foreignness—as if they were trying to find out what the devil their dear friend had seen in a woman like me that would cause him to do something so outrageous as marry and have a child with her.

The butler announced that we could go through to the dining room. With a quick count, I confirmed that there were exactly a dozen of us sitting down for dinner. In addition to our hosts, there were three other couples. One was Fiona, the daughter of the house—talkative and somewhat strident, dressed in lavender silk and wearing a string of sapphires around her neck—and her husband, a man named Evan. There were two other couples: beautiful Alexia and quiet Adrian, and agitated Harriet and her husband, Bruce. And two single—or at least temporarily unpaired—men who, I knew from Marcus, had been his close friends when they were young. Raymond was a self-assured financier for the city, and Dominic, the Hodsons' son, was the instigator of the gathering.

It was between these two that I found myself sitting. The dinner began with smoked salmon and conversation with my table neighbors. The Hodsons were hardly extravagant, but the grim postwar frugality and troubles were less acutely evident in this Belgravia residence than they were at my mother-in-law's home. Raymond spoke at length about the state of the stock market, and Dominic, who was less talkative, mentioned that he'd only been in London for a few days and planned to return to Nairobi once he'd finished tending to some arrangements. Other equally innocuous conversations flowed around the table: the recent rise of the Thames, Mountbatten's appointment as Viceroy of India, complaints against the Labour government and its tax hikes.

The dinner continued smoothly, with voices kept at an appropriate volume. Next we were served duck in a berry sauce. Over the delicate glassware and candles, I noticed the butler filling the glass belonging to Fiona—our hosts' daughter—at a faster rate than the rest.

She had emptied it four or five times when her exclamation broke through the quiet.

"I propose a toast!"

Her husband let out a ridiculous guffaw, and her mother, from the head of the table, gave her a piercing look. Fiona had flouted the rules of etiquette: toasts must be proposed by the host and were reserved for the end of the dinner. Out of the corner of my eye, to my left, I saw her brother grip his cutlery, clearly uncomfortable. The patriarch, at the opposite end of the table, carried on eating like a little bird, as if he hadn't heard her. The rest of our voices were left suspended in the air, our faces wavering between expressions of shock and humor.

"I propose a toast in memory of our dearest friend Mark Bonnard!"

With varying amounts of zeal, we all ended up obeying her. But Fiona didn't seem prepared to settle for that.

"I propose, also, that we remember him! Dominic! Raymond! Bruce! Adrian! Tell us a story from your time with Mark at Harrow!"

Obligingly at first, and then with growing enthusiasm, the men recalled moments from their childhood and youth: pranks, exploits, and incidents. Between anecdotes, Fiona continued to empty her glass.

The guests reacted to the stories with smiles, approval, the occasional exclamation or burst of laughter. However, those entertaining tales of the Old Harrovians, masters and school friends, celebrations, sport, holidays at country houses, and double-barreled surnames meant nothing to me and simply sounded like rain on asphalt. I'd met Marcus in Tétouan when he was thirty or so, and our life together had been so rushed, so secretive—so rocky, complex, and uncertain—that we'd always focused on the now, barely allowing ourselves to detach from the present. The portraits the others were painting of him seemed, on the face of it, like stories about a stranger, someone remote to me.

I looked at Olivia, some distance from me at the table. In her magnificent, completely out-of-fashion crystal-embroidered dress, with her bony features and great head of white hair, she looked splendid in the candlelight.

"I suppose the Marcus Logan you knew was nothing like this one."

I turned at once toward Dominic. *Marcus Logan,* I thought I'd heard. He'd said *Marcus Logan.*

"Don't be surprised I know his other name," he added. "Life made us drift apart for a few years, but at one point we got back in touch."

Dominic had a warm voice, was mild mannered and polite, but his attractiveness ended there. Apart from that, he was an ugly man in the strictest sense of the word. Bulging, watery eyes, with virtually no eyelashes and with premature bags under them; sparse hair styled with more effort than success; a fleshy nose, reddish skin, and large ears—all on a head that was both too small and too round.

Dessert had been served, and our glasses had been filled with port. Fiona continued to absorb wine like a sponge. Her complexion, meanwhile, was taking on an increasingly blushed hue as her voice gained in speed and power.

"And now! And now! Attention, everyone!"

The conversations stopped once more, and we turned to her again.

"Now! Now let's talk about Mark and his loves!"

I noticed that Dominic, to my left, was about to stop her.

"Be quiet, Dominic!" she howled, cutting him off. "Don't be a spoilsport!"

All eyes remained fixed on her flushed face, expectant, questioning.

"Tonight we've met the mysterious foreigner who ended up stealing our most handsome boy's heart. But tell us, Alexia Burke-Landon, née Durbin . . ."

She was addressing the person before her, seated on the same side of the table as me and so outside my field of vision. I'd noticed the woman when I arrived. In a butter-colored gauze dress, with mahogany hair and delicate features, she was undoubtedly the most beautiful woman there.

"Tell us, tell us, dear, how did you feel when Mark confessed to you that he'd given his heart to another woman and broke off your engagement?"

A dense silence slithered over the table, slipping between the silver candelabras and the plums in syrup. The next thing we heard was a chair falling to the floor. Alexia Burke-Landon had gotten up to rush out of the dining room.

It was Dominic who immediately took control.

"Coffee in the living room," he announced, plopping his napkin down on the table.

While everyone began to stand in silence, relieved that the embarrassing scene was finally over, he turned to me and whispered a sober and sincere "I'm sorry."

25

The workroom where Ángel Ara received me was very different from the Colombian director's office, both in size and degree of elegance. The place was a bit of a shambles: piles of books, librettos, records, notepads. Still, he managed to clear two armchairs, offered me one, and sat opposite.

"Please excuse the mess. At the start of the war, to get away from the bombings, much of the Latin American Service was moved along with other sections to the countryside, to Wood Norton Hall, the Duke of Orléans's country house in Evesham, northeast of London. Now we're being reunited with the rest of the foreign-language services. Almost all the BBC's Overseas Services are now here at Bush House. What used to be called the BBC's Empire Service changed its name once the range of broadcasting languages went beyond the confines of the empire."

We were in fact at that moment in Bush House, a building at the end of Kingsway in Aldwych that appeared less damaged, at first glance, than Broadcasting House. An entrance supported by two massive columns led to a large marble lobby; the splendor ended there, however. The inside was a functional labyrinth of corridors, offices, and studios.

"I'm delighted you're joining us, truly," he added. "We're badly in need of women contributors in our language. There are some female announcers, but few of them bring their own stories to the microphone."

"It's only going to be three appearances," I reminded him.

"Even so . . . Well, first off, so I can take note of it, will you use a nom de plume or jump into the arena as yourself?"

A nom de plume. I was reminded of Fran Nash, and our hybrid name for Télam: Frances Quiroga.

"Think about it," he insisted. "Almost all of us here have one."

"May I know yours?"

He smiled at my spontaneous request. He was thin, not very tall, with a pointed face and nervous mannerisms. He must have tried to tame his curly hair before he left home; no doubt he'd used a good dollop of cream to keep it tidy. At midmorning, however, his efforts were beginning to unravel, and this gave him a somewhat youthful appearance.

"My pseudonym couldn't be more obvious or generic: Juan Español."

I looked at him wordlessly, waiting for more.

"What is it you are asking, my friend, with those big, lovely, inscrutable eyes with which you're staring at me? The reason for my disguise?"

I was the one who smiled now. He wasn't trying to flirt with me, despite the compliment. He was simply a friendly fellow.

"If you don't mind me asking . . ."

"If that's your question, you should know that, behind such a common name, there's simply a lawyer with a soul that belongs to the former republic. A man who, like so many others, was swept off his country's map by a pitiful war. Now I earn a living as a programmer for this blessed corporation's Latin American Service, and when I say *blessed*, don't mistake that for sarcasm. Many of us Spaniards who came to this island with one hand behind our back and the other held out are now filling our stomachs thanks to its coffers. After years as an occasional contributor, I'm proud to say I now have a very decent permanent contract, which is why many Spanish friends with less luck and too much wit have taken to calling me the 'Prince of the Airwaves.'"

His final sentences were punctuated by a clattering in the corridor that grew nearer. We heard a singsong voice through the open door and turned our heads at the same time. I saw a young woman behind a metal trolley loaded with tin teapots.

"Would you like a cup of tea?"

I declined. He said goodbye to the girl in his rather awkward English. The clattering resumed, and I assumed the employee's role was to offer her mobile service to all the staff.

"Please, no more tea, for the love of God . . . ," he whispered sarcastically.

I was about to burst out laughing when he leaned forward and drew closer as if to share a secret with me.

"Wouldn't you love a nice coffee with milk like we have back home, the ones we had before the war? The coffee freshly roasted and filtered, lovely and black. The milk creamy and hot, a couple of sugar cubes . . . and to go with it, a good *magdalena*," he said, referencing Spain's traditional lemon-flavored cupcakes. "Or no, perhaps not. Perhaps a couple of *rosquillas*, fried in oil." Fluffy Spanish doughnuts.

He threw his hand in the air, as if his nostalgic thought was a fly he wanted to bat away.

"Anyway, as I was saying, I'm going to mentor you all through this process. From now on—"

But there was something I had been curious about since the tea trolley interrupted us, and I wanted an answer before we continued.

"And why does Juan Español work in the Latin American Service and not on the broadcasts for his own country?"

"And where have you been, my señora, that you haven't heard about the censorship suffered by those of us who oppose our Generalísimo's regime?"

His question could've seemed brusque—rude, even—had it not been asked with an expression of exaggerated astonishment and concluded with a burst of laughter. Though they resembled each other neither physically nor in manner, for a moment he reminded me of my old friend Félix Aranda from Tétouan: witty, sharp, and quick tongued; equally well educated; both grimly defiant, with a touch of wryness that was completely forgivable.

"I'm sure you know the objectives that this blessed—yes, I will say it again, blessed—radio broadcasting corporation aims to meet . . ."

He held up four fingers and made them dance in front of me.

"To accurately inform, to stimulate new interests among listeners, to educate, and to entertain. These, in theory, are its cornerstones."

He added a thumb and showed me his empty hand.

"But in the overseas services we have another powerful raison d'être. And it's none other than—"

I finished the sentence for him.

"Propaganda."

He nodded with satisfaction, as if I were a brilliant student.

"That was why these foreign-language services were created in the years leading up to the war, to build support for the British cause. And they couldn't have found a better medium than radio. It goes beyond borders; leapfrogs battlefronts, rearguards, and trenches; penetrates the privacy of homes and human brains . . . a sure bet."

"I know this is the case in European countries, but how is that the case for the Latin American Service?"

"Well, both Germany and Italy have had effective radio propaganda networks throughout the South American continent since the midthirties. The Nazis, you may know, were fanatical about radio and used it as an extremely powerful weapon both to indoctrinate and to arouse passions within Germany and to intoxicate people outside it. And the Italians, albeit without the same vigor, were also using radio to gain sympathizers for the fascist cause. That is, until the BBC arrived with broadcasts in Spanish, with all the service's know-how and good reputation, and became the most respectable voice during the conflict, especially among the educated and well-off classes. Since then, the Latin

American Service has become iconic. Last year, our director, Camacho, went on a tour of several countries, giving talks, and wherever he went he was hailed as a victorious general. The main national newspapers put his visit on the front page, as if he'd won the Battle of Normandy with his own blood and sweat."

He let out another burst of natural, contagious laughter. Ángel Ara seemed a genuinely nice man. I was even grateful for his talkativeness—the more he talked, the less I would have to lie about myself.

"Though officially it's an independent corporation, the BBC was created, as you know, under the direct, effective, and careful control of the Foreign Office, the Ministry of Information, and their intelligence services. And because these British don't do anything for nothing, the results have been fabulous from the start. Their admirers now include tens of thousands of listeners across the pond."

He checked the time, frowning.

"It's still early for lunch if you ask our Iberian stomachs, but I'm afraid we must yield to the ways of the locals. May I invite you to eat in our formidable canteen?"

I accepted without knowing whether the adjective "formidable" was just more of his irony. As we negotiated the warren of galleries and corridors, Ara continued to speak, unfiltered, shrewd, and convincing.

"The service for Spain, however, works with its hands infinitely more tied than does the service that broadcasts for Latin America. In Spain, it's not about sowing seeds to harvest later, because the BBC has always had a peremptory, urgent political mission there. During the world war, the essential task was to firm up Franco's neutrality at all costs so he didn't side with Germany."

We'd reached an elevator and were waiting for it.

"And now?" I asked.

My curiosity was sincere. I'd been away from my country for almost two years. I'd left at a pivotal moment, when the two nations that were friends of the regime—Italy and Germany—had been defeated. Since then, all I knew about our domestic politics had come from the little I read in my father's letters and the rare newspapers that reached us in Jerusalem back when Marcus was still alive, out of date and duly censored.

The elevator doors opened; it was full of people of various sizes and ethnicities, heights and styles. They all took a step back or to the side to make room for us.

We stood in silence as the contraption descended, packed in with the others.

"The British Foreign Office has changed its policy," Ara went on as we exited. "The exiles from Spain were heartbroken. We all had faith that the victors of the world war would topple Franco after the conflict, but that hasn't been the case, and in the end, all they did was issue an official statement condemning the regime. They decided not to intervene in internal affairs. *The Spanish people must carve out their own destiny,* they declared. As we Spaniards say, 'Every mast must hold up its own sail.'"

A kind of melancholy passed between us as we walked on into the depths of the building. We were both thinking the same thing. *Our poor country. Poor Spain.*

"Even so, Britain is maintaining an ambiguous position and is determined to avoid offending Franco. Which is why the Foreign Office forbids the BBC from having politically compromised staff. So when someone well known to have anti-Francoist baggage is involved as a contributor or guest, they always participate under a pseudonym. And those of us who aren't very inclined to keep our mouths shut, they prefer to assign to the Latin American Service."

He stopped, stepped aside for me, and winked.

"That way we're less problematic."

We were in an enormous underground hall filled with smoke, the murmur of conversations, and the sound of cutlery clinking on dishes. A lot of men, some women. Skin of every color, from pale white to the blackest gloss. Blond, curly, red, frizzy, brown, straight, and dark hair. Tall, average, short. Indecipherable languages coming from mouths as fast as spoons, forks, and cigarettes were going in. Many people were already sitting, and others were standing and waiting, forming a line to collect a tray that would be filled farther down by women in white hats holding big ladles.

"Welcome to the Bush House canteen, my dear, the most cosmopolitan place in all of England. Urdu, Russian, Swahili, Norwegian, Malay, Farsi, Greek, Polish, Burmese . . . thirty-something languages. Call out any language and you can be certain some editor, translator, or announcer will raise their hand."

He lowered his voice and drew closer to my ear, as if to pass on some artful secret.

"It wouldn't surprise me if there was more than one spy among them."

26

The fire was lit, and Víctor was playing on the rug, throwing some wooden blocks I'd bought for him in Woolworths, the shop I discovered in Chelsea on the way back from my meeting with Ara. Later, I'd learn that there were lots of identical outlets all over London, all over Britain, all over the United States of America. The chain, in fact, formed a gigantic empire. On that first visit I gathered a handful of functional things: little toys, two sets of cotton pajamas, socks, a plate and cup made of tough Bakelite so that my son could eat and drink, then throw them on the floor without fear of destroying Olivia's crockery.

It was a peaceful afternoon, there was still some natural light, and through the big windows I could see the days slowly growing longer. A game of bridge at one of her friends' houses was keeping my mother-in-law out, and as soon as Philippa walked through the door, I'd given her a few hours off. I sat on a sofa with my notebook in my hands and a pencil between my teeth, my mind retrieving details from Jerusalem, trying to string together content for my radio appearances. This was what I'd agreed to with Ángel Ara: I would think up some ideas, discuss them with him, and together we would shape and organize them.

A few moments before, I'd heard the doorbell and assumed that Gertrude would open it. She did, and here she was now, with her odd eye and arm outstretched, handing me an envelope. To my surprise, it was from Dominic Hodson. First, he apologized for the embarrassing evening at his parents' house, then he proposed a meeting, suggesting tea at Fortnum & Mason. *I need to speak to you,* he indicated. Not *I would like,* nor *it would be a pleasure.* No. I "need."

For some impulsive reason, I didn't mention the invitation to Olivia. The journey back from the Hodson house after dinner had been uncomfortable, tense. I'd had no desire to revisit the events of the evening, but she'd insisted.

"Try to forgive Fiona," she'd said as soon as we were in the car. "She was always a charming girl, perhaps she just—"

I cut her off.

"I'd have been grateful if you'd spared me this unpleasant encounter," I retorted curtly.

Her response was evasive.

"I had no inkling, dear, that Alexia might've returned to London, and anyway, her and Mark, it happened such a long time ago, and she's fabulously married with the Burke-Landons' youngest now. They have two girls, her mother told me last time I saw her, at a concert at the Royal Albert Hall, I seem to remember . . ."

I let my mother-in-law continue her chatter filled with places, surnames, and scathing adverbs while my memory relived the mortifying question that had been asked by that drunk, provocative woman, the sound of the chair falling, the gauze of the yellow dress flying through the door. Neither Alexia nor her husband had stayed for coffee, and the revelation of the called-off engagement had continued to resound inside me like a malicious echo. Now that the memory of that dinner-turned-sour was beginning to fade, I'd made up my mind to accept—without saying a word about it to Olivia—the invitation from the man who'd been my neighbor at the table. I would decide whether to tell her about it after the meeting.

The next morning I hurried out in search of clothes. I didn't have anything intermediate between my everyday sweaters and trousers and my one evening dress. A few days before, a shop I happened to come across among the streets of Kensington had caught my eye. DIGBY MORTON. READY-TO-WEAR read the engraving on a bronze plaque on the facade. The shopwindow was as simple as it was refined. An atmosphere of restrained subtlety greeted me as I walked through the door. The saleswoman showed me several impeccably finished dress models, a novelty to me, accustomed as I was to creating each of my pieces at the customer's personal request. I tried on several superbly cut two-piece suits. *Exquisitely fashionable,* the shop assistant said. I marveled at their pure, stylized lines: simple, clean, devoid of ostentation or extravagance, a vivid reflection of the austerity the country was under in every sphere of life. The prices, on the other hand, stood in stark contrast to the economic constraints and rationing. I decided on two outfits, adding a pair of shoes with slender heels and a hat as neat as a pillbox.

At half past four, I walked into the tearoom at Fortnum & Mason in my grayish-blue tweed trouser suit. My hair was gathered in a low bun, and I wore dark eyeshadow: muted elegance to meet a stranger with unknown intentions. Dominic Hodson was waiting for me at a table against the wall and stood as soon as he saw me. He was wearing a bland suit and a subtly patterned tie and had the same aqueous eyes and lack of good looks that I remembered from the dinner.

We shook hands. The waiter showing me to the table pulled out a chair for me to sit on. The tearoom, decorated in pastel tones, was packed with identical tables. Around them were groups of two, three, or four, some men but mostly women, chatting after doing their shopping, drinking teas with exotic aromas, and eating delicate pastries. Like the price tags at the couturier Digby Morton, everyone in this sophisticated setting seemed frivolously oblivious to Britain's coupons, queues, and shortages.

"I don't know whether you're familiar with this place and if it's to your liking," he said timidly. "It's a classic tearoom very famous among the usual ladies. I chose it thinking you'd feel comfortable here, but to be honest, it's the first time I've been."

I appreciated his frankness, the gesture of leaving his own environment—whatever that was—to meet me somewhere that he supposed suited me.

"First of all, allow me to reiterate how profoundly sorry I am for my sister Fiona's shameful behavior. Her indiscretion was extraordinarily inconsiderate of Mrs. Burke-Landon and, equally, of you."

I nodded without answering, as if accepting his apology. And he nodded back, as if accepting my reply.

"While there's no justification whatsoever for her actions," he went on, "allow me to divulge to you that my sister is going through a difficult time in her own marriage. On the outside they keep up appearances, but she drinks too much and seems to be developing a certain . . . let's say, sourness, a certain amount of verbal aggression, even, toward other women who're perhaps more . . . more attractive or more on an even keel or . . . Please forgive my ineloquence. I'm a bachelor and I don't handle these matters very well."

Once again I was touched by his unfiltered honesty. The resolute colonial official, hardened in Africa, was stepping in puddles as he trod the turbulence of the feminine soul, in front of a stranger and surrounded by ladies who were discussing curtains and cushions, spring trends, or ridiculously complex problems with their domestic staff.

We ordered our teas—his black and strong, mine a Darjeeling, a little tribute to my slippery friend Rosalinda.

"I'm doubly ashamed because I was the one who suggested the evening. I wanted to meet you in person and thought that would be a more relaxed setting. I deliberately left my mother in charge of organizing a small dinner according to my instructions but, in the end, and unbeknownst to me, my sister intervened and added some guests."

I couldn't contain myself.

"Guests like Alexia Burke-Landon, for example."

He nodded slowly. Then he weighed his words with extreme caution.

"I don't know whether you're aware of how close she and your husband were when they were both still unmarried."

"Not really," I admitted.

I was sure there had been other women in Marcus's life before me. But I'd never met any of them, and I'd never known he'd had a firm commitment with any.

"At the risk of being indiscreet, I must tell you that I suspect that, in their relationship, the balance of interest, shall we say, always tipped in the direction of Alexia."

I smiled, but the corner of my mouth turned down with sadness. This was a subtle way for him to tell me that Marcus might not have loved her all that much, an elegant attempt to soothe any potential retroactive jealousy.

"Sentimental matters aside," he added, "I imagine it must've seemed strange to be summoned like this."

Incredibly strange, I almost acknowledged. But I opted to let him continue.

"I must admit, I too was taken aback by the matter that led to you and I being here together today." He cleared his throat, as if mustering his courage. "You see, what I must tell you is that your husband, my old friend Mark Bonnard—Marcus to you—decided some time ago to make me the executor of his will."

My back tensed. I frowned. What? What was he saying?

"It's why I came to London, to see you and make the necessary arrangements."

I remained incapable of putting my bewilderment into words. A waiter appeared with a three-story stand of finger-shaped sandwiches, pastries, and delicate cakes. The man took only a few seconds to arrange everything on the table and serve us with deft ceremony, but the pause in our conversation seemed as dark and immense to me as a winter night.

Dominic picked up where he'd left off as soon as we were alone again.

"At the beginning of last year, after a long time with no contact, I received a letter from your husband from Jerusalem. He informed me of your marriage in Gibraltar, and of the fact that you were waiting for your first child to be born. In view of the burgeoning violence in Palestine, and to make provision for . . ." He paused; his Adam's apple swelled. "To make provision for potential adverse outcomes, which sadly ended up transpiring, he'd decided to leave his legal and financial affairs in order. And to do so, he opted to name me as executor, despite the years that had passed without us seeing each other."

He looked down at his cup, fixing his eyes on the dark tea, as yet untasted.

"Once I'd gotten over my initial surprise, I must admit I felt honored that Mark was placing his trust in me." He looked up again with eyes that were as ugly as a fish's but profoundly sincere. "So here I am, honored to be assuming a firm commitment to safeguard your and little Víctor's interests."

He finally lifted the cup to his lips. I copied him, trying to swallow both the hot liquid and my bewilderment. I didn't understand what Dominic Hodson was saying to me. I'd closed Marcus's and my accounts at the Barclays Bank branch in Jerusalem myself. All our remaining money was now in an envelope in my bedroom wardrobe. I was also waiting for the authorities to finish working out the official pension we would receive for Marcus's service to the empire—Olivia was taking care of it. Beyond that, apart from some of my son's features and his straw-colored hair, I wasn't aware of any other inheritance from Marcus that was due to us.

"But . . . ," I stammered. "But couldn't I have . . . ?"

He finished the sentence for me.

"Taken care of everything yourself? He didn't want to worry you. He was only trying to protect you. First of all, though you may have sensed it, he didn't want to explicitly convey to you the feeling that his life was in danger. And at the same time, in the event that such an awful thing should happen, he wanted to spare you the administrative complexities of a country whose workings and institutions you're unfamiliar with. You would've been embroiled in tiresome legal proceedings, you would've needed a professional to advise you—"

I broke in.

"His mother could've helped me."

He reached for the triple stand and took an egg mayonnaise sandwich. Before putting it in his mouth he said, "I'm afraid, my dear, that Lady Olivia Bonnard, more than being the solution, could be a significant part of the problem."

27

I received a call from Ángel Ara the next morning. It pulled me from my ruminations and forced me to plant my feet back in reality, stopped me from thinking about the episode at Fortnum & Mason, about Dominic Hodson, and about Marcus's will, the existence of which had come as such a shock to me.

In my role as executor, he'd told me, *my job is to put your husband's affairs in order, and that's what I'm doing. Please, don't think we're dealing with an enormous estate or anything like that. Just give me a few days to go through some paperwork, and I'll contact you as soon as everything's ready.* I'd agreed. How could I not?

My fellow Spaniard's voice sounded brisk and jovial through the receiver.

"So, my friend, how're those Palestinian notes coming along? When do you think we could meet? Tomorrow? Day after tomorrow? The day after that?"

Ara was an unflagging fellow, dynamic and persevering in his unique way.

"I'm working on it," I assured him. "But if you could give me a couple more days I'd be extremely grateful."

"Very well. Two days' time, then. Shall we meet at Bush House again? At ten in the morning?"

"I'll be there."

"Great. We'll go over your work and I'm sure we'll be able to adapt it to our format."

I was about to hang up when I heard him yell at the other end of the line.

"One more thing! Do you like art? A most esteemed friend of mine, a compatriot of ours, is opening an exhibition tomorrow. Would you like to drop by?"

Without waiting for an answer, with an urgent "Note it down, note it down!" Ara gave me some directions on the fly.

A taxi left me on Bond Street outside the Lefevre Gallery. Nearby I could make out other art galleries, antique shops, and auction houses. I hesitated for a moment at the entrance. I had no invitation or anything to identify me as an acquaintance of a friend of the featured painter. All the same, I walked in with a firm step, cool and erect, as I tended to do whenever insecurity or doubt bared their teeth.

The gallery was bright and spacious with central pillars and broad white walls. Hanging from them, distributed symmetrically, were numerous framed drawings: simple black outlines with no internal details, plain human forms that were both expressive and modern.

It wasn't difficult to find Ara, with his curls and mustache, among the large crowd. He was with a small group talking animatedly in Spanish, rather more loudly than was the norm in phlegmatic England.

"My dear, don't you look dazzling in that design, the color of the wine from our vines . . ."

He planted a couple of kisses on my cheeks, a thoroughly Spanish gesture. I was slow to react, accustomed as I was now to simply shaking hands or exchanging stiff greetings with a slight bow of the head.

"Come, come with me, take my arm and I'll take you for a mosey to show you who's who among our own."

I didn't protest—in his words and suggestions there was never a hint of flirting, only straightforward friendliness. And so, linked together, we began to move around the large room, between artistic works, pillars, and people.

"Look," he announced to me not overly discreetly. "Him in the blue tie, that's Rafael Martínez Nadal, the celebrated Antonio Torres from *La Voz de Londres*, very well known in Spain for his programs during the war. Ring any bells? He works for the *Observer* now. He's a clever chap, never backs down. He gave the BBC itself the Iberian slap when they asked him to try to sound a little less Republican when he was on air. The young woman smoothing down his pocket square, though she's young enough to be his daughter, is in fact his wife, Jacinta Castillejo, a dancer—daughter of the great Don José Castillejo. You know Castillejo? He was one of the scholars who was purged after Franco's victory, quite the intellectual. He ended up here in England, giving a few measly classes and living like an ascetic at the University of Liverpool. He even fixed the soles of his children's shoes sitting on a cobbler's stool while talking through matters of philosophical significance with his students."

We continued to move around the room as more people arrived. The welcomes and congratulations grew louder.

"Look, that beautiful woman is Nieves Mathews, daughter of Salvador de Madariaga. She's quite the art expert. Her father must be around here somewhere, too. You might've heard of him. He was a minister and diplomat and remains a highly respected thinker. He works with the BBC from time to time, but for our transoceanic service. They don't want him anywhere near the broadcasts for Spain.

"Look, the chap with the protruding belly is Deric Pearson, owner of the Atlantic-Pacific Press Agency, which distributes news all over Latin America. His business employed a lot of Spaniards as editorial staff and saved them from hardship. Manuel Chaves Nogales, the magnificent journalist from Seville who died a few years ago, was editor there. You've heard of him?

"Look, that tall, elegant lady is Natalia de Cossío, the wife of Alberto Jiménez Fraud, once director of Madrid's celebrated Residencia de Estudiantes. He's one of the most successful academics, a lecturer at Oxford.

"Look, him with the big nose, that's Salazar Chapela. He looks very serious but he's a very funny man, from Malaga. He's about to release a novel in Buenos Aires in which, apparently, all of us appear. He has us a little alarmed—who knows what it reveals?

"Look, that's Luis Portillo, who held the chair of civil law at the University of Salamanca. Now he does translations and writes articles, but the poor man has had a terrible time trying to survive, even peeling potatoes and digging ditches at an airfield for a living.

"Look, the fellow with the look of a melancholic dandy, with his thin little mustache, that's the poet Luis Cernuda. He's been here almost a decade but can't adapt to England for love or money. He's been offered a position at an American university and will be gone soon.

"Look, that tall gentleman, the bald one with glasses, is Pablo de Azcárate. He was ambassador for the Spanish Republic during the war, and now it looks like he'll be back in Geneva with a big role in the United Nations. He's quite the luminary, hugely respected, and we all stand to attention here whenever we see him.

"Look, that gentleman with dark, slicked-back hair is Arturo Barea. He works with us and has an enormous audience all over the Americas under the pseudonym Juan de Castilla. He also writes books—excellent ones, they say—but so far he has only been published in English, so not many of us have read him. He doesn't show his face much around here because he lives in the countryside with his wife, Ilse, the lady with her back to us.

"Look, the young man with a limp is Pepito Estruch. He's wonderfully funny and wild for the theater; the poor chap spent six months in a concentration camp in France. Once he got to England, he devoted himself to the children who were sent here after the bombing of Guernica. There were a great many poor wretches left. No one claimed them so they could go back after the civil war.

"Look, that man speaking Spanish with an accent, that's Tomás Harris, art dealer and expert on our great masters. It's said that his father, an English antiquarian, was quite the plunderer of churches and monasteries in Spain.

"Look, that priest is Padre Onaindía, a Basque nationalist who causes a stir on the microphone under the pseudonym James Masterton."

We continued greeting people, barely stopping to admire the exhibition. Ara knew everyone, and everyone seemed to know him. Someone came up to us, the group grew larger, he carried on introducing me, and I was received with warm gestures and words. Some of those present then suggested going for dinner at Martínez, but few of the others joined them.

"Martínez is the most famous Spanish restaurant in London," my new colleague explained in an aside, almost in my ear. "Even Franco had lunch there when he came in early '36, before his insurrection, to attend the funeral of King George V. Despite that awful detail," he added with a sardonic wink, "we all love eating there."

He scanned the room, rapidly swiveling his head left and right. Then he lowered his voice as if speaking in confidence.

"When you hear someone making an excuse for not going to Martínez, you can bet it's not because they don't want to. Rather, it's a question of numbers."

He rubbed his thumb against his forefinger several times in an eloquent gesture. In that illustrious group there could be found plenty of wisdom, culture, brains, talent. But money was lacking, unfortunately. Before the civil war, they'd all been financially solvent, to a greater or lesser degree. Public figures with assets, prestige. Now, more than a decade after leaving their country, stranded in a foreign land, they were slowly accepting that the chances of returning were dwindling and that their exile would be long lived.

Finally, Ara introduced me to the artist: Gregorio Prieto, a vivacious man from La Mancha, handsome and well mannered, who received praise and congratulations from all corners.

In the middle of this hubbub, lulled by the sound of voices speaking my own language, I felt a warm sense of well-being, something I hadn't felt for an incredibly long time. All these people were unfamiliar to me, as were their lines of work; politics, poetry, art, and academia were spheres I'd never come into contact with—far from it. Even so, it was as if simply being among fellow Spaniards had brought me a sense of peace.

It was a fleeting sensation, however. Like almost everything in my life of late, the feeling quickly disintegrated.

As I made my way through the increasingly busy room, I saw George Camacho, the director of the Latin American Service, my mentor, in a manner of speaking. He noticed me too and gave me a sideways look, raising his eyebrows with emphasis. I understood his message: *Wait*.

He managed to reach the painter to congratulate him. Apparently Prieto also contributed to the service. Camacho didn't stop there for long. As soon as he'd dished out a hug and said a few words, he left the artist with the rest of his circle of admirers and headed to Ara and me at the edge of the room.

"May I trouble you for a moment of your attention?"

His voice still retained its Colombian melody, but his expression was serious. He led us to a corner, by the cloakroom. He looked around to be sure that no one but us would hear him.

"I'm sorry to tell you, Señora Bonnard, but it appears we've come up against an unexpected setback."

The racket in the room suddenly sounded muffled, as if it were merely an undercurrent.

"The BBC's hiring department has rejected our proposal for you to be a contributor. We received a flat refusal. No explanations. Nothing."

28

Ara insisted on accompanying me outside. George Camacho was wanted by someone inside who probably intended to ask him for a role in his service, the bread and butter of so many of those present.

It was drizzling when we went out, the lights were already off in the shopwindows, and there were hardly any pedestrians or traffic. In the meager light of a streetlamp, I saw that my compatriot was frowning.

"This . . . it's rather . . . it's rather . . ." He stopped dead, as if his mind needed clearing. "Are you in a rush? I'd like to talk. I know a pub nearby."

He went in to gather his things and quickly returned, pulling up the collar on his raincoat.

Unlike on the half-empty streets, in the Coach & Horses there was no shortage of locals. The place was full of smoke, voices, and the effusions of humanity, but we found some space in one of the corners. The paneling on the walls and furniture was of dark wood. I rested my hands on the tabletop and snapped them back—it was greasy. Ara took the handkerchief from his top jacket pocket and tried to clean it without much success.

"Don't lean on it. I'll be right back. What would you like to drink?"

"Whatever you're having."

"Perfect."

He approached the bar. A few solitary men were spread out along it, sitting on stools. I watched the proprietress, a woman with enormous breasts and graying curly hair, serve him. When he returned, he was carrying two pints of ale and a glass of water. He dipped part of the handkerchief in the water and started to clean the table with the wet fabric.

"Milady offered me one of her bar towels, but I thought it would be more sanitary to use my own materials."

The beer was a dark copper color, lukewarm, sickly sweet, dense. Ara was left with froth on his mustache.

"The thing is, my dear friend," he said after his first sip, "sometimes hiring has proven to be a little complicated because of the nature and baggage of the speaker."

I cut him off.

"It doesn't matter. Honestly, I promise you, it doesn't matter."

I was lying, of course. It did matter. My indifference was fake. And not because of what the broadcasts meant to me—a complete upstart who'd nominated herself brazenly and with one or two lies—but because the rejection had been so drastic, so arbitrary. I wondered on what they could have based the decision. On my exploits in Madrid? On the fact that I was Marcus's wife?

Ara's voice cut through my brooding.

"May I ask you a rather nosy question?"

I nodded, and he cleared his throat.

"Is there some political reason why the BBC would censor you?"

I took another sip, reluctantly. I'd never liked beer.

"If by political reason you mean links to a party or organization that has something to do with Spain or our war, the answer is a categorical no. But look, Señor Ara . . ."

"You can call me just plain Ara."

"Look, Ara," I repeated. I paused, trying to decide where to begin my story. "You see, there are a lot of things you don't know about me.

In fact, you know almost nothing, other than that we're from the same country, I had an English husband, and I lived in Jerusalem for a time."

Now it was he who nodded. In our meetings, due to his overwhelming warmth and charming way with people, he had always monopolized the conversation, but perhaps he now understood that he should listen instead.

"But I'm going to fill you in," I went on, "in case you'd like to pass these details to whoever it may concern, in the upper echelons of the BBC or wherever you think advisable."

He nodded again. Neither of us touched our beer.

"For five years of my life, for the entire duration of the world war, I worked very closely with the British intelligence service. I'm not going to tell you the nature of my activities, or where and how I carried them out, but believe me, in the role I was entrusted with, I excelled."

Absent the sparkle they'd had when he was chattering, my compatriot's eyes now studied me, intrigued and alert.

"After the war, my husband, a loyal protector of his country's interests, was assigned to Jerusalem, and that was where we went, to fulfill his nation's will. And do you know what happened? He was killed, that's what happened. While he was breaking his back to help Britain behave moderately well in the trap it had walked into in Palestine, as he was working in his office, a monstrous quantity of explosives placed by Jewish terrorists took his life. They destroyed him, butchered him completely. I was pregnant. The explosion made me go into labor. My son was born while they collected bits of his father from the rubble."

Now I did drink half a glass in one gulp, to help me swallow the bitter lump stuck in my throat. Ara murmured a hoarse "I'm sorry." I planted the palms of my hands on the table, now indifferent to the layer of filth. I leaned forward so my words would have a shorter distance to travel.

"I don't know why your corporation disapproves of me, but be aware that this country, when doing so has served its interests, has used me capably. And what its institutions owe me, for my own sake and for that of my husband, isn't unjustified censure, but a modicum of consideration and gratitude."

Now he slowly lifted his glass to his lips.

"Do you know what we are to them, Sira?" There was a trace of melancholy in his tone, a sudden sadness. "Pawns. Mere pawns on their board. You, me, everyone working in the overseas services. Everyone you saw the other day at Bush House. All the men and women you passed in the canteen, in the elevator, and the corridors. Human beings from near and far—we're all the same thing: simple pawns whose role is to be useful. We act for and on behalf of the British government. We submit to their interests and their propaganda efforts, to their criteria and instructions. That's what we did during the war, and in the interests of global democracy and lasting peace, we continue to do so. Within their machinery, however, as individuals we're just minor parts: controllable, expendable, fleeting."

The commotion in the pub remained intense. Almost all the tables were taken. One group had started a game of dice. Behind the counter, the buxom proprietress was drying glasses with her dubious towels.

"For all that, we enter the game freely and voluntarily—grateful, proud, even." He took another drink, almost finishing his beer. "They're arrogant imperialists, but even so, for almost all the people you saw a moment ago at the exhibition, who've been driven out of their country, the BBC has been a gift from God. First of all, because it provides them with a paid position, and with those three and a half guineas, or four, or five—or however much they're paid per contribution—they can clear part of their rent or afford coal and food. For some of them, it's meant they can replace the pick and shovel with the word and the pen. But it's not only that. Finances aside, they're interested in the role of broadcaster because it enables them to use their intellect, their knowledge, their talents, even their poor bruised ego. Stripped of their professorships and positions of responsibility, deprived of their professional lives or of their audience, in front of the microphone, for a moment they feel—we feel—useful again. And that, my dear friend, in these uncertain times, is a boost for our morale and self-esteem that can be more nourishing than a good steak."

He finished off his drink and picked up the damp handkerchief with his fingertips, folding it meticulously and putting it back in his pocket.

I understood his arguments. They were solid and convincing. But they were of little use to me. I wasn't an intellectual in exile or a political refugee.

"In any case, we'll look into it, don't worry. We'll ask them what their grounds are for such an incomprehensible rejection. It's the least you deserve."

He insisted on accompanying me in a taxi to the Boltons. If he was surprised that I was living in such an opulent neighborhood, he kept it to himself.

The street was deserted when I got out of the car. All I could hear were dogs barking in the distance. I said good night to Ara from the pavement. I was about to go through the little gate when I realized there was a light in Olivia's bedroom window. Light, and a silhouette.

29

The household routines were maintained with detailed precision. At half past eight every morning, we sat at the table once again. It was no longer as atrociously cold as it had been when I arrived, and my mother-in-law had over time dispensed with some of her woolen shawls. Now she wore just a long cardigan with a beautiful cashmere stole over it. Her ash-gray plait, which she continued to wear over her shoulder, now almost reached her waist.

"Did you have a pleasant evening, dear?"

"Fabulous. I went to a Spanish artist's exhibition."

She feigned an expression of pleasure as she cracked the shell of her boiled egg.

"And did you manage all right going there and back in a cab by yourself?"

She was aware I hadn't returned alone; she'd definitely seen me saying goodbye to Ara from her window. I pretended to concentrate on Philippa arriving with Víctor in her arms before I responded.

"Perfectly."

I sat the boy on my lap and put my own teaspoon full of soft-boiled egg in his mouth. I knew Olivia disapproved of such close contact with my son, skin to skin, saliva to saliva. I'd have been lying if I said I didn't secretly enjoy going against her.

"I saw that you bought some things in Woolworths, that popular department store that's so . . ."

I didn't know the meaning of the word she said next, but I didn't ask.

"I've never been in one of those shops," she admitted after a sip of tea. There was obvious scorn in her voice.

"They sell all sorts of things," I replied simply. "And at good prices."

"Oh, I don't doubt it. It's just not the kind of establishment I'm accustomed to."

I continued to share my egg with Víctor, laughing at the different faces he pulled when he was disgusted by the white and happy tasting the yolk.

"The heiress must be about your age, and she's on her third or fourth husband already. She lived here in London for a while, but I read that she ended up selling her Regent's Park mansion to the United States government for one dollar."

She fell silent, as if waiting for a reply from me.

"I don't know who you're referring to, Olivia."

She shook her head in her characteristic way, as if enduring my ignorance took significant effort.

"Barbara Hutton, my dear. The millionairess from New York. Granddaughter of the owner of the Woolworths chain, a socialite who tries to pass herself off as an aristocrat, though her grandfather was nothing more than a common farmer turned modest shopkeeper who invented the dime store formula. She, Barbara . . ."

An unexpected presence entered, saving me from her prattle.

"Yes, Gertrude?" I said.

"Telephone for you, madam."

With the boy in my arms still, I apologized to my mother-in-law and went out into the hall. At the other end of the line, Ara sounded hurried.

"I spent the night chewing things over, my friend. We've just asked the director of the overseas services for a formal explanation of why they vetoed you. In the meantime, I think we should carry on as before, just in case we manage to resolve the issue."

"You want us to work as if nothing had happened?" I asked, doubtful.

"That's the idea. I propose that you finish writing the material on Palestine, we meet as planned to give it the best possible structure, and we start recording without delay."

I was silent for a few seconds.

"And what if the answer is still no?"

"In that case, we'll write off the disks of your voice as a loss but offer the text to Atlantic-Pacific Press, the agency that distributes written reports all over Latin America. They'll accept it, I'm sure."

I fell silent again, trying to process his proposal. Víctor was writhing to free himself, so I crouched to put him down on the floor.

"Hello? Sira?"

"I'm here."

"So, what do you think?"

"Are you sure, Ara?"

"Positive."

"Then let's do it."

I shut myself away to work that very morning while Philippa took Víctor out for a stroll, and while Gertrude and Olivia prepared to try to reverse the garden's decline after the awful winter. Through the window, I saw a pair of men arrive who'd seemingly been hired to lend a hand in the task. One was clumsy and overweight, the other puny and rather hunched. Both were over sixty, wearing grubby flat caps and clenching crude cigarettes between their teeth. They clearly lacked the energy needed for a struggle against nature's onslaught, but there they were, stoically enduring my mother-in-law's orders. The four of them made quite a picture: Olivia with her peculiar style, with the addition of a pair of mud-covered Wellington boots; Gertrude, wearing an old military coat over her uniform; and two poor devils, eager to earn a few shillings by any means possible.

In reality, I thought, this was simply a picture of the world without men of working age that had emerged after the Second World War. Britain and other countries had lost almost an entire generation of young males, men who'd lost their lives bravely serving as soldiers, sailors, and aviators. There were plenty of women, children, and old men left, but they were aging fathers and mothers, like Olivia, who'd unnaturally outlived their sons; girls without sweethearts, like Philippa; young widows like me; or little ones like my Víctor, who hadn't had time to meet their fathers.

I shook my head as if trying to throw off the emotions that rocked me from time to time. I didn't want to feel Marcus's absence again. *Jerusalem,* I told myself, picking up my pencil. Jerusalem, seen through unfeeling eyes, was what I had to focus on. Without personal wounds or passions. Without rage or fury or resentment.

I didn't stop working until the telephone rang again.

"Mrs. Bonnard? Sira Bonnard?"

It was Dominic Hodson, Marcus's friend. This was the first time I'd heard from him since the afternoon at Fortnum & Mason.

"I'm near the Boltons and would like to see you. Would you be so kind as to give me half an hour of your time?"

I looked out of the window again before putting on my coat. The four awkward gardeners were still there. I saw that they'd lit a bonfire. The men were throwing armfuls of branches and spadefuls of dry leaves onto it, Gertrude was still pulling up weeds, and Olivia, wearing a pair of enormous, dirty leather gloves, was raking debris into a pile. I felt a stab of guilt for not helping them, but now wasn't the time.

I agreed to meet Dominic outside St. Mary, the church we continued to attend on Sundays. He was there waiting for me. We started to walk, following one of the paths. The sun was shining half-heartedly, but the temperature was agreeable. Spring was just beginning to show itself in the trees and flowerbeds.

"It's a very lovely place, the Boltons," he said. To say something, I supposed.

It was indeed a lovely place with its large houses and serenity. Two curved streets and an oval garden in the center, the basics of its existence. At this time of day, almost noon, there were only children playing outside, nannies watching over them, and one or two people out strolling.

"A century ago, this was just countryside, did you know? Now it's a sought-after urban enclave, and it will be even more desired in the future when everything stabilizes and the property market bounces back."

I nodded, though I couldn't have cared less about these observations.

"Supposedly these gardens are for the exclusive use of residents," he went on. "There even used to be a fence around the entire perimeter. Like in many other places, it was removed at the start of the war so the iron could be used to make armaments. Another small part of the war effort."

That was something I already knew—Marcus had told me about it—but I made a special effort to keep quiet and listen to his praises and historical details, until finally I couldn't contain myself anymore.

"Sorry to be impatient, Dominic, but what news is there about the will?"

He was about to reply when we saw Philippa appear around a bend in the path, pushing Víctor's pram.

"My son," I mumbled.

He greeted me with his usual joy, laughter, and open arms, so that I'd pick him up. I showed him to Dominic, incapable of hiding my pride.

"It's a friend of Papa's, say hello," I said to Víctor in Spanish.

Víctor didn't, but he looked at him with his green eyes, curious and serious. Philippa took a few steps away. Dominic looked back at him for a moment, then slowly, clumsily, placed his hand on top of Víctor's woolly hat. Clearly, he wasn't used to dealing with infants.

"This boy and you," he announced soberly, "are the heirs to the Bonnard estate. The only heirs."

I frowned. He continued to speak, slowly, doing his utmost to make sure there wasn't a single syllable I didn't understand.

"To my surprise, among Mark's papers I found some related to his father's—Judge Bonnard's—will." He paused, as if preparing himself for what came next. "Apparently, owing to some regrettable circumstances that occurred decades ago, your mother-in-law doesn't own a single brick of the house she is occupying. For this same reason, she doesn't even have the right to use the property."

He diverted his gaze to the house, which, from the gardens where we stood, could be seen in its entirety through the still-leafless trees. There it was: white and dirty, with its withered pillars and flaking stucco, faded but beautiful.

"This Boltons residence and its contents were entirely your husband's property, my dear. To put it simply, your mother-in-law has enjoyed the benefit of its use over the years, courtesy of her own son, as a mere guest."

I didn't manage a response. Víctor stretched an arm out toward Dominic and grabbed the brim of his hat. Impassive, Dominic continued.

"Now that Mark—Marcus—is no longer with us, the situation has taken a different turn." He paused again, swallowing. "I'm sure the need would never arise but, legally and without any justification required, as of now, you could show Olivia Bonnard the door whenever you wished."

30

I tried to put my boy back in the pram and return him to Philippa so she could take him home. I needed to speak to Dominic undistracted. Everything he'd just told me was so unexpected, so difficult to process and so lacking in logic, that I needed detailed explanations. But Víctor refused and threw a noisy tantrum. Philippa and I tried to calm him down, without success. At some point Dominic checked his watch.

"I'm afraid I'm going to have to excuse myself. I'm expected for lunch at my club in half an hour. If it's convenient for you, though it's not in my purview as executor, I'd like to gather some precise information so I can give you more details. If you could give me a little more time, I'd be most grateful."

I agreed—how could I not?—while Víctor continued to cry and kick out like a colt, intent on getting out of the pram by any means possible. I had no choice but to give in.

"All right," I said to Dominic, picking up my baby again. "But please, don't be long, because all this is so . . . it's so . . ."

I struggled to find the right word, but in neither English nor Spanish could I find a sufficient adjective to describe my state of shock.

"I understand perfectly. Believe me, I'm as bewildered as you are."

We went home. Víctor gradually stopped crying, he ate his vegetable purée, and I put him down for a nap. By then, it was time for Olivia and me to sit at the table to have our meager lunch, as we did every day: boiled cabbage, half a boiled potato, maybe a miserable piece of ox tongue. I heard her come in, protesting angrily about the incompetence of the two laborers and lashing out at Gertrude. The prospect of what would happen next suddenly seemed too much. While she was still downstairs, I scribbled an excuse, left the note at the entrance, and crept out.

I had nowhere in particular to go, but I simply didn't have the strength to face her. Olivia Bonnard, my mother-in-law—formidable, exuberant, domineering, grandiloquent Lady Olivia Bonnard, the heart and soul of the Boltons—was for some mysterious reason residing in that mansion like a phantom, dispossessed of the very entitlement she displayed so imperiously every day.

I walked through South Kensington, chewing over Dominic Hodson's words in my mind: the revelation that the legitimate owners of the house were a boy born in the Near East, who hadn't yet celebrated his first birthday, and an uprooted and confused foreigner.

Tired of asking myself questions without finding answers, I decided to sit on a bench outside the Natural History Museum. I took out my notebook and tried to concentrate on my notes for the radio recording with an uncertain future. Ultimately, it could end up in the bin, without reaching anyone, either at the BBC or the press agency Ara had mentioned. But at least for the time being it was something to engross myself in, a way to banish my demons and center my attention on something concrete, in the naive hope that doing so would give me some respite from the worries of the present.

When I returned to the Boltons, Olivia luckily wasn't there. Gertrude informed me that the lady of the house had gone out for dinner, and relief washed over me. Once Víctor was overcome by sleep, and without my mother-in-law's vibrant presence, the house was lifeless and silent earlier than usual. Gertrude and Philippa took themselves off to their rooms and I went to mine, using the time to continue working on my notes. It was about ten o'clock when the telephone rang downstairs.

I was tempted not to move, certain it wasn't for me. Who in their right mind would call at such an hour? But it kept ringing until I decided to go down in the dark with a thick shawl over my shoulders, cursing the culprit for his or her untimely insistence.

"Please forgive me for disturbing you so late. I'm calling from a telephone box in the street and didn't want to leave it until tomorrow."

It was George Camacho, the Colombian director.

"You see, my esteemed friend, I've just come from a meeting with some BBC colleagues and, surprisingly, someone answered our queries."

There was interference on the line, and he sounded far away.

"The matter of your contract has taken a most unexpected turn. As far as I understand, you weren't turned down for any political reasons relating to the Spanish situation. In fact, until this afternoon, there wasn't even any record of your application having reached the overseers at the Foreign Office."

"Then what was the reason?" I asked, amazed.

"It seems that someone in a certain position of authority made the decision unilaterally and in a personal capacity to reject the request. It's that simple."

I pressed the receiver against my ear.

"Are you familiar with the name Cora Soutter?"

31

I fell asleep that night mulling over the absurd ability we humans have to complicate our lives unnecessarily.

All my assumptions had turned out to be wrong; how naive I'd been. Nobody at the BBC had vetoed me because of misgivings of a political nature. Nor had I been rejected for my undercover work with the SOE in Spain during the war, let alone for being the wife of an agent who'd died while performing his duties. No, I wasn't facing censorship by the hallowed intelligence service. I was simply the victim of a jealous woman's reprisals. A woman who was jealous without any reason or grounds. Or so I believed.

Still, despite the apparent frivolity of the matter, I did not take it lightly. Far from it. As the hours passed, my indignation grew. After getting up I tried to decide what to do. I was aware of my bleak situation as I stood in the bathroom. I had no one to share my confusion with, no one to consult about my doubts or from whom to receive advice. No family, or partner, or friends. The woman the mirror threw back at me was the only person who could help me make decisions: me, the same person I had always been—and at the same time, different.

The face I saw in my reflection had lost the rounded smoothness of the girl who'd crossed the Strait of Gibraltar eleven years before, clinging to a crook's love. Neither was there any trace of the light I'd radiated when I was pregnant, and when Marcus was still by my side. The woman in the mirror was heading toward maturity now, with sharper, more angular features, pronounced cheekbones, eyebrows high above a gaze full of unknowns. Only in her would the answer be found.

I continued to ponder as I washed, as I sank my face into my son's cradle to say good morning. Should I leave things to be straightened out at the BBC through the official channels, through George Camacho and his people? Or should I confront Nick Soutter's wife myself?

I'd received letters from Nick the whole time I'd been in England and missed our friendship terribly. I missed his confidence, his lucidity and his charisma, his judgment. Under different circumstances, our long late-night talks in front of the stove in my apartment at the Austrian Hospice in Jerusalem would certainly have helped shine a light on the darkness of my confusion. Him listening to me, me listening to him, exchanging our thoughts, comparing perspectives—together we would've been able to examine the conflicts that plagued me, with wisdom and a sense of balance. But those conversations were in the past. Now there were three thousand miles between us. And for no apparent reason, I'd found an opponent in his wife.

The morning started out slow and calm. The two poor souls returned to clear the weeds from the garden, and through the window I could hear my mother-in-law's high-handed demands again. At half past nine I reached the conclusion that I wasn't going to confront Cora Soutter. At ten, when Philippa took Víctor out for a walk, I decided I would—I at least needed to know her reasons. At half past ten, I persuaded myself of the opposite. At eleven, tired of debating, I considered what the women who meant something in my life would've done, the friends who had, with their courage and boldness, become role models for me. Rosalinda Fox, Fran Nash, even Candelaria the smuggler with her working-class fighting spirit. Would they have kept quiet? Or would they have shown their claws, even if only to assert their dignity and not allow themselves to be trod upon?

Still reflecting, I looked at myself in the mirror again, picked up a deep-red lipstick, and applied it to my lips. After brushing my hair, I left my bedroom, slamming the door behind me.

I didn't want to ask for her when I arrived at Broadcasting House, so I simply stood to one side of the main entrance and waited. It was almost midday, and a lot of employees were beginning to pause their work and go out for lunch at one of the establishments in the area. I didn't know Cora Soutter's exact professional rank, but I was certain she wasn't a telephone operator or mere typist; she was more senior than that. Her worldly background, her style when she planted herself in front of me on the day I went to collect my radio, and the confidence conveyed by her voice and movements all suggested that she wouldn't be leaving the building with a group of chattering colleagues. It wasn't long before I confirmed as much: in less than half an hour, she was outside.

She was alone and this time wearing an aubergine skirt and jacket. She cut a good figure from behind, with her shoulder-length blond hair, her slender legs. She walked with a firm step, covering a stretch of pavement before crossing between vehicles. The ends of her hair bounced as she looked from side to side. I followed her at a conservative distance. At no time did she seem to hesitate or slow down, as if she'd repeated the route many times. She turned left and strode into a small restaurant, and I stopped a few yards away. I looked at the exterior, which had dark-green wooden panels and curtains covering its little window. Chez Louis, I read on the sign above the door. I waited a couple of minutes before going in after her.

The restaurant, narrow and deep, was almost full. It took me a moment to locate her. When I finally did, I saw that she was sitting at the back, opposite a man, at a small table against the wall. She had her back to me again. Her friend, or whoever it was, stretched an arm across the table and stroked her right hand.

The head waiter offered me one of the few remaining free tables, but I turned it down and indicated another, farther from the street and closer to the couple. He agreed with a shrug, handed me a menu, and went off in his incredibly long apron to see to some other customers. From my table, I could still see her shoulders and the back of her head, but not her face. The man, on the other hand, was practically facing me. Aged between forty and fifty, with a delicately striped suit and a tie with a geometric pattern. He exuded confidence, his hair was slicked back, and his looks were average, neither good nor bad.

I ordered a *soupe à l'oignon*. The waiter offered me a glass of wine, and I was about to say no when I thought, why not? My initial impression of the place had been wrong: despite the narrowness of the building and its understated exterior, the clientele's appearance and the prices on the menu suggested it was a French restaurant of some standing. And as I observed the complicity between Nick's wife and her companion, I sensed that their clandestine lunch à deux was repeated here with some regularity.

Having been subjected for so long to the frugal cuisine of my mother-in-law's home, I found that the wholesome soup and sips of claret nourished my soul, but I tried not to allow myself to be softened by delicacies. I was there for a reason, and I had to keep my eye on the ball. So I brazenly began to entice Cora Soutter's companion. It wasn't long before he noticed. At first he disregarded my behavior, as if he couldn't believe himself the object of the attentions of an audacious dark-haired woman who was having lunch alone. When I smiled at him flagrantly, he was finally persuaded, and each time Cora looked down at her plate, he took the chance to exchange glances with me. That is, until she began to sense something was amiss. She turned her head to find out what it was that kept causing her companion to divert his gaze.

Her face contorted when she recognized me. In reply, I subtly raised my glass. *Here I am,* I was signaling, *waiting for you.* I couldn't hear her, but she craned her neck and said something to him—undoubtedly nothing very pleasant. They quickly finished eating, barely exchanging a word, clearly uncomfortable. They ordered neither dessert nor coffee, and they didn't even ask for a bill. He just left some notes beside his napkin.

I waited for them to get up before I did the same. Only then, before they began to walk to the exit, did I take four strides and plant myself by their table.

"That's a lovely tie you're wearing, my friend," I said with ease. "Forgive me for staring at it. It's not you I'm interested in, however." I turned to her. "A pleasure to see you again, Mrs. Soutter."

She didn't refuse when I asked her to sit down again. I did the same in the chair he'd just vacated, opposite her. Hesitant, the man searched for a sign from his friend or lover. By way of goodbye, she just mumbled, "We'll talk later."

"I wanted us to meet somewhere neutral. Better than at your workplace, don't you think?"

She held my gaze; she was anything but timid. Her eyes were a very light blue, beautiful, perhaps a little too close together. Her eyebrows were plucked, too much for my taste. Still without saying a word, she took out a snakeskin cigarette holder. She offered me a cigarette, but I said no, thank you. An obliging waiter held a lighter out to her, and she took a deep drag. I remained silent, patient, waiting. There was no need for questions.

"I don't appreciate your closeness with Nick," she admitted after slowly blowing out the smoke. "I simply don't like it. I don't appreciate him sending you packages from Jerusalem. I'm unhappy that he's concerning himself with you and trying to please you."

"And so you interfere with my work?"

"I don't want him to repeat our past."

She took a second puff, her words now coming out enveloped in rings of smoke.

"I can't bear him reliving our past with another woman."

I raised the corners of my mouth in an expression halfway between disbelief and sarcasm. The head waiter approached and offered us coffee. We both accepted.

"As far as I knew," I said, "you and he led independent lives."

"That's right. And it won't be long before we're divorced, I hope."

As she said the last word she flicked the ash from her cigarette. Her fingernails were painted bright coral. In that tiny movement, I thought I glimpsed a trace of ferocity.

"I'm sure it's for the best, for both of you," I replied calmly. "And though I shouldn't have to tell you, I would like to. Know that I'm not in any kind of relationship with the man who is still, even if only for a short time, your husband."

She shrugged.

"That may be so. To be honest, it's the least of my worries."

"So why treat me like this?"

She sipped her coffee, as if giving her answer careful thought.

"You may not have consummated the relationship," she conceded as she separated her lips from the rim of her cup. "But you *have* taken my place in his affections."

I watched her, waiting expectantly.

"He admitted it to me himself. He was here last Christmas, you may recall."

Indeed, Nick hadn't spent the festive season in Jerusalem. He detested Christmas carols, but he had gone to see his children in England. It had been a terrible time for me, without Marcus, with my baby, my grief. I had at least been comforted by Fran Nash and by her daughters, so full of warmth, who'd come from Cairo for the school holidays. We'd had some respite from the savage violence, and we'd even attended Christmas Eve mass at the chapel of the Notre Dame of Jerusalem Center. Nick had not been there. He'd spent almost two weeks away, and I'd missed him terribly.

"Nick has fallen in love with you, my dear," she said, stubbing out the cigarette.

She'd only smoked half. She pressed it down hard until the unsmoked paper broke off and tobacco strands were left in the bottom of the ashtray.

"He's deliriously in love. And even if not so much as a glimmer of what there once was between us remains, it still turns my stomach and hurts me deeply."

32

I wasn't surprised to find Dominic in conversation with Olivia when I arrived back at the Boltons. At this point, anything seemed possible.

Her greeting sounded abnormally warm.

"You're here at last, dear!"

They'd finished their tea, but Gertrude hadn't cleared away the crockery yet. In front of them were empty cups, a cold teapot, plates covered in crumbs, and the remains of a plum cake.

"Divine *tailleur* you're wearing, my dear. You look like a different woman," she said.

Dominic's face clearly showed relief when he stood to greet me. I imagined that my mother-in-law had occupied him for too long and, being a dependable man, he'd found it difficult to get away.

I saw, in front of him, a leather folder on the table. I felt a pinch in my insides: I assumed it contained the documents that related to Marcus's will and its consequences.

He cleared his throat before speaking.

"It's been a pleasure, my Lady Olivia. Now I'd like to speak to Mark's wife alone, if you don't mind."

I'd made myself comfortable between them, in the very center of the sofa that separated their armchairs. They both turned their heads toward me when they heard me speak.

"I'd rather she stayed."

She sat back with a look of satisfaction, as if I'd just proposed a most appealing plan. Dominic gave me an inquiring look, and I reaffirmed my words with a subtle gesture.

"If that's what you wish, it's fine by me." He rested his fingers on the folder's fastener. "Right. Well. To put you in the picture," he said, addressing Olivia, "what we're going to discuss here is your son's last wishes. He named me executor of his will, and I've had the honor of fulfilling his wishes, making use of my powers in accordance with his interests."

He spoke in the bureaucratic tone of the senior colonial official that he was, sitting with his spine straight, away from the back of the chair. His not-very-attractive face wore a serious expression, his knees were together, his hands lined up on either side of the papers.

"Despite it being held in a domestic setting," he went on ceremoniously, "this meeting shall be regarded as a formal succession hearing."

I glanced at my mother-in-law out of the corner of my eye. Her expression was drastically different. The numerous wrinkles that were usually spread all over her face seemed to be concentrated around her mouth and between her eyebrows.

"But, Dominic . . ."

We looked at her in silence, waiting for her to go on. But she said nothing else. For good measure, he reemphasized the terms.

"This is the matter of Mark's final will, and this is how I must proceed, legally and morally. Honoring his intentions. And his memory."

"In that case . . . ," Olivia said drily.

We heard the slap of her palms against the upholstery as she let her hands fall. Then she lifted her shoulders and chest, as if filling her lungs with air. She also tried to raise her voice and keep it steady.

"While I didn't anticipate that you would be the one who ended up undertaking it, dear," she said to Dominic, "I imagined all this would come to pass sooner or later. In any case, and before you say anything," she went on, "perhaps I should speak first and save you from having to make what evidently will be uncomfortable explanations."

She allowed her gaze to wander the room for a few moments, over the shabby wallpaper and tired curtains, without coming to rest anywhere in particular. Her mind seemed to be traveling back to a time decades before our present.

"Sometimes," she continued in a somber tone, "we make bad decisions without foreseeing that their consequences will stay with us for the rest of our lives, like long, black shadows."

She pushed herself up with her arms and went to the dresser where, by way of a bar, there stood a tray of the bottles that her friends always brought to their Thursday gatherings. She picked up several and examined them closely. They were all almost empty. In the end, she found one of Plymouth gin that was a little fuller. She showed it to us as if to offer a glass. Dominic and I declined, but she served herself a generous quantity.

Back in her chair, she took a slow drink. After that, in only a few brief minutes, she gave a summary of a period of her life that had changed the family's future forever: Three small children and a husband who was too busy and lacking in affection. During the First World War, an attractive American businessman who'd traveled to England to take charge of a company that was involved in the arms industry. Irrepressible passion and a story of deceit, turmoil, and adultery. Upon learning of the infidelity, Judge Bonnard, deeply hurt, had set in motion the legal machinery at his disposal in order to separate her from the children and deprive her of assets and rights. She'd accepted the terms in exchange for her freedom, but she came to regret her decision. After a long absence, she returned to the family home, but by then, the marriage had been officially dissolved. The usual order was mostly restored, but the legal terms of the separation were never reversed. Neither did her husband ever change the restrictive testamentary decisions that he'd made in her absence.

She didn't speak with melancholy. Olivia wasn't given to showing her emotions openly, and sometimes I even doubted that she felt any.

Marcus had not ever mentioned the episode to me. I'd always assumed his parents were a stable and conventional couple. Another box from my husband's past that he'd never opened.

"That's how the ownership of this house and the rest of the estate went straight from the father to the children," she explained after another drink of gin. "And all to Mark, since the two little ones died without descendants."

They hadn't been young children when they left this world, that much I knew. The only daughter, Ann, had died from meningitis at age fourteen; the middle child, Hugh, had enlisted in the air force and was killed in combat shortly before Marcus and I were reunited in Lisbon. Nevertheless, that was what they remained in her memory: her two little ones.

Dominic's formal tone brought us back to the business at hand.

"In that case, the terms are clear, and we can rule out any further inquiries. Regarding Mark's instructions, however, I must inform you that, among his wishes, there is a clause for the provision of assets on his behalf."

We both looked at him with curiosity.

"Mark stipulated that his mother must receive a sum from the estate that allows her to live with dignity," he explained, holding up one of the documents. "It will not be a fixed amount paid in advance. Rather, it will consist of an annuity whose amount must be decided between the testator's widow and me."

Good heavens. Good heavens. Despite Dominic's formal language, I could see the crux of the matter: the provision of means for Olivia's subsistence lay in my hands. I didn't know whether to laugh or cry. Why had Marcus done this to me? For what reason had he placed such a responsibility on me? Had he distrusted his own mother? For all that he hadn't revealed, had he in the end trusted me with too much?

Olivia reacted with astonishment. First she blinked, perplexed. Then, with her lips pressed together, she smiled with satisfaction.

"Splendid," she muttered, raising her glass as if drinking a toast to her son, wherever he was.

The pieces of the puzzle were beginning to come together in my mind. Some of them, however, didn't quite fit. She had been surprised to learn that she would be paid a regular sum of money, which meant that she hadn't expected to receive anything at all. What on earth, then, was the explanation for her earlier actions?

Since we were uncovering the truth, I decided to raise my doubts directly.

"Olivia, I have a question. If you already foresaw this outcome, why did you bring an architect here?"

She let out a rasping burst of laughter.

"Oh . . . that!"

"Was it to persuade me," I persisted, "before I found out about the situation myself?"

"Well, if you'd been receptive to the idea, I would have known how to approach the matter of the formal ownership of the property later. By then, with a bit of luck, I would've gained a small piece for myself: a flat from which you would have found it difficult to evict me. But I misjudged you. I was entirely wrong."

She paused, as if retrieving the memory of that meeting. Then she smiled with bitter irony.

"You weren't interested at all. I thought you far more banal and whimsical than you've proven to be, my dear. You've taken me by surprise, I must admit."

I was about to protest, to justify myself, but she cut me off.

"Two summers ago, on the afternoon when I met you, you seemed an altogether different person. Superficial, insubstantial, utterly dependent on Mark. What on earth, I wondered, had happened to my son, such an astute and intelligent man, that had caused him to end up marrying a . . . some sort of exotic doll?"

Dominic let out a disapproving growl.

"I was just trying to please you," I muttered.

My memory of that afternoon was still vivid. I'd arrived in a foreign country feeling awkward, trying to speak a language I only half knew, anxious to make a good impression, hoping Marcus would be proud. What I'd found, instead of an attentive mother-in-law, was someone with an overbearing personality who'd treated me with supreme disdain, barely giving me the chance to say a word.

"In any case," I concluded, trying not to lose my composure, "that's all in the past. And now that your son's final wishes are starting to become clear, I suppose you won't have to put up with me for much longer. As soon as you've sorted out the matter of the pension that's still—"

Dominic interrupted me.

"I'm sorry?"

Ignoring him, Olivia got up to pour herself another drink. His expression was of uneasy curiosity.

"What's this about the matter of the pension?"

I told him about the letter I'd received, the sinking feeling I'd had when faced with such complex bureaucracy, and her offer to take care of the matter. While I explained, she kept her back to us, serving herself the dregs of another bottle. I started to ask her about it, but Dominic raised his hand to stop me.

"Lady Olivia?"

His voice was firm, but she didn't turn around.

"Olivia?"

Nothing.

"Olivia?"

When she sensed from Dominic's taut tone that she had no option but to face the consequences, she turned around slowly, with resignation.

"The official notification your daughter-in-law mentions, which you are supposedly taking care of . . . ," he said. "Could you explain to me what it's about?"

Still standing, she shielded herself behind another sip, remaining silent. There she was: aloof, proud, feigning weariness and indifference, once more dressed in one of her long outfits, her hair ash colored, her bearing regal.

"Because," Dominic went on without altering his grave tone, "as far as I'm aware, nothing of your son's affairs is still pending. And I can assure you, I've gone through every detail with the utmost rigor, as I was entrusted to do."

We sat watching her, waiting for an answer.

"Olivia?" Dominic repeated, darkly serious.

Cornered, she finally threw a hand in the air, as if making light of the matter. As if all of it—the will, her son's memory, our presence—had suddenly made her feel profoundly bored.

"What was it about?" he insisted. "Was it an important matter?"

Realizing Dominic wasn't going to give up, she slowly shook her head.

"So, it was just some minor business? An unimportant administrative step?"

Now she nodded, slowly once more, without parting her lips.

That was when it became clear. Clear as daylight. How stupid I'd been. How ridiculously naive.

I got up and approached until I stood before her wrinkled face, her extravagant appearance, her conceit, her insolence. The questions poured out; my indignation was fierce.

"Are you telling me you didn't have to do anything on my behalf? That we're not waiting for them to resolve anything important relating to Marcus's pension? That you've kept us in London all this time for no reason whatsoever, only to make sure I didn't look into whether something was due to me and claim inheritance? Are you trying to tell me that you've been deceiving us, and that you haven't let us go, only because of your . . . because of your . . . nothing more than your selfish schemes?"

33

Perhaps the attack on the King David had affected my ability to see things clearly. So much so that I hadn't even realized that my mother-in-law had been manipulating me so blatantly. Neither had I managed to pick up on Nick Soutter's true feelings, nor, perhaps, my own. Bit by bit, however, I was finally beginning to see clearly.

Marcus's death had torn me apart, destroyed my life. But, for my own sake and for the sake of my son, I couldn't allow the catastrophe to rob me of my capacity to perceive reality, with all its creases and contradictions, its brutalities and its subtleties. I had to change my attitude, no matter how hard it was to do so. I had to change my behavior radically, I realized that now. No more passive resistance and allowing myself to be dragged along. No more docile waiting: the time had come to make decisions, bring chapters to a close, and go my own way. To that end, my first order of business was to wrap up my work with the BBC. My second was to buy tickets to leave London immediately.

The previous evening, after confronting Olivia, I'd asked Dominic to take care of everything. To liquidate what Marcus had left me and my son, to assure Olivia that I had no intention of throwing her out of what had been her home. To pay her whatever amount he considered appropriate and deposit the rest in a bank account for a time, until I knew where I was going to settle. I had no desire to stay in England, thank you. I'd had enough.

The first thing I did the next day was call Ángel Ara.

"I've finished my notes and I'm ready. If the matter of the approval has been sorted out, we can start right away. I don't have long. I'm leaving London soon."

"It's as if you read my mind, my friend. I was just about to call you. We start tomorrow at nine."

I arrived five minutes early and he was already there waiting for me. I told him my ideas, and he accepted all my notes enthusiastically.

"They're fabulous images of present-day Jerusalem. Our listeners are going to be captivated. Magnificent, real, fresh, incisive, illustrative . . ."

I let him go on, though his flood of superlatives didn't give me much pleasure. I'd simply described what the city was like in the year and a half I spent there, without fig leaves or artifice. I hadn't gone into painful private matters like Marcus's death, or personal details of any kind. Nor had I mentioned the reality of the attacks, the everyday conflicts, the controversies, the different sides of the argument, the anguish, and the hardship.

We worked without rest, first structuring the notes, him sitting at the typewriter, me offering suggestions, making changes and corrections as we went—preparing, essentially, the text that would later become a voice recording. We were putting the finishing touches to it in the office adjoining the studio when there came a knock on the door. Through the glass we saw George Camacho. He came in and greeted us with his usual amiable courtesy before, to my astonishment, asking Ara to leave us alone for a moment.

He got straight to the point.

"I have a message for you. Highly confidential. I ask that you treat it with the utmost discretion."

A cold sweat broke out all over my body.

"I must confess that this whole business is taking a most surprising turn. During the investigation into the matter of your approval to work with us, it seems some aspects . . . some unusual particulars emerged."

His tone was as modulated as ever, but even so, he sounded serious.

"There are certain people who, having learned of your presence in London, would like to speak to you, Señora Bonnard. I will take the liberty to ask you, please, to listen to them."

I was alarmed, taken back to a time when my work involved clandestine messages, furtive meetings, and secrecy.

He concluded his message.

"If you'd be kind enough to accept, a car is waiting for you at the entrance."

There were no windows in that room next door to the recording studio, nowhere to allow my gaze to wander while I tried to take in what he was saying. So I focused on my hands, examining them while I weighed up what my intuition was telling me.

A few long moments passed as he waited patiently.

"All right, my esteemed friend," I said finally, looking up from my fingers. "I suppose I'll listen to those gentlemen, as you ask. But we'll do it on my terms, no orders or demands. I'm not going to get into any car right now. Nor will I meet anyone where they tell me to."

George Camacho was looking at me with astonishment. I stood up so that we were on the same level.

"If it's not too much trouble, please tell the people who sent you that they'll have the chance to see me at the Dorchester at three o'clock this afternoon. In fact, no, sorry—half past three would be better."

I remembered the name because it was the hotel I'd visited in my search for Rosalinda, when I'd found no trace of her. I rounded off my effrontery with a smile as false as it was luminous, a trick I also had to rescue from the depths of my memory, as I hadn't used it for a very long time.

He left bewildered, unable to understand me. Ara was back at once with a couple of tasteless sandwiches: our lunch. I neither explained nor did he ask, and we continued as if nothing had happened. At ten minutes before three, we'd finished. I managed to flag down a cab, and at twenty past three I was at the entrance to the Dorchester. My legs were almost out of the car when I drew back and asked the driver to start off again.

"Where shall I take you, madam?"

"Let's go for a quiet drive," I replied. "Anywhere you want to show me."

Through the window I contemplated Buckingham Palace, the legendary Big Ben, the broad, dark Thames, the Houses of Parliament. At forty minutes past three we drove along Park Lane again, and I finally got out of the taxi in front of the hotel. I was usually a punctual person, but this time I was late on purpose. If the meeting was going to be what I suspected it would be, this time it would be me who decided the time that it would happen.

They were waiting for me in an out-of-the-way area, and they stood as soon as they saw me walk into the Dorchester's elegant lobby. They were wearing suits, their hair neat, and their faces clean shaven. One of them was blond, in his thirties; the other, more mature, had some elegant gray hairs and was wearing glasses and a beautiful silk tie. I didn't know either of them, but I'd met a few of their style, so they seemed in a way familiar. I greeted them with outward confidence and sat down gracefully, crossing my legs as I always used to do. They both had cups of coffee in front of them. I declined when they offered to get me something.

The nearby tables were unoccupied, but even if they hadn't been, they were distant enough for the risk of our conversation reaching ears beyond our own to be minimal. After our introductions, they offered me their condolences for Marcus's death and reiterated how sorry they were for the deplorable incident of my rejection by the BBC.

"A section manageress made an imprudent mistake," the elder one said, "but it's all resolved now. The plus side, for us, is that thanks to this error, the director of the Latin American Service asked for an explanation, assuming it was a political veto, and the matter was passed through the relevant authorities until we learned of it. Which is how we located you. I must admit, finding that you'd settled in London came as a complete surprise to us."

The younger man removed some papers from a clipboard and passed them to his superior, who lowered his gold-rimmed spectacles to the tip of his nose and proceeded in a soft, articulate tone.

"To refresh our memories a little, according to our files, you, the British subject Sira Bonnard, previously the Spanish citizen Sira Quiroga, were employed by the Special Operations Executive from 1940 to 1945 under the assumed identity of a Moroccan dressmaker, Arish Agoriuq, with code name Sidi. Your base of operations was in Spain, with occasional relocations to Portugal. You performed your duties with the utmost competence, thoroughness, dedication, and integrity at all times."

I confirmed as much without opening my mouth. The other man then spoke.

"You should know that, to verify these points and obtain a more personal appraisal, we took the liberty of consulting the officer who originally recruited you."

A tiny hint of a smile appeared at the corners of my mouth as I whispered a surname.

"Hillgarth."

The terrace of the American Legation in Tangier came to mind: it was where I'd met him and where my training began. He'd issued orders and guidance to me with efficient aplomb, instructing me on how to communicate using Morse, the norms for transmitting messages, rules for sending and receiving. He'd also provided me with the list of Nazi wives who were to become my customers, and he'd advised me on how to behave so as not to arouse suspicion: whom to approach and whom to steer clear of, the places to go and those to avoid at any cost.

Drawing me from my torrent of memories, the fair-haired man spoke again.

"That's right. Captain Alan Hillgarth, naval attaché at our embassy in Madrid during the war, gave you a glowing report. I don't know if you're aware that, after the war, he decided to retire both from the navy and from our activities. He now lives in Ireland, from where he was pleased to respond to our inquiry and sends you his warmest regards. He also requested a postal address at which to write to you personally."

People were beginning to sit at the tables around us, and the murmur of conversation was louder, albeit muted. The waiters were beginning to push trollies and serve tea. Teaspoons clinked, voices multiplied. The older man saved me the discomfort of admitting to them that I had neither fixed residence nor any current prospect of finding one.

"Are you sure you won't have anything?"

Perfectly sure. Given the privations of life on the Boltons, if I hadn't felt so tense, I might have appreciated a full afternoon tea like the one at Fortnum & Mason, with sandwiches, scones, and cakes. I might have even snuck a few into my handkerchief to take to Víctor, who would've been delighted to have them. But I declined again. All I wanted was for them to get to the point without further delay. They, however, continued to take turns speaking in some sort of coordinated preamble.

"As you know, Mrs. Bonnard," the older man began, "everything has changed radically these past two years. There is a new world order, and we must adapt to situations with wholly different dynamics than those from the war years. We no longer face troubles as worrying as the ones that occurred in wartime, but there are other scenarios that require close attention."

Of course I knew that. All too well. I knew that neither the locations nor the conflicts were the same as they'd been. How could I not know it, having lost Marcus in one such inferno? But I said nothing and waited for them to finish.

They continued with their verbal choreography.

"Which is why, for one of our new missions, we need someone with a very specific profile."

"A judicious and worldly person who knows the terrain in which she must operate, who has a command of the language and is able to act with discretion, shrewdness, and tact."

"The tasks we require such a person for are urgent."

"The problem is that, until now, we hadn't managed to find anyone who meets our criteria."

One, two, three . . . five seconds of silence. The one with the gray temples broke the suspense.

"Until, Mrs. Bonnard, you suddenly appeared."

34

I felt dizzy, as if instead of turning down their offer of a drink, I'd had three or four martinis. There it was. There it was, entering my life again. The British intelligence service, casting its hook into me once more.

The more mature man spoke.

"This being the case, Mrs. Bonnard, we would like to propose a new mission in Spain."

As they waited for a reaction, the two strangers' eyes were fixed on me like magnets. I didn't so much as blink. I remained impassive, legs crossed, mouth closed, back straight. Under my jacket's soft fabric, however, my pulse was furious.

The two men had taken turns during the introduction, but now the elder and higher ranking of the two seemed unwilling to relinquish the floor.

"It would be a very specific operation, performed during a limited time—over about three weeks—though we expect the work will also be intense. The risk will be managed, with no political controversy whatsoever that might compromise your safety. In fact, your cover would be so watertight that even the government would approve your participation."

I finally managed to string a few syllables together.

"What would it involve?"

Inflexible when it came to procedure, they didn't answer. They still had some background to lay out.

"Do you have any personal links to Argentina?"

Argentina? Why on earth were these individuals from the secret service interested in Argentina? In a drawer of my wardrobe at the Boltons house, I had a Télam press card that Fran Nash had given me when I left Palestine. Télam had sent her two of them plus a rubber stamp so she could add her photograph and certify her connection to the news agency. She'd decided to issue one in my name, for no particular reason. "Who knows, Sira?" she'd said. "Sometimes a press card can open doors for you."

I didn't disclose any of this to the pair. I just answered, "None that I know of."

"And do you have any knowledge of the current situation in the country, its leaders?"

I knew something about it. During my last few months in Jerusalem, Fran had arranged to receive copies of the newspapers in which the reports I'd translated appeared. She probably did it just to cheer me up—she didn't understand a single word of Spanish. But lacking anything else to read in my language once the papers from Madrid stopped arriving after Marcus's death, I'd often leafed through them. And so I'd familiarized myself with certain names and circumstances, events and important figures.

I opted, however, to be cautious.

"Very little."

"If you could give us a few moments of your time, we can give you some background."

I agreed, though my voice was barely audible. The senior man took off his fine-rimmed glasses, as if they hindered his ability to speak.

"Right. Well. For a long time, relations between Britain and Argentina were very fruitful, particularly as far as trade was concerned. Since the end of the last century, we've been the recipients of the majority of their exports, especially meat. Entire generations of British people lived on beef from the Pampas. Likewise, over time we made huge investments in their country: railways, the refrigeration industry, loans to the state, public service companies, insurance, banking . . . Thanks to all of this, our links with their most powerful classes have been incredibly fluid and cordial, and there is also a large British population there. In fact, some of the country's past leaders even stated that Argentina was, in economic terms, almost part of the British Empire."

He spoke in a low monotone, though his diction was crystal clear. He paused while he folded the arms on his spectacles, measuring his words.

"In recent times, however, the situation has taken a drastic turn. The war, as you know, laid waste to Britain's finances, whereas Argentina has a buoyant economy and, after supplying us all these years, is one of our biggest creditors. So we froze both repayment of the debt and Argentine funds deposited in London, knowing that at some point we would have to sit down to negotiate. The elections last year gave victory to General Perón, who was already leading the policy of the previous government. This confirmed the country's nationalist orientation, and negotiations have been rather difficult ever since. The Argentinian state's expropriation of railways and gas and electricity companies marks the end of an era for our interests in the country, and the nationalization of the financial system has been very challenging for our banks and insurance companies. There have also been changes in other areas, such as foreign trade. All of this, in short, has led to a huge loss of British capital, been a blow to our businesses, and generally weakened our influence both in Argentina and in much of South America."

He put his glasses back on, his forefinger sliding up the bridge of his nose until they were in place. *"Sic transit gloria mundi,"* he said in conclusion. Thus passes the glory of the world.

I took the information with a grain of salt. I was sure everything he'd said was accurate in broad terms. I also knew, however, that the British were hardened negotiators, seasoned traders and industrious entrepreneurs who'd long been roaming the world with a voracious appetite, arrogantly imposing their rules, and always earning fat returns. But I said nothing about that, of course.

"To put it mildly," he went on, "this situation is detrimental to us and disconcerting. But we won't throw in the towel and prefer to remain quietly optimistic and think that smooth relations can be restored, at least in part. And with this in mind, we might just have one last card to play."

I raised my eyebrows in a faint questioning expression.

"From the midst of the Peronist government's efforts to keep our presence in the country's economy to a minimum, a figure is emerging around whom there are many questions that need answering."

The waiter approached the table again, but the younger man waved him away.

"I'm referring to Eva Duarte," the older man declared, lowering his voice. "Señora Perón, the president's wife."

Yes, I'd read about her. And seen her blurry image in the press. A woman neither beautiful nor beauty's opposite, quite a bit younger than her spouse, somewhat over the top in terms of her choice of attire.

"We know she's gaining prominence in political affairs, which even within her own milieu pleases few and angers many. She's also involving herself in several government matters, seems to have a great deal of influence over her husband, and is growing in popularity among certain sections of Argentinian society, particularly the working classes. But while we know this much, we also feel we're short of firsthand information, more reliable and direct details about her."

He paused, as if piecing together what he was about to tell me next.

"It's hard to admit, but sometimes the diplomatic reports we receive are rather dubious. We get the impression that our staff aren't moving very well in the new circles of Argentine power—plus, depending on whom they speak to, we receive conflicting reports. As I mentioned, we have some great friends in Argentina, families we've had close and lucrative ties with for many years. Sadly, however, many of them, whom we used to consider reliable, are no longer useful as informants. This is because most belong to the opposing elite, a highly critical section of society that is resistant to the Peronism that claims to favor the working class and hopes to put an end to the oligarchy, or to at least reduce its privileges. Because of this, we can't rely on them in this urgent matter."

I understood everything the gentleman was explaining in his professorial tone. I knew the meaning of every noun, adjective, and verb. But I still hadn't the slightest idea how they intended me to fit into this fantastic tango.

As if reading my thoughts, he added, "Which brings us to the matter at hand."

I clenched my fists in an attempt to remain calm.

"Señora Perón is planning a visit to Europe soon. General Franco initially extended the invitation to General Perón himself, in gratitude for the generous economic assistance the Argentine regime is offering Spain, so badly needed after the civil war. Perón couldn't accept in person. Keeping close relations with the Franco regime after the defeat of Franco's Axis friends would be a delicate matter for any government. But rather than turn down the offer, Argentina's president had the idea of sending his wife to represent him."

He gave an almost imperceptible signal with his jaw. The younger man understood it at once and pulled from the clipboard several folded newspaper front pages. He handed them to me so I could read the headlines.

"Some of her itinerary has already been made public. She'll start in Spain, where the overall tone of the tour will be set, and from there she'll head to Italy, where the Pope will receive her. There is additional talk of visits to France, Portugal, and Switzerland. There's also a potential stopover that nobody mentions."

I refolded the pages and tried to give them back, but he waved them away.

"The Argentine foreign minister has queried our embassy representatives about the possibility of Señora Perón meeting our monarch as an elegant finishing touch to her expedition to the Old World. They've even proposed a date of around mid-July."

He paused, turned his head to the left again, and whispered something. The other man gestured to a nearby waiter and ordered water. The lobby was quiet again after the teatime rush, waiting to fill up again when it was time for predinner cocktails.

"Faced with this possibility, I must tell you that we're plagued by significant economic uncertainty, but that's not the only issue. We're equally concerned about the political situation, given that, while Argentina's president was democratically elected, our Labour government considers him to be very close to the fascist regimes we fought so hard to defeat in the war. A paradox, considering that Perón won the elections as the candidate for the Argentine Labour Party, proclaiming him a champion of the working class."

His voice was beginning to fail. I realized that speaking for so long was wearing him out. Despite his confidence and impeccable outward appearance, he was most likely older than he looked. He didn't let up, however.

"Considering the current state of our relations, an agreement by King George and the Queen to receive Perón's wife with the honors due the spouse of the Argentine head of state could be perceived as a humiliating change in stance toward Argentina on Britain's part. At the same time, we're forced to recognize that the visit could yield a good return."

His voice was growing fluty. He reddened, and I noticed some minuscule drops of sweat on his brow.

"Despite the precarious state of our economy, there are things we are still interested in selling them: warplanes, naval supplies, machinery of various kinds. And of course, we still need meat from them to feed our long-suffering people. For all these reasons, we believe that, if carefully orchestrated, Señora Perón's visit could serve to ease tensions, smooth things over, and mend ties between the two countries. In a nutshell, it could prove to be an interesting strategic opportunity for us."

The waiter arrived with a glass of water on a silver tray. The blond man indicated that he should leave it in front of his boss.

"With this in mind," the older man said as he delicately picked up the glass, "and with the aim of obtaining specific information that could help us make the most appropriate decision before submitting a report to Parliament, we're in urgent need of someone who can be our eyes and ears during her trip around Spain. Someone to absorb and retain information, assess it, filter it, and transmit it to us."

He sipped the water. Anticipating what was coming, I suddenly felt a terrible urge to snatch the glass from his hands and drink it all down.

"We would also like to size up her entourage. Numerous people will be accompanying her in various roles. If you accept our proposal, we'll brief you on all of them. We expect that, one way or another, most will be valuable sources of information relating to Señora Perón: what she's like; how she acts, behaves, speaks, reacts; what her opinions are, if she has any; and most of all, what she thinks, if she thinks at all, about Britain and her potential visit."

He cleared his throat and drank again. As he did, he gestured at his subordinate to continue for him.

"It would be a mission under the Foreign Office, and of course, you would be appropriately remunerated and receive diplomatic protection should anything unfortunate happen."

"Could you be more explicit, please?"

The senior man picked up the thread again, his voice restored. "Señora Perón's visit to Spain will be covered by numerous news organizations both Spanish and foreign. Which is where you would come in."

He leaned forward so that his eyes were level with my eyes, his nose with my nose. He gave me a sharp look through the lenses of his spectacles.

"We want you to infiltrate the pool of international correspondents. Undercover as a BBC reporter."

35

When, years before, Rosalinda Fox met me at Dean's Bar in Tangier to propose that I work with the British secret service, I'd thought what she was suggesting was absurd, utterly without merit. In the dark seclusion of the establishment's storeroom, among sacks of coffee and crates of bottles, she'd raised the possibility of me inserting myself into a web of covert sources for the purpose of obtaining information on the Nazi contingent based in Madrid. I would have to move to a different country, falsify my past, alter my name. I flatly refused in the beginning, believing what she suggested to be beyond my abilities, thinking I'd be able to contribute very little to such an enterprise, as daring as it was grandiose. Rosalinda and my mother, however—each with their own arguments—made me see things from different angles. They gave me rationale and evidence; they spoke to me about loyalty, commitment, and a sense of duty. In the end, they persuaded me to take on the task and do my part.

Unlike then, in this strange London to which life's unhappy winds had dragged me, I had nobody to give me confidence. There was no one now who could listen to my worries and doubts or throw light on the shadows that had floated in my mind ever since my meeting with the intelligence service men at the Dorchester. No Rosalinda or my mother. No Marcus, Fran Nash, or Nick Soutter. Nobody to hear my cry for help in the middle of the storm.

I was conscious, however, that my lack of sympathizers must not paralyze me. Now more than ever, alone and responsible for my son, I had to muster the little courage I had left and turn it into something productive, find my spirit and move forward again. Getting away from Olivia would be a relief, but the closer the time came to leaving, the more I realized that escaping from her only to take refuge under my mother's wing wasn't the best idea. And so, after calmly considering the disconcerting proposal, I finally decided to say yes.

Yes, I would agree to infiltrate the journalists who would travel Spain for three weeks chasing the shadow of a former radio actress turned first lady of the only country in the world that was holding out a hand to my poor starving country. Yes, I would agree to pass myself off as someone I wasn't again, cloaking myself once more behind brazen lies and false identities. What would I personally gain from my efforts, aside from the information I obtained for the unflagging British? Apart from a financial reward, I didn't yet know. All I knew at the beginning was that I would be able to rebuild myself and feel that I was capable of doing something productive. That I was still useful and worth something.

A couple of days later, we finally made the recordings on Palestine. During our rehearsals and preparations, I absorbed with the utmost attention everything that was around me: technicians, equipment, work methods, body language, and procedures. Finally I was ready to get in front of a microphone, a device with the BBC's initials on it, in burnished steel. To everyone's relief, I was calm and clear, with no trace of nerves, no shadow of insecurity or stammering. And so my voice was recorded, alternating with Ángel Ara's, on the grooves of three disks that would later be transmitted via shortwave across the Atlantic and reach listeners in a dozen or so countries. An account of what was happening in Palestine, narrated by someone who'd suffered and loved, cried and given birth, in that troubled Holy Land on the very brink of its bloodiest days.

Everything went smoothly. I was tempted to ask about Cora Soutter, but I hid my curiosity and never learned whether her knee-jerk decision to veto me had had repercussions for her. I preferred not to give too much thought to her confession about Nick. It was too unsettling and made me question feelings that no longer made any sense. I decided therefore to simply leave her testimony sealed off in some corner of my heart or mind, I didn't know which.

As soon as we'd finished the recording for the BBC's Latin American Service, and as spring set in, preparations began for my next assignment. A thick envelope with no return address on it arrived every morning at the house on the Boltons, containing the leading Argentine newspapers, all of them out of date, of course, and offering varying treatments of the figure in question. Papers such as *La Prensa*, *La Nación*, and, when it came, *La Vanguardia* were ostensibly critical. The latter even printed satirical cartoons and merciless caricatures on the front page. Others like *Democracia*, on the other hand, heaped effusive praise on the Perón regime and on the woman whose tour I would cover in Spain. The papers were ironed before reaching me, but I realized nonetheless that the pages had already been thumbed. Sometimes there was a tear, or even a section cut out with scissors. On occasion, I could make out ink or grease stains, even imprinted circles that suggested a cup of coffee or glass of wine had been carelessly placed there. In other words, they were newspapers that had been read and were ready to be thrown away—copies, perhaps, that someone had been tasked with stealing from the Argentine embassy before they ended up in the wastepaper basket, kitchen stove, or—in the absence of hygiene goods—in some more private nook.

The intelligence service placed at my disposal a car and driver for my movements around London. The purpose of the next few days was to train me to operate among journalists with at least a shred of credibility. The aim wasn't for me to learn the inner workings of the trade— we were aware that I wasn't going to metamorphose overnight into a seasoned foreign correspondent. But there were a lot of little holes in my knowledge that I could fill, superficial details that would help me to get by without arousing suspicion.

One of the first activities was an accelerated typing course taken in one of Whitehall's dark offices. At my shoulder at all times, tasked with teaching me, was a thin and surly secretary of mature years with a tightly wound bun. While I grappled with the intricacies of the carriage speed and key pressure, sad echoes of another time came to mind. It was in a typewriter shop that I had first met the lowlife Ramiro Arribas, after my boyfriend at the time, kind Ignacio, decided that I should become a civil servant. And it was from Argentina, coincidentally, that the franchise for a chain of those innovative centers was supposed to have come: a network of Pitman academies in which Ramiro and I were to have invested the money I was given by my father when he decided to get to know me after many years. Stern Miss Crossman, with the strict manner of a Victorian governess, cut short my mind's wanderings, demanding full attention on my task. In this way, I managed, luckily, to keep the melancholy at bay.

So that I wouldn't appear completely ignorant to photographers, at a studio in Fitzrovia I was instructed in the operation and nomenclature of various cameras, films, and lenses: how to use the shutter release and the timer, how to change the roll. In another studio at Broadcasting House, I was taught to operate a reel-to-reel tape recorder, in case the need to use one ever arose. I worked the controls, handled the heads, and inserted and removed the rolls of magnetic tape over and over until I was able to repeat these actions with mechanistic ease.

I also had to familiarize myself with the names and duties of some of the members of the Argentine first lady's trusted entourage: her right-hand woman, her brother (who was also General Perón's private secretary), the shipowner who would bear the cost of the tour beyond Spain's borders, her military escort, her priest, her dressmakers, and her hairdresser and confidant. The intelligence service didn't have the full list yet. I would have to monitor developments and locate additional individuals as soon as they arrived.

I was also given a foundational knowledge of the world's major newspapers, magazines, and agencies: Reuters, France-Presse, Continental, Associated Press, United Press. I even learned about the Spanish news agency EFE. We had to work in broad brushstrokes, because the intelligence service also lacked precise details about which news providers would cover the first lady's tour. They anticipated, however, that there would be quite a few. Both a supremely isolated Spain and the visiting celebrity were sources of morbid fascination among the international press.

They also arranged for me to meet people they deemed relevant to my work. At the Press Club near Fleet Street, I met a reporter from the *Evening Standard* who'd covered the presidential elections the year before in Buenos Aires. At the Argentine Club on Hamilton Place—a bona fide gentlemen's club where I was given permission to access a small private dining room—I had lunch with the majority shareholder in one of the Anglo-Argentine railways, a venerable old man with an opulent surname who ended up half-drunk, shedding nostalgic tears for his lost enterprise while trying to kiss me to the strains of the tango song "Cuartito azul." At a dinner gathering, they sat me beside an official from the Argentine Consulate General, a mind-numbing fellow from whom I extracted nothing more than descriptions of the beauty of Bariloche's forests. With yields of varying degrees, I had several more meetings in which no one ever uttered my real name, and we never let on a single clue about me, my past, my future, or my intentions. A slippery customer, I listened to everyone with complete attention, asked the occasional question, memorized an abundance of information, and left without making a sound or leaving a trace.

Amid the relentless comings and goings of my final days in London, I found time to say goodbye to Dominic Hodson. We didn't ever become friends; he'd been courteous, dependable, and dutiful, but impenetrable. He suggested a goodbye lunch, but I made my excuses. As a counteroffer, and taking into account that I had a meeting to attend at the Dorchester, I suggested another walk, this time in Hyde Park instead of the Boltons. After half an hour of us strolling under the now bloom-filled trees, he held out his hand to say goodbye. Feeling genuinely grateful for the efforts he'd made to watch over Marcus's wishes, our son, and me, I couldn't contain myself and I gave him a hug. He almost blushed, and he stammered a little.

"My friend Mark was lucky to have you," he mumbled without making eye contact. Then he looked up with his round, faded, lashless eyes, like a sea bream's. "Do you know? I loved him very much, too."

Without saying anything else, he touched the brim of his hat, turned away, and headed off in the direction of Marble Arch. *I loved him very much,* he'd admitted—that unadorned, elusive word, "love." Confused, touched, I stood watching him walk away, the back of his raincoat shrinking in the distance as he advanced along the broad pavement. Dominic loved Marcus very much, and he was still single, and he was awkward around women. He loved him very much, but Marcus had separated himself from Dominic for years, and he had not spoken to me about him. Perhaps that was why.

Just before leaving, I finally found some time to organize everything that fell outside the remit of the intelligence service. Going to the hairdresser, for instance. Buying clothes for my son, for the almost twenty pounds he already weighed, and for the days of moderate warmth that awaited us in Madrid in early June.

"Your son? I'm sorry?" was what Kavannagh had said, knitting his distinguished brow. Sir Nigel Kavannagh was the name of the gentleman with the gold glasses and silver hair who'd made the proposal to me to work with his people again. I'd taken a firm stance.

"My son and his nanny come with me, or I go nowhere."

Philippa had agreed to come with us, and I'd arranged everything for our stay in Madrid. I'd assured Kavannagh that their presence wouldn't affect my work in the slightest. They would be kept completely out of things, and I would appear to the world as an Anglo-Spanish BBC correspondent, fully committed to my role, competent and autonomous. He didn't like my offer in the least, but the dapper senior officer had had no option but to accept it.

It would be inaccurate to say I refreshed my wardrobe, because in truth I scarcely had old clothes to exchange for new ones; the suitcase I'd brought from Jerusalem contained only winter wear. To stock up, I returned to the Digby Morton boutique in Kensington, where I was fortunate enough to find the designer himself, and we chose the garments together. He swallowed my story that I was the wife of a Portuguese diplomat, and I said nothing about my past life as a dressmaker. With the benefit of his judgment and mine having worked in concert, I came away with a magnificent wardrobe for which I paid an obscene sum of money. I confessed the sin to my conscience and absolved myself at once: I was going to receive a splendid fee for my mission in Spain, and I was awaiting the unexpected settlement from Marcus's estate. The designer accompanied me to the car.

"You have superb taste, my dear," he said. "Return whenever you like. You'll always be welcome."

As my car was pulling away, I threw a question at him. "Where is the best place for stationery?"

"Smythson, on Bond Street, without question."

I went there to buy leather-bound notebooks, writing paper and envelopes, notepaper, and a professional-looking yet elegant briefcase. I had in mind some of the women journalists I'd met in Jerusalem through Fran Nash after Marcus's death: hardworking, charismatic, diligent women like Clare Hollingworth of the *Observer*, Ruth Gruber of the *New York Times*, and a few others. I intended to copy their ways and mannerisms, their expressions, their worldviews.

Turning a blind eye to Kavannagh's rule of avoiding contact with Spaniards or Latin Americans before my departure, on my last night I had dinner with Ángel Ara and George Camacho at Martínez. I wanted to treat them to say thank you for believing in me, for being in my corner. They didn't know the precise nature of what I would be doing, and I made up a story about Kavannagh's interest in my husband's past. I doubt they believed me, but dinner proved to be very enjoyable at that restaurant which, despite its location within a stone's throw of Piccadilly Circus, was decorated with Talavera tiles, wrought-iron lanterns, and a fighting bull's head hanging from a wall.

Outside, while Camacho flagged down a cab, I handed Ara an envelope containing a thick wad of pounds sterling and whispered a message in his ear.

"Get this to the children that escaped the bombs in Spain, the ones nobody claimed after the war."

We'd been in London for four months. We had arrived with the snow and ice of the cruelest winter in decades, and we left after spring had fallen upon the city, making its hardness more bearable. Olivia came out to say goodbye. For all her usual lack of affection, she pressed Víctor hard against her chest. Due to my constant coming and going, we hadn't crossed paths much over recent weeks, and when we'd had no choice but to do so, we'd both kept our composure: diplomatic and cordial but always maintaining a distance. What would happen to the house, we would see. She and Dominic could decide between them. I had other priorities now.

We arrived at the airport with our bulky luggage on a trolley pushed by two porters. We were met by Dean Haines, Kavannagh's fair-haired subordinate whose acquaintance I'd made at the Dorchester and with whom I'd met several times since. With the utmost discretion, he handed me an envelope. Inside there were three impeccable passports bearing our false names and two copies of my press pass. Another smaller envelope contained five, ten, hundred, and thousand peseta notes.

And last, I found a little card holder. On the cards was printed the Broadcasting House address and a telephone number that, logically, would connect not to the BBC but to the intelligence service, in case anyone made inquiries, so that they would be the first to know. At the precise center of each carboard rectangle, in elegant print, appeared the new name with which I had chosen to rechristen myself.

LIVIA NASH

BBC

REPORTER

I'd stolen five letters from my mother-in-law, the surname from my friend. In all likelihood, neither of them would ever know.

PART THREE

Spain

36

I was awake until the early hours. Question after question shouted for my attention. Would I manage to perform my duties? Would I come up against an obstacle that blew my cover? Would Víctor be all right at his grandfather's house, separated from me?

As I lay there alone in that strange bed, sleep insisted upon eluding me and I saw my travel alarm clock's minute hand turn until it marked one, two, three, almost four in the morning. At some point I heard voices on the floor below, footsteps on the stairs, a nearby door opening when someone turned the key. Then, just silence.

We'd arrived in Madrid that afternoon a day ahead of schedule. Once we were in the terminal, Philippa stayed back with the boy while I walked out with the air of the self-assured radio reporter I was supposed to have transformed myself into.

Right away I located my driver but pretended I'd missed him in order to scan the entire room. I was relieved when I saw another man waiting patiently to the side and had to make an effort not to run into his arms. There he was, my father, Gonzalo Alvarado, a little older, a little thinner in his three-piece suit. He saw me too of course. But as we'd agreed in our telephone conversation, we ignored each other. Beside him, dressed simply, was Miguela, the lady from Extremadura who'd taken over from old Servanda to run his house. They would take

Philippa and my son to their home on Calle de Hermosilla, where the two would stay while I played reporter.

I didn't exchange a word with the driver as we drove into the city, instead taking refuge in the solitude of the back seat. A flurry of images of the recent past, all with Marcus in them, hounded me as I was reunited with places, advertisements, posters, and buildings. Once or twice my eyes welled up; fortunately I was wearing a large pair of sunglasses to protect me from both the early-June light and untimely surges of melancholy. Marcus and I had left the city two years before—elated after the Allied victory, proud to have served, and excited to begin a new life in which we could be together openly, without lies or subterfuge. Now I was returning with a boy who had his eyes and skin color, while his shattered remains lay under a slab of marble on a Palestinian hillside. Trying not to fall into despair, I searched the streets and people for changes, clues, some trace of hope in this poor ruined country of mine.

The first thing I noticed was that the Germans and their garish manifestations had disappeared as completely as if they'd been swallowed up by the earth. As we drove along Paseo de la Castellana—now named Avenida del Generalísimo—I saw none of the red, white, and black flags that used to display their swastikas on every corner.

Outside what used to be the German embassy, very near Plaza de Colón, there were no longer crowds of officials and diplomatic representatives going in and out. Inside, the Allied Control Council was now working on Operation Safehaven, whose aim was destroying any trace of the Nazis. To this end, they were carrying out a painstaking process of identifying and expropriating dozens of official properties, restricting all kinds of organizations and institutions, blocking hundreds of companies from operating, and freezing capital and assets, including the famous Nazi gold that had been plundered from various parts of Europe.

As we drove on, conspicuous signs of the fall of the Third Reich could be seen among the mansions and villas. We left behind the empty shell of the German Transatlantic Bank. A little farther ahead, at number 18, the Gestapo headquarters were under lock and key with thick chains intertwining the door knockers. On the opposite side of the road, the shutters were down on the once-elegant offices of the Nazi business conglomerate Sofindus, while the gates of the Deutsche Schule on the corner of Calle de Zurbarán were held shut with a sturdy padlock. The front garden of the imposing structure that had been the German Cultural Institute, on the corner of Paseo del Cisne, was overgrown and wild. Near the Castelar Roundabout, rust was beginning to sink its teeth into the iron railings of the German Press Office.

Though I didn't manage to see them on my route, I assumed the rest of the always opulent, well-positioned buildings of the Nazis in Spain were in a similar state of decay. I'd been in some of them, as a guest at events and receptions. The ambassador's residence on Calle de los Hermanos Bécquer, or the bustling social club next to the Church of San Fermín de los Navarros. The Nazi Party's headquarters opposite them, on the corner of Calle de Zurbano. The Tourist Office on Calle de Alcalá. The German Chamber of Commerce on Calle de Claudio Coello. The Transocean News Service at number a hundred and something on Calle de Serrano. All these properties and many others distributed around Spain were now under Allied control and subject to negotiations with Franco's government. The two sides were in a tense tug-of-war, each one wanting to come away with the best prize.

The car continued its route to the press club, a place that was unfamiliar to me and where it had been arranged for me to stay. We also passed the residence of Sir Samuel Hoare, the former British ambassador. I wondered from which of his open windows he'd watched his counterpart Hans Adolf von Moltke's funeral cortège. Von Moltke had died three months after taking charge of the German legation. From inside his house but in public view, in meticulous formal dress, Sir Sam had doffed his top hat as the coffin went past and had bowed his head in a solemn gesture of mourning, displaying impeccable diplomatic etiquette, even as war raged.

A little farther on, near the Altos del Hipódromo area, the car turned right into the narrow Calle del Pinar, and we stopped outside number 5, a building that was halfway between a large house and a mansion. "We've arrived, señora," the driver announced. When I got out, something knotted inside me as I contemplated the entrance. I knew this place; I'd been here at least a couple of times. And no, at the time it hadn't housed anything like a press club. Far from it.

As soon as I was inside, I realized it still smelled of fresh paint. In the reception area in the right wing, where my former customer Helga Henke once exhibited her mediocre floral paintings, several groups of armchairs were now arranged around a large radio. In the stairwell, where portraits of Hitler and Franco had hung in cordial harmony, there was a large oil painting of a hunting scene. An austerely dressed lady came out to receive me, her style somewhere between that of a governess and a housekeeper. She introduced herself by her surname, Cortés, and welcomed me and showed me around the communal areas: the library and reading room, the telephone booths, the dining room with windows that looked out onto the rear garden, and an adjoining room with a small bar and a selection of liquor bottles.

Everything had been repositioned, but the rooms were the same as they'd been back when Serrano Suñer, fiercely pro-German, decided to lease the property to the Baron of Sacro Lirio to create the brand-new Hispano-German Association. To set everything in motion, they had ordered furniture and fixtures, put together a large library of books written in German or about Germany, and expanded the kitchen area, installing modern electrical appliances that were donated by German companies. One company even contributed a full dinner service decorated with both the swastika and the yoke and arrows of the Falange, Spain's fascist party. Throughout the world war, patriotic lectures and concerts, exhibitions, and talks testifying to the greater glory of the

Third Reich and its harmonious relations with Spain had been held here.

Now, two years after the Nazis' defeat, there remained no trace of those speakers, artists, and guests. After giving the premises a face-lift and carefully removing anything that smelled of Nazis, in the run-up to the first official visit from an overseas dignitary to Franco's Spain, they'd converted the cultural institution, on the spur of the moment, into a refined club for foreign journalists. I was reminded of the press center the British had set up in mandatory Jerusalem for the convenience of international reporters, the bar where I'd had my first drink with Fran Nash, when I learned that she and Nick Soutter were friends. Keeping the press happy seemed to be a primary concern that transcended borders.

By the time stern Señora Cortés finished showing me the facilities on the main floor, I still hadn't seen any sign of another resident. Then she gestured toward the stairs.

"Allow me to show you to your room. Only the lady journalists will stay here. The gentlemen have been accommodated in hotels, though this will be the meeting place for everyone."

Someone had brought up my luggage. When I entered, it was already against the opposite wall. The room's furniture was contemporary, almost modern. A bureau with its chair, an upholstered armchair by the window, a built-in wardrobe, a small bathroom, and a single bed with a crucifix above the headboard. On the bedside table I found a bouquet of white flowers and a card. *Diego Tovar, director of the Diplomatic Information Office, welcomes the BBC reporter Livia Nash to Spain.* Beside it there was a schedule for the next day. We were to convene in the meeting room at ten o'clock to be briefed on the tour's opening ceremonies.

"Dinner will be served at half past eight," I heard the housekeeper say behind me.

She closed the door softly and left me alone in my room. I checked the time: twenty minutes past seven. I hesitated. My very soul was begging me to run downstairs, shut myself in a telephone booth, and call my father. But I restrained myself—no, I wasn't going to make any calls from the press club. To banish my worries, I started unpacking.

When I went down to the dining room an hour and a quarter later, only two tables were occupied. At one of them was a lady, advanced in years, with a compact build, short hair, and thick-rimmed glasses hanging from her neck on a silver chain. She was reading a magazine while she held a fork in the other hand. She barely looked up when I said hello to the room. She clearly didn't have the slightest interest in meeting me, let alone in inviting me to eat with her. At the other table, looking out toward the garden with her back to the entrance, was a second woman whose face I couldn't see. She seemed slender, young, I supposed, because of the natural shade of her chestnut hair, not particularly well styled. She also ignored my greeting, as if she hadn't heard me. Given the universal indifference, I opted to sit alone in a corner.

I was served by a silent waiter wearing a short white jacket buttoned up to the neck. I was finishing my starter when the young woman stood and said good night in American English, without even looking at us. "Good night, sweetheart," the lady with the glasses on a chain said with the same accent and without looking up from her reading. My hake in breadcrumbs with mayonnaise had arrived by the time she also said goodbye, no less succinctly.

After the austerity of my mother-in-law's house, those dishes should've tasted out of this world to me. But I left them half-eaten. I never would have imagined that I'd miss the Boltons, London, even Olivia. But I missed the proximity of her, the confidence and solidity she and her compatriots exuded, the whole country working as one to rebuild—austere, valiant, and admirably stoic, facing the hardship together, and bearing the sacrifices with collective effort. Whereas Spain, my poor homeland, was trying to rebuild while still divided by a sinister Nationalist-Republican rift.

After turning down the dessert of custard, I went out into the garden and sat on one of the white metal chairs. All that could be heard away from the bustle of central Madrid were the crickets and cicadas. There was still some light, the smell of jasmine was in the air, and the temperature was pleasant, all the ingredients for a perfect evening. And yet I was plunged into a loneliness as deep as a ravine, ignored by those haughty Americans, asking myself for the millionth time why I'd said yes to another crazy commitment.

Back in my room, to ward off the phantoms, I took out the folders Kavannagh had given me and started rereading what I already knew by heart. They'd insisted that, in addition to the Argentine first lady, I should probe her entourage as much as possible. Judging which members would be useful—sorting the wheat from the chaff—was left to my discretion.

Lillian Lagomarsino de Guardo, I read again. Thirty-five years of age. Sister of the Argentine magnate and secretary of industry Rolando Lagomarsino, and wife of the president of the Chamber of Deputies, Ricardo Guardo. Mother of four, personal escort, adviser on matters of protocol and etiquette. *Juan Duarte*, brother, thirty-three, single, the president's private secretary, former traveling soap salesman, lover of entertainment. *Alberto Dodero*, sixty-one, twice married and divorced, shipping tycoon, free-spending socialite, delegation coordinator, and financial backer for much of the tour. *Julio Alcaraz*, married, fifty or so, hairdresser. *Asunta Fernández*, age and marital status unimportant, trusted dressmaker employed by the haute couture house Henriette. *Juanita Palmou*, age and marital status unimportant, trusted dressmaker employed by the Paula Naletoff house.

There were other names and roles: military aides, a doctor, a photographer, even a priest, and three journalists I would do well to avoid. One was the radio scriptwriter Francisco Muñoz Azpiri, sent as a speechwriter. Another, a young photographer, Emilio Abras, whose task was to take as many pictures as possible of the first lady. And finally, one Valentín Thiebaut, reporter for the *Democracia* newspaper, who had been authorized by the Presidential Information Secretariat. Given their professions, they could make my work difficult. Best to keep them at arm's length. It was the others who interested me: a lady of high society, a dissolute brother, an older rich man with a taste for high jinks, a hairdresser, and two dressmakers as efficient as I'd once been. One way or another, I would have to contend with all of them. How I would do it and what results I would achieve I did not yet know.

Unable to sleep, I looked at the alarm clock. The fluorescent-tipped hands marked five minutes before four. I pressed my eyelids together and turned over yet again.

37

I arrived just in time to have coffee before the meeting. Unlike the evening before, the dining room was now crowded, mostly with men. Voices, exchanged greetings, and dense cigarette smoke filled the air. Feigning confidence, I headed to the only table that remained free. No sooner had I been served than the room began to empty, but I was in no hurry. I wanted to wait, observe, see how my future colleagues conducted themselves. And so I was among the last to arrive in the adjoining reception room. At the front, there was already someone waiting to speak.

I had with me one of my leather-bound notebooks and the pen I'd bought in Jerusalem. I was wearing a lightweight wool suit with elbow-length sleeves, neither too formal nor too informal. The room fell silent. I saw that there were some twenty of us, and I was relieved to find that everyone had notebooks in their hands. From my chair at the back, I saw the two American women from the night before arrive separately and sit in front of me. I saw another female head, belonging to the woman I'd heard arriving late at night, I supposed. The rest were men.

A staid gentleman in his thirties greeted us and asked us to call out our names and organizations. Some did so with willing enthusiasm. Others with an overtone of weariness. I supposed those must have been correspondents based in Madrid who were fed up with having to constantly prove their identities. A couple of journalists said they worked for

Argentine newspapers, *La Tribuna* and *Democracia*. The rest were shared between the *New York Herald Tribune*, the *Christian Science Monitor*, the magazine *World Report*, the *New York Times*, Lisbon's *Diário da Manhã*, *Time*, and the German magazine *Der Spiegel*, as well as the news agencies Associated Press, United Press, and Reuters, all of which had offices in Madrid. There were no Italian or French publications for the time being. They would cover Señora Perón's tour once it arrived in those countries, but the organizers avoided any mention of that detail so as not to take the shine off the glorious visit to Spain.

While the genuine journalists offered up their credentials, I prepared myself by trying to keep my nerves under control. I cleared my throat imperceptibly, swallowed several times, kept my knees pressed together, and gripped my pen as if it were a life preserver until it was my turn.

"Livia Nash. BBC London's Latin American Service."

It was done. I'd said it. Several heads turned toward me; it wasn't a service well known to many of them.

After the introductions, an extremely thin man with neatly slicked-back hair stepped up to the front. He must've been forty or so years old, and he wore an impeccable pearl-gray suit. The fellow who'd acted as presenter moved to one side, ready to listen dutifully.

"On behalf of the Diplomatic Information Office, as its director, I would like to welcome you, ladies and gentlemen . . ."

This was Diego Tovar, the signatory of the flowers I'd found in my room the previous evening. He proceeded in Spanish, delivering the inevitable formalities, extolling the generosity and considerable effort made by the Spanish and Argentine authorities to organize the visit, as well as his profound gratitude to the news organizations that would strive to cover the event. He repeated the same message in more-than-decent English.

"Though we plan to provide you with all the relevant information in detailed notes, allow me to outline the Argentine first lady's itinerary as it stands now."

I looked left and right out of the corners of my eyes, confirming that everyone had opened their notebooks. I imitated them.

"As for the means of transport, Señora María Eva Duarte de Perón and her retinue are flying in a brand-new DC-4 four-engined plane owned by the Iberia company, acquired by order of the Generalísimo expressly for this tour and specially fitted out to afford the utmost comfort to our distinguished guest. The cabin has two bedrooms decorated in the Moorish style, a living room, a dining room for eight, a kitchen, and utility areas. Another plane from the Flota Aérea Mercante Argentina airline will accompany it carrying the support staff and baggage."

Tovar spoke with ease, his manner a far cry from the exasperated barking of many other high-ranking officials. Barely glancing at the papers he held, he continued to alternate seamlessly between the two languages. Almost everyone around me was taking notes, so I copied their behavior again.

"They took off from the Presidente Rivadavia Airfield in Castelar, Buenos Aires province, at around half past four in the afternoon on Friday the sixth of June in the presence of President General Don Juan Domingo Perón, his government, numerous senior officials, and a large crowd. After flying through the evening and night over South America, the aircraft stopped over at the Parnamirim Air Base near the Brazilian city of Natal, in the country's northeast."

Pens and pencils scurried across paper. I was unable to match their pace and hoped that the promise of detailed notes wasn't just lip service. Tovar, meanwhile, continued his report.

"Having refueled, they began the Atlantic crossing. The passengers raised glasses of champagne as they crossed the equator to celebrate the symbolic moment. Then, after almost twelve hours of transoceanic flying, the plane landed at the Villa Cisneros Airfield on the Spanish Sahara's Atlantic coast at a quarter past eleven last night. After being received as guest of honor at a gala dinner at the Officers' Club, and then resting at the governor's residence, Señora Perón and her retinue continued on their journey this morning to Las Palmas de Gran Canaria Airport, where they are expected to land"—he paused, bent his left elbow in an elegant gesture, and checked the time—"in approximately twenty-five minutes. After visiting the Island Council and hearing mass, at two o'clock the delegation is expected to depart for Madrid. Estimated arrival, eight thirty."

Diego Tovar concluded by going into the practical aspects of the itinerary. That he did so himself rather than leave it to a subordinate was quite the gesture. He informed us about our transfer to the airfield, extended an invitation to lunch at the press club to all who wished to attend, and stressed that his office was at our complete disposal concerning any contingency that might arise. The final details were being provided when I also glanced at the time. It was ten minutes after eleven. He'd just announced to us that a bus would collect us at five o'clock. I calculated how long it would take to slip over to my father's house and return in time.

As soon as the speaker had finished, a few journalists rushed off. The two Argentines stepped forward to introduce themselves formally to Tovar, while others talked among themselves or remained seated, engrossed in their notes. I waited a little while. Once the noise and voices quietened and I thought the entrance would be clear, I went out onto the street.

The end of Calle del Pinar was quite near Calle de Hermosilla—I could've walked. However, I hadn't expected to run into the director of the Diplomatic Information Office at the door. He was giving some final instructions before getting in a car in the shade of the acacias. Seeing me, he dismissed his subordinates and asked the driver to wait.

"Señora Nash," he said, approaching. "What an honor to finally meet you in person. I wanted to greet you earlier, but the Argentine correspondents held me up and then it was impossible to find you."

He took the hand I held out to him and kissed it chivalrously while I cursed myself for not waiting a little longer, until I was completely sure I could leave without being seen.

"We're very privileged to have you with us, my dear friend. Please don't hesitate to ask if there's anything you need in the performance of your duties."

I made a subtle gesture of gratitude, but all I wanted to do was leave.

"I'm in a tremendous rush right now. There are still a lot of details to finalize for the afternoon, and I must drop in at the ministry first. But I can take you to wherever you're going. Where are you heading, if you don't mind me asking?"

I hesitated. I hadn't considered that I might need to lie. I berated myself again for my lack of precaution.

"I'm going . . . I'm going to look for a church to hear mass. There's no need to trouble yourself."

I had just heard him mention this very activity in relation to Señora Perón, and it was the first thing that came to mind. He nodded with pleasure, giving my intention his approval. Diego Tovar was a handsome man, with sharp features and very pale eyes that gave him an almost youthful appearance, despite the presence of his first gray hairs.

"I'm afraid you'll struggle to find what you're looking for in this area, but I can drop you at the Cristo de Ayala if you like. It's a wonderful parish church. You'll be there in good time for the noon Eucharist."

I recalled that Calle de Ayala ran parallel to Calle de Hermosilla and accepted his offer without thinking twice. On the plus side, at some stage it could prove useful to have made this initial contact with the man who was in charge of pampering the foreign press.

Within minutes he left me outside the church, repeating as he departed how sorry he was to be unable to devote more time to me. Worshippers were pouring in, dressed elegantly for the big day and in keeping with the fashionable Salamanca neighborhood. Almost all the women were wearing veils of fine lace over their salon curls, and none of the men was missing a hat or a tailored summer suit: Sunday mass in National Catholicism Spain was the most important social event of the week. I followed them in with outward devotion and sat on one of the pews at the back. As soon as the priest intoned his *In nomine Patris, et Filii, et Spiritus Sancti,* I made my escape.

I was received with joy by everyone on Calle de Hermosilla. I was finally able to confirm that Víctor had fit in well in my absence, hug my father, make sure Philippa had set up the little camp of baby things, and see that Miguela was coping with the new guests without difficulty. The hours went by in a blink. I wished I had more time to take my son out to El Retiro, to chat with Gonzalo. But it wasn't possible; I had to get back without delay. Miguela had the idea of using the porter's cat to distract Víctor while I slunk off. I jumped in a taxi and went to the press club where some reporters were already waiting outside.

The bus to Barajas Airport left on time. I sat by myself in the middle of the vehicle and, without removing my sunglasses, gazed out of the window as we set off.

The deprivation in the country at the time, mid-1947, was a little less pronounced than it had been in the initial years after the war, but there was still a shortage of almost everything in the cities, villages, and countryside. There were no supplies to live on and no way to obtain them. In addition to the ruin that was occurring from within, the United Nations General Assembly had decided to slam the door in the face of a Franco regime that had been imposed by military force with the support of the Axis powers.

Only one foreign head of state was now holding his hand out to the starved and friendless country. General Perón—president of Argentina and head of its new Justicialist Party—with his regime and prosperous economy, was offering wheat, meat and eggs, leather, loans, and a tiny bit of hope to the motherland. This wasn't entirely altruistic generosity, mind you: the regimes shared certain ideological affinities, as well as an interest in strengthening ties with countries that fell outside the two blocs into which the world was dividing itself. Put succinctly, this economic support provided bread for the people of Spain and a boost for their leader Franco, and he'd decided to show his gratitude by sparing no expense. The Generalísimo wasn't going personally unrewarded, either. His intention was to sanitize his image and open a crack in the wall that stood between Spain and the world, aided by the interest of the foreign press.

In the days leading up to the visit, Madrid's city council had published several edicts calling on the people to decorate their balconies and inviting residents to take to the streets en masse.

As the bus drove on, I saw that my compatriots had been obliging. Crowds filled the streets and squares, even the side of the road that led to the airport, despite the presence of the strong sun.

38

I watched the plane land from the press box, surrounded by my supposed colleagues in the foreign press and by a good number of Spanish journalists from various provinces. The latter were tended to not by Diego Tovar's refined Diplomatic Information Office but by the General Press Directorate, a rather less pleasant censorship body whose responsibility was ensuring that the tone and substance of their reports aligned with the regime's version of events.

The invited guests occupied the large terraces and the inside of the airport terminal. The citizens who'd come on their own were farther away, around the outside perimeter or even on the arid land nearby. Everyone was fervently cheering and waving Spanish and Argentine flags, mixing whites and light blues, reds and yellows. The airport had been decked out with wall hangings and carpets, flags and floral garlands. In front of the main tower, they'd constructed a platform draped in deep red, with three lavish armchairs on it. The giant banner serving as a backdrop displayed the head of state's coat of arms. The entire government and several hundred top military and civilian figures fanned out to the sides, having been summoned to witness the grand arrival.

We were kept informed about the plane's progress through the loudspeakers—its speed, how long it would be before we could see it. The buzzing crowd roared the moment the two squadrons of air force planes escorting the DC-4 appeared on the horizon. At that precise moment, Franco and his wife descended from the platform onto the runway. The silvery Iberia aircraft then emerged from the afternoon sky, turned gracefully by way of a salute, and landed cleanly. The ovation from the onlookers was so deafening, I almost had to cover my ears.

Once the plane had stopped, an air of expectation suddenly silenced the crowd as the operators attached the stairs. The door slowly opened. First, two stewardesses came out and immediately stepped to one side. Then she appeared. The clapping and cheering, the euphoric cries, and the handkerchief- and flag-waving turned wild.

There she was, dressed in a blue skirt and jacket with a matching hat: First Lady María Eva Duarte de Perón—none of the Spanish news organizations would dare to shorten her incredibly long name. Blond, young, slight, splendidly styled. She wore a flower on her lapel and a smile on her mouth that didn't fade for an instant. She waved her right hand in greeting, then she descended from the plane, escorted by the minister for foreign affairs.

Franco and his wife, Doña Carmen, were waiting for her at the bottom of the stairs: he, joyful in his olive-green uniform, and she, dressed in a black wide-brimmed hat and white summer gloves. The cheers and applause remained impassioned as the Generalísimo introduced the guest to the various dignitaries. One by one they kissed her hand; she did the same with the bishop's. They reviewed the troops of the First Air Force Region. Salvos of artillery fire resounded. Someone gave her a gigantic bunch of flowers. Once the dignitaries were on the platform, the military band performed both national anthems with great verve.

We all watched the show attentively from the press box. "My goodness," exclaimed a young female reporter from the International News Service, who was sitting beside me, amazed by the display. A little farther away, a stout, smirking American from United Press made a joke, and the journalists nearest him guffawed. The Argentine from the *Democracia* newspaper asked me what he'd said, and I shrugged, as if I didn't know. But yes, I'd understood him, which was precisely why I'd laughed inwardly and decided I'd better keep the joke to myself.

The crowd was still clamoring as the organizers ushered us back to the buses, separating the foreign and Spanish journalists. Meanwhile, the dignitaries began to file through the terminal to reach their vehicles. Franco's was an impressive Mercedes Pullman limousine, identical to the one that Himmler and the SS chiefs had tended to use. He hadn't yet had time to replace it with the British and US models he would alternate between in later years, depending on the status of his changing friendships. He and his illustrious guest got in, flanked by an escort of white-helmeted motorcyclists. His wife and the foreign minister went in the car behind, followed by the cream of the Argentine entourage and the Spanish grandees. We journalists brought up the rear of the motorcade, with children and youngsters yelling excitedly behind us, running until the vehicles outran their legs.

As we drove on through Madrid's outskirts, the crowds grew. Up ahead, near El Retiro Park, an infantry company was waiting in formation. Opposite them, on horseback, was the Guardia Mora, Franco's ceremonial escort drawn from Spain's Moroccan Army Corps. Evening was setting in by the time the procession reached the Alcalá Gate, where the mayor and the entire city council were waiting for us, along with another enormous group of officials, other important figures, and crowds. Forty fighter planes passed overhead. Once again, the cheers and cries were deafening, and scarves and handkerchiefs waved by the thousands. Banners, flags, and Manila shawls hung from balconies.

Franco and the Argentine first lady exited the Mercedes and reviewed the troops, surrounded by military marches and constant cheering. The mayor presented her with another huge bunch of flowers. A few minutes later they climbed into a different vehicle—this time open topped—and set off again. The Cibeles and Neptune Fountains, and many other squares and roundabouts, had been decorated with colored lights. Rumor had it that it had taken eight days and three hundred thousand pesetas, nine engineers, a dozen technicians, and two hundred workmen to set them up. The result was a spectacular display of electrical illumination in a country where almost everyone, in private, used bare, feeble lightbulbs and endured constant power outages.

So that they might salute and be saluted, the caravan drove through the crowds on Calle de Alcalá, Gran Vía—named Avenida de José Antonio at the time—and Plaza de España, and from there headed to Madrid's university district. There, the motorcade finally broke up, and Franco, his guest, and their closest aides continued on to El Pardo Palace, the Generalísimo's residence, where Señora Perón would be staying. The rest were sent their separate ways, thank goodness.

I was extremely relieved that the proceedings were over. Everything had been so agitated and frenetic—so noisy, gaudy, and excessive—that my poor head needed a little peace. It had proven to be an incredibly long day. The heat in the press box had been terrible under the sun. Dust and grime had poured in through the open windows of the bus. The fervent cries, the sounds of the aircraft and motorcycles, the salutes of honor and the trumpets of the military bands. I'd also slept badly the previous night. I was completely exhausted and deeply grateful for the respite, anxious for the bus to leave me at the press club, where I could take off my creased suit, have a cold shower, and get into bed. I didn't foresee, in my naivety, that the chance for the rest I craved would go up in smoke the minute I arrived.

The envelope was handed to me by the reserved Señora Cortés. I opened it while sitting on an armchair in my room as I took off my shoes. Upon reading it, I let out a cry of irritation. Diego Tovar, director of the Diplomatic Information Office, was inviting me to dinner that night. He would collect me at ten o'clock, and it was exactly—I checked the time and let out a groan—twenty minutes to ten.

I noted an admiring look in his eyes as he saw me come down the stairs, but he quickly hid it, conscious of his role and purpose for being there. The meeting was of a professional nature, not personal, let alone romantic. Even so, it was a night out, and I'd opted to dress according to the etiquette appropriate for any high-society event held after six. In the little time I'd had, I had managed to take a shower, do my makeup with reasonable care, and put on a beautiful, low-cut, sleeveless patterned dress that I'd bought at Digby Morton in London. So that I wouldn't be late, I had left my hair down.

"You don't know how pleased I am that you've accepted my invitation. I trust you're not too tired."

I lied blatantly, assuring him that I too was delighted, without making mention of my tiredness or the inconvenient time. He too had changed, now wearing semiformal attire of dark trousers and a pale jacket. I recognized the hand of a good tailor in his clothes, and in him, an undeniable charm. Even so, I would have given anything not to have to go anywhere with him.

"What do you fancy? Outdoors or in? I booked tables at two places, just in case."

I preferred the first option, of course. Out on the street, I saw that he'd dispensed with the official car and brought his own: a two-seater Mercury with the top down. It certainly wasn't a family man's vehicle, nor did it seem in keeping with the austerity of the nation he served.

"I don't know how well you know Spain. I don't even know whether I ought to call you Señora or Señorita Nash," he said, holding the door open for me.

It took all my effort, but I managed to tear the words from my throat.

"You can call me Livia."

He hadn't been with us in the press box at the airport—he'd been in another box, one for top officials—but he'd come by to greet us cordially before the landing, accompanied by a couple of waiters in short jackets carrying cold drinks and trays of snacks from the Viena Capellanes patisserie. I hadn't seen him again since then, but he seemed tremendously pleased with how the event had gone. He wasn't responsible for the organization of the tour, but he did play an essential role: ensuring that the international press covered everything accurately and without rancor. It was very likely that he would try to sound out all the reporters in one way or another, as he was doing with me now. Clearly he saw me as easier to manipulate than the headstrong journalists from the other news organizations.

We left Madrid, heading up Cuesta de las Perdices, and found very little traffic. Before long he turned left, toward a cluster of lights. VILLA ROMANA, I read on a neon sign. There were several dozen cars parked at the entrance to the premises. After opening the door again and holding out a hand for me, he gave the keys to a porter. Inside we were greeted by a large garden with pergolas and lush vegetation, a terrace restaurant, and a dance floor. I even thought I could make out a swimming pool in the background. An orchestra was playing light music, and despite it being a Sunday, there were plenty of customers.

"Did you know this place?"

"I didn't even know it existed. I haven't set foot in Spain for a few years."

They showed us to a table, and we ordered, talking while we waited.

"But you have been to Madrid before, I imagine?"

"Many times, yes. I have . . . ," I stammered. "I have some family here, though I don't see them very often."

He fixed his eyes on mine.

"I talk to a lot of foreigners," he said with unexpected familiarity. "I travel constantly, to many destinations outside of Spain. Even so, I can't locate your accent."

How would he, if everything about me was a sham? As part of my cover, I had decided to speak good Spanish but, from time to time, introduce English words, or feign an affected cadence, or articulate words with a pronunciation that I pulled out of my hat.

"I'm originally from Tangier, and my family derives from various nationalities."

Diplomatic as he was in every sense of the word, he didn't probe further. But with his silence he discreetly left his interest on the table. To polish off my lie, I added another detail.

"At the Latin American Service, I work alongside people from many different places. Perhaps that's why the way I speak seems somewhat unorthodox."

"Nash is your paternal surname?"

I could have laughed. Besides wanting to know where my people were from, he also wanted to know whether I'd acquired my surname at marriage or birth. I'd dodged his previous question about whether I was titled señora or señorita, but he wasn't giving up. Faced with his curiosity, I decided to offer a small deception.

"Nash is the surname I took from someone who's now out of my life."

In truth it wasn't such a big lie, despite my misleading answer. Only that the person was a female friend, not a husband.

Beyond these lighter matters, the director of the Diplomatic Information Office had a serious interest in the BBC and the service I was supposed to be working for.

"Let me be frank now that we're getting to know each other. You see, Livia, in this new era for our country, contact with the nations of Spanish-speaking America is of enormous importance to us. Before . . . I mean, during the world war, there were other more pressing matters. But now, absent that conflict and with new players coming to the fore, we're aware of where our true allegiances lie."

I already knew all of that. From the reports Kavannagh had sent me in London, and from what I'd had the chance to learn from my father that afternoon, I understood that this was one of the regime's new priorities. Ever since the end of the civil war, there had been a great deal of interest in restoring the concept of the Hispanic world and of reviving the grandeur of the old empire. After the kick in the teeth that had come from the United Nations, and with Argentina's hand extended to them, Francoist thinkers saw this as the perfect time to try to rebuild ties with Spain's old friends across the pond. It wasn't going to be an easy task: several governments there were radically against it, and the presence in the Americas of thousands of exiled Spanish Republicans complicated matters.

Without his having asked me openly, it was obvious that Diego Tovar was eager to know the format my work would take, its tone, how it would be distributed, and how many people it would reach. And though he was careful not to say so explicitly, he made it clear that he would appreciate it if, beyond reporting on Señora Eva's comings and goings, I would be sensitive enough not to speak badly of Spain. Though I was a brazen impostor, at that moment it fully dawned on me that it would be my personal impressions, my judgment, and my viewpoint that would end up reaching tens of thousands of listeners on the other side of the Atlantic. The filter I applied would determine what they heard.

We finished dessert. Unexpectedly, it had been an enjoyable dinner. Villa Romana had proved to be a pleasant place, with its greenery and the music under the June sky. Far from winding down, by around midnight the atmosphere was beginning to come alive. The guests, well dressed and well groomed, were having a wonderful time, enjoying mixed drinks and sparkling wine, eating tournedos, seafood cocktails, and monkfish roulades. It was this Spain, and not any other, that Tovar undoubtedly wanted me to report on.

A group of ten or so people arrived, laughing and chatting loudly. The waiters started to put two tables together to accommodate them.

"Argentines," Tovar explained with a slight gesture with his cigarette. "Madrid's suddenly full of them."

"Did they come with Señora Perón?"

"Not exactly. She brought her own entourage. We're not sure who all these spontaneous visitors are. They don't fit the usual mold, and there hasn't been time yet to investigate. But certainly they're here under her wing. We assume they're just opportunists, individuals gambling on a chance to achieve personal or commercial gain under the banner of the first lady's visit."

He finished his cigarette and stubbed it out in the triangular Cinzano ashtray. The orchestra was playing the opening bars of Agustín Lara's "Solamente una vez." I thought he was going to suggest leaving when he spoke again.

"Might I be so bold as to ask you for a dance?"

I wrung my fingers under the tablecloth but mustered my courage and said, "Of course."

We headed to the dance floor, which was full of couples. I hadn't danced since the final stages of my pregnancy and was now flooded with memories of Marcus. I tried not to drown in them as I moved my body closer to this stranger's. Diego Tovar proved to be an excellent dancer: graceful and natural, not at all tiresome. We danced the first bolero, and then there were two more. Then the singer asked for our attention. There was silence, and everyone turned to the stage. He cleared his throat, raised his voice, and informed us with pleasure that they were now going to play a tango, in tribute to the newly arrived wife of General Perón and in honor of the Argentine customers who were with us that night.

"Shall we go?" I whispered as the audience applauded enthusiastically.

We headed to our table while the pianist played the first notes of "La cumparsita." *The little parade.* Some of the Argentines took to the dance floor. They were all smiling, seemingly delighted with the tribute to their country. The rest of the dancers stepped aside, still applauding, to make way for them.

I observed the first two: a man with a sturdy neck and a slender brunette. After them came a bald fellow and a peroxide blond with her hair styled in kiss curls. When the third couple went out onto the floor and the man's eyes met mine, I felt as if an iron fist had split my soul.

Tall, handsome, beaming, brilliantined, he was holding hands with a woman in her thirties who had mahogany-tinted hair. It was Ramiro Arribas, the son of a bitch who had once left me for dead.

39

The municipal edict had summoned all of Madrid's inhabitants to fill Plaza de Oriente that Monday. Students' classes were canceled, and civil servants were given the day off. Businesses and shops were ordered to grant their employees leave to go out midmorning.

Our bus was to collect us from the press club at half past ten. Mindful of the torrent of activities ahead of me, I decided to get up early. By around eight o'clock, I was in the elevator in my father's building, hoping to see my son for at least a few minutes before I became busy with my duties. The flat was just starting to come awake, and Víctor was still asleep. Philippa gave me an exhaustive report and assured me the boy was still very happy. He'd become inseparable from the porter's cat and didn't seem to notice my absence too much. Miguela served me and my father coffee, him still in his pajamas and dressing gown, me dressed for the day in sea blue. Breaking all protocol, and despite the splendidness of the flat, since I was in a hurry we opted to sit in the kitchen. I briefly wondered what Olivia would've thought if she could have seen us.

I recounted snippets of my dinner with the head of the Diplomatic Information Office, and Gonzalo cast light onto some shadows in my understanding.

"This Diego Tovar you speak of, given the position he holds, must be one of the Acción Católica propagandists."

Since the fall of the Nazis and Italian fascism, he explained after sipping from his cup, the Falange had been losing influence in certain important spheres, particularly those concerned with foreign relations. From among the various families buzzing around him, the Generalísimo had begun making political appointments to compensate for this shift. These appointees were members of a devoutly Christian movement—Acción Católica, or Catholic Action—that was just as anticommunist as the Falange, but less radical.

"Despite the changes," he added, "not that much is different. The aim now is to make the regime more palatable. The fascist salute has been dispensed with, and supposedly we have a law of succession in place. But there's a joke making the rounds, with the people turning to humor, as they always do, so they don't go to pieces. The joke goes: everything's essentially the same, only now, instead of raising one's arm and giving a passionate cry of 'Up with Spain!' whenever we set foot in a government building, our officials are content to hear us offer a whispered 'Hail Virgin Mary.'"

I laughed lazily as I finished up my coffee. It was time to go.

"Martín-Artajo, the minister for foreign affairs, is presently Acción Católica's most prominent member," my father concluded, standing to see me to the door. "Presumably he has granted appointments to people who are of the same mind. Your new friend, for example."

With that word—"propagandists"—etched in my mind, I headed back. I felt a pang of sadness at having seen Víctor only while he was asleep, along with the peace of mind of knowing that he was happy and well looked after. Beyond all these thoughts—about the Catholics implanted in politics and my son's sleep—there remained something else that unsettled me profoundly, that had left me shaken: Ramiro Arribas. The man who, looking dashing and confident, had arrived in the early hours to dance a tango under the stars on Cuesta de las Perdices.

Our eyes had met only for an instant, but it was enough for us to recognize each other. It had been almost eleven years since he left me his crushing letter in our room at Hotel Continental in Tangier, before running away like a rat. I had been left behind, abandoned, pregnant, with neither money nor the jewelry I'd inherited, loaded down by fear and debts. Neither of us had any idea how the other had rebuilt their life. I'd never tried to find him, and it would've been very difficult for him to follow my trail given my changes of identity and location. And yet, without question, we'd both known who the other was at once. Shaken, I had gripped Diego Tovar's arm, wanting to leave the place as soon as possible. Ramiro had stood there watching me while his eye-catching companion pulled on his sleeve to drag him to the middle of the dance floor. I'd arrived back at the press club after my early-morning outing with his face still in my mind.

The bus left us in the courtyard of the Armory of the Royal Palace. I would've liked to have had some time—twenty minutes would've been enough—to drop by my neighborhood, my square, and my street, the place where I'd grown up, so near to there. But it wasn't to be; I couldn't detach myself from the group. We filed up the imposing marble steps flanked by halberdiers, and everything opened up majestically around us: immense rooms, tapestries, rugs, lamps. The war had left the building battered, but two years of repairs had healed its wounds and the scars were less visible now. After the royal family's hasty escape into exile, only Azaña, in his role as the last president of the Spanish Republic, had inhabited the palace temporarily. The Nationalist Franco, of more austere tastes, had decided to move into El Pardo Palace, located farther outside the city center and more modest. He only used the Royal Palace for occasions that required pomp and ceremony. Like this one.

The press was accommodated in a room near the one where the formal ceremony would take place. We were surrounded by gilded furniture, pastoral frescoes, and walls draped with greenish silk. A sustained, harsh noise like a rough sea was coming from the other side of the balconies. Some of us, curious, pulled back the curtains to see. It was a dramatic sight: thousands, tens of thousands, perhaps hundreds of thousands of people were gathered in the great Plaza de Oriente and its surroundings, masses of bodies crowded together, holding placards and flags. There wasn't a single cloud in the sky, and the heat was beginning to take hold. I could only imagine how that compact throng of people felt, there being little in the way of shade to protect them.

At some point Diego Tovar appeared, impeccable as ever. He greeted everyone warmly, kissing female hands and shaking male ones. Some people he gave friendly pats on the back, and he even joked with some of the most seasoned American journalists until they laughed with him. His talent for public relations was undeniable, and I wondered how much I would ultimately profit from him. He left me until last, not as a snub but as a courtesy, to be able to devote a little more time to me. He asked how I was, whether I'd rested. After the sudden encounter with Ramiro the other night at Villa Romana, I'd pleaded exhaustion on the way back to disguise my disconcerted state.

Before long we began to hear the sounds of orders and rushed activity. They were arriving, General Franco and his guest. We journalists were escorted through to the Throne Hall and positioned out of the way on one side. The curtains were closed, shielding the room from the midday light. Candles burning in candelabras and wall lamps with weak bulbs gave the room a gloomy feel. It was because of this murk, perhaps, that I thought my eyes were playing tricks on me as Señora Perón entered alongside Franco, who was dressed in his uniform. But no. As they approached the middle of the room, I saw that I hadn't been mistaken. On that sweltering June 9, on top of her taffeta dress, the Argentine president's wife was sporting a lavish sable coat that I would've liked to have had during my first weeks in London, when the temperatures remained stubbornly below freezing. Averse to simplicity, the illustrious first lady had paired the unique garment with a sort of cap from which striking plumes hung down to below her shoulders.

An interminable formal reception followed, with the two dignitaries in the center of the room. A veritable royal court of civilian notables in morning suits, military men in full uniform, and ladies in wide-brimmed hats passed before them. There were some lapses in concentration and mistakes, elbow pokes, and even shoves. "Move, please, that's my place," more than one person whispered, everyone wanting to be as close as possible to the stars of the show. Staff had to intervene at one point to restore order. Once the tedious sequence of greetings was complete, the Spanish head of state, with the Chain of the Order of the Liberator General San Martín pinned on his shoulder and the corresponding sash across his sizable belly, by God's grace, positioned his spectacles on the tip of his nose and proceeded to read a pompous speech crammed with allusions to faith, harmony, affection between nations, and the great Spanish-speaking family.

Next it was time to pin the Grand Cross of Isabella the Catholic on María Eva Duarte de Perón's chest in the form of an ornate brooch. The decoration was intended to have tremendous symbolic value, and the piece's material value, too, could not have been inconsiderable, with its solid gold, rubies, pearls, and numerous diamonds. In the center, on enamel, the two pillars of Hercules were linked with a ribbon that bore the inscription *Plus Ultra*. Very few people received such a high distinction—it was a grand gesture.

Following thunderous applause, the Argentine first lady responded with her own equally turgid speech in which she linked the spirit of the Catholic queen to still more allusions to faith, divine providence, and love between peoples. She read with ease—although the Spanish press had diligently omitted any mention of her past, from Kavannagh's reports I knew that Eva Perón had for years been an actress, or an aspiring one, at least. She'd never found success, but the time she'd spent performing on the stage and, even more so, in radio plays, had prepared her to operate confidently in front of audiences, cameras, and microphones.

In broken but comprehensible Spanish, during the bus journey, the *New York Herald Tribune* correspondent had asked Valentín Thiebaut, the reporter for the Argentine newspaper *Democracia*, whether it was true that the scriptwriter had been put on the plane at the last minute by order of the Argentine president himself, because he was nervous about his wife's oratorial abilities. By now, we all knew that *Democracia* was the Argentine newspaper most supportive of the Peronist regime, and someone even went so far as to say it was owned by the first lady.

While she continued to reel off the high-flown phrases that had been written for her, and as the photographers' cameras flashed away, I focused on implementing my plan. The first objective I'd set for myself was identifying the members of her entourage I was to get close to. I located them in the front row, off to one side, surrounded by generals, clerics, and bigwigs. None of them was particularly distinctive, everything about them was in order, but somehow they seemed different from the Spanish officials, less stiff and uptight. The lady wearing mauve with an understated headdress of flowers I assumed to be Lillian Lagomarsino, companion and adviser. The older broad-chested gentleman I identified as Alberto Dodero, the shipping magnate who was coordinating and financing the unofficial later stages of the tour. And the younger man with slicked-back hair and pencil mustache I guessed was the brother, the womanizer who'd recently been a soap salesman and was now a vital cog in the presidential machinery. *Juancito*, they called him.

She finished her speech to another resounding ovation. At last, the staff hurried to open the balconies, and a deafening roar arose from the square. Franco and Eva walked out, followed by the most important officials and ministers. Radio Nacional de España microphones awaited them. The crowd seemed to be in a frenzy, the people euphorically waving flags and handkerchiefs, caps and placards. They began to chant with a pulsing rhythm that grew in force.

"What're they saying?" my colleagues asked me.

We were packed together. I pricked up my ears, but it was hard to make out the exact words in the chanting that sounded more like drumming. Once I had the phrase, I turned around and repeated it, before translating. *"Franco, Perón, un solo corazón,"* the mass was singing in unison. Franco, Perón, a single heart. Finally, she took the floor.

Her speech was brief but extremely effective, and she expressed herself with passion and charisma. Off the cuff, without any notes now, she spoke about the poor, the disadvantaged, and laborers, about workers' rights, social renewal, and justice for the people. Some of the Francoist officials at the back of the main balcony had sweat running from their temples. I imagined that to a few of them, her words echoed those of La Pasionaria, the exiled Republican heroine Dolores Ibárruri.

The hundreds of thousands of Madrileños, indifferent to the searing heat, continued to clap and cheer. The first lady's actual words probably didn't matter an awful lot to them, and they would've applauded just as fervently no matter what message came from her mouth. This was simply a jamboree, a free circus, a day off, plus they'd been told that the señora would bring bread and meat to Spain by the shipload, and that was all that really mattered. Franco, despite his guest's rather subversive language, appeared jubilant as he took in the public's response. This was precisely what he wanted: massive popular acclaim, a picture of a people united around their leader. For the world to see Spain celebrate him.

They were waving goodbye and we were about to return to the Throne Hall when a melody began to rise from the plaza.

"What're they singing?" my supposed fellow journalists asked again.

It took a few seconds for me to realize it was "Cara al sol." The massive crowd, spontaneously and unstoppably, with right arms held high, was now belting out the Falangist anthem, oblivious to the fresh image the new Acción Católica appointees were trying to project beyond Spain's borders. To show her gratitude, or simply because she was caught up in the moment, Eva Duarte seemed to join with the crowd, and just for an instant, she appeared to give the old fascist salute. A grumble of disapproval came from the foreign journalists behind me. I looked around—the foreign minister's face was transformed, Diego Tovar looked like he was going to bury his head in his hands, and other senior propagandists were either mumbling complaints or showing irritation in their expressions. The masses, meanwhile, continued to sing with fevered enthusiasm in the square. Inside the palace, some were already anticipating the reports that would appear in the international press the next day. *Nothing has truly changed in Spain despite the outward reversals,* the North American, British, and French newspapers would say. *The new shirt that was once embroidered with the yoke and arrows of the Falange is still being worn. The terrible Rome-Berlin Axis of fascism had disappeared after the Second World War; but now,* various reporters would note, *another with a similar ideology seems to be emerging between Madrid and Buenos Aires. And Eva Perón,* some would write, *has come to Spain to ratify it.*

The occasion was brought to an end. People gathered into small groups, exchanging opinions and saying their goodbyes, but no one dared leave until the Generalísimo and President Perón's wife had gone out through the door. I watched the scene closely and waited for my chance, until I decided that yes, now was my moment. "Go get him," I whispered to myself as I smoothed down my skirt. I put a huge smile on my face and walked gracefully toward my prey.

"Livia Nash, from the BBC Latin American Service," I said, holding out my hand. "It's a real honor to meet you, Señor Dodero."

40

The shipowner asked me to meet him on the Riscal terrace. I would've preferred somewhere more secluded—an office at the Argentine embassy, or some tucked-away corner of his hotel's lobby instead of the balcony, for example. After my encounter with Ramiro, I wanted to avoid public places at all costs. Especially the busiest and most famous ones.

Oblivious to my concerns, Alberto Dodero arranged for a car to collect me from the press club: a sumptuous black Cadillac that made heads turn on its way through the streets. He was waiting for me, drinking a whiskey on ice and talking to two men who made themselves scarce as soon as he gave the sign. Around him, unsurprisingly, the place was crawling with curious bystanders. It was said that the entire city was on the lookout for the Argentine dignitary or members of her delegation. He kissed my hand, held my chair, and praised my appearance. He said he'd never been interviewed by such a beautiful woman. I accepted his gentlemanly courtesies with a neutral smile—I had little choice.

"As a matter of fact, Señor Dodero, it's not going to be an interview in the usual sense of the word," I explained while I placed the napkin on my knees. "It'll be more like a relaxed conversation, if you don't mind. We're doing background work for an extensive radio report that will cover President Perón's wife's visit to Spain, to be broadcast on our service."

"A lot of people listen to the BBC in Uruguay and Argentina," he said, raising his glass in a gesture of appreciation. "It will be a pleasure to talk to you . . . Do I call you señorita or señora?"

I employed the strategy I'd used with Diego Tovar again.

"You can just call me Livia."

He was over sixty and the most powerful shipowner in Río de la Plata—in fact, one of the most important shipowners in South America. He headed a group of family enterprises that owned hundreds of vessels, from huge freighters to ocean liners, tugboats to river launches. Far from becoming impoverished during the war, he had profited from it, thanks to the rise in freight prices. And since the conflict, he had in recent years been buying up former US Navy vessels at bargain prices, converting them from troop and weapons carriers to passenger and cargo ships. My companion that evening was rich, terrifically rich. Openly and unashamedly so.

He ordered for both of us without bothering to look at the menu. "The paella" was all he said. Someone must've recommended it. I did well not to point out that in Spain we usually ate paella for lunch and not for dinner at almost eleven o'clock. At Riscal, it seemed to be the star dish.

"All right, Señor Dodero, let's start . . ."

"Please, call me Alberto," he said. He had aplomb in spades, bags of skin under his eyes, and jet-black hair, which must've been dyed because not a single gray strand could be seen. "If you want me to call you Livia, I'll simply have no choice but to be Alberto."

"Let's start then, Alberto, with the preparations for the tour. How was . . . ?"

I barely had to ask anything more because, from that point, it was all him. He paused only long enough to praise the paella that would be brought to us: a dish as colorful as a garish modern painting, made for two, but crammed with so many langoustines, lemon quarters, and strips of red pepper, it could have fed more than half a dozen.

With that tendency so common to self-assured men, Alberto Dodero dominated the conversation and spoke at length about *I, my,* and *me* almost until dessert. Born in Uruguay, he was the child of Italian immigrants with the sea in his blood: a son, grandson, and great-grandson of Genoese sailors. He'd taken all his tenacity and boldness to Buenos Aires as a young man and, together with his brothers, had managed to build an empire that connected the ports of the Río de la Plata with the rest of the planet. He'd been married twice, and his love life followed the pattern typical of a mature man with money pursuing eternal youth: his first wife had been a woman of his own age who gave him children; the second, a head-turning actress almost thirty years his junior. A lover of luxury and everyday elegance, he had properties and friendships all over the world. The former included the lavish Villa Betalba in Montevideo, Hotel Cataratas del Iguazú, and a summer mansion on the Côte d'Azur, overlooking the Mediterranean. The latter, a certain Ari Onassis, and the Peróns, of course.

Kavannagh's report suggested, and my fellow journalists had confirmed, that Dodero was the supplier of the first lady's jewelry—currently opulent pieces by Walser Wald and Ricciardi of Buenos Aires, soon to be replaced by items from French jewelers Cartier and Van Cleef & Arpels. He presented the pieces to Señora Perón, and she accepted them and sported them in public with enormous pleasure. There didn't seem to be any conflict whatsoever between the shipping magnate's business interests and his sumptuous generosity toward the president's wife. It was said that she had a weakness for gold, whereas Franco's spouse preferred pearls: different tastes and desires.

"And as I understand it," I managed to ask when he held his glass of wine to his mouth, "when the tour leaves Spain, you will cover the cost of the European trip. Is that right?"

Dodero continued to speak openly without the slightest embarrassment.

"It's a great honor for me that General Perón has accepted my backing for those stages. It means we won't have to incur unnecessary expenses for the state, and I am paying from my own pocket with the utmost pleasure. Unfortunately, not all the European countries have been as generous as this one."

He let out a loud burst of laughter, a langoustine's head held between his fingers. Everyone around us looked at him, yet again. On any other day, every customer, every group, every couple at the restaurant would have minded their own business, keeping their attention on their food and their own conversations, indifferent to the buzz from the other tables. That night, however, the rumor had spread among the clientele that the sixty-something gentleman with the raven hair was an Argentine tycoon who was traveling in the company of Eva Perón.

"And on the subject of the latter stages of the tour, could you tell me what plans you have?"

That was the direction in which I wanted the conversation to go: to his immediate future rather than to his past, as worthy and as extraordinary as it was. But a couple of bystanders interrupted us, approaching for the sole purpose of shaking the magnate's hand, perhaps to have something to boast about the next day. *Welcome to Spain, señor! Give our thanks to President Perón! Viva Argentina, our great sister nation!*

As soon as they'd gone, the shipowner went on to discuss the presidential party's future visit to the Holy Father. Then he mentioned France, potentially Switzerland, perhaps Portugal. I had the impression that, at that point, Rome was the only guaranteed destination. It seemed that beyond the Pyrenees, no one was willing to stomach Señora Perón's presence.

I listened until the waiter interrupted us with suggestions for dessert. As soon as he'd gone away with an order for flambéed soufflé, I stuck my pointed question in like a lance.

"And Britain? How are the plans for visiting London working out, Alberto?"

He diverted the conversation back to himself, his own dealings with British associates, his many trips to finalize operations there, the unused seaplanes he'd recently bought from the United Kingdom with the aim of dipping his foot into commercial aviation—a new and risky venture.

"But Señora Perón," I insisted, "does she really have an interest in Britain, or do you think . . . ?"

He looked at me intensely while he held his solid-gold lighter to the tip of a Dunhill. There was a click, the flame popped up, and I immediately regretted my overenthusiasm. Perhaps I'd been too direct, but the dinner was reaching its end and I needed an answer, some firm response, before I could wrap up the meeting. I had to be careful, however, not to try his patience. I had no choice but to concoct a lie to get out of trouble.

"Because if you do end up traveling to England, perhaps the first lady would do us the honor of speaking on our service."

He smiled with satisfaction, slowly letting smoke out through his nose, his eyes still fixed on me.

"I like determined women—"

He didn't have the chance to go on—at that moment someone else approached the table. The man appeared behind me, so all he'd have seen of me was my bare shoulders, my dark hair gathered in a bun, and the back of my patterned outfit.

"My esteemed Señor Dodero, what an immense pleasure it is to find you here in Spain. Román Altares, at your service," he added, holding out his hand. His accent sounded even more Argentine than the shipping magnate's. "Please forgive my intrusion, both you and your beautiful companion . . ."

He looked to me, and sweat broke out on my back. His smile turned to stone. The greatest of my fears had been realized. Wearing an elegant three-piece summer suit and with brilliantined hair, attractive, a snake charmer, there was Ramiro Arribas. Again.

He reacted quickly, turning his eyes from me to Dodero. He cited a long string of names, places, and events. My companion gave a slight frown, as if trying to recall him without much interest. After a few seconds, and without much conviction, he muttered, "Yes, yes, I remember."

Unable to remain calm, I got up from the table.

"If you'll excuse me for a moment . . ."

I headed to the bathroom. I would've liked to scream, swear, stick my face under the faucet. But no, I couldn't lose control. I couldn't allow that pig's presence, his mere existence, to affect me. I clenched my teeth, breathed deeply.

Ramiro Arribas had become Román Altares, his new name different but relatively similar to the original. He was no longer speaking our language the way I did. Rather, his was now a fluent Buenos Aires Spanish. Things weren't going too badly for him, judging by his appearance and the fact that, at least tangentially, he knew Alberto Dodero. But what the devil was he doing in Madrid if he supposedly lived in the Argentine capital? And what was he hoping to obtain from the shipowner, beyond a chance to introduce himself? I recalled Diego Tovar's words at Villa Romana: Madrid was full of unclassifiable Argentines—opportunists, in all likelihood. And that profile fit Ramiro like a glove.

I washed my hands and looked at myself in the mirror. The person I saw was not the unsuspecting girl that swine had manipulated at his will, the twenty-something he'd cheated and abandoned without a trace of remorse. Before me was the reflection of who I was now: a battle-hardened woman with a scarred soul, the world on her shoulders, and a tiny family in her care. "Do it for your son," I whispered. But I immediately made a correction. *Do it for your children,* I told myself. For my little Víctor and for the child who'd never been born, the one that *he* had fathered and then destroyed when he abandoned us, the baby I lost among blood clots as I fled Tangier on a bus, alone and terrified after he left. For that ill-fated child, for my living boy, and for myself, I couldn't allow Ramiro to upend me.

I walked back to the table with feigned ease and saw the bastard still speaking enthusiastically while Dodero fiddled with his lighter between his fingers, not paying much attention. Ramiro gave me his splendid smile when he saw me, the sly fox even starting to say something—to give a compliment to make an impression on the magnate, perhaps. I didn't give him the chance. Ignoring him, still standing, I asked, "Could we leave, Alberto?"

The shipowner stood, leaving his napkin scrunched up on the table. The head waiter quickly arrived, and in three words they agreed to something. To send the bill to the palace, I supposed. Men of his status rarely bothered to take out their wallets in public. He gestured dismissively at Ramiro with his chin. *Another pest,* he must've been thinking. *Another social climber trying to get in with the right people.*

I allowed Dodero to lead me to the exit with his hand planted on my waist, leaving behind us the untouched soufflé and a terrace full of whispering people with their eyes fixed on us. For a moment I wondered what Ramiro would be thinking of me, what feelings were bubbling inside him.

That very night an event was being held in Plaza Mayor—an extremely long tribute to the illustrious visitor, offered by Spain's provinces. Popular dances, songs, parades, and gifts . . . a tedious multitudinous affair that would go on until only God knew when. The next day, the newspapers would praise the first lady's grace once more, as well as the affection she showed for the people and the impressive white fox coat she wore on the verge of summer. So that she wouldn't be left alone in her extravagance, the Generalísimo's wife and other distinguished ladies had quickly retrieved their own furs from the back of their wardrobes, and they too would wear them for the evening, boiling themselves to death in order to keep up with the Argentine. Dodero would attend the final stage of the occasion after leaving me at the press club. On the way back, I managed to compose myself and put on a charming face.

"It was a very enjoyable dinner, Alberto. Your remarks will certainly enrich my report."

He smiled with pleasure, oblivious to my hypocrisy. In truth, it had been anything but enjoyable: he hadn't told me anything significant and had spent the evening talking about himself, barely touching on any subject that mattered to me. And Ramiro's unwelcome arrival had prevented us from continuing our conversation during dessert and coffee, at which point—who knows—I may have been able to extract something. With things as they were, with our meeting about to end and no results, I had one more shot to take, a final opportunity to get the millionaire to at least open up another door for me.

"At the risk of imposing on you, there is something I wanted—"

"Anything you like, *preciosa*," he said emphatically. "Anything in my power."

"So that I may give an accurate account of Señora Perón and her circle, it would be most useful if I could speak to her dressmakers. As I understand it, they're also staying at El Pardo. Perhaps if . . ."

Alberto Dodero wasn't a man to waste time.

"Consider it done."

41

The original schedule of activities had revolved around the main monuments to the spirit of Spain: El Escorial monastery, Ávila and its medieval walls, the heroic ruins of the Alcázar de Toledo, and other glorious settings of this kind. However, the program had to be changed several times. At the request of the Argentine first lady, the organizers had been obligated to include a few visits of a more prosaic nature. Eva Perón couldn't care less about Spain's art, history, and past imperial power; what she wanted, above all, was to see the workers and learn what provisions the state afforded them. If the people in charge could bring them to her, perfect. If not, she warned, she would go and find them herself.

They quickly organized a parallel itinerary to satisfy this unusual demand. With Franco's wife for company, she was taken to a children's home run by the state's welfare institution, Auxilio Social, as well as to a public medical center's inauguration, a training college for laborers, and a state-subsidized housing development. In Toledo, they even allowed a group of construction workers to approach and shake her hand. Wherever she went, she had something to say; each time they heard her assert the need to continue fighting for social justice whatever the cost, Señora Franco and the officials accompanying the guest were visibly unsettled.

I continued to juggle attending these events with escaping to see my son and writing my reports for Kavannagh. After the first few days, I realized that the foreign journalists were thinning out. To the annoyance of Diego Tovar's Diplomatic Information Office, after the event on Plaza de Oriente, the international press had once again lambasted Perón's and Franco's regimes, recounting the pseudo-fascist scenes they'd witnessed in the Royal Palace, as well as touching upon both the repression and misery in the country and the exorbitant cost of the visit. In order to soften the attacks, references to the first lady focused on harmony, joy, and friendship. To give color to the visit, the press gave it the sickly sweet name "the Rainbow Tour."

A rumor spread that from time to time, Señora Perón ignored the protocol, ducked off to visit poor neighborhoods, and gave out handfuls of money. I never witnessed this, and with her packed schedule, I couldn't have said when she would've managed to do it. It was also said—and it seems this part, at least, was true—that she persuaded Franco to pardon a communist who'd been sentenced to death for attacking the Argentine embassy using explosives, causing a lot of noise but no victims; Juana Doña was the woman's name. Rather than have her executed by firing squad in front of the Carabanchel Cemetery wall like her comrades, His Excellency commuted her death penalty to a magnanimous sentence of thirty years in prison.

Every evening was equally crammed with events, to which Eva Perón invariably began to arrive late as the week progressed. There was also a gala at El Pardo Palace with performances by artists just beginning to make a name for themselves, including a certain Carmen Sevilla, and the duo made up of Manolo Caracol and the dark-skinned girl who went by the name of Lola Flores. Another formal dinner was held at Casa de Cisneros, and a performance of Lope de Vega's seventeenth-century play *Fuenteovejuna* took place at the Teatro Español. Next on the schedule was a grand event in El Retiro Park, the largest of all the soirees to be held in Madrid.

Though I tried, I didn't manage to get out of it. Diego Tovar, who'd noticed my absence on some of the previous evenings, suggested that he collect me personally from the press club. Many of the international newspaper correspondents had already filed their stories about the first stage of the visit, while I, supposedly, was still gathering information for my report. As director of the Diplomatic Information Office, perhaps he thought there was still time to win me over to their cause.

The gala was to start at half past ten, and before ten o'clock more than a thousand guests were already waiting: leading figures, the entire government, the city councilors. Franco and Señora Perón's car, however, didn't arrive until twenty minutes past midnight. Everyone seemed amazed when word spread that the first lady had kept the Generalísimo and Doña Carmen—who'd been ready in their chevrons and necklaces—waiting for almost two hours at El Pardo while she preened. A man of military punctuality who was used to ruling with an iron fist, Franco must have been infuriated by such ill manners. However, he swallowed his pride and appeared smiling with his guest on his arm, showing no sign of displeasure. *A small price to pay,* the general must've thought. That very morning the *Río Santa Cruz*, the first ship of the Argentine merchant fleet to arrive since the end of the world war, had docked at the Port of Barcelona. It carried in its hold a thousand tons of wheat, almost two hundred of beans, and as many again of sugar. Its arrival would mark the beginning of a continuous to-and-fro of goods. Only for this was Franco prepared to put up with as many delays as were necessary.

Anyone who was anyone in Madrid was at El Retiro that night, waiting patiently for the evening to begin. There was talk of shady dealings used to obtain invitations, that some people had sold theirs for tidy sums or exchanged them for favors. Businessmen, political leaders, artists, black marketers, great men and their spouses, and plenty of gate-crashing social climbers—the whole catalog was there, everyone dressed to the nines. While we waited in the park for them to arrive, the air was thick with comments and gossip about *Doña María Eva Duarte de Perón*, as the press unanimously continued to refer to her. She'd been a variety-show performer and she used too much peroxide, the ladies cackled. She had a magnetism that could control even a headstrong macho man like General Perón, the gentlemen remarked with a touch of envy.

The cream of society, quite naturally, had also been invited to the event: titled aristocrats, wealthy men of distinction and ancient lineage. It was known, including by Franco himself, that this distinguished minority liked to have it both ways. Behind closed doors they remained monarchists at heart, anxious for the restoration of the crown to Juan de Borbón, and considered the Generalísimo an uncouth boor without merit or class. Publicly, however, they'd installed themselves comfortably in the regime that reinforced their privileges.

Many of this select group had some connection with Argentina, so they were aware of the tensions that existed in that place between its oligarchy and its first lady. Buenos Aires's high society had branded her a coarse and spiteful social climber, and she in turn had launched an all-out attack on that opulent elite, so remote from her humble origins and her efforts in the entertainment world. She was famous for her slights against those who possessed vast cattle ranches, had English governesses for their children, did their shopping at Harrods, and traveled to Europe every year. She even claimed that the richest among them took cows along on the ship. People with surnames like Álzaga, Anchorena, Unzué, Larreta, Martínez de Hoz, Blaquier, Uriburu, and Lezica, who lived in Frenchified mansions, traveled in sumptuous Bentleys, played golf and polo at the Tortugas Country Club, danced on the roof garden at the Alvear Palace Hotel, and had a box at the racecourse. Families whose holidays, parties, and marriages were photographed for *El Hogar* magazine; clans whose men were members of the Jockey Club and whose women took tea at the Café de Paris or the

Confitería del Gas and did charitable work in the exclusive Sociedad de Damas de Beneficencia.

Having been battered by the civil and world wars, the Spanish upper classes were far removed from the lavish Buenos Aires of that time. Most of its members were as rich in breeding, land, and titles as they were poor in pocket cash and their bank accounts. But the two groups were of similar stock, rich from the cradle, and so these elite looked down on Spain's guest of honor with a touch of contempt.

An enormous central stage had been erected between El Retiro's trees. Around it were dozens of chairs, tables laid for dinner, waiters, and strings of lights. As soon as Franco and Señora Perón made their entrance, the national anthems were sung. The entertainment and dinner followed, everyone ravenous by now.

They were serving coffee when I sidled off in search of Alberto Dodero. Warm and gallant, he introduced me to two key figures in Eva Perón's retinue whom I'd identified at the Royal Palace and was enormously curious about: her female companion and her brother.

The woman, Lillian Lagomarsino—a lady of refined, wealthy, and conservative origin—had embraced the Peronist creed alongside her husband and subsequently found herself obligated to become the first lady's loyal attendant on her journey. Lillian accompanied her patiently wherever she went, advised her on matters of etiquette, instructed her in good manners, and acted as a moderate counterbalance to Señora Perón's often tempestuous character. As we exchanged a few words, it became obvious that she wouldn't be much use to me: disciplined and discreet to the extreme, she stubbornly resisted my questions.

The other specimen was Juan Duarte, "Juancito." A couple of minutes in his vicinity was again enough for me to rule the former soap salesman out. There he was in his vanilla dinner jacket, with his little mustache, his cigarette, and his glass of brandy in his hand, admiring the derrières of the youngest ladies, bored stiff and indifferent to everything. He didn't know where the next stages of the tour would take him, nor did he care. His only thought now was to get out of there as soon as possible and enjoy the rest of the night. In the past days, he'd met a Mimí in Villa Rosa de Chamartín, a Monique in Pasapoga, a Lupe in Chicote. The three of them were waiting for him, and he had only to decide which he would opt for or whether he would take the trio as a package to his room at the Palace Hotel.

With no prospect of getting anything out of either of them, I turned my attention back to the magnate. I complimented him on his tie, accepted a Dunhill and a few flattering comments, laughed at a couple of his jokes, and let him brush my shoulders with the excuse of rescuing me from a bug that had fallen from a branch. After waiting a prudent amount of time so that I wouldn't seem too brazen, I pounced again.

"And the dressmakers, my dear Alberto. Do we know anything of them?"

"Of course, the dressmakers . . ."

He had no interest at all in the matter, of course. But he'd promised to help. And there I was in front of him, reminding him: insistent, smiling, waiting.

"Do you like bullfighting, my dear?"

"Not really."

"We have a *corrida* tomorrow, at five o'clock if my memory hasn't failed me. They won't attend, that's for sure. Perhaps that would be a good time to go and see them."

Then he drew a little closer, as if to speak without the loyal companion and the brother hearing him. He smelled of smoke and too much aftershave lotion: French and expensive, I presumed.

"Let's keep it between you and me. I don't know whether Evita would like the idea. I, on the other hand, am sure it will be good publicity for her and the tour. I'll send you my car at half past four."

He couldn't say anything else; we were interrupted by a group of gentlemen. Like so many others, they wanted to meet General Perón's friend, smile at him, flatter him, shake his hand with manly affection. As soon as I saw that Ralph Forte, the United Press journalist, was about to leave, I joined him and slipped away.

I also managed to get away the next day and have lunch at my father's house. Víctor welcomed me with his usual joy, wrapping his arms around my neck with delight. To my sorrow, every time he did so, the uncomfortable memory of Ramiro returned to my mind, and somewhere deep in me I felt a stab of grief for the child I'd lost.

My father listened in astonishment as I confided in him.

"Do you really intend to waltz into El Pardo with no official permission to speak to some dressmakers?"

That was indeed what I was going to do, as strange as it seemed. The shipowner's Cadillac did not collect me at half past four as we'd agreed, but at a quarter to six, it arrived. The driver, a skinny man in an oversized peaked cap, greeted me with his Buenos Aires accent. *Armando*, I remembered he was called.

"Sorry for the delay, señora, but the delegation has only just left for the bullring."

I almost burst out laughing; Eva Perón was as cool as steel. After keeping Franco and the cream of Madrid waiting for two hours the night before, now she'd done the same thing again, testing the patience of both the bullfighters and the leader.

"Is there a message for me from Don Alberto?" I asked, containing my nerves. It was clear that I was heading to El Pardo Palace, but I didn't have the slightest idea what to do once I got there, whom to speak to, or if anyone was aware I was coming.

"Nothing, señora."

At the end of the civil war, Franco had chosen as his residence that old palace that was surrounded by scrubland, a place that for centuries the Habsburg and Bourbon monarchs had used for hunting and recreation. Just a few miles from Madrid, it was a stark but majestic building with slate roofs and a big wrought-iron gate at its first entrance. To my surprise, Dodero's chauffeur only had to wave to be granted immediate access, as if he had at least a government minister in the back instead of a fake reporter. Once we were inside the grounds, after driving through the gardens, we passed through a broad stone arch. We stopped outside what had once been an entrance for horses. Armando quickly got out to open the door for me.

At the same time, Doña María Eva Duarte de Perón was waving as she exited an equally opulent car at Las Ventas bullring. The crowd outside, fired up after waiting for an hour and a half, fervently cheered her once more, jumping up and down to catch a glimpse of her black mantilla, remarking on the claret-colored double carnation she wore at her ear. She was accompanied by Franco, dressed in an everyday suit, and Doña Carmen and their daughter with *madroñeras* covering their heads, all three hiding their annoyance at yet another delay, smiling at the audience as if nothing had happened.

The evening would begin with a Goyaesque parade marched to the beat of paso dobles. Gitanillo de Triana, Pepe Luis Vázquez, and the Argentina-born Raúl Acha, known as Rovira, were to be the matadors. The ring was decked out with coats of arms and floral shawls, and the stands were packed to the rafters. No one cared in the slightest to remember that just a few years before, during Himmler's visit to Spain, it had been swastikas as big as bedsheets that adorned the arena while the band played the German national anthem, and the spectators all raised their arms as one.

"The lady is visiting Señora Perón's rooms," Armando announced to the two soldiers guarding the entrance. He sounded confident, as if he'd been through the same process many times.

The pair stood to attention to allow me in. They neither asked questions nor requested identification.

My heels clicked loudly against the great courtyard's paving stones, but nobody came out to meet me. I hesitated, even turned my head to ask the driver if he knew where I should go, but he was already back at the wheel. Slowly, I walked on.

Rumor had it that the presence of Eva Perón and her entourage had turned this grand house upside down. Before their arrival, the organizers had had to renovate rooms, tile some old bathrooms from top to bottom, replace the mattresses, and move a mass of furniture and objects. They'd installed electrical connections, light switches, and sockets, as well as new telephone lines, passing cables over the roofs and through the windows. Since Señora Perón had settled in, cars had come and gone at all hours, transporting people, messages, orders, and gifts back and forth.

The switchboard was practically giving off smoke; day and night, calls to Buenos Aires were requested so the first lady could speak to her husband or the cabinet ministers.

The dressmakers, hairdresser, and companion were the only ones staying here with Señora Perón. However, Dodero and Juancito came and went from El Pardo as they wished, as did the military aides, various attendants, the official photographer, the speechwriter, Father Hernán Benítez, and the embassy staff. They could request anything from the kitchens at any hour; the sound of orders being placed, people running, and doors slamming was constant, and organizational changes had been made everywhere. It was the first time someone from outside the family had stayed in the palace, and the lively troop of Argentines had blown to pieces the quiet bourgeois comfort in which the Francos lived. It was said that Doña Carmen was frothing at the mouth while swearing by all that's holy that she would never host strangers in her home again.

It was also rumored that, though they shared the same residence, the guest preferred to keep to a bare minimum the amount of time she spent in the company of her hosts. With distance between them, in her rooms she behaved in her usual way, ranting and raving whenever she liked. There, among her people in her private space, she continued to refer to the Generalísimo's wife as *la Gorda*, Fatty, though Doña Carmen was as thin as a rake. Of Franco, she maintained that he had the look of a shopkeeper, and their daughter, Carmencita, she renamed *la Nena Mirona*, Nosy Girl, on account of the young woman's habit of observing her with fascination.

That evening, however, at that bullfighting hour, the atmosphere at El Pardo was unusually calm. I kept going, but still, nobody appeared. It was hot, and the late departure to Las Ventas must have been tense and unpleasant. But finally they'd left, and the staff knew the bullfight would last several hours. Another gala dinner had been organized by the mayor that evening, so the household had no preparations to make. I supposed the workers were enjoying a moment's respite, some calm amid the storm, perhaps dozing in their quarters, doing crosswords, or listening to a serial on the radio. I continued slowly, my throat dry and my stomach tight. I was entering the official residence of the Spanish head of state, one of the world's most controversial figures, with a reputation for showing not the slightest bit of mercy to those who crossed him. In my handbag I carried a British passport with a made-up name and a BBC card, credentials from a foreign corporation I didn't really work for. No one had invited or authorized me to enter the building, other than an Argentine fat cat who was used to doing whatever he pleased, with the boldness that wealth brings. And my mission was to find two anonymous dressmakers, two simple workers, hardly illustrious guests.

If this had been some contest in sinister behavior, I would've taken all the prizes.

42

I entered a dimly lit corridor. The only sound I could hear was a heavy *ticktock, ticktock, ticktock*. A dozen paces on, I found its source on top of a chest of drawers: a splendid clock on a marble base. The time was twenty minutes past six.

From the walls hung banners and coats of arms, oil paintings and large tapestries. I opened a door, slowly turning its handle. Inside I found a palatial room with low tables and armchairs, a large ceiling chandelier, and frescoes on the walls. I assumed that this was a waiting room for nobles. I closed the door carefully and continued along the corridor. My footsteps were silent now on the thick carpet. I gripped the next door handle and again turned it slowly. The door creaked and I held my breath—this room was even bigger, with an enormous damask-draped table equally suited for feeding thirty people or hosting large meetings. I went on, detecting no trace of a human presence. Three doors later, I had to hold my hand to my mouth to contain a scream—I'd just peered into what I assumed was Franco's office.

I retraced my footsteps in a hurry, intending to return to the courtyard. I was putting my head into the lion's mouth, and I had to get out of there no matter what. But I heard voices in the distance, men's voices—moving toward me or not, I couldn't tell. Distraught, I decided to head back into the corridor, walking quickly, quickly, and looking over my shoulder. I dodged and turned, going down more corridors that went on forever, no longer stopping to open doors. I finally found a staircase and guessed that it would lead me to the private areas, away from visitors. I tiptoed up the steps without stopping. There was now silence again except for the constant ticktock, as if there were hundreds of clocks spread around the palace. Without pausing, I let myself be guided by my most primitive intuition: if I'd just been in the area meant for formal receptions, perhaps logic dictated that Señora Perón and her entourage would be staying in the diametrically opposite direction. After covering a long distance, I began to notice a thick smell of flowers. I sensed with relief that I hadn't been wrong.

On top of every chest of drawers, console table, and shelf were enormous centerpieces, bunches, and arrangements of flowers, all competing to be the showiest and most colorful. Most had ribbons across them identifying their senders. *The Spanish Trade Union Organization, the Provincial Court, the Guild of Printers, the Railway Workers' Association* . . . tokens of affection by the dozen for the Argentine first lady, giving off an almost nauseating fragrance.

The furniture and decorative objects were still sumptuous here, but something seemed different. Before long I realized that the walls and ceilings were newly painted in a much brighter white than the lifeless tone of the rest of the building's interior. A ton of flowers, fresh paint, and a location at the opposite end of the palace. Everything indicated that now I was finally where I needed to be, even if no one was waiting for me.

I started knocking on the doors, but no voices came from behind them. I knocked harder. I waited. Nothing. *In for a penny,* I must've thought. As I had done downstairs, I opened them one by one. The first, a wide double door, led to a living room too elaborately furnished to be comfortable. The second opened onto a private dining room with a round table large enough for eight people. I imagined Eva Perón had breakfast or lunch there when she wanted to escape the tedious company of the Francos. I found nothing personal in either of these two rooms except another load of floral gifts.

The third room, however, was quite another matter. Still clutching the door handle, I contemplated the interior for a moment, lost for words. They'd turned this space into a sort of wardrobe, salon, and dressing room. Barely aware of what I was doing, with no thought to the possible consequences, I slowly went in. There was nobody here, either.

More than a dozen evening gowns, mantles, and shawls hung from the curtain rails. Waves and folds of silk, satin, lamé, and velvet spilled from up high, floating in the air, as if this were a dressing room at the opera. I cast my eyes over the pieces, and in a few brief seconds I was able to make out two very different styles. Some were sober and elegant, worthy of any dignitary on an official visit to Europe. Others were gaudy and overelaborate, more appropriate for stage productions than for a first lady.

Over the brocade upholstery of the sofas they'd spread out fur coats and stoles: sleek fox, smooth mink, a long ermine cape, sables. An enormous wardrobe with its doors open revealed her everyday outfits, in impeccable order. To the left were the two-piece suits, in plain tones with big shoulder pads, as straight and as sober as soldiers and reminiscent of the recently ended war. To the right, the day dresses, in an array of summer, floral, and polka-dot patterns.

Dazzled by the display, I approached a desk acting as a dressing table. On it sat tubs of cream, compacts, lipsticks, and talcum powders. Though I'd only seen her from a distance, I had the impression that Eva Perón had excellent skin, that she barely used makeup and only painted her lips bright crimson. I picked up a lipstick, recognizing the brand. I took the lid off, turning the base until a cylinder of pearly tangerine came out.

Another table, whose original function had perhaps been the serving of dainty refreshments, had been covered with a white towel. On top of it, hairdressing accessories were impeccably lined up. Brushes and combs with different uses. Crimpers, curlers, hairnets, rollers of all shapes and sizes. I found several hairpieces in the form of buns and chignons hanging from braided wire stands. There were also bottles of nail polish and a few more of perfume.

Against a wall, two Empire-style chests of drawers were home to the hats. Each one had its own stand: bonnets, caps, elaborate tiaras, headdresses with tulle or feathers, wide-brimmed summer hats of raffia, abaca silk, and pleated horsehair. With great difficulty I resisted the urge to try one on. The shoes were arranged in a long row on the floor, made-to-measure, no doubt, and numbering more than twenty pairs. The plainer day shoes were at one end, in python, lizard, or dyed leather. Then there were the evening models, jet black and sparkling.

They'd removed a pair of candelabra from a console table in the corner to set down a small blue leather trunk. I tried to open it, without success. I supposed it was the jewelry case and that someone was jealously guarding the key.

Back in London, Kavannagh's reports had barely touched on the first lady's "humble origins." *Cinderella from the Pampas*, America's prestigious *Time* magazine would later name her. The reference to the fairy tale, given what I saw in that reception room, would make perfect sense to me. No one who did not know otherwise could ever have suspected that such a display could belong to a woman who was not yet thirty, a daughter born illegitimately and raised in poverty in a dusty town, an ordinary-looking woman, with no great talent or education. Pursuing her childhood dream of becoming a performer, she had packed her handful of rags in an old hardboard suitcase and put on her hundred-times rewashed blouse, her skirt of cheap percale, and a shabby pair of shoes inherited from her mother. With this modest gear plus her dogged audacity, she took a train to the capital. She was fifteen and dark haired, with neither contacts nor money. Nevertheless, she managed to elbow her way into the world of radio drama, where she remained until her relationship with Perón changed the direction of her interests and she became one of the most powerful women on the planet.

Some people branded her a despotic upstart, others a benevolent angel. Some spurned her and others adored her. I didn't know enough to be able to align myself with either of these two positions, but right then, looking at that scene, I became aware, fully aware, that Eva Perón was indomitable and afraid of nothing.

"Can I help you?"

I almost screamed. Behind me, I'd just heard the voice of an Argentine man. My presence had undoubtedly surprised him. Surprised and angered him, judging by his tone. A brand-new carpet had been laid in the rooms renovated for the guest, and this was why I hadn't heard his footsteps. I pressed my eyes shut and wished for the ground to swallow me up. Then a light turned on in my mind and I exclaimed, "Don Julio!"

The entire file was suddenly available to me in my mind. Julio Alcaraz, Señora Perón's personal hairdresser. Of mature years, serious about his profession, a family man. They'd met when she was aspiring to stardom. She'd never managed it, but along the way she had made some friends, and this stylist of actresses was one of her closest. From his hand came the elaborate pompadour hairstyle the first lady wore.

I strode toward him. He hadn't moved from the doorway. A gray-haired fifty-something, I saw, not very tall. He was wearing pale trousers and a shirt unbuttoned at the chest, and over his shoulder he had draped a towel. I did more than just offer him my hand—I gripped his and practically forced him to shake it.

"It's a pleasure to meet you. I'm here on Señor Dodero's recommendation. He gave me permission to meet you and your colleagues."

He remained silent, motionless, a stern look fixed on his face. *Who the hell is this intruder invading our sanctuary?* he must've thought. I hadn't bargained on encountering him either, but now I was aware that I had to win him over.

"Don Alberto insisted I should meet you. The work you're all doing—to amplify Señora Perón's elegance and make the tour a success—it's magnificent."

Dodero. Don Alberto. Don Alberto Dodero. I had a feeling that he was the key to not raising suspicion. I had to press home that I was there with the magnate's blessing, though he seemed to have forgotten, or not deigned, to inform them. But the hairdresser remained unmoved. Emerging from his shirt pocket, like an identity badge, was the end of a comb.

At his lack of reaction, my brain began to race. Friendliness clearly wasn't going to pay off. So I opted for another strategy, remembering the old adage that attack is the best form of defense.

"I'm very glad you're finally here for our appointment, because I've been waiting for you quite some time."

Now his expression did change, and he questioned my words with a frown.

"You didn't receive the message from Don Alberto?"

Now I was the serious one, with a touch of irritated disbelief in my voice and feigned reproach on my face.

"These messengers are hopeless," I mumbled with supposed indignation. "They should've told you I was coming. Our meeting's scheduled for six o'clock sharp. I was very surprised not to find you here."

He finally reacted, shrugging uncomfortably.

"We didn't know . . ."

I tried not to show my delight. I'd done it. But just to be sure, I tightened the screw.

"It may not be your fault, but the delay has made me feel tremendously uncomfortable. I don't know if there will be some consequence . . ."

I was sorry to be so impertinent, but I couldn't think of any other way to get him on my side. Eva Perón was famous for her temperamental character and impetuous reactions. It was clear the hairdresser Alcaraz had no desire to anger her.

"I'll fetch them right away . . . ," he sputtered.

I followed him, any trace of my discomfort now gone. He went to the door at the end of the corridor, and I stopped a few paces behind him to wait. When he opened it, in the foreground I saw three enormous trunks, and a tall pile of hatboxes behind. Farther back still, I spotted the foot of a bed, Alcaraz's own, perhaps. Maybe he was accommodated there so he would always be near Doña Eva, to do or undo her hair whenever needed.

He opened a window and waved his arm energetically. No one seemed to respond, so he tried again, moving both arms now like a windmill's sails. Still no answer. In the end, he had no option but to stick his fingers into his mouth and whistle loudly across His Excellency's regal gardens.

43

The personal stylists arrived a few minutes later in a fluster. They had been alarmed by Don Julio's urgent gesticulations from the window, a sign that something wasn't as it should be.

Asunta Fernández, from the Henriette fashion house, was in her forties and wore her hair gathered in a silk headscarf. Juanita Palmou, of the Paula Naletoff house, was of a similar age and was holding a pair of sunglasses and a light-colored, wide-brimmed hat in her hands. The former was tall and slender; the latter, curvy with a flushed complexion. I'd assumed the women tasked with ironing garments and doing up fasteners would be two tender young assistants I could easily have eating out of my hand, so I was surprised to find myself facing a pair of seasoned professionals, like the one my mother had been when she was employed at Doña Manuela's workshop. Except these women were from Buenos Aires, where there was a great deal more money and glamour than there had been in an impoverished prewar Madrid. As a dressmaker, I'd skipped this intermediate step and gone from young seamstress with potential to owner of my own businesses, first in Tétouan and then in Madrid's Salamanca neighborhood. But they didn't need to know any of that.

I greeted them without the flippant insolence I'd used to neutralize the hairdresser's mistrust. However, I continued to pull the necessary strings to win them over.

"I'm here on Don Alberto Dodero's say-so," I insisted. "I'm very sorry that nobody informed you I was coming."

I waited for a reaction but they both remained stonily silent and were clearly uncomfortable. It had been a busy, complicated day for them, as every day had been since their arrival. Or, more likely, as all the days since long before that. It had been a busy, complicated day as every day had surely been since their respective fashion houses received the request to designate an employee to take care of the first lady's wardrobe on her tour of Europe. She hadn't been a regular customer of either house before that and had used their services only occasionally, since General Perón secured the presidency the year before. And of course, those dealings were rarely welcomed. As reputable ateliers and boutiques, both Henriette and Paula Naletoff had been dressing the ladies of the Buenos Aires aristocracy for many years—women of tremendous taste, class, lineage, discernment, and wealth. The very ones against whom the president's wife was waging a merciless war. Or vice versa. Either way, the result was the same.

The request had been a catastrophe for both businesses. Neither wanted to risk upsetting or perhaps losing their exclusive clientele by having their names openly associated with the president's wife, but refusing would be reckless. Nobody refused Eva Perón anything. Anyone who dared would face the consequences. The houses had agreed, of course, and prepared several exclusive outfits. And they put forward Asunta Fernández and Juanita Palmou as assistants, two trusted, prudent, and highly regarded employees who would perform the task with complete professionalism.

On the day of my visit, the planned itinerary had required four wardrobe changes: day wear for both the indoors and outdoors, two more outfits for an evening at the bullfight and a gala dinner. Which was perhaps why, once they'd finished their work and the official delegation had rushed off to Las Ventas, they'd allowed themselves to take the small liberty of visiting the palace swimming pool. Now, judging by their demeanor, they were convinced that it had been a bad idea. No one had given them permission, because there hadn't been anybody to request it from; their only boss was the first lady, and occasionally Don Alberto Dodero. In their absence, they'd authorized themselves, and now, standing dumbstruck in front of me, they appeared to regret their mistake.

"I'm here from the BBC in London to cover Señora Perón's tour of Spain. I'm preparing a report that will deal with various aspects of it, and Doña Eva's styling is an important one. Señor Dodero gave me the go-ahead to speak to you. Don Alberto also stipulated that the first lady mustn't be troubled about this meeting."

I sounded convincing—no duplicity or sweet-talking, just the truth. A truth that contained within it a tremendous lie about who I was, naturally. They seemed to relax a little, but they neither moved nor uttered a word.

"You should also know," I added, "that I have no ties to the Spanish authorities or this palace. Like you, I'm just a professional doing her job."

"And what is it you want from us, specifically?"

Finally, the tall one with the headscarf spoke. She didn't have the look of someone who liked to waste her time. Once again she reminded me of my mother as she'd been years before: dignified and serious, always proper. I knew the woman's identity from Kavannagh's reports, but I kept it to myself.

"Are you Señora Palmou or Señora Fernández?"

"Asunta Fernández, studio manager at the Henriette house, Buenos Aires, at your service."

She spoke with a mixed accent, some Argentine notes over a base of Peninsular Spanish. I assumed she was an emigrant, like so many others who'd left for those prosperous lands. I also noticed the look she gave the hairdresser. I sensed what their roles were in the trio. Julio Alcaraz was the eldest and the closest to Señora Perón, which was why before agreeing to my request, the stylist wanted to consult him—more out of fear of him letting the matter slip while he was doing Doña Eva's hair than out of hierarchical respect. Of the two fashion stylists, Asunta Fernández was the one who called the shots. The crazy idea to spend some time at the pool that evening must have come from Juanita, who appeared to be less dour. It had been an absurd notion, the three of them now seemed to realize. But they'd been cooped up for a week, working under pressure from the first lady and ignored by everyone else. Kept out of sight, isolated, and often performing minor tasks that fell well outside their usual roles because Señora Perón was traveling without a housemaid or personal assistants, and she hadn't been offered an attendant at El Pardo. Nobody had bothered to take them out for a walk in Madrid or a single glass of horchata; no one even remembered they existed. In Buenos Aires they'd lived independent lives, coming and going, making decisions, earning good salaries, and running their own departments. Now they were sleeping in servants' quarters, the hairdresser surrounded by empty trunks, the stylists sharing a small room furnished with bare beds.

The hairdresser finally assented with a quick nod, and the stylists proceeded to describe their most important designs for the various occasions the first lady was attending. At first they were reserved, stiff, then a little more fluid. I wondered whether to take out my notebook, to at least pretend to take notes. In the end I decided to keep it in my bag, sensing they would feel more comfortable that way.

From the start it was clear that, with a few exceptions, they were not working from a fixed plan. They proposed outfits depending on the schedule for the day, and Señora Perón chose them in the moment. I recognized some of the garments they showed me from events I'd attended where the first lady had sported them, but others were new to me. The stylists appreciated my occasional comments, and we agreed on various points of view. In short, we understood one another—how could we not when we spoke the same language? Mongol crêpe, silk charmeuse, chiffon, opaque satin.

As we talked, it became increasingly obvious that the creations we were looking at fell into two categories. The two stylists' houses and a few other select brands had provided the haute couture, the more sober and elegant designs. From other, very different creators—they mentioned one, Jamandreu—had come other, more extravagant models made with sparkles, flounces, and drapery, some even finished with marabou feathers.

Thanks to our common vocabulary, little by little the seamstresses grew more trusting, and when Don Julio was out of the room for a while, they let slip a few mild secrets. That they and Doña Lillian had tried to persuade the hairdresser to give the first lady less grandiloquent, cinematic hairstyles, featuring neither a profusion of ringlets nor bouffants, hairpieces, rolled quiffs, or banana buns. That they and Doña Lillian were trying to advise her to opt for more harmonious and less flamboyant outfits. And that in the end, Eva Perón always, without exception, did whatever she pleased.

"She should dress more like you," Juanita noted, assessing my outfit with expert eyes.

Asunta looked me up and down approvingly. I was wearing a grainy crêpe dress for the first time, a far cry from the stiff designs imposed by the world war, but free from frivolous details. Softer shoulder pads, a fitted waist, and an airier skirt. It wasn't my own creation, but I appreciated the compliment, coming as it did from those women.

"And this one?"

I held up an extraordinarily long sky-blue lace dress studded with sequins. The two women checked the door to be sure the hairdresser hadn't returned.

"It's a rather special design by Ana de Pombo. Señora Perón is keeping it back in case they go to London," Asunta announced concisely.

"In case—"

Juanita cut in.

"In case the king and queen receive her after all."

I pricked up my ears. This was precisely what I needed to know. And I hadn't even had to ask.

"But . . ." I probed, "that part of the tour's still up in the air, isn't it?"

They looked at each other, as if coming to an agreement.

"This business," Asunta admitted, "is making Doña Eva's life a misery, if we're honest."

This was where I needed the conversation to go. I honed my attention, sharpened my senses. To hide my interest, I continued to examine the outfit, focusing now on the accompanying cloak. It was finished with ostrich feathers and, when worn, would drag at least a yard along the floor. The striking ensemble was a bit much, almost carnivalesque.

"And what will determine whether she goes to England?" I asked while I allowed the fabric to slide through my fingers.

Asunta sighed, as if weary of the subject.

"She hasn't said as much publicly, but she's waiting for a formal invitation from Buckingham Palace. She hopes they'll accommodate her, and that there, as here in Spain, she'll be treated as a head of state. They're looking into dates. I heard it could be before July 20, after Italy and France."

I once again lifted the folds of the outlandish cloak in which she hoped to walk the halls, stairways, and corridors of Buckingham Palace. So that was it: Evita demanded regal protocol, tête-à-tête with the monarchs.

"And the first lady says that, if the king and queen don't agree, she won't go."

I couldn't hold back a sad smile. The audacious Eva Duarte de Perón had lofty aspirations, with that supposedly majestic cloak of hers that looked like something taken from a Hollywood melodrama. Perhaps no one in her circle had told her about the times of hardship and austerity Britain was going through, about how the main concern of the government and the people at this time was survival. Or maybe she did know, and she didn't care.

"London's one of her main preoccupations," Juanita reiterated. "She's always mentioning it and constantly asking whether an invitation has been received when she calls Argentina to speak to the president or ministers."

"She knows she's triumphed in Spain, so her work here is done," her colleague explained. "Now what interests her is London and the Pope."

I raised my eyebrows. I barely had to ask anything now. Luckily for me, the long days they'd spent in isolation without exchanging a word with anyone, my apparent friendliness, and their slight weariness had loosened the stylists' tongues.

"Look, this is the dress she's going to wear to the Vatican."

They showed me an extravagant black robe hanging from the curtain rail. It consisted of a cloak, hood, and enormous hem and looked as if three Evas could fit in it.

"It's a design by Madame Gres for the Bernarda Meneses house. She'll wear it with the Grand Cross of Isabella the Catholic on the chest during her audience with Pope Pacelli. She intends to see if she can persuade him to make her a marquise," Asunta explained. Her face remained deadly serious, but I thought I could hear a hint of sarcasm in her tone. Then she said again, "For the Holy Father to grant her the title of papal marquise. That's what she wants."

"And beyond that, for the whole tour to be a resounding success," Juanita went on. "The only thing missing if she gets what she wants in Rome would be to walk into Buckingham Palace through the front door."

"And . . . she wouldn't be content with a less regal invitation?" I probed.

Together they were rehanging the sky-blue cloak, their movements coordinated, working without looking at me, using their four skilled hands. A couple of sequins fell to the floor, and Asunta bent to pick them up. From there, crouching, she looked up at me.

"The Crown will receive her, or she won't go at all."

44

As soon as I arrived back at the press club, I started to transcribe everything the stylists had said about Señora Perón and Britain. Sitting at my desk with the window open onto the garden, I first jotted down some quick notes that I later set fire to with a match over the lavatory bowl. Then I uncovered the typewriter I'd brought with me from London, recalling the typing skills I'd learned from the strict tutor I was assigned. It had been only a few weeks since I underwent that accelerated learning. I'd since made the leap to Madrid, leaving behind Olivia and the Boltons, Ara and Camacho's BBC, and Kavannagh and his people. Everything that came next had happened in the very recent past, but at times it felt as if several long months had gone by. To my surprise, however, far from feeling relieved that I'd left that London that was so foreign to me, as time went by in my unfortunate and dispirited Spain, I was becoming increasingly aware of how much I valued England and the English. Though my stay among them had been brief, I'd learned important lessons from them about pragmatism, dignity, and integrity.

But this was no time for nostalgia—I had to concentrate. As the sun came down on one of the longest evenings of the year, I began typing at speed, using the organizational method I'd adopted in my work at the Núñez de Balboa studio and with my Nazi customers. I detailed the interests and demands of President Perón's wife, her insistence on an invitation from the king and queen. I also thought to mention her desire, after having been fêted in Madrid with the Grand Cross of Isabella the Catholic, to be granted the title of marquise by the Pope; the British might wish to start preparations to offer her a similar important honor. Once I'd finished, I extracted the page from the carriage, folded it, put it in an envelope, and hid it in the false bottom of my suitcase alongside other brief reports I'd written up over the previous days. They'd planned for me to meet my contact the next morning, the final day of the tour in Madrid. I still didn't know who the link would be, and neither did I know the meeting's time and place.

I flung open my wardrobe doors but, while plenty of style and good taste was represented there, it suddenly seemed tremendously bare. I quickly reconciled, though, that I had neither time nor a personal hairdresser nor a pair of skilled stylists to help me spruce myself up. That evening's dinner at the Ritz was being offered by Señora Perón in gratitude for the Generalísimo's hospitality before the tour continued its itinerary to other places on the Iberian Peninsula.

The Diplomatic Information Office sent several drivers to collect us. This time Diego Tovar didn't search me out to deliver me personally, but I found him waiting when I arrived at Plaza de la Lealtad, impeccable in his tailcoat and with his hand held out, ready to help me out of the car. Forever correct in his manners, he knew this was no time for flattering remarks. His appreciative gaze, however, spoke volumes.

Once more, a mass of people had gathered near the hotel to catch a glimpse of the Argentine first lady. While they waited for Doña Eva to arrive—whether late or on time—the onlookers entertained themselves by watching her guests. Residents from nearby neighborhoods out on their evening stroll, telephone operators, students, entertainment hopefuls, salesgirls, manicurists and apprentices, children, hustlers, and masses of maidservants from the distinguished houses nearby: all of them and more made up the throng that clapped, cheered, and shouted compliments indiscriminately to whoever was going in.

"The lady in the blue dress, in the blue dress!" they yelled as I went past. "Sensational! Sensational!"

The public display didn't seem to amuse my companion one bit. But in those days when almost everything else was banned or censored, the authorities had issued an emphatic order to allow any spontaneous expressions of fervor. So Diego Tovar, in his formal dress and with me on his arm, had no choice but to set aside his diplomatic preciousness and run the gauntlet.

The crowd grew denser as we approached the great doors of black iron. There was, however, some control there, as it was one thing to give the mob free rein to shout and cheer, and quite another to let them inside. To stop this from happening, a group of men stood firm near the entrance. Silent, serious, with cold gazes, they were there to make sure things didn't get out of hand.

When we reached the doors, a photographer emerged. He was about to take our picture when the crowd's collective enthusiasm caused him to be inadvertently pushed. He stumbled with camera in hand and trod on the hem of my long dress. This time I was the one who was thrown off balance. Stopped short, I had no option but to let go of Diego Tovar, and for a few moments, in my high heels, I thought I was about to fall. For a few agonizing seconds that seemed to go on forever, I remained teetering until someone I couldn't see behind me held me firmly by the waist and prevented me from toppling over. A wave of relief washed over me once I was vertical again. I composed myself and, still flustered, turned to thank my rescuer.

"Don't mention it."

His voice sounded deeper than I remembered. His face seemed thinner. He was wearing a rather creased suit of middling quality, and he had a receding hairline that presaged baldness in the not very distant future. Other than that, he was the same. Ignacio Montes, the boyfriend of my youth, had just stopped me from falling in public using his own hands. The same hands that had once caressed me, the ones that had welcomed me at the studio door every evening when I finished my work, and had given me paper cones of roasted chestnuts in winter and little bunches of jasmine bought for two *reales* in summer. The hands that would've worn a wedding ring that bound us together had it not been for the lowlife who came between us and who now, having returned to Madrid, was with great impudence passing himself off as an Argentine.

We didn't say another word to each other. Standing dumbstruck amid the crowd, we simply held one another's gaze until, by way of a goodbye, Ignacio raised two fingers to the rim of a hat he wasn't wearing. I could only pull my eyes from his and walk on, holding the arm of yet another man who wasn't him. I could hear more compliments being shouted, the sounds of flashes going off, yelling, clapping. Behind me, I was leaving a piece of my past: a man who was doing his job, supervising his subordinates, to make sure nothing went wrong that night. Somewhere within me, I felt a pinch of deep nostalgia.

Oblivious to my reunion with the past, Diego led me into the lobby, tucked under his protective wing.

"I took the liberty of requesting that you sit at my table. There's someone I think you'd like to meet for your report."

Typically, I was allocated a place with my press colleagues, the international journalists gradually diminishing in number and the Spanish ones unfailingly present. As head of the Diplomatic Information Office, Diego, on the other hand, usually occupied a more prominent seat. I nodded distractedly, the close proximity of my dear old Ignacio still in the forefront of my mind.

Our feet were beginning to ache from standing for so long when the nerves and excitement that heralded the arrival of His Excellency and the first lady, late as usual, began. Fortunately, since the Argentines were hosting the evening, after the inevitable national anthems there was no more official pomp, and before long we were able to start dinner. From a distance, I saw that for this farewell evening, Señora Perón had ignored her personal stylists' advice. She'd dressed and styled her hair as her whims dictated, as if for an MGM gala instead of a formal dinner in the staid Madrid of 1947. A mermaid silhouette dress in iridescent silver with a long matching shawl coming down from her hair. Enormous earrings, a striking necklace, rings, bracelets, a sash, and a brooch. Don Julio had outdone himself with his own hair gel, his blond coif rising several inches from the top of his head. The Generalísimo was in a tailcoat instead of a military uniform and wore the insignia of the Order of the Golden Fleece around his neck. The rest of the guests were sparkling in their family jewels and emblems of distinction, sashes, insignia, and medals of honor. Surrounded by this display of honorifics, I overheard a whisper: it seemed Franco was not at all amused that, on her last day in Madrid, his guest wasn't sporting the Grand Cross of Isabella the Catholic that he himself had conferred upon her.

Everyone at our long table of twenty or so diners seemed to know one another. The person Diego Tovar had thought would interest me turned out to be a stout gentleman with a plump face and curly hair slicked back with a copious amount of cream. It wasn't the first time I'd seen him, as he'd been a fixture at the events. This was Agustín de Foxá, second secretary of the Spanish embassy in Buenos Aires and 3rd Count of Foxá. "Agustín de Foxá, count of the same" was how he liked to introduce himself.

The great dining hall of the Ritz dripped with ostentation that farewell evening. Filled with lush plants and resplendent chandeliers, it made quite a display in that gray postwar capital where the streets were scarcely lit, and where the people stole bulbs from the streetlights and cables from the urban network in order to extract the copper wire to sell at Madrid's flea market. Despite the solemn regard commanded by the presence of the head of state and his guest, the atmosphere was jubilant, with many people breathing a sigh of relief because, after tonight, responsibility for the visit would be passed on to other cities. *Goodbye, good lady,* they must have thought. *And good riddance.* Farewell to the preparations and arrangements, the demands, urgency, hysteria, and anxiety of making sure everything was perfect in order to dazzle the wife of the Argentine president, to glorify the image of the Generalísimo, and to try to send the world the message that the regime was in excellent health.

With Diego Tovar to my right and a boring high-ranking official of some ministry or other to my left, the banquet got underway. My neighbor at the table, upon learning that I was with the BBC, began a long soliloquy about hunting in England. I pretended to listen with interest, while in truth my eyes and ears were tuned in to the rest of the table. Foxá was certainly the most talkative. With a lively, jocular manner of speaking, he went on to describe a recent tour of South America. "Lima is a Seville with earthquakes," he said as he made short work of the appetizers. "Lake Titicaca, a Mediterranean held in the air like a glass. From the air, at night, Rio de Janeiro is marvelous, incredible, superior to Constantinople." Everyone around him applauded his comments, and between verdicts, he voraciously dispatched wine and food.

"Spain is a nonentity as far as Argentina is concerned," he then proclaimed, his glass of wine raised like a flag. "The wealthy and educated of Río de la Plata either adore the Anglo-Saxon snobbery or look to France and everything French for inspiration. For Spain, in contrast, they feel only indifference, as if we didn't exist. What we were to those lands for centuries is a distant memory, and to them we're just a country of emigrants now, rough *gallegos*, as they call us. Stubborn, miserly halfwits, whether Andalusian, or Leonese, or Valencian, we're all *gallegos*, fit only to be porters, waiters, storekeepers, or bricklayers with knotted handkerchiefs on their heads. Do you know how Perón's ministers usually receive Ambassador Areilza? 'Here comes the poor starving *gallego*,' they say. 'Let's see what he has to say.'"

Foxá went on like this, captivating his audience without taking a single break. By the time the River Bidasoa salmon arrived, he'd won the attention of the entire table as skillfully as any prima donna might have done. Those closest to him gleefully passed on to those out of ear-shot the words and opinions belonging to the 3rd Count of Foxá and Marquis of Armendáriz, an old hand of the Falange, career diplomat, newspaper columnist, writer, and poet. Even guests at nearby tables pricked up their ears to listen to his witty remarks. With a few rare exceptions, like me, everyone in the dining hall had undoubtedly read his novel *Madrid de Corte a Checa*, which recounted the ups and downs of Franco's nationalist supporters in Republican Madrid during the war, the suffering experienced by the side that all those present that evening had been on, of course.

"How could I not be right-wing?" he bellowed proudly. "I'm fat, I'm a count, and I smoke cigars!"

There were only two people who seemed uninterested in his incisive monologue. One was my neighbor, who was still prattling on about pheasant and partridge, boar and deer. The other was sitting diagonally across from me. I had seen her before too, though only from a distance, at other events and visits that had been part of the program. She was a tremendously attractive young woman who stood out because of her height and her style, classier than the other well-bred ladies who made up Doña Carmen Polo's entourage. While Foxá extracted another wave of laughter with one of his irreverent comments, I observed her dis-creetly. Impassive, she kept her eyes on her plate, scraping it with her fish knife. Distracted, focused on herself, she wasn't even eating. She was wearing a cherry-colored sleeveless dress. Her neck was long, her hair dark chestnut, her features were beautiful, and her eyelids, lowered with a trace of sadness.

Our plates were taken away, the chateaubriand with duchess pota-toes arrived, and the gluttonous diplomat took the chance to move on to a new topic. While he demolished the meat and gulped down the red, Eva Perón herself became the theme of his performance. He knew what he was talking about—he'd been posted to the Spanish embassy in Buenos Aires for six months and knew the workings of the Peronist system firsthand. With ornate irony, he then proceeded to describe the first lady's efforts for social justice.

She was in the habit of spending hours at the Ministry of Work and Welfare, where she was as likely to receive the poverty-stricken, the underprivileged, and old women as she was ambassadors and bishops. From this location, President Perón's wife exercised her power, balancing hard bargaining, the saintliness of Our Lady of Lourdes, and a most magnificent generosity. By sheer force of will, she secured bicycles, pensions for widows, false teeth, mattresses, and bridal trousseaus, roof repairs, surgical operations, prosthetic legs, and thousands of cans of powdered milk.

While jumping from one anecdote to another, urged on by the comments and guffaws from the distinguished guests, Foxá still managed to polish off his meat and ask a waiter to fill his plate again as he finished another glass of wine. My neighbor to my left offered me his umpteenth observation about fox hunting with dogs, but I barely paid attention. The beautiful, inexpressive young woman, meanwhile, remained impervious, as if the chatter that everyone else was enjoying so much bored her to death.

"Isn't that right, Mery? Tell us if what I'm saying isn't true."

The diplomat had raised his voice, and, to my surprise, all eyes turned to the young woman. In response, she shrugged her shoulders without even looking at him, as if she couldn't have cared less about the question or the man. Her disinterest didn't seem to bother Foxá. Undeterred by the lack of reaction, he carried on talking, regaining the attention of the diners.

Our section of the table, however, was left with an uncomfortable atmosphere. Diego Tovar tried to lighten it.

"Mery, are you all right?"

She remained silent while the sound of voices, the clink of dishes and cutlery, and the popping of the first bottles of Spanish champagne, as the printed menu called it, ricocheted around the opulent dining hall of the Ritz.

Diego persisted.

"Mery?"

Finally, she looked up, her eyes big and dark, full of melancholy detectable even through her long eyelashes. She smiled mechanically, then muttered, "Perfectly all right, darling, thank you."

By then we had a swarm of waiters upon us taking away our plates and serving the dessert and the sparkling wine in coupes. Foxá's runaway mouth had dropped the subject of Eva Perón in favor of the imminent farewell bullfight of the celebrated matador Manolete. As a result of all the food, drink, and fierce verbosity, his chubby face had turned red, and he wiped sweat from his grandiose jowls with a crumpled handkerchief. There was a blotch of sauce on the white piqué of his waistcoat.

Indifferent to all of this, Mery slowly got up, straightening her body.

"Don't tell me she's his wife . . . ," I whispered to Diego, hiding my disbelief behind my napkin.

He nodded. To my surprise, she then addressed me, asking in excellent English if I would accompany her to the powder room.

45

"Your husband has a way with words," I said, to break the ice.

We'd left the great dining hall together and walked through the lobby. We'd powdered our noses and necklines together in front of the mirror, touched up our lipstick at the same time. But until that moment, we hadn't exchanged a word.

"My husband's an imbecile."

She spoke without drama, as if she'd simply mentioned the day of the week or an appointment with the optometrist. Then she sat on an upholstered bench, crossed her legs under the red gauze of her dress, and lit a cigarette. She didn't appear to be in any hurry to go back to the table. As a couple, she and Foxá were so ill matched that their pairing still struck me as inconceivable. She was young, of exquisite manners, beautiful, and composed. He was flamboyant to the extreme, a voracious eater, undoubtedly intelligent, but ugly, loudmouthed, and brash.

The interest she hadn't shown her husband she now directed at me.

"So. You live in London?" I didn't know when she'd learned this detail; I hadn't seen her pay any attention to me all evening. "I lived there for a few years, before I had the misfortune of moving to Spain."

She took a long pull on her cigarette, leaving a ring of red on the tip.

"I can't stand this country, or its people."

I remained in front of the mirror, pretending to return a lock of hair to the coil at the back of my head.

"And Buenos Aires?" I asked after a few seconds. "Do you like it?"

"At least it's the capital of a young, prosperous country. Do you know they even have a Harrods?" she said with a sardonic look. Then she was serious again. "At least I can swim there, play tennis, go around by myself without being branded as sinful. Or mad."

Her tone remained dispassionate, faintly frivolous. Even so, I was aware I had a potentially useful source of information in front of me. If she could tell me without a care that her husband was an imbecile, she might talk to me openly about other things.

"And do you know Señora Perón well? Have you had the chance to meet her?"

She looked at me while she puffed on her cigarette, her eyes fixed on the blue taffeta that enveloped me.

"Are you really preparing a report on her? You don't look like a journalist. I don't think you could afford an evening dress like that on a reporter's salary."

I reached for her cigarette case without asking for permission and put one of her cigarettes in my mouth. If she wasn't shy, then I wouldn't be.

"A full-time reporter for the British Broadcasting Corporation," I assured her brazenly after blowing out the smoke. "The genuine article."

She uncrossed her legs and crossed them again the other way. Ultimately, she didn't care who I was.

"Everything that bigmouth Agustín said about Eva Perón is true. She likes to appear ostentatiously generous in public, make extravagant displays of her devotion to the unfortunate, and browbeat anyone with means into supporting her cause." She spoke Spanish with a strange mixture of accents. "She's in a class of her own, Evita," she added. "To some she's shameless, resentful, arbitrary, impertinent, and despotic, with no restraint, culture, or class. Whereas to others she's a fairy god-mother fighting tooth and nail for the dignity and welfare of workers, women, children, and all the poor wretches that no one else ever cared about."

Yes. I was already aware of those contrasting perceptions. But I wanted someone to go a step beyond that, to give me a more balanced opinion, a midpoint between those who adored her as if she were the Virgin Mary and those who wanted her to go to hell.

"Do you know what I think is truly admirable?" she went on. She stood and took a final puff on her cigarette, narrowing her eyes so the smoke wouldn't go in them. "That she's a free woman."

I nodded slowly. I thought I understood her.

"At fifteen, Eva Duarte decided for herself what her future would be and went in search of it. In her early twenties, she chose the man she wanted to be with and made him hers. Once she'd done so, she didn't settle for living under the wing of the most powerful man in one of the most prosperous countries on earth. By his side but never subdued, she forged her own path and made something of herself through her own efforts."

Beautiful Mery then pushed open the door to one of the cubicles, lifted the toilet lid, and threw in her cigarette end with good aim.

"Nothing intimidates her," she added, coming out of the stall. "She bows to no one. Look at her now, sitting next to the tyrant Franco, dressed however she pleases and completely confident in herself. I've never known a woman so free, so autonomous in her opinions, decisions, and actions." She came closer. "Can you say the same thing about your life, my dear?"

I didn't answer. And the obvious was implied by my silence.

"Nor can I."

We checked ourselves in the mirror one last time and picked up our handbags to return to where we should be: dependable, obedient.

"Say it on the BBC. Tell the world," she concluded as our heels clicked on the marble floor of the lobby. Raised voices came from the dining hall. The waiters were now serving coffee and liqueurs. "Broadcast on your airwaves that Evita is unique and will go down in history. When there's nobody left that remembers you, me, or my husband's clowning, when Franco's glory has evaporated and everyone who adulates him now fades into the background, Eva Perón's memory will live on."

46

We were almost alone as we drove along Paseo de la Castellana, the night air lashing our faces. Plaza de la Lealtad and Neptune with his trident were behind us, and we passed the goddess Cybele while Diego Tovar informed me of the next stages of the tour.

"The flights to Granada will take off at half past five tomorrow evening. Señora Perón will travel in a plane with her delegation, and our official escort and the press will follow. As soon as we land, the events will start."

We'd passed only two or three cars going in the opposite direction. At Plaza de Colón two workers were watering the road with enormous hoses, and Diego had to swerve so that we didn't get wet. We continued along the broad avenue lined by greenery, public buildings, and old mansions. I closed my eyes for a moment while my skin's pores and the roots of my hair absorbed the cool of the night.

"I wanted to apologize, Livia. Perhaps it wasn't such a good idea to seat you at our table," he admitted, completely changing the subject. "Foxá wasn't at his best this evening."

I thought about the unusual couple. They'd left the Ritz the same time we did. She'd walked ahead, upright, tall, and beautiful, sheathed in gauze. He'd followed a few paces behind her, drunk and sweaty, moving with heavy strides, his shirtfront dirty, his tie knot half undone.

Over the purr of the engine, Diego gave me a brief account of Mery Larrañaga de Foxá's background. The daughter of a Peruvian executive at Shell and a Spanish lady of noble ancestry, she'd been transferred at a young age, at the family's behest, from London to Seville. Before long, she was being pressured to marry a man twice her age whom everyone found exceedingly charming. Everyone, that is, except her. But he was an aristocrat, rich and famous. And a diplomat. That was perhaps the only thing she'd been faintly attracted to: the possibility of being taken far away from that dusty, impoverished Spain.

"When we attended the wedding in Seville, all her friends could see that the marriage was a farce. I'm no authority on marital matters, I have no experience, but there in the Church of the Hospicio de los Venerables, and at the reception afterward in the courtyard, it was obvious that the match made no sense." He stopped for a moment, as if retrieving fragments of memories. "She didn't so much as look at him the entire time. He ended up drunk as a lord."

His expression fell somewhere between melancholic and sarcastic. I observed his profile for a few seconds while he continued to grip the wheel. The wind had ruffled his hair, and his brown fringe flapped over his forehead, giving him an almost youthful appearance despite his forty or so years. Diego Tovar de las Torres was an attractive man. Handsome, of good family, successful. A good catch, all in all. I wondered why he was still unmarried.

"But Agustín adores her," he went on, as if to exonerate Foxá.

"She can't stand him. She thinks he's an imbecile."

He gave a bitter smile.

"He's an extravagant bon vivant and idler, he never shuts up, and he's a disaster in matters that require discipline and methodical work. But he's a man of brilliant wit who loves his wife. He loves her badly, but he loves her. Deeply."

We overtook a junkman's cart pulled by two mules. It was piled high, crowned by precariously balanced cardboard and bundles of paper. That was when he confided in me.

"She has decided to make up for her unhappiness by being unfaithful to him. She doesn't even bother to hide it, does it in full view of everyone. We all know about it."

I remembered her smoking on the bench with her legs crossed, the back of her head resting on the tiles. I wondered if she'd had one of those affairs with Tovar.

"And him. How does he react?"

Diego guffawed.

"With admirable stoicism. He says without any embarrassment that he would prefer to share a diamond than have a turd all to himself."

We both laughed into the night air. There were few lights at that last section of the Castellana, near the racecourse, the vacant lots, and the leveled land.

"Afterward, to console himself, he attacks his rivals with scathing wit and dedicates poems to them."

We turned right into a dark and deserted Calle del Pinar. He stopped the car outside the press club. On any other occasion, he would've quickly climbed out to open my door, but this time he didn't move.

"They're strange, relationships between men and women," he said, turning off the ignition. It was a banal statement, but something in his tone made it seem sincere.

"Why have you never married, Diego?"

I immediately regretted my question. Our association had been easy, he had just confided in me about the marital affairs of a friend, but our relationship was purely professional, and that is where it had to remain. Yet the question had popped into my mind, perhaps because it was very late and because I was exhausted from all that pretending to be someone I wasn't, or perhaps because the complexities of the human condition were growing ever more incomprehensible to me.

My curiosity didn't appear to bother him. Or even to surprise him.

"I came close, but the war broke out. She had to leave because she was a diplomat's daughter and . . . well, a reunion wasn't in the cards. After that, I was posted outside of Spain, I was in Brazil, Chile, the Philippines, and later, when I returned to Madrid . . ."

He suddenly stopped talking and laughed bitterly through his teeth.

"Lies, Livia. Everything I just told you was lies. Excuses I make for myself. The real truth is that I haven't considered marrying again because I haven't found anyone who has captivated me enough."

Still parked outside the press club, we could see nothing but weak lights in the doorways of the nearby villas, the star-speckled sky, and in the distance, a pair of yellowish streetlamps. The only sound was crickets and cicadas, the occasional bark of a dog.

"I haven't found anyone . . . ," he repeated, "yet."

At that moment I knew I had to go. I had to get out of that car at once. But he stopped me. His hand covered my hand. His voice sounded assured, a husky whisper.

"Wait."

The rest happened by itself—his fingers on the back of my head, his mouth on my mouth. I couldn't refuse. A sudden weakness overcame me, as if the world were vanishing around me. As if my body were disintegrating and I had no more substance than a mass of foam.

Afterward, I tiptoed up the stairs, trying to collect my thoughts. Once I was in my room, I found an envelope that had been slid under the door. Written in innocuous terms, under the guise of an innocent meeting, was an invitation to breakfast at Embassy, the tearoom on the Paseo de la Castellana, at ten o'clock. Something crackled inside me. Embassy. It had been a long time.

I slept badly that night, dreaming a lot of strange dreams. Ignacio's hands on my back and me about to fall into an abyss. Foxá's bloated face bellowing with laughter. His wife sitting on the lid of a toilet smoking an interminable cigarette. Diego Tovar's kiss transforming into a long whistle. I woke early, and with my head still in a muddle, I gathered my belongings.

The last thing I did before setting off for Embassy was extract the reports hidden in the bottom of my suitcase. I decided to walk—it wasn't hot yet—so I could think to the rhythm of my steps. They hadn't specified who would be waiting for me, whether a stranger or someone I already knew. This didn't worry me, I'd become accustomed to this practice in the past, and it was how we'd proceeded many times. I recalled the person I'd been back then: younger and more fragile, more vulnerable, and more zealous about my own glamour, in keeping with the demands of my customers. Now I was walking in light trousers. Few women in Franco's puritanical Spain dared wear such a thing, but I could take the liberty, disguised as I was as a foreigner. I wore them with a linen jacket, my big sunglasses, and my hair gathered in a silk handkerchief. It had been a little over two years since my operations in Madrid, and a new world order had emerged since then. Both in form and content, I too was a different woman.

There was nothing juicy in the information I was going to pass on to the British secret service, but for the time being, I was obediently carrying out my duties. I had described my conversations, what I'd seen with my own eyes, and my general impressions of the Argentine first lady and the visit's progress. The rest of the tour of the Iberian Peninsula awaited me, and at the end of it, on my return to London, I would deliver another quantity of reports. With that, this unexpected chapter of my life would end, and I would return to the present. A present still undefined that would lead to a hazy future I didn't want to think about for now.

Embassy's entrance was on the corner of Paseo de la Castellana and Calle de Ayala. On one side, a bootblack was talking with a lottery ticket vendor; on the other, an old woman in a black woolen headscarf was begging with a filthy hand stretched out. A young uniformed employee opened the glass door of the tearoom for me, and without taking off my dark glasses, I saw that there were already customers inside. A handful of early risers drawn from the few foreigners who remained in Madrid at that time, some Spaniards who'd dutifully attended mass first thing and wanted to take home a tray of pastries for the family's breakfast or a lemon tart for dessert. Well-dressed ladies with cups of hot chocolate in front of them, gentlemen sitting down to drink a *café con leche* while they read the *ABC* or *El Alcázar*, one or two young men who hadn't been to bed yet, on their way home from carousing.

Just a few years before, when the Germans were still strutting around Madrid, this small premises had been the epicenter of intrigue, tension, conspiracies, and the transfer of refugees. I'd operated in the middle of all that, passing coded messages to Captain Alan Hillgarth or one of his men, sharing innocent teas with my customers, and conveying clandestine words of warning to various contacts.

The delicious smells reached me at once: trays of freshly baked Swiss buns, pastries, plum cakes, and croissants made with white flour and fresh butter. No, in this distinguished establishment they weren't in desperate need of the wheat that Perón's generous Argentina was promising to send to ease the hunger of so many. Rather, its owner, the admirable Margaret Taylor, used her skills to coax consignments of essential goods from various sources, with the help of her contacts. And so while most ordinary Spaniards started their Sunday with a glass of watered-down milk, an ersatz coffee made from chicory, or just a chunk of hard bread—while millions of families had barely enough to eat—at Embassy, hardship was an alien concept.

As soon as I took off my sunglasses, I saw him from the entrance, and my heart skipped a beat. It was a familiar face. Reading an out-of-date copy of the *Times*, smoking his pipe, waiting for me at the counter was Tom Burns, the former press attaché at the British embassy. We'd never had the opportunity to become close, but I knew that Marcus had worked shoulder to shoulder with him in the fight against the Nazi threat. I knew that he had been aware of our marriage, and that the two of them had held each other in high esteem. Remembering all of this, I was struck by a heavy wave of melancholy. I managed to compose myself and hide my feelings as best I could, drawing on the skills of deception I'd once used in other situations in this very place. With feigned coolness, before I burst into tears or hugged him, I held out a languid hand. He looked me in the eyes.

"Delighted to see you again, my dear."

My dear, he'd said. Not *Livia,* or *Arish,* let alone *Sira.* There were no Germans at Embassy anymore, nor informers or collaborators, it was presumed. Even so, it was wise to be prudent.

We sat at a table beside a pillar and ordered tea. Once the waiter was gone, Tom Burns extended his condolences for Marcus's death while a knot formed in my throat. He offered some words of praise for my husband but was tactful enough to stop just before I fell to pieces. He no longer worked for the British legation; like Sir Samuel Hoare and so many others from that time, he'd returned to London. In fact, very few people remained at the embassy now that, following the United Nations' decision to deny Spain membership, most of the ambassadors had been withdrawn from Franco's Madrid, and diplomatic missions were operating at minimum capacity. But Tom Burns's wife was Spanish, daughter of the celebrated physician Dr. Marañón, so the couple frequently returned. And on these occasions, for old times' sake, his friends in the secret service occasionally asked him for a favor. A favor like meeting me that morning, for example.

We made small talk, neither of us mentioning anything to do with Germany's surrender, the Nazi legacy in Spain, or the bloody King David bombing. We spoke only about the rising heat of the day that was already making itself felt, his profession as an editor in England, the Martínez restaurant in London, and the dreadful cold of the previous winter. No one noticed that, as we talked, I took the reports from my handbag while I pretended to look for a handkerchief. Nobody saw me inserting them between the pages of the *Times* that he'd left on top of the spotless tablecloth beside the sugar bowl. The procedure completed, we said goodbye with no further delay. I watched him leave with the newspaper under his arm and his pipe in his mouth. Through the glass I saw him rummage in his pocket and bend to give money to the black-clad old woman with the dirty hand.

I waited a couple of minutes after his departure, my tea now cold, and felt overcome by immense loneliness. Tom Burns, of the same age as Marcus and with a similar sense of duty, was going back to his life, his family, and the prospect of building a future and was looking ahead. Meanwhile, thanks to one of those sinister twists of fate, his friend Marcus Logan—Mark Bonnard—was no longer in the land of the living.

I managed to pull myself together and slowly stand up. I would've liked to buy a tray of cakes to take to Hermosilla, some sweets to delight Víctor with, some chocolates with which to thank Philippa and Miguela for their devotion to my son. But I didn't have the strength. I started to head up Paseo de la Castellana, seeking out the shade of the acacias. Behind my dark glasses—my being neither able nor willing to stop them—a few tears welled from my eyes.

47

"There's someone waiting for you in the garden. A gentleman, an old friend. He didn't give his name."

I clenched my fists. For days I had sensed this moment would arrive. I hadn't known when or where, but I'd been certain that, sooner or later, I would have to face him.

I was tempted to go back onto the street and run. Or go up to my room, barricade the door, lower the shutters, and hide there until he left. I didn't want him back in my life. I didn't want to speak to him or see him. I didn't even want to know that Ramiro Arribas still existed.

"Thank you, Señora Cortés," I replied in a quiet voice. "Would you be so kind as to request a car to collect me in half an hour?"

He was sitting under the patio awning, on one of the cast-iron chairs, his legs crossed, with the arrogant posture of someone who was capable of feeling comfortable anywhere. He'd been served something on ice, and the glass was half-full. He was perhaps less slender than he had been, but he remained an extremely attractive man in his white shirt and seersucker summer jacket. Like me, he was wearing dark sunglasses, which he took off when he stood up to greet me. I, on the other hand, kept mine on as protection, as a shield of sorts, or a shelter.

I had once turned my life upside down for my love of this man. He had stirred up an obsessive passion in me, irrepressible, deaf, blind. I had left my world behind for him, ended my relationship with my boyfriend Ignacio, distanced myself physically and emotionally from my mother. I'd left my neighborhood and my future, my support, and my country. I had put on a blindfold and taken his hand, diminished my free will, and allowed him to sweep me along. I'd trusted him, I'd allowed myself to be dazzled by his intentions, I hadn't questioned his actions or decisions, and I'd never resisted his foolish dreams. I had given myself to him completely: my body, my mind, and my recently inherited wealth. And he had let me down on every count.

"What do you want?"

"To know how you are, Sira, is what I want first and foremost," he said in response to my abrupt question. "Although maybe I should ask how you both are."

He'd lost the Argentine accent I had heard at the restaurant with Dodero.

"I'm fine, as you can see," I replied sourly. "And if you're asking me about the child I had inside me when you left, it doesn't exist. The pregnancy miscarried and it was never born."

I blinked behind my sunglasses, containing myself. I'd never spoken out loud about the baby that never came into the world. I'd thought a lot about it over the years, an awful lot—I still did. But since those distant days when I'd fled Tangier and arrived in Tétouan, when the blood had started dripping down my thighs on the La Valenciana bus, and Commissioner Vázquez had admitted me to the civilian hospital to recover from the loss, I'd never mentioned it again to anyone.

We were both standing, away from the sun of the approaching midday, under the black and white stripes of the awning. There was nobody else in the garden, for the time being.

"Please, Sira, let's sit down. Just give me five minutes, ten at most."

I hesitated but ended up agreeing. The press club wasn't the best place for me to make a scene. For my own benefit, I would be wise not to react, though it took all my effort.

"I want you to know first of all how much I regret the way I behaved in Tangier," he continued once we'd sat. "There are things I preferred not to tell you at the time, but I made mistakes. I was forced, pressured—"

I raised a firm hand to stop him. At this stage, explanations were superfluous.

But with apparent seriousness, he added, "The last thing I wanted to do was hurt you."

Son of a bitch, I thought. But it was in the past. Now wasn't the time to get into a fight. I just wanted the conversation to end, for him to go and leave me in peace.

"I'm glad to know that life has treated you well," he added, easing back onto the cushion behind him. "To see that you've become a . . ." He gestured, taking in all of me. "A formidable woman."

A waiter arrived, the same one who'd served dinner on the first evening. I told him I didn't want anything. I refused to drink so much as a simple glass of water with Ramiro.

"I always thought you were special. Unique," he went on as soon as the waiter had turned away. "I've wondered many times what became of you, how you had—"

I didn't let him finish.

"From Tangier I went to London, while the war was still going on in Spain. I was offered a job, I settled, I progressed, and I've done well for myself, thanks."

The lie came to me on the spur of the moment. I needed a wall between us, even if it was one built of falsehoods. I was reluctant for him to know what had really become of me. He had no right to invade my past, as he was trying to do now with my present. Tétouan, Marcus, Madrid and my covert activities, Jerusalem, and Víctor—Ramiro had to stay away from all of it. There was no question in my mind about that.

"To say you've done well is an understatement. You've done very, very well," he insisted. "It's obvious. You're still beautiful, but now you also have an air of sophistication and confidence, style, and . . ."

He reacted quickly to the displeasure on my face and stopped the flattery about my appearance, but he carried on complimenting other qualities.

"But most of all I'm amazed at how well you handle yourself."

"It's necessary in my line of work," I stated.

"Well, being in the service of the BBC isn't just any old job . . ."

It was obvious: he'd been checking up on me. How and through whom I couldn't say. Nor could I know how much he'd learned about me, how far he'd gotten with his inquiries. Still protected by the bulwark of my dark glasses, I observed him closely. He had gray hairs at his temples, more than a few, but he wore them well. I already knew that from when I'd seen him at Villa Romana on my second night in Madrid. His clothes were impeccable, and he had a barbershop shave. A fine watch with a snakeskin strap was poking out from under his immaculate shirt cuff, though I couldn't make out the brand. He'd gained a few pounds, perhaps, but apart from that, he'd barely changed. He was still handsome in his mature years, the lowlife. Handsome and dangerous.

"My work is none of your business," I said sharply.

He made an apologetic gesture.

"It's not. You're right. But the truth is, I *am* interested in the company you keep." He leaned forward. "I know you're busy, and I don't want to waste your time, so I'll come straight to the point. I need a favor, Sira," he announced seriously. "One, just one, a single favor is all, and then I won't bother you anymore. I'll disappear from your life again, forever."

He held his right hand to his heart as if to seal his pledge. I almost told him to shove his promise where it hurt most and stop talking nonsense. I wasn't going to do any favors for the wretch. Whatever it was he wanted, no. Never, not anything. But before I could refuse, he laid his cards on the table.

"Dodero. I need a private meeting, on your recommendation, with Alberto Dodero." He paused, then as if the statement required clarification, added, "The Argentine shipowner. Your friend."

I held back a bitter burst of laughter. Here he was, living up to expectations—exceeding them, even, the same old crook. He'd seen me first dancing with Diego Tovar at Villa Romana, then sharing a paella with Dodero outside the Riscal restaurant. Perhaps, without me realizing it, he'd also seen me going in and out of other events. Who knew what he hoped to gain from all of this?

"I came with a group of businessmen from Buenos Aires. In recent years I've been working on investments and projects in Argentina, I'm a . . ."

If there was any trace of truth in these supposed affairs of his, it would undoubtedly have been thanks to the money and jewelry that my father had passed on to me and that I, with huge naivety, had left in Ramiro's care. Those wads of notes and valuable jewels that he'd taken when he fled Tangier, leaving me pregnant, penniless, and with a big bill to pay at the Hotel Continental.

"I'm a serious businessman, Sira. I have partners and companies. And to be able to extend the reach of these enterprises all the way to Dodero would be a singular opportunity that would enable me to expand exponentially. I won't bore you with the details, I just want you to know . . ."

Detached from his words, I was retrieving memories. It had been eleven years since he filled my head with nonsense about yet another entrepreneurial fantasy: the Pitman academies. We had planned to introduce them to colonial Morocco together. It was to have been a resounding success, one that would make us rich in no time. More than a decade later, Ramiro Arribas—or Román Altares or whatever he called himself now—was still around, no less shameless, fanciful, and sure of himself. He'd simply changed the size of his ambition. He used to be content with typewriters and typing methods, but now he wanted to do business with one of the most powerful shipping magnates in South America. Other than that detail, his desire for easy and immediate gain seemed unchanged.

He was still talking about his advantageous operations when I stood up. I'd had enough.

"I have to go, I'm expected somewhere."

He stopped abruptly and fell silent for a moment, as if thinking. "Sira, Sira . . ."

I made as if I couldn't hear him and turned my head. At the other end of the garden, the waiter was about to go inside after serving the Portuguese correspondent a drink.

"Excuse me, Secundino!" I called out. Obligingly, he approached our table.

"The gentleman's leaving. Could you please accompany him to the door."

He positioned himself beside my visitor with an upright, almost military posture.

In the end, Ramiro got up, albeit reluctantly, but he had no choice. I walked around the table until we were facing each other, just a few inches apart. I raised my face up to his, to those harmonious and masculine features that I'd adored during that time of foolish passion. I was so close that I almost brushed against the lips that had kissed me so often. I noticed the scent, unnerving and toxic, of the body that had once made my feelings go haywire. Slowly I moved my mouth to the ear into which I'd poured so many words on those nights of reckless love.

My voice, as it had been then, was a whisper.

"Forget I exist. I don't want to see you again."

48

My bags were packed, the taxi was at the door, and I felt like I was about to jump out of my skin. The encounter with Ramiro had shaken me, thanks to both his present impudence and the fact that he'd forced me to return to a painful past. His visit had also delayed my visit to my son, making the little time I had to see Víctor even shorter.

I was leaving the press club when the always serious Señora Cortés appeared behind me and asked me to wait a moment. I barely contained my irritation. I considered telling her that, in my absence, they should turn away anyone who said they were my friend or acquaintance or anything else. Crooks like Ramiro had the audacity to adopt any disguise.

I took the paper from the envelope she held out to me and quickly unfolded it.

> *I forgot to ask you how your parents are.*
> *I know your mother left the neighborhood a while ago.*
> *Does Don Gonzalo still live in his big apartment in*
> *the Salamanca area?*
> *To contact me:*
> *Román Altares, Hotel Buen Retiro, room 417*

A flash of rage ran through me like the lash of a whip. Ramiro had been back to my street. He'd been asking after my mother and me.

Fortunately, my mother, always prudent and cautious during the war, hadn't told anyone where she was headed when she left for Tétouan. We'd moved away years ago, the residents of Calle de la Redondilla must have told him. No one there had any more information than that, thankfully.

As for my father, that was a different matter. Ramiro had never gone to his house because at the time, Gonzalo Alvarado and I had had little contact. But Ramiro did know of the existence of the distinguished gentleman whose paternity of me had been kept quiet for so long. He was also aware of Gonzalo's splendid flat in the Salamanca neighborhood, his wealth, and of course the inheritance he'd unexpectedly given me when the war was about to break out and he thought he was going to be killed. But I couldn't remember the exact details I'd shared with Ramiro. Had I told him that my father lived on Calle de Hermosilla? Had I said he lived at number 8? Had I described Gonzalo Alvarado to him? Would Ramiro recognize him if he saw him? All these uncomfortable questions went with me as I headed out to see him.

The few hours I spent with my family flew past, just enough time for me to have lunch with Víctor sitting on my lap and to play for a short while on the rug. We tried to distract him again so that he wouldn't notice me leave, but this time the trick didn't work. Neither the porter's cat nor the thousand other things we tried had any effect. Fed up with my constant absence, his child's intuition warned him I was trying to pull the same ruse again. And so to stop me, he brought out the big guns: a colossal tantrum thrown at the very last minute.

The taxi to take me to the airport was waiting downstairs at four o'clock sharp, but I refused to leave with my son in such a state. Meanwhile, the clock ticked on to five, ten, fifteen, twenty minutes past the hour. At four twenty-five, Víctor seemed to calm down, and he fell asleep on the sofa. I started tiptoeing out to the hallway, my shoes in my hand. But the thick oak floorboards creaked before I reached the living room door, and my son, wary and on guard, opened his eyes.

Seeing that I wasn't beside him, he burst into tears again: a heartfelt cry that pierced my soul. Containing my anguish, I had no choice but to keep going. I knew he was in the care of Philippa and Miguela, under my father's wing, but even so, as I walked down the hall, his despair resounded in my ears. While I picked up my luggage and went down in the elevator and hurried into the taxi, unpleasant words echoed in my mind. *Traitor. Deserter. Selfish woman. Bad mother.*

I was late, extremely late. To make matters worse, the road to the airport was jammed with cars. Naively, I hadn't banked on the fact that, with Eva Perón's stay coming to an end, thousands of residents would be out on the capital's streets again. We moved at a snail's pace, and the taxi driver cursed and honked his horn. Torn by nerves, I insisted he try to push his way through.

"Speed up, please! Pass that van!"

I was going to be late. I was going to miss the flight. To the organizing committee, to the Diplomatic Information Office, and to my colleagues, I would look like someone who can't be relied upon, a lazy professional.

"Go right! Now left!"

The most important events were scheduled for that evening in Granada. Given the state of the old Spanish trains and ruined railways, if I traveled by land I wouldn't make it to Andalusia until the next day. I'd die of shame when I had to inform London that I'd been too slow and missed one of the stages of the tour.

"Try to get ahead, please!"

"I can't go any faster, for God's sake!" the driver yelled. "Can't you see, woman? Don't you realize it's not possible?"

I searched in my handbag. I tapped him on the shoulder and waved a hundred-peseta note in his face.

"It's yours if we arrive on time."

He veered off the road. Over arid fields, holes, and wasteland, with the car sweltering but with the windows up to keep out the hot dust and dry straw, we lurched into Barajas after the planes already had their engines going.

The band had finished playing the anthems, and the distinguished crowd was stirring in the stands. All around, as they had on the day of her arrival, both invited guests and casual observers had gathered under the fierce afternoon sun, and all were anxious to leave as soon as the first lady's aircraft took off.

I ran into the terminal with my briefcase in my hand and my steps hammering on the terrazzo. Behind me, the unfriendly taxi driver carried the rest of my luggage in exchange for an extra twenty-five pesetas. Diego Tovar roared with relief when he saw me. Outside the planes, just three or four men were still standing with him, the rest of the delegation and escort already in their places with seat belts fastened—a few, no doubt, whispering the Lord's Prayer in fear of the flight.

"Come on, come on!" Diego exclaimed, snatching my suitcase from the taxi driver's hands.

We hurried on a few steps in the direction of the second airplane until a yell cut through the roar of the engines.

"Livia!"

We both turned. It was Alberto Dodero calling me. As organizer and jack-of-all-trades for the tour, he was giving out final orders to the embassy staff remaining on land. Then he raised his arm with an urgent gesture, waving me over. Diego Tovar frowned, and I hesitated.

"Come with me! Come on our plane, there's plenty of room!"

I searched Diego's eyes. Without the need for words, we agreed that I couldn't refuse.

Dodero and I climbed the steps and boarded the aircraft. A mechanic sealed the door behind me now that everyone was inside. Dodero told a hostess to show me to my seat and Juan Duarte to inform Doña Eva of my presence. She was sitting in a window seat at the front, next to her uncomplaining companion Señora Lagomarsino, wearing a rather plain short-sleeved dress. On her head, however, she'd gone all out with another of Don Julio's hairstyles, crowned with an indescribable hairpiece with more flowers than a garden. The hairdresser and her personal stylists were in the second plane, fortunately, so we wouldn't have to pretend we'd never met.

The first lady was watching the farewell through the glass when her brother approached and bent down to speak to her. He must have told her that I was a trusted journalist or something similar, though I couldn't hear his exact words. Hers, after she'd looked me up and down, were louder.

"I know who she is. She's been with the tour from the start. Do you think I'm blind?"

He moved to one side, ceremoniously serious with his mustache and double-breasted three-piece suit. I stepped forward.

"Good afternoon, señora," I said respectfully.

"Nice outfit" was her reply. "All the clothes you've worn have been beautiful. Were they made for you here, in Spain?"

"In London, señora. An English dressmaker."

"I see!" she exclaimed in surprise. "Lilliancita . . . ," she said then, addressing her companion. "Lilliancita, since you have such good handwriting, would you note down the name of the lady journalist's dressmaker? Remind me to visit him when we go to London."

Several dubious but attentive faces turned toward her from nearby seats. The military aides. The Argentine ambassador Pedro Radío. The Spanish ministers of justice and agriculture with their wives. Dodero himself. Even Juancito, who usually couldn't have cared less about such matters.

"Yes, I said when we go to London! Don't look at me like that! When we go to London to see the king, if they ever send us the official invitation! And if they don't, I'll tell them all to go to hell!"

I managed to sit down while the plane was taxiing to the runway. As I fastened my seat belt, through the window I saw the masses applauding and enthusiastically waving hundreds, thousands of handkerchiefs.

Separated from the euphoria outside, I rested my head against the seat and closed my eyes while the aircraft took off. Little by little, I relaxed as we flew south through a clear sky over fields parched by years of terrible drought. *A prolonged drought*, the regime's officialdom called it. Finally, I was able to sort through my memories. I recalled my meeting with Tom Burns at Embassy and my nostalgia for Marcus, my son's crying and my distress at leaving him, the fear that I wouldn't arrive at the airport on time, the taxi's daring gallop over rocks and holes. All of that was behind me now, thankfully. I trusted that Víctor, with his good nature, had regained his eagerness to play, that he was laughing at everything and pulling the cat's tail. I imagined that the taxi driver was going around telling everyone that some daft woman had given him the extravagant sum of 125 pesetas to take her to the airport. Deep within me, however, I continued to feel the painful sensation of something profoundly unpleasant. A sharp splinter that went by the name of Ramiro.

It would've been very easy to solve the problem right there, a breeze. Given the fondness the Argentine magnate seemed to have for me, I could've stood up right then and gone to speak to him. Within minutes, no doubt, I could have secured what Ramiro had asked me for: a private meeting in which he could propose God knows what. If I asked, I was sure Dodero would even give him preferential treatment. But I refused to do so. Ramiro had no right to such a favor. After being so cruel, he didn't deserve for me to lift a single finger to help him now.

We landed at the Armilla air base at around half past six. As we descended the steps, we filled our lungs with the pure air of the nearby Sierra Nevada. Nobody could've foreseen the hard night that lay ahead.

49

There came another round of mass clapping and cheering, troop inspections, crowds, and artillery salutes. So that she wouldn't disappoint at the evening events, Eva Perón changed in her suite at the Alhambra Palace Hotel into another of her sumptuous outfits. To avoid repeating the mistake of the previous evening, especially in a city with such close ties to the queen herself, this time she didn't forget the Grand Cross of Isabella the Catholic. To the astonishment of everyone present, she also arrived at the city hall sporting an Alaskan mink coat over her shoulders.

The dinner in the assembly hall began with the now customary delay caused by the guest's late arrival. And once it started, it was extremely long, filled with anthems, speeches, food, and hundreds of diners. It was terribly hot in the improvised dining hall. At that time, a medium-sized city like Granada lacked large public spaces for such momentous occasions. The ladies brought out their classic fans while the men cooled themselves with the printed menus. Little air was entering through the open balconies, and only the noise of the crowd on Plaza del Carmen made it through. Dessert was being served when some distance from my place I saw that Eva Perón, feeling hot like all of us, was taking off the capelet she wore over her gold lamé dress. To do so she also had to remove the Grand Cross brooch that was on top of both garments. I noticed that she tried without success to put it back on and wanted Lillian Lagomarsino to help her, but the minister of justice had appropriated the companion a few yards away with his chatter. In the end, the first lady had no option but to turn to her brother, Juancito, the only person who was nearby. After a quick exchange of words and hands, he took possession of the badge.

At around half past one we were taken to the marvelous, illuminated Alhambra. A tour of several stages began. In the Lindaraja courtyard, a pianist performed the maestro Albéniz's serenata "Granada," and in the Leones courtyard, a string quartet delighted us with another exquisite concert. Magic, history, and a penetrating aroma of myrtle were everywhere, the ideal atmosphere from which to send us exhausted to our beds, overflowing with a sense of beauty. But no, it was not to be. There was still the grand finale to come: in the Partal gardens, everything was ready for a gypsy *zambra*. Resigned to it, we took our seats and tried to hide our tiredness. Holding back my yawns, I watched Dodero and Juan Duarte speaking to some men I didn't know, over by the cypresses to one side. The shipowner, with a fat cigar between his fingers, checked several times from afar to make sure the first lady was seated with the appropriate honors. The brother puffed on a cigarette, indifferent to the charm of the place, looking first at his watch and then out into the void. The lights dimmed, a master of ceremonies took to the stage, and there came shushing sounds from the audience. It was dark, finally, and the first guitar chords were played. I didn't see the Argentines again.

The performance under the stars began: flamenco dancing with Moorish echoes, the dancers in long ruffled skirts and white shirts knotted under the chest, dark-haired, barefoot women who performed their legendary art as if floating. There was singing, clapping, and strumming, and then it was the turn of the ballet corps from the Liceo de Barcelona, visiting the city for the Corpus Christi celebrations. It was after three in the morning when the final ovation came to an end. We left the gardens after the senior officials and guest of honor.

The Alhambra Palace lobby gave us a splendid welcome, with its softly lit lamps. The hotel was used to receiving a high class of tourists and visitors, but never a guest like Eva Perón. To embellish the hotel, Granada's most distinguished families had temporarily loaned furniture and coats of arms, tapestries, bronzes, oil paintings, and porcelain. I was heading to the lift with another couple of journalists when Diego Tovar requested my presence with a vague excuse. Both of us had been so hard at work, we hadn't been in each other's vicinity since we'd separated on the Barajas runway, when Dodero had made me switch planes.

"Will you drink a whiskey with me outside? I think we've earned it."

I was so exhausted I didn't have the strength to refuse. Taking my silence as a yes, he led me to the beautiful mirador decorated with Moorish tiles that projected over the city, the fertile lowlands, and the sky. We were the last customers, and a sleepy waiter served us. We savored the first sip in silence, and once more I remembered his kiss in the car outside the press club. It had happened only the previous night, but it felt as if entire weeks had passed between then and now.

In theory, all the stars and extras in the cast were in bed at last, the lead and the supporting players: the first lady and her self-sacrificing attendant, the military aides and the stylists, the reporters, the priest, the hairdresser, the doctor. All of them sleeping the sleep of the just. Or so we believed.

There was more silence than talk between us, but neither of us was uncomfortable with the other's quietness. I was aware, however, that Diego felt some obvious attraction toward me. Whether I did for him, I couldn't say.

"The thing is, Livia—"

Something suddenly broke the peace of the night and caught him up short. There was some commotion inside, words crisscrossing, loud voices. Then the waiter appeared on the terrace looking awkward, making way for two men in everyday suits who looked a little worn out given the time of night.

They identified themselves as members of the General Police Corps. The shortest one—Inspector Gallardo, he said—addressed Diego. Man to man, of course.

"Are you associated with some Argentine gentlemen going by the names of . . . ?"

He looked at his subordinate, who read from his notebook.

"Juan Gualte and Alberto Durero."

"Juan Duarte and Alberto Dodero," Diego corrected them, standing up in alarm. "What is this about?"

He had no authority to speak for the men—his role wasn't to oversee the guests' security, only to coordinate the foreign press. But he sensed a problem, and all his diplomatic alarm bells were going off. Something far from desirable was happening. And there was no one he could turn to at that hour without raising tensions. It was wise to proceed with caution.

"They've gotten themselves into trouble in a cave in Sacromonte," the policeman explained uncomfortably. "The gentlemen went to a gypsy party and got into an argument that turned violent. We've arrested three locals: a gypsy prostitute and her two brothers, riffraff. The three of them robbed Señor Juan Gualte or Duarte or whatever it is, but his belongings have been recovered, there's no problem with that. The supposed friends who took the Argentines there fled, but, out of discretion, we didn't want to move the victims. One of them is severely inebriated, neither one is carrying formal documentation, and they're refusing to give the names of anyone who can vouch for them. They just want to be allowed to go because they say they have a close relationship with Señora Perón. We can't agree to that, however, until we confirm that this is true."

The inspector swallowed. An Adam's apple as big as a fist moved up and down in his throat. Stubble was showing on his face. He must have spent the entire day organizing the operation so that nothing got out of hand during the illustrious visit. And now, two crackpots out on the town were stirring up trouble.

"If you'd be so kind as to come with us to identify them and take responsibility for them, we would be most grateful," he pleaded with Diego.

"Right away."

He finished his drink while he pocketed his cigarette case and turned to me.

"If you'll excuse me, Livia . . ."

I stood up, too.

"I'll go with you."

He was about to refuse, but I insisted.

"There're two of them. I might be able to help."

I didn't let him say yes or no, I just took him by the arm.

We went down into the city and drove alongside the river in the deep of night, the four of us in a dilapidated Lancia. The policemen were in the front in their plain clothes. Diego and I sat in the back, him in his exquisite dinner jacket, and me enveloped in fine layers of organza. We started to climb once again, the road appearing in front of us between agaves and prickly pears, narrow, winding, stony and unsurfaced, full of dips and sharp bends. The old car managed to sputter its way up, while inside we lurched back and forth, my body and Diego's constantly colliding.

Through the window I could see moonlit slopes and clearings, crumbling adobe walls, hollows and caves with grimy curtains in place of doors. These were the gypsy houses that foreigners in search of local color found fascinating, squalid homes where hundreds of poor souls struggled to survive amid filth, ignorance, lice, and hunger. I didn't feel the slightest attraction to the place, but Sacromonte was certainly a quaint and exotic poor quarter where tourists came to listen to pure flamenco or to enjoy a good time with dark-skinned prostitutes.

The inspector stopped the car outside one of the caves, somewhat smarter than the previous ones. Its front was whitewashed, and red geraniums had been planted in cans on each side. Despite the time of night, fifteen or twenty curious neighbors were nearby, including a few ragged children. A little farther on I saw another parked car—it belonged to the policemen who were guarding Juancito and Dodero, I assumed. The four of us got out of the Lancia. The others started heading into the cave, but I opted to keep back. "I'll wait here for now," I whispered to Diego. I didn't know what state the Argentines would be in, and I sensed it would be prudent to give them at least a few moments before I entered.

From outside, I heard Dodero's voice when he recognized Diego Tovar. Gruffly, he demanded to be let out of there at once. Meanwhile, two barefoot girls approached me, their hair tangled, their faces smudged. They must've been eight or nine years old, and no one seemed to care that they were wandering around. They looked at me, amazed, giggling nervously. No doubt I seemed to them a bizarre presence in my long dress, delicate sandals, and makeup.

"Is it true the men in there are friends of that Perona lady?"

They had to repeat the question three times before I understood, but once I did, I almost burst out laughing. Electricity, running water, and basic education hadn't reached this poor quarter, but the news that Eva Duarte de Perón was visiting Granada had, even though these youngsters knew neither who the lady was nor how she was really named.

I heard the shipowner sounding a little calmer, Diego in a serious tone, and the inspector, but I couldn't hear Juan Duarte. I was trying to sneak a peek through the curtain when I felt a tug on my dress. "Through there, through there," the girls said. They pointed at a cavity to one side, another door of sorts. Then they each pulled one of their lower eyelids down with a dirty forefinger, and I understood at once. If I went in there, I would be able to see what was happening inside. Without a second thought, I did exactly what they were suggesting.

50

The dark space we went into had a low ceiling and an opening in the back wall that led to the main room. With the girls clinging to my legs, the three of us in total silence, I peered through it at an angle. Diego Tovar, the two policemen who'd brought us here, and the other two who'd been guarding the Argentines were all standing. Dodero, with his bow tie unknotted and his face flushed, was sitting on a wooden chair while Juancito was out cold on a stone bench. I saw that he was wearing neither his shoes nor his jacket. The others seemed to be discussing what to do with him, whether to wait for him to perk up or take him back to the hotel despite his condition.

On a table in the center of the room, in the light of a kerosene lamp and in perfect order, I could make out his patent leather shoes, a watch, a gold cigarette lighter, a pair of cuff links, a wad of notes, and the ruby ring that President Perón's private secretary always wore, evidence of the fact that it had all been stolen but later recovered. I felt a nag of doubt then. Something, by omission, wasn't right. Almost without intending it, my memory spun me back to a few hours before, to the sweltering dinner at the city hall. I'd seen Juan Duarte put an object in his pocket, something his sister Eva gave him after she'd been unable to attach it to the lamé of her dress. That was precisely what was missing from that table.

I heard a match being struck behind me and quickly turned my head. Sitting on a ledge coming out from the wall, a bench of sorts, an old woman dressed in mourning was lighting an oil lamp. The quivering light made orangey shadows dance on the cave walls, and I felt a shiver when I saw her severe face with its wrinkled skin. "Good evening," I managed to mutter. I owed her that much, at least, seeing as I'd sneaked in there without permission. The girls, suddenly frightened, shot out of there like bullets. I was left alone in that place with the woman.

My eyes quickly adjusted to the light and shadows. I saw that the room was rather bigger than I'd imagined, with a few low tables and stools, and I supposed it was a modest tavern. I saw demijohns of wine on the earth floor, a shelf lined with unlabeled bottles, and some dirty glasses. Everything in order, all the paraphernalia for a lowly business.

The old woman kept her eyes fixed on me while I continued to scan the shadows to escape her gaze. Even so, with her just three yards away, I couldn't help but notice her appearance. Serious, well built, with a straight back and tight bun, her hand on the grip of a walking stick, and possessing the look of a matriarch. At once I suspected she was the owner of this den, the mother of the three siblings, perhaps—the whore and her two brothers—who'd ended up in a cell after fleecing Juancito. It occurred to me that, if she was who I thought she was, she might know something.

I worked up some false courage so my voice would sound firm.

"There's something missing from the gentleman's belongings," I said, indicating the neighboring room with a thumb over my shoulder. "The watch, lighter, cuff links, ring, shoes, and money are there. But there was one more thing."

Her expression was unchanged, and she gave no indication of whether she knew what I was referring to or not.

"Something he had in the right-hand pocket of his jacket is missing."

She continued to stare at me, unblinking, wary. I realized she wasn't so old, simply a mature woman who'd been ill treated by the miseries of a rotten life.

"And this thing the gentleman had in his pocket," I added in a severe tone, "no one's going to be able to sell it."

I was standing, exquisitely dressed in evening attire; she was clothed in black from top to bottom, remaining motionless on her simple seat. If my outward appearance surprised her at all, she didn't show it. She must've been used to all kinds of people passing through that squalid place.

"It has no value on the street," I insisted, "because—"

"It's worth a tidy sum. Do you think I don't know?"

My nerves crackled when I heard her go on the attack, her accent broad and her voice as coarse as dry esparto grass. I fought to draw my voice from my throat to reply.

"But it's a gift with serious political implications. From Franco to Doña Eva Perón, the visitor. It's been in all the newspapers, which is why, if you intend to sell it, you won't find anyone who will buy it." I paused, then in a somber tone, I added, "Whoever's caught with it, they'll have the book thrown at them."

She remained silent, as if chewing on my words. The men's voices could be heard coming from next door again. It seemed they now wanted to bring Juan Duarte back to the world of the living. I realized I had to be quick, make progress before they moved from that room.

"Five years in prison at least," I added forcefully. "Or they might well send you to the execution wall. You know the Generalísimo doesn't mess around. His people did away with quite a few here in Granada, or don't you remember the war and what came after?"

I didn't know precisely what the civil war had brought to Granada, but I assumed everything that happened there had been as cruel and appalling as in the rest of Spain, and so I took the gamble. This seemed to have some effect on her because she contorted her parched lips with displeasure. She surely knew that Sacromonte, with its complex geography, had once become a refuge for guerrillas and fugitives. In the hunt for them, there had been many betrayals, tip-offs, confrontations, and gunfights. Blood had been spilled; there had been captives and casualties.

"I can make sure the piece is returned to its rightful place. And I can do it without being noticed."

Her only response was another silence. But it was not a no.

"It would all remain between you and me, I give my word." Without moving, I gestured behind me with my thumb again. "The alternative is that the four policemen in the other room—Gallardo and his men—will be back, and they won't give up until they find it. This is an ugly business, and they're very anxious about what punishment might fall on them if they mess up. Mixing politics and theft in this Spain of Franco's is not a good idea, as I'm sure you know."

We heard Juancito slurring his words next door. *Leave me in peace, jackasses,* or something like that. I continued to brazenly pile on the pressure—I was running out of time.

"I won't say a single word to anyone," I assured her. I gestured at the other room with my chin, toward the sound of the voices. "None of them know I'm here, in fact. They think I'm still outside waiting. I'll pretend I found it by chance, on the road or wherever, it will be on me. There will be no repercussions for you."

The protests Eva Perón's brother was making were growing louder. He was refusing to be moved. *Why the fuck won't you just leave me here, you Spanish pieces of shit, sons of fucking bitches.* Turning a deaf ear to the Argentine's insults, I stuck to my task.

"Make up your mind, señora. There's no time."

In the lamplight, I saw her mouth preparing to reply.

"And what will you give me in return?"

Her voice creaked, severe, forceful, and I felt my heart miss a beat. The wizened matriarch knew what she was doing.

"How much do you want?"

"Let's see what you got."

I opened my little gem-encrusted purse and found a few notes inside. No documentation or accreditation of any kind, just a financial precaution. Money had worked with the taxi driver, and I guessed it would have the same effect here.

I could hear the men lifting Juancito up as if he were a bundle to be transported, and he directed numerous insults at the policemen's mothers. I had to be quick; it was now a matter of seconds. I took out two hundred pesetas, approached, and left them beside her on the bench. She shook her head. I added a third note with the brother's complaints still reaching my ears, but the old woman rejected it again. I put a fourth and fifth note on top, took out my clean handkerchief and lipstick, and turned over the open bag so that she could see it was completely empty.

"That," she muttered, pointing to the lipstick with a finger as twisted as a vine shoot.

Dodero was bellowing at his friend now, and Diego was trying to bring about order. The old woman pointed at the handkerchief, then the handbag: "That and that." I nodded; it was all hers. I had to wrap up the exchange as soon as possible. I held the palm of my hand out to her in an eloquent gesture, then folded my four fingers back toward myself. *You have what you want,* was the message. *Now, quickly, give me what you owe me.*

Without getting up, she put her stick down on the bench and bent forward until her hand reached the hem of the skirts that almost touched the floor. Then she stuck it all the way up inside there, moving past her calves and thighs, rummaging through layers of dark, dirty material, until she reached her groin. She dug about in her private parts for a moment while I contained my disgust. Finally, she found what she was looking for, and her hand retraced its route until it was out again. Slowly, she held it out to me. There, extracted from the depths of her filthy crotch, was the Grand Cross of Isabella the Catholic, sparkling in the light of the oil lamp.

The men's voices grew even louder. They were ready to get Juancito out of there and put him in one of the cars. Fighting back my nausea, I plucked the decoration from her hand with the tips of my fingers. I wanted to retrieve the handkerchief to clean it with, but the old woman was quicker than me and snatched it up before I could get hold of it. With that option lost, unable to ignore my overwhelming revulsion, I lifted the skirt of my dress, gripped the lining, held it to my mouth, and tore a piece off with my teeth. I wrapped the honorary cross in it while the gypsy woman mumbled some words I couldn't decipher. Cursing my ancestors, no doubt.

I slid the little package down my cleavage until it reached the strap of my brassiere, so that it was held in place by the stretchy silk. Finally, I spat on my hands and rubbed them together to try to clean them with my own saliva. With a final look at the old woman, I saw that she'd put away all my belongings, who knows where.

In exchange for five hundred pesetas, an imitation handbag, a handkerchief, and a lipstick, I'd managed to recover the award that Franco had bestowed upon Eva Perón at the Royal Palace.

The old woman turned off the oil lamp, leaving the cave in semidarkness.

I pulled open the curtain and went out into the night.

51

No one from the tour went down to breakfast the next morning. The local organizers and journalists, the officials with knots in their stomachs, and hundreds of onlookers were waiting in the lobby and the vicinity of the hotel, assuming that the Argentine first lady was the cause of the delay. Madrid had alerted them in advance that she was constantly behind time. Ambassador Radío was forced to take responsibility. He came out of the elevator at almost eleven o'clock, went to the middle of the lobby wearing a grave expression, and made his announcement: Señora Perón was indisposed, so for the time being all events were canceled. *Please excuse the inconvenience. We will keep you informed of any changes.*

It was true that Eva Perón suffered relatively frequent discomfort. She ate little and was often tired, her ankles tended to swell, she sometimes looked too pale, and her doctor was constantly advising her to rest. That morning, however, her state of health was merely an excuse. She had no physical ailment. Her only upset was the one her brother had caused. And this wasn't the first time—he'd made trouble for her before.

Gossip spread about Juan Duarte's arrival at the Alhambra Palace despite it having been facilitated with the utmost discretion. He'd been driven there in Inspector Gallardo's car with Diego Tovar and Alberto Dodero on either side of him. It had been a strange scene: the refined diplomat, General Perón's personal secretary, and the powerful ship-owner, all squeezed into the back of an ordinary car like three common criminals. I had been taken in the second vehicle by the other police-men. To save him from embarrassment, I made sure Dodero never noticed my presence. I got out at the main entrance, but Juancito was taken in through a service door for the kitchens, like a consignment of meat from the slaughterhouse. Still, even from a considerable distance, I caught the tail end of his drunken cries, some incomprehensible gib-berish about Isabella the Catholic and that halfwit gypsy Rosario.

With only a few brief hours of bad sleep in my body, as soon as I got up just after nine o'clock, I saw that an envelope had been slipped under my door. I tore it open: Diego Tovar was informing me that the ministry had summoned him, and that he was immediately head-ing back to Madrid by car. He added nothing else, likely playing it safe. Reading between the lines, I sensed that news of the incident in Sacromonte had reached the capital and caused serious concern among the highest authorities. And as an eyewitness, he had to make his report.

The handwritten note in my hand, I threw open the doors to my beautiful balcony with the view of the Alhambra Forest. I eagerly breathed in the clean air, then I sat on the end of the bed. Diego's unexpected departure had thrown me off balance. I'd been relying on him. I needed him. As head of the Diplomatic Information Office, as an adept professional with aplomb to spare, he would've known what to do. Now, with him gone, my fate was entirely in my own hands.

I threw the note onto the sheets and headed to the bathroom. The washbasin was still full of water, but the mass of bubbles that had been left on the surface—the lather I'd made when I rubbed the bar of soap between my hands before going to bed—had dissolved. On the white porcelain bottom, strange and outlandish, was the Grand Cross of Isabella the Catholic. Remembering again where it had come from, I retched. I dipped my hand into the water, pulled out the plug, and waited for the sink to empty. Then I turned on the tap, letting the fresh water from the Sierra Nevada wash over the insignia's solid gold, the pearls at its tips, the little diamonds and rubies, the *Plus Ultra* inscription, and the enamel of the pillars of Hercules. Surrounding the badge's center was a laurel wreath and a legend: *A la lealtad acrisolada por Isabel la Católica*. For proven loyalty to Isabella the Catholic. I couldn't help but give a wry smile. Thank goodness the poor queen had been underground for centuries and couldn't witness the scant loyalty with which her memory was passed from hand to hand. I rubbed it furiously again with the bar of Heno de Pravia to remove any trace that might remain of the old woman's nether regions, then I wrapped it in a towel. With the decoration hidden between folds of fabric, I sat on the toilet lid. I had no idea how I was going to proceed. I couldn't think straight.

Only a few customers remained, and the staff was starting to clear the tables when I arrived in the dining room dressed and made up like the resolute reporter I was pretending to be. I thought I could see the back of Alberto Dodero's head in an out-of-the-way corner. This was certainly not a good time to offer him my company, as I was sure he'd prefer to bemoan his hangover and his irresponsible behavior alone. For all intents and purposes, he was the boss of the delegation, and General Perón had entrusted him to take care of everything, banking on Dodero's political loyalty, maturity, and worldly savoir faire. And, of course, the shipowner was responsible for ensuring that the whole group of Argentines conducted themselves impeccably, and that his own behavior be faultless.

As a bon vivant and lover of debauched recreation himself, however, he'd ended up tolerating too much of Juan Duarte's wild behavior, laughing along with him and going with him on many of his benders. Until last night, when it had gotten out of control. The Sacromonte incident itself hadn't yet had any serious repercussions. It was thought that everything the prostitute and her brothers had pinched from Juancito had been recovered, and they'd managed to get him out of that filthy cave before dawn, transport him to the hotel, and put him in his bed. No doubt to the annoyance of the shipowner, this hadn't been the happy ending he might have hoped for. In the following hours, the Granada police had informed their superiors in Madrid of the incident, they in turn had told the Ministry of Foreign Affairs, and the minister Martín-Artajo himself had ordered Diego Tovar to return immediately and give a step-by-step account of what had happened. This wasn't Eva Duarte's brother's first blunder. In the capital I'd heard about past fixes involving prostitutes, bums, booze, and powdered substances. And Juancito, the black sheep of the entourage, was making the authorities extremely nervous.

I imagined Dodero was reflecting on the situation that morning while he chewed on the two Optalidon pills they'd given him to combat his headache after the excesses. The glorious march of Evita's tour was on the verge of being derailed, in large part because of his indulgence of the mad brother. Worst of all, however, wasn't that, but a much more serious problem whose existence the shipowner would have begun to suspect upon their return to the hotel, something he would have confirmed when he got up. A problem that, in the final stages of the tour, had the potential to stir up conflict, even bitter discord, with Franco himself. And the fool Juancito, Dodero surely suspected, was to blame. The magnate would have gone to the brother's room smelling a rat, shaken him to wake him up, and searched with him every pocket of his crumpled suit, but there would have been no trace of the medal.

I crossed the restaurant floor while I was thinking of all of this, ready to inform the shipowner of the missing Grand Cross's fate, ease many of his worries, and restore peace to his afflicted soul. I approached with carefully prepared words and my best morning smile, but the latter turned to a grimace as I rounded the table, saw its occupant face-to-face, and realized my mistake. This individual wasn't the Argentine magnate but a gentleman with a sizable mustache, finishing his breakfast alone.

I spoke to the head waiter, who informed me that Señor Dodero had had only a double coffee early in the morning.

I quickly headed to the hotel reception.

"He left over an hour ago."

"By himself?"

The employee hesitated before finally nodding.

"Yes, señorita. The gentleman was alone."

"And do you have any idea where he was going?"

He stalled again. He looked like a good person, an honest father of four or five children, perhaps, who needed shoes and schoolbooks at a time when workers earned a pittance. Thank goodness the pragmatic British had given me a thick wad of notes before I flew to Spain. Another hundred under the palm of my hand slid over the desk.

"The hotel car took him to the airport," he announced while the note disappeared into his pocket.

"With or without luggage?"

The receptionist was honorable enough to answer without even asking for another tip.

"Señor Dodero had a good-sized suitcase with him."

My nerves began to jangle. Diego Tovar had gone. Alberto Dodero had gone. And there I was, alone in Granada not knowing whom to trust, with the blasted Grand Cross hidden in my room, stuffed between the cotton balls I used to remove my makeup at night.

I anxiously scanned the lobby. Despite the unexpected cancelation of the day's events, the place was still busy with journalists, officials, and spectators who didn't dare leave in case there was a turn of events. Behind the reception desk, I noticed a door. *Centralita*, I read. Switchboard. Without a second thought, I went in and closed the door behind me. The two operators recognized me at once as a member of the group traveling with Eva Perón and welcomed me with the utmost courtesy, barely containing their delight at being face-to-face with one of the show's bit players.

They were both in their forties and must've worked in the hotel half their lives. I sensed they wouldn't be tempted by a hundred pesetas, or even a thousand. And so I tried another ruse, an improvisation I made up as I went along, in which I passed myself off as the vaguely foreign wife of Don Alberto Dodero, the man responsible for Doña Eva's well-being. Dodero was several decades older than me, but they, like me, knew that the world was full of couples of dissimilar ages, especially ones composed of women who did not lack in beauty and men who had power, fame, and money.

Attempting an Argentine accent, I played the role of a glamorous bimbo, cursing myself for oversleeping and acting upset that I hadn't been able to speak to my husband before he left for the airport. By sweet-talking them with vacuous patter, I eventually managed to persuade them to note down all the calls that had been made that morning both to and from the shipowner's room. To my satisfaction, not only did the telephone operators provide me with the numbers, but one of them, in pointed handwriting, jotted down that two of the calls had been to Granada's airport and the rest to Madrid. The Argentine embassy had been one of those calls; the Palace Hotel, another. And three—exactly three calls—had connected the shipping magnate to an establishment named Cejalvo.

I rooted around in my memory. "Cejalvo, Cejalvo . . . ," I repeated to myself. But the name didn't ring any bells. As if reading my mind, the darker of the two operators volunteered what she knew.

"It's a jeweler, silversmith, and medal maker, Señora Dodero. That's what it says in the telephone directory for Madrid. Perhaps," she added with a look of mischievous complicity, "he's planning to buy you a gift."

The three of us laughed in unison—the pair of them genuinely amiable, me cynical to the extreme—while I put two and two together in my mind. Why would the shipowner contact such a place if it wasn't to search for a replacement? Surely that was why he'd decided to fly back to Madrid, to take care of the matter himself. With no intermediaries. With total discretion.

I said goodbye to the friendly telephone operators, pledging my eternal gratitude. It was up to me to stop Dodero now that I knew what he was doing. Having the insignia in my possession was also a risk. Deciding how to get rid of it was the next step.

Back in my room, trying to think, I sat on the edge of the still-unmade bed. If Dodero had called the medal maker, then it was likely that neither he nor anyone else was prepared to report the loss to the authorities. The blunder was too embarrassing, the negligence too shameful, to be admitted officially. But someone could still let the cat out of the bag. The police could probe the gypsy clan in Sacromonte again. The old woman might talk and point her scabby finger at me. At any rate, knowing that the badge was still in my toilet bag disturbed me.

After weighing the options, I understood that there was only one way to return the Grand Cross to where it belonged: I would have to get it to the first lady myself. The problem—the big problem—was how. One possibility, I thought, would be to hand it over unnoticed to the stylists Asunta and Juanita, or to Don Julio the hairdresser. They knew me. I could speak to them without any pretext, explain the situation, leave the decoration in their safekeeping, and let them do the rest. But this would compromise them too much, I concluded. They'd find themselves in a dangerous bind in which they could be suspected, their story disbelieved, and their involvement might even incriminate them. Another alternative, I considered, would be to hand it in to the police, to go in person to the station, ask for Inspector Gallardo, tell him the truth as it happened. But in that scenario, I could be the one who was jeopardized if they didn't believe me. I could just imagine the headlines: *BBC correspondent jailed for grand theft*. No, that certainly wasn't an option, either.

Fed up with forming and discarding ideas, I went into the bathroom, lifted the top of my elegant toilet kit, and poked through the beauty products, a tub of cold cream, and bobby pins until I found the packet of cotton wool in the bottom. I rummaged in the fluffy white mass and took out the Grand Cross. I didn't even stop to look at it; I just squeezed it in my fist. *Let's do this,* I said to myself, and headed for the door.

Señora Perón's suite was on the first floor of the hotel, in its grandest area. I walked there at an unhurried pace, trying to soften the sound of my footsteps. The corridor was cool and dark despite the splendid weather. I encountered no one. I was firm in my conviction, ready to settle the matter, prepared to deliver the badge to its owner in person. I would simply say I'd found it while strolling around the Alhambra. The explanation was so uncomplicated that it almost seemed absurd. But it would have to do: the truth was too complicated.

When I was just a few yards away I began to hear the woman's voice, growing louder and more furious. Eva Perón, though I wasn't aware of it then, had just finished a telephone meeting with the deeply Catholic minister Alberto Martín-Artajo. Without waiting for Diego Tovar to reach Madrid, the head of Spain's foreign affairs had decided that what the Granada police had told him, plus what he knew about previous soirees, was reason enough to muster his courage and request a call to the Alhambra Palace.

"It fills me with the most profound unease, señora . . ."

The foreign minister must have begun with these or similar words, after first swallowing his pride. People were hearing about the incident, the press was hearing about it, rumors were spreading that could reach His Excellency. The madcap brother had to be stopped, no matter what, and censured for his unacceptable behavior.

After hanging up, María Eva Duarte de Perón had begun tearing into her husband's private secretary as I approached her door. She was no longer the timid little girl with whom her brother had grown up in poverty in Junín. She was a powerful woman now, thundering at an unruly subordinate. And it wasn't because of the Grand Cross's loss, I sensed. At this point, she was not yet aware of that.

I was standing outside the double oak door, about to knock, when I heard her let out a cascade of expletives, furious over Juancito's penchant for boozing, brothels, and trouble. Her brother, meanwhile, didn't dare open his mouth.

Once it seemed like things had calmed down, I raised my arm, hesitating for a moment. I was almost touching the wood when a yell made me stop.

"One more whore, you hear me! One more and you go straight back to Argentina!"

Still clutching the Grand Cross, I decided to turn around, and I hurried back to my room.

52

If Granada's Alhambra Palace evoked Andalusia's Nasrid past, the newer Hotel Alfonso XIII in Seville was a spectacular Neo-Mudéjar fantasy—a bit artificial, but no less splendid. Señora Perón and her closest circle were taken straight to the royal accommodation, while the rest of us waited patiently to be allocated our rooms.

"Welcome, Señora Nash," the receptionist said when it was my turn. "Would you be kind enough to show me your passport?"

I held it out to him with a fixed grin, then I had to wait for them to fill out my details on the corresponding card. It was almost nine o'clock, and we'd just arrived by air from Granada. I waited patiently for the employee to hand over my key, which was attached to a heavy cast-iron fob. And he gave me something else, to my surprise.

"A telegram arrived for you from Madrid a few hours ago."

I practically snatched it from between his fingers; I moved to one side while I tore open the folded and sealed piece of blue paper. *Víctor.* It was for him that I feared.

> BEAUTIFUL BABY.
> FATHER IN GOOD HEALTH.
> SWEET ENGLISH NANNY.
> WE ARE ALL ANXIOUS FOR YOUR RETURN.

WITH LOVE.

R. A.

I screwed it up into a ball and almost let out a stream of expletives. *Bastard, son of a bitch, lowlife.* I barely managed to contain myself. I wandered away from the reception area, ending up in a beautiful central courtyard whose charm I didn't even bother to appreciate. Overwhelmed, I slumped into one of the wicker chairs.

The initials R. A. could have stood for Román Altares, as he now called himself, or the name familiar to me, Ramiro Arribas. Either way, he was reminding me that he was still waiting expectantly. My doubts had been dispelled, and now my fears were real—yes, he knew my father's precise address. Worse still, evidently, he'd turned up there. He'd learned that there was a child of mine in the world and knew the boy had a nanny. Had he managed to lay eyes on them, or had the porter innocently let on about their existence? Had he gone up to the apartment and rung the bell with some excuse, or had he just waited patiently and seen them come outside? These questions bounced around in my head.

I didn't even go up to my room. Instead, I retraced my steps to the lobby and requested a call to Madrid. I went into one of the wooden booths and waited anxiously for the telephone to ring. *Your call's ready. I'll put you through, señora.* I held my breath until I heard Miguela's voice on the other end of the line. "All's well," she said. No, no news. Yes, the boy's fine, happy. Yes, Philippa's also perfectly well. No, no strangers had been there. The boy had gone out for a stroll with his nanny, my father was at the Gran Peña, and they would all be home for dinner soon.

I finally went back to my room, somewhat relieved but still on edge. I checked the time; in theory I needed to be ready in twenty minutes, but if I assumed that Señora Perón would be as late as she usually was, I might take a little longer. I hesitated, then finally decided not to open my suitcase yet, and collapsed onto the bed like a deadweight.

The trip later was made in calashes drawn by horses that seemed to dance on Seville's cobbled streets. The first lady traveled with the mayor in the main carriage. As ever, the masses fervently applauded her and shouted compliments, hurrahs and bravos on every corner, and the ships anchored in the port blew their horns. All along the route to Plaza Nueva, thousands of carnations flew down from balconies and rooftops, and rose petals covered the pavements. There was even a release of five thousand doves, which flew off in all directions. So began another act in the fabulous Hispano-Argentine operetta, with all the performers dressed to the nines again, albeit without Dodero this time, and with Juancito taciturn, sitting in his carriage stiff as a board.

After the reception at the city council's Colón Hall, we made our way with difficulty through streets still packed with high-spirited onlookers. The next stage took us in fits and starts to the Mudéjar Pavilion at one end of the María Luisa Park. Another lavish dinner was served there, after which we went out onto Plaza de América, which thronged with people. Everything was ready for a great dance in which flamenco groups and more than six hundred dancers performed sevillanas into the early hours, in the light of thousands of lanterns.

I struggled to fall asleep. Even after I was in bed, my head echoed with the clapping and heel stamping, the guitar strumming, and the cries of "*Olé!*" and "*Arsa!*" of that ostentatious reception, excessive, wild, offensive to an impoverished Spain and to the city of Seville so full of hungry people. I felt as if I'd just fallen asleep when the telephone's ringing woke me. I leaped up and snatched the receiver from its stand. *Víctor, something's happened to Víctor* was my first thought again.

"Yes?" I demanded.

I heard a response: a man's laughter.

"Relax, Sira, relax. Don't worry, woman, everything's fine . . ."

Ramiro Arribas was speaking in a supposedly friendly tone. I didn't have the strength to ask him for explanations, to insult him, to beg him to forget me.

"I just wanted to make sure you received my telegram yesterday."

Sitting on the bed, I nodded with my eyes closed, oblivious to the obvious fact that he couldn't see me.

"So?" he persisted. "Did you receive it, Sira?"

I swallowed and took a deep breath.

"I received it, Ramiro. And I wasn't happy to read that you've been stalking my family."

"No, no, no," he replied cordially, almost cheerfully. "I was simply passing through Hermosilla and remembered your father lives there."

"Leave them alone. Speak to me and only me. Don't even go near them."

"All right, all right, relax," he said in a conciliatory tone. "I'll just ask you, then, how are things progressing with our friend Dodero?"

"They're not progressing at all. He's not here, in Seville. I have no way to speak to him."

"Don't lie to me, sweetheart. I know he's part of the tour, I've just seen the photographs of him in Granada's *Ideal*, with Evita in the Alhambra."

His "sweetheart" pierced my soul like a rusty spike. I quickly shook off the feeling. This was no time to struggle with emotions, and I had to keep a cool head.

"He was in Granada, yes, but I didn't have the chance to say anything to him. Now he's back in Madrid. You can check. Ask for him at the Palace."

He was silent for a few seconds, as if reflecting. When I heard his voice again, it was more forceful, less friendly.

"Listen, Sira, this business I'm working on, it requires an urgent solution. I'm not asking for anything outrageous. It doesn't compromise you in any way, it's just a small favor."

He was silent again, as if choosing his words. I just stared at my bare feet on the rug and said nothing.

"I need that meeting with him. Things are getting complicated with my associates, and it's very important, I repeat, very important that he hears about my project before he leaves Spain. If he departs for Italy, the door will close on me and there won't be another chance."

No. No. No. I repeated the word to myself as I shook my disheveled head. I couldn't allow myself to be dragged into something by this rat. For the sake of my own dignity, I couldn't help him.

"It'll be a breeze," he insisted, "I'm sure—"

"I have to go, Ramiro. I'm expected for work. I need to earn a living too, you know."

"But you—"

"Dodero isn't in Seville. I'm being honest with you. Find another way to reach him because I can't help you with this."

I slammed the receiver down and put my face in my hands, as if I could shield myself from what was happening. And I partly did: I distanced myself from the present, yes, but my treacherous memory took me back to another time. Images, feelings, and sensations passed through my mind in fierce waves. The way Ramiro had seduced me with his masculine attraction and his charisma. The way in which, with skillful subtlety, he'd gotten me to come away from my world. The decadent life we'd led in Madrid and Tangier, his ambitions and his lies, the castles he'd built in the air, only to, without warning, set fire to them, casting me into oblivion.

I longed to have someone close to me in whom I could confide, a hand outstretched to stop me from falling into the abyss. Someone with whom to share my doubts and fears, my uncertainty, my unease. I missed Marcus and his sober lucidity, Fran Nash and her resilience. I yearned for Rosalinda Fox and her nerve, and Nick Soutter with his solidity, even Diego Tovar, with his efficient diplomacy. But no, in this Seville, which would soon resume the grotesque carnival it had prepared for the Argentine president's wife, on that hot morning in that wonderful hotel, there was only me in my nightdress, confused, anguished, and immensely lonely.

I was still punishing myself with bitter memories and thoughts of absences when the telephone rang again.

"Tell me one thing, Sira, just one thing, angel. What do you think your boy and the nanny would most like to do with me? A walk in El Retiro or a boat ride on the lake?"

I hung up unceremoniously for the second time and leaped to my feet. The fun was over, enough was enough. I shoved handfuls of tubes, sticks, and tubs into my toilet bag while I brushed my teeth. Under a brief shower I made my first decisions. "Get back to Madrid," I repeated to myself as I yanked my clothes from the wardrobe. "Stop that bastard Ramiro," I insisted while I stuffed garments into my suitcase. "Find a way to get rid of him," I concluded as I quickly put my hair up. I requested a call to the room of another correspondent while I put on my shoes. I told him an unavoidable commitment had come up and I'd be stepping away from the tour for now.

The lobby was packed with uniformed officials, photographers, and reporters, men with brilliantined hair and impeccable suits, beautiful local women in their mantillas—all waiting to join the first lady's retinue. A busy day lay ahead: a solemn Hail Mary at the cathedral, a visit to the Brotherhood of the Virgin of Macarena where she would be named as an honorary patron, another Hail Mary in the Church of San Gil before the image of Our Lady of Esperanza, a visit to the Torre Pavadel estate and to the tobacco factory to be cheered by the campesinos and cigarmakers. And more clapping, and more yelling, and more cries of *olé*, and more dinners . . .

Followed by the porter, I all but elbowed my way through the mob. I couldn't see a taxi in the vicinity, and the area around the entrance was entirely taken up by shiny official cars. Beyond the perimeter wall of the grounds, a noisy crowd was already gathering. I looked left and right. I needed to get out of there, fast.

"One of those, señora?"

The young man helping me gestured to one side of the garden, to a small caravan of horse-drawn cabs. Another crisp note worked the miracle, and within seconds the lean coachman had adjusted his hat, clicked his tongue, and pulled on the horse's reins. With a clatter, he delivered me to the station on Plaza de Armas.

53

I got off the train at Atocha station after midnight, leaving behind the jostling, jolting, and soot, the suffocating heat and smell of sweat. I'd also had time—a long time—to think, set aims, and decide my next steps. As soon as the passengers climbed down onto the platform, the porters descended on us like flies. I chose an older man with a kind face.

"Do you know of a guesthouse nearby?" I asked as he loaded my luggage onto his cart.

"But of course, señora. I'll take you there right away."

The building was near the start of Paseo de las Delicias; on the second floor, we were received by a woman in her fifties with curlers in her graying hair and a faded floral housecoat over her nightdress. Resting on her chest, I noticed, was a scapular of the Virgin of Carmen. I followed her as she shuffled down a long, dimly lit hallway in her espadrilles, both of us silent. The apartment may once have been elegant, had perhaps been inhabited by a well-to-do middle-class family. The ceilings were high, the exterior more than decent, but now it was a drab, partitioned property, one of the many cheap converted boarding-houses located close to the station, lodgings that droves of unfortunates from all over Spain arrived at in their search of an illusory future. The landlady opened a door at the end of the corridor, turned a knob on the wall, and a bulb illuminated the room with a weak light.

"Fifteen pesetas a night, for you."

The bedroom was modest, with two small beds that weren't even twins, a washstand at their feet, and a stick chair on either side of the balcony. As soon as I was alone, the first thing I did was fling the doors open.

The Alfonso XIII in Seville, the Alhambra Palace, the press club on Calle del Pinar . . . if they'd had lives of their own, those places where I'd slept the previous nights would have burst out laughing if they had seen me now in this fifteen-peseta guesthouse. Even Candelaria's hostel in Tétouan had possessed more sparkle. My body was crying out for a good bath, but I had to make do with the bucket of water that Señora Eusebia brought to fill the chipped ceramic washstand. She was about to close the door after muttering a paltry good night when my voice surprised her.

"Fifteen more pesetas if you give me clean sheets."

She was back in no time with them and remade one of the beds with skilled hands. After slapping the pillow a few times to give it shape, she left again, carrying the bundle of dirty linen in her arms.

The day was breaking when the bustle of the street woke me. Once my mind found its bearings, I went out onto the balcony and gazed at a long line of carts pulled by Percheron horses, their hooves and the carts' wheels rattling on the cobbles—ten, twelve, fifteen carts advancing one after the other at a steady pace. They were all carrying an identical load, which I managed to make out, looking closely. EL ÁGUILA, I read on the signs on the sides: The Eagle. They were transporting vast quantities of beer barrels from a nearby brewery, distributing them nice and early to the bars and taverns all over Madrid.

I didn't go back to bed. I stood watching the local life beginning to flow along the road that sloped down almost to the bank of the Manzanares—men in white shirts with wet hair, heading out to work, greengrocers arriving from the market gardens of Villaverde, the dairy opposite receiving its customers, the melodious song of a roving knife sharpener's ocarina.

"Do you happen to have a telephone, señora?" This was the first thing I asked the landlady after saying good morning from the door to her kitchen. She was wearing the same curlers, the same nightdress, and the same housecoat, but over those clothes she'd put on a stain-covered apron. I'd already dressed after washing in the communal bathroom. Reluctant to leave it between the walls of that cheap guesthouse, firmly held under the waistband of my skirt, in contact with my very flesh, I had with me the Grand Cross of Isabella the Catholic, the badge that almost everyone believed to be in Eva Perón's possession.

She continued to labor with her dishes at the sink, not even bothering to turn around to respond.

"There's a phone in the bar downstairs. Do you want your coffee white or black?"

There were no other guests in the kitchen, but traces of them remained: a scabby metal ashtray with several filterless cigarette ends in it, a couple of dirty china cups, a checkered rag wadded up into a ball. If she'd seen me there, my mother-in-law would have split her sides laughing.

I was tempted to turn down the offer; who knew what kind of brew the woman was prepared to serve me? Toasted chicory, in all likelihood, mixed with watered-down milk and barely a pinch of sugar. I didn't say no, however. When she set a cup of ersatz coffee and a piece of burnt toast down on the table, I became aware of my accumulated hunger and stopped being choosy.

We didn't exchange a single word until, once I'd finished, I asked, "And would you happen to know where I could buy some mourning clothes?"

The excuse I then gave was that a close relative had died, I had to attend the burial, and this was why I'd arrived so late the night before. My lie was a cover for a very different intention: I'd decided to transform myself as much as possible in an attempt to go unnoticed.

"Go a good way up Calle Atocha. On the right you'll see a clothes shop. La Gloria, it's called."

Though I went down to the bar early, making the calls I needed to make took an eternity. I had to inquire, get it wrong, and try again. I had to give my place up to a woman so she could call her village for news of her dying mother-in-law, and to a man who needed to resolve some business with plots and boundaries. Finally, in that narrow space at the back of the premises, facing a flaky wall on which customers had penciled or carved various messages, names, and numbers, I managed to complete my tasks one by one.

The first thing I did was to call my father, who much to my relief assured me that Víctor was well. Through the Diplomatic Information Office I confirmed that Diego Tovar was still in Madrid. This was a double-edged sword. On the one hand, I ran the perhaps remote risk of bumping into him. On the other hand, the favorable side, since he was away from Seville, he didn't know that I, the competent BBC reporter, had suddenly stopped covering the first lady's tour. My third call was to verify that the magnate Dodero was back in his suite at the Palace, and the next was to check that Ramiro was still registered as a guest at the Hotel Buen Retiro under the false name of Román Altares.

At La Gloria I found everything the perfect widow of the new Spain would need: all the mourning clothes I hadn't worn when Marcus died. A black calf-length skirt, under whose waistband I once again inserted the Grand Cross. A modest black blouse buttoned up to the neck, closely woven black tights, and a headscarf of the same color. They allowed me to change in the back room, the excuse of the burial working to good effect once more. I went back out onto the street, transformed into one of the many wives who'd lost husbands in the war and now had years of mourning and an uncertain future ahead. Ultimately, I wasn't so different: I too had lost the man in my life to a bloody conflict.

I took a taxi to the corner of Hermosilla and Serrano, a short distance from my father's house. I entertained myself by looking at the flowers of a hawker who sat on an upturned bucket while she shouted her wares. *I have fragrant spikenards, azaleas for the señora, going like hotcakes, my dear, believe me.* In reality I had little interest in her flowers, but I took the opportunity to subtly look around. My father had told me that Philippa tended to go out with Víctor at around midday. It was ten minutes before noon, and I had to find somewhere from which to observe them.

A nearby haberdashery provided the solution. It was opposite the house and had a small shopwindow that was crammed with edgings, buttons, satin ribbons, and bobbins. From behind it, I could see them without being seen, the perfect place. When I pushed the door open I found no other customers in the shop. The owner behind the counter was a tall man with gray curly hair who welcomed me without asking any questions. I lingered for a while, pretending to studiously examine some rolls of braids hanging from a bar while, in reality, I was looking through the glass to the other side of the road.

My heart skipped a beat when I saw them come out; there was my boy. It took all my effort to stop myself from running to him. He was sitting in his pram, the hair that was the same color as his father's hidden under a white sun hat. I could hardly see his face, but I could make out his hands enthusiastically batting the colored balls that hung from some elastic. I was comforted, at least, to see that he was full of his usual joyful energy. Pushing him along was Philippa, the nanny who'd been uprooted from London and brought to a sweltering Madrid. She was in a floral dress that was new to me, and instead of wearing her hair up as she usually did, she'd let it down to her shoulders, a style I'd never seen on her before. My suspicions grew. I hated that I couldn't go to them and warn her openly, pick Víctor up and squeeze him tight, kiss him all over, call him my love, and make him laugh, take him away. But I couldn't. And within moments I confirmed that I'd had good reason to be suspicious.

They'd barely begun advancing along the pavement when I saw him from behind, crossing the street. He was leaving a nearby bar, where he'd undoubtedly been waiting, with a folded newspaper under his arm. He wore a light-colored jacket and piqué trousers, impeccable as ever. In his left hand he held a small bunch of flowers, surely bought from the same vendor I'd seen minutes before. He reached them in a few strides. She stopped when she saw him, and my mouth filled with bile.

There was the predator Ramiro wooing poor Philippa, the hypocrite flattering the efforts she'd made to improve her bland appearance, with her freshly washed hair and her dull Sunday dress. *Son of a bitch.* I had to grip the frame of the shopwindow when I saw him bend over. Fury rose from my belly when he stroked my son's cheek. Víctor must have offered a funny response because both adults burst out laughing— Philippa's laughter sincere, Ramiro's no doubt false.

All the anguish in the world washed over me when I saw them set off. From behind they could have been mistaken for a happy family: the daddy handsome and mature, the young mummy plain but loving, the two of them proudly strolling with their beautiful little boy. A disgusting, bitter lump blocked my throat, and I bit my lip to stop myself from crying. *Son of a bitch.*

But no, I wasn't going to follow them. I was certain that Víctor wasn't in any danger. They would merely go for a walk, perhaps sit outside a bar and have a drink. What Ramiro wanted was to win Philippa over so that he could blackmail me with fear, intimidate me, force me to help him. Which was why I had to be firm, not give in. Once I'd lost sight of them, I bought just a handful of safety pins from the haberdasher in gratitude for his patience. I didn't even wait for the change. Adjusting my headscarf, I left the shop.

I looked up at the elegant building that housed my father's flat but resisted the temptation to go up and knock on the door. With his mettle and experience, he would've helped me tackle the imprudent situation I found myself in. Perhaps he would have tried to persuade me to abandon the foolishness I had planned. But I wasn't going to back down now. After the scene I'd just witnessed, I did not doubt for a moment that I had to get Ramiro Arribas out of my life: because of his deceitful machinations today and because of the pain he'd caused me in the past; because of what he'd stolen from me; for the child I'd lost, and for Víctor; even for Philippa the dope, blithely unaware of her supposed suitor's maneuvers. Dressed as the ordinary widow I essentially was, I overcame my impulse to visit Gonzalo Alvarado and kept walking.

My next step was to go to the Hotel Buen Retiro. I'd thought I didn't know it, but I learned that it was on Calle de Alfonso XI. My soul dropped to my feet when I had it in front of me. The establishment, with its rationalist architecture, turned out to be Hotel Gaylord's, renamed: a place that harbored many memories for me.

After my return from Tétouan years before, I'd learned that during the civil war the building had become the Russian headquarters in Madrid. The Russians had installed their staff there, accommodated spies, Soviet agents, and military officers. Even Hemingway, the celebrated author, had used it as a setting in one of his novels. It was said mockingly that Franco had a profound dislike for the place and that he would seize the first possible opportunity to demolish it, to erase any trace of those loathsome communists. For the time being, however, it was still operating, with nearly equal distinction to the classic Palace or Ritz Hotels, but with an added touch of worldly modernity. During the world war, it had been a favorite of the Americans and the British, and Marcus had frequented its cubist-styled bar, and his embassy had organized numerous events in its function rooms, which I never attended because of my required closeness to the Germans.

For all that, I'd managed to enjoy it briefly, and still etched in my memory was the weekend he and I once spent together in a top-floor suite after our unexpected reunion in Lisbon, arriving at different times to enjoy two full days with each other, making up for lost time, reconciling our souls' yearnings with our bodies' impulses, going no farther from our room than the balcony with its views of the Puerta de Alcalá. This would be the first of our many secret encounters—how could I forget it? Now, however, it was the creep Ramiro Arribas who was passing himself off as someone else: a solvent Argentine businessman. My Marcus, meanwhile, no longer inhabited this world, and I, dressed in the black I hadn't worn to mourn him, was incapable of preventing a rebellious tear from sliding down to my mouth, where it left a strange salty taste on my tongue.

I tried hard to keep my sadness in check and, sheltered behind a convenient newsstand, I watched the hotel entrance and the customers milling around there, the row of taxis, the uniformed porters carrying suitcases and belongings. I still didn't know how I was going to do it, but sooner rather than later, I had to go in through that door, to get to room 417.

54

I returned to the guesthouse, and the landlady invited me to sit down for lunch. My intention had been to say no, thank you, but my mouth played a trick on me, and I accepted. At the table were a railway worker with soot under his fingernails, a candidate for a position at Telefónica, Señora Eusebia herself, and no one else. I supposed the other guests were eating out, at their own expense. Or not eating at all, perhaps. I was struck by flashes of the hostel in Tétouan again: the old master, the ugly sisters, the fool Paquito with his tyrannical mother, all of them sharing a pot of stew, a dish of sardines, or a watermelon in the courtyard, with Candelaria among them, serving them one by one and acting as arbiter in their bitter verbal disputes, putting out fires with her irresistible energy. The atmosphere here was unlike that at my first Moroccan home: it was infinitely duller and more impersonal. Neither was the *cocido* that the owner of the house served me very good: barely a handful of chickpeas boiled with some noodles, a small piece of potato, and some slices of carrot. No chorizo or *morcilla* or belly pork, no chicken. This tasteless, meager stew was what was eaten daily in most houses in Madrid. And to accompany it, some lettuce leaves with a drizzle of cheap oil and a pinch of salt. That was how postwar Spain fed itself in winter and summer, the time of year made no difference; for both the defeated and for many who were on the winning side, there was nothing else. I thought with disgust of the banquets the authorities had held in honor of Eva Perón, the sprawl of succulent delicacies, insulting to the millions of bodies whose bellies creaked when they went to bed, poor wretches who tried to trick their hunger with mouthfuls of water, potato peelings, heartbreaking guile, and the hope that one day everything might be better. Yet again I wondered whether such shameful extravagance was really needed to obtain Argentina's wheat. And yet again I admired the dignified stoicism of the British.

As soon as I could, I shut myself in my room, took off my sad black clothes, hid the Grand Cross under my pillow for the moment, and took out my most unremarkable outfit from my suitcase. That afternoon I wouldn't need to be in disguise, as I was going to an ordinary neighborhood where there was no danger of anyone recognizing me. I shook out my suit and hung it up, trusting that the creases would fade away by themselves—I didn't want to ask the landlady for the iron, I didn't want to see anyone. I lay on the clean sheets in my slip. Looking up at the damp ceiling, I set myself to thinking.

It was almost seven o'clock when I reached my destination at number ninety-something of Calle Santa Engracia, very near Glorieta de Cuatro Caminos. He'd told me himself during that other time that he lived there. It was not common in those days for people to move, so I assumed he still had the same address. Crossing my fingers for it to be so, I sat on a bench on the street to wait.

But at half past seven he hadn't arrived. Nor at eight o'clock. Or half past eight, nine, or half past nine. Fed up, frustrated, at around ten o'clock I was about to leave when I saw him appear. He was coming from the entrance to the Metro, skinny, with his shoulders slumped and his tie loose, walking the dispirited walk of someone who was in no hurry to go home. I noticed again that he'd lost hair and gained a hardness in his features. Unlike Ramiro—unlike me, even—time had not been kind to him.

He walked past without seeing me, his head bowed and his hands in his pockets, keeping to his thoughts. Or worried or exhausted after a long day.

"Ignacio."

I said his name to his back, but he didn't hear me. After I'd spent so many hours alone and silent, my voice was barely audible. I cleared my throat and tapped his shoulder.

"Ignacio," I said again.

He spun around, almost menacingly. I raised my hands, as if to show my innocence.

"It's Sira. It's me."

The ferocity disappeared from his face, but he said nothing. He didn't even move.

"I want to tell you something that might be of interest to you given your responsibilities. I'm sorry to turn up without warning. I'll be quick. I just need a few minutes of your time."

"I'm not in a hurry."

He gestured at the nearby building with his chin.

"The family's at my parents-in-law's village for the summer. We can go up to my flat."

I hadn't been expecting the invitation, and I would've preferred not to go into his private space. We could have gone for a walk around that working-class neighborhood like we'd done so many times before, or sat outside a bar sharing horchata, surrounded by noisy anonymous people. But Ignacio was right, as ever. This wasn't just a courtesy visit, and away from the street, I could fill him in more prudently.

The flat was in semidarkness. As soon as we were in the living room, he proceeded with the centuries-old routine southern peoples used to combat the sun. When it was beating down without mercy, the shutters were lowered, the curtains were drawn, and the windows, doors, and balconies were shut tight. When it went down, everything was opened again. Disciplined and thorough, Ignacio repeated the sequence while

I surveyed his middling home. Neither too humble nor in any way luxurious, it was the home of a civil servant with a meager salary and good sense. It could've been his home or his neighbor's or anyone else's. There was nothing in it that gave it its own personality.

"I'm afraid I can only offer you a glass of tap water."

I remembered then that he'd never liked to drink, nor had he ever smoked.

"I don't want anything, thanks."

"Have a seat, at least."

I perched on the edge of an armchair. He sat opposite me, on a chair he pulled from under the dining table. Unhurried, he rolled up his shirtsleeves, leaned forward, and rested his elbows on his knees.

"Tell me."

I would've liked to have begun with a brief chat about our lives, to hear about his children, for instance, and to announce that I was a mother, too. In reality, we were both indifferent to the other's offspring. I wasn't interested in whether his were good at math or drawing, and he couldn't have cared less that Víctor now had eight teeth. But at least this would've helped to break the ice and given the situation a false sense of normalcy, nothing more than two old friends reunited and exchanging news.

But that wasn't the case, it was clear, and there was no reason to pretend otherwise. Ignacio and I weren't friends. We had gone our separate ways more than a decade before, when I left him to embark on my turbulent relationship with Ramiro. We'd had one brief encounter later, on my return from Morocco, after he followed me incognito through the streets of Madrid and slipped into my studio on Calle de Núñez de Balboa. That stormy night, I'd learned that he worked for the Directorate-General for Security of the Ministry of Governance. Using the powers he had in that role, he had forced me to show him my documentation, inspected my home from top to bottom, and fired a barrage of intrusive questions at me. After he'd scared the life out of me, there was also time that night for other things: for us to update each other on the preceding years with some degree of honesty, for him to admit that he performed his duties with bitter skepticism in a political regime with which he didn't agree. For him to unsparingly open my eyes to the painful reality that my neighborhood and its people experienced after their side was defeated in the war.

I'd never imagined that we would meet face-to-face again, yet there we were once more, together in his living room.

"I imagine you were surprised to see me at the entrance to the Ritz, among the guests at Eva Perón's banquet."

He shrugged, saying neither yes nor no—we were both recalling that moment when he'd held me amid the commotion. I could almost feel his firm hand again, on my waist, stopping me from falling.

"I've been abroad for a couple of years. Now I'm back in Spain to cover her visit as a BBC reporter."

"I know." Of course he knew. How could he not? "But I assumed you'd be in Andalusia now," he added.

"I arrived from Seville last night. It's a quick visit, and confidential. Nobody knows I'm in Madrid."

He didn't bat an eye. I observed his thin, pale face, the dark rings under his eyes, his receding hairline. I'd better get to the point, I decided, not waste any more of his time, or mine.

"The decoration that Franco awarded to the first lady, the Grand Cross of Isabella the Catholic, has been stolen. That's what I came to tell you."

"I know that, too." I hid my surprise as best I could. "No one in the Argentine delegation has reported it," he explained, "but we understand that the shipowner Dodero is trying to obtain a duplicate of the badge. The Cejalvo house informed us. They're the ones responsible for making all official decorations. They sensed that the request was irregular and wanted to make us aware. So we gathered that the badge is missing, though we can't openly confirm that with anyone in the Argentine entourage. We have express orders not to disturb them."

The confusion on my face must've been telling. He leaned forward a little more, as if he wanted the gesture to embolden him.

"We don't miss much, Sira. Or so we hope."

"And will Dodero manage to acquire an identical piece before the end of the tour?"

"We've given the go-ahead to Cejalvo, and they're working on it. It's a complex and laborious job and will take a long time. We know they're against the clock, but it's still not certain that they'll finish."

"But it will be essential that Señora Perón wear it for her final event before leaving Spain, won't it?"

"I would say so."

"And if she didn't wear it, it would be a direct affront to Franco, an unacceptable lack of consideration, don't you think?"

He nodded, serious, while he loosened his tie until it was completely unknotted, then undid the top button of his shirt. Despite his efforts to keep the flat cool, the place was still hot.

"We're conscious of all of that."

"And it doesn't worry you?"

"It does, a great deal."

"And do you have a contingency plan?"

He paused, rolling the long fabric of his tie in his hands before replying.

"If I'm honest, no, not as yet."

We were both silent for a moment, thinking. The sound of the few vehicles on the roads outside reached us through the balcony doors. An ugly cuckoo clock hanging over the sofa ticked wearily. Ignacio was the one who broke the silence, veering off topic abruptly.

"You never cease to amaze me, Sira. You appear, you disappear, you reinvent yourself, you mystify me. Now you're back as a supposed reporter, rubbing shoulders with leaders and involved in murky business. Last I knew of you, you were working for Nazi customers. Then when Germany fell, you vanished. I've often wondered where you ended up."

"I was doing my duty by sewing for those women," I said simply. "For reasons that are beside the point now, it was what I was required to do."

"You were hanging around with an English agent at the time."

I didn't like his airy tone, but Ignacio being who he was, I forgave him.

"I wasn't just hanging around with him," I explained, weighing my words carefully. "We were in a serious and sincere relationship, but in secret because of the circumstances. That English agent became my husband, and it will soon be a year since he died. I'm his widow, I have a son by him, and I'm trying to carry on with my life."

"I'm sorry," he muttered in a dry tone.

I perceived sincerity in those three syllables.

"Let's get back to the present. What I came to tell you is that I think I know where you'll be able to find the Grand Cross. The real one."

He straightened, with a look of disbelief on his face.

"But I want something in exchange," I added.

I stood and took a few steps. The room was not very attractive, but I was moved by its simplicity, with its magazine rack and its workbox and its calendar, its mediocre prints of still lives and sea storms dotted around the walls, and its crocheted back covers on the armchairs. My home would've been like this, no doubt, if our lives hadn't been thrown off course by the same cretin I was now trying to rid myself of. I was certain that if I'd carried on snooping around the flat, I would have found a mirror-fronted wardrobe in the bedroom, a canary in its cage, and in the kitchen, a pot of parsley and an apron hanging behind the door—the everyday things that people possessed.

Standing in the middle of the living room, wearing my Digby Morton suit, grotesquely out of place in that home and neighborhood, I made my demand.

"It's essential that the person you find in possession of the badge goes to jail for a time."

"That's what will happen, of course, if we find whoever stole it."

I shook my head.

"No. The person you'll seize the decoration from isn't the person who took it, but that must make no difference to you and your people. Even if he has alibis, even if they defend his innocence, it's vital that he spends time in detainment."

"Perhaps that's something a judge should decide."

I laughed cynically.

"Don't talk rubbish, Ignacio. You put whoever you want in cells and prisons. In this dark Spain, that's how things work. In any case, this is an embarrassing matter for everyone involved, humiliating and compromising both for the Argentine side and for Spain. For the sake of both countries, you and I know that nothing will ever be officially brought to light. It'll be as if the Grand Cross never left the first lady's neckline." I clicked my fingers, the action of a conjurer about to do a trick. "Now you see it, now you don't. As if nothing had happened."

He looked at me thoughtfully, weighing my proposal, wondering, perhaps, what on earth the dressmaker's apprentice he fell in love with in the Parque de la Bombilla was doing mixed up in this mess. The daughter of Señora Dolores, the girl from Calle de la Redondilla to whom he'd insisted on giving a typewriter back when he was still a naive and innocent young man.

"Promise me a month in jail for the person involved," I said emphatically, "and I'll give you all the details."

He shifted position, crossing his legs.

"I could guarantee you that, and you could tell me, right now."

"You could, but I'm not ready to share anything with you yet. I need a few days."

"It's not long before the gala dinner in Barcelona, the official farewell. The Generalísimo will be there, of course," he reminded me. "It'll be the visit's crowning moment and the last chance for Doña Eva to wear the Grand Cross in public."

I saw that, like me, he had the tour schedule memorized.

"You'll have it by then."

"Are you sure?"

I swallowed. No, I wasn't sure. Far from it. My ideas were still hazy, a reckless plan riddled with pitfalls that could lead to disaster. But there was no sense in going forward if even I didn't have faith in myself.

"You can count on it," I reaffirmed. "But you must leave me to handle this. Don't follow me or have anyone else do so. Don't try to verify anything or probe anyone, anywhere. Just leave me be."

He accompanied me to the door. How could he have guessed that I was carrying the coveted badge under my clothes? The simplest, the most sensible thing to do would have been to hand it over to him and explain what had happened with Juancito in the Sacromonte cave. But I didn't, and I left him knowing no more than he'd already known, that at some stage Doña Eva had lost the Grand Cross, and Dodero, instead of crying over spilled milk, had raced off to demand a new jug. Instead of trying to find a badge whose whereabouts were uncertain, he'd decided to replace it with another one.

Spilling the beans, in short, would've been the most advisable action, would have gotten me out of the picture and allowed me to forget about the uncomfortable situation forever. But some new words had entered my vocabulary in recent days, and it was Ramiro who'd injected them into me with his demands and low tricks and baseness of today, and with the painful memories of the past that he'd dug up. And these words were stalking me now, to the point that they'd become my prime objective. *Justice. Revenge. Retaliation.* With his persistence, he'd awakened the bitterness in me.

From the Castilian cabinet in the entrance hall, Ignacio took out a card.

"Here are my phone numbers, at the Directorate-General and my private one. Call me when you think we can go ahead."

I looked at him for the last time in the semidarkness; he hadn't turned on the light. My Ignacio, who'd nearly become my lifelong companion and the father of my children. The man I'd caused to suffer so much.

I started off down the stairs.

"Take care, Sira," I heard him say behind me.

It may have sounded like just a polite goodbye, but I was aware that his warning was sincere. Despite his coldness and cutting detachment, Ignacio's feelings remained unwavering. Though I didn't love him like he still loved me, I had to contain my longing to go back, hug him, and beg him not to forget me. He was the only person who connected me to the girl I'd once been, the girl I'd lost along the way.

For Ramiro, I was a fancy that had quickly gone out of date; for Marcus, I'd been the end of a journey; for Nick Soutter, I was a counterpoint, perhaps; while for Diego Tovar I might have seemed a bright extravagance in a gray world. But among all these men who'd at some time felt something for me, the one closing his door now was, without a shadow of a doubt, the one who'd loved me most. And the one who still did love me, despite how badly I'd repaid that love.

I resisted the urge to return to his side, however. If I'd asked him to hold me in his arms to give me courage, his reply would've been an emphatic no.

55

"It looks like the nanny has a suitor."

I knew this all too well. Even so, when my father confirmed it to me the next day over the telephone, I felt as if I'd been punched in the stomach.

"Have you seen him?"

"No, but Miguela suspected something, says she's in and out more often now, more dressed up, more cheerful. And today she asked for the afternoon off."

I held my breath.

"To go to a swimming pool, it seems," Gonzalo went on. "The Stella Club. It's just opened on Calle Arturo Soria. He must be a boy with a good job or of some means because, from what I hear, it's a stylish, modern place. Maybe he's the son of a local family, a kid who wants to practice his English or—"

"It's all right," I said, hiding my unease. "It's all right, give her permission. In fact, make it the whole day, not just the afternoon. Víctor can stay at home with you and Miguela today."

"Righto, whatever you say."

"Tell Philippa that it's an order, that I said to take the whole day off to relax. But please, don't mention the . . ." I stopped before saying the word that was on the tip of my tongue. *Suitor.* "Behave as if you don't suspect anything."

I hung up the receiver on the dirty wall at the back of Casa Prudencio, in that spot squeezed in between crates of soda bottles and demijohns of Valdepeñas wine. I was relieved that Ramiro wouldn't be going near Víctor today, but his courting of innocent Philippa stung like vinegar in an open wound. For her sake, because of the hurt that her fraudulent admirer could cause. And even more so because the girl was my employee, my responsibility, a foreigner in my care. But I needed her to keep Ramiro distracted, to give me time.

My next call prompted another breath of relief.

"Señor Tovar left for Santiago de Compostela in an official car early this morning."

The Diplomatic Information Office confirmed to me that Diego was already on his way to rejoin the tour on its brief visit to Galicia. I would work out how to justify my absence later, after he learned of it. For the time being, and to shore up my peace of mind, I considered his absence another obstacle checked off my list.

I had to step aside to let a half-deaf local call a relative, and then again so the owner of the bar himself could track down an order of God knows what. Once I had my place back at the grimy wall, I called the Palace Hotel.

"Good morning, Alberto, it's Livia Nash, from the BBC in London. I'm calling from Seville. I trust you remember me."

"I'm offended, dear. How could I forget you?"

His gallantry was just good manners. At that early hour and in his situation, the shipowner must have had little desire to flirt.

"I realized you were no longer in Señora Perón's entourage and was simply wondering whether everything is all right and if—"

"No problems, my darling, everything's fabulous." He spoke with too much force, aware, perhaps, that although I was a woman, and an attractive one, I still worked for the press. "I just had to return to Madrid unexpectedly to attend to a business matter," he added. "Nothing important."

"I trust we'll see each other again, in that case. Before the Rainbow Tour continues around Europe, I'd like to hear your final thoughts on Señora Perón's stay in Spain. You know, for my report."

"Of course, Livia. I'll join you as soon as possible. I don't think I'll make the Galicia visit, but I'll be in Barcelona . . ." I thought he sounded doubtful. "In Barcelona, soon, without fail."

I waited a couple of seconds, as if considering his tone.

"Forgive me if I seem nosy, Alberto, it could just be these dreadful Spanish telephone lines, but your voice sounds a little—"

"It's probably the heat, it's not good for my stress levels," he cut in before I could finish. "In Argentina it's the middle of winter right now. The contrast is stark."

My criticism of the nation's infrastructure, however, seemed to set him at ease a little because he proceeded to complain openly.

"The diabolical heat, and these hotels without air conditioning . . . ," he grumbled.

I smiled. An unexpected chink in his armor had opened before me. He didn't know my real identity, so I played upon my supposed foreignness.

"Almost everything's rather dreadful in this country. The infrastructure, the facilities, amenities . . ."

"All of it, all of it," he replied, vehement and conspiratorial. "The authorities are trying their best, I don't doubt it, but even finding some good ice and a decent whiskey for a drink on the rocks is a chore."

I felt a little disloyal. My country had just suffered a cruel war, and his was rich, with grain and meat coming out of its ears. *What did you expect, Dodero? To find yourself in New York, or Monte Carlo, or paradise?* I contained myself as an idea suddenly took shape in my mind. If Ramiro was intending to take Philippa to the Stella pool, perhaps I could try another angle.

"Still, if you're not too busy, there are some places in and around Madrid that make the heat rather more bearable."

"Not to worry, Livia, I don't think—"

"Have you had the chance to go to Villa Romana, for example? There's a fantastic swimming pool. Beautiful gardens, plenty of cool shade and comfortable deck chairs, an elegant atmosphere, excellent bar service and . . . and very lovely girls," I said with a burst of laughter as singsongy as it was hypocritical.

"Sounds tempting," he said. And he didn't sound insincere.

I punched the air, as if my team had scored a goal. I pressed on.

"Why don't you get out of Madrid for a day and relax? Forget about the heat. It'll seem like a different universe."

I emphasized my words with a lilting tone, exaggerating everything. In truth, I'd only been there once, with Diego Tovar, and that had been at night—the night Ramiro had reappeared among the strains of tango.

"Then when you're back at your hotel, in the evening . . ."

The shipowner bellowed with laughter, regaining his old optimism.

"You've convinced me, dear. What did you say the place was called? Villa Romana? I'd planned to drop by . . . that is, drop in to see how a delicate matter I'm dealing with is progressing, but I doubt I'm going to be able to resolve anything today, so I may as well postpone it. In fact, I think I'll head to this paradise you mention right away before the heat gets the best of me."

I left Casa Prudencio with my spirits high and rushed up the stairs to the guesthouse. As things stood, all the men who could hinder my plans were going to stay out of the way. It was time to worry about myself.

When I arrived in the kitchen to say goodbye to the landlady, she was hanging laundry, half her body leaning through the window into the well of the building. She turned when she heard my voice. She had an enormous pair of underpants in her hand and a couple of wooden pegs between her teeth. When she saw me, astonishment painted itself across her weathered face. I'd put on one of my plainest suits, done my makeup impeccably, and gathered my hair into a strict bun with a simple headpiece at the back. After looking me up and down in disbelief, she noticed my suitcase and frowned.

"I'm off."

I left another of my hundred-peseta notes on the table.

"I don't think I have enough change," she said, depositing the underpants on a stool and feeling her apron pockets.

"There's no need, it's fine."

I left her uninclined to go back to the clothesline, scratching her head, wondering once more what on earth a woman like me was doing in her miserable guesthouse.

The taxi driver held two fingers to his cap when I gave him instructions.

"Wait!"

He'd just started driving when I made him jam on the breaks.

"I'll just be a moment," I said, darting out of the car.

I'd noticed the little optician's next door to Casa Prudencio. I went into the narrow shop and examined the glasses on display.

"Those ones, please."

The optician in a white coat sounded surprised.

"They're for gentlemen, señorita."

"I want them for my fiancé. May I see them, please?"

He shrugged and took them out. I searched for a mirror with them in my hand and found one hanging on the wall. I tried them on. The frames were black, square, and large. The lenses were dirty, covered in fingerprints and dust. Who knows how long they'd been there?

"I think they're two-diopter lenses. He would have to come himself to be tested. He could come—"

I didn't let him finish.

"They're perfect as they are. I'll take them, thank you."

Back in the car, the driver had lit a stinking hand-rolled cigarette. The stench was infernal inside the old gasogene taxi.

"Excuse me, my friend," I said with my new spectacles in my hand. "Would you be able to find a slightly sleeker car than this one? It'll be a short journey. I'll pay whatever's necessary."

He looked at me in the mirror. His eyebrows were thick, and his greasy skin was covered in blackheads.

"My brother-in-law, maybe . . . How much are you prepared to shell out?"

I shot the magical figure at him. A hundred pesetas, as usual. He scratched his unshaven chin, thinking.

"A hundred for him and another hundred for yours truly?"

"If you don't make me wait, deal."

He put his foot down on the gas. We found the brother-in-law nearby, at the Ministry of Agriculture's garage. I stayed in the taxi, cleaning the scabby lenses with a handkerchief while he got out. They exchanged a few sentences I couldn't hear, punctuated with a great deal of gesticulation.

"Good to go, love," he said afterward through the lowered window. "But the car has to be back at three o'clock sharp."

56

The driver got out to open the door for me when we reached number 5 of the narrow Calle de la Cruz, a stone's throw from the plaza of Puerta del Sol, in the heart of the city. Permitting me to be driven in that government-owned Hispano-Suiza was certainly a risk for the driver's brother-in-law. But the undersecretary had a lunch planned at the ministry itself and wouldn't need it until later, and with my tip I was sure his subordinate would be able to plug one or two holes in his meager finances.

As soon as I got out, I put on my new glasses and looked up at the sign on the exterior wall. The blurred inscription read CEJALVO. JEWELRY. SILVERWARE. HERALDRY. MEDAL SPECIALISTS. I swallowed. "Let's do this," I whispered. My high heels clicked loudly on the floor. I was the only customer in the shop.

Three pairs of men's eyes turned toward me. One of the men, the eldest and highest ranking, came out from behind the counter to welcome me. They'd seen my splendid automobile through the shopwindow, no doubt. They didn't know who I was, but based on the car, I had to be someone important.

"Allow me to introduce myself. I'm in charge of protocol at the Embassy of the Argentine Republic in Spain," I announced in a serious tone. "I'd like to see the manager. It's an urgent matter."

He looked at me for a few seconds, as if processing my words. My accent had been perfect. I must've sounded like a true Argentine, because the assistant nodded in an almost military fashion and scurried to the back of the shop. He knocked on the door, went in when he was given permission, and quickly returned.

"Señor Cejalvo will see you right away, señora."

The office was neither large nor luxurious, and the man who was manager and owner of the business welcomed me courteously, looking a little stunned, while I adopted the demeanor of an efficient professional, my back straight, my hair gathered in a headpiece at my nape, and wearing my formal glasses. I neither cleared my throat nor hesitated. I acted as if I was used to these situations—confident, convincing.

"Our ambassador Dr. Pedro Radío is accompanying the first lady on her tour of Spain. In the interim, I'm responsible for dealing with any eventualities that arise at the embassy. I'd like you to know, however, that I speak on his behalf and that he shall be kept informed at all times."

In another environment, one wouldn't have needed to know much about how a diplomatic mission operates to have questioned my intentions. But in that Spain, isolated from the world and in a fever because of Eva Perón's visit, the Argentine authorities were seen as beneficent angels sent from heaven, indulged and protected by the regime. Not to be questioned or challenged.

"We have received news from the Ministry of Governance's Directorate-General for Security," I went on, improvising by citing Ignacio's organization, "that a supposed Argentine citizen has been visiting this establishment, attempting to obtain a replica of the Grand Cross of Isabella the Catholic that the Generalísimo awarded to Doña Eva."

I continued to imitate the accent I'd heard so many times over recent days.

"As representatives of the Argentine Republic, we're obliged to officially inform you that Don Alberto Dodero, who is in fact

Uruguayan-born, has no authority whatsoever to take formal measures concerning official gifts received by our first lady. Neither can he request duplicates, reproductions, or copies whose ultimate purpose we do not know. Least of all," I stressed to touch on a sore spot, "of an object the Generalísimo Don Francisco Franco himself gave to her."

I was surprised at my own nerve, though what I'd said wasn't a complete lie. In truth, the shipowner didn't have any official public role. He was just a well-known businessman whose organizational and financial contributions did not give him the right to meddle in diplomatic matters. I continued to speak, maintaining my same tone and posture. The jeweler listened intently, the tips of his ten fingers planted on the desk.

"We therefore ask you, señor, to stop the production of the new Grand Cross in your workshops, with immediate effect."

Cejalvo nodded slowly, understanding.

"To avoid any undesirable tensions, and given that Señor Dodero is a gentleman of a certain age and close to those who hope to fête Doña Eva, we advise you not to give him a flat refusal."

The jeweler raised his eyebrows.

"Fob him off," I suggested. "Stop the work he commissioned, but when he presses you for it, make excuses. Delays, difficult circumstances, unforeseen events . . . He'll stop bothering you soon and will have no choice but to leave Madrid. We know that he intends to follow Señora Perón first to Barcelona and then to Rome, where—as you may be aware—the Holy Father will receive her at the Vatican."

He nodded again, more emphatically this time. Pius XII was to receive Doña María Eva, and all of Spain knew it. How could the owner of this elite business not have heard?

He accompanied me all the way to the front door. My parked car had blocked a horse-drawn cart and another couple of automobiles from passing, but no one dared protest. Who would dare confront the driver of an official vehicle in that high-handed Spain? From the shop's entrance, he watched the chauffeur deferentially help me into the back seat.

Despite its success, my fraudulent performance left a sour taste in my mouth. It didn't sit well with me to cheat an honest business owner or to put a stop to the plans that meant so much to Dodero. But the situation called for it, necessary evils in the pursuit of my objective: ridding myself of Ramiro.

"To the Hotel Buen Retiro, please" was my next instruction for the ministry driver. "Once we arrive, take out my luggage and accompany me inside. As soon as you've left it at reception, you can go."

On the way, I took off the simple dark headpiece and put on an eye-catching velvet turban that I pulled from my handbag. I replaced the spectacles with my sunglasses.

The lobby of the former Hotel Gaylord's was almost empty at lunchtime. From the dining hall at the back, however, came the echo of conversations, cutlery, and dishes. There was just one receptionist behind the desk, a hollow-chested young man.

The procedure proved to be extremely simple. Well-married Spanish women weren't allowed to open bank accounts, obtain their own passports, or perform any kind of formality without their husband's permission. Working outside the home was considered improper, and checking into a hotel alone, an unacceptable audacity. But with my British passport, fake chauffeur, big sunglasses, and turban, I was a bona fide foreigner. And foreigners like me had carte blanche.

"My husband airplane arrive tomorrow," I said in broken Spanish as I collected the key.

I swallowed my sadness as I went into the elevator with a porter carrying my luggage. The very same contraption had taken me up to meet Marcus years before, on the weekend that would mark the beginning of our short and ill-fated story as a couple. This time, however, I was not heading to a suite with a balcony; neither was there an enamored man waiting for me. Now, passing myself off as an extravagant outsider, I ascended for reasons that were infinitely less pleasant.

The hotel had given me room number 514. It seemed comfortable and functional, in keeping with the building's rationalist architecture. Patiently, so I'd grasp what he was saying, the receptionist had informed me that, with the exception of the corner rooms and top-floor suites, the rooms were all identical. As soon as the porter had left with his tip, I got to work.

The first thing I did was change. I flung off my heels, turban, and suit, and put on low shoes and the anodyne mourning clothes I'd bought on Calle Atocha—no trace remained of the elegant Englishwoman. Seeing my new look in the mirror, I felt the bite of fear. What if it all went wrong? What if everything, due to my own rashness, to my own foolishness, turned against me? The Diplomatic Information Office, the BBC in London, the secret service itself: I would betray them all, look like a contemptible person. No one would stand up for me.

I tried to banish those dark thoughts like blackbirds. "For God's sake, focus," I told myself through clenched teeth. Back when I'd collaborated with the British, while Madrid was crawling with Nazis, I had been given some basic training in the art of seeing without being seen, of sticking one's nose into other people's business. One of these skills was to open locks with a simple hairpin. I tested my old expertise on my own door and was relieved to find that I could still do it effortlessly.

I saw no one either in my corridor or as I walked down to the next level. As soon as I set foot on the fourth floor, I heard men's voices coming from the corridor to the left. Someone waiting for the lift, I assumed. Motionless beside a pillar, I waited until the mechanical doors closed and silence returned.

I knew more or less where to find the room; the floor plans were identical. I stepped forward cautiously, holding my breath, without giving panic the chance to sink its fangs into me again: 409, 411, 413, 415. When I reached 417, I knocked. As I expected, there was no response.

Hand in pocket, hairpin, door handle, door. In seconds, I was inside. Only then did I breathe easily again.

I stepped forward into a room darkened by drawn curtains, uncertain until I confirmed that the layout of the furniture was the same as mine. I approached the desk, pulled the little chain on the table lamp. There was an address book with a dark cover, and I opened it with the tips of my fingers. I recognized Ramiro's small, neat handwriting in the names, addresses, and numbers. None that I read at a glance were familiar and neither were the street names: Posadas, Tucumán, Belgrano, Ayacucho. Curious, I looked under *S* and *Q*, confirming that Sira Quiroga appeared in neither place. There was also a Waterman pen and promotional leaflets for motors and machines—I supposed for the business in which he supposedly had a stake. I found handbills for clubs and bars in Madrid—Pasapoga, Le Cock, Molinero, Pidoux—and some business cards bearing his new name: Román Altares, Riobamba, 952, Buenos Aires. For some reason, I took one.

My plan had been to act as quickly and as efficiently as possible: choose the ideal place, carry out my task, and leave right away. But I didn't behave that way. It was as if my feet had turned to lead, and my hands were refusing to obey me. I headed slowly to the head of the beds; Ramiro hadn't been a reader when we were together, and the absence of books indicated that he still wasn't. On the bedside table, beside the alarm clock and a bottle of unlabeled pills, I found only a few news magazines. Among these, with each relevant page marked with folded corners, were a couple of copies of the Argentine *El Hogar* magazine. I flicked through them, and in both cases I found articles with photographs in which Eva Perón appeared alongside Alberto Dodero.

Then I opened the wardrobe. I found three suits made from excellent fabric, several sport jackets, more than half a dozen shirts. I unhooked one that seemed to have been worn and held it to my face. The familiar scent, the one I'd hoped to forget, filled my nose, a man-smell as enticing as it was unsettling.

"Stop being an idiot," I said to myself. "Stop looking and rummaging. For heaven's sake, Sira, hurry up and find a place."

I retraced my steps to the desk and pulled on the little chain again, leaving the room in semidarkness once more. I then went into the bathroom, hit the switch, and the lamps on each side of the mirror came on. I resisted looking at my face; I couldn't have borne seeing myself. On a shelf I found an elegant toilet bag. I picked it up delicately, stroking the caramel-colored leather with my fingertips—soft Argentine leather of supreme quality, I was sure. I put it down on the toilet lid, unfastened its clasp, and it unfolded into two halves, like an open book. Inside, tidily arranged and held in place with bands of the same leather, were little bottles with silver caps for eau de cologne and lotion, a soap dish, a shoehorn, shoe cloths, a clothes brush. As vain as Ramiro was, and as laughable as Spanish prices were, he undoubtedly had his shoes polished by a bootblack and his face shaved by a good barber every day. Hence, almost all his utensils were stored in the toilet bag and only his toothbrush, toothpaste, and a comb were missing: the essentials.

The idea came to me all of a sudden: I'd hidden the badge in my own toiletry case in Granada; perhaps his could be a good hiding place, too. I picked the case up again to weigh it, holding it on the palms of both hands.

"Perfect," I whispered.

Thanks to the glass of the grooved bottles, their metal lids, and the rest of the contents, the case wasn't light, and adding a new object would make little difference. I felt the bottom of each side until I found the most appropriate spot. There: under the shoe cloths. From my pocket, I took the little sewing kit I'd carried around with me for years and extracted my minuscule scissors from it. With just the tips, I popped the stitches on one side.

I pulled the Grand Cross of Isabella the Catholic from my bra strap, the same hiding place I'd used on the first day when the old woman handed it over to me in Sacromonte. Without stopping even to look at it, I inserted it in the newly opened seam and, with my skilled dress-maker's fingers, slid it inside and pushed it against the bottom. Once I'd ensured that it was in the right place, I removed my hand and proceeded to redo the stitches with a needle I'd already threaded. The opening was sealed with an undetectable seam.

"Perfect," I murmured again.

I examined the inside and outside of the case with a meticulous eye. Nothing looked strange. I held it again, caressing the almost silky leather. The additional weight was barely noticeable.

I was about to put the case back in its place when a distant sound broke the silence. I got goose bumps and a wave of terror flooded through me. It wasn't my imagination, my fears playing a sinister trick on me. It was a faint but unmistakable click: a key turning in its lock. I stealthily placed the case on the shelf while with the other hand I turned off the light and closed the door from the inside.

My heart beat furiously. Someone was entering the room.

57

I couldn't see them, but their voices reached me clearly through the wood. What an idiot, what an imbecile I'd been, taking for granted that they'd spend the whole day at that Stella pool, cooling themselves down in its blue water, lying with faces to the sun, on hammocks. Naively, I hadn't considered that events might proceed differently.

"Here we are, you'll feel better here, no sun here, no sun in this room, see?"

He was mixing Spanish from two continents with a smattering of English. She replied in little more than a murmur.

"Here," Ramiro indicated. "Here on the bed, lie down."

The frame squeaked, and Philippa, always so Britishly correct, said a "thank you very much" in an incredibly weak voice. Once she was lying down, I heard the sounds of him moving around the room: the key clunking on a surface, the hinges of a wardrobe door, the catch closing. Meanwhile, I sat in the dark with my heart in my mouth, curled up behind the shower curtain, hidden in the bathtub.

My immediate assumption was that Philippa wasn't well. No doubt the sun, too fierce for her pale English skin, was to blame, heatstroke at the worst time of day. Perhaps he had given her some alcohol— vermouth for their aperitif, sangria with lunch, who knows. And she never usually touched it. Finding himself responsible for the girl, albeit reluctantly so, Ramiro had no choice but to keep her in his hotel room until she felt better. Heaven only knew what ploys he'd used to get her in without her being registered with reception. Feeling dizzy and faint, Philippa would've imagined, I was sure, that the best thing to do would be to go back to my father's flat. But Ramiro would've taken charge, and the poor girl probably didn't have the strength to resist. Or perhaps she was dying of embarrassment.

I was speculating about these things when Ramiro threw the bathroom door open. He slapped the light switch, and I sunk my head between my legs, wanting to dissolve, to disappear down the bathtub drain. I heard him turning a tap. Water gushed from the pipes, then he rubbed his hands together beneath it and filled a glass. After that, I sensed, he was wetting something, a towel or a handkerchief perhaps. He went back into the bedroom, leaving the bathroom door open and the light on. He must've given Philippa a drink, then pressed the damp material to her brow. She muttered another feeble thank-you.

A stretch of time that felt infinite went by. Now and again he asked her how she felt, but without any enthusiasm and without feigning any affection. I noticed growing annoyance in his voice. At some point he picked up the telephone and gave the operator the number of a room in the same hotel, but when she tried to connect him there was no answer. Then he requested another call, but the same thing happened. He slammed the receiver back in its cradle. He was clearly upset. Nothing was going as planned, and he was starting to lose his temper.

Another stretch of time passed that seemed no less eternal. He'd lain on the other twin bed, and I heard him moving restlessly as if struggling to find a comfortable position. I heard him leaf noisily through one of his magazines, then throw it on the floor. I remained in the bathtub, my arms wrapped around my legs, my back arched, motionless in the fetal position. I couldn't help jumping when the telephone rang. Ramiro snatched up the receiver.

I caught only scraps of the conversation; his fake Buenos Aires accent made it difficult for me to follow. But I grasped the substance, and the substance was a string of lies about his supposed future meeting with Dodero. That everything was almost ready, the decisive meeting would soon be confirmed, they just had to agree to a time. That success was a foregone conclusion, and the shipowner was going to accept everything they were offering—spare parts and components for seaplanes, a range of supplies. There was nothing to worry about, he insisted, because the caller's sizable investment—a juicy sum by the sound of it—would be repaid twofold, multiplied by three, four, or even five.

"Chicote at ten o'clock. All right, see you there. Perfect."

He hung up and huffed, letting out an expletive. Then, unable to do anything else, powerless and fed up, with Philippa nearby—more serene now—he allowed himself to be caught up in the tide of sleep.

There were 268 tiles on the three walls surrounding the bathtub. I counted them one by one several times. They were glossy, perfectly symmetrical in their layout, with a bluish-green tone. On a shelf there was a bar of soap and a sponge. The shower curtain was made of a vanilla-colored fabric, machine stitched. I fixed my attention on all of this with extreme concentration to try to keep my fear at bay.

When I thought Ramiro had fallen asleep, I slowly, silently, got up, listening. As I drew back the curtain, I looked up to make sure the metal rings didn't hit one another or slide noisily along the bar. Hitching up my skirt, I lifted one leg out of the tub and then the other, leaving just my tiptoes on the floor. I patted my thighs to make sure I had the sewing kit and my room keys in my pockets. Then I flicked the light switch as slowly as possible so that it barely made a sound, guessing that the darkness would work in my favor should he wake up.

I crept into the bedroom, approaching Philippa's bed with cautious steps. As I passed her feet I saw her shoes and handbag on the floor. I left the former but bent to pick up the latter and hung it from my shoulder. When I reached the headboard I bent down toward her. Counting to three so I'd move my hands at the same time, I firmly covered her mouth with one to stop her screaming, and with the other I pulled her arm to get her up.

"It's me, Mrs. Bonnard," I whispered in her ear before she could react. "We have to get out of here right now. For God's sake, don't say a thing."

Despite the fright, in a sudden flash of lucidity she seemed to recognize me. I managed to get her onto her feet, weak and wobbly.

"We're going, Philippa, you hear?" I insisted in a barely audible voice. I was still holding her with her mouth covered.

She nodded emphatically.

"Good girl, let's go," I whispered an inch from her ear.

I finally took my hand from her mouth, held her by the shoulders, and pushed her forward. One step, another step, one more, another. In seven we were at the door, in nine we were out in the corridor. I didn't close it completely, to avoid making noise. Behind us we'd left a pair of sandals, a sleeping Ramiro, and the Grand Cross of Isabella the Catholic hidden in his toilet bag in the bathroom.

I took her quickly to my room, submerged her in lukewarm water, and she seemed to begin to recover. I consoled her when she cried and apologized to me, contrite. She mentioned the heat and the sun and the red wine and some sweet drinks whose alcohol content she didn't know. I soothed her, made her stop talking, told her that everything was all right, and put her in bed again. At around eleven o'clock that night, I made two calls. One to reception, to confirm that Ramiro had gone out. Another to my father, for him to come in a taxi to collect the hungover, sunburnt, and shoeless nanny.

A porter took my note to Ramiro the next morning.

In your hotel restaurant, in half an hour.

In exchange for ten pesetas, the young man had promised that he would keep knocking on the door to room 417 until he'd personally handed the message to its occupant. It was almost ten o'clock, and by then I'd already made a few arrangements. The easiest was to confirm that Philippa had slept well, that she was up and taking care of Víctor. Her skin was red and sore, but she was all right.

Rather more uncomfortable was my conversation with Diego Tovar. With his office's assistance, I located him in Vigo. Following a brief visit to Santiago, the tour's Galician stage was moving full steam ahead, and the sheer number of engagements and activities was dizzying. Señora Perón and her entourage had slept at Castrelos House, the rest of the delegation at Hotel Universal. To justify my absence, I made up some small excuses.

"When do you think you'll be able to rejoin?" I heard him say through the interference.

He sounded sincerely concerned. Because of the BBC report, no doubt. Maybe also a little because of me.

"I'll try to be in Barcelona as soon as possible."

"Contact my office and ask for whatever you need. Tickets, a car, anything."

There was no way he could know that I was about to meet an undesirable who'd put me through hell years before, but his voice sounded as if he did.

"Take care, Livia." He paused before adding, "You're missed."

I was replaying the conversation with Diego Tovar in my head, regretting that I'd had to lie to him as well, when Ramiro arrived in the restaurant. I was waiting for him in a discreet place against the wall with a cup of tea in front of me. He saw me right away. He was wearing one of the shirts and one of the light-colored jackets I'd seen in his wardrobe. His hair was wet and neatly styled, fresh from the shower where I'd spent a few terrifying hours the previous afternoon.

"Before I even say good morning, Sira, I want to apologize . . ."

He bent toward me, as if wanting to press home his excuse and greeting with a single kiss on the cheek—in the Argentine way, I supposed. I recoiled, refusing it. He sat opposite me and continued with his lies.

"I just wanted the girl to enjoy herself a little, but when I took my eye off her she disappeared. I looked everywhere for her but couldn't—"

"Don't bother," I cut in.

He looked at me, feigning bewilderment.

"You really don't want to know how—"

A waiter in a white jacket approached the table. He offered Ramiro a breakfast menu, which he refused, almost ramming it into the man's kidneys when he unceremoniously handed it back. He knew what he was going to have; Ramiro always knew what he wanted. He reeled off his order of eggs with underdone pork belly, bread rolls with butter, fruit salad, black coffee in a large cup, a double orange juice. Once we were alone again, I closed my eyes and breathed through my nose. I opened them again as I blew air slowly out through my mouth, arming myself with patience.

"I'm sick of you, Ramiro. Your pressuring and intimidation, your demands."

"You've got me wrong, sweetheart. The English girl's dull but pretty. I genuinely like her, I'm serious."

"And now that you've gotten the poor girl drunk and almost given her second-degree burns, what's next? Where would you intend to take my father? What plan do you have for my son if I don't agree to your wishes?"

"My God, Sira—"

"I know you, Ramiro. It's been more than ten years, but you're the same person. Nothing stops you when you want something. Obstacles don't even exist as far as you're concerned."

"I don't want you to think that of me, I don't—"

I planted my hands on the table and leaned toward him, sober and serious.

"You win."

He raised an eyebrow, just one, as if he were a Hollywood heart-throb. Even fresh out of bed, the lowlife was attractive.

"I don't want you to bother my family again. I don't want any more problems. I don't trust you an inch. I surrender. It's hard for me to say this because you don't deserve it, but I'm throwing in the towel. You'll have your meeting with Dodero."

He looked at me, taking in my unexpected decision. Satisfaction may have been running through his veins, but he contained himself and didn't show any jubilation openly. He was a scoundrel through and through, but not a reckless madman. He knew what was needed in any given moment.

"I appreciate it, Sira. Really. Thank you."

To emphasize his words, he held his right hand to his chest. He was convincing, and he seemed honest in his reactions. But I ignored the gesture and concentrated on finishing my tea with apparent indifference.

"All we need to do," I said, separating my lips from the cup, "is set a date. I'll try to make it as soon as possible, so you can stop pestering me and I can forget about this whole unpleasant business."

I left the cup on the saucer and got up. Like a gentleman, he stood too and approached to pull the chair out for me. Then he went to take a step forward beside me, but I stopped him in his tracks.

"There's no need for you to accompany me. Enjoy your breakfast." My back was turned when, without looking at him, I added, "I'll let you know what agreement I come to with the shipowner."

58

The National Theater Company exceeded all expectations. The actors, the set, the lighting, and the sound effects made for a magnificent performance of Shakespeare's *A Midsummer Night's Dream*. But at almost four in the morning, the audience, though they tried, couldn't stop the involuntary closing of eyes, the nodding of heads, and the yawning.

We were in Barcelona, in the gardens on the great hill of Montjuic, where a big stage had been set up under the stars. Some fool had had the idea to schedule the performance for after midnight: half past midnight, in theory. But as always, the delays piled up and it was after three before we took our seats. I'd returned to my duties at last, and by all appearances I was focused on gathering impressions for my future report. That facade, however, was only a half-truth, and if anyone had been able to see inside my head, they would've found my brain working in two dimensions. One part of my mind was operating right there in the preferential seats reserved for foreign correspondents, while the other was galloping someplace else, at a hundred miles per hour.

A couple of days before, I'd come out of my meeting with Ramiro at the former Hotel Gaylord's convinced that everything was ready: the Grand Cross was hidden in his toilet bag, he'd been placated by the promise of a meeting, and Ignacio was waiting for my signal to arrest him. Events would begin to unfold as soon as I wanted them to. Once the Argentine national Román Altares was detained for possessing the badge that had been taken from the first lady, everything else would fall into place. True, he hadn't stolen anything in this case. But he had in the past. And now he'd deviously coerced me, behaved miserably with Philippa . . . who knows how far he would've taken things if I hadn't stopped him? The punishment he received, for whatever reason he received it, would be more than justified.

And yet, surprisingly, I'd felt no satisfaction after leaving him with his succulent breakfast. Feeling uncomfortable, I'd taken a taxi to Hermosilla. I was on edge, tired after that turbulent night in Granada, Seville and its confusion, the return journey to Madrid by train, the run-down guesthouse in Atocha, all my comings and goings, the constant telephone calls, the toing and froing in and out of the Gaylord, my lies, my deception, my machinations and dissembling. I needed rest, a bit of calm and fresh air before the next step. A physical rest, but not just that. Above all, I needed to give my poor soul a bit of peace.

Víctor had welcomed me with delight. He threw himself into my arms, laughed his head off, pinched my face, pulled my hair. We'd only been apart for a few days, but I had the impression he'd grown. He hadn't started walking on his own yet, but he could do it with a little help. With him gripping my little finger, we went up and down the incredibly long hall in my father's flat half a dozen times. I fed him a plate of rice with chicken, and he sat on my lap while I finished my lunch. Then we lay on the sofa together to take a nap in the semidarkness of the living room while my father was out for lunch at the Gran Peña. I started singing "El Señor Don Gato" in a low voice, and within a couple of verses he was out, lying atop my body. Seconds later, I too fell asleep, under his weight.

I thought I was dreaming when an insistent murmur began to circle my head. "Señora, señora, señora . . ." I noticed I was being shaken, opened my eyes, confused, and found myself looking at Miguela's wizened face a few inches from mine.

"Señora," she whispered again, so as not to wake Víctor. "There's a call for you. They say it's urgent."

I slid off the sofa to receive the call at the desk in my father's study.

"You almost pulled it off, my girl. I almost believed you."

I was standing in bare feet. I swallowed. It was Ramiro.

"I don't consider a job done until I've tightened all the screws, Sira. Maybe you don't remember that about me, or perhaps it's something I've learned to do later, over time. So to make sure your promise was solid, I dropped by the Palace, where you told me yourself Dodero was staying. In fact, I'm calling you from here right now."

There was a soft whirring in the background; he could equally have been telling the truth or lying.

"The shipowner should be there," I said. "I spoke to him yesterday."

"He was. He *was*. Past tense of the verb 'to be.'"

"What do you mean he 'was'?"

"He 'was' because he's not anymore. He's gone."

"Gone? Where?"

"You tell me."

It took me a moment to fit the pieces together; I was still shaking off the cobwebs of sleep. If the Argentine magnate had given up on Madrid, the logical thing would be for him to proceed to the next stage of the tour.

"I suppose he's on his way to Barcelona, then, to prepare for the arrival of—"

He didn't let me finish.

"How sure are you of that?"

"Almost completely."

"And you'll be there, too?"

I could've told him it was none of his business but preferred not to show my irritation.

"Of course. I have to continue covering the tour."

"Good. Get me a meeting with him in Barcelona, then."

All the calm politeness he'd shown me that morning seemed to have vanished. Ramiro's tone was demanding and detached now, as cold as a knife plunged into ice. I sensed that this was more than a simple mood change. The way he spoke suggested something darker.

"Leave a message with reception at my hotel, but don't bother asking to speak to me. I'm not there anymore. I've gone away, too."

I slumped into my father's leather armchair with the heavy receiver pressed against my ear. *Oh God. Oh God. Oh God.* Ramiro had left Hotel Buen Retiro. And he would've taken his luggage, naturally. And his toilet bag would be in his luggage, with the Grand Cross inside. And I didn't know where he was staying now, and he didn't seem to have any intention of telling me.

"I'm losing my patience, Sira," he went on, unrelenting. "And worst of all, I anticipated it. I knew you'd try to put me off with false promises and anger, so hurt, so wounded by my behavior. You've reminded me you were always like this, touchy, unbearably sensitive. That's why I tired of you and left, I should think."

I sat back and closed my eyes.

"I don't know exactly what you are now," he continued without stopping to take a breath. "Your past is a mystery. If I'm honest, since I left Tangier I've been too busy to take the slightest interest in you. I've had businesses, women, ups and downs, good times and bad. I haven't had time to spare. I've also had friends. And one of them, would you believe it, has been in London for a few months, it turns out. As it happens, he owed me a favor, and he just repaid me with a bit of information that alarms me."

He continued with a serious tone, relentless.

"Nobody knows you at the BBC, as Livia Nash or Sira Quiroga or however you prefer to be called. No one has ever heard either the name you use now or the one you had before. The friend I'm talking about is Argentine and well connected, and the Latin American and Spanish crowd isn't so big. Everyone knows everyone or they've heard of one another, not least of all someone who's supposed to work in radio. But curiously, nobody has ever heard anything about you."

I didn't bother to reply. The excuses and cover stories I used with others wouldn't work with Ramiro. The fact was, he now knew what no one else in Spain must know. And with that knowledge, he had the upper hand.

"So, to be clear," he added forcefully. "Barcelona. Dodero. I need concrete progress. And it's no use just offering me a place and time, and then you disappear. I don't trust you. I want you to be at the meeting, to come with me, to push him, find a way to make the shipowner accept my proposals."

He knew I was listening, just as he knew I wouldn't reply. He finally paused, and I could hear faint piano notes in the background. Perhaps he hadn't been lying when he said he was at the Palace.

"You'll work out how to do it, Sira. I'm mystified by the arts you use with those people. I don't know whether you win them over by playing innocent or by exciting them between the sheets. It's neither here nor there to me. Either way, you know what I need. Cooperate, or I'll make sure those concerned know that the supposed BBC reporter they treat with such deference, the one who parades around with grandees and pokes her nose in everywhere, is nothing but a fraud."

Two days later, I was recalling that conversation, as I had so many times in the intervening days, while I contemplated the Montjuic Park stage full of characters penned by Shakespeare. I hadn't heard from Ramiro since the call, and I didn't know whether he was still in Madrid or was now in Barcelona like me, waiting for his appointment with the shipping tycoon. As we applauded the performance and got to our feet, two mysteries were still hounding my thoughts. First, where was Ramiro—and, with him, the Grand Cross? And second, where the hell had Alberto Dodero disappeared to?

I'd assumed that I would find the shipowner there, attending the first engagements of the final days of the tour. But no, he hadn't shown up. The first lady was escorted by her good-for-nothing brother, by her personal companion, by the ambassador whose orders I'd pretended to be following at the jeweler's, and by other loyal followers. But not by Dodero. He hadn't shown his face at those initial events in Barcelona where, to the delight of those attending, Evita wore another over-the-top cabaret-star hairstyle and her white lamé dress, cascading jewelry, and an ermine stole that almost reached the floor. She wasn't sporting the badge that the Generalísimo had pinned on her, but expectations regarding the farewell dinner hosted by Franco were another matter.

They put us up at the Hotel Majestic on Paseo de Gracia—quality and luxury for the foreign journalists, as ever. Only three or four of those who'd been at that first meeting at the press club in Madrid remained, but for the Barcelona visit, in preparation for the leap to the rest of Europe, a few new ones had joined us. A well-dressed correspondent from *Il Giornale d'Italia*, a slender gentleman from the French agency Havas, a Pathé News reporter, and three or four more whose particulars I didn't concern myself with. I had other problems.

I woke early despite the late night, and the first thing I did was ask reception whether any messages had been left for me.

"No, none, Señora Nash."

"And Señor Alberto Dodero? Has an Argentine gentleman by the name of Alberto Dodero checked in in the last few hours, by any chance?"

"No, Señora Nash."

A few minutes after I hung up, the telephone rang. I answered anxiously—perhaps the receptionist had made a mistake and there was something for me. Or the shipowner had arrived after all.

"Livia? Good morning, it's Diego Tovar. I'm calling to let you know that this morning's engagements have been canceled. We'll try to rearrange the activities for a later date. The first lady is exhausted, and it's better that she rests. We have another busy schedule lined up for the afternoon and evening."

I didn't know if he was aware of my relief when I thanked him. To hell with the trade fair visit, the applause, the anthems, the rushing around! I was about to say goodbye when he interrupted me.

"It's a luxury on this tour to have some free time. Do you know Barcelona? Can I persuade you to come for a walk and I'll show you around?"

I hesitated. It was the first time I'd set foot in the city, and the idea of a morning off was tempting. But no, I had to stay focused. At the same time, however, it wasn't wise to turn him down, particularly after the fright I'd had in the last few days. Wavering, I made a counteroffer.

"How about we meet for lunch? I'd like to make the most of this breather and get ahead with some work."

If I'd been a real reporter, that was what I would've done. As nothing more than an impostor, however, I threw myself into my other matters. I went down the big hall and found the switchboard. I remembered how wonderfully the operators at the Alhambra Palace had treated me and hoped they would do the same here. In keeping with the size of the hotel and the upbeat tempo of the city, instead of two employees working the lines, I found five.

Barcelona was a big city where anything could happen, and the Majestic was a hotel that catered not just to relaxed tourists but also to all kinds of visitors with more urgent business and problems. I wasn't going to get away with playing the charming but scatterbrained young wife of an older millionaire. Feigning an Argentine accent once again, I adopted a different role—it was all I could think to do. In a serious, almost severe tone, I mentioned the Diplomatic Information Office, Señora Perón, and their busy schedule of activities. I threw every name I could think of into the mix, but without identifying myself as holding any particular official position. In any case, they eventually took me to be someone with a certain amount of authority, and I achieved my objective.

"So what is it you need exactly, señora?"

"To locate Don Alberto Dodero as soon as possible. Please start with Pedralbes Palace and then all the city's five-star hotels, as well as the four-star ones. Please be as careful as possible. And contact me in my room as soon as—"

Something caught the attention of my left ear and I stopped dead. Sitting with her switchboard plugs in front of her at the last station, one of the youngest operators had just said some compelling words.

"I'll put you through to Señor Duarte right away."

I took a couple of steps toward her and redoubled my air of authority, even raising a finger for emphasis. I didn't know who was calling the brother or why, but I was going to find out.

"If the gentleman doesn't answer, please keep trying."

She nodded obediently. She would keep up the effort until she managed to get Juancito out of bed, the bathtub, or God knows where else.

"Señor Duarte, a very good morning to you," she said at last. "It's an international call. I'll put you through to the ambassador of the Argentine Republic in London."

I don't know where I found the nerve, but by the time the conversation had started, I had the girl's headphones over my ears.

59

I heard everything, of course. I even noted down some details with a pencil on the pad that the operator put in front of me when I requested it by scribbling in the air.

I hadn't received any news about Señora Perón's visit to London since her stylists had put me in the picture about the outfit she was planning to wear there, or since the first lady herself had mentioned the invitation she was longing for, while on board the plane to Granada. At times, I felt pricks of guilt like pins in my conscience—faced with this lack of information, perhaps I should have been more probing, found other ways to discover how things were progressing. But the last few days had been so frenetic that this hadn't been possible.

"First of all, I hope you will allow me to extend my good wishes for your saint's day tomorrow."

Despite the shortcomings of the telephone lines, I could hear maturity and judiciousness in the man's voice.

"Everyone at the diplomatic mission in London wishes you a very happy day, señor, as we do our president."

Sure enough, it was June the twenty-third, Saint John's Eve, the night of festivities that preceded the Feast Day of Saint John the Baptist—when Juan Domingo de Perón and Juan Duarte himself would celebrate their saint's day. Hence the ambassador Dr. Ricardo Labougle's good wishes.

"We wished to contact you," he went on, "to update you and to request that you pass on some particulars to the first lady."

The ambassador was astute—astute and wary. What he was about to communicate was not, I was sure, welcome news. And foreseeing Evita's furious outburst, he preferred to use an intermediary to shield himself.

"If she decides in the end to add the United Kingdom to her tour," the diplomat went on, "the British Government insists on welcoming her with the appropriate etiquette for the first lady of a friendly country. But the visit, it seems almost certain, would not be granted the desired official status in any way."

There was irritation in Juancito's voice.

"And what does that mean, Labougle? That the king and queen won't receive her?"

"I fear as much, señor. His Majesty's government does not believe it appropriate for the king or queen or prime minister to issue an official invitation. If the first lady still wishes to come, they propose receiving her with the usual courtesy that is extended to any distinguished foreign visitor. A schedule of visits would be drawn up for her, but with a low, almost private profile. The wife of Prime Minister Attlee would, however, be pleased to take tea with her . . ."

"Where? At Buckingham Palace?"

"I regret to inform you, señor, that such an option would be impossible. Buckingham Palace is the official residence of the Crown. Only the king and queen themselves receive guests there, and they are soon to take up residence at Balmoral Castle, in Scotland, where they will spend the summer. They won't even be in London on the dates the first lady has proposed."

A sharp sound reverberated on my eardrum: Juan Duarte, making a noise of displeasure.

"The king and queen will be on holiday when my sister arrives, is that what you're saying? Have the English not heard how she's being received here in Spain, as if she were a princess?"

"That's precisely why, señor. With all due respect to your host General Franco, London has no interest in doing anything that would liken Britain to the Spanish regime."

I was fascinated by the ambassador's patient attitude, the unruffled courtesy with which an official of his rank handled a commoner like Juancito, who'd been propelled to the top of the pyramid by nothing more than a leg up from a family member. Nonetheless, the ambassador preferred to contend with him rather than with her—a hundred sharp retorts from Juan Duarte were better than facing the first lady's fury.

"Are you serious, Doctor? How do I explain to Eva that they won't receive her in the manner she deserves? Do you have any idea of the hell that'll break loose here? Don't do this to me, Ambassador. Tell me there's still a way to persuade them to have the king and queen receive her . . . or at least the full government. Use the negotiations for procuring planes and ships from them as leverage, tell them those deals can fall through, put pressure on them regarding the agreements on meat imports they want to renew. Who do they think they are, these people?"

He raised his tone, flaring up. The ambassador remained stoically silent.

"Almost half of all the meat those down-and-outs ate during the war was sent by us! Have they forgotten? I'm serious, Doctor, those degenerates need to understand who they're dealing with. Or sparks will fly here, and if they do, we'll all suffer for it . . ."

There was whistling and interference on the line. The operators continued to bustle with their plugs and messages while I remained absorbed, holding my breath, headphones on.

"While I understand your position, Señor Duarte, I must ask you to inform the first lady of the need to make her final decision public as soon as possible. The British press won't stop publishing conjecture, and our credibility as a nation is being gravely damaged. If you would allow me to make a suggestion, señor, both Foreign Minister Bramuglia and I, even the president himself, believe that, for the sake of our bilateral relations, this kind of private visit would be preferable to no visit taking place at all."

Juancito was silent for a moment, seemingly reflecting.

"Prime Minister Attlee's wife, Lady Violet," the ambassador went on, "is a mature and magnificent woman. She has always been a huge support for her husband, just as Doña Eva is for our president. During the war she was a nurse, she did great work for the Red Cross, and—"

Juan Duarte cut him off with a somewhat menacing tone.

"It seems we don't understand each other, Señor Ambassador. Do you really think that Doña María Eva Duarte de Perón, wife and special envoy of His Excellency the president of the Argentine Republic, will be content with being received in London by nothing more than a fat old woman, to go for a stroll and have tea and cakes?"

Heroically, the ambassador stood his ground.

"Allow me to explain, señor . . ."

But the former representative of the Guereño soap company, now presidential secretary, had had enough.

"Not one more word. I'll pass on the information to the first lady because you've asked me to, but know in advance that you would be wise to insist to the British. Either they receive her in the manner that befits her—with the highest honors and sparing no expense, as they've done here in Spain—or we don't go. It's in your hands, Dr. Labougle, you'll work out what to do—"

The connection was abruptly cut. I pulled off the headphones and held them out to the young woman, mumbling a brief thanks. It was interesting to know what the two sides were feeling about the London issue, very interesting. In front of the operators, however, I didn't show any sign of the conversation's impact on me.

"Any news on Señor Dodero?"

"Nothing yet, señora. We've just confirmed he's not staying at the Pedralbes Palace, or the Ritz on Avenida de José Antonio. We'll keep trying and let you know."

I slipped out onto the street. In a nearby bakery, I learned where the closest telephone booth was located. While the agile operators continued their search of the city's most notable hotels, I set out to find Ramiro in another class of accommodation, convinced he wouldn't stay somewhere well known if he intended to go unnoticed. Shut away in my cubicle, sitting on a stool with the telephone guide on my lap, I soon threw in the towel: it was an impossible task. Barcelona had hundreds of run-of-the-mill establishments—hotels, hostels, boardinghouses, inns, guesthouses. Locating him would've been as difficult as finding one of my needles lost in an immense haystack, and time was against me. And in any case, he would soon find me, as he always did.

I returned to the Majestic and poked my head into the switchboard room. Nothing. Not a trace of Dodero anywhere, they confirmed. I was still mulling over Juan Duarte's conversation when the idea occurred to me to ask him for news of the shipowner, his drinking partner. I was trying to think of some absurd excuse with which to approach him when I heard a commotion behind me.

As if the stars had aligned, when I turned I saw the man I had in mind striding across the lobby toward the exit in his white twill suit and cream-colored shoes, with his thin pencil mustache, his streaks of brilliantine, and his usual cigarette. He didn't appear as nonchalant as usual; he was pressing his lips together, and there was a different urgency in his stride. Was it because of the ambassador's call? Or because there was only a day left before the farewell event, and the matter of the item *he* had lost in Granada was still unresolved?

He was surrounded by embassy and consulate staff, local journalists, reporters, and photographers, a few officials, and more than a few onlookers, all swarming toward the door.

Diego Tovar detached himself from the group when he saw me.

"I've been calling your room, but you didn't answer."

I frowned, suddenly disoriented.

"Change of plans. The activities are resuming sooner than expected. The first lady gave the order out of the blue. We're going out right now, they just informed us." He lowered his voice, inching toward me. "Lunch with you would've been a hundred times preferable, but duty calls." He touched my elbow. "Shall we go?"

I didn't even have the chance to go up to my room to change, collect my notebook, or wipe the disappointment from my face. A minute later, I found myself sharing the back seat of a car with two foreign would-be colleagues who'd recently joined the circus.

The tireless masses—undeterred by the delays, the blistering sun, and the threats of cancelations—had been waiting in the vicinity of the National Palace of Montjuic since early morning. Outside the grand classical facade, enormous Spanish and Argentine flags were flying atop dozens of masts. The mayor, governors, the president of the provincial council, a long line of the most senior officials—all men, of course— were waiting there for the first lady.

She arrived in the company of the minister of labor, wearing a wide-brimmed hat the size of a parasol and a dress with a deep neckline. Doña Carmen Polo and the industrial minister got out of the car behind hers.

The ovation Eva Perón received when she walked into the impressive assembly hall was deafening. The public were bunched together in the rows of seats, in the corridors and stairways, crowded against the walls, occupying every possible space. The heat was sweltering, but everyone was eager to hear her, see her, be near her. Before the event began, a choir of suntanned Argentine sailors sang the anthem of their far-off homeland. An enthusiastic murmur spread through the crowd: the sailors' ship had arrived two days ago full to the brim with wheat and was now anchored in the port.

The speeches ensued, and Doña Eva finally took the floor. Her words were to be broadcast on Radio Nacional, so she addressed the entire nation.

"I leave part of my heart in Spain. I leave it for you, workers of Madrid, cigarette makers of Seville, farmers, fishermen, workers of Catalonia, of the whole country. I leave it for you. This bridge of brotherhood, inaugurated by my visit to this land of labor, will not be broken. All workers of Spain, know that for as long as there is an ear of wheat in our fields, that ear will be shared with you in an expression of solidarity, Christianity, peace, and social justice."

The applause was deafening. While it continued to ring out, I remembered the beautiful Mery de Foxá and her prophetic words. Everyone packed into that auditorium would leave the world having barely left a mark. The woman speaking vibrantly from the stage, however—the twenty-something peroxide blond who said and did whatever sprung from her soul—would leave a loud echo in history.

60

The rockets whistled, the firecrackers crackled, and the flares left trails of bright light in the sky. At the street intersections they'd lit bonfires, and music, revelry, and people flowed everywhere. It was the Night of San Juan, a night of parties.

Despite the shortages, the repression, and the restrictions, and although the recent war was still on the minds of those who'd been on both sides, each neighborhood, each group, managed to celebrate with overflowing optimism. Locals came out to see the flames dance, boys and young men leaped fearlessly over the bonfires, and couples held each other to the sound of the bands playing in the street. All of Barcelona was celebrating the summer solstice, and as night fell, the city transformed into a vast festival.

The Royal Tennis Club was holding the most illustrious of the events. The aristocracy and high bourgeoisie gathered at the large premises on Calle Ganduxer: elegant, worthy citizens who'd lived in fear during the civil war in Republican Barcelona and who had, after the war ended, enthusiastically embraced the victorious regime. Fervent Germanophiles during the subsequent world war, they now—following Franco's suppression of Spain's regional languages—no longer spoke Catalan, not even a single word.

The orchestra was playing in high spirits when we arrived, with hundreds of couples dancing on the enormous dance floor into which the courts had been transformed. Strings of lanterns and colored bulbs illuminated the grounds, with garlands and paper chains, streamers and bunting everywhere. The most high-ranking and distinguished party-goers were dining and watching the scene from the central boxes. We were led to one of these, relatively near the presidential box, which was still empty. Our group was made up of a handful of international correspondents in the care of Diego Tovar, as always. Dressed in his white dinner jacket, he was explaining in English to a newly arrived reporter from the *Daily Telegraph* what the Night of San Juan meant to many towns on the Mediterranean coast.

I went to sit in the most secluded corner of the box, but Diego—able and attentive, even though he was still talking to the British man—managed to usher me to a more favorable seat. The waiters from the Ritz offered us cocktails and Perelada sparkling wine, delicate appetizers, the traditional *coca de San Juan* pastries, soft drinks with ice. I avoided speaking to anyone while I sipped my drink. Absorbed in my worries, I pretended to watch the bustle of the party. We were surrounded by well-cut dinner jackets and dresses made of divine fabrics from the town of Santa Eulalia on the island of Ibiza, beautiful creations by Catalan designers and fashion houses—Asunción Bastida and Pedro Rodríguez, Pertegaz and El Dique Flotante. The young and the not-so-young chatted breezily under pergolas, laughed in circles, spun to the sound of the orchestra under the stars. Jorge Sepúlveda was singing "Mi casita de papel" at the microphone. The newly arrived correspondents were frowning, wondering what on earth all this splendor was about, whether it was a faithful representation of Spain's true reality or merely a small island of good living situated within the great leaden ocean of the postwar period. The singer's sugarcoated voice continued to spill out from the loudspeakers dotted around the grounds.

A short while later, something in the air changed. Faces and bodies began to turn in the direction of the entrance. People rushed around nervously. The music stopped as the clapping multiplied, becoming thunderous applause. A booming, colorful burst of fireworks peppered the night sky. The illustrious guests were now there: the Generalísimo's wife and the Argentine first lady had arrived at the Royal Tennis Club.

Dodero. That was my first thought. Despite my limited faith, I sent a prayer up to the heavens. *Please, God, let him be there with them.* But no, he didn't appear. I searched the usual entourage, but there was no sign of the shipowner. Accompanied by the Count of Godó, the foreign minister, and others, the two dignitaries passed in front of our box on the way to theirs, larger and raised higher, decorated with tapestries, flags, and a profusion of flowers. The dark blue of Doña Carmen's suit contrasted with Eva Perón's extravagant display of lace and paillettes. Over their shoulders, as ever, both wore sumptuous furs. As had happened elsewhere, no one in Barcelona had had the courage to tell the first lady that mink and ermine were ill suited to that short festive night on the Mediterranean. Not only had nobody dared point out her mistake, but worse still, as I saw when they stood to compliment her, just like in Madrid, many ladies had dug their own furs out from the bottom of their winter wardrobes and shaken off the mothballs so they could imitate her.

Following behind them, I saw Lillian Lagomarsino, the eternal companion. Unlike the striking furs the great men's wives were sporting, she was wearing just a short, sleeveless sable jacket. I observed her while the rockets, ovations, and cheers continued to thunder around us. I was amazed by her supporting role in the hilarious comedy sketch, by her restrained attitude, always three paces behind, reserved, inconspicuous.

I was still watching her as she moved away with her back to me when I noticed something unusual on her guipure lace dress, something loose or hanging down. I looked closely and saw what was happening: a section at the back of her skirt had become detached without her knowing it—it must've been trod on, ripped in the crowd, or gotten caught somewhere—and was threatening to leave her underwear, or an indecorous part of her body, exposed. I reacted instinctively. The applause was still going as I deposited my drink on the table and left my place.

I managed to stop her just before she went up into the box behind the star of the show as she always did. She turned and, recognizing me, smiled without parting her lips. She must've been around my age, with thick eyebrows and a large nose. She wasn't beautiful, but she had a pleasant aura.

"There's a problem with your skirt," I whispered in her ear. "Something's come unstitched and it's hanging down. If you'll allow me, I think I can help."

We'd never exchanged a word before, but we'd spent many hours chasing about together, and that must've reassured her. We withdrew to a stone bench to one side, near a garden wall. Out of occupational habit or mere precaution, once again I was carrying my little sewing kit in my bag. Inside it, I had just what I needed to save the situation.

She remained standing and I sat on the bench behind her. I managed to find the defect in the yellowish light of a lamppost and reassured her that I could fix it.

"How fortunate that, as well as being a journalist, you have a seamstress's hands."

We both laughed, she genuinely and I frivolously. She had no idea how much truth there was in her joke.

"Though it's no surprise," she said, looking back at me, "with the good taste you have in clothes."

I muttered a barely audible "thank you," focused as I was on my task.

"Señora Perón and I have commented on it more than once. You saw how she praised your outfit on the flight to Granada. I insist to her as emphatically as I can, respectfully of course, that she pay attention to you and your clothes, even the way you do your hair, nothing too elaborate, or even a low bun. I think a style like yours, an elegant professional woman's look, would work very well for her. Even Don Alberto mentioned it to her once or twice."

I stopped my backstitch dead. *Don Alberto,* she'd said. Don Alberto Dodero. I tried to make my tone light, as if it were nothing.

"Speaking of the gentleman, I haven't seen him for days. It surprised me that he wasn't in Barcelona."

"Oh, of course he's here."

I was doing the final stitches along the rip, and my fingers holding the needle were left hanging in the air. I wanted to hold my tongue, but the words came out of their own accord.

"And where is he, if he hasn't shown his face anywhere?"

"Relaxing on his ship, the freighter that arrived a couple of days ago with one of the first shipments of wheat. Did you see the sailors singing the anthem at the National Palace? That's the crew. Not a very professional choir, but it was nice to hear them, don't you think?"

I had so many questions, but I contained myself. *Relax, Sira. Slow down. This lady is the height of discretion. Don't draw the bowstring too far.* Fortunately, I was still joined to her back, and she couldn't see me.

"Very nice, yes. But tell me, Lillian, is Don Alberto all right? Is everything in order?"

"Well, he's not young anymore and he has a few minor ailments. He's also responsible for everything going well on this tour. I guess the excessive demands and the heat got the better of him because in Madrid the other day, at a swimming pool, he blacked out for a moment."

Good heavens. Dodero had fainted at the pool *I* had sent him to. The infernal sun and high temperatures, probably along with some drink and his old age, had played the same nasty trick on him as they had on Philippa—except the Argentine tycoon was over sixty, and the nanny was only twenty or so.

I tugged on the skirt a couple of times, so she'd think I was still working. I was almost done, but I wanted to keep her talking for a moment.

"And has he recovered completely now, or is he still . . . ?"

"He's fine, he's fine," she said in her soft Argentine accent. "The doctor traveling with us accompanied him on the journey from Madrid to Barcelona, but he preferred to withdraw to his ship and regain his strength there, in the captain's cabin, surrounded by his people. The hotels, as you know, are a little indiscreet."

We remained on the secluded bench, in the soft light and the trees, surrounded by hydrangeas in pots. The band and singer had started up again. I pulled on the material once more.

"All done."

I got up so I was level with her. She smiled and thanked me warmly.

But it was I who was grateful, immensely so. Lillian Lagomarsino de Guardo, a well-bred girl from Palermo Chico, educated at Le Cordon Bleu, wife of the president of the Chamber of Commerce—and disowned by her own social class because she'd embraced the Peronist couple—couldn't imagine the enormous favor she'd just done me. A mother, forced to accompany Señora Perón on this hectic journey around Europe—closer to the first lady than anyone, complicit in her nocturnal fears, witness to and occasional victim of her excesses, suspicions, and distrusts, massager of her swollen ankles, and writer of the letters that Evita then copied and sent to the president—without knowing it, this fairy godmother had cast a ray of light onto my darkness that night. She would never become a true friend of Eva Perón's, only a stoic companion who, like so many others, including her own husband, would soon plummet from the steep cliff from which politicians who're no longer useful tend to fall. And yet, noble woman that she was, she would always remain faithful to the time she shared with Evita, as would be made clear when she wrote her memoirs in the years to come.

I accompanied her to her box, just as the guests were getting to their feet. The visit to the Tennis Club had been extremely brief, a fleeting but eloquent gift to show the regime's gratitude to all the eminent Catalan families who'd remained loyal to the nationalist side despite the cost.

"Give my regards to Don Alberto if you have the opportunity," I said by way of a goodbye.

I believed that we journalists would continue to cover the visit that night, but she and I would each be in our respective places, with no further chance to speak to each other. She quickly shook my hand, and they all set off again, to another big party at Pueblo Español, a more popular, less plush event, but unmissable.

"Of course. He's holding a lunch in honor of the first lady tomorrow, aboard his ship, the *Hornero*."

I returned to our box trying to contain my euphoria. I'd located Dodero and he was in good condition. On his ship, at the port. Everything could get back on track if I played my cards right, though I would have to be careful and shrewd. But as of this moment, the main piece was in its place and the game could start.

I was surprised to see that my group was still enjoying the occasion and hadn't gotten up to follow the delegation.

"We're not going?" I asked.

Diego Tovar shook his head.

"No more activities today." He gestured at the new correspondents, raising an eyebrow. They were chatting among themselves, relaxed. A couple of *La Vanguardia* journalists had joined them. "They want to stay."

My blood was fizzing. *Dodero has resurfaced*, I kept repeating to myself. Everything, finally, was going to come to an end. I approached Diego. He looked handsome in his dinner jacket. I held my hand to his and delicately took the glass of whiskey from him.

"Shall we dance?"

If my boldness surprised him, he didn't show it at all. No, it wasn't common for a woman to ask a man to dance, but he gladly accepted. After all, I was supposedly a foreigner, a novelty in that milieu of illustrious Catalan families who possessed boxes at the Liceu Theater, stately apartments in Ensanche, mansions in Pedralbes, Sarriá, or San Gervasio, prosperous businesses and assets in the bank. I was a rare bird in the middle of that excellent evening that marked the beginning of summer, that time before all the families fled to their houses at the beach, to sunbathing, ice cream, and languor.

The couples drifted across the crowded dance floor to the steady rhythm of a bolero. With my body paired with Diego's, we joined the flow. Set to the sounds of cloying lyrics, maracas, and guitar chords came the sight of rockets, crackling of fireworks, fleeting flares traversing the sky. I would've liked to have invited Diego into the relief I felt at having finally located the shipowner. To embrace him, even, to whisper in his ear that I was one step closer to easing my fears. Though I'd never been entirely honest with him, in those uncertain times we were living in, the man I was dancing with was the closest thing I had to a friend. Perhaps he sensed something, because he drew me even tighter.

"If you'll allow me . . ." The voice stopped us dead. "Would it be too bold on my part to ask you to part with the señorita for this number?"

It was as if a stray burst of fireworks had fallen on my skin, burning me alive. That was how I felt: scorched, wounded, holding back an urge to scream into the night, while Diego Tovar, with his diplomatic courtesy, let me go and ceded me to Ramiro Arribas.

61

"Tell your people to tread carefully. He's clever and audacious. And at the same time, he's well prepared, calculating, cautious. When you find out where he's staying, search his toilet bag and pull out the bottom of the left side. You'll find the Grand Cross there."

Ignacio, in his flat in Madrid, was noting down everything I was telling him from the other end of the line. I'd returned to my room at the Majestic after leaving the party in a rather hasty manner, the final events of the night still tearing at my soul. Ramiro's nerve at gate-crashing the Tennis Club, his effrontery in asking Diego Tovar to allow him to dance with me, the strangeness of my skin when I'd felt his so close to mine. His shamelessness when—by way of farewell, in front of everyone present, and just a few paces from Diego himself—he whispered goodbye in my ear and kissed me on the lips.

"Give this description to whoever's going to head up the operation: Forty-two years old, sophisticated appearance, tall, good looking. I imagine he'll be wearing a light-colored jacket and trousers. A tie as well, because he's supposed to be going to an important meeting. His hair is straight, dark, thick, styled with a side parting, some gray hairs."

"Spanish or Argentine accent?"

"He uses both, depending on what suits him."

"Understood. The final thing I'll need is his name. Or names, if he uses more than one identity, as it appears he does."

I swallowed.

"One is Román Altares. That must be the one he used in Buenos Aires in recent years, and the one that probably appears on the passport he entered the country with and uses to travel around."

"Román Altares, all right. And the other one?"

"The other one . . ." I tried to swallow again, but my throat felt blocked, as if a ball of phlegm were obstructing it. "The other one is Ramiro Arribas."

Eleven years after I'd left Ignacio, the mere mention of that name sunk him into a heavy silence. I considered adding something, an explanation, an argument, an apology, perhaps, for again pitting him against the man who once turned his life upside down—the attractive manager of the Hispano Olivetti firm in whom he'd naively placed his trust. The man who'd sold him a typewriter with one hand and with the treacherous other hand had torn me from his side.

But Ignacio didn't give me the chance. Coming to terms with the information, he adopted a neutral tone again and simply said, "Noted."

"Perfect. He said he would call me at eleven o'clock so I can give him instructions. I'll do everything I can to arrange the supposed meeting with Dodero at noon, half past at the latest, because there's to be a lunch later with Señora Perón on the ship."

"Very well."

"I'll leave you a message with the details at the hotel switchboard. Ask for a message in your name, it will be from—"

"Livia Nash. Don't worry."

Through the half-open window came the crackle of a solitary burst of firecrackers, the death rattle of the Saint John's Eve party. Before going to bed, I prepared what I would need to have first thing in the morning: plain, inconspicuous clothes.

"I must speak to Diego," I repeated to myself as I drifted off. I needed to tell him who Ramiro was, explain his intrusion and insolence. Or perhaps I did not. Perhaps it was better to say nothing. Strictly speaking, nothing firm beyond my supposed job tied me to Diego Tovar, and I was under no obligation to explain anything to him. But his behavior toward me was more than just the usual courtesy afforded to a journalist in his care. And as confused as I was about my own feelings, the truth was, I hadn't resisted his advances.

Day was breaking weakly when the alarm clock went off. I got up and washed, then dressed without making a sound. There was no one who could hear me, I was alone in my room, but caution was already in my bones. A solitary taxi driver was waiting at the entrance to the Majestic, hoping for an early-rising traveler on the way to one of the railway stations, or El Prat Airport, perhaps. Or, as in my case, the port.

"Have you heard about the Argentine ship that docked recently, loaded with grain?"

"You're kidding, right, señora?" the driver replied in a southern accent. He was one of the many migrants who'd arrived in prosperous Catalonia since the end of the war. "Near the ferry terminal, two thousand tons of wheat they say it's carrying. The Perona's wheat."

I grinned. The Perona, he'd said, like the little girls in Sacromonte. It must've been what the common folk were calling the woman they said was traveling around Spain, dispensing charity with generous, open hands.

"Then take me there, please."

We descended along the beautiful Paseo de Gracia. To make sure no one was following us, I looked through the back window several times. As we traveled along Las Ramblas, I took everything in with a voracious attentiveness. After years of conflict and postwar hardship, this old part of the city looked faded, exhausted, and dirty. The only people we saw were one or two road sweepers, a newspaper deliveryman with his load on his back, a few poor wretches collecting cigarette ends from the ground. When we reached Portal de la Paz, I saw a gigantic monument with Christopher Columbus in bronze pointing to the sea.

We entered the port, and the driver took me to the most convenient place to get out.

"One of those monsters must be the one you're looking for."

We found just two ships berthed sideways along the quayside. There were other smaller vessels at the nearby wharves: old sailing ships, peeling fishing boats, leisure boats, courier boats. But few goods or passengers traveled by sea at that time. The two recent wars—civil and global—had finished off many large ships, and the shortage of means and materials meant that few old ships were being repaired and even fewer new ones were being built. It wasn't a good time for the shipping industry. Though there were exceptions, of course. Exceptions that flourished in countries that hadn't suffered the ravages of war, Argentina being the best example. As a result, there were also shipping companies that were expanding their fleets by buying vessels that had survived the war, converting them into ships for migrants and cargo, and introducing new routes, services, operations, customers, and revenue. The *Hornero* was a symbol of the success Dodero's company had experienced: a bargain from the world war, one of the many Victory-class ships that had been manufactured nonstop in the United States to replace those vessels sunk by Nazi submarines. After the Allied victory, they'd become part of the country's navy reserve. Now, having been exchanged for a few thousand dollars, this one no longer flew the Stars and Stripes but flew the Argentine flag instead.

"Would you wait for me? I have a hundred pesetas for you if you can."

"That's what I'm here for, señorita. You're the boss."

I walked along the wharf's broad esplanade without anyone bothering me. The day was starting with a light silvery mist, the sky and sea seemingly joined, like two connecting layers. In the distance, I saw some early-rising fishermen with rods over their shoulders; there being little movement of ships here, the fish swam freely in the port's waters. Amid the gulls' wild screeches, I confirmed that the first of the two gigantic ships wasn't the one I was looking for. The letters on the black hull were unintelligible to me, and I guessed they were of Nordic origin. I went on, stepping in puddles, dodging dead fish, orange peels, sharp pieces of broken glass bottles. I knew nothing about boats, was unable to distinguish between port and starboard or bow and stern. I did, however, know exactly what I was searching for. And when I found it, I shouted to make myself heard.

Catching the attention of the young sailor was easy. Persuading the just-out-of-bed captain to invite me on board was another matter.

"I need to see Don Alberto Dodero. It's urgent."

I didn't playact—the pot-bellied, gray-haired, weather-beaten seafarer didn't look like someone who would swallow a tall tale, let alone accept the notes I'd been giving out to my miserable compatriots as freely as if they were playing cards.

"I'm a reporter for the BBC," I said calmly. "It's in his interest to see me. I can help him solve a problem of his."

The captain wasn't smoking a pipe, as the stereotype invites one to expect. Instead, bright and early in the morning, what he held between his fingers was a fat Havana cigar, already half-smoked. He brought it to his mouth and squinted, sizing me up while he puffed.

The shipowner received me in a cabin that was nothing like the hotel suites where he usually stayed. But this was a refuge, far from the deafening noise of everything associated with the first lady's visit. He was still in his pajamas and a silk dressing gown, his gray chest hair poking out through the triangle of his neckline. He hadn't had time to shave, though he'd combed his hair and brushed his teeth in my honor. Despite his efforts, and though they'd opened a porthole to air out the space, the cabin smelled of stale tobacco smoke, the secretions of a man getting on in years, and a menthol mouthwash mixed with fragrance.

"I know you must be puzzled by my visit, but I needed to speak to you about the Grand Cross."

"Good God, Livia, no, quite the contrary," he said, offering me a chair. "Anything you can tell me about it . . ."

He stopped when he saw me turn my head toward the captain. The man was standing at the door to what had been, until a couple of days ago, his own cabin, legs apart, cigar in his mouth, and his dark, hairy arms crossed over his belly. Dodero nodded, and with that brief signal I understood that I could speak freely. The captain was fully informed.

I summarized the story in a way that suited me, delivering information that I'd supposedly obtained from fellow journalists and other contacts. I distorted some details and kept others to myself, as I considered appropriate. He listened with a frown, without interrupting. I must've been convincing because when I finished he didn't ask for any additional explanations. Or perhaps he simply had no interest in asking. His prime object was to recover the badge, and he didn't give a damn about the rest.

"Let's get on with it, then," he said firmly, slapping the deep-red silk of the dressing gown covering his thigh to underscore his words.

"Where would you like to hold the meeting?"

The two men looked at each other again. The captain gave a brief sign.

"Invite him here."

"If you send a car to my hotel, I can bring him myself."

"Consider it done, my dear."

When I was back at the Majestic, I left the message for Ignacio at the hotel switchboard: *Meeting scheduled for twelve noon, the ship* Hornero, *Port of Barcelona.* At eleven sharp, as we'd agreed the night before, Ramiro called my room.

"Is everything ready?"

"I'll pick you up in forty minutes. Tell me where."

"Where will we go?"

"You'll know in good time."

Ready and waiting in the lobby, I saw the shipowner's sumptuous Cadillac arrive outside the hotel. I stood and headed to the door. I acted naturally when I recognized the chauffeur: under the gray cap, in a uniform that accentuated his stout build, wasn't the fellow Armando who'd driven me on other occasions, but the ship's captain. Dodero had decided to leave nothing to chance.

"We'll stop on Plaza de Cataluña, please."

We collected Ramiro from outside Café Zurich, a place that could be seen by all and sundry. It was impossible to know whether he was staying near there or far away. We were silent throughout the journey. I remained unsmiling, cold, my muscles tense, looking straight ahead. At one point he slid his left hand toward me over the leather seat. He tried to stroke my little finger with his, a conciliatory gesture. As soon as I felt the contact, I snatched my arm away. As we drove into the port area, out of the corner of my eye I saw him looking disconcerted, but he said nothing.

We stopped a short distance from the ship's imposing hull.

"Don Alberto will receive us on board," I finally explained. He frowned, not at all amused. "It's one of his ships. It was he who suggested meeting you here."

The captain courteously opened my door, and Ramiro got out on the other side. The wharf was empty—conspicuously empty for the first midday of a radiant summer. There were just two fishermen in the distance, minding their own business, their backs to us. My body flushed with sweat. What if nobody came? What if Ignacio hadn't set up an operation? If he'd backed out after discovering that the target was Ramiro?

"Follow me," the supposed driver directed.

A uniformed crew member emerged then from the ship and descended the ladder.

"Documents, please," he said when he reached the bottom.

As if that had been a password, the sequence of events began in an instant. The captain grabbed Ramiro from behind, twisting his arm, and the placid fishermen transformed into athletic officers. A car's engine roared behind us, tires skidded, brakes screeched. I heard brusque voices, yelling, frantic orders.

It all happened in seconds, as if in flashes. Ramiro did not know precisely for what he was being arrested. He was guilty of so many things, however, that he knew it was in no way in his interest to be caught. He was fit, agile, and slippery, and without much difficulty he managed to escape the grip of the captain, who was stouter but less nimble.

Someone grabbed me roughly by the shoulders.

"Come on, get in, quickly."

The car that had just arrived had its doors open. I looked at the stranger in confusion. He was trying to push me into the back seat. When I resisted, he placed a hand on my head and with the other forced me to bend down, and in seconds we were both inside. The driver stepped on the accelerator, but over the racket outside I heard the first man say, "We have to get her out of here, Montes's orders."

Montes was Ignacio, Ignacio Montes. The same one who, at that precise moment, more than four hundred miles from his own Madrid, was pursuing Ramiro with a pistol in his hand.

62

The afternoon I spent shut away in my room was agonizing, but I didn't risk returning to the port. I didn't know how things had ended up, whether they'd arrested Ramiro, whether they'd found the badge among his belongings, or what had happened afterward. At around five o'clock, feigning the voice of an overbearing Argentine once more, I asked the operators to put me through to the Pedralbes Palace. To my surprise, they didn't object when I asked to speak to Señora Lagomarsino.

"Yes, Don Alberto's in fine fettle now, my dear," Lillian responded in her friendly tone when I pretended to still be concerned about the shipowner's health. "Yes, yes, we had lunch with him on his ship," she added. "We just got back. He seemed to have recovered completely and was in incredibly good spirits, too."

I hung up and slumped onto the bed, feeling as relieved as I was overwhelmed. The fact that Dodero was happy suggested that everything had gone well. I would've liked, nonetheless, to have confirmed the facts with Ignacio, but there was no sign of him, and I hadn't the slightest idea where to find him.

The hours until the farewell dinner felt like an eternity. Finally, at half past ten, we crossed a crowded Plaza de San Jaime to be received with pomp and ceremony. There was scarcely any delay that evening; perhaps Eva Perón wanted to say goodbye to Spain without leaving a bad taste in its mouth. But the ritual was once again pompous and excessive, exhausting. We were all boiling hot. I was nervous. After the protocol of greetings was over—having included mace-bearers, sergeants-at-arms dressed in eighteenth-century attire, and an endless procession of guests—it was announced with great formality that Franco and his guest of honor would be entering the beautiful Patio de los Naranjos, which was illuminated by spotlights and hundreds of silver candelabra. I held my breath, stretching my neck to see them from my place. There they were, walking in.

The Generalísimo, proud and paunchy, was wearing his commander-in-chief's uniform with the Laureate Cross of Saint Ferdinand. She was in sky-blue satin with an empire coiffure, and a long white mink cloak covered her shoulders and back. As she stepped forward, I saw a striped band across her body. Pinned to it, at chest height, the Grand Cross of Isabella the Catholic gleamed brightly.

My fears relieved, I allowed my wine glass to be refilled at the table several times, I chatted animatedly with my supposed fellow reporters, and though the dark shadow of Ramiro's arrest was still looming over me, for the most part I managed to forget about it. The badge was back with its owner, the pieces were fitting together, and I'd gotten rid of him.

Unlike on other occasions, Diego Tovar sat not by me, but at the other end of the table. From a distance I saw him converse with a couple of journalists, as professional and as attentive as ever. The dinner was a relaxed affair. An orchestra delighted us with tangos, waltzes, and music by Falla and Granados, and the palace's carillon played the national anthems and a popular Catalan lullaby. I ate heartily: Malossol caviar with blinis, foie gras from Strasbourg, chicken from the Catalonian town of Alp, and fresh mushrooms. My stomach finally seemed to relax after several days of tightness. They served the dessert and coffee, but there was no time for after-dinner table talk, and before long the host and guest of honor stood. The festival was beginning on Plaza de San

Jaime, and the masses were waiting for them to appear on the grand main balcony.

The guests started to follow the dignitaries out, the courtyard gradually clearing. Left behind us were crumpled napkins and drooping floral arrangements, breadcrumbs, and crockery covered in the remains of strawberries and vanilla ice cream.

I stopped Diego as he was heading to the exit with those who were leaving, practically blocking his path.

"I wanted to ask if you think it necessary that I stay for the farewell tomorrow at the airport."

He smiled before answering, showing his usual pleasantness. I could see in his eyes, however, that it wasn't sincere.

"There's no need. You're free to go if you want," he assured me. "There won't be anything new. Excitement, protocol . . . you know, same as always." He smiled again, no less falsely. "Anyway, if you'll excuse me, Livia, I have to—"

"Wait." As if my voice were not enough to stop him, I grabbed him by the wrist. "Give me a few minutes."

I led him back to my former table near the colonnade, where the waiters were beginning to clear leftovers, dishes, cutlery. I asked one of them for a couple of clean glasses and held several bottles of local sparkling wine up to the light until I found one that wasn't empty.

"To a perfectly organized tour and unbeatable hospitality," I said, proposing a toast. "My heartfelt thanks for your efforts, Diego."

The spotlights illuminating the beautiful Renaissance courtyard suddenly turned off, and the waiters cursed. We were left only with the light from the candles, almost completely melted now. I held my glass to his. He clinked it without much conviction.

"And I'd like to apologize."

"There's really no need—"

"There's no need," I cut in, "but I want to." We both sipped our wine; it was warm, flat, dreadful. "The man who separated me from you last night, the one who ended up kissing me at the Tennis Club, he means nothing to me, nothing whatsoever. He did in the past. He meant a lot for a time. Now, however, I feel only contempt for him."

He ran his forefinger around the rim of his glass, two, three times, with his eyes fixed on me, attractive and serene in the near darkness. With his usual grace, to avoid any awkwardness, he changed the subject.

"When are you going back to London?"

"As soon as possible."

"Will you spend the summer there?"

I shook my head slowly.

"I'll go to Morocco. My mother lives there." I paused, hesitant. "She hasn't met my son yet."

He raised an eyebrow, half-surprised, half-incredulous.

"His name's Víctor, and he's going to be one next month. Right now he's in Madrid, in my father's care." I finished my drink and slowly deposited the glass on the table. "He was born the same day my husband died." He didn't say I'm sorry, he didn't say anything. He just kept his eyes on me. "And seeing as I'm coming clean with you, Livia Nash isn't my real name, either."

He shook his head slowly, a resigned look on his face.

"Will we have the BBC report all the same?"

"By all means. But I won't be complaisant."

He also finished his drink.

"I wouldn't expect anything less of you." He gave a complicit wink of one blue eye.

The waiters continued with their work in virtual darkness. We heard dishes clanking together as they were piled up, the metallic clinking of forks and spoons, muted laughter, orders.

We might've made a good couple, Diego Tovar and I, in other circumstances. He was undeniably attractive with his lean build, harmonious face, and way with people. A man born for diplomacy, he held a coveted position, and his manners displayed good lineage. He would have been quite the catch for the daughter of Dolores, a seamstress and single mother from Calle de la Redondilla. Or perhaps, without formally becoming a couple, we could have enjoyed the final evening together. Our work was coming to an end, our mission accomplished. Eva Perón was leaving, and why not celebrate her departure together? At my hotel for example, in my bed, our naked bodies delighting in each other, unhurried and with no strings attached until the sun rose. But no, it wasn't possible, and I'd been wrong not to stave off his interest from the beginning. I liked Diego, and he liked me, but the wound from Marcus was still raw. I wasn't ready yet.

He slid his long fingers across the tablecloth toward mine until they almost touched.

"Excuse me, are you Señor Tovar?"

The waiter emerged briskly from the shadows.

"They're looking for you, they're waiting for you in the gallery. They say to hurry, please, something's happened."

Diego slowly withdrew his hand, getting to his feet without hiding his profound reluctance. He could guess at the nature of the incident: a journalist couldn't find a car to return to the hotel with, or he'd drunk too much, or his wallet had been stolen in the crowd. At any other time, he would've delegated the task of sorting out the mess to a subordinate. This being a part of the first lady's official visit, however, he was the only option.

"Will we see each other again?" he whispered in my ear.

He tried to kiss me lightly on the cheek, but I turned my head until his lips touched mine. Then in a low voice, I simply said, "I don't think so. But it's been nice to know you."

63

Getting to the back of the building where the cars were waiting took a huge effort; the crowd was immense. On Plaza de San Jaime, on an enormous central stage, were the choirs and dancers of the Sección Femenina—the Women's Section of the Falange—entertaining the officials and an audience of thousands.

I reached the Majestic exhausted, eager to take off my shoes, my evening dress, and my makeup. It was the end of my stay in Barcelona, almost the end of my time in Spain; the end of the ludicrous farce with the Grand Cross, of what might have happened with Diego but had not.

My room was dark. I was about to turn on the light when the desk lamp came on, flooding the room with its soft light.

"For God's sake, Ignacio . . . ," I whispered, shaken.

"Sorry to have startled you," he said, getting to his feet. "I didn't know what time you'd be back and preferred to wait for you inside."

It wasn't the first time he'd invaded my space without permission or warning. He'd done it at my studio on Calle de Núñez de Balboa after I returned from Morocco. That time, it had unsettled and scared me, but this time it did not. Now, worn out as I was, after the initial fright I was pleased to find him there.

My sincere feelings bubbled over.

"I am so grateful to you—"

"Sit down, Sira. We need to talk."

His tone was unsettling, and I nearly retched. The lukewarm sparkling wine, the excessive dinner . . . it all threatened to make the return trip from my stomach.

Slowly, I settled into an armchair in the corner.

"Things didn't go as planned."

"But . . . Señora Perón . . . she was wearing the Grand Cross this evening."

"That matter *was* resolved. We recovered it from a cheap hostel in the Barrio Chino. In the toilet bag, as you said."

"And so?"

"The problem is him."

"Ramiro?"

"Yes."

Ignacio had sat down again on the desk chair, turned to the side so he would be able to see me. The light was behind him, outlining his silhouette. His face was lost in the shadows.

"We were unable to detain him. The arrest would've taken place on an Argentine ship, legally considered the sovereign territory of Argentina. And as I'm sure you'll understand, this is not a good time for international scandals."

With my lips pressed together, unable to utter a word, I recalled the image of Ramiro freeing himself from the captain's grasp, pushing him, springing onto the gangway to go on board. I remembered Ignacio arriving and rushing after him with a gun in his hand while his men tried to get me out of there. Had Ramiro been aware of what he was doing? Or had it just been an impulse? Did he know all along that if he was caught on land he would be accountable to the Spanish authorities? Had he preferred to intentionally throw himself into the arms of his generous adoptive country?

"He is, however, unofficially detained on the *Hornero*. They plan to set sail in a few days for Buenos Aires and take him with them. But no one's going to press formal charges against him, and they've flatly refused to arrange for him to be left in our hands. Having recovered the

Grand Cross, Dodero considers the matter settled. That was his only interest. The means by which it came into your friend's possession are of no consequence to him. He has no intention of making inquiries, probably because putting two and two together would end up implicating Juan Duarte, or simply because he doesn't want anyone to know that the badge was mislaid for a while. Dead dogs don't bite, as far as he's concerned. All we've managed to do is get them to guarantee that they'll remove him from Spain, and that's it."

The bathroom door was open. The sound of water bubbling in the cistern was all I could hear while my brain took in everything he was saying.

Ignacio got up from his chair and came over to me.

"I did everything I could, Sira." His tone had changed; he sounded less formal, more human now. "But nobody's going to allow an incident like this to mar the visit of Franco's guest in any way. Neither my superiors, nor the Argentines. No one."

I slowly stood until I was level with him. Unable to stop myself, I fell against his chest, and he had no choice but to hold me. His warmth felt strange. I didn't recognize the smell of his forgotten male body, or the shape of the back I placed my hands on. But it comforted me to feel him close. And there we stayed in the semidarkness, together like before, for an eternity.

Eva Perón and I left Barcelona on the same day. She reached the airport escorted by motorcyclists and accompanied by the Generalísimo and his wife, senior officials, troops, and thousands of onlookers. From the open door of the Douglas DC-4 belonging to Flota Aérea Mercante Argentina, wearing a hat as flowery as a garden, she said farewell to the mother country with a smile, waving like mad. At almost the same time, I was heading to the train station to take the express to Madrid. None of the men I'd had anything to do with in the last few days were with me.

Evita was leaving Spain with a bittersweet impression—she was moved by the workers, but her hopes for the Generalísimo had deflated like a popped balloon. She was also saddened by the misery of the postwar hardship. For all the adornment and the luxury the authorities had lavished on her, the poverty of the people appeared around every corner, and she had a trained eye for detecting it. Orphans with hunger in their faces, the children of the defeated, ragged beggars with hands held out, widows in mourning selling tobacco and individual cigarettes. Crippled, silenced, punished, poverty-stricken people who turned up wherever she went. All of it pained her, without question. But for all that, she didn't leave behind even one of the trunks that were filled to the brim with the hundreds of sumptuous gifts that had been given to her from here and from there—jewelry, rugs, regional attire, embroidery, tapestries, tableware, works of art. Something still remained in her of the poor village girl she'd once been, and she loved receiving gifts.

All the authorities breathed a sigh of relief when they saw her plane take off. They'd hailed her, lauded her, glorified her to such an extreme that the excessive adulation had worked against them, and Señora Perón, defiant and contemptuous, had made the tour an unbearable nightmare for them. Nobody would have to suffer her delays, no-shows, and sudden changes of plan anymore. Nor would they have to listen to her populist harangues, her fervent recognition of the worth and rights of the working class, which, far from resonating with the regime's National Catholicism and anticommunism, seemed closer to the cause of the Republicans who'd lost the war.

The people, for their part, also idolized her, but not so much for what she proclaimed about the virtues of her Argentina and Peronism. To ordinary Spaniards her references to *descamisados* and *justicialismo*— to her "shirtless ones" and "social justice"—sounded like music from another planet. What excited people about Eva Perón was her exoticism, her sumptuous style—an unprecedented novelty in that prudish, gray, poverty-stricken Spain; a colorful walking extravaganza with her enormous hats, elaborate coiffures, and outrageous furs in the heat of

June. She was young, spontaneous, as dazzling as a movie star, a breath of fresh air that came and went. A passing distraction. A glimmer of light in the darkness.

In the international press it was repeatedly stated that Spain had spent more than a million dollars fêting her, a patently excessive display considering the country's empty coffers. Those on the inside, however, knew that despite the painful drain on resources, the books would be balanced. As a result of the visit, more than five hundred million dollars in loans would be secured, and the great permanent convoy that would be established from Argentina's Río de la Plata to half a dozen Spanish ports would continue until 1950. In the next few years, ship after ship would cross the Atlantic loaded with wheat, maize, and rye, meat and leather, eggs and little pasta stars. Vital help, in any event, for an isolated and hungry Spain. As a reminder of her visit to Barcelona, a shanty town grew up in the city, which would be known as La Perona for decades.

Her next destination was Rome, where, at the Vatican—far from awarding her a papal marquisate—Pius XII would bestow upon her a simple silver rosary. Nor would she receive the treatment she expected in the rest of Italy, and the tour was forced to cancel visits and there were protests in the streets. Tomatoes were even thrown at her car. Italians couldn't forgive Perón's support for Mussolini and took exception to his wife's visit. The rest of the Rainbow Tour would keep a lower profile. The extravagances of Spain would not be repeated.

But all of that would take place in the days to come; that day, at almost the same time, while her plane crossed the Mediterranean on its way to Ciampino Airport, and while Ramiro was supposedly waiting to return to Buenos Aires on board the merchant ship *Hornero*, a train took me to the city that had once been my home.

She would be received with pomp and ceremony by the authorities. He would be received by perhaps nobody.

For my part, my father and my son were waiting for me. We would fly to London together the following night.

PART FOUR

Morocco

64

The London I found on my return was both the same and different from the one I'd left. The deprivation was ongoing, but the faces and streets seemed less subdued, as if postwar life was a little more bearable in the summer's light.

We stayed at the Dorchester, the hotel where the British intelligence officers had convinced me to undertake the clandestine mission from which I was now returning. My collaboration with the secret service had resumed in that exclusive establishment, and it was there, I had decided, that it would end: a full circle. The fact that my father was traveling with us had also provided the perfect excuse not to return to the Boltons. In any event, it wasn't long before Olivia came to see us, dressed in one of her shabby but majestic outfits, her plait over her shoulder, her stride firm. As ever, she was hardly effusive, but it was obvious how happy she was to see Víctor again. She even treated me with relative warmth, which I preferred not to question. One person on whom she really made an impression, however, was my father. He wasn't accustomed to seeing ladies like her in his impoverished Madrid.

My plan was to be in England just long enough to submit my final intelligence report and to record the BBC piece about Eva Perón's tour, before leaving again. I did not anticipate that, although that would be the general scheme of things, I would end up having to negotiate more stumbling blocks than I'd anticipated.

We had lunch that day in the hotel grill, the three of us sharing a table for the first time while Philippa took Víctor to Hyde Park to see the squirrels. Without the slightest embarrassment, my mother-in-law ate with a laborer's appetite. A delectable white bread roll that I hadn't touched even disappeared from the table, slipped into her handbag or hidden in her tunic, up her sleeve or between its folds. I left them having coffee, Olivia chain-smoking the American cigarettes my father offered her, which he'd bought on the black market back home, the two of them striving to keep a somewhat complex conversation going despite his middling English and her nonexistent Spanish. Meanwhile, I met Kavannagh in the Promenade, one of the hotel's sumptuous lounges. The veteran secret service officer had received the results of my work the night before. As soon as I landed, I had passed them to an anonymous individual before leaving the airport.

"We're grateful for your excellent work, Mrs. Bonnard. We've read your report closely, and it has given us a clear impression of how events unfolded."

He didn't know about the shadier part of the operation—it hadn't crossed my mind to mention the business with the Grand Cross. In any case, I wasn't about to contradict him, so I pretended to receive his comments with satisfaction. This time it was just Kavannagh, without the blond subordinate from previous occasions. He was as immaculate and as distinguished as ever, with his impeccable suit, fine gold-rimmed spectacles, and comb lines above his gray temples.

"The cabinet is still deliberating on the terms of Mrs. Perón's possible visit to London, but you can be certain that the information you provided will be taken into consideration when it comes to making the final decision."

I couldn't see the stiff British wanting to battle with Evita's volcanic temperament, or organize extravagant receptions for her, or lavish her with gifts as expensive and as absurd as the ones she'd received in Spain. Even so, so that they would have an unfiltered, uncensored picture of how the tour had unfolded, I had prepared thirty-nine pages full of informative details about the first lady and her behavior, reactions, and entourage. In exchange, I would receive a considerable sum with which I would pay the bill at that luxury hotel and live comfortably for a few months in some less exclusive, still undetermined accommodation. A fair exchange. Agreement fulfilled. My association with Kavannagh and his people would end that afternoon. And once I'd recorded my story through a BBC microphone, I would forget about the whole Peronist chapter, forever.

He finished his glass of brandy and left it on the table, then stood up.

"Allow me to say, my dear girl, that it has been very pleasant working with you."

I held out my hand, replying with some vacuous courtesy. This elegant servant of His Majesty, and his duties, was no longer my concern.

"I hope you enjoy the English summer."

"I don't intend to stay, but thank you."

"In that case, my best wishes, wherever you go."

"To Morocco," I said. And right away, I saw a keen reaction on his face.

"Ah," he replied. Restrained, terse. I withdrew my hand from his as he asked, "To Tangier, by any chance?"

"Only passing through" was all I said. I wasn't going to give any more explanations. The next phase of my life was my business and no one else's. Kavannagh didn't need any more hints.

"In any event, I reiterate my very best wishes, Mrs. Bonnard."

I watched him head to the exit holding his hat by its crown. At that precise moment, Philippa came in with Víctor in his pushchair. They crossed paths, ignoring each other. My reunion with my boy immediately banished any thought of the officer from my mind.

That afternoon I spoke to George Camacho, the director of the Latin American Service, on the telephone. He asked me to do the recordings as soon as possible, now that Eva Perón's tour had moved on to Italy and while the media was still reporting on it.

"It would be good to meet. How about lunch tomorrow?"

I made a counteroffer: I would go to him. I wanted to keep lunchtime free for my father, for him to enjoy his short stay in London as much as possible. The city had fascinated him ever since he'd visited it a couple of times years before, on his way to Manchester to meet a machinery supplier, back when he was still working and Alvarado e Hijos—the foundry in Madrid that had been requisitioned from him when the war broke out and that he'd never reopened afterward—was still in full swing. He was also a great admirer of the empire, Churchill, the Industrial Revolution, and Chesterton, of the Savile Row tailors and the hats of Lock & Co., the punctual trains, and Atkinsons' cologne. Which was why, on the face of it, I had suggested he accompany me on my brief return. I didn't tell him there was another underlying reason for my invitation: to get him out of Madrid. Sheer precaution, in the event that something changed on Dodero's Argentine ship before it left Barcelona. Or that Ramiro managed to slip off the vessel at some other port and went to look for me in Madrid to call me to account. I didn't want Gonzalo Alvarado to find himself having to confront that nasty piece of work if anything went wrong.

We sent Miguela to her village in Badajoz for a few days, and we closed the balcony shutters of the flat and triple-locked the front door. My father told the porter he was going away for a long while. After London, he would spend the rest of the summer in a little hotel in the northern coastal town of Fuenterrabía, as he usually did, fleeing the heat of central Spain's flat Meseta plains, escaping to the shores of the Bay of Biscay. Perhaps I was being overly cautious and would never see Ramiro again. But knowing him as I did, I preferred not to let my guard down.

I returned to Broadcasting House the next morning. The sun was glowing softly and the people milling around seemed more buoyant than before, the women wearing bright colors, bicycles everywhere, and flower stands on some corners. There were still plots that had been turned to rubble, holes, and a great deal of damage. But in several places I saw builders working and painters perched on scaffolding, moving their brushes up and down the facades.

I'd left those offices months before with my radio, unsettled by the reaction of Nick Soutter's wife, and returned there a few days later to see her again. In his last letter, Nick had told me that his work in Palestine was coming to an end. He didn't know his next destination, but he was working on figuring that out. I'd just had news from Fran Nash too: everything, they both said, was plunging into the abyss in Jerusalem, the violence growing more bitter and more extreme. My memory took me back to Marcus and the attack on the King David like a knife in the back. To shield myself from the pain, I grabbed hold of the memory of my friends who were still alive—how far away they were now, in physical distance and in my thoughts. We'd separated just half a year ago, and yet I often felt as if decades had passed.

"Everything you're proposing for your recording is fabulous, Sira my dear." Camacho's words sounded sincere, and I didn't detect any duplicity. "Thrilling! If only I'd been able to go with you, my girl. Quite an experience."

Ángel Ara, my likable compatriot, had also come to the meeting, and he joined in on the praise. I was overjoyed to see him.

"We've been reflecting, and we think we can organize it into four parts, one for each stage of Doña Eva's visit," the Colombian director went on. "It would be interesting for the audience if we alternate the report on the tour itself with information about each city. A bit of history, geography, idiosyncrasies, art . . ."

We continued to talk, considering alternatives until we settled on various options.

"We'll start tomorrow, then," Ara concluded.

"And so that you may embark on this new radio adventure in good spirits, we have a surprise for you." Camacho picked up a large pile of open envelopes, leaning forward to offer them to me over the table. "They're for you," he said in his soft cadence. "They've arrived from Mexico, Venezuela, my beloved Colombia, Uruguay, Argentina . . ."

I took them from him, skeptical. Ara couldn't contain himself.

"Your first admirers from across the pond."

I frowned.

"They're reactions from listeners to your pieces on Palestine, which we aired a few weeks ago. It's usual to receive letters, we always do," Camacho explained. "In this case, they're all positive, every last one. You should be proud. And when they start arriving in such numbers, you can be sure there're more to come."

I flicked through the envelopes, quickly passing them from one hand to another. All unique, with diverse handwriting, stamps, and postmarks, varying types and colors of paper, different inks.

"We'll receive a lot more from those countries. The ones from Chile and Peru will take a little longer, and later they'll come from Bolivia, Ecuador . . ."

I stopped hearing him at that point. I didn't know exactly what the messages said; I cared only that their senders had appreciated my work, that here was evidence that my efforts had meant something.

I left the office with my handbag full of letters and a strange feeling of satisfaction flowing through my veins. I passed a multitude of people in the corridors, men and women walking with purpose, with urgency, most of them, with direction to do something concrete with their lives. At once, I found myself fantasizing about being one of them—professionals engaged in a job that took up portions of their time, their concerns, their thoughts. Valuable, useful people who were committed to their tasks, just as I was at that moment. I preferred not to remember that, as soon as my next recordings were done, this purpose of mine would disappear in a puff of smoke.

I was surprised to find Kavannagh sitting in the lobby when I returned to the hotel. Alone, like the day before, having an early drink.

He had a cigarette between his fingers, and his crossed legs revealed skinny ankles wrapped in silk-knit socks. He could've been any customer of the exclusive Dorchester, a smart gentleman of mature years like so many others. Except his eyes were too aware of the door. When he saw me walk in, there was a minuscule movement at the corners of his mouth.

My footsteps clicked rhythmically; I was in a hurry after the meeting at the BBC had gone on longer than expected. I'd arranged to meet my father for lunch and was afraid I'd be late. Simpson's in the Strand was the place he himself had chosen, we had a reservation, and he was waiting for me there with Olivia, who was clinging to us like a limpet. And so I tried to avoid the officer, walking past, pretending I hadn't noticed him.

"Mrs. Bonnard?"

It hadn't worked, of course. And I had no option but to stop.

"Mr. Kavannagh," I muttered half-heartedly. "I'm sorry, I hadn't seen you there."

I made little effort to disguise my lie, but he didn't challenge me.

"Could I have a moment of your time?"

"I thought my work with you was done."

"Indeed."

"What then?"

"This is about something different."

"The thing is, right now I'm not interested in—"

"Five minutes, no more. I promise."

We moved to a corner, away from the bustle of customers and visitors.

"Would you like anything?"

"No, thank you."

He held out his silver cigarette case.

"Cigarette?"

"No, thank you."

He lit one, breathing out.

"I'm sorry, Mr. Kavannagh, I'm in rather a hurry."

"I guessed as much when I saw you come in," he said, letting out curls of smoke. "Forgive me, I'll try to be brief."

"I'd be grateful."

"There's someone who'd like to meet you."

I raised an eyebrow.

"You see, sometimes we receive inquiries from certain people or organizations of a nature that fall outside, shall we say, our official duties. They're looking for some advice, often a contact, a place, a name, a particular . . ."

I had no idea what he was talking about; he was being too obscure. I cleared my throat to indicate as much.

"I'm sorry, I'll get to the point. In short, let's say a friend has asked me for a reference to give another friend."

Considering who Kavannagh was, his work, I supposed the word "friend" had a double meaning.

"And in this chain of friends," he added, "the final link is a private client."

His hand slid to his pocket, and he took something out, which he handed to me. A card.

"In this case, it's a solvent insurance company, nothing to do with our operations. They need some assistance with a matter of the utmost urgency. In Tangier, to be precise."

65

We made the recordings about Evita's visit almost in one go. With Ángel Ara's efficient help, everything went smoothly, though we did work long hours. We worked for three days, during which time I managed to get home to see my family only in the evening, shortly before Víctor went to bed. There was just enough time afterward for me to have dinner with Olivia and my father, to go to a concert with him at the Royal Albert Hall, or to talk for a while about his trips around London, his visits to museums, parks, and monuments.

Throughout this time, Kavannagh's card remained on the desk in my hotel room. Printed on it were the name of a business, the name of a person, and an address in the city. On the reverse, handwritten in ink, was a telephone number.

Ending with Eva Perón's farewell in Barcelona, we completed our work in the recording studio, my voice now etched into the grooves of three slate disks. My next step was to go back to Broadcasting House to say goodbye to George Camacho. We exchanged the usual courtesies, giving each other our best wishes.

"And let me remind you that payment for your—"

I interrupted him.

"Consider me paid already."

He wouldn't accept my refusal. He insisted.

"I'm serious, George. The amount I've already been compensated for my assignment in Spain—think of that as payment for my work with you, too. After all, the content's the same. Use the money to hire another compatriot of mine. I'm sure they'll need it more than I do."

With his Colombian courtesy, he accompanied me to the end of the corridor. Only when I was in the elevator and the doors had closed did his kind face, the face of a good man, disappear from view.

That July morning, the elevator was practically empty. Which was why I immediately noticed a presence that I might have missed on another occasion when it was crammed with other bodies. Her hair had grown, its wavy tips now resting on her shoulders. She was still slender, wearing a muslin dress with a deep-red belt, and white heeled sandals with her toenails brightly painted. She was carrying some folders but no handbag, so I supposed her destination wasn't the street but some other office in the building. Now that I was inside, I could only look at her out of the corner of my eye. Both of us faced the door, standing almost shoulder to shoulder, while the contraption slowly descended. We both feigned impassiveness, but I imagined we were equally uncomfortable.

There she was again, Cora Soutter, Nick's wife or ex-wife—I still didn't know the exact status of their ill-fated marriage. This time, however, we both brazenly ignored each other, without saying a single word.

She had no option but to look at me, however, when I got out on the ground floor and she remained inside. The doors began to close. I headed toward the exit and tried to make my walk seem casual. My apparent composure, of course, was entirely affected. I hadn't been able to prevent the proximity of that woman from perturbing me—because of her connection to Nick, because of their shared past that I knew nothing about, and because of his feelings for me that she had previously laid bare. I sped up my pace and breathed more easily once I was sure the doors had closed completely behind me and she couldn't see me anymore. Mixed with my relief was a slight bitter taste in my mouth. It came, I knew, from a degree of envy: she was staying and I was leaving.

I left Cora Soutter behind me, with her folders and her duties, going down to the basement, perhaps, to receive or give out orders, or heading to an office to take part in a meeting or to conduct some negotiation or another. Meanwhile, I'd just said goodbye to the director of the Latin American Service and was heading nowhere in particular. Only to put up with my mother-in-law, to make small talk with my father, to cheer on my son's entertaining ways. And then, once I was in Morocco, to reunite with my mother and allow myself to be dragged along by the gentle passing of the days. One after the other, and then another, and on and on. Empty and slow.

Olivia and Gonzalo were waiting for me, enmeshed in one of their confused conversations, each with a glass of sherry in front of them. They didn't even notice me when I arrived in the large restaurant, but I saw them. At that moment, as I approached their table, my father leaned forward slightly to say something, and hearing him, Olivia let out a guffaw. I was still chewing over my departure from the BBC and my unpleasant encounter with Cora Soutter, which was why, perhaps, out of sheer distraction, I failed to see the red flags.

They both ordered Welsh lamb, but I just had the asparagus with mayonnaise. Each in their own language, they told me about the locations they'd visited that morning: Saint James's Park and the National Gallery. For the evening, they had planned a play at the London Palladium and dinner out somewhere.

"What's it called, Sira, that Spanish place you told me about?"

"Martínez."

"Martínez, that's it. I think Olivia would like to go there."

With great difficulty, I contained a burst of sarcastic laughter. Olivia would like to eat Spanish food? I very much doubted it. In all the months I'd shared a roof with her, she had never once showed any such interest. She'd never asked about Spain, my family, my language, or the cuisine of a country that she saw as being estranged from the civilized world, half-wild.

And yet, to my surprise, my mother-in-law responded with an outburst of enthusiasm.

"Yes, yes, Martines, Martines!"

She even clapped her hands a couple of times. And Gonzalo laughed along.

I took in a mouthful of air. I had no desire to go to a Spanish restaurant—I'd just returned from Spain where, while the people's bellies creaked with hunger, Eva Perón's delegation had been catered to with obscene extravagance. But I gave in. What else could I do? I wanted my father to enjoy himself, and if showing such courtesy to Olivia was what he wanted, I wasn't going to refuse.

"Very well. I'll book a table."

"You don't have to come with us if you're busy."

"I've finished."

"Maybe you'd prefer to stay with the boy, then."

"We'll see. You know we don't have much time left before we leave."

A waiter arrived pushing the dessert trolley. They both asked for the *coupe dame blanche*. I just had seasonal fruit.

"Well, about that . . . ," my father added once we were served. "About leaving London, I don't think there's any hurry."

I'd just pricked a little strawberry with my fork but didn't put it in my mouth.

"Yes, yes, there is. I'm going to buy the tickets this afternoon, in fact. There are plenty of boats from Gibraltar, and just yesterday a Spanish friend at the BBC told me there are several weekly ferries from Plymouth to Santander. From there, it will be easy for you to get to Fuenterrabía."

The friend I referred to was Ara. A veteran expatriate in England, he knew all the possible routes to Spain. But my father barely took any notice, instead concentrating, like Olivia, on his glass of ice cream, whipped cream, and molten chocolate, an undreamed-of delight for two stomachs that had suffered equally cruel postwar hardships.

"The thing is, my girl, we thought—Olivia and I, that is . . ."

I frowned. We? *We thought,* he'd said? Had I heard right? Them? Olivia and my father had thought something behind my back?

It was she who spoke next.

"Yo invitar Gonzalo to stay in London," she announced in a mixture of English and bad Spanish. As if punctuating her sentence with a flourish, she set to finishing off her ice cream. The clinking of her teaspoon against the glass penetrated my ears.

None of us said a word on the way back. Only once my father and I had gotten out of the taxi outside the hotel, and she'd continued on to the Boltons, did I confront him, unable to contain myself.

"Would you care to explain to me what on earth you and my mother-in-law have been scheming?"

"She's a remarkable woman, Sira."

"*Remarkable,* that's exactly the right word. You couldn't have chosen a better description. Now tell me, what are you planning to do with your remarkable friend?"

His answer was curt.

"Let's go inside."

He took my elbow to lead me into the hotel, but I stopped him.

"Here, right now, Gonzalo. Please tell me what I've missed, what's happening?"

We were under the big canopy at the entrance. The doorman looked sidelong at us. My father took a few seconds to decide what to say to me, his gaze wandering over the road to the treetops in the park. Finally he turned to me again and fixed his eyes on mine.

"Do you know how long it's been since a woman made me laugh, Sira?"

I didn't know and I didn't care. Nor was I in the mood to play a guessing game.

"I might not be exaggerating if I told you the last to do so was your mother."

I couldn't help but do the math. My mother, for God's sake. That must've been more than thirty years ago.

"Olivia is wonderful," he went on. "She's . . . she's different, unique."

I cut him off straightaway.

"Listen to me, Gonzalo . . ." I'd never called him Papá, or Father, or any other term of endearment. "Listen carefully. She is Marcus's mother, Víctor's grandmother, you're . . . you're practically family."

"Don't try that on me, Sira. It won't work. You and I aren't even registered anywhere as daughter and father. Officially, Olivia and I have no ties."

He was right. He was completely right. I seemed to have lost my powers of reasoning. I needed more solid, credible causes for objection, but I was so angry I couldn't think of anything. And so I resorted to the naked truth.

"She's egotistical, intrusive, manipulative, and a liar."

A guffaw came from his throat.

"She's your mother-in-law, that's all."

"She's a hypocrite. And she can't stand me."

"You just bemuse her. She doesn't know how to behave with you. She doesn't know what to make of you."

It didn't matter, in any case. My relationship with Olivia was our business, hers and mine. What worried me now was her involvement with my father. Whatever absurdity they were cooking up between them.

"All right then. I take back what I said. I'm the difficult one, and Lady Olivia Bonnard is a charming person, accommodating and uncomplicated. Now, tell me, what are you going to do with her?"

He shrugged.

"Honestly? I don't know. All I know is that, for now, I don't want to go anywhere. I don't want to leave her side."

"But, but . . ."

My throat was dry, my tongue tied. A luxurious car stopped nearby, a couple got out, a young porter ran to take care of their luggage. They headed inside speaking to each other rather more loudly than the English tended to. The woman—blond, graceful—burst out laughing. Rich Americans back from doing their shopping on Bond Street. The hotel was full of them.

"We've spent many hours together these last few days," Gonzalo went on, "while you were recording and going to meetings and getting on with your life. And we got along."

I was about to remind him that his English was mediocre, and that Olivia couldn't string three words together in our language. But he was one step ahead of me.

"When you reach a certain age, you don't need to talk so much."

They must've been starting to serve tea in the hotel lobby. Private cars and taxis continued to arrive, spitting out customers who practically brushed against us on the way in. We hadn't moved. There we were: me, standing in front of Gonzalo Alvarado, the engineer who no longer engineered, the elderly man from Madrid who read the conservative-leaning *ABC* newspaper, a man of fixed routines who liked to live a quiet life. And there he was, coming clean to his natural daughter under the Dorchester's canopy, in the alien London to which I'd dragged him without foreseeing the consequences of my doing so.

"For God's sake, Father . . . ," I muttered. It was the first time I'd called him that, the first time in my life. "Don't tell me you've fallen in love with Olivia."

66

The Brax Insurance Ltd offices were located in an imposing building in the city. On King William Street, to be precise, very near the monument erected to commemorate the great fire that had ravaged London centuries before.

There were no flower vendors on the corners there, or girls in sandals and summer dresses. Men were in the majority, circumspect, wearing dark three-piece suits as somber as ones worn in winter. They walked quickly in their shiny shoes, always black, in obeyance of the strict "no brown in town" rule: any man who made the mistake of wearing that color in the financial district would be frowned upon. The few women I saw I guessed were secretaries running errands, their outfits no less austere, their superiors and the environment having rubbed off on them. In my sinamay hat, pale gloves, and light-colored suit, I suddenly felt as if, rather than merely getting out of a taxi, I'd descended to another planet.

Gregory Sacks had offered to meet me at a place of my choice, but once more I preferred to be the one who traveled, hoping physical distance would help ease my disquiet. My father and Olivia together, for the love of God. I couldn't get it out of my head. In fact, the shock of my learning about this was, to a large extent, what had driven me to take the next step: a sort of leap into the dark to get away from that uncomfortable situation. And so, the previous afternoon—after the announcement, while Gonzalo got ready with boyish excitement to take my mother-in-law out for dinner at Martínez—I had made a call from my room.

The conversation had been brief and neutral. I had no idea what kind of man I was going to find myself face-to-face with the next morning. He proved to be a tall, skeletal fellow of fifty or so in a plain three-piece suit, with a plain tie and a plain face whose skin was nearly transparent. Restrained in manner, tremendously serious. In his office, as if it were an extension of him, there seemed to be no room for levity or freshness, whether in the wood-paneled walls, the thick curtains, or the oriental rug. A desk presided over the office. Behind it was a revolving Chesterfield chair, and in front of that, two armchairs. He offered me one of them. I obediently sat down.

"We've been duly informed of your operational effectiveness, your extreme discretion, and your reliability."

How much of my credentials had Kavannagh revealed to this individual? Only Evita's Rainbow Tour? My collaboration with the British in Madrid during the war? What did he know about Rosalinda, Beigbeder, and my long-ago encounter with Hillgarth at the American Legation? I didn't ask, and he didn't give me any clues.

"That being the case, we believe you could be the right person to handle certain tasks relating to an extremely delicate matter we're dealing with. I won't burden you with internal details, but I can disclose that it's to do with a very specific insurance policy, unique both in terms of the nature of the item to be insured and the environment in which the item will be handled."

I nodded, though I didn't have the remotest idea where this Sacks was heading with his spiel.

"Allow me first of all to give you some background. You'll have heard of the Romanov family I presume."

The Russians, yes. My time in school had been short, but my knowledge did stretch that far. But what on earth did the Russian czars have to do with this guarded Englishman and me?

"We must hark back to them to give you a full picture of the matter. You see, after the outbreak of the Bolshevik revolution, many of the magnificent jewels the dynasty had hoarded for more than three hundred years were seized by the new state. Others were sold on the black market within Russia, and there were additional pieces that vanished without a trace. This suggests that certain covetous hands may have taken them apart to get rid of them bit by bit, almost stone by stone."

I nodded slowly, indicating that I hadn't lost the thread.

"Besides all that," he went on, "a significant number of jewels left Russia, leaving a trail that could be followed. Once they crossed the borders, many were sold or auctioned off. They ended up in the hands of anonymous buyers and sometimes public figures—millionaires, celebrities, or even members of other royal houses. In fact, our own Crown now owns some of them."

My impassive face caused the left corner of Sacks's mouth to twitch.

"Please don't think I'm fluent in the intimacies of the czarist dynasty, Mrs. Bonnard. Everything I'm telling you I learned very recently, out of sheer necessity because of the matter that brings you here today."

I nodded for the fourth, fifth, or sixth time. I'd lost count.

"And so we come to the assignment at hand. Among the jewels that survived and made their way west are those that belonged to the widow of the Grand Duke Vladimir Alexandrovich, uncle of Czar Nicholas II. The duke and duchess, it appears, were one of the most notable couples in the court in Saint Petersburg. When circumstances became difficult for them, she was able to flee to Crimea, taking with her just a few items of everyday jewelry. The rest, of enormous value, she left hidden in a secret compartment in Vladimir Palace, in Saint Petersburg. In the end, the grand duchess managed to escape to Venice, the last Romanov to leave Russian territory."

He paused and changed his tone. "Sounds like a novel, doesn't it?" he said. I shrugged; I had no answer to that. He continued his soliloquy.

"Meanwhile, a British antiquarian—an art expert and acquaintance of the royal family, a man named Albert Spotford—apparently managed to gain entry to the palace disguised as a simple worker, to retrieve the jewels, and, in two big leather bags, bring them to London, where the children of the grand duchess lived in exile. A few years later, after her death, the family divided the inheritance, and each of them did as they pleased with their part. Some pieces remained in the family, and others, the most valuable ones, ended up being sold. The legendary Vladimir Tiara, for instance, is now the property of Queen Mary. And the magnificent suite of emeralds the duchess received as a wedding gift from her father-in-law, Czar Alexander II, passed into the hands of the jeweler Pierre Cartier for a sum that was unrevealed at the time, but was without doubt extremely high."

On the desk was a dark-red leather folder, which Sacks opened delicately. He took out a photograph the size of a sheet of paper and handed it to me.

"The Grand Duchess Maria Pavlovna's fabled emeralds were set like that when they left Russia. It's even said that they may once have belonged to Catherine the Great."

The absence of color in the black-and-white photo didn't prevent me from seeing that the items were as beautiful and as sumptuous as anything I'd ever seen: a large brooch with an enormous hexagonal emerald and a necklace with a good number of stones.

"To dispose of the rather imperial air the pieces had, and to adapt them to the fashion of the time, Cartier, when he bought them, reset the jewels in this long art-deco-style necklace. It's called a sautoir, a term I didn't know until now, so please excuse my ignorance."

He held out a second photograph over the desk. Sure enough, the same stones now formed a wholly different piece: a beautiful, twenties-style long necklace, with the large emerald at the bottom and the rest appearing in descending order by size, largest to smallest, all the way back up to the clasp.

"This design was acquired by the eccentric Chicago millionaire Edith Rockefeller McCormick, and it is estimated that she paid almost half a million dollars for it. That she was eccentric isn't my assessment, please understand—I'm not someone given to making such frivolous judgments. I mention that detail only because it is on record that the lady claimed to be a reincarnation of the pharaoh Tutankhamun."

I didn't know whether to burst out laughing or run away. Everything I was hearing was so extraordinary, so extravagant, and so alien to me that I suddenly felt as if I were in an operetta. Secret compartments hiding treasure, antiquarians in disguise who made off with the same, and crazy Americans who thought they'd once been Egyptian pharaohs. And this tall, serious gentleman, his face like wax, telling me everything in an asphyxiating London office that little outside light entered, despite it being a splendid July morning. *What're you doing there, young lady?* my mother would've said to me. *Stop listening to that nonsense and go find your son. Separate your father from that scorpion of a mother-in-law, and go home.* "Go home." That is what Dolores the dressmaker from Calle de la Redondilla would've told me to do, as upright and as pragmatic as she always was. Home. As if I knew where that was.

Oblivious to my thoughts, Sacks continued his story.

"To conclude the sequence of events and bring it into the present, Cartier purchased the emeralds again after their previous owner's divorce. And it's said that they returned to him in Europe freed from the necklace setting and shipped in a manner that was, shall we say, unorthodox. Do you know how?"

I raised my eyebrows. No, I had no idea what absurdity would come out of his mouth next.

"It seems that they were hidden inside some tea shipments, in the holds of two merchant ships. The main gem was in one of the shipments, and the rest in the other. They say the seller's fortune had been beginning to dwindle, and she'd wanted to avoid customs issues, insurance, and taxes. Once the jeweler had reacquired the emeralds, they were sold again. The piece now comprises just seven stones. They were recut into an octagonal shape by a Cartier designer named"—he took a card from the table and read it out loud—"Lucien Lachassagne, who created an entirely different piece. At the request of the new buyer, they're now part of a tiara that can also be worn as a choker. Look . . ."

I was handed a third image.

"You can't see it without color in the picture, but the mounting is yellow gold, not platinum like before. It seems the design was inspired by Indian art, by the crowns of the—"

"Mr. Sacks?"

He looked up at me in surprise.

"Would you mind coming to the point and explaining why you've approached me about this business?"

"I'm sorry. Sorry," he mumbled. "I'm going off on a tangent. Let's get to the point, yes. Despite my long-winded introduction, I'm sure it's clear that I'm not a jewelry expert. My area is insurance. I know little about purity or beauty, cutting or shaping, or even karats. I'm concerned only with numbers—how much risk can I assume to make selling a policy worthwhile? And since we've been offered the chance to insure these emeralds, we at Brax Insurance are assessing what the coverage limit should be. Which is why we need to consider potential contingencies."

"And what would I have to do with this?"

"We've been informed that the emeralds' next destination, for a time at least, will be Tangier. Their owner has acquired a palace there, and her intention is to wear them at the party that will serve as its unveiling. And this event is the circumstance that worries us. Before agreeing to the policy, therefore, we must conduct an exhaustive risk assessment."

"Could you elaborate a little more?"

He cleared his throat, prepared at last to make his point.

"We need a detailed analysis of Sidi Hosni Palace, its surroundings, and peculiarities. We need to know who's going to move in that circle, from the domestic staff to anyone who might occasionally visit the residence. We would also be interested in knowing more about the function that is to be held, as well as many other details that we must consider as part of our assessment of our policy limit."

At last. So that was what all this was about. Finally, I was beginning to understand. It was nothing to do with state affairs or anything that might lead to disagreements between countries. It was a purely financial matter.

"And what you want . . . is for me to produce the report?"

"That's right. For you to gain access to this milieu and provide us with detailed information. After that, based on the particulars and the potential vulnerabilities of the place, we'll make our decision. Assuming that, as payment for your work, you would accept the sum of 2,500 pounds."

I swallowed. It was a tremendous amount of money.

"Allow me to be frank, Mrs. Bonnard. Brax Insurance is very . . . extremely interested in this client. Though she's a New Yorker by birth, her interests and properties in Britain and on the Continent are growing in number. And while her insurer until now has been a New York firm, we hope to, little by little, assume the coverage of these assets, and to develop a much larger portfolio for her. However, in this first instance involving the emerald tiara, we want to tread carefully. You see—"

I cut him off. I didn't care about his company or its procedures. There was something else I needed to know.

"And do you have in mind anything specific for the, shall we say, pretext, or cover, or guise with which I'm to get close to the proposed target?"

When I had become a supposedly Moroccan dressmaker the first time, and a fake BBC journalist the second, the decision had been made on my behalf—someone had decided in advance what my cover would be. The insurance industry, however, proved to be rather less imaginative.

"We'll leave that to you to decide. We expect that you will be able to find the best way, of your own accord."

I started to feel a thick heat. I was tempted to go over to the windows, draw the curtains back, and open them. But I didn't move from the armchair.

"There's one last thing you haven't mentioned," I said instead. "The name of the current owner of the emeralds and palace in Tangier."

"Indeed. I understand you don't live permanently in Britain, but you may be familiar with the Woolworths stores."

"Yes, I know them."

It was the place where I'd bought some things for Víctor a few months before.

"In which case, you'll be able to make the connection. The lady is Barbara Hutton, the heiress of the Woolworth empire."

67

Tangier began to unfurl before my eyes, white and compact, set against the bright sky like a heap of little cubes. Though I tried to resist, I couldn't help but remember another similar arrival. Eleven years and a few months had passed since Ramiro and I crossed the Strait of Gibraltar together on the same route, back when I was still a submissive and unsuspecting young woman. Now I was traveling not with a man by my side, but with a child, a nanny, and a large amount of luggage. With scars on my soul. And a specified task I needed to complete.

I was overcome with emotion when I identified the figure waving his arms wildly on the wharf. The man waiting for us was dressed in light-brown linen, with a fancy bow tie and new glasses: Félix Aranda, who'd been my neighbor back when I had the studio in Sidi Al Mandri. We'd kept in touch over the years, and I knew he'd moved from Tétouan to Tangier after his mother died. He worked in some sort of office, and—inspiration and life permitting—he hoped to take his first steps in the art world. I'd sent him a cablegram from London announcing our arrival.

"It's so good to see you again, queen of impersonation!"

I couldn't stop myself from laughing—it was what he'd called me back then, when he'd tried to teach me manners, knowledge, and skills to help me pass for the cosmopolitan and glamorous couturier that I quite evidently hadn't been.

Félix gave out hugs, compliments, and praise. He yelled at the porters in Arabic for them to take our baggage. An hour later, we were enjoying a gin fizz together on the terrace of Hotel Cecil. Curious as ever, he fired question after question at me.

"And our dear Mrs. Fox? Do you know anything of Rosalinda?"

"I tried to find her, to no avail."

"The little bird's flown off . . ."

"Yes, but I have no idea where."

"And our sorely missed high commissioner, any news of him? He's never mentioned in the papers anymore."

I hadn't heard anything of Beigbeder, either.

"Nothing," I said.

We sipped our drinks, then fell silent, as if we were concentrating on the beach stretched out below us or the Spanish coastline on the other side of the strait. Our minds, however, had gone back to the days when my friend and her lover Beigbeder were the most controversial couple in the protectorate, a young, uninhibited Englishwoman and an older Francoist military officer, powerful, scheming, and rather eccentric. They'd flirted with glory and, once they'd found it, squared up to the Francoist establishment, leading to their downfall. He'd been discarded like a broken toy; she, perhaps, had managed to change her fortunes.

"And Marcus, my dear . . ."

Félix knew about everything, which might've been why he didn't finish the sentence. Instead he just raised his glass to toast my dead husband. I copied him, trying to stop a tear from escaping from behind my sunglasses.

"Anyway, let's set our melancholy aside and turn to practical matters. So tell me, are you just here on holiday as a proper lady, or do you intend to stay?"

I smoothed the pleats on my white cotton dress while I organized my thoughts.

"I'm here, among other things, to offer you something akin to a partnership."

He looked at me quizzically. We'd remained in contact over the years, certainly, but only superficially. I'd never mentioned my collaboration with the British, or the truth behind Marcus's supposed journalistic endeavors. As astute as he was, however, he surely suspected rather more than I'd told him.

"And what do you have planned for me? Backstitching and hems? Or sketches like that tennis outfit, remember that?"

"For you to be a sort of assistant, that's what I'm offering."

His laughter echoed around the terrace, and several heads turned toward us. The nineteenth-century Hotel Cecil was a somewhat decadent place that overlooked the sea, and it was full of British tourists, for the most part, a little on the old side and bleary eyed, but certainly distinguished. The kind of people who refused to change their annual summer habits.

"Shhh! Quiet, Félix! Listen carefully. I'm here for a job. For my work I need help, reinforcements, connections. And I'd be glad if you could give me a hand."

"A hand, another hand, a foot, another foot . . . anything you need, my queen."

"Perfect. Now answer me this: How well do you know Tangier these days, beyond your own circle?"

"My circle? What circle? Since my mother died and I left Tétouan, I've been a free agent, dear. No ties to anything. I come, I go, I move—"

"Wonderful, my dear. You're hired. Let's take matters one by one, then. The first thing I need is for you to help me find a house while I go to Tétouan to see my mother for a few days."

He opened his mouth so wide I could almost see his uvula.

"Are you seriously intending to buy—"

"Not buy. Are you mad? Rent, is all. Just for a few months. I don't know how long we'll stay, but I'd rather be prepared. A house with a garden, for the boy. Furnished, spacious, comfortable, beautiful."

"Well, let me investigate and I'll get back to you. Although, they say prices are shooting up, so be warned. After the Spanish left and the world war ended, the fun started, and the place is turning into Monte Carlo."

Félix then gave me another of his characteristic lectures, as he had on those Tétouan nights when he'd crossed the landing that separated our homes and installed himself in my living room, after leaving his mother to sleep off the Anís del Mono. I would still be sewing and he, indefatigable, would talk to me excitedly about American films or great literary figures, about gossip concerning our neighbors, celebrities, high society, his and other people's dalliances and dramas.

"Latching on to the small print of the Tangier Protocol, which established Tangier's status as an international zone, as soon as the war in Europe broke out Franco sent our battle-hardened Spanish troops here for a period of time, and let his Nazi friends come and go as they pleased. Everything was suddenly Hispanicized under Francoist regulations. Even the use of languages other than Spanish or Arabic was regulated. Gambling was banned, and they cracked down on the nighttime mayhem the city was famous for. There was a rigidness like the city had never seen before, and the atmosphere became much staler and more subdued, if you know what I mean. Spanish through and through, for God and country, arms raised high."

That certainly wasn't the image I was seeing now from my wicker chair. The beach was full of people in brightly colored bathing costumes, the sand dotted with colorful deck chairs and parasols. The terraces and beach clubs were packed with customers, and modern cars were flowing along Avenida de España between the palm trees.

"Fortunately, before the war was over," Félix went on, "the Generalísimo realized that the Allies might end up winning, and he ordered his troops to ease off. The earlier privileges and responsibilities of the international zone were restored. Between that and the conflict's end, as you can see, the place is now buzzing. Everyone says it's the best

Tangier has ever been—divine, prosperous, marvelous. It's been filled with banks, import-export agencies, new businesses . . . With Europe devastated and starving right over there, we're an attractive destination. People are even saying that an American multimillionaire has bought a gorgeous palace here."

"You don't say," I mumbled. I didn't want to get into that matter just yet. "Right, well, we must get started, Félix. We'll have plenty of time to talk about millionaires and palaces. For now, let's get organized . . ."

Half an hour later, Víctor, Philippa, and I set off for Tétouan in a taxi. We took just a couple of suitcases, and the rest we left at the Cecil: more suitcases, a trunk, my radio, and some packages containing the last shopping I did in London. Though there were hotels in Tangier that were more modern, and classier, with its faded opulence, the Cecil was the perfect place for us to begin.

With a knot in my throat, I traveled the familiar road from Tangier to Tétouan, on which every bend brought back another memory. The terrifying journey on the Valenciana bus when my first pregnancy miscarried. The toing and froing in Rosalinda's convertible, first to negotiate the debt that Ramiro left in my name at the Continental, then to beg the British consul to help us get my mother out of Madrid and bring her to Morocco. Holidays and day outings with Marcus.

I pulled myself together when I saw the city ahead, passing a handkerchief under my eyes in case my mascara, mixed with my emotions, had left a telling mark.

"Mohamed Torres, 17," I told the driver.

My mother was waiting for us on the balcony. I'd called Casa Ros, the nearby shop, and left a message announcing that we'd arrive at around eight o'clock, but she'd probably been looking out for us since the afternoon. All the tears I'd managed to contain in front of Félix on the Cecil's terrace and on the way to Tétouan now flowed. There my mother was, dressed in mauve without a trace of makeup. Fortitude incarnate, the voice of my conscience. Dignity itself, the woman who had brought me into the world alone and who'd made so many sacrifices to bring me up, until the day that I, her child, had decided to leave her side to follow a cretin. My mother, Dolores, forever stoic, now showered my son with affection while she gripped my arm, almost digging her nails in, as if she feared I would run away again.

The flat was simple and spotless, the furniture austere, with a round table, a basic kitchen, and muslin curtains. Her husband, Sebastián, proved to be a calm and quiet man, a widower, recently retired from the postal service, from Granada originally but a resident in the protectorate ever since the armistice that marked the end of the Rif War, which had been declared sometime in the twenties.

We took Víctor for a walk up and down Calle Generalísimo, then back to Plaza Primo. My mother and her husband said hello to people, and she was proud to show off her grandson to the friends or neighbors we came across. Meanwhile, I reacquainted myself with places from my past, seeing flashes of hidden nostalgia. Tétouan was crowded as evening fell, beautiful and warm with its white buildings, its touches of green, and its extraordinary light. Couples, families, groups of friends; soldiers of the infantry, the artillery, the air force, the Regulares: they were all strolling the streets or sitting outside the bars and cafés, having a lemon ice or a beer, an ice cream at La Glacial, or simple cones of sunflower seeds and toasted nuts. Among them were Moroccan men in their djellabas and Moroccan women in their haiks. We ended up eating some of the city's famous kebabs in a little place near the high commission. I had to fight to stop the melancholy from choking me as I ate.

We would've been a lot more comfortable at the Hotel Nacional or the Dersa, but I didn't want to refuse my mother's efforts. A neighbor had lent her a cot for Víctor prepared with pristine sheets, freshly ironed. I was given a narrow bed in the same bedroom, and Philippa had a sort of opened-out divan in the interior room where the sewing machines were kept, my mother's and one that had been mine, both

clean and silent, frozen in time. When no one could see me, I slowly
ran my hand over them.

It had been a long day, and I was exhausted. But I gathered my
strength and stayed up to chat with my mother after everyone was
asleep, the dining room balcony wide open onto the night, the sky full
of stars in front of us, the imposing silhouette of Mount Gorgues in
the background.

"And your father, have you heard from him? Seen him recently?"

To my annoyance, Gonzalo had stayed in London. At the Boltons,
to be precise, in the same bedroom I had occupied for months. When
he'd informed me of his decision, I hadn't been able to believe what I
was hearing. "But . . . how? You . . . you . . . you," I'd stammered. "How
is it you're going to move into . . . to . . . to . . ."

"As a simple guest, Sira," he'd insisted. "Olivia suggested it, and I
think it's a good idea. More comfortable and economical than a hotel,
and we'll be able to keep each other company."

In our prudish Spain, such a situation wouldn't have been
tolerated—a man and a woman unconsecrated by marriage must
never share the same roof. This was even more true when they were
well-to-do, mature, conservative, and formal members of the middle class. Even in London, less stale than Madrid, the arrangement
would have seemed improper.

"And you won't go to Fuenterrabía?" I'd asked, trying to lure him
away.

"We'll see later on," he'd said simply.

I had decided not to push him, and I'd said nothing about the
details of Marcus's will. If I'd wanted to, I could've put an end to their
act of madness by exercising my legal rights as the owner of the property. Dominic Hodson left it all sewn up before he returned to Nairobi,
all the formalities completed. But I said and did nothing. I simply had
dinner with them to say goodbye, in the dining room where Olivia and
I had eaten so many times. I supplied the wine and food, bought during

another visit to Fortnum & Mason, and snuck down to the kitchen so that Gertrude could serve them. I didn't want to be the one to disenchant my father on our last evening together. I was certain that reality would take care of that.

At any rate, Gonzalo Alvarado and Olivia Bonnard were now a good distance from the reunion I was having with my mother.

"He's well," I merely replied. Why give more explanations? "Getting older like everyone, but fine."

We were still having breakfast the next morning when there came a knock on the door. Sebastián opened it.

"Where are the most hardworking hands in all of Africa? Where is the best dressmaker in the world? And where's the little boy I'm going to smother with kisses?"

The person yelling wildly as her heels clicked along the hall could only have been Candelaria, the loud, shameless, and likable smuggler.

"I was simply dying to come last night. I even went to the hairdresser! But I didn't want to be inconsiderate and intrude on the family. But this morning, as soon as I opened my eyes, I thought, 'I can't wait any longer.'"

She finished her speech as she appeared in the doorway to the dining room, then finally, she was standing in front of me. Older, rounder, with her lips painted in my honor and her worn handbag pressed under her arm, she was holding a big pack of churros. A leopard never changes its spots, and my old landlady was as formidable as ever. She told me that, billeted at her guesthouse in La Luneta, only the dried-up old sisters from my time there remained—like remnants of a shipwreck.

"The rest of the guests," she admitted after hugging me, "either left or died. And new ones are in short supply."

We spent the day together, she and my mother competing to push Víctor in his chair. My son, initially a little overwhelmed, soon grew in confidence and then deployed all his charms to make them laugh, the two women swelling with pride, enraptured. At the end of the afternoon, it was time to leave Tétouan. Eight, ten, twelve times, I had to repeat to my mother that we couldn't stay any longer, but not to worry, we would see her constantly over the summer. She wasn't convinced, and she struggled not to show it.

The taxi was pulling off when Candelaria slapped the roof a couple of times and yelled to me through the open window.

"You find me a husband or a job or anything you can think of there in Tangier, all right, Sirita? I'm stone broke. Anything will do, my love."

68

I ruled out the first house I went to see with Félix. It was on Monte Viejo, owned by the wife of a Dutch official, who, once widowed, had decided to return to the Netherlands. She maintained it, however, in case she ever wanted to return, when the rain became unbearable, perhaps, and she missed the bright skies of the strait. It was certainly a good house, large and with land around it. But I turned it down because its location was too far out. I didn't like the idea of Víctor being left there alone with Philippa while I was in Tangier.

The second was a villa in Marshan, owned by a wealthy Jewish family, at the end of Paseo del Doctor Cenarro. It was gorgeous, surrounded by a garden of bougainvillea and palm trees. I would've snapped it up had it not been empty, awaiting someone with their own furniture. The third option, luckily, was perfect. The place was located in an area of new buildings, very near the Italian Hospital and a club I hadn't known about until then. It had opened recently, I was told, and was frequented by a lot of Americans, of whom there were many since the end of the war. Seeing the pool at the Parque Brooks, as the nearby club was called, was enough to persuade me that it would be the ideal place for my son and Philippa when I wasn't there. Water, shade, people around, a restaurant service. That afternoon, we left Hotel Cecil and moved into our new house.

We had more than enough space in every part of that beautiful villa, with its tall windows, fancy molding, and cool geometric-patterned floor tiles in its rooms. It was newly built and there was little in the way of furniture, but we immediately felt at home. To Víctor's delight, two cats that lived in the garden also became residents. While I hung up clothes and put away our belongings, Félix, eager in his role as assistant, kept reappearing with the most unexpected acquisitions: a pair of hammocks for the veranda, provisions for the first few days, some beautiful lanterns for the bottom of the stairs. I was organizing the last few drawers when he arrived with a different discovery: two young Moroccan women in their white headscarves.

"Your new house corps, my dear."

I didn't want to complain and tell him that one pair of hands would be enough. They both became members of the household, just like sweet Jamila had been when I lived in Tétouan; just like our dear Sharifa, who'd done so much for us after we moved to the Austrian Hospice in the Old City.

After a couple more hours of domestic chores, I called it a day.

"Let's go out for dinner," Félix suggested.

I didn't feel like it; I barely had the strength. I would've gladly eaten any old thing—a slice of watermelon, a tomato with dressing—and stayed home to chat with my old friend under the stars on one of the new hammocks, carefree, without a drop of makeup on, hair let down. I was aware, though, that I needed to get moving. I'd finished chapters one and two: Nostalgia and Housekeeping. It was time to start chapter three.

I got dressed and carefully did my makeup and hair. It was the first evening of a new phase—I had to make an effort—and I let Félix lead the way. He chose the terrace at La Parade, another new addition in Tangier, and one of his favorite haunts, I supposed. He assured me that, for the beau monde of Tangier, this was the place to be.

La Parade turned out to be a villa on Calle Fez that had been converted into a restaurant, with a leafy garden bordered by white walls and with twenty or so small candlelit tables. A pianist livened up the atmosphere, and the Moroccan waiters in red fezzes nimbly moved around with their trays. The clientele was varied, judging by its attire and languages: French, English with British or American accents, some Spanish (albeit not much), one or two flurries of Italian—the general pattern of the city, on a small scale.

Félix didn't say hello to anyone, however. And no one seemed to know him. I was surprised. From what he'd told me in his letters, from his ease of manner when he met me at the boat, and from the way he spoke about various people, I'd assumed he was well connected in the city, with no shortage of friends and contacts. I was amazed he went so unnoticed in the colorful crowd around us. Regardless, I focused on the menu. Who knew where the dinner would take us?

I decided in seconds that I would just have the sole. He, on the other hand, took his time, enthralled by the list of dishes, which he read meticulously, as if savoring them—hesitating and correcting himself until he opted for beef: tournedos Rossini. He then enunciated the word "champagne" syllable by syllable, before placing his hands on the tablecloth and taking in the surroundings and citizenry with fascination.

"Oooh, look . . . ," he whispered. "Him in the yellow jacket, the one with the silk neckerchief, that's the great David Herbert, a big cheese among the English expats. And her, in the turban, she must be—"

"Félix . . ."

He didn't let me interrupt.

"And look, look . . . that tall blond man, the dashingly handsome one heading toward the piano, I think that's one of the owners of this place, Jay Has-what's-his-name."

"Félix . . ."

He paid no attention.

"And them, at the table in the back, behind the fountain," he said almost voicelessly, overcome with joy. "They're the writers from New York. They arrived not long ago. They're evidently very modern, liberated. They live here in a little place on the Monte, writing wonders, no doubt."

"Félix, will you listen to me?"

"I'm sorry, darling. It's just I'm so, so, so . . ."

"Listen to me. All these people, you don't know them personally?"

"Me? I wish. I know who they are, but they move in their own circles."

"And what about you?"

My life had done so many somersaults in recent years that, irrationally, I'd assumed that both of us, Félix and I, had performed similar acrobatics in high society. In my letters, I'd told him about my comings and goings between Madrid, Jerusalem, and London, about events, grand hotels, a miscellany of people, the strangest of specimens, the most eye-catching aspects of my experience, the top crust that hid the less pleasant parts. From his letters I'd learned about his move, and I had imagined that it had been a springboard to a better life, that he'd left behind the stifled existence he'd led with his mother to join the most cosmopolitan and sophisticated stratum of Tangier society. But now, reality was making me question my assumptions. Seeing Félix's reaction in that garden, I was realizing that his move had been only a physical one, a purely geographical leap. These people surrounding us at La Parade—foreigners with a hedonistic je ne sais quoi and expatriate professionals; some frivolous, others formal, variously wealthy and similarly self-assured—lived in an entirely different world than my ex-neighbor.

"Félix?"

I didn't want to ruin his moment, but I needed to know.

"Provisioning Office, Statistics Department, from nine o'clock to two o'clock, and from four to seven. And in my free time, like I said, I try to paint—though I must admit, I haven't progressed a lot. Oh, and three evenings a week I go to the cinema."

There it was, laid bare: my friend's life. Freed from his mother's tyranny, he'd fled Tétouan in search of the myth of a magical city and had found himself alone among strangers, trapped in a job as tedious as his previous one and shut out of the circles of the extravagant artists he so admired.

"So, you don't actually mix with any of these people . . . ," I mumbled, as if I needed to persuade myself of this truth that radically reduced my prospects.

"Look, Sirita," he added, setting aside his usual effervescence for a moment. "What they say about the legendary international Tangier—it exists, yes. But at the same time, it's a myth. I have all the figures in my head thanks to my work. Shall I recite them?"

I didn't strictly need the numbers, but it was a fact that knowing them would give me an idea of the makeup of the place.

"So, of the city's hundred thousand inhabitants, there are almost seventy thousand Moroccan Arabs, properly speaking, and some eight thousand Moroccan Jews. Among the Christians, we Spanish take the cake, with around fifteen thousand registered, excluding those here illegally. We're the largest foreign population by far and the ones who, to a large extent, define city life. Did you know there's even been talk of building a bullring? Next there's the French, who—being as they are and having their own protectorate to the south—give the appearance of numbering more, but are really no more than three thousand. Then it's the Italians and British, followed by the Portuguese, Belgians, Dutch, and a smattering from the rest of the world."

He swept the room with his eyes.

"And here we all are, living in harmony, but at the same time, each associating with their own. Under the surface, the city is divided by invisible lines. Not urban ones, but lines related to nationality, religion, class . . . And while some people cross over, most move within their boundaries. French with French, British with British, Jews with Jews . . . even the large Spanish colony has its dividing lines. On the one hand, there are the government officials, businessmen, top professionals—you know, the doctors at the hospital or the managers of Banco de Bilbao or Español de Crédito. And on the other, there are droves of exiled or migrant Andalusians working as laborers or waiters and living in humble houses, around little courtyards full of geraniums and laundry blowing in the wind."

I was beginning to understand, more or less.

"In short, my dear, people are respectful with each other within this hodgepodge. They cross paths all the time, of course. There are Spanish children at the Lycée Regnault and the Liceo Italiano, just as there are Jewish and Arab children at the Colegio Español. There are families of different nationalities living together like good neighbors on different floors of the same building. There are even mixed marriages. But at the end of the day, birds of a feather flock together, you know? They each read their own newspapers, go to their own churches, go to the cinema to watch films in their own languages, and go about their business as they would back home."

He'd given me a terrific overview. There was something, however, that I'd begun to suspect from the moment we arrived at La Parade. And I needed him to corroborate my understanding.

"So you never go to parties organized . . . I don't know . . . by that Englishman in the yolk-colored jacket?"

"David Herbert invite *me* to a party?" He looked as if he were about to choke. "Of course not, are you mad? Not him nor anyone else in those circles."

The laughter he himself had managed to contain suddenly burst out among a group sitting at a nearby table. We looked at them quite openly.

"That noisy bunch are Americans. Like I said this morning at Parque Brooks, they've flocked here in droves since the Allied victory.

We haven't accounted for them in any detail yet in our department, but they number quite a few now. I believe they have a military facility nearby, and several new radio stations, and they're beginning to open a few businesses—"

I cut in unceremoniously.

"So, Félix, let's get this clear. What you know about this international fauna beyond figures comes simply from what you observe because you like knowing who the movers and shakers are and—"

"And because, deep down, I'm an incorrigible busybody—you know me. But yes, dear, with great regret, I must inform you, that's where my connection ends."

I put my fork in my mouth so that the flavor of the fish might soothe my disappointment. While making my naive plans, I'd imagined that Félix would be able to introduce me to the milieu in which I was supposed to carry out my new mission in Tangier. Hanging from his arm, I would pass myself off as a traveler with a vague past and no ties, operating with my usual brazenness and duplicity, making lighthearted comments, telling ambiguous stories, and mentioning scenarios I'd plucked from nowhere. Now, however, that plan was deflating like the soufflé glacé that had just been served at the next table.

I contemplated my friend while he ordered his dessert from the waiter in an affected French, like a diligent student, happy regardless to have been taken out of his daily grind as an office clerk in charge of surveys and reports, folders and blotting paper. And while I looked at him, I wondered when his wings had failed, when he'd found that he couldn't fly, as he'd always wanted to do. All his hopes, his dreams of living a different life as the brilliant artist I'd thought he would become back when he drew sketches for my designs, seemed to have vanished. His mother was dead and buried; he was free, in theory. But he was limited to the experiences of what he read in newspapers and books, what he heard on the radio or in other people's conversations, and what happened in front of his eyes, always at a distance. Never involved himself. A mere spectator, a simple voyeur of other worlds.

"You were expecting more of me, weren't you?" he said while he attacked his crème brûlée without looking me in the eyes, as if he'd read my thoughts.

I lied, out of sheer habit.

"I don't know what you mean."

He looked up then, slowly wiping his lips with his napkin.

"Yes, you do."

The voices of the other diners masked our silence. The pianist began to play a lively piece, two or three couples got up to dance, a photographer snapped a shot.

"I was the clever one when we met, do you remember? The well-versed, well-informed, cultured one. The one who had ideals, ambitions—who knew what he wanted. You, on the other hand, were a young girl with nowhere to go. Fragile, vulnerable, with no vision or prospects. I longed to be free from my mother, and you longed to be reunited with yours. And now look at us. The old hag Encarna's pushing up the daisies in the civil cemetery in Tétouan, and I'm still cowed under her shadow. Meanwhile, you found the courage not only to be with Dolores once more but also to separate yourself from her again with no bad blood, and to follow your own path. And here you are now, a formidable woman with a purpose, alive inside and turning heads."

The tone of the atmosphere had changed, and more couples took to the little dance floor. Laughter, loud voices speaking several languages, bottles uncorking, vibrant music.

I took my friend's hand and squeezed it hard.

"I still need you, Félix. I'm counting on you. I need you by my side."

69

Finding the palace of Sidi Hosni was my next objective. I went out early the next morning before Víctor woke up and the house became filled with movement. The sky augured another bright day as I left my new neighborhood, part of an Englishman's large estate that was being broken up and sold so the modern city could continue to grow. Parallel to the Muslim cemetery's wall, the long street of Sidi Bouarrakia led me to the market known as Afuera Souk. I passed the Las Palomas bar and the Mendoubia Garden, and as I walked through the Bab Al Fahs gate, I saw the Moroccan traders working in their *bakalitos*, arranging pans and feather dusters, flyswatters, pots and washbowls, preparing their wares for the customers that would arrive throughout the day.

From there, I headed down Avenida de Italia with its beautiful curved balconies, quickening my pace as I came to two cinemas, the Capitol and then the Alcázar. I didn't want to loiter. I'd been here several times with Ramiro on those idle and flighty days I'd spent blinded by his love, while at the Hotel Continental, behind me, a bill had been building up that I would end up having to pay. Shaking off the unpleasant memories, I strode up to the kasbah, the citadel up on the hill. I was wearing flat sandals, light-colored trousers, and a silk headsquare covering my hair, my eyes hidden behind sunglasses. I could've been any tourist. Except there weren't any tourists in that part of the city, not at that hour or at almost any other. In those days, they stayed at the beach clubs and hotel pools. At most, they went to see the Caves of Hercules or sat outside a café at a market like the Chico Souk to enjoy the picturesque views of the city. Only adventurers and eccentrics ventured into the citadel in the high part of the historical district that was the medina, the old part of the city with narrow streets and market stalls below it.

Which was why I was so surprised that it was precisely here that the millionaire Barbara Hutton had decided to buy a palace. The seller, as the languid Sacks had informed me in his insurance company office, was a certain Maxwell Blake, a US diplomat high up in the consular corps in Tangier. After decades of service in Morocco, retirement had meant that it was time for him to go home—to Kansas City, of all places. Over the years, the palace's various owners, spending money and patience in equal measure, had successively added seven more houses to the property, joining the buildings together to create one home as labyrinthine as it was beautiful. Its original owners had included Sidi Hosni himself—the Muslim saint whose name the place bore and whose remains, it was said, lay under the building. Another famous owner had been the legendary *Times* journalist Walter Harris, who'd later built himself a villa in the Malabata area of Tangier, on the other side of the sands. Finally, after having undergone all these transformations, the palace was passed on to Barbara Hutton.

All the visible building materials were original. Local artisans had worked the plaster, mud, metal, and wood with skilled hands, using age-old techniques. Or at least, that was what Sacks's two-page report had stated. The transaction had been completed for the sum of a hundred thousand US dollars, and the original furniture and fittings were included in the price, the report further informed me. And that was it. That was all the information I was given. The rest, I would have to find out myself.

I tried to ask a Muslim woman in her haik where the palace was located, but she ignored me and walked on. Then I stopped some children. "Sidi Hosni?" I asked. They shrugged, laughed, and asked me for a coin. I continued to climb, negotiating narrow streets, mounds of melons and potatoes, holes in the ground, grime, and cats, wondering what had possessed one of the richest women in the world to buy a house there. Had the cautious Gregory Sacks of Brax Insurance Ltd been with me, he would've died from fright. In the end, it was an old man in a grubby djellaba who, with a crutch crudely fashioned from a stick, pointed me in the right direction: up and right. After leaving ten pesetas in his rough hand, I headed to my destination.

Instead of attendants, guards, or watchmen, I found a couple of sacks of earth beside the open gate. There being no one to ask, I crept forward into a wide open-air corridor. There was no one in the first courtyard I found, just an impressive wooden door with polished studs, left ajar. In the vicinity there were signs that someone had been there working: a hoe, a rudimentary wheelbarrow, half-rusted pruning shears. And farther away, flowerpots and planters, cuttings and plants ready to sink their roots into soil. I found myself thinking of Olivia, working in the garden on the Boltons, firing orders at her clumsy pair of helpers. If my dictatorial mother-in-law had been responsible for the work here, she wouldn't have let the gardeners out of her sight. Far from stopping me, the absence of people spurred me on. Without asking permission from anyone, in three steps, four steps, five, I was inside.

The first thing I found in the hallway was a pile of large boxes covered in foreign labels. I bent down to see where they came from and found the emblem and address of an interiors shop on Sloane Street, Knightsbridge, London. Some of the boxes were open. Large pieces of fabric stuck out from one. I couldn't resist, and I caressed them delicately between my fingertips. A quick feel was enough to tell me they were magnificent velvets intended to dress windows, arcades, balconies.

The soles of my sandals allowed me to move with stealth around the maze of rooms and courtyards, terraces, and unexpected flights of stairs. Now I understood how the original seven houses had been incorporated: with fluid harmony, but without following a logical order. Even so, the palace exuded peace and beauty. There was some furniture, and also a lot of empty spaces which seemed to have been recently emptied, now ready to be occupied by pieces that were to the new owner's taste. There were rolled-up rugs, unhung paintings and mirrors, items out of place. Reception rooms and bedrooms unexpectedly followed one another, each displaying carved wood-paneled ceilings, scrollwork-covered skirting boards, wrought-iron railings.

Without following any particular pattern, I ended up in a beautiful courtyard, the main one of the house, I imagined. In the center, an enormous fig tree provided shade for what I guessed was a summer dining area. Another staircase led me to the scullery, the kitchen, the larder, the laundry room. Climbing still more unruly stairs, I found myself on the flat roof—out in the open air, on a succession of connected terraces that had views of the entire medina and its laundry-covered rooftops, plus some sections of the modern city, the sea's splendor in the background.

The Sidi Hosni wasn't a monumental palace. It was neither ostentatious nor grandiose. But I could see why the millionairess from New York had fallen in love with it. It had magic and charm, soul, its own personality.

The metallic sound of tools being used pulled me from my rapture. Someone, a gardener probably, had started working downstairs; it was time to get out of there. My objective now was to find the exit. Slinking noiselessly, I started to head down the stairways, retracing my steps and getting lost several times. Finally, I reached the main hallway and sighed with relief. I was almost there, back at the half-opened boxes of fabric. Within seconds I'd be in the first courtyard, and in half a minute, on the street, heading down into the kasbah.

I was tiptoeing toward the door when a murmur made me freeze, a soft growl of annoyance. I identified its source right away: the mouth of a woman who at that precise moment was emerging from behind one of the big boxes. She had been crouched, which was why I hadn't seen her. Now she was three paces away and there was nothing I could do.

"*Mon Dieu*, what a fright!" she said, holding her hand to her chest. She was as thin as a reed, with high cheekbones, a long neck, and transparent skin. A tiny pair of glasses perched on her nose and a fringe full of gray hairs hung over her brow, the rest of her hair gathered in a bun.

"I . . . I'm sorry, I didn't mean to . . . ," I stammered.

"Oooh!" she exclaimed then, relieved. "You're the seamstress!"

I said neither yes nor no. I was too stunned to speak. Who *was* this foreign woman? Why did she know who I was? How did she know me if we'd never met?

"Finally you're here!" Her voice was dry, her accent heavy. She started moving carefully between the boxes. "I'm Ira Belline, the housekeeper. I was expecting you yesterday. Toni—the housemaid—said you'd be here in the afternoon."

She worked her way through the packages to the empty part of the hall, where I was standing motionless. She was holding a small notebook in one hand and a mechanical pencil in the other. She paused, looked me up and down, and frowned.

"I didn't expect you to be . . . I thought you would be a woman of . . ." She threw a hand in the air with a vague gesture that suggested it didn't matter. "Anyway, the important thing is you're here. Let me explain . . ."

Sure enough, she spent the next few minutes describing the situation. The exclusive establishment in London from which a famous interior designer had ordered curtains for the whole house had made a hash of the measurements. They'd gotten in a tangle over centimeters, inches, feet, and yards. The result was that the curtains were too long, and they had to be shortened and repaired. The new proportions were written on a card, which she handed to me.

"When do you think you'll have them ready?"

That was when I should've corrected her mistake. *It wasn't me you were expecting, I'm afraid, señora. I was once a dressmaker, but I'm not anymore. Now I'm just an intruder who's shamelessly wandering around the palace without permission, someone who's been hired to secretly assess the place and the people in it.*

What I said, however, was something very different.

"How soon do you need them?"

"As soon as possible, of course. But it's a lot of work, you'll need help. The princess arrives in two weeks and there's still a lot to do. If we could get through this before they start with—"

I cut her off.

"Give me a couple of days."

The expression on her face showed something between disbelief and confusion.

"Are you serious?"

"Absolutely. I just need the boxes taken to my house."

"C'est merveilleux . . ." She was so relieved that her French came out without her realizing it.

"I live in the Parque Brooks area. You can tell whoever's transporting it that there's a big pine tree at the entrance to my villa."

She still hadn't changed her expression when I headed to the door and went out into the courtyard. I saw a gardener, a Moroccan man as old as his tools, turning soil over in the pots. A couple of boys were helping him, others were carrying boxes from the street. Sidi Hosni was beginning to come alive.

I heard a throat being cleared behind me.

"Excusez-moi, madame . . ."

I turned. Ira Belline had followed me. I looked at her through my big sunglasses.

"And your name is . . . ?"

I held out my hand, languid, false, almost feather light. The woman who was not me had arrived, my new identity plucked from nowhere.

"Arish Bonnard, pleased to meet you. I'm a couturière, arrived recently from Buenos Aires, though I lived in Tangier for a time some years ago. I specialize in haute couture, and I don't usually do decorative projects, obviously. Consider it a special favor, seeing as it's for . . ."

I was going to say Barbara Hutton, the name that had been present in my mind for days, but opted instead to use the moniker the housekeeper had used moments before.

". . . for the princess."

The contrast once I was back in the medina was extreme. Noise and yelling, smells, flies, people, as if the city's old quarter had woken up in a fury while I was inside the palace. I started to make my way downhill, between men and women in djellabas, robes, and haiks, and old men in rags. There were market stalls, peddlers, rugs hung from windows, cages, puddles, squatting beggars wearing hoods, their scabby hands outstretched. Life—real, sprawling life—poles apart from the cosmopolitan sumptuousness of Tangier's international zone.

A little farther on, however, one person stood out from the crowd. A Christian woman of mature years, dressed in dark clothes and a little overweight. She wore a look of dejection on her face. When she was a few paces away, I noticed her relief the moment she saw me.

"Excuse me, señorita, do you speak Spanish? I'm looking for a house called Sidihoni or something like that."

I quickly assessed her. An Andalusian seamstress, uprooted from her village by the cruelties of life and transplanted to Tangier as so many others had been. Ready to earn a few francs, pounds, or pesetas doing any job that was offered to her.

"Are you the seamstress? Did Toni send you?"

"Yes, señorita, at your service. I was here yesterday, went round and round like a spinning top but never found the place."

That was how Maruja Peña came into my life.

70

We put the borrowed sewing machines in one of the ground-floor rooms, a space with little furniture and with two high windows in the corner to let in light and air. We had long hours of labor ahead of us.

"With the heat, señorita, there's little in the way of work, as you can imagine."

Maruja's current lack of customers, undesirable to her, served me perfectly. She, a neighbor of hers, and a niece set up camp in the room just as soon as the fabric arrived.

The boxes appeared piled up on the back of a cart. I tried not to laugh at the contrast: the sumptuous velvets bought at the price of gold dust from a prestigious interior designer in London had completed their journey under the steam of two Moroccan youths and a pair of donkeys. Overseeing the operation was Paco, who I was informed was the husband of the previously mentioned Toni. *Paco*, *Toni*, and *Ira Belline*: I already had three names for my report, people connected to the palace whose precise roles at Sidi Hosni I would have to delve into.

The women threw themselves into the work with dedication. They weren't great seamstresses, and they lacked finesse. But when well directed, they operated with no problem whatsoever. I worked with them at first, led by example, established the guidelines. It wasn't a complicated task, but it had to be done with sound judgment and delicacy. At no time, however, did I reveal to them the skulduggery with which I'd landed the job. I intended to pay them well—more than they would've received had they done the work of their own accord without me acting as a shadowy go-between. And for me, the arrangement opened the doors to the palace in the citadel and its people. Everyone was a winner. Plus, holding those beautiful fabrics in my hands—and being surrounded by material, needles, scissors, and thread once more—was thrilling. A pleasant reminder of the woman I'd once been.

"What in the blazes is all this?" Félix asked from the door to the improvised workshop. He had to shout to make himself heard over the noise from the machines.

It was almost six in the evening. I left my new operatives to finish their work and asked Daniya, one of the Moroccan girls, to make Félix and me some mint tea. We sat on the veranda while we waited.

"So that's why you wanted such a big house. Not for a holiday but to set up another studio. It all makes sense now."

I didn't confirm it or contradict him, so he went on enthusiastically.

"My girl, these divine fabrics, where did they come from? You didn't bring them with you, it wouldn't have fit in your luggage. And you haven't had time to buy it, as far as I know."

Since I'd arrived back in Tangier, I'd been pondering how to explain my situation to Félix. I still wasn't sure what parts I should come clean about and what I should keep to myself. After the unexpected twist that morning, however, I now had an excuse that would make the lie a little less mendacious.

"What brought me to Tangier, Félix, was some work for Barbara Hutton."

"Barbara Hutton?" he asked with exaggerated bewilderment. "The American millionaire? The heiress they say has bought a palace here?"

I smiled innocently while, inside, my conscience gave me a kick.

"That's right."

He clapped loudly three times and bellowed with laughter. Víctor, who was playing with some scraps of fabric on the floor at my feet, imitated him, giggling along. For some incomprehensible reason, my son found Félix, who had no understanding whatsoever of children, enormously funny.

"I knew you were up to something, you rascal! And I've been biting my tongue, waiting for you to decide to tell me."

"She's going to be here in a few weeks' time, and I'm going to help with the . . . let's call it the textiles."

Daniya arrived with the tea on a polished tray. She served it in little glasses, the boiled water still bubbling. It smelled glorious.

"Hey, hey, hey, and have you seen the place inside? Will you let me go with you? Will you—"

I cut in.

"We'll see. First, I need you for something else."

Barbara Hutton, born in New York in 1912. Will be thirty-five in November. Granddaughter of a rich merchant. Lost her mother when she was a child. Father absent. Raised by nannies. Given a lavish debutante ball in 1930. Resident of Europe since the age of twenty, when she'd first married, divorcing soon after. Married again the next day, settled in London, had a son, and divorced again in 1941. When the war broke out in Europe, she returned to the United States. In 1942 she married the actor Cary Grant, her third marriage, before divorcing him in 1945.

These cold facts and dates from the insurance company's report were all I knew about the owner of the emeralds. My earlier visit to what would soon be her house, however, had stirred my curiosity. I wanted to know more about her, to investigate, to somehow get closer to her, but I lacked the time and resources.

"Can you take a few days off work, Félix?"

"As many as you like, my queen. There's not much to do in the summer. We spend days at the office twiddling our thumbs."

"Perfect, because I need you to do something for me."

I knew he would be intrigued by my plan, nosy gossip that he was. Finding out as much information as possible about Barbara Hutton, that was the aim, to give me as complete a picture as possible of her life. My old neighbor's obvious delight made Víctor practically cry with laughter again.

"You'll have to search the British and American papers, mostly. I imagine they'll let you see them at the consulates."

"I'll find a way. I'll get straight to it."

Keeping my promise, two days later I unloaded the finished work at Sidi Hosni. I'd even managed to get a son-in-law of Maruja's to transport the material in a wagon that was narrow enough for the streets of the medina and kasbah. It took some time for me to decide what to wear for my second encounter with Ira Belline. I would've liked to show up dressed in something different, exotic, in keeping with the place and with the fraudulent identity I'd created. But my London wardrobe didn't give me that option—its clean lines and neutral textures were far from extravagant.

The effort would've been for nothing, in any case, because my target wasn't there at that moment. The housekeeper, confidant, or whatever else Ira Belline was, wasn't at Sidi Hosni the afternoon when we arrived with the finished, ironed, and folded curtains wrapped in manila paper and tied with deep-red silk cord. I did find the gardener and his helpers, and I heard noises and voices inside, but this time I didn't stray from the hallway, preferring instead to be cautious.

A few hours later, back at home, Víctor refused his dinner, pressing his lips together and vigorously shaking his head. Philippa and I tried together, but he fought both of us off, and in the end I asked her to leave me alone with him so he'd be less distracted. He didn't seem to like the purée one of my new housemaids had made for him, and I hadn't had time to get involved in domestic matters and find something more appetizing. Focused as I was on my new task, I hadn't even given instructions on what to buy and how to cook it, or on any other aspect of running the house. Sitting in front of my son in the kitchen, I tried again with another spoonful, doing the airplane, singing "Cinco lobitos" and trying several other silly things, none of which worked. I persisted, but he continued to refuse. My boy was certainly stubborn when he wanted to be. And I was exhausted. To keep my word and finish on time, in the end I'd had to join the seamstresses and spend the entire day stitching. I took a deep breath and made one more attempt. Fed up with my perseverance, Víctor batted away the spoon. Only then did he open his mouth, to burst into laughter when he saw the blob of purée on my pale blouse—over my left breast, to be precise.

Just then the doorbell rang. Trying to clean myself with a damp cloth, I went to the door. I'd assumed it would be Félix, or perhaps one of the girls, having forgotten something. The one person I never would've anticipated finding there was Ira Belline.

"I wanted to say an enormous thanks for your excellent work," she said, putting a hand to her heart and tapping it. Then she smiled as I invited her in out of sheer politeness, not expecting for one moment that she would accept. But she did.

"We've just moved in, we're still—"

"C'est une jolie maison."

I called Philippa so she could take over with Víctor, and I apologized for the state of my blouse. I was far from pleased that Barbara Hutton's confidant was seeing me in such a state, unkempt, struggling with a child who was in full rebellion.

"And you'll have to forgive me, but I don't have anything to offer you."

She was indifferent.

"Was it here you sewed all the curtains?"

Fortunately, Maruja and her colleagues hadn't taken away their sewing machines yet. They were too heavy, and we had agreed that they would send someone to fetch them the next day. Everything had been tidied, however. Spare material, fabric scraps, reels, bobbins, all in perfect order, like a tiny army of objects. So I asked Ira to follow me and showed her the corner room. The windows were still wide open, the sun was going down, and the room was in semidarkness. With its high ceilings and the resting machines, it exuded a strange beauty.

"It was our first job in Tangier" was all I said.

"I have no doubt you'll have more work soon."

I tried not to allow myself to be dragged along by the current.

"No, I don't plan . . ."

I left the sentence hanging, and she didn't press me. We headed back toward the living room and were about to go in when I changed my mind and suggested we go out on the veranda. The temperature was pleasant, the air smelled of lady of the night, jasmine, the white roses in the flowerbeds, and the sea in the background. Before I'd invited her to sit, she slumped into one of the hammocks.

"Organizing Sidi Hosni must be a complicated business."

I'd spoken cautiously while striking a match to light the lanterns that Félix had brought. The candles sprouted flames with a beautiful glow.

"You can't imagine," she admitted.

A lively group passed by on the other side of the garden fence—boys, girls, speaking Italian. No doubt they were heading to the nearby Parque Brooks, where there was to be a dance that evening.

"You know, I always thought of myself as an effective organizer. I've worked in a lot of places, I've been a partner in businesses in Paris, Cannes, Marrakech . . ."

"But you're not French, are you?"

"Not originally. I was born in Russia, but I arrived in France young. The Revolution, you know . . ."

Yes, I did know. It was precisely because of some stones that had left the same country during that turbulent time that I was now in Tangier.

"But this is pushing me to my limits," she added in little more than a murmur. "This was supposed to be a minor endeavor, a temporary refurbishment until the princess, once she'd settled in, could make the decisions."

"And things got complicated . . ."

She sighed deeply. We heard more noise coming from the street, this time the click of heels alongside flat footsteps. It was completely dark out now. I guessed it was a couple that was walking past. Perhaps I should've gotten up to turn on a light, but I didn't. We remained in the shadows with only the lanterns for light.

"Everything's multiplying by two, by three, by four, by five . . . ," she continued, counting in a low voice as if talking to herself. "She keeps changing her mind. What was good yesterday is no good now. Then there's the added difficulty of the distance. The requests, orders, instructions—they all go back and forth in telegrams and telephone calls, letters, packages. Commands and retractions cross each other. They don't understand in London that things happen at a different pace here."

I wished I had a bottle of something, wine, champagne, even a soft drink. Anything to offer Ira Belline so that she'd feel at ease, so she'd keep talking and fill my ears with details about Sidi Hosni and its owner.

"Mrs. Hutton must be a very special person."

"You can be certain of that, *chérie*."

"And she must be enormously excited about the palace."

"*Évidemment*. But many can't understand it, can't fathom why she'd set her mind on a residence that's undoubtedly beautiful but so, so complex." She let out a short, dry burst of laughter. "No one even knows how they're going to get her car through those narrow streets!"

I recalled the surrounding area—the holes, the puddles, the humble people, the scattered debris. It had certainly been a strange whim that had led her to live in such a house.

"Anyway, *mon amie*, I don't want to take up any more of your time. Let's get to the point."

I straightened my back. The point? What was this "point"? I'd thought she'd come to thank me for my work, perhaps to pay me. A mere formality, in any case.

"I believe you said the other day that you had lived in Tangier before, so I suppose you know the nature of this world well."

Without knowing what she was referring to, I just muttered, "More or less."

"You see, another requirement has been added to the princess's list. She wants a wardrobe in keeping with the location. Not just any wardrobe, *naturellement*, but something with soul and quality, if you know what I mean."

She'd explained badly, but I believed I understood what she was saying.

"I'd planned to go to Marrakech," she continued. "I know someone there who makes just such clothes, an exquisite French designer, albeit rather extravagant. But I'm so busy now that I'm not going to be able to make the trip."

I let her go on without interrupting her, my eyes fixed on the flames.

"Which was why I was wondering if you, Madame Bonnard, with your style and that efficient team of yours, could perhaps prepare a line of Moroccan-inspired garments for the princess to wear this summer."

I was still trying to digest the offer when Ira Belline sighed loudly.

"I know this is another eccentricity, and please forgive my boldness in proposing such a thing, but she's determined that the clothes should be ready for her when she arrives. Mrs. Hutton's new property acquisition has inspired in her a deep passion for the traditional and the authentic. It even seems that she intends to bring with her valuable jewelry of a certain exotic flavor—which, between you and me, I find perplexing. You know the palace's surroundings. Let's hope the pieces are well insured, at least. Otherwise, God help us, as her compatriots say."

71

I had the hardworking hands of Maruja Peña and her colleagues from Patio Pinto at my disposal. I had my good judgment and my background as a dressmaker. And I had an objective. With these three factors, I was close to gaining access to Sidi Hosni and its world. However, I still needed a fourth component.

Fabric, textiles, cloth. That was what was missing: material to work with. And that was precisely the problem—I couldn't find it anywhere, despite all my traipsing around Tangier. I spent an entire day trawling the little artisan shops in the medina where the Moroccan population did its shopping, but all I found were coarse, everyday fabrics, with no body, lacking refinement. The next day I headed to the modern area where businesses catered to international clientele. These were almost all owned by Jews. My skin prickled when I saw, in various places, Hebrew signs that reminded me of Jerusalem.

But it wasn't fair to associate these decent traders with the terrorists who'd ended Marcus's life at the King David. Forcing myself not to invent sinister connections that did not exist, I went from shop to shop on Boulevard Pasteur, Calle Velázquez, Calle Murillo, and Calle del Estatuto, as well as Rue Jeanne d'Arc, Rue Delacroix, and anywhere else that was recommended to me. But all I found were rolls of fabric of a European sort—plain wools and common cottons, cretonnes, gabardines and flannels—for making ladies' and gentlemen's outfits, children's clothes, and uniforms. There was nothing here that I could use for the line of sophisticated kaftans I'd decided to create to meet the demands issued by Mrs. Hutton, the princess without a principality, the extravagant heiress.

Someone told me about an elderly antiquarian in the Fuente Nueva neighborhood, but each time I went to that corner of the medina I found only a locked door. Another person also told me there was an old merchant in Fez who sold antique Persian fabrics, but for a thousand different reasons, that place was beyond my reach. I returned home frustrated and sweltering shortly after two o'clock. Outside, the east wind was battering the buildings and spoiling people's day at the beach. As soon as I opened the door, I heard yelling and Víctor crying in the kitchen. I rushed in to find a disastrous scene. Everything was in disarray, and my son was sitting in his high chair, angry because they were trying to feed him some new baby food that, once again, he didn't like. Philippa and one of the Moroccan girls were arguing without understanding each other. The other girl, with her back to me, was stroking one of the cats, which was perched on the bench, while the other animal, with no one paying attention to it, was licking a plate.

"What is going on here?"

My raised voice was followed by a sudden silence. Even Víctor stopped crying, while the cats slipped away to the rear patio with guilty stealth. Within seconds, however, the racket started up again: the Moroccan girls yelled in unison in their native dialect of Darija, a cowed Philippa complained tearfully in English, and my son continued his wordless tantrum. With the boy on my hip, I tried to mediate between the three young women, but it was impossible—how does one resolve an argument over a vegetable purée between two girls from the outskirts of Tangier and a placid subject of the British Empire? Fed up and unable to get them to reach an understanding, I asked the former to tidy the kitchen and go home, and the latter to get out of the way and do whatever she pleased. Then I gave Víctor a banana and we went upstairs to get changed. Half an hour later, the two of us were in a taxi on the way to Tétouan, and this time there was no opportunity to slip into melancholy or longing on the way. I had enough problems in the present: my despair at not being able to find the fabrics I needed for my work, my frustration at not being able to get my own house in order. I was indignant, angry with everyone else, and with myself. I hadn't even managed to persuade Víctor, asleep now thanks to the bumpy car ride, to finish his damn banana.

My mother welcomed us with open arms again and soon had her grandson eating gluttonously. Infected by her composure, I began to feel calmer. I didn't mention my worries, however. I didn't want her to see me in a fragile state. We went out for another walk while Sebastián stayed at home reading the *Diario de África* and listening to a broadcast on Radio Dersa, the local Francoist shortwave station. We strolled along the usual streets and down to the park.

"How about we drop by La Luneta on the way back and say hello to Candelaria?"

I agreed right away. How could I refuse? We started at the street's southern end, the one opposite to Plaza de España. Inwardly, I was retracing the steps I'd taken on that foolhardy night long ago when—at Candelaria's behest—I'd walked under the stars wearing a haik stuffed with pistols. I'd never said a word about that episode to my mother, but I broke out in goose bumps remembering that night now. The weight of the guns pressed against my skin all the way to the station. The terror that had gripped my stomach when the military patrol stopped me for a moment. The walk back, once day had begun to dawn: me dirty and barefoot, loaded with money but unable to feel even a pinch of satisfaction. The terrifying feeling I'd had when I imagined what might become of the man who'd untied the cache of guns from my body.

Walking unhurriedly, we crossed paths with Moroccans and Spaniards, vendors selling hot buns and cones of toasted chickpeas. We passed the Teatro Nacional, the Monumental Cinema, Café Oriente,

Bar Levante, and Callejón de Intendencia, seeing a variety of establishments I knew, and others that were more recently opened. I felt a stab in my gut as we arrived at the guesthouse where I'd once lived, about halfway up the road. I saw myself there again: thin, fragile, clinging to my little suitcase, terrified of Commissioner Vázquez's authority.

The door was open, so we walked into the cool, gloomy hallway. "Candelaria!" my mother shouted. No one came, but the residents of that long-ago time began to appear in my mind as if the past had suddenly returned. The teacher Don Anselmo with his phlegmy coughing, the fool Paquito and his despotic mother, sweet Jamila with a basket of chard. "Candelaria!" I heard again. Víctor protested. He didn't seem to like the place. I, on the other hand, couldn't resist stepping forward over the floor tiles of that past life.

We found her in the courtyard behind the kitchen, crushing ingredients for gazpacho in a bowl. Sitting on a decrepit bullrush chair, in a threadbare apron and espadrilles, she was alone in that space that had always been so full of life. Her hair was undyed and her face expressionless. Around her were only remnants of the greenery there had once been. The previously bountiful flowerpots were now empty, only a few lifeless geraniums were poking out from food cans. No life remained even in the canary cages.

"Holy Mother of God! What a surprise to see you here!"

There was a mixture of genuine joy and barely concealed discomfort in her voice. She was none too pleased that we were seeing her and her house in such a state of decline. All the same, she bit the bullet and invited us to sit down. She wiped the filthy table with the end of her apron. She gave Víctor a hunk of bread, which he gladly accepted; my mother and I accepted glasses of cool water from a *botijo*.

Then she slumped into her chair, the wood creaking under her weight as she slapped her thighs loudly.

"Well, you can see how things are here. In a bad way, let's not kid ourselves."

We tried without much conviction to lighten her pessimism—we couldn't make ourselves blind to the obvious reality.

"These days visitors all go straight to the new guesthouses in the suburbs, flats with balconies over the street and hot water, and rooms without leaks or dampness. But that's just one part of my situation. At least without them, I don't have to spend all day toiling like a draft horse. My bones aren't up to much running about these days. No, I don't miss having guests. The worst part, the thing that's left me wasting away, is my other business."

Her shady dealings, I assumed she meant. The buying and selling under the counter, the wheeling and dealing, the exchanges. All that must've been in decline as well, judging by the state of the place.

Candelaria picked up her pestle again, fixed her eyes on the broken tomatoes and pieces of cucumber, added a splash of oil, and set to work on them, almost viciously. Without looking up, she added, "It's the Indians. It's all their fault, this mess."

I frowned. The Indians? What Indians was the smuggler talking about and what was their fault? I didn't have to wait long for answers because she reeled them off.

"They had one or two businesses before, but after the war ended, in no time they were running the show. The fountain pens I used to shift, the imitation stockings, the watches and perfumes, all the goods we brought in from Gibraltar hidden in our petticoats to resell . . . they all have it now, nicely arranged and set out for purchase. After all the running up and down we did, me and my friends, for a few measly pesetas, after all the trouble we had dodging the police . . . You remember, Sirita, that Commissioner Don Claudio, how he made my life a misery, the old bastard."

I recalled Commissioner Vázquez with a touch of nostalgia. And I also remembered the Indians' emporiums, though they'd been nothing special at the time. My ex-landlady, meanwhile, continued her energetic wrist work, pounding the vegetables for the gazpacho.

"They even sell radios now, right here, in La Luneta. And nail varnish and those Pond's face creams, and cameras and Lux soaps from the Americans. They sell just about everything, those swine."

"And why are these people here?" my mother wanted to know. Her curiosity was genuine—she didn't know much about geography or the ways of the world.

"There's problems in India, they say, with those pesky British. That's what people who know about these things are saying."

It was my mother, again, who cautiously asked me about it.

"You've lived with those people, dear, you must know a bit about the empire."

Indeed, the matter was discussed on the streets of London and in the press. Fran Nash and Nick Soutter mentioned it in their letters. The great, powerful, majestic British Empire was springing leaks, and word was it would fall sooner rather than later. The pro-independence uprisings in India were constant; the negotiations, arduous. Perhaps that was why some, anticipating turbulent times, had opted to leave. Even so, I still couldn't see the connection between Tétouan and the British Raj.

Candelaria, using an increasingly rough hand to pulverize tomatoes, peppers, and garlic, immediately clarified.

"They arrive in Gibraltar, that's their first destination. Some stay there, and others come here or head to Ceuta, or even to the Canaries, I hear."

Then she thumped the pestle into the bowl with such fury that she cracked the bottom. The liquid mixture ran down her apron and legs, pieces of ceramic fell onto the floor, and she let out a profanity that made my son burst out laughing.

We got up to help her. My mother gave her a hand with the greasy apron, and I crouched to pick up the pieces from the smashed bowl. Víctor, meanwhile, seemed to be enjoying the spontaneous show.

"What're you laughing at, kid?" the smuggler asked, arms akimbo. "Is it because, half a little Englishman as you are, you don't want me to pick on those people?"

As if he understood, from where he was on the floor, he threw a stone at her feet and laughed at her again. The three of us couldn't help but follow suit. The mess was far from a laughing matter, but the boy's reaction at least gave us an excuse to distract Candelaria from her worries.

We waited for her to wash and change, then we went out again and, out of deference, let her push the chair along La Luneta. A few yards on, she stretched out her arm, pointing.

"There, right there's where the emporiums start."

My mother and I hadn't reached this section of the street—between the guesthouse and Plaza de España—during our earlier walk. It was the busiest and most commercial stretch.

"Look at them, my girl, they're one after the other; count them, there must be six or seven. They sell all sorts of things, just look at those beautiful shopwindows. Glassware, porcelain, gentlemen's ties, fine stockings, Swiss watches, those Jantzen swimsuits. And you wouldn't believe the fabrics they have. Silks, brocades, gold thread . . . enough to drive you crazy. There's nothing they don't have, love."

I desperately wanted to go into one of the establishments right then, but I didn't want to rile her up even more. We slept at my mother's that night, and I woke when the muezzin called the faithful to the dawn prayer. Before the Indian shops had drawn up their shutters, I was back on La Luneta.

Candelaria hadn't been wrong—some of the Indian fabrics they showed me were splendid. Among the miscellaneous goods, I found sumptuous cottons from Jaipur, silks delicately made by the legendary weavers of Varanasi, lengths of material worked by the skilled hands of spinners, dyers, and embroiderers, using centuries-old techniques. The owners of the emporiums provided me with all these details, pleasant shopkeepers completely unlike the pitchfork-wielding demons they were in Candelaria's furious mind.

I didn't buy anything, however. I preferred to wait. And that was precisely because of the tip one of them gave me in his unusual Spanish.

"All these fabrics, good. But if you, señorita, want to buy more better, you must go to Gibraltar. To the warehouse of my family on Main Street. From there distribute. There, you find wonders."

72

Félix arrived just before dinner, when the salad was ready and the smell of what would be a plump *tortilla de patata* was spreading to every room. The table, on the veranda, was laid with freshly ironed napery. There was even a candle in the center and a little vase of white roses picked from a flowerbed.

"And how did this miracle happen, my girl? Did you get Hotel Valentina to come and serve you? Or win a guardian angel in the lottery?"

"This miracle has a name. Come in the kitchen, come on."

The howl of astonishment that followed reverberated off the walls. My friend had just found Candelaria with frying pan in hand—it was she who'd turned the domestic situation around. The idea, like almost everything sensible in my life, had come from my mother. "Why don't you take her to Tangier to give you a hand, dear? I'd go with you if I could, to take care of the boy and sort the house out, but with Sebastián, you know . . . Candelaria, on the other hand, you'd be doing her a big favor. You'd keep her busy, which is what she needs. You can pay her whatever you think fair. The poor woman, as you've seen, is penniless. And you'd have someone you can trust."

That same midday, Candelaria came with me, elated. The rickety old women, her only remaining guests, she left to their own devices in La Luneta—after all, they were as much a part of the guesthouse as was the furniture. On the way, she spoke unstoppably about the girdle she intended to buy from Monoprix and the *tocinos de cielo*—heaven's bacon—she was looking forward to sampling at La Española. She had with her a shabby cardboard suitcase; God knows how many times it had bumped and jolted along with her as she'd negotiated bends and potholes over a lifetime. As soon as we reached Tangier, she swung into action. She shouted her appreciation when she saw the new house in which water ran from the taps, there were plenty of lightbulbs, and there was even a refrigerator to keep food fresh. She chose a room at the back and hung up her meager belongings in the wardrobe: drab clothes, even one or two garments I'd sewn for her more than a decade earlier, before we'd opened the studio in Tétouan's modern area, and when my neighbors were still my only customers.

Once she had her bearings, the next step was to assume her role as housekeeper—like the diligent Ira Belline at Sidi Hosni, but on a smaller scale. She gave orders in Arabic to the girls, set their working hours, and gave them specific tasks to do starting the next morning. Though she had only a smattering of English, she even managed to bring sweet Philippa into line, since the girl was always so timid and lacking in impetus. Having given out orders and warnings, Candelaria then tied an apron around her waist, planted herself at the stove, and in twenty minutes' time had made a little stew for Víctor, which he wolfed down. After that, she moved on to the grown-ups' dinner, which was simple and authentic—not even Martínez in London could've made such a juicy tortilla. It was just as she was skillfully flipping it that my old neighbor arrived in the house, which from that point on would be her domain.

I listened to them with pleasure from a distance: the cries, the laughter at being reunited. Candelaria's arrival had certainly taken a weight off my shoulders. It relieved me of responsibilities and ensured there would be order and leadership under the roof that was supposed to be, at least for a while, my home.

"And now, my dears, if you'll excuse us, I must speak to the lady of the house about work matters," Félix announced.

The three of us plus Philippa had finished eating dinner in the garden, the English girl amazed to have been invited to join the group of old friends. My mother-in-law would've been horrified to witness such familiarity with the staff.

Candelaria started clearing the table.

"In a quarter of an hour, I'll leave the kitchen sparkling, and five minutes later I'll be between the sheets and down for the count."

The nanny, with fewer explanations and more discretion, also got out of the way. Félix took some folded pieces of paper from his jacket's inside pocket.

"Well, well, well, my dear. You'll never believe what I've found out about your heiress."

By going here and there, checking publications at the British Consulate and the American Legation, and investigating in God knows what other crevices, my friend had come away with a stack of notes written in the meticulous hand of an accomplished clerk.

"I'll type it all up tomorrow, if you want, but for now I'll just give you the short version, *d'accord?*"

Félix loved inserting French words here and there, little nods to the cosmopolitan existence to which he aspired.

"All right, go."

"Well, let's start with the origins of the family: her grandfather. Frank Winfield Woolworth was his name. And can you guess what the fine fellow did for a living?"

"Make money."

"Before that, I mean. Before he built up his empire."

"No idea."

"He was the son of a humble farmer, and he started work as a store-keeper's apprentice, without even taking a salary. There, he saw that the fabrics and other goods that didn't seem to be very popular ended up on a table, offered at a single price of five cents. Bright as he was, this gave him an idea, and he opened his own business selling just that: low-cost items at a fixed price. Thirty years after that first venture, the modest chain he'd managed to set up at the beginning had become the modern Woolworths stores, of which he owned more than five hundred. And, thanks to them, he had enough money to build what was the tallest building in New York at that time."

We were still in the garden, just the two of us now. My friend had brought a bottle of French wine with him that evening, and we finished it with the music from Parque Brooks playing in the distance, another night of live music and dancing.

"Let's go on to the next generation, then," he said, moving his written notes closer to the candlelight. "After marrying his longtime girlfriend, the gentleman had three daughters, Helena, Edna, and Jessie. Of the three, the one that interests us is the second. I've seen a photo or two, and I wouldn't say she was a stunner exactly. But a fortune like hers always helps to make an ugly girl beautiful, and she ended up marrying a handsome fellow who had a few dollars himself and who, no surprise, wandered right from the start. At the time, the couple lived lavishly with their four-year-old daughter in a sumptuous apartment in the Hotel Plaza. And one night when Daddy was likely out with one of his lovers, and the nannies and governesses were who knows where, the little girl missed her mum and must've been running around the hotel shouting *Mommy, mommy, mommy—*"

"Félix, please," I cut in. "Stop messing around and get to the point."

"*Pardonne-moi, chérie*, it's just it's all so dramatic, I couldn't resist."

"So what happened?"

"Mother had taken a bottle of pills and snuffed it in the bathtub."

"She was dead? The girl found her there?"

"It was sweet little Barbara that found her, yes, the Barbara who'll be wearing your creations before long. She'd lost her mum, her father didn't take a damned bit of notice of her, and because of prudent legal measures, he couldn't touch the fortune that his spouse left behind. It wasn't long before the grandparents gave up the ghost too, leaving a thousand stores still operating and many millions of dollars. Little Miss was left alone and stinking rich, living between boarding school and relatives' homes."

"A hard childhood, I'm sure, despite the money."

"Well, as they say, money softens the blow. Given the choice, I'd have swapped my old bat of a mother for a few million without thinking twice."

"Don't be such a brute. Come on, what happened next?"

He finished off his wine and looked back at his notes.

"At eighteen, she was presented to New York society at a debutante ball that cost sixty thousand dollars. First thing tomorrow I'll go to the moneychangers on Calle de los Siaghin to see what price the dollar's at and convert that number to pesetas. But it must've been an awful lot because they say it was a real scandal. It was 1930, can you imagine, in the middle of the Great Depression after the crash of '29. Everyone was bankrupt, businesses were closing, workers were without jobs and having a rotten time . . . But the fat cats were sparing no expense with their bottles of champagne and fur coats and luxury cars at the Ritz-Carlton, with Maurice Chevalier dressed as Santa Claus handing out lavish Christmas presents to the guests as if they were peanuts. In short, the press tore them to shreds, to the point that they decided to get the girl out of the way by sending her to Europe. And then the big changes came."

"In whom? In her?"

"In her body, to be precise. She went from robust to emaciated. She'd been chubby until then, but she grew thin as a rake. And there was the leap from being plain rich to becoming a supposed princess."

"That's what Ira Belline calls her: *princess* here, *princess* there. What did she do? Don't tell me she bought a title."

"No, silly. What she bought was a husband. Wait, I have the name here somewhere . . ."

A bolero began to play in Parque Brooks. The still night brought its verses to us intact.

"Here, here it is. A certain Alexis Mdivani was the lucky man. She was twenty; he, twenty-eight. His princely lineage is, it seems, dubious. From what I've read, his was a wellborn family that left Georgia for Paris when Russia invaded. Who knows where their noble blood came from? In any case, it's neither here nor there because the marriage lasted only a couple of years. Our Barbara got rid of the young man in an agreement that cost her a few million, but she kept the title. Phony or not, she still uses it."

"So, first marriage kaput. What about the second?"

"Immediately after, she married a Danish count with an unpronounceable name, changed her nationality to his, built a mansion in London, had her son, Lance. Meanwhile, problems were mounting. It appears the new husband was a horrid man who made her life a misery, she still suffered from anorexia and other disorders, and she started hitting the bottle and pills hard, until she ended up in a sanatorium. And taking advantage of the situation, he tried to disqualify her from managing her fortune."

I didn't know what to say. The singer's voice filled my silence.

"Anyway," he went on, "it all ended in another scandalous divorce that was red meat for the press. And of course, he didn't go away with empty hands. Here, I'll read you what the fellow said, let's see, where did I—"

"It doesn't matter, Félix, I'm not interested in that. Come on, let's move on to the next one."

"For that we'll have to hop over to California. She went there in '39 when the war broke out in Europe. And it was there that Cary Grant led her to the altar. What a bomb they let off in the middle of the war! The Hollywood star and the richest woman in the world, both divorced, now suddenly a couple. Apparently they met during an advertising campaign to raise funds and sell bonds for the Allies. In the eyes of the public, they became almost heroes."

"But that didn't work out, either."

"No, they divorced three years later. She, it seems, was still rather unstable upstairs from the previous husband, and his nature wasn't exactly easygoing. But at least he was a classy kind of gent and didn't ask for a single dollar in their divorce agreement. Though she, who still had money coming out of her ears, decided to compensate him anyway."

"Very generous . . ."

"Indeed. In fact, that's one of the repeated descriptions in most everything I read. It seems she's generous to a sometimes almost absurd degree. She gives lavishly, as if wanting to buy affection. The 'poor little rich girl' the press has called her since she was a child."

"To summarize then, Félix . . ."

"To summarize, your future client is, like I just said, excessively freehanded, and also chronically depressed, temperamental, unstable and fickle, something of an alcoholic, addicted to various substances, anorexic, and obsessive about her own physical appearance. Today, a palace in Tangier has taken her fancy, but tomorrow it could be an estate in Seville, a piece of the Great Wall of China, or a Comanche fort. What's clear is that whatever she wants, she gets. So, duckie, you'd better start sharpening your scissors."

73

"Maybe we could start with half a dozen day outfits and, let's say, a couple of evening ones. What do you think?"

My intention had been to go back to Sidi Hosni so that Ira Belline could give me precise instructions before I went to Gibraltar in search of fabrics. And, while I was at it, I could carry on identifying the complexities of the palace and its surroundings, which was what I was really in Tangier to do. But she got in ahead of me, and first thing the next morning a young Moroccan woman arrived with a message from the Russian housekeeper. It asked me to meet her at the Madame Porte tearoom. I went at the arranged time.

Eight creations. This was what she proposed I make all at once. Eight outfits for Barbara Hutton in less than two weeks. I almost burst out laughing and asked her if she was crazy. It would be a colossal undertaking, almost unfeasible. But I held my cup to my mouth and didn't refuse her request. I'd find a way.

We were sitting under a large mirror at a little round table with a vanilla-colored tablecloth. Around us, there were barely any customers. On a summer's afternoon in Tangier, enjoying the beach or a siesta was more appealing than having a chocolate éclair in that famous place on Calle del Estatuto then, before it moved to the more modern Calle Goya. But Ira Belline, like Candelaria, was tireless despite her age. She mentioned some of the tasks she was working on at that moment, from finding Berber rugs according to the dimensions of the rooms, to contending with decorators, blacksmiths, and builders. She didn't ask from where I planned to obtain the fabrics for my work, and neither did I give her any explanations. She had enough on her slight shoulders without me adding my problems to the load.

The instructions she gave me revolved around three cornerstones: quality, charm, and a trust in my judgment. Once all had been agreed upon, she asked for the bill and opened her handbag to pay, but seeing what was inside, she let out a sigh of exasperation.

"Since word spread that the princess is about to settle in Tangier, all kinds of requests and proposals keep arriving at Sidi Hosni—people offering to work or to sell her a plot of land, others begging for a loan, some wanting her to be godmother to a newborn, or to entrust her with a herd of goats. You can't imagine the ridiculous number of requests. *Généralement*, I don't even bother to answer, but I'm afraid there are some matters it wouldn't be wise to overlook. Like this invitation that arrived a few days ago, for example."

With two fingers she took out a cream-colored postcard and left it on the table. I had no choice but to read it. *The International Press Association is honored to invite Mrs. Barbara Hutton or a representative to the Summer Gala to be held at the Emsallah Garden.* Time, ten thirty. Date, that very night.

"I have no desire to go," she admitted, letting her eyelids drop. "But I'm afraid I don't have much choice. I've had clear instructions from Paris to be on good terms with the local press. Apparently the princess worries about these things."

I remembered Félix's explanations from the night before. He'd mentioned that the American press had gone for the jugular because of the outrageous excesses of her debutante ball. Afterward, they had laid bare her marriages and divorces. He had also said that she'd been praised for her generous support of the troops during the war. Yes, Ira Belline might well have been right. The famous socialite, though she threw caution to the wind when she wanted to, was concerned about her image. We weren't talking about the *New York Times* now, of course, or any other newspapers of a similar weight, but just local publications in one small corner of Africa.

"Anyway," she concluded, gathering up the change. "I'll try to muster my strength."

"It might not be too boring," I said. I only intended to console her. My time as a fake reporter had ended before I left London.

She closed her change purse with a click and looked me in the eyes.

"I don't suppose you'd like to come with me, *chérie*? After all, we're both associates of the princess."

I certainly didn't have the slightest interest. But I wasn't quick enough inventing an excuse, and she interpreted those seconds of silence as a half-hearted yes.

"I don't know if you're familiar with the place. It's a beautiful open-air garden, and I'm sure they'll serve a delicious dinner. We can relax for a while, at least."

Emsallah Garden turned out to be another of the recreational establishments that had emerged after the world war. And luckily it was quite near to my house, the consulate, the Spanish Hospital and School, and Plaza del Obispo Betanzos.

It was an elegant gathering, featuring lanterns and hanging bulbs, tables and waiters aplenty, distinguished summer attire, and an orchestra that was playing a melodic piece as we walked through the broad, plant-covered entrance arch. Most of the journalists were men, but they were accompanied that evening by wives, fiancées, or girlfriends. Ira Belline and I weren't the only women present, though we were perhaps the most unusual. She'd dispensed with her day wear and was wearing an evening dress somewhat out of fashion but magnificent. I'd opted for the most striking of my English designs, leaving my back and shoulders uncovered. I hadn't managed to wear it during Eva Perón's tour, too audacious for our demure Spain. Now, on the other hand, it seemed perfect for a Tangier night on the Atlantic shore. No one here knew me, after all, and for the first time in a long while, I naively thought I wouldn't need to lie or pretend.

I was wrong, however. As soon as it became known that we were there on behalf of Barbara Hutton, everyone showed a marked interest in meeting us. In short, in the eyes of those people, I was immediately seen as someone very close to the famous heiress who'd had the crazy idea to buy a house in the kasbah.

Out of habit, perhaps, and although I was supposed to be at leisure that evening, I engaged my brain and registered the names of the organizations to which the people who approached us belonged. I was questioned by the incredibly refined editors of the French-speaking newspaper *La Dépêche marocaine*. The talkative American who headed the *Tangier Gazette* fired a barrage of questions at me while brazenly staring at my cleavage, and the reporters from the *Cosmópolis* weekly asked me whether I could confirm the rumors that the opulent American was planning to hold a party for hundreds of guests who would be arriving from all over the world. I was greeted by the veteran Alberto España, senior among Tangier's reporters, and the Franciscan monks who published the *Mauritania* magazine asked with the utmost respect whether Doña Barbara would be kind enough to take pity on the most disadvantaged on this side of the strait and make a generous donation to their cause. I also spoke to people who broadcast on the airwaves, unaware, until now, that Tangier had so many radio stations.

The accents and tones of all these people's voices varied, but their questions were basically the same: When would the princess arrive, how were the preparations going, how long did she intend to stay, what did she plan to do in Tangier, would she be prepared to grant an interview, was it true she'd managed to buy the place by doubling the offer that Franco himself had made to the previous owner? The interest in the heiress of the Woolworth empire was more considerable than I'd imagined, and it was evidently genuine—perhaps because everyone predicted that her presence could be a powerful magnet that might bring greater prestige, renown, and wealth to a city that was already quite prosperous.

We were still standing for the aperitif—wine, canapés, and croquettes. Without us realizing it, at some point Ira Belline and I ended up in separate groups. A moment later, I was introduced to the management of the *España* newspaper and chatted for a few minutes to its editor, Gregorio Corrochano, and with a pleasant journalist named Jaime Menéndez, whom they called by the nickname El Chato. I didn't admit to any of them that, back in 1938 during the civil war, I had been present as Beigbeder's guest at their newspaper's inauguration. It had been the high commissioner himself who'd injected a hefty sum of official money into the venture so that his friend Corrochano could launch the publication, an effective propagandist weapon to support Franco. Beigbeder was no longer in Morocco, however, and while the editor hadn't changed, the newspaper had evolved toward a more open, internationalist approach that included little censure, a more truthful worldview, and a somewhat broader ideological perspective than before. So much broader, in fact, that its editions were eagerly awaited in mainland Spain.

"If there're no storms on the strait," El Chato informed me with pride, "by about midday they can be found in Cadiz, Seville, and Malaga, and by midafternoon they reach the newsstands in Madrid, where they fly off the shelves."

A photographer from the newspaper approached then to take a picture of the group. Ira Belline was still talking in another huddle, and I was the only woman in mine at that moment. All of the men insisted on me occupying a prime spot, perhaps so there would be proof that someone connected to Barbara Hutton had really been there, or because my dress and appearance would be a welcome change from all the ties. *Wait for it, wait for it, one, two, and three.* The flash went off.

I continued like this for a while with a soft drink in my hand, giving my attention to their requests without committing to anything. At no time did it occur to me to mention my talks on the BBC. Having dispensed with my reporter's disguise, I simply dodged awkward questions, made up lukewarm answers, and acted as if I were there purely to serve as decoration amid those respectable professionals and officials of the protectorates, businessmen and senior employees, Jews and Christians alike, only a few Arabs among them. All I said about myself was no, I didn't live at Sidi Hosni, but in a villa near Parque Brooks. Among the many people who were present that night, however, there was no trace of the frivolous foreigners wearing colorful foulards or yellow jackets like the ones who dined at La Parade and who so fascinated Félix. Just as he'd explained, they must've inhabited a different world.

"Those must be the new fellows from Gibraltar," someone said. "They're just arriving."

Heads turned toward the backs of three men. Something about the one in the middle was vaguely familiar. His gait, perhaps, the back of his head, the shoulders, the neck. But I didn't stop to connect what I was seeing to my memory bank, as the mere mention of Gibraltar had quickly returned me to my more urgent duties.

"Excuse me, gentlemen, perhaps you could help me. What is the easiest way to get to the Rock?"

I'd assumed that the fastest and most logical way would be by boat. After all, it was a short stretch of sea—cross the strait and you're there.

"There are the Bland Line ferries," someone pointed out. "But recently the British established a daily flight. They must have a surplus of planes after the war."

The group's laughter was accompanied by the announcement that it was time to take our places at the tables.

"*Je suis exténuée,*" Ira Belline whispered to me as the guests started to move toward their chairs.

Her exhaustion was more than reason enough for us to go. After excusing ourselves, we headed toward the exit together and, enveloped by the night, we left behind affairs to which we would return in due course.

Though I didn't know it, of those three men's backs, there was one that I knew all too well.

Neither was I aware that inside the *España* newspaper photographer's camera was an image whose existence would have sinister consequences for me.

74

Félix was in the seat beside me. I grabbed his hand and squeezed it hard. A donkey-driven cart was crossing the runway as the little plane, perpendicular to the cart, was about to land. Both the old man in a beret and espadrilles leading the animal and the pilot flying our aircraft were, however, unmoved. This must've been a common occurrence in Gibraltar—pedestrians, animals, cars, and bicycles, smugglers and airplanes, contrabandists and carts all moved in different directions on that sandy isthmus of uncertain sovereignty that separated the mass of the Rock from the rest of the Iberian Peninsula. Each one minding its own business, moving at its own pace. Resident British and Spaniards both coming and going, crossing the border daily for work, or to get their hands on assorted goods they would resell later. Postwar southern Spain was still suffering serious hardship.

There were two reasons why I'd asked Félix to go with me. The first was to give me a hand with the transactions. My intention was to buy fabrics and take them back with me on the return flight that same afternoon. I needed to start work as soon as possible; Mrs. Hutton's outfits couldn't wait any longer. I needed someone I could trust to help me with the buying and the carrying. That explanation was the one I gave him, and he was elated to have been asked. It was the first time he'd been on a plane, the first time in his life he'd set foot outside of Africa. My friend was a Spaniard only by upbringing and passport. Apart from those ties, he was distinctly colonial, detached from the motherland, a *criollo*—an inhabitant of Spanish descent, living in a current or former Spanish colony—on the fringes of his ancestors' lands.

What I didn't mention was the second reason why I wanted him with me. I preferred to keep that to myself and not admit to the pain I anticipated feeling. Marcus and I had driven to Gibraltar from Madrid in order to marry as frugally and as discreetly as possible. With no flowers or church or guests, no rings, even, we'd sealed our plans for a family, for the future. Now he was dead, and I had—as I'd done so many times before—pivoted to adopt yet another vague and false identity.

Fortunately, the contrast between the leaden winter's day when Marcus and I married and the summer morning Félix and I descended in the BOAC plane was so sharp that my sadness was kind to me and called a truce. The last time I'd visited the Rock it had been tightly militarized, closed for business, the population having been evacuated to Northern Ireland, to Jamaica, to Madeira. Now, more than two years after Germany's surrender, although Royal Navy officers were still present in abundance, the civilian residents had returned, repatriated, and the streets were full of everyday life and movement. Union Jacks were blowing in the breeze; the pubs, cafés, and shops were open; deliverymen and ice cream sellers circulated advertisements and posters everywhere.

The taxi left us on Main Street, right outside the establishment whose particulars appeared on the card I'd been given in La Luneta. M. DIALDAS & SONS. DEALERS IN WHOLESALE & RETAIL, with head office in Hyderabad, India, and branches across the world: Hong Kong, Canton, Port Said, Bombay, Sierra Leone, Tenerife, Panama, Casablanca. And Tétouan, from where I'd been sent, of course.

In the large shopwindow hung dozens of tapestries, shawls, rugs, and garments. Félix and I went in. The place smelled of incense. We were led to a storeroom where an attentive Indian shopkeeper with copper-colored skin, jet-black hair, and beautiful white teeth began to show us stock that met my requirements. Sure enough, my eyes were wide with admiration at the beauty and quality of what he put in front of me. Spun viscose, exquisite silk in both bright and muted tones. Fancy threads, bobbins in a wide palette of colors, ribbons, buttons, embroidery, brocades, beading. A paradise for a dressmaker who hadn't sewn for a long time and who, by a twist of fate, had been asked to make a whimsical wardrobe with a Moorish flavor. None of the materials were, in essence, Moroccan—they had come from the other end of the world—but I would find a way to make them seem so.

I took my time. There was a prodigious selection, and I had to choose wisely. The shopkeeper, patient in the face of what he sensed would be a good sale, withdrew to the front of the premises to leave us in peace. Félix, bored, decided to head out onto the street—he didn't want to waste his big day stuck between those four walls. I was left there in that dimly lit room, going in and out with the fabrics to see them in the sunlight, wavering, debating. And it was during one of these times when I went out, when the front part of the bazaar was packed with customers, that I perceived something that gave me another feeling of déjà vu, much like I'd experienced the night before, at Emsallah Garden, with a man's back. Now it might've come from a face, a mannerism, a vague smell, some floating words. Something in the middle of that melee suddenly seemed close, as though it were touching my soul as I walked through darkness.

I ended up leaving a good-sized stack of pounds sterling on the counter while the staff began to wrap my packages with skilled hands. We agreed that they would take them to the airport for me. It was lunchtime, the shop was empty, the customers had gone, and it was just us there, with the radio playing. The announcer mentioned the imminent independence and partitioning of India and Pakistan, Lord Mountbatten and Nehru; that seemed to be the latest news. The staff stopped working for a moment. It was their country of origin that had been mentioned, and the story interested them. At the same time, surrounded by those unusual wares, I felt something tighten inside me. And then, suddenly, I realized. It wasn't the message itself but the voice on the radio that transported me to another time and place. The person speaking with poise about the last gasp of the British Empire was Nick Soutter. It was his voice I was now hearing.

"Station? Which station?" The questions tumbled out of my mouth, and it was a few seconds before the men understood me.

"Aah . . . ," the shopkeeper finally said with his big, peaceable smile. "GB. Gibraltar Radio."

What they weren't sure of was where exactly the broadcast was coming from. That was what we were discussing, the men trying to agree on an answer, when Félix returned with a bottle of Scotch and two cartons of Craven A, his gleaming purchases.

"Are you ever going to finish, angel? I'm famished and I've seen a restaurant called El Sombrero that looks fantastic."

Still without replying, I quickly said goodbye to the friendly Indians.

"You go and eat by yourself," I said once we were outside. "There's something else I need to do."

"At this time of day? There isn't a soul on the street, my girl. These people might be as British as you like, His Majesty's subjects and all that, but they spend the hot part of the day in the shade just like their Spanish neighbors in La Línea."

I managed to shake him off, then I approached one of the local bobbies, identical to the policemen in London.

"Wellington Front, madam," he told me.

The taxi driver didn't know that a radio station had installed itself in the old military fortification, so he stopped and started a few times before leaving me at what seemed to be the entrance. I didn't see anyone as I went in, nor as I walked on, until I found a dark, silent corridor that was in stark contrast to the brilliance of the Bay of Gibraltar. The premises were a far cry from the splendid PBS building in Jerusalem, even more so Broadcasting House or Bush House in London. As I walked on between walls of bare rock, all I found was a sign pointing the way to a studio. Unsure about everything, I followed the arrow.

I saw him through the glass panel, and for a few seconds I couldn't believe my eyes. There he was. His disheveled hair, loose tie, shirtsleeves rolled up to his elbows, revealing his big hands, his tanned wrists, the same old Orator with a leather strap. The sturdy shoulders that had held me so many times in my grief. The same ones, I now realized, that I'd seen from behind the night before at the journalists' dinner in Tangier, when he had arrived and I was leaving. We'd crossed paths without seeing each other.

A few paces away, separated from me by only a pane of glass, was the man who'd been my friend and comfort in Palestine, the large frame I'd accidentally bumped into as I walked into Barclays Bank on my first morning in the Holy Land, the feet onto which I'd thrown up when my pregnancy hadn't yet been confirmed. The professional who'd trusted me despite my inexperience when I had suggested working with his radio station. The husband of the woman who'd tried to sabotage me in London out of a jealousy that had made no sense.

He was sitting at the microphone, but he wasn't speaking; the news program had ended a while ago. He was, however, still concentrating on his papers, engrossed and serious, eyes down. Between his fingers he held the remnants of a cigarette. He was about to take a final puff when I knocked on the glass. He looked up, frowned. He didn't see me at first in the dark corridor. But somehow, little by little, he seemed to slowly recognize my silhouette. Without bothering to look at what he was doing, he squashed the cigarette end in the full ashtray, rough in his movements like he so often was. Then he began to stand. Slowly. Disbelieving.

75

As it turned out, Paseo del Doctor Cenarro wasn't far from my house. I followed the directions given to me on Boulevard de Alejandría by a gap-toothed little boy in shorts, with an Andalusian accent. I set my course by his outstretched finger and headed in search of Maruja Peña.

I was more or less clear about the general style of the garments I was going to make, but my concepts were missing a few details. To help me with this, on the return journey from Gibraltar I gave Félix a new task: to do some homework on traditional Moroccan attire meant for lavish events, much as he had once done in Tétouan, when a demanding German customer requested a tennis outfit, and I didn't know what either the game or the clothing consisted of. Once I'd added Félix's information to my intuitions, I would be able to adapt my creations to my new client's gaunt figure, giving the designs made from Indian fabrics a sophisticated and unique elegance. I should've been reflecting on all of this as I went in search of my workers. But I wasn't. All I could think of was my reunion with Nick Soutter.

In that dark corridor, our first mutual impulse had been to hug each other. Moved to my core, my face buried in his chest and my arms around his back, I'd been unable to stop myself from crying. For the shattered Jerusalem we'd left behind, for Marcus and for my boy, who'd been born without a father. For what Nick had meant to me while I grieved, and for how I'd missed his support since leaving Palestine and his side.

We brought each other up to date, both of us still stunned by the coincidence, amazed at how small a place the world could be. It all had a logical explanation, however. The PBS, Palestine's public radio service into which Nick had poured all his efforts in recent years, had been another victim of the increasingly deadly conflict between Jews, Arabs, and British. It was no longer the solid organization it had once been, and as a result, little room had remained for a professional like him, bound to the colonial mandate that was about to collapse. And so he'd considered other destinations, but the prospects in the rest of the empire had been no less bleak. Nobody doubted any longer that British power was reaching its end.

And so his good sense and his gut had told him to return to the West.

"But I ruled out London," he said, "while the divorce is ongoing."

The possibility had arisen of setting up a civilian radio station in Gibraltar, making use of an old military facility, with links to the BBC, but independent. He'd taken on the role just a few weeks before.

"It's a small project with few resources, just news three times a day. But I'm looking at this as a transitional phase. We'll see what the future brings."

Sitting face-to-face in that bland studio, we continued to talk about me, him, Víctor, his children, and our mutual friend Fran Nash, who refused to leave her flat at the Austrian Hospice in the Old City while she covered the conflict as a sought-after freelance journalist for a grow-ing number of newspapers. He filled me in on the unbearable tension in Palestine, the worsening violence and the increasingly extreme stances, on the American Colony and Bertha Vester, Katy Antonius and other people from my time there. I, in turn, recounted my London adventures and my days spent following Eva Perón around Spain, as well as my unexpected contract with a London insurance company and my new role in Morocco. Unable to contain myself, I also told him about my encounters with his wife. There in front of the microphones—neither of us having had lunch, and with no notion of the speed at which the hours were passing—we continued to talk until I realized I was about to miss the plane that was supposed to take me back across the strait.

"Come on, my car's outside."

We hurried out of the Wellington Front, and he drove fast to the nearby airport. As we approached the terminal, I saw Félix pacing outside, beside one of the Indian shop attendants and stacks of packages, his hair and the coattails of his jacket flapping in the wind. He must've been wondering where on earth I'd gotten to; it was just twenty minutes before our flight was to take off.

There were no more embraces between Nick and me but, just before I opened my door, our hands joined between the seats. It was only a moment, my slender fingers interlocking with his thick ones.

"Would you like it if I came to see you in Tangier?"

The answer got stuck in my throat. He had to settle for a slight nod.

We landed at sundown, and Víctor was already asleep when I arrived home. I was famished, and Candelaria, formidable in her new role, had dinner ready and the table laid on the veranda. Before sitting down, however, I went up to see my son, and in a low voice, whispering almost into his ear, I told him that our friend Nick Soutter was close by again.

It was all of this that I was mulling over as I climbed the slope of Paseo del Doctor Cenarro the next morning in the direction of the Marshan quarter, or the Marchán, as my compatriots pronounced it. As I walked, I passed the offices of the *España* newspaper; however, I didn't yet know they were located there. Neither did I foresee the chain of events that the photograph taken of me at Emsallah Garden would set in motion. I also saw a house that looked vaguely familiar. It was then that I remembered I'd been there with Rosalinda a long time ago, to place an order for some headpieces with a woman known as Mariquita,

a rather unique hatmaker whose shy son Antoñito had sat at her feet
doing calligraphy and watching the customers with round, nearsighted
eyes. We hadn't suspected then that later, as a man, he would end up
telling the story of the city's future decline in a novel.

I walked on. There were a lot of middle-class villas with front gardens on that long avenue, but I was looking for a different kind of
home. After asking another couple of girls, I managed to find the place
where Maruja lived: the Patio Pinto.

Such residential courtyards were common in opulent Tangier, evidence that this was not a time of plenty for everyone. There was this
community, Patio Pinto, plus Patio del Inglés on Calle San Francisco,
Patio Marché, Patio Benchimol, Patio Eugenio . . . their names paying
tribute to the property owners who, in exchange for a few pesetas or
dirhams per month, provided families—large ones, often—with a tiny
living space. Society's unfortunates lived together there in close proximity: Christians, Jews, and Moroccans whom the thriving city had mer-
cilessly forgotten, people who had nothing to do with the flourishing
import-export businesses, the grand banks, and the tax-free dealings.
I entered a flat area of dirt that surrounded a big central palm tree.
Laundry hung from wire, and a few chickens were loose. I asked some
little children where I could find Maruja.

The seamstress accepted my offer, of course. She could barely hide
her relief when I told her what I would pay her.

"But it will be difficult work, Maruja. We have a few hard weeks
ahead of us."

"Right you are, señorita. I'll muster my neighbor Luisa, my niece
Higinia, my sister-in-law Prudencia, my kid's godmother Paca, and my
homegirl Pepa. That's six of us, like you asked for, ready to do what's
needed."

"Each with their own sewing machine," I added.

"I'll get my son-in-law to take them to your house at lunchtime,
and we'll start work this afternoon."

Next, I headed in the direction of Sidi Hosni to confirm to Ira Belline that everything was moving forward. I found the kasbah unchanged from my previous visit, a scene irreconcilable with the palatial mansion it surrounded. I discovered the housekeeper in one of the reception rooms, perched on a ladder alongside a couple of electricians, trying to hang an enormous Moorish lantern from the ceiling. I said hello before taking the opportunity her awkward task presented to slip off into the house—I couldn't forget the other role I held besides couturière. I took out the little notebook I always had with me and the Biro I'd bought in Jerusalem. As it had done so many times that day, my mind returned to Nick Soutter.

Room after room, I noted down all of the ways in and out, the number of windows, balconies, miradors, and doors, where they led, which rooms or courtyards they opened onto, how easy or difficult it would be for an intruder to enter without being seen and make a clean getaway. To my annoyance, I had to stop before too long, when I'd only managed to cover part of the palace. Ira Belline wanted my opinion regarding where to hang a Persian tapestry in the main dining room and was unsure whether it should go on the left or the right wall. I tried to escape again after that, but I barely had time to inspect one more room before she called me back with another question. We continued this game of cat and mouse until midday, when it was time for me to go home.

At three o'clock, we had all the sewing machines in place and the six women were ready to receive orders. At half past three, I sent the Moroccan servants home and Philippa took Víctor to the Parque Brooks pool with instructions to return at around seven. We needed to be without distractions; it was time to start work. I organized two teams: Maruja, Higinia, and Paca; Luisa, Prudencia, and Pepa. To start with, each group would be responsible for making a different kaftan, beginning with the daytime ones. Félix had obtained, among his other finds, a magazine from the French Protectorate that contained photographs of

Moroccan princesses taken at the extremely rare official occasions when they'd been seen. Lalla Abla bint Tahar, second wife of Mohammed V, their eldest daughters, Lalla Aisha and Lalla Malika, and her sister, Lalla Hania bint Tahar. Their garments seemed heavy and overelaborate, but they were a good starting point from which to work.

Candelaria joined us as my assistant. The room was filled with the sounds of treadles operating, scissors clicking, fabric rustling, and voices speaking a vocabulary that I hadn't heard for a long time, and which tied me to that past. I was so absorbed, so focused on my task, that the afternoon flew by.

"We'll get going, señorita," Maruja announced after finishing the last backstitches. "The family will be wanting dinner soon."

It was almost dark outside, and Candelaria turned on the ceiling light.

I looked up, holding my needle in the air. And that instant, something exploded inside of me. A macabre premonition, a stab of terror in my belly.

I leaped to my feet. The silk I'd been working on slid to the floor. I pulled the door open and went out calling to them. I checked the big living room and the small one, the dining room, the kitchen. I flew up the stairs two by two until I reached the bedrooms, then rushed back down shouting their names over and over. I checked Candelaria's room, dashed out to the veranda and the garden, ran across the plot to the rear courtyard.

Nothing. They weren't there.

It was after nine o'clock, almost completely dark.

And Philippa and Víctor hadn't come home.

76

Trying to hide my anxiety, I quickly said goodbye to the seamstresses. It was best that they not notice my anguish. As soon as they'd started heading back to their courtyards and their domestic chores, I bolted toward Parque Brooks, where the nanny and my son were supposed to have gone to spend the afternoon. Candelaria wanted to go with me, but I shouted at her to stay at home and wait, just in case.

They'll be there, I'm sure, I kidded myself. *They must've lost track of time and fallen asleep or been distracted by something. It's fine, I'm going to find them in a minute.* I shot in without so much as a hello to the doorman. The lanterns were lit inside the open-air enclosure, the lawn and the garden were devoid of towels and bodies, and a few tables on the terrace were occupied by early-dining Americans. I slipped past the siren sculpture at the entrance, and a waiter with a bushy mustache and red fez approached graciously. I practically shoved him aside and rushed down to the pool area. The surface gleamed like a sheet of dark steel, the enormous concrete diving board projecting a disquieting shadow. Not a single bather remained, only a pair of young Moroccan men arranging the deck chairs, preparing for the next day. I asked them nervously, "Nanny, boy . . ." In response they simply shrugged.

The children's play area was deserted. There was nobody on the slide, and the swings were still. I went into the changing-room huts, the ladies', the gentlemen's. I screamed their names and slammed doors.

Nothing. I ran breathlessly around the perimeter of the site, parallel to the garden walls decorated with modern murals. I zigzagged through the cafeteria and restaurant, questioning every member of staff I came across. Nothing. I returned home with my heart in my throat. Félix had arrived while I was out. He and Candelaria were waiting for me by the gate, pale faced. Again, nothing.

I asked Candelaria to stay and watch out for them once more, and Félix and I scoured the nearby streets. "Perhaps they've gotten lost," I stammered, knowing that this was impossible—it was no more than a hundred yards door to door, one of the reasons I'd chosen the house. Even so, we both ran to look for them. I combed the route to the Italian Hospital. Félix went as far as Calle Inglaterra. Nothing.

We left Candelaria crossing herself with the repetition of an automaton. She wasn't a deeply religious woman, but she did tend to invoke the Almighty when adversity bared its teeth. We rushed to Plaza del Obispo in search of a taxi. The driver turned out to be a man from Malaga who took on my anguish as his own and drove around the nearby areas with urgency, ignoring the speed limits and highway code. Not finding them, we continued to Plaza de Francia and drove along Boulevard Pasteur with our heads practically out of the windows, trying to spot the two figures among the crowds of pedestrians. Nothing. We carried on the search down Boulevard Anteo, returned in the opposite direction, went up and back down again. Then we were in Calle del Estatuto, the Grand Souk, the edge of the medina. Nothing.

We returned home. I was unable to contain my tears. Félix had the next idea.

"We must go to the Sûreté."

I didn't know what he was talking about.

"The International Police," he explained. "They have a branch nearby, in a passage at the end of Calle América del Sur, near the Afuera Souk. I'll go."

It made me shudder to hear the word "police," but perhaps it was the most sensible thing to do. This wasn't simply a case of them being lost. Something had happened to my son and Philippa. I had no doubt about the nanny's innocence—where would such a reserved and timid soul like her go of her own accord in that strange city? As painful as the mere thought of it was, the situation was clear: someone had taken them.

Once Félix had left for the police station, Candelaria asked me for permission to go to the nearby Church of San Francisco; her fit of religious fervor seemed to have taken a firm hold. I was left alone in the dark of the garden, sitting on one of the stone steps. As it did every night, the music began to play at Parque Brooks, the place from which they should've returned, where they perhaps had never gone in the first place. I closed my eyes and covered my ears with the palms of my hands. The notes and lyrics of the boleros made me retch.

It was half an hour before my friend returned with someone who introduced himself as Sergeant Renard, a quite young, inexpressive, and skinny young man. He spoke mediocre Spanish with a strong French accent.

"He's Belgian," Félix clarified quietly from behind me.

I gave him the facts in detail, and he took notes without altering his expression. He didn't interrupt me once or show the slightest sign of empathy. Then came his questions, one after the other, delivered with the precision of a methodical officer.

"The boy's father?"

"He died."

"Anyone else who is a paternal figure?"

"No."

He spoke in a neutral tone, without enthusiasm, as if asking whether I preferred tea or coffee, a first- or a second-class ticket.

"Are there any personal reasons why someone would want to kidnap your child?"

I felt as if someone had driven a butcher's knife into me.

"No, not that I know of."

He finished questioning me, stood up, and put his notebook in a jacket pocket. He still hadn't uttered a single word of compassion.

"We'll get to work on it first thing in the morning and will keep you informed," he said by way of a goodbye.

I leaped up like a cat that had been kicked.

"What do you mean you'll get to work tomorrow?" I cried. "You're not intending to do anything tonight?"

"We'll try to make some inquiries, but it will be difficult. We're just three men on duty."

I yelled, protested, demanded, ended up grabbing him by the lapels. Candelaria, who in the meantime had returned, and Félix had to separate me from him. The cold officer moved away, wished us a terse *bonne nuit*, and left without closing the door.

"Now what?"

I was sobbing. I tried to calm myself and think with a cool head, but my thoughts led nowhere. Head out into the streets again—that was the only idea that occurred to me. Walk the pavements, the avenues and slopes, the boulevards, the squares, until my feet bled. Go down to the beach, climb up to the citadel, to Monte Viejo, search every nook and cranny, walk until I dropped with exhaustion.

Candelaria cut short my ravings with her instinctive wisdom.

"They are wherever they are, and whoever has them has them. By this time the little boy will be fast asleep, I bet. Going around in circles out there won't achieve anything, my girl. You're not going to find them no matter how much walking you do."

"We shouldn't have gone to the police, Félix, but the consulate," I said, convinced this was true. "The two of them, my boy and Philippa, they're British subjects, I'm sure there they could—"

"I can't see how right now, my queen." He looked at his watch. "It's almost one o'clock. They're not going to answer the phone at this hour."

I gathered my composure and weighed the resources I had at my disposal. It was frustrating that I couldn't think of anyone who could help. My contacts in the intelligence service would be of no use to me in Morocco, nor would my role with the insurance company. I didn't see much progress being made on the basis of my official nationality, let alone my Spanish one—to hide my connections, I hadn't even kept my passport up to date.

I had Ignacio in Madrid, but the Spanish authorities had little to no influence in Tangier. It would've been a different story had this happened when Beigbeder was overseeing the protectorate, but no trace remained of the high commissioner's fleeting glory. *And yet . . .* , I suddenly thought. And yet. Back when I was visiting Madrid, among the top officials of the new regime, I'd believed I had at least one friend: Diego Tovar, director of the Diplomatic Information Office. *Perhaps,* I thought with a glimmer of hope. Perhaps if I called him he could intercede to make something happen urgently among the diplomatic corps in Tangier. Diego Tovar and the Spanish legation. Diego Tovar and the Spanish consul. I swallowed. That was who I'd have to speak to as soon as the sun was up.

"Say, I wonder . . . ," Félix mumbled.

I turned my attention to him in a flash.

"You wonder what?"

"I wonder if the highest authorities could intervene, like they did in the Perdicaris incident."

"Who's that?"

"A man who was involved in something that seems like fiction, but it's real, and it happened right here in Tangier. Raisuli, a sharif from Jebala, sent his men to kidnap the American businessman Perdicaris and his wife's son. President Theodore Roosevelt himself intervened to get them released."

"And the kidnappers let them go?"

"I'm sure they did."

"And when was that?" I asked anxiously.

He took a couple of seconds to answer, his voice subdued.

"At the turn of the century, I think."

The closest thing to my hand was one of the sandals I'd just taken off. I threw it with fury and hit him in the head.

Other than keeping me company, beyond Félix going to the useless police and Candelaria visiting the parish church to plead with the Almighty, I sensed that my old friends would be of little use. I didn't anticipate how wrong that impression would prove to be.

I didn't want to go upstairs—it would make me fall apart even more to see Víctor's empty cot, his folded pajamas, his cuddly rabbit, and the woolly sheep that was missing an ear. The three of us stayed in the living room, silent, dismayed, unable to bear the uncertainty. Candelaria made coffee and rolls with cold cuts and butter. I drank a couple of cups but ate nothing. At around three o'clock, she started to nod off. I insisted she go to bed but she refused. She ended up snoring in the armchair, thighs apart, neck twisted, and mouth half-open. Her eyes, not completely closed, were blank. Félix lasted a little longer, trying hard to orchestrate conversation to keep me distracted. But I didn't want to talk; I didn't want anything. Before four, he too succumbed to sleep, with his head against the back of the sofa and his glasses tilted, one lens on his cheek, the other over his eyebrow.

It was after five when I came out of the ball I'd curled myself up into. My back was hurting. I stole my friend's packet of Craven A and book of matches. Leaving the two of them asleep, I went out into the garden in search of air. The temperature had gone down as it always did in the early hours, and I felt a damp Atlantic freshness in the air. Only the sounds of nature could be heard in that recently built-up area, near the old Bueyes Souk, stretches of countryside, and reedbeds.

My son's absence tore viciously at my soul. Where was he, who'd taken him, why hadn't Philippa protected him? I tried not to punish myself, tried to let the hours pass until I could go to the consulate. I lit a cigarette half-heartedly, breathing in the smoke. I was blowing it out again when I heard some footsteps on the pavement. Slow footsteps that crunched lightly on the gravel, as if someone were placing the soles of their shoes on the ground with great care. Someone was out on the street, out of my view. Close by, on the other side of the garden wall.

I heard another step, and another, and a third. Whoever it was, they were undoubtedly approaching the garden gate.

Within seconds, I could make out a silhouette.

77

"Son of a bitch."

The words left my mouth like viscous phlegm. I threw the cigarette on the ground and rushed toward the gate, asking for my son, cursing the man, demanding that he return my boy to me.

"Shhh. Shout one more time and I'm gone."

His voice was harsh. I lowered mine instantly.

"Where is he, where did you take him, how is he? Has he eaten, has he slept? And Philippa, what've you done with her?"

The questions came out in furious spurts. In front of me was Ramiro, ripping my life apart again. Ramiro Arribas: it was he who'd taken Víctor and the nanny. He knew them all too well. God knows what tricks he'd used this time on the unwary English girl.

I didn't know why he was in Tangier or how he'd found me. I didn't know, and at that moment I didn't care. I was still in the garden, gripping the gate's iron bars. He remained on the street, albeit practically within my reach. I stretched out a hand to try to grab him, wanting to shake an answer out of him. He took an agile step backward and I didn't touch him. Lamps on each side of the gate cast their dim light on us.

"You thought you'd never see me again, didn't you? You thought you'd gotten me out of the way with your dirty trick."

"Give me back my son," I begged. "Give the boy back to me, give him—"

"Shut up!"

I tried hard to calm myself, literally biting my tongue.

"It was very clever what you pulled on me, Sirita. You're learning. The Grand Cross in my toilet bag, your scheming with Dodero . . . I never would've guessed you'd become such a resourceful woman, given how innocent you were when I took you to Tangier the first time. Speaking of which, hasn't the city changed?" His whistle of supposed admiration cut through the early-morning air. "I haven't had time to see much since I arrived at midday, just passing through. But the new hotels on the coast, the beach clubs, the banks on the boulevard, the modern shops . . . So many cars and tourists, some seeking the sun, others cheap gratification for their bodies. And all these newly developed areas . . . I bet this place is full of good business opportunities these days. A much more positive outlook than when you and I were trying to get that license for the Pitman academies . . . remember that?"

He was speaking in a feigned tone of indifference now, as if he were merely a visitor to the city. I didn't dare keep asking after Víctor. I suspected it wouldn't be wise to annoy him.

"It's a shame I can't stay to size up the situation. But, as you know, I have business to take care of in Buenos Aires. In truth, you may have done me a favor by sticking me in your friend's ship. It'll ultimately save me the fare."

A cockerel crowed in the distance, though it was still dark out. The sound reminded him to cut his spiel short.

"Well, let's not waste any more time. Ten thousand dollars. That's what I want if you want them both back. And I need it now, immediately."

He might've asked me for ten million dollars or ten cents, but it was all the same—I was incapable of thinking in terms of sums.

"Tell me where my son is, tell me how—"

"Stop asking me about the fucking boy!"

I bit my lip, driving my teeth into the flesh inside my mouth almost until I bled. He went on, authoritative in his demands.

"I'm not going to tell you anything, I'd rather let you squirm. I repeat, ten thousand dollars. Keep that figure in your head. And I need it now, at the end of the day, as soon as it gets dark. Right here. I'll come to collect the money from this corner."

He gestured to one side with his chin, and I made out the dark form of a car.

"Ten thousand dollars in legal tender, banknotes," he insisted. "Hard cash. Some can be sterling, and I'll also accept some French francs. Moroccan francs and Spanish pesetas, on the other hand—don't even think about it. They can't be exchanged anywhere, and I don't intend to return to these parts."

My mind was incapable of doing the math, but I knew the amount he'd named was beyond my reach.

"I don't think . . . ," I stammered.

I closed my eyes for a second, trying to clear my head. It was then that he took the chance to slip his hand through the bars. Before I could react, he grabbed my neck and squeezed hard.

"You listen to me," he growled as he pulled me toward him like a ragdoll, jamming my face against the space between two iron bars. "I have every reason to do away with you, bitch. To smash your little brat's head in and fuck the little English girl till she breaks."

I couldn't breathe, I needed air. He could've choked me to death if he'd wanted to. But I didn't even move, or defend myself, or do anything to free myself from his hooklike fingers. I simply looked down, away from the demands of his eyes.

"But maybe I shouldn't get my hands dirty."

He suddenly let go, shoving me at the same time. I took a few awkward steps back, stumbling, unbalanced. Then I bent over, my hair falling over my face, and coughed up strings of saliva.

Ignoring me, he continued, unmoved.

"If you let me down, perhaps the best thing to do would be to put them in the car I rented when I arrived and head out of town, anywhere. I'm sure I'd find a turn somewhere that would lead to some wasteland. I could simply leave the daft nanny and the tender infant there in the parched wilderness with no trace of life nearby. No food, no water, not even a miserable bit of shade in which to take shelter from the sun. The two of them all alone in the hands of God, waiting for nothing." He paused, as if doing a mathematical calculation. "How long do you think they'd last, Sira? Two, three days? Who do you think would drop first, the nanny or your little prince?"

I managed to straighten myself. My eyes were stinging and I still felt the pressure on my throat. He gave a cynical smile.

"I'm sorry if I've upset you, treasure. I got a little agitated. Let's finish up here. It'll be light soon and I want to get out of here."

I nodded. We'd better come to an agreement, yes. Before Candelaria or Félix woke up, before there was movement on the street. Just the two of us, without anyone else involved.

I coughed for the last time and wiped the saliva, tears, and snot from my face with my bare forearm.

"I'm not resentful, Sira. I took you for a ride back then when I ditched you. And you paid me back, selling me out to the authorities. Tit for tat, we're square. But you refused to give me a hand when I begged for help with Dodero, and that blocked my path to a good deal and made me lose a very large amount of money. And now, you're going to compensate me for that cash that I didn't earn and that I urgently need."

Some dogs barked in the distance. There was the sound of an engine and the rattle of a van, perhaps delivering early-morning milk and eggs. It would be light soon, and life was beginning to stir.

"It wasn't so hard getting off the *Hornero*, you know," he said, picking up the pace. "Once Evita had left Spain, the Argentine sailors stopped caring about me. And so, as luck would have it, in the end the ship left without me."

"And you went in search of me, I suppose," I said, my voice little more than a croak.

"Of course. On the first Barcelona-to-Madrid express, wasting no time. But being the clever, farsighted girl that you are, you'd already taken precautions, and there was no trace of you or your family in Hermosilla. Luckily your father has a rather useless porter, and thanks to his stupidity, I managed to have a nose around the big flat. It was so easy to get in that I went back and stayed there a few nights. It was helpful to not have to pay for a hotel, and it gave me time to conduct some deals. If Gonzalo Alvarado wants to get back some of his oil paintings—say, if they're family heirlooms or he's fond of them—tell him I sold them at the flea market. The watches, pens, and a few pairs of cuff links, I'll keep as a souvenir. There wasn't much else—surprising, considering how impressive the flat is."

I didn't bother to ask how he'd found me. He offered up the information willingly.

"Since you weren't returning to Madrid, I admit I decided to throw in the towel and head back to Argentina. You almost earned another victory. A travel agency on Gran Vía told me there was an Ybarra company ship that would put in at Cadiz on its way to Buenos Aires, so I headed there by train to wait for it. But its departure was delayed, and I had to stay in Cadiz for a few days, in a filthy guesthouse near the port. I was sick of it all, sick of Spain, and stewing in my anger toward you, when on the fourth day after I arrived, while I was having a coffee to pass the time, bored and leafing through a newspaper, I found this."

He took something from the inside pocket of his jacket, unfolded a newspaper page, and held it out to me. Had it not been such a sinister situation, I would've burst out laughing.

The photograph took up half a page. Eight men, and me in the middle—one of the images that accompanied the report on the

International Press Association's dinner. My light-colored dress with its narrow waist, my cleavage and bare shoulders, were in stark contrast to the formal males on either side of me. At the foot of the picture was an eloquent caption.

> The editors of the *España* newspaper with Mrs. Arish Bonnard—collaborator of Mrs. Barbara Hutton—who recently took up a summer residence in a villa near Parque Brooks to prepare for the American millionairess's arrival in the international zone.

What was supposed to have been a merely informative tag couldn't possibly have given more clues as to my whereabouts.

Stacks of the *España* crossed the strait from Tangier every day, El Chato had explained to me in detail. Once on the Iberian Peninsula, they were devoured by readers, even when, after choppy crossings, copies arrived wet. That, in essence, was how I'd ended up in front of Ramiro in a Cadiz café.

What had started out as an innocent bit of descriptive text had come back to haunt me, with cruel fury.

78

Candelaria burned the toast on the stove.

"That son of a bitch has made my blood boil. Even my hands are trembling!"

It was starting to get light, and she'd woken up when she heard me come in from the garden. And when she began asking questions at the top of her voice, Félix, still sprawled on the sofa, had woken up, too. In a few words, I told them about Ramiro's visit. When I'd finished, so that I wouldn't collapse again, Candelaria set about making breakfast.

"Do you think he's capable of doing something to them?" murmured Félix as soon as our friend was back at the stove.

My voice was hoarse. I could still feel his hand on my throat.

"I don't know, Félix. He's desperate for money, he must be up to his neck in debt. And he's also full of bitterness and resentment."

I took barely two bites of the toast with oil and sugar. Unable to eat any more, I rubbed my eyes and announced, "I have to get moving."

Neither the British nor the Spanish consulate. Neither Ignacio nor Diego Tovar nor the apathetic Belgian policeman. I wasn't going to turn to any of them for help. I would deal only with Ramiro. This matter was between me and him—a one-sided contest, given that I was prepared to surrender from the start. When he'd come to Spain, I'd gained the advantage, but now, I would lose without even putting up a fight. I would give in to his demands. I'd look for the money under stones, if I must—anything to get my son and his nanny back. It didn't have to be the whole ten thousand dollars. I knew Ramiro well and, in his eagerness and ambition, he always aimed high. I sensed he would be content with an approximate amount. The problem was how to obtain it.

"Candelaria, how was the workshop left last night?"

She held her hands to her head, cursing her forgetfulness. Broom in hand, she set off to sweep up the loose thread, trimmings, and fabric remnants left on the floor. I followed her, picking up my notebook full of jottings and measurements. It wouldn't be notes about sleeve lengths and back widths that I would write down now, but figures of another kind.

"When Maruja and her women arrive," I warned, "don't say a word. See to them. Tell them to carry on following yesterday's instructions. Get them working as if nothing's happened."

I finally ventured upstairs, crept into the bedroom, and ran my fingers over the cot's rail. Tears returned to my eyes, sharp and painful. Even so, I was no longer up against the unknown but rather an opponent with a name and a face, and that fact had lifted a little of the weight from my shoulders.

Sitting at the foot of the bed, I started doing some quick calculations, one after the other. I had Marcus's and my money that I'd brought from Jerusalem, the sums that Dominic had paid into my account from the will, and what I'd been paid for my work as a supposed BBC reporter following Eva Perón's tour. The problem was that it was all in England. Plus, the insurance company had only paid me an advance, and I wouldn't receive the bulk of my money until I finished the job. There was also Ira Belline and what she would pay me for my creations for Barbara Hutton. Again, it wasn't yet in my hands.

I turned to a new page and wrote a single word: *loans.* The first person I thought of was my father, but I immediately recalled that, following his foundry's closure and the war, he had few assets beyond his flat. Even Ramiro had noticed how little there remained of value in it. That was, in any case, a property his legitimate children would inherit, and in principle, I wasn't entitled to even a part of it. My next thought was his beloved Olivia, my mother-in-law. I'd written to them both at the house on the Boltons when I arrived in Tangier but still hadn't received a reply.

Remembering the London mansion, something stirred inside me. Perhaps that was where my salvation lay. Legally, as Marcus had stipulated and as his friend Dominic had confirmed was the case, the house was ours: mine and Víctor's. I would never throw my mother-in-law out, but she herself had once had the idea to sell it. Perhaps now I could use it as a guarantee for a loan.

With my head full of numbers, I took a shower. Wrapped in a towel, I untangled my hair in front of the mirror. In my reflection I saw a dejected face, dark rings under my eyes, and some ugly marks from a man's fingers around my neck. I gathered my hair in a bun, dressed plainly in a gray dress, and tied a silk scarf around my throat to hide the sinister evidence.

As I went downstairs I heard sewing machines. My new employees were there already, reliable, early. Candelaria was clanging around in the kitchen; Félix was waiting for me in the living room. He'd half-tidied his hair, redone his tie, and tucked his crumpled shirt back into his trousers. Despite his best efforts, it was obvious he'd had a bad night.

"I need a list of the banks in Tangier."

"What for, angel?"

Instead of giving the explanation he wanted, I persisted with my request.

"Start with the biggest ones."

"Hmmm . . . there's the State Bank of Morocco in its big house at the Chico Souk. There's the Banco de España, Bilbao . . ."

I remembered Ramiro's instructions: no pesetas.

"Not the Moroccan or Spanish banks. What are the British ones?"

"Well, there's the Bank of British West Africa, and one or two others."

"Is there a Barclays Bank branch?"

"Not that I know of. But I think I remember seeing one in Gibraltar the other day."

In Gibraltar the other day, he'd said. And memories of the Rock flooded back. With all the rushing about, it felt as if our visit there had happened weeks, months, years, centuries ago. I thought of Nick Soutter again. I'd have given another ten thousand dollars to have him close to me right then.

Oblivious to my thoughts, Félix continued with his list.

"And there are the French ones, the Banque de France and the Banque de l'Algérie et de la Tunisie, and at least two or three more—you know what posers the frogs are. And there's also the Jewish banks. There are two large, serious institutions, the Banca Salvador Hassan and the Banca Pariente, which has just moved into some classy premises on Calle del Estatuto."

I was barely listening, still immersed in my thoughts.

"Apart from that, since the end of the war, a multitude of other banking firms have opened, but I'm not sure how trustworthy they are. There're a lot of smart people out there who have very little shame. There are posters everywhere, just look on the boulevard and the streets around there. The Tangero-Suisse, the South Continental Bank . . ."

"Félix . . . ," I said while I opened my handbag and rummaged inside.

"They must see Tangier as an easy mark, and smart alecks have come here from all over the world. No one checks the transactions, there's no taxes or laws, no regulatory bodies—"

"Félix," I repeated. "Can you do me a favor?"

He stopped his blathering. In his eagerness to be useful, he'd gone a bit overboard.

"Sorry, not one," I corrected myself. "Two. Two favors."

"I'm all yours, my queen."

"First, before you do anything else, go to the police and tell them they've shown up, that it was all a misunderstanding, whatever comes to mind. Just get them out of the way."

His face was a picture of astonishment, but I didn't give him the chance to question my reasons. Before he could react I handed him Nick's card, the one he'd given me at the radio studio.

"And straight after that, go somewhere with a telephone, call this Gibraltar number, and ask for this name."

He pushed his thick glasses to the top of his nose and held the card a few inches from his eyes.

"Nicholas Soutter," he slowly enunciated.

"Speak to him in French if that's easier. Tell him you're calling on my behalf. Tell him to please come to Tangier, urgently. That . . . that it's"—the six letters of his name were stuck in my throat—"it's Víctor."

I slammed the door on my way out, heading into the unknown. It was a splendid morning in Tangier, with a clear sky and a light west wind. All my efforts, however, made it feel to me as bleak and dismal as a dreadful winter's night. In the first, the second, and the third bank I visited, I achieved absolutely nothing. Arranging for my money to come from London would be a lengthy process, they informed me. If I wanted a loan, I needed guarantors, assets, or income. My claim that I owned a mansion in the Royal Borough of Kensington and Chelsea must've sounded like a tall story, and my mentioning the sum of ten thousand dollars in cash made more than one of them smile condescendingly.

I was sure Félix was right, and that Tangier was a paradise for individuals who were moving money—a free market with no restrictions, where it was possible to speculate with currency, to traffic gold, and to open and close businesses with nothing more than a scribble. Checks from anywhere in the world could be cashed, money from contraband could be laundered, and financial transactions could take place without scrutiny. But nobody seemed prepared to give a penny to a woman like me, alone, unknown, with a desperate look on her face.

Frustrated by the refusals from the British banks, I decided my next option was to try one of the Jewish banks that Félix had mentioned, the one owned by the Pariente family. I didn't spend a second remembering the attack on the King David as I put the soles of my sandals on the marble floor of the splendid premises into which they had just recently moved. Without wasting time, I attempted to explain myself to one of the employees on the other side of the mahogany desk. I asked to speak to the manager, the deputy manager, someone who was in charge. But it was summer, it was early, and again, no one seemed to feel any urgency in that city where "live and let live" was the norm. Disappointed once more, I headed to the exit, containing my urge to beg, scream, curse the world. I was about to leave the building when an unexpected presence pushed the door open from outside.

"There you are, my queen. Finally! We've been looking for you for an hour!"

The volume of my voice when I saw Félix made heads turn.

"What's happened? Has Ramiro been back? Did he bring Víctor? Any news?"

"Nothing new, relax. But someone who might be able to give us a hand has arrived."

I must've been in a daze. The sleepless night and devastating morning were taking their toll. Félix pulled me and then pushed me from behind to make me walk.

"Come on, let's go. He's waiting for you outside."

His hat was casting a shadow over his face, but even so, I recognized him as soon as he raised a couple of fingers to the brim. Waiting for me to come out of the Pariente Bank was Commissioner Vázquez, the man who had once trusted me when he had no reason to do so, the one who'd watched over me, who had kept me on a tight leash with one hand while allowing me to fly with the other.

He'd just come from Tétouan at Candelaria's request. The first thing he did after greeting me was send Félix home.

"Someone needs to be there, watching for anything unusual. Please keep an eye on the perimeter of the property, go out onto the street at regular intervals, and take note of anything that seems out of the ordinary."

As soon as my friend had left to follow his orders, Don Claudio came clean.

"Candelaria could've done those things, in all honesty. But I wanted us to be alone."

He offered me an arm, and we started crossing to the other side of the road.

"Let's go to El Minzah over there. You look like you urgently need a coffee, señorita."

79

"Not one cent."

I almost choked on the omelet the commissioner, concerned by my haggard face, had insisted on ordering for me.

We were sitting in the hotel's central courtyard, the only customers remaining as the waiters cleared the last breakfast tables. The guests had returned to their rooms, and before long they'd head out to the beach again, or to buy souvenirs and rugs, or to go on excursions. It was a time for rest and relaxation, in other words, for the patrons of the distinguished El Minzah. Meanwhile, I was being eaten up from the inside by anxiety.

"Forget about trying to find the money. We'll have to fix this another way."

"I won't get the police involved," I insisted. "I already told you. I know this wretch. I know it's better if—"

"All right, we'll forget about the International Police if you prefer."

"You must keep out of the way as well, Commissioner. You mustn't interfere. Advise me, guide me, but let—"

"There's no need for me to get out of the way, Sira. I'm not officially active anymore. A couple of months ago, I moved into the reserves."

He must've been over sixty, but he didn't seem to have aged at all. He was somewhat grayer, his eyes a little narrower, his body a bit slighter, perhaps, but the calm elegance he conveyed in that light-colored linen suit of his was unchanged.

Candelaria had called him the night before—she'd lied when she said she was going to the church. She had in fact taken matters into her own hands and gone in search of a telephone to try to locate her former adversary, the veteran servant of public order who'd put a stop to so many of her shady deals and plagued her with his steely diligence. After several attempts, she'd managed to find Don Claudio in Tétouan, and she'd told him about my situation. He'd had no idea I was back in Morocco. To her surprise, he had offered to come to Tangier. And now, here we both were, face-to-face.

"I don't think tackling a matter like this by ourselves is the best idea, but we can do it privately if you insist."

"You don't know how grateful I am."

More than a decade had passed since he came to arrest me at the La Valenciana station, when I was still miscarrying my pregnancy by Ramiro. It was he himself, Claudio Vázquez, who had taken me to the hospital in his own car, and who'd then brought me out of there once I'd managed to recover, who'd put me under Candelaria's protection at the guesthouse on La Luneta, and who'd watched over all my subsequent movements with shrewd eyes.

"Without wishing to pry into your private life, there're certain things I need to know," he then said. "First off, who is the boy's father?"

"Do you remember that supposed English journalist who arrived in Tétouan to interview Beigbeder?"

"Logan was his name, wasn't it?"

He was aware of Marcus's stay in Morocco. What he didn't know was that our paths had crossed again.

"His real name was Mark Bonnard and, as I imagine you suspected at the time, he wasn't a reporter but a British intelligence service officer."

I speared the last piece of omelet. It'd gone cold, but it was doing me good, breathing a little life into me. Before holding the fork to my mouth, I added, "After some toing and froing that I don't need to go into now, we ended up getting married. He's my son's father. He died a year ago in Jerusalem, the same day the boy was born."

I suspected he had a lot of questions, but he contained his curiosity and let them go. Concentrating, he took a sip from his cup and, with an eloquent gesture, waved off a waiter who was about to take my plate.

"All right. Let's focus on the present, then, and recap, so everything's clear. Let's see, the individual we're dealing with now is the same man who, when I met you, had just abandoned you, taking all your assets and leaving you with a bill at the Hotel Continental. Correct?"

"Correct."

"And just a month ago you came across each other by chance in Madrid, and he asked you to intercede on his behalf with an Argentine acquaintance on a matter of business. Correct?"

"Correct."

"And you refused, and he started accosting your son's nanny. Correct?"

"Correct."

"And you, afraid things could get out of control, took the law into your own hands and managed to get him arrested for a crime that, in reality, he hadn't committed."

I hesitated. Put that way, I sounded like the cruel and vindictive one, and Ramiro like a poor devil who'd had someone else's misdeed pinned on him.

"More or less, but—"

He held up his hand to stop me.

"You don't need to explain yourself. I can imagine the pressure he must've put you under to make you do what you did."

Grateful for his understanding, I tried to smile with relief. The feeling, however, lasted barely a few seconds.

"Just as I understand the grudge this man must have against you."

The courtyard was now completely empty, with all the tables cleared except ours. The first bathers were beginning to cross it on the way to the pool.

"I imagine there are a thousand more details that you'll tell me some other time, but right now, let's review what happened last night."

I repeated the story that I'd first summarized for him while we walked to El Minzah. This time, I recounted it with less haste and more cohesion.

"And you say he grabbed your throat?"

I lowered my silk scarf to my collarbone so he could see the marks. They probably seemed trivial compared to the stabbings and beatings he must have seen during his long career. Still, from his grimace, I could see that he didn't take the matter lightly.

"Tell me, what do you know about his situation in Tangier?"

"Only that he hadn't been back here in all this time. Since . . . since . . ."

"Since he abandoned you without a penny, leaving you to deal with the consequences of his chicanery and his debts, I understand. Let's suppose then that he doesn't have any contacts or friends here, let alone accomplices."

That was what I believed to be the case, yes.

"And he's in a hurry," I added. "He told me he arrived at midday. From Algeciras, presumably. He's doing everything in a rush, on the fly."

"He told you himself he'd rented a car, didn't he? Did you see it? Color, make, model?"

I shrugged. "I couldn't say. It was on the corner some distance away, and it was dark."

We fell silent for a moment, each of us worrying about a different side of the same coin. He, about the modus operandi of an unscrupulous man acting on pure instinct. I, about the whereabouts and well-being of my son and Philippa.

"And his physical appearance this morning, what can you tell me about it? Was there anything that caught your attention?"

I shook my head. There was nothing I could say about that, either. Even at that time, even after crossing from one continent to another to abduct two innocents by force, Ramiro was dressed correctly, his hair in place, the same bearing and elegance as ever.

"Although . . ."

"Yes?"

"Let me think. There was something. Something fleeting that caught my attention . . ."

I closed my eyes, trying to concentrate. There had been something. When he'd grabbed me by the neck, when he'd wanted me to look at him, I had lowered my eyes, instinctively refusing to play along. There was something I'd noticed then, while I was choking, that seemed out of place. What was it, for God's sake, what was it . . . ?

I clenched my fists in an unconscious action, as if digging my nails into my palms would help me think clearly, until a lucid image formed in my mind.

"Mud," I said. "He had mud on his shoes."

The commissioner frowned, trying to understand.

"He had dirty shoes. He usually keeps them gleaming."

80

We remained at El Minzah until the tables in the courtyard began to fill with the first relaxed tourists, arriving to cool off with beers, colorful cocktails, and modern Coca-Colas in ice-filled glasses. We then decided to head back to headquarters: my house. And we didn't go empty handed, but with a stack of newspapers.

It had been my idea to ask for them.

"Just a second," I'd said to the commissioner, squeezing his arm.

The doorman had already been holding the door open. In his red tarboosh, gold waistcoat, and velvet breeches, he was obligingly holding the bronze bar to let us out onto Calle del Estatuto. But I'd seen something that lit a spark in me: a customer engrossed in a copy of the *España*, the newspaper that had innocently revealed to Ramiro where I was.

"Make use of your former authority, won't you?" I'd whispered almost in the commissioner's ear.

He had raised an eyebrow.

"Ask at the desk for copies of the last few days' newspapers. All the information that rat has about me and Tangier as it is now will be in there. Maybe it's worth taking a look."

We found everything in order on our return, not counting a lack of fresh news and the obvious absences. The seamstresses, having finished their morning's work, had gone back to their courtyards for lunch, to serve their families the stews they'd made at sunrise. Candelaria, well prepared as ever, was making something for us. But nobody seemed to be hungry. Félix, the commissioner, and I opted to sit in the living room, forming a triangle. Candelaria, with one eye on the stove and another on us, stood in the door's threshold, ready to come and go. Although, tending to lunch might've just been an excuse, and she may have preferred not to sit down because the presence of Don Claudio still filled her with feelings of both respect and distrust.

"All right, señorita, we're going to try to think clearly, without getting carried away by our emotions."

Perhaps because I was feeling particularly sensitive, I was touched by the fact that he still called me "señorita." With his impeccable manners, it was how the commissioner had addressed me back when I was a frightened and penniless young woman, and I was still a señorita to him a decade later, despite my now being a mother and a widow, despite my past woes and present misfortune.

"It was a good idea to bring these newspapers. If this Arribas disembarked yesterday in Tangier and headed straight here, the one reliable source of local information that's been available to him is, as you rightly supposed, the press."

"Straight here to kidnap, that's why the son of a bitch came, may he burn in hell . . . ," Candelaria brooded, tea towel in hand.

The commissioner contradicted her.

"Not necessarily, Candelaria. I'm inclined to think he arrived without a fixed idea of what he would do, but rather to see what options were open to him. And he suddenly found himself with easy pickings—the nanny and the boy, alone in the street."

"It was . . . I . . ." My voice faltered. "They never go out at that time, they're usually at home for a nap. But yesterday . . . yesterday . . . the workshop . . . there was a lot of work to do . . . I shouldn't have—"

He raised a hand, stopping me.

"Please, don't blame yourself. It will only hurt you. Had things not happened as they did, he would've found another way to coerce you. This way was just especially easy. Having already accosted them in Madrid, he simply used the same strategy again. Don't punish yourself for what happened yesterday. Our aim now is to try to find out where he's keeping them."

I opened the newspaper from the previous day and started to turn the pages. The Indonesian issue, the tensions in Palestine, the violent Greek guerrilla attacks in Thrace. An alarming slump in the London Stock Exchange, the search for a Gestapo torturer in France.

Don Claudio went on, taking charge as he had so many times before.

"Let's focus on accommodations, then. That's the first thing he needed to spend the night in Tangier."

The advertisements for hotels were scattered among articles about international current affairs, columns, sports news, and information about Morocco.

"Ramiro's not stupid," I warned. "I don't think he would consider taking them anywhere well known, where everyone would see them."

"He certainly wouldn't have gone back to the Continental," he agreed. "It would've been too imprudent."

"There's an ad for the Rif here, the new one at the beach."

"No, no, no . . . ," he said sharply. "Let's see, we don't need to read the advertisements one by one. We need a method. You said his shoes were muddy, didn't you? Let's start by ruling out any hotels that are in the more urban locations, on public roads where he'd be less likely to get them dirty."

"Villa de France, El Minzah, the Rif, the Cecil, and Hotel Valentina are all out, in that case," Félix chipped in. "In any case, they're too classy, too visible."

"Exactly," confirmed the commissioner. "Go on."

My friend's instinct for observation enabled him to continue confidently.

"The ones at the Chico Souk are no good, either. Neither the Bristol nor the Fuentes, nor any of the others. And anyway, that would be like going into a mousehole—you can't even get a car in there."

I kept flicking through the newspaper. Not the city hotels, not the beach ones, not the ones in the medina—those three locations were ruled out, and we were running out of options. Perhaps we were wrong and the mud wouldn't lead us anywhere, but we were desperate. There was no time to waste.

And then my eyes stopped on a small advertisement in the corner of an even page. A cheap ad, judging by its size and position, which didn't portend a great deal of luxury.

"Félix, have you heard of El Fahrar?"

"Of course, my queen. On Monte Viejo. But it's not a hotel. It's more a place where one stays for a longer period. It's quite far out and—"

The commissioner's brusque voice cut him off.

"Have you ever been there?"

My friend took a couple of seconds to respond, a short pause in which I sensed he was hiding something he felt guilty about.

"Only once, months ago. When . . . when that American writer moved in there." He lowered his voice a little. "Bowles, the one who plays the piano. He was with a group the other night at La Parade, do you remember? I drove past the place after he moved in."

Everyone is perfectly free to have their weaknesses, and Félix's particular vulnerability was for somewhat extravagant foreigners—even if he limited himself to admiring them from a distance. This time, however, it seemed his fetish might prove useful to us.

"Peace and quiet," I read, returning to the advertisement. "Views of the strait and the two seas. Inexpensive. Long and short stays."

"They have bungalows of a sort, spread around the garden and—"

Don Claudio's incisive voice was sharp again.

"What kind of garden?"

"Big, green. With mimosas, eucalyptuses, and—"

"And is there anywhere with . . . with . . . you know . . . plants that need water, where there might be mud?"

"*Bien sûr.* The owners are English. You know how extravagant they are with their flowers. They have a marvelous rose garden."

If I'd had it my way, I would've headed there immediately. The commissioner, as shrewd as ever, was one step ahead of me.

"Don't rush into anything, señorita," he said seriously. "For starters, it's a possibility, not a certainty. And in any case, we must tread very carefully, bide our time, and act with cool heads. Let me think about the best way to proceed. And to that end, if you'll excuse me . . ."

He stood, snatched up his hat.

"You're not going to stay for lunch, my señor?" Candelaria's shocked voice reached us again from halfway between us and the pots and pans. "Hey, I've made a divine squid stew."

The one time she'd had a chance to ingratiate herself to the man who'd given her so much trouble, the plan had fallen flat.

"No, I won't stay. I'm going to find a friend, an old colleague." Then he faced me, so that I'd listen carefully to what he was going to say.

"The man I hope to see was also a policeman, and like me, he's not in active service anymore. But I need to speak to him before doing anything, to plan the next steps. This is a delicate business. I want to ask him about a few things, perhaps have him help, even."

I nodded like a diligent student who's just understood a complicated lesson. He turned to leave, and I started to get up to go with him.

"Don't move, it's not necessary."

I obeyed, wringing my hands.

"Eat something," he suggested. "Take it easy. Try to sleep for a while."

A bitter burst of laughter rose from deep in my belly.

"How do you expect me to sleep, Commissioner? Good heavens . . ."

"Relax, at least. Everything will be all right, trust me. But first let me consider the best way to proceed, the way to achieve optimum results with minimum risk. And be patient because, whatever I decide with my colleague, we won't do anything until nighttime."

Before putting his hat on, he gave Candelaria and me another emphatic look, like the one he'd given us long ago, back when he left me at the guesthouse on La Luneta. "I don't trust either of you one bit, so I'm going to watch you closely," he'd said that morning in August of 1936, shortly after the civil war had broken out.

The warning was different now, but the delivery was the same.

"Be careful, ladies. For your own sake, keep your wits about you."

81

"Keep your wits about you." I was determined not to let Don Claudio down, and I repeated the sentence to myself six or seven times. "Keep your wits about you, keep your wits about you, keep your wits about you . . ."

I sent Félix home to wash, change, and recover his energy for the coming hours. Then I dropped by the improvised workshop and saw that the dressmakers had come back to work at siesta time. Fortunately, the tasks I'd given them the day we started were laborious, so they were still busy with the first of Barbara Hutton's kaftans and didn't need any more instructions. I did ask Candelaria to stay with them, so that if there was a problem she could take messages back and forth between them and me. And, to a lesser extent, so that I could be alone, out of the way and without distractions.

I took some sewing from the room in the vain hope that it would keep me distracted. But I left the fabric, scissors, and reel on a side table and forgot about them. It was best, I decided, to listen to the commissioner. I closed the living room shutters, leaving only enough space for the light to filter in through the cracks. I took off my shoes and sprawled on the sofa, as stiff as a post, with my hands on my chest and my jaw clenched, as motionless as if I were made of wood, of stone, of bone. *Relax.* That was what the commissioner had told me to do. To stop thinking about my boy: how he was, what state he was in. How the lowlife Ramiro was treating him, and how he was coping with my absence. "Keep your wits about you," I whispered again through clenched teeth, my eyes closed. "Keep your wits about you."

I must've been so exhausted, so physically and mentally depleted, that for a moment my brain detached itself from reality and filled with blurry images—until something snatched me from my daydreaming. The sound of an engine, close by. A car's engine, that was it. Out on the street. A car had just stopped at the gate.

I jumped up as if my life depended on the car's arrival and ran to the garden barefoot, my hair disheveled and my skirt ridden up. Could it be Ramiro? Had he regretted his actions and brought Víctor and Philippa home? I ran down the steps from the veranda, dashed across the garden to the gate through which I'd spoken to him in the early hours, and yanked it open.

A man was getting out of a taxi. He had a leather bag in his hand, a cigarette between his teeth, and a crumpled pinstriped jacket. It wasn't Ramiro, but instead someone I now held on to with all my might. "Don't let the taxi leave" was the only coherent thing I managed to say. In English, of course—Nick Soutter wouldn't have understood me had I used my own language.

He wanted to know what was happening and asked me several times with urgency.

"Wait a second" was my only answer.

I ran back in and collected my shoes from near the sofa to put on in the car. In the rush, I bumped into the side table on which I'd left my sewing. Silk, thread, and scissors fell to the floor. Operating on reflex, I picked everything up and put it all back, except for the scissors, which, for no particular reason, I dropped into my pocket.

"To Monte Viejo," I ordered the taxi driver a moment later. "Do you know a place named El Fahrar?"

It was a fellow Spaniard behind the wheel, one more of the many Andalusians who toiled away in the protectorate. Lean, dark, with sharp features and eyes as black as the coal they sold at the Afuera Souk.

"I have an idea where it is, more or less."

"Then get us there quickly, please, but slow down as you approach."

I'd tried with all my strength and would swear as much to anyone who asked, on all that was sacred to me. I had tried to submit to the commissioner's orders, to be meek and obliging, even. He would know what to do. He was guided by a mind furnished with cool lucidity and decades of experience, and I was just an anguished woman whose son had been stolen from her. This was why I'd had every intention of following his orders, on my honor. Of being responsible, reliable, judicious, obedient. But I'd been unable to do it, despite my best efforts. My sense of duty was offset by my mother's instinct. And that instinct was what, in the end, tipped the scales in the other direction.

We gradually left the urban area behind us and climbed toward Monte Viejo, where dozens of Europeans had built residences, most of them magnificent, many with views of the Strait of Gibraltar. Finally, the paved road came to an end and the route turned into a winding lane flanked by thick vegetation. On the way, as we jolted along over the potholes, I explained the situation to Nick in fits and starts.

"Are you sure you want to do this?" he asked when I finished telling him.

"Yes, if you'll help me."

I didn't need to ask. The two of us were in the back seat. He put his arm over my shoulders and pulled me toward him.

The car continued to climb before taking a turn to the right. Suddenly we had the gates to a couple of villas in front of us. But we couldn't see the buildings; they must've been hidden behind the vegetation and walls. We left them behind and continued down a stony path.

"We're nearly there, señora," the driver informed us. "What shall I do now? Go in or stay out here?"

Wait, was my answer. Then I spoke to Nick—quick sentences, instructions. He agreed to everything without questioning me. The car slowed to a stop outside a double gate. A modest sign on a marble

plaque announced that we were in the right place. On the right, a bougainvillea draped from the garden wall, and on the left were the pads
and fruit of an overgrown prickly pear.

Nick grabbed his leather bag and started to open the car door.

"Just a moment," I said.

Almost wrenching it from him, I made him take off his jacket.
Once the garment was in my hands, I gave the driver his instructions.

"You and I will stay here and wait."

Holding my breath, I watched Nick go through the gate and walk
away with his back to me, along the path inside the property, his stride
confident and neutral. His bag was over his shoulder. He looked like
just one more disoriented visitor searching for accommodation, an
anonymous Englishman, one of the many who milled about the area
and who would be perfectly comfortable staying in the company of
some compatriots among the cool leafiness of Monte Viejo.

He came back half an hour later, retracing his steps with the same
easy walk, his appearance that of a new guest going out to stretch his
legs, unhurried and with no particular destination in mind. As soon as
he was outside the gate, however, he rushed to the car. I was waiting for
him with the door open, fear eating away at me.

"They're inside."

I held my hands to my mouth to stop myself from screaming.

"They're inside and they're fine, Víctor and the girl, both of them."

My whole body was trembling; Nick had to hold me.

"They're fine, they're fine, they're fine . . . ," he repeated, stroking
my head to calm me down. "I saw them through a back window. They're
happily playing, the nanny and him, sitting on the floor. There're toys,
wooden blocks."

I still had my hands over my lips, one clamped on top of the other,
tightly, as if I was afraid something might escape: a shriek, a retch, my
last breath. My son was all right, building, like he so often did, unstable
structures that he would later knock down with a slap, bursting into

laughter at the destruction. My son was all right. Imprisoned, forcibly held, even if his child's mind didn't know it. But content and unharmed.

"And Ramiro?" I managed to ask in a faint voice.

"He's in the same bungalow, in the adjoining room, the one at the front. He goes in and out, can't stay still. He walks a short distance and goes back in. He seems . . . I'd say he looks uncomfortable. Fed up, even."

I wanted to ask more questions, learn more about the situation, get the full picture.

"Did you see food, water, a bed or cot?"

"Listen, Sira. Listen."

"Is air getting in, is it clean, are there animals or anything dangerous nearby?"

He didn't want to get into details. A master of informative brevity at the microphone, he'd been quickly efficient while he was inside this place as well.

"Listen to me. I spoke to the owner, an American by the name of Buckingham. His English wife and his children are in Brighton right now. We've been lucky. I explained the situation, and he hadn't suspected anything at all. There are four bungalows, modest accommodations spread around the garden. They're in the last one, the one closest to the cliff, sufficiently far away from the main house. Two of the other bungalows are occupied by American writers, but they've left for the Atlas Mountains for a few days, apparently. So no one's heard any crying or screaming, if there's been any."

Screaming, crying . . . So that those words wouldn't tear me apart, I preferred to push on.

"And this Buckingham, is he prepared to help us?"

"Of course. Straightaway, he offered to call the police."

The "no" left my throat several times.

"It's the most sensible thing to do, Sira."

"No, not until we get Víctor away from that lowlife. Not until I have him with me."

We were in the back of the car. The driver had gotten out and was smoking idly some distance away, admiring the horizon, unconcerned by our doings. He was probably immune to his customers' eccentricities.

"Did you see any way to get into the bungalow without being seen?" I persisted. "I don't know . . . a back way in?"

"No. There was just a path that goes down to the sea, narrow and sloping."

"Let me think, let me think . . . ," I mumbled through clenched teeth. "You say . . . you say Ramiro seems fed up. That doesn't surprise me. He's a social animal, urban, intense, always active. Guarding a rural bungalow must be torture for him, and he's surely being eaten up by the uncertainty of how this insanity will end."

We racked our brains for a few seconds.

"What if I offer a bit of distraction?" Nick suggested.

"That's exactly what I was thinking. And meanwhile, I'll—"

"Not you. I'll get Buckingham to help."

I practically shouted my protest.

"What do you mean not me?"

"It's better if you keep away from him. You're his ultimate target."

"I'm going in, Nick," I said forcefully. "You keep him away, at least for a few moments. We'll play it by ear."

"Sira, I insist. We must let Buckingham call the police, it will all—"

We had reached an impasse, and though it was hard for me to admit it, he was probably right. Perhaps the police were the best solution. But knowing that my son was so close, within my reach, was more than I could bear.

"How is Buckingham physically? Energetic? Vigorous?"

"He's not as big as me but he has a booming voice, and I doubt he lacks strength."

Even so, they might be two against one, but Ramiro was agile and as slippery as a snake.

Through the window I saw the taxi driver approach. He must've grown tired of wasting time. Our eyes met for a moment. I didn't know what he saw in mine, but I perceived a lot in his—accumulated hunger, suffering, hardship. The uprooted life of a man who'd had no other option for moving forward, who was in exile after having joined a cause that once promised the unfortunate a little hope. Surely he was tired of slaving away, day and night, just to put a few lentils on his children's plates.

"Excuse me, amigo."

"Yes, señora."

"Would you help us with something, in there?" I gestured with my chin at El Fahrar, then added, "For a fee, of course."

He took a couple of steps closer. His hands were in his pockets, doubt was on his brow, and the very end of a cigarette hung from one side of his mouth.

"What is it you want?"

"To put a detestable crook in his place."

"Has he played a dirty trick on you? Has he behaved badly?"

"Like a pig."

"Well then, for a hundred pesetas, sweetheart, I'll pull his teeth out for you if you want."

82

It all happened in a flash, like a gust of wind that forms a dust cloud and, just as quickly as it swept in, subsides again.

Ramiro's impatience worked in our favor. Passing himself off as a new guest, Nick—for all practical purposes a solitary man Ramiro didn't know—easily persuaded him to step out and have a drink. I started creeping toward the bungalow as soon as Ramiro turned his back to the door. With cautious steps, taking extreme care as I turned the door handle, I managed to get inside. There was joy on Víctor's face, and he even went to throw a wooden block at me but saw me with a finger over my lips, begging him to be quiet. Philippa was trembling when, without saying a word, I gestured at her to move silently toward me.

But Ramiro was no fool, and the fact that he'd accepted a whiskey from an English stranger didn't mean that he would take his eye off the ball. And so the predictable happened the moment I had them with me at the door, ready to run to the big central house, with Philippa on one side and Víctor in my arms under Nick's jacket, pressed against my chest as if we were playing some sort of hide-and-seek, like the game we'd played so many times before.

Ramiro must have heard or suspected something and turned around to see us. An animal cry came from his mouth when he sensed what was happening. As quick in body as he was of mind, he rushed at us to cut off our escape before it had begun. His face was contorted, just a few dozen paces between us. He didn't shout, swear, or threaten me—his only thought was to charge, frenzied and violent, with the sole intention of snatching my son back from me. It was then that, with my free hand—the one that wasn't holding the boy—I patted the side of my skirt and dug in my left pocket.

"One more step and you'll have these stuck in you."

It might've been the conviction in my voice that made him pull up, or perhaps it was the sinister gleam of the sun on the scissors. Either way, he stopped dead, then raised both arms to stop my flight. And it was at that precise moment that Nick and the taxi driver, who'd emerged from the rosebushes, grabbed him from behind, their four arms holding him firmly. But Ramiro was accustomed to evading problems, both tangible and immaterial ones. And he used that skill one more time in his attempt to shake off the two men. They were resorting to brute force, but he opted for slippery agility. And he won the battle and got away.

He didn't have many options about what to do next, however. The owner of the place, Buckingham, joined the two men, and between the three of them they blocked the way back to the road. Ramiro opted to give up on me, at the bungalow, perhaps knowing that my threat hadn't been empty, and that if he pushed me to the limit I wouldn't hesitate to gut him with the scissors to protect my son. And so his only option was to head down the path that led to the sea: an escape to nowhere.

He stopped for a few seconds, his hair falling over his forehead, and looked at us all with restless eyes, as if assessing the extent to which he was penned in. All we could hear were cicadas and the breeze rustling the eucalyptus leaves, a stifled sob from Philippa behind me, the sea against the rocks. Finally, in the middle of the silence—with me on one side of Ramiro, pressing Víctor against my body, and the three men on the other, making his escape impossible—in the midst of that tense stillness, we began to hear the hum of engines.

Before long, we saw them arrive at speed through the gate, the gravel crunching as they hit the brakes. Out from the first car came the

Belgian policeman from the night before and another officer of a similar age, each holding a pistol. From the second emerged Commissioner Vázquez and what must've been his old colleague, a sturdy man with no hair.

"Don't move, Arribas!"

Perhaps Buckingham had called them, or my own disappearance had alerted Don Claudio. Either way, the arrival of the two young officers and two retired policemen had just helped us to close the net.

"Don't move!"

The path to the beach really was Ramiro's only option now. Perhaps he imagined that from there he could find a junction to help him escape. He hurtled off in that direction but hadn't accounted for the roughness of the terrain. Within seconds, the sound of him falling reached our ears. Had the cliff been steeper, he could have killed himself, broken his neck as he rolled down, cracked his head open on the rocks. Luckily for him, it wasn't that sheer. But he wasn't unhurt—far from it.

The younger policemen went down to fetch him, the insipid Belgian and his partner ultimately proving to be efficient types. Since he was unable to walk by himself, the two of them brought him up by his armpits, dragging him roughly even though he must've fractured at least one leg. He was bleeding down one side of his face, and judging by the way he was bent over, his abdomen or ribs were causing him acute pain. His usual tidiness was in ruins, his fine clothes and sophisticated style torn to dirty shreds. Below the cliff, empty and half-hidden, lay Merkala Beach, the stretch of sand that could have been—but had not, and never would be—his salvation.

I refused to look him in the eyes. I wasn't tempted to insult him or challenge him or claim revenge. All I wanted was for him to forget about me again. I had never imagined, after he abandoned me the first time, that he would return, but meeting him again had been an even more cruel blow than the first. Now that I had my son back, I just wanted to be free of that nasty piece of work forever. And so I avoided looking him in the face, and he didn't search for mine, either. As ever, his main concern was himself.

Once I'd seen from a distance that they were starting to drag him to one of the cars, I quickly took Víctor and Philippa inside the main house. Nick followed us with the taxi driver right behind him while the owner finished talking to the police about the ugly turn of events that had shaken his peaceful lodge. We'd been enormously lucky that neither his family nor any of his guests were there at that moment.

It had been six months since Víctor last saw Nick, since we'd left Jerusalem for London. Nonetheless, perhaps because his little memory had formed some connections that remained unbroken, he seemed to recognize him. At the very least, he cheerfully welcomed the man who'd meant so much to us at our darkest time. He was so pleased to see him, in fact, that within minutes he'd gone from my arms to his with a confidence that allowed him to pull Nick's tie and hang it over his ear. Being held captive by Ramiro didn't seem to have affected my son, and that impression eased my worries and filled me with profound relief.

I walked up behind Nick and stopped beside him, resting my cheek for a moment against his shoulder. As I slid my hand into his pocket, I said into his ear, "I'm stealing your wallet."

I took out five one-pound notes. In my rush to get to Monte Viejo, I hadn't even stopped to pick up my handbag or money. All I had with me were the dressmaking scissors, which had gone back into my pocket. I would not have hesitated to drive them into the body of the man I once loved, if I'd needed to.

The sum I ended up paying the taxi driver was, at an exchange rate of ninety-eight pesetas per pound on Tangier's free market, five times what he'd asked for. He narrowed his eyes and nearly dropped his cigarette end from his mouth, but he didn't turn the money down. He simply folded up the notes and put them in his shirt pocket.

Philippa, meanwhile, had slumped into an armchair beside the family's piano and a silent parrot in a cage. Her gaze was absent, her expression blank, showing neither anguish nor relief, fear nor satisfaction. Nothing. I took her hand and pressed it between mine.

"I'm desperately sorry you had to go through this, my dear. And I thank you from the bottom of my heart for taking care of Víctor with such dedication. Tomorrow, without fail, we'll buy you a ticket home."

She nodded. Her only family was an aunt in the West Midlands; nothing desirable waited for her in England. But going anywhere else would be better for her, I sensed, than staying with us in Morocco. She could never have imagined that looking after a child would bring her so many tribulations.

I let go of her hand just as I saw Commissioner Vázquez's silhouette coming through one of the arches that opened onto the patio. The sea was in the background, and on that clear afternoon, we could see all the way to the dunes of Tarifa, on the other side of the strait. As he walked in, I heard the first car start. The officers of the International Police were taking Ramiro away, finally removing him from his hideout and his prey. They would take him to a Sûreté cell first. I had no idea where he would end up after that.

I walked slowly over to Don Claudio.

"I'm sorry to have let you down again, Commissioner."

Years before, he'd told me to search for a decent salaried job in Tétouan, and I'd gone against him by opening a business using shady money. Now, he'd asked me to do nothing until I received his orders, but the moment he turned his back, I'd disobeyed him and gone off to resolve the situation in my own way.

"You learned to take care of yourself a long time ago, señorita. I should've realized." He used plain words, the kind he'd used in the role he held for so many years. In his authoritative face, however, I thought I perceived something like admiration. "And as for that undesirable," he added, "he won't bother you again, you can be sure." He turned and gestured toward the terrace. "My friend will make sure he disappears. He still has clout."

83

Candelaria didn't set the table for dinner on the veranda that evening, but in a corner of the garden illuminated by one of the lanterns and sheltered by the honeysuckle. The table she prepared was a small one, with just two chairs.

Félix brought out another bottle of wine but disappeared with the excuse that he was going to the opening of a new place that would be full of the foreigners that allured him so much—who knows how he'd managed to get invited. Candelaria, for her part, announced that she was sore to her tailbone after the long day and the previous night. "I've been dreaming about hitting the sack for hours, my girl," she swore before getting out of the way. Earlier she'd taken a tray up to Philippa with a glass of milk and some fruit, as the poor nanny was reluctant to leave her room.

It was dark by the time Nick arrived, freshly showered, wearing clean clothes, without his leather bag. He'd decided to check in to El Fahrar for the weekend, to begin with. We still hadn't determined exactly how, and for how long, he would end up staying in Tangier. I was waiting for him with Víctor on my lap. I refused to be separated from him. It was as if I needed, with his presence, to fill a hole that his brief absence had left.

The gate squeaked when Nick came in, carrying some flowers for me that he'd picked from a garden wall on the way and a rustic drum for my son, which he'd bought from a Riffian Berber's stall. Before I got up, before we'd said hello or congratulated each other or said a word to one another, he finally did what he had never dared do in Jerusalem: he left a long kiss on my mouth.

That was the first of many nights, the first of many dinners, we would share together under the stars with the smell of jasmine and the sea in the air. The prelude to the two of us becoming closer, as we inevitably would.

We had the whole rest of the summer ahead of us. We weren't concerned about what would come after that.

EPILOGUE

By the time Barbara Hutton landed in Tangier in early August 1947, her beautiful kaftans were hanging in her wardrobe. On the desk at Brax Insurance Ltd in the City of London was the detailed report I had sent them: twenty-three typed pages giving a precise account of all the strengths and vulnerabilities, the weaknesses and potential risks, of Sidi Hosni. The information was used to establish the policy that covered the Romanovs' jewels; I knew they'd reached an acceptable agreement because, together with one of my creations made of sumptuous Indian silk, the millionairess wore her emerald tiara at her housewarming party at the palace in the kasbah. Nick and I attended together, and thanks to Ira Belline, I even managed to obtain an invitation for my friend Félix, who practically melted with delight.

It was an occasion that marked the beginning of a tradition that would continue over the years on those terraces that overlooked the sea and the roofs of Tangier, and which would define an era. Celebrities, aristocrats, and people of worldly sophistication would circulate there to the music of various bands—local or from New York, or from wherever the princess desired. What did it matter, if it was only a question of paying a price? With that same impulsiveness, she would have decorative items from Paris, floral decorations, hundreds of crates of champagne, and other enticing delicacies flown to her in a private plane. Tangier's hotels would fill up with guests from all over the world, and then the bills would be sent to Ira Belline at the palace—the host always covered their travel costs. Later, I would often hear the housekeeper complain about the many guests who shamelessly abused Mrs. Hutton's hospitality, adding indulgences for themselves to their travel expenses.

Over time—in parallel with a flow of changing friends, servants, and hangers-on—the rich heiress's turbulent life encompassed a succession of marriages, divorces, and diverse lovers. She married seven times and took almost all of her husbands to Sidi Hosni. The fourth was an impoverished Russian prince; the fifth, a Dominican diplomat named Porfirio Rubirosa, as famous for his likable impudence as he was for his skill at lovemaking. These spouses were successively replaced by an elite tennis player and a struggling French noble who was believed to own properties in Indonesia. Among those who visited her heart or her bed without ever signing a contract were a young roaming guitarist, numerous anonymous men for whose services she paid, and even the bullfighter Ángel Teruel, who she pursued around half the bullrings in Spain when he was still in his twenties and she was over sixty.

She was by that time so prematurely decrepit that she could barely move, and she often had to be carried. Alcohol addiction, substance abuse, insomnia, depression, and eating disorders drove her to attempt suicide several times. She failed in those bids to end her life, but the efforts made her increasingly vulnerable. She died at the age of sixty-six, emaciated and alone in a Beverly Hills hotel. Of the immense fortune she'd inherited in her childhood, little more than three thousand dollars remained. By then, her son had been dead for some years, so creditors, ex-husbands, and supposed heirs descended like vultures in search of carrion. They didn't even leave enough to fulfill her final wish—to be buried in Tangier.

The city that Barbara Hutton's remains never reached in the late seventies was by then no longer the place she'd known. A great deal had changed in the intervening decades.

That summer of 1947 proved to be the beginning of the end of the British Empire, the breakup of the biggest global power in history. The changing of the times, the emergence of other powers, aspirations for freedom, and Britain's inner conscience itself were what altered the course of things. The devastated and exhausted United Kingdom that had emerged from the war finally faltered, and on August 15 that same year—while the candles, drinks, and rugs were being readied for Sidi Hosni's debut into society—India, the jewel of the empire, gained its independence. Two states emerged, India and Pakistan, from a bloody beginning.

The same thing would happen in the coming months in Palestine. Nick and I followed the news with growing concern. In late November of the same year, the United Nations General Assembly adopted a resolution in favor of the partitioning of Palestine into two states, one Jewish and one Arab. And so the state of Israel was born. Predictably, the former group welcomed the decision with jubilation, and the latter rejected it outright. As for Britain, it was time to get out of the way. Time to distance itself from the outbreak of a civil war that was ravaging the region with increasingly brutal and cruel horrors. In the early hours of May 15, 1948, the British Mandate over Palestine expired, and officials and armed forces alike left the territory. The bitter Arab-Israeli conflict would cause tens of thousands of deaths and continue for decades.

Meanwhile, in that thriving, golden, and ebullient Tangier that existed following the world war, nobody could yet anticipate the spread or effect of that contagion. But yes, the decolonization that began that year would trigger a chain reaction that would spread around the world. It would be just nine years before foreign control of Morocco came to an end. But in 1947, that was a horizon that couldn't yet be seen. In the prosperous international zone, promising opportunities continued to emerge, as if that morning would never arrive.

In parallel to these historic events that filled the newspapers that summer, some disturbing developments also happened closer to home. The first surprise came by ship from Southampton in the form of my father and my mother-in-law. They didn't even warn me—as bold as two wild youngsters despite their age, Olivia Bonnard and Gonzalo Alvarado decided to turn up in Tangier to give me two pieces of news. First, they informed me that someone had made a tempting offer to buy the house on the Boltons. Then they announced their decision to marry.

Certain that my opinions would make no difference, I kept my thoughts to myself, threw caution to the wind, and simply put them up in Hotel Cecil on the beachfront and made the necessary arrangements for them to fulfill their wishes. They were of different religious denominations, but my father was gentlemanly enough to concede. They ended up marrying in the Anglican Saint Andrew's Church in front of a small group of invitees: Víctor, Nick and me, Candelaria and Félix, the vicar, the British consul, and Buckingham—the owner of El Fahrar—on the piano. We confirmed their vows with a lunch on the terrace of Hotel Villa de France. They drank a toast to their future, brimming with happiness. I, though I hid it, toasted with little conviction. In principle, their idea was to settle together in Madrid, but they continued to put off their return. In time, delighted with the pleasant life of North Africa, they even looked at houses where they could stay for a long period. Neither showed the slightest interest in leaving that warm land where there were no rationing cards, and where they could each speak their respective languages, read newspapers from their own countries, and be near the grandson they shared.

By then, Nick had become someone essential to me, the companion who brought light and support into my life. His coming and going between Gibraltar and Tangier was constant, and he was endlessly crossing the strait to spend as much time with me as his work allowed. With tenacity and deftness, he managed to persuade Cora, his ex-wife, to allow his children to spend a couple of weeks with him, and so Víctor and I met Paul and Ashton, and threads of genuine affection were woven between us. With the children, we enjoyed sunny days on the beach and outings to the Forêt Diplomatique—meeting place of sand and trees—sunset strolls to the city walls on the boulevard, and dinners in the garden made of mint lemonade and Candelaria's delicious kebabs. We also went several times to see my mother in Tétouan, but to the pool at Parque Brooks, we never returned.

The end of August saw the departure of Nick's children, Barbara Hutton, and a great many holidaymakers. On the other side of the Atlantic, however, it wasn't "goodbyes" that were heard, but "welcome home." After a Rainbow Tour that had lasted two months, Eva Perón had just returned to Argentina where the reception was euphoric. Her visit to Spain had been a sparkling success, but in the rest of the countries—Italy, France, Monaco, Portugal, and Switzerland—the reaction had been more muted. In London, the king and queen had not received her, despite her fervent wishes. In the eyes of her country's people, nonetheless, the European tour had been a resounding success.

No mention was made of the succession of cancelations abroad, or the hearsay that circulated regarding some of her destinations. Malicious tongues had spread rumors that she'd passed through Switzerland to deposit millions in murky bank accounts and that she'd had an affair in Monte Carlo with Aristotle Onassis, a great friend of Alberto Dodero and a fellow shipping magnate. Whether those stories were true or not, the fact was Evita returned to her country having enhanced her credibility and image. What nobody suspected yet was that the exhaustion she'd felt during some stages of the tour—the bluish tone of her skin, and those ankles that tended to swell up, and which the long-suffering Lillian Lagomarsino massaged at night—were the early signs of something tragically serious.

Within a few days of her arrival in Buenos Aires, the Chamber of Deputies would approve the law that established universal suffrage and equal political rights between men and women in Argentina. She'd devoted herself fervently to that cause and shortly after, she would address the masses who packed Plaza de Mayo with a speech that began with the words "My fellow countrywomen . . . ," and in which she would speak of a long history of struggles, setbacks, and hopes, failures to understand, refusals, and justice. The photographs taken of her showed that she no longer wore the theatrical hairstyles she'd paraded in Spain, or the garish and ornate clothes I'd seen at her public appearances and in her rooms in El Pardo Palace. After returning from Europe, Evita had decided to adopt a style free from excesses, which would give her a more becoming and respectable look of restrained elegance. In the newspapers and magazines I saw at that time, I thought I could detect a hint of my suits from Digby Morton.

Listening to her shouting with such unashamed passion in front of thousands of citizens, no one could have anticipated that within five years she would be dead; she wouldn't reach the age of thirty-four. Ravaged by cervical cancer, but active and spirited until the end, she was mourned by her people in a monumental funeral that claimed every flower in Argentina and filled the country with tears, mass processions with torches, ceremonial honors, and queues many miles long made up of those who wished to say goodbye to her. Thereafter, she would become an icon with defenders and detractors, and her name would continue to raise passions and furious hatred in people despite the passing of time. What happened later to her embalmed body would be story enough for another novel.

But it was still a few years yet before Evita would die, then, and my concerns at that time remained tied to that present. And that present also brought new prospects to my horizon. I'd drawn so close to Barbara Hutton's universe that, much like what had happened with the Press Association party, I received invitations to various events. Sometimes I accepted, other times I turned them down, depending on my mood and the type of gathering. Until one Friday evening, at a dinner party at a villa in Marshan that Nick and I attended, someone left a proposal on the table: launch a new radio station.

The end of the world war had made North Africa one of the world's great focal points, a bridge between the Americas and dozens of European nations. Through the use of old military infrastructure and new buildings, advances in electronics and antennae, and messages and ideas, propaganda and intrigue had begun to flow between radio stations and receivers. America's powerful RCA had just installed a relay station on the nearby Charf Hill. Radio Tangier International and Pan American Radio were already broadcasting their programs, sharing the airwaves with other more modest stations. Through serials, innocent competitions, advertising, and seemingly innocuous music—in Arabic and French, English and Spanish—radio's power to shape opinions was continuing to grow.

With that proposal, we said farewell to the summer.

Without having said either yes or no, with our arms around each other's waists, we walked back to my house. Nick had the experience. I had the money that would come after the house on the Boltons was sold. Neither of us disliked the idea of undertaking something together. The world was preparing for a cold war, and we would all have to find our way through it, among stitching or among the airwaves.

AUTHOR'S NOTE

When the Spanish edition of *The Seamstress* came out in June 2009, I was an unknown writer, and the protagonist—a dressmaker involved in espionage—was a rarity among the latest titles. The warm reception from readers propelled the novel on a completely unexpected trajectory, and as a result, recurring questions were asked: Would the story continue? Would there be a second part? Would we have a sequel?

I never answered with an outright no, but I knew, right then, that Sira Quiroga and I needed some time apart. Almost twelve years later, however, we were reunited, and as before, I once again drew on many sources and received the generous support of various people.

Of great interest in my efforts to sketch the atmosphere and events taking place in Jerusalem in the final years of the British administration were the books *Palestine between Politics and Terror, 1945–47* (Motti Golani, 2013); *One Palestine, Complete: Jews and Arabs under the British Mandate* (Tom Segev, 2000); *Ploughing Sand: British Rule in Palestine, 1917–1948* (Naomi Shepherd, 2000); and *Mandate Days: British Lives in Palestine 1918–1948* (A. J. Sherman, 1997). The workings of the Palestine Broadcasting Service are detailed in *This Is Jerusalem Calling: State Radio in Mandate Palestine* (Andrea L. Stanton, 2014). As for the attack on the King David Hotel, a meticulous reconstruction can be found in *By Blood and Fire, July 22, 1946: The Attack on Jerusalem's King David* (Thurston Clarke, 1981).

The author Amos Oz's books also touch on this period, particularly the pages about his childhood in his moving autobiography, *A Tale of Love and Darkness* (2002), as does Dominique Lapierre and Larry Collins's *O Jerusalem!*. Though they stretch beyond the timeframe of the novel, to understand the unraveling of the British presence in Palestine, the memories and reflections of those who performed their duties there during that time are illuminating. *The End of the British Mandate for Palestine, 1948: The Diary of Sir Henry Gurney* (Motti Golani, 2009) is one such account. Another important witness is my fellow Spaniard Pablo de Azcárate, a diplomat and United Nations official who held successive important posts in the region. His book *Misión en Palestina. Nacimiento del Estado de Israel* was republished in 2019 by Cuadernos del Laberinto in the La Valija Diplomática collection in a new edition with an excellent preliminary study and notes by Jorge Ramos. More personally, to help me ensure the coherence of the regional terminology, I'd like to thank *El País* journalist Ángeles Espinosa, an old college friend and a true Middle East expert.

During his time as ambassador of the Spanish Republic to the United Kingdom, Pablo de Azcárate also witnessed the trials and tribulations of the Spaniards exiled in London, and he undoubtedly met some of the Spanish expatriates mentioned in this novel. They were the subject of Luis Monferrer Catalán's complete study *Odisea en Albión. Los republicanos españoles exiliados en Gran Bretaña (1936–1977)* (2007). As for the involvement of some of them in the BBC, there are also pertinent details in Rafael Martínez's books *Antonio Torres de la BBC a The Observer: Republicanos y monárquicos en el exilio, 1944–1956* (1996) and *José Castillejo, el hombre y su quehacer en La Voz de Londres, 1940–1945* (1998). With a lighter tone, in *Perico en Londres* Esteban Salazar Chapela provides many details of this expatriate community in his novelized account of the Spanish exile originally published in Buenos Aires in 1947 and republished by Renacimiento in 2019 with an interesting introduction and notes by Francisca Montiel.

The founding and reach of the BBC's overseas services is documented in works such as *Let Truth Be Told: 50 Years of BBC External Broadcasting* (Gerard Mansell, 1982) and *A Skyful of Freedom: 60 Years of the BBC World Service* (Andrew Walker, 1992). A detailed reconstruction of the legendary broadcasts in Spanish can be found in the "Locutores y presentadores del Servicio Latinoamericano de la BBC de Londres. Lista histórica" section of Uruguayan journalist Horacio A. Nigro Geolkiewsky's La Galena del Sur website.

To frame all this within the bleak backdrop of London after the Second World War, David Kynaston's book *Austerity Britain 1945–48* (2007) is enormously informative and evocative. On this topic, I'd like to thank Professor Elizabeth Murphy, a dear colleague from my academic days, for her help ensuring the coherence of the text in its place and time.

I'd also like to express my gratitude to Jimmy Burns—the Anglo-Spanish author of *Papa Spy*—who years ago welcomed *The Seamstress* to London and whom I still look forward to meeting. Without his involvement, Tom Burns—his father—would never have had breakfast with Sira at the Embassy tearoom.

To travel back to World War II–era Spain and find the precise locations of the Third Reich's properties and institutions, Peter Besas's exhaustive book *Nazis in Madrid* (2015) is essential reading.

The itinerary of Eva Perón's visit to Spain can be followed closely thanks to reports in newspapers such as *ABC* and *La Vanguardia*, and the work of various Argentine authors. The tour is also covered in detail by Enrique F. Widmann-Miguel in *Eva Perón en España. Junio, 1947* (2014) and in Jorge Camarasa's book *La enviada: El viaje de Eva Perón a Europa* (1998). The account of Lillian Lagomarsino in her memoir *Y ahora . . . hablo yo* (1996) is also illuminating. With a broader perspective, to shed light on the woman and her career, titles of note include Marysa Navarro's *Evita* (1994), Vera Pichel's *Evita íntima* (1993), *Santa Evita*, by Tomás Martínez Eloy (1995), and Abel Posse's *La pasión según*

Eva (1994). Felipe Pigna's book *Evita: Jirones de su vida* (2012) is among the most up to date and well documented. From a Spanish perspective, the chapter devoted to her in *Así los he visto* (1974) by José María de Areilza, Spanish ambassador to Argentina from 1947 to 1950, is enlightening.

On a more personal note, I'd like to thank Mercedes Güiraldes, senior editor at Planeta Argentina, for her sound and congenial observations; the journalist Catalina de Elía—author of *Maten a Duarte* (2020)—for ingratiating me with the first lady's brother; Diego Arguindeguy, for marveling me with his wisdom and taking the whole novel under his erudite wing. And my dear Nacho Iraola, the Planeta editorial director for the Southern Cone, for laying the first bridge to allow Sira to cross the Atlantic and for always treating me just as Evita would've liked to have been treated at Buckingham Palace.

As for the fourth and final part, I would single out the biographies *Million Dollar Baby: An Intimate Portrait of Barbara Hutton* (Philip Van Rensselaer, 1979) and *Poor Little Rich Girl: The Life and Legend of Barbara Hutton* (C. David Heymann, 1983), as well as the intimate account *In Search of a Prince: My Life with Barbara Hutton*, written in 1988 by Mona Eldridge, her personal social secretary who spent long periods with her in Tangier.

To reconstruct those glorious days, the many articles by Domingo del Pino in various publications and the books *Historia de Tánger: Memoria de la ciudad internacional* (2009) and *Tánger, Tánger* (2015) by Leopoldo Ceballos are magnificent.

Equally valuable are the accounts shared with me by a few Tangerines—both by birth and adoptive—for whom the memory of that microworld's splendor and decline is still fresh. With this in mind I'd like to extend my gratitude to Vicente Jorro, who lived in the Parque Brooks area, bought paintings from Sidi Hosni when the building was emptied, and always has fascinating stories to share with me; Ramón Buenaventura, who learned to play tennis at the Emsallah, and who loaned me his grandfather Alberto España—author of *La pequeña historia de Tangier* (1954)—for the International Press Association event; Manolo Cantera, who occupied the bungalow at El Fahrar and could write reams about the people who passed through there; Sonia García Soubriet, who described the city's decadence beautifully in her book *El Jardín (Al Bustán)* (2007); Chema Menéndez, who in his book *Diario España de Tánger* (2020) recounts his grandfather Jaime "El Chato" Menéndez's career as a journalist.

Turning toward Tétouan, I'm eternally grateful to Ricardo Barceló for our many walks and his forever companionable nature, and to my aunt Estrella Vinuesa, for continuing to share with me her stories of a time from which she still remembers the scent of sandalwood in the Indian bazaars on Calle de La Luneta. On the sad subject of those who will never be able to relive these scenes again, I pay tribute to the memory of Paco Trujillo and María Rosa Temboury, who were indefatigable in their efforts to keep the Spanish presence in Morocco alive through the La Medina Association. And to the memory of my uncle Enrique Vinuesa, who lived there in his childhood and youth, and my cousin Elisa Álvarez Moreno, who grew up among a nostalgia for that protectorate, the place through which our grandparents and then our mothers passed, before she and I did, holding their hands.

This novel would never have reached the bookstores without the efforts, as ever, of the publisher Planeta's magnificent teams; my infinite gratitude therefore to all of them and in particular, for their constant closeness and involvement, to Belén López Celada, Isa Santos, Laura Franch, Ferran López Olmo, Sabrina Rinaldi, Marc Rocamora, Lolita Torelló and Silvia Axpe, and to Dolors Escoriza and her team. And a very special thanks to Lola Gulias, who was the first to meet Sira, and to Raquel Gisbert, who allowed herself to be drawn in and left a piece of her heart in the Jerusalem of this novel. To my agent Antonia Kerrigan and her formidable coworkers. To my family and friends, whether immediate or less so.

Much of this story was written during the pandemic that has plagued the world. With it I would finally like to honor all those whose eyes closed—as Gardel's famous tango says—while the world moves toward some longed-for normality. It is to them and to all the readers who kept *The Seamstress* alive over the years to whom Sira and I dedicate this reunion.

ABOUT THE AUTHOR

Photo © Carlos Ruiz

María Dueñas is the author of the *New York Times* bestselling novel *The Time in Between*, which has sold more than three million copies. It has been translated into almost forty languages and adapted into an acclaimed television series that became a phenomenon in the Spanish-speaking world. María holds a PhD in English and was a college professor for almost twenty years. She is the author of five novels and participates in book fairs and literary events all over the world. She is currently involved in audiovisual projects and is working on the adaptation of *Sira* to a new television series.

ABOUT THE TRANSLATOR

Photo © Colin Crewdson

Simon Bruni is an award-winning literary translator with a focus on contemporary Spanish and Latin American fiction and a wealth of experience translating books and articles within the humanities and social sciences. Simon combines his profound knowledge of the Spanish language with a supple command of written English, working creatively to bring Spanish voices to life in their new host language. His translations of Paul Pen's *The Light of the Fireflies* and Sofía Segovia's *The Murmur of Bees* have both become international bestsellers.